Garden Open Today

HER MAJESTY QUEEN ELIZABETH THE QUEEN MOTHER
PATRON
THE NATIONAL GARDENS SCHEME CHARITABLE TRUST

Garden
Open Today

A GUIDE TO GARDENS OPEN TO THE PUBLIC
THROUGH THE NATIONAL GARDENS SCHEME

EDITED BY MARTYN AND ALISON RIX

PHOTOGRAPHS BY JACQUI HURST

MERMAID BOOKS

MICHAEL JOSEPH LTD

Published by the Penguin Group
27 Wrights Lane, London W8 5TZ, England
Viking Penguin Inc., 40 West 23rd Street, New York, New York 10010, USA
Penguin Books Australia Ltd, Ringwood, Victoria, Australia
Penguin Books Canada Ltd, 2801 John Street, Markham, Ontario, Canada L3R 1B4
Penguin Books (NZ) Ltd, 182-190 Wairau Road, Auckland 10, New Zealand

Penguin Books Ltd, Registered Offices: Harmondsworth, Middlesex, England

First published in Great Britain by Viking in 1987
First published in Mermaid Books in 1988

Text and photographs copyright © The National Gardens Scheme Charitable Trust,
1987
Maps drawn by Reginald Piggott
Botanical line illustrations on pp. 21 and 112 are reproduced from *Victorian Floral
Illustrations*
(ed. Carol Belanger Grafton), Dover Publications, Inc. 1985
Other line illustrations copyright © The National Gardens Scheme Charitable Trust,
1987

Typeset in 8/9½ Palatino by
Wyvern Typesetting Limited, Bristol
Colour origination by Colorlito, Milan
Printed and bound in Spain by Graficromo S.A. Cordoba

Designed by Judith Gordon

British Library Cataloguing in Publication Data

Garden open today: a guide to gardens open
to the public through the National Gardens
Scheme.
1. Gardens—Great Britain
I. Rix, Martyn   II. Rix, Alison
914.1′04858   SB466.G7

ISBN 0-7181-3066-9

Contents

NOTICE TO READERS

Readers will undoubtedly be aware that the storm which swept southern England in October 1987 caused widespread devastation to gardens in the area. In view of this fact it is *essential* to consult the National Gardens Scheme's annual publication 'Gardens of England and Wales' as mentioned on page 12 before planning to visit any of the gardens described in this book.

On page 42 we regret that the caption is incorrect. It should read 'The garden at Penn, Alderly Edge, in June'.

KENSINGTON PALACE
LONDON W8 4PU
TELEPHONE 01 937 6374

The Gardens Scheme was started as a memorial to
Queen Alexandra who was Patron of The Queen's Institute of
District Nursing for the relief of District Nurses in need
through old age or illness.

The success of The National Gardens Scheme has enabled it
to extend its charitable work over the years to include many
others and this book is a commemoration of all that has been
achieved.

It is a tribute to garden owners and all who support
The National Gardens Scheme that in its 60 years it will have
raised over £3½ million, an amazing figure when the admission
charges to most gardens remained at 1 shilling a head until 1964.

As a lover of gardens I wish every success to this book,
and feel sure it will appeal to all those who struggle to keep
their gardens, however large or small, as they used to be in
the past.

Alice

PRESIDENT

Barnwell Manor, Northamptonshire, the residence
of Her Royal Highness Princess Alice, Duchess of
Gloucester GBE.

History of the
National Gardens Scheme

Despite its title, it was the care of people rather than the care of plants that led to the creation of The National Gardens Scheme. The story really begins in Liverpool in 1859 when one William Rathbone, a wealthy business man, employed a trained nurse to care for his dying wife at home. This was such a comfort to his family that it made him think about the sick poor in Liverpool for whom the only available nursing care at that time was in hospital – and in the mid-nineteenth century there was every chance that one would leave that institution feet first. Mr Rathbone employed the nurse who had cared for his wife to go out into one of the most deprived districts of Liverpool and to nurse sick people in their own homes. After two weeks the nurse told him it was too distressing and the conditions too appalling for her to continue. But he persuaded her to persevere; and he also got nurses to work in other deprived districts in Liverpool, and from this small beginning stemmed the district nursing service as we know it today; it spread first to Manchester and then to London, and to other big cities with problems similar to Liverpool.

At an early stage Mr Rathbone enlisted the help of Florence Nightingale and later of Queen Victoria, who took a keen interest in nursing; and by the turn of the century there was a nation-wide service for nursing the sick poor at home, with the Queen Victoria's Jubilee Institute for Nurses, established in 1887, to conduct the training and set the standards. Both the district nursing service and its governing body were run entirely on voluntary funds, and by the early 1920s more money was needed for both; also many of these splendid nurses themselves were in need of care and assistance in their old age after a lifetime of service, caring for others.

Queen Alexandra had succeeded her mother-in-law as Patron of the Institute (subsequently re-named the Queen's Institute of District Nursing). She took a passionate interest in all aspects of district nursing and when she died the Institute suggested to King George V and Queen Mary, by then its Patron, that a fitting memorial might be a Fund devoted to the further development of the district nursing service and to care for its nurses in retirement; the King and Queen agreed and so the National Memorial to Queen Alexandra was launched on 7 January 1926, with the Duke of Portland as Chairman.

People all over the country pursued all sorts of ways of raising money, and one of the most successful, and certainly one of the most long-lasting, was the inspiration of Miss Elsie Wagg, a member of Council of the Queen's Institute, and of the Memorial committee. Tradition has it that she said 'We've got all these beautiful gardens in this country and hardly anyone sees them except the owners and their friends – why don't we ask some of them to open next year for the Appeal?' This suggestion may not seem strange today, accustomed as we are to visiting other people's private gardens, but when made in 1926 it no doubt caused the cynics to raise an eyebrow or two. Nevertheless in 1927 a small committee of noble ladies succeeded in persuading the owners of many stately homes to open their gardens to the public, and charge a small fee for the privilege. A booklet was published (there is just one precious copy in the N.G.S. archives) with the title *The Gardens of England and Wales* listing gardens to be opened in what was described as a 'June Garden Month', and this was so successful that many more gardens were opened in July and August. The fact that King George V allowed his private garden at Sandringham to be opened was a tremendous encouragement to other owners, and it has been the mainstay of the Gardens Scheme ever since. Among other gardens opened for the Appeal were many of the most famous in the country such as Blenheim, Chatsworth and Hatfield House; and others belonging to such renowned gardeners as William Robinson of Gravetye Manor and the intrepid Miss Willmott with her one hundred gardeners at Warley Place. Arrangements were made with rail and transport companies for the running of special trips and literally thousands of people, including a large number of visitors from overseas, took advantage of the opportunity provided for viewing many of the principal gardens of the country and a splendid sum of £8,191 was raised from the 'shilling a head' admission fee.

Altogether 609 gardens were opened that first year, some on more than one day. When the report on the National Memorial to Queen Alexandra was published it stated that on the closing down of the Appeal 'the whole machinery of the Gardens Scheme was handed over to the Queen's Institute of District Nursing, so that in addition to all the direct and indirect benefits received as the result of the National Memorial Appeal, the Institute inherits a Scheme which should ensure a substantial annual income for the cause of District Nursing, as it is intended that the Opening of the Gardens should be an annually recurring event so far as the Garden-owners will agree'. Time has proved this hopeful intention to be well-founded and ever-increasing support from a great many generous garden owners has provided not only a continuing source of funds for the district nurses, but has also enabled the Scheme to add other charities to its objects over the years.

To organize what was at first called The Gardens of England and Wales Scheme the Queen's Institute set up a sub-committee, headed by the late Hilda, Duchess of Richmond and Gordon and composed of Miss Wagg, the Lady Georgina Mure and Mrs Frank Stobart (who together had organized the garden openings for the Memorial Appeal), Mrs Pepyat Evans, Sir William Lawrence (treasurer and Council member of the Royal Horticultural Society) and Mr Avray Tipping (of *Country Life*). Honorary County Organizers were appointed, including the late Pamela, Lady Digby who carried on this work in Dorset until 1966, a wonderful link with the early years, as was the Duchess, who continued as Chairman for twenty years and still took a keen interest in the Scheme right up to her death in 1971, just before her hundredth birthday.

Since its inception, the Scheme has had only four Chairmen; the Duchess handed over to Mrs L. Fleischmann (in 1947) who was succeeded in 1951 by Lady Heald, and in turn by Mrs Alan Hardy in 1979.

The growth of the Gardens Scheme during pre-war years, and the steady increase in the number of gardens open is reflected in the mounting annual totals from £8,000 in 1927 to £15,000 in 1938. Even during the war the garden openings continued, albeit low-key, with half the counties managing to carry on, though on a reduced scale. After the war there was much rebuilding to be done but the Scheme quickly adapted itself to meet the challenges of those early post-war years including petrol shortages, and the changes which lay ahead.

In 1948 came the National Health Service which made many people think that the Gardens Scheme would no longer be needed to raise money for district nursing. This was true in so far as the running of the service was concerned, but there was still a great need for funds to care for the nurses both young and old when in difficulties through illness. No sooner had this fact been established than it was learnt that The National Trust had started a new project – the preservation of certain gardens which were of importance in their own right and not just as adjuncts of an historic house. The first such garden acquired, in 1948, was Hidcote in Gloucestershire and the Trust was seeking a source of income specifically for such gardens. Following an approach by the Trust to the Queen's Institute, it was agreed that from 1949 the Trust would receive for its Gardens Fund a share of The National Gardens Scheme proceeds, in return for the Trust's help and support for the Scheme.

By the time the Gardens Scheme reached its half century in 1977 the number of gardens open each year had risen to 1,400 and annual takings to nearly £100,000. During these years too the Gardens Scheme, while still constitutionally a part of the Queen's Institute, had developed its own identity, and by 1979 the Institute recognized that the Scheme had become a fund-raising organization of such national stature that it now deserved its own independent status. So in 1980 The National Gardens Scheme Charitable Trust came into being, with Her Majesty Queen Elizabeth The Queen Mother as Patron and Her Royal Highness Princess Alice, Duchess of Gloucester as President. From that year, too, garden owners have been able, if they so wish, to help an additional charity especially dear to their hearts with a share of the money raised through their garden openings.

The continuing success of the Gardens Scheme had led by the early 1980s to a situation whereby the share earmarked for the Queen's Institute was more than was needed for its welfare and benevolent work. So from 1984 the balance of the money not needed for these Institute activities has been given each year to Cancer Relief, to assist with the training of district nurses as Macmillan nurses for the continuing care of cancer patients and their families in their own homes. An even more recent change, in 1986, has been the merging into the Gardens Scheme of the Gardener's Sunday organization, as a result of which elderly gardeners and gardeners' dependants now get a share of the proceeds.

In sixty years The National Gardens Scheme has grown from the seed sown by Miss Wagg to a national charity of consider-able standing and one now able to help many worthwhile causes. But despite its broader charitable face these days, our Founder's great interest in district nurses is still the moving spirit behind all the Gardens Scheme Activities.

From the Scheme's earliest days its Committee and the County Organizers have been energetic in seeking publicity for the garden openings and the support of other organizations, and both have been freely given, perhaps because it was for 'the nurses'. In early days, it appears, newspapers and magazines had to be encouraged to regard garden openings as news-worthy, but gradually this came to be accepted as the interest in gardening and garden visiting took off.

The A.A. and R.A.C. played an early part in the success story and while their patrols still used motor bikes they could always produce from their side-cars a Gardens Scheme guide. The Royal Horticultural Society has supported the Scheme from its earliest years, so too has *Country Life*, and from 1932 to 1939 it published an illustrated guide book for the Scheme with a foreword by Christopher Hussey. The guide books produced by the Scheme from 1940 to 1948 were strictly economy-style, but in 1949 the book started to appear in the now-familiar yellow cover. Never in the whole history of the Scheme has a garden owner been taken for granted; each year the County Organizers update the information and the book is compiled afresh. To get the new book out on time is a challenge for everyone concerned, 'rather like climbing Mount Everest in a hurry'!

There have inevitably been changes in the type of garden open under the scheme; in the pre-war era it was the larger gardens, generally of three or more acres, which were the mainstay of the Scheme – often gardens surrounding castles, manors and great halls. Today, while there are still many 'grand' gardens opening for the Scheme – including nearly fifty of that first six hundred opened in 1927 – the backbone of the scheme is now formed by the small to medium-sized garden; and yet the addition of small and even really tiny gardens, far from being a drawback, has increased the Scheme's popularity, maybe because people can relate to them more easily.

But no matter what the size of garden, large or small, the message is the same as it has been over the past sixty years: throughout the length and breadth of this country there are generous-hearted people who not only love their gardens, but are willing to share them; they invite us into their private world by displaying a yellow poster which states quite simply 'Garden Open Today'.

Miss Rachel Crawshay MBE

Rachel Crawshay was appointed Organizing Secretary of the National Gardens Scheme in 1956. She devoted the whole of her professional and private life to the furtherance of the Scheme which flourished under her direction. Many tributes were paid to her during twenty-seven years of dedicated service and Council bestowed its greatest honour on Rachel Crawshay on her retirement in 1983 when she became a Vice-President of the National Gardens Scheme.

C.H.

Editors' note:

This book is designed to be read in conjunction with the 'Yellow Book' (*Gardens of England and Wales*) published annually by The National Gardens Scheme. Dates and times of opening, which vary from year to year, will be found in the annual book, and have been deliberately omitted from the main body of this book in the hope that it will thus remain a useful reference work for many years. Full directions for reaching each garden will also be found in the 'Yellow Book', and their general location only is given here; the sketch maps are designed to enable the reader to see at a glance the concentration of gardens in selected areas, and due to the large number of gardens to be mapped one number will sometimes mark the position of several gardens in close juxtaposition.

The majority of descriptions in this book have been forwarded to us by the owners of the gardens themselves (thus accounting for the variety of styles) and we have made as little alteration as possible; we hope that, like us, you will enjoy reading their accounts of the often gruelling work involved in creating and maintaining a garden, and of the pleasure with which one is rewarded when a colour scheme is successful or a favourite plant flourishes. The point most frequently made by owners, however, is that the greatest joy comes from sharing their gardens with other people; we hope that you will be one of them!

Alison and Martyn Rix

Please note:

Those gardens marked with an asterisk were the original ones opening for the Scheme in 1927. Where a 'National Collection' of plants is mentioned, this refers to a scheme organized by the National Council for the Conservation of Plants and Gardens (NCCPG) which may be contacted c/o The Royal Horticultural Society, RHS Garden, Wisley, Nr Woking, Surrey.

The Editors would like to thank the following people for their valuable advice and assistance in the preparation of this book:

The garden owners, for their descriptions
The NGS County Organisers for their help and encouragement at all stages of the book
The staff of the National Gardens Scheme, particularly Mrs Amanda France and Miss Fiona Macleod
Miss Rachel Crawshay, for her knowledge of so many gardens
Mrs Carolyn Hardy, Chairman of Council, The National Gardens Scheme
Beverley Behrens, for so patiently typing much of the book
Val Biro, for permission to reproduce the line drawings, originally used as covers of the NGS annual book
Christopher and Prunella Scarlett, for their encouragement
Eleo Gordon, Judy Gordon and Clare Harington of Viking
Bob Vickers for assisting in the design of the book

Photographs

The majority of photographs reproduced in this book were taken by Jacqui Hurst; in addition the following people have kindly donated pictures:

Jonathan Clark
Roger Phillips
Charles Quest-Ritson

We should also like to thank Norman Parkinson for permission to reproduce the photograph of Her Majesty Queen Elizabeth the Queen Mother on the frontispiece.

Previous spread: **Frogmore Gardens, Windsor Castle. The gardens are described on page 28. By gracious permission of Her Majesty The Queen.**

AVON

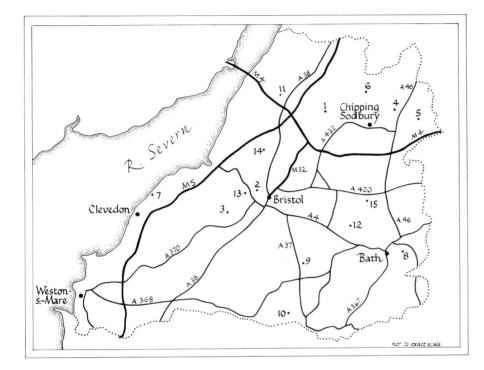

not to exact scale

Directions to Gardens

Algars Manor and Algars Mill, Iron Acton, 9 miles north of Bristol, 3 miles from Yate Sodbury. [1]

45 Canynge Road, Clifton, Bristol, near Bristol Zoo. [2]

Church Farm, Lower Failand, 6 miles southwest of Bristol. [3]

Cox's Hill House, Horton, 2½ miles northeast of Chipping Sodbury. [4]

Essex House, Badminton, 5 miles east of Chipping Sodbury. [5]

Goldney Hall, Lower Clifton Hill, Bristol, at top of Constitution Hill, Bristol. [2]

Hill House, Wickwar, 4 miles north of Chipping Sodbury. [6]

The Manor House, Walton-in-Gordano, 2 miles northeast of Clevedon. [7]

Orchard House, Claverton, 3½ miles east of Bath. [8]

Parsonage Farm, Publow, 9 miles south of Bristol. [9]

Pear Tree House, Litton, 15 miles south of Bristol, 7 miles north of Wells. [10]

Severn View, Grovesend, 1½ miles east of Thornbury, north of Bristol. [11]

Springfield Barn, Upton Cheyney, Bitton, 5 miles northwest of Bath, 8 miles southeast of Bristol. [12]

University of Bristol Botanic Garden, Bracken Hill, North Road, Leigh Woods, 2 miles west of Bristol. [13]

Vine House, Henbury, 4 miles north of Bristol. [14]

Wick Manor, Wick, 5 miles northwest of Bath. [15]

◆

Algars Manor, Iron Acton

DR AND MRS JOHN M. NAISH

The manor house is built on a rocky outcrop above the valley of the River Frome and the mill house spans the mill stream. The garden north of the house features two lawns, one of which is partly enclosed by a red pennant wall. A hundred-year-old weeping lime, a *Cedrus atlantica glauca* and a massive *Robinia* dominate the main lawn, while an eighty-foot balsam poplar, only thirty years old, occupies a corner of the walled garden. Other notable plants in this area are a well grown *Poncirus trifoliata*, very large specimens of *Acer pensylvanicum*, *Cornus mas* and *Viburnum × bodnantense*.

Leading from the walled garden, by mill-stone steps, is a circular path through a two-acre oak wood planted during the last thirty years with rhododendrons, camellias, eucalyptus and magnolias. The bank of the mill-stream has clumps of bamboo and dogwood as well as two secluded lawn-like areas. There are two rustic wooden bridges, one of which leads to a river garden, which in spring is thick with daffodils, and which has, as its centrepiece, a large pond connecting the mill-stream with the main river. Here there are many different types of willow as well as two stately scarlet oaks. On the steep north bank of the millstream is the magnolia walk where twelve different cultivars are planted, the largest of which is *Magnolia kobus borealis*, thirty-foot tall and forty-foot in span.

◆

Algars Mill

MR AND MRS J. WRIGHT

Algars Mill garden, over the road from Algars Manor, has been more recently developed from old woodland. The red stone walls, a bridge, the tail-race emerging from under the mill house and the banks of the river fill the garden with interest, while in the mill itself visitors can inspect old milling equipment and copies of ancient miller's accounts.

As well as a great variety of wild flowers, the winding walks offer, as one visitor put it, a 'surprise round every corner'. To encourage wild flowers the owners offer this advice: don't be too tidy!

◆

45 Canynge Road, Clifton

JOHN AND GEORGIANA NYE

The main features of this small garden of a Victorian town house are the mature mulberry tree and a yew hedge. Until the recent changes its lines were severely rectangular, with a central straight flagged path and narrow flower beds. In the new design the yew hedge has been used as a background for a semi-circular pond, in which stands a lead statue of Mercury; a weeping willow surveys it from a discreet distance. The path has been made winding and more functional, and the borders shaped to billow in more ample curves. The plan has been influenced by the fact that the main window of the house looks out from well above the garden level. The planting is intended to be labour-saving and consists mostly of shrubs, including a variety of hydrangeas and *Pieris forrestii* with alstroemerias prominent in July. We prefer blues and yellows, and try to avoid harsh colours; one of our favourite combinations is that of bluebells and astilbes. In late summer nets are laid out to help collect the abundant falling mulberries.

---◆---

Church Farm, Lower Failand
MR AND MRS N. SLADE

Church Farm was purchased by us in 1975. It is a smallholding of about two-and-a-half acres, previously worked as a market garden for some years but latterly neglected, and there were many old apple and plum trees. The site is slightly north-facing with extensive views across the Bristol Channel to Wales.

For the last five years the garden has been worked on organic lines with a large vegetable garden on the raised-bed system. A new orchard of dwarf and semi-dwarf top fruit is now well established, and there are various outbuildings for poultry and pigs. It is, therefore, a 'working' garden, but much of our time and energy has been put into the development of shrub and herbaceous borders and plantings of interesting trees such as *Metasequoia glyptostroboides, Gingko biloba*, and *Cytisus battandieri* which are already semi-mature. The soil is almost neutral, so that by raising up some beds and by the addition of large amounts of lime-free compost, many ericaceous plants are doing well. There is a small water-garden which at the moment is being extended. We think that the large number of visitors who came last year (our first opening for the National Gardens Scheme), reflects a growing public interest in organic methods and in a smallholding run on semi-self-sufficient lines.

Algars Manor, Iron Acton, in May. Part of the oak wood with rhododendrons, bluebells and young male ferns (*Dryopteris filix-mas*). For a description of this garden see previous page.

Cox's Hill House, Horton
MR AND MRS I.R. DUNKERLEY

Requiem for a gardener . . . and a dog
Come on John, let's walk round the garden. Come on, Trampas – good boy. Under the yew tree to the Little Garden, peaceful and serene, guarded on the north bank by the tall Leylandii, and open to the south across the fields to the Manor. Along the drive and under the towering wall, its foot ablaze with *Aubrieta*, tulips and wallflowers, to the shrubbery and the wood behind. This is our 'shop window', open to the road for all to see.

Up the steps and across the terrace to the Top Garden, the lawn sloping steeply up to Widden. Just listen to the birds! This is where the gifts of love and friendship are – the paeonies from my mother's garden, my husband's camellias, a friend's lilies, the weeping pear from a lorry driver, the rhododendrons bought with prize money from the Village Hall draw, the 'Esther Reed' your father gave me when he was gardener at the Hall. You have tended them all, John, with Trampas at your side.

You chose the pink 'Ralph Tizzard' roses and 'Clara Butt' tulips – I chose the yellow 'Malmesbury' (my husband's mother came from Malmesbury) and the Appledoorns. Up now to the herbaceous border, ninety-three feet long and 'as good as any stately home' you said. Look at the view! It still takes my breath away, even after twenty years.

Go with gratitude, John, through the top gate and the wood to whatever lies beyond. Trampas left before you – if you see him give him a pat from me. You leave me my garden, the kiss of the sun, the song of the birds!

Essex House, Badminton
MR AND MRS JAMES LEES-MILNE

This is not a garden for all seasons. Within half an acre, a large part of which is dominated by three ancient cedars of Lebanon, there is no room for much in the way of autumn- and winter-flowering trees and shrubs; anyway I like to concentrate on spring and summer. True, there are the autumn-flowering *Cyclamen* which have at last established themselves under the cedars, a fine bush of *Lonicera×purpusii*, *Clematis balearica* on the house, and two winter-flowering *Prunus subhirtella* 'Autumnalis' – not much to boast about.

I started remaking the garden in 1976. I brought with me from a former garden several clipped box bushes which, with others added at strategic points, plus a lot of box edging, give a certain form which I find most necessary. There are many old shrub roses underplanted with perennials, alliums and hostas. I fear I belong to the cramming brigade, and cannot resist an interesting plant. As the garden is so small I have had to resort to standards. Two *Euonymus radicans* 'Silver Queen' flanking some steps have been a great success. Then there are several standard roses, 'Little White Pet', 'Iceberg', 'The Fairy' and, best of all, a newish rose called 'Pearl Drift'. *Clematis* do well and in late summer, 'Perle d'Azur' and many Viticellas abound. *Clematis* 'Minuet' has taken over a large *Rosa glauca (rubrifolia)* which seems a good combination.

There are a few stone troughs and many large terracotta pots, some planted with lilies or just clipped box, others with annuals and some with spring bulbs.

With only casual untrained help it is increasingly difficult to do what one would like, but if I am able to keep it reasonably tidy and weed free, it helps the general effect. There is quite a lot of grass and on days when this gets mown the whole place looks quite different.

There is no doubt that more than half my time is spent 'house-maiding' in the garden, clipping, staking, tying-up and weeding; the jungle is all too ready to take over.

---◆---

Goldney Hall, Lower Clifton Hill, Bristol
UNIVERSITY OF BRISTOL

Goldney gardens are a fine example of a mid-eighteenth-century garden of nine acres. Laid out in the 1730–1770s by Thomas Goldney II, the original extent of the gardens has been diminished by sales of land, but many of the features remain, including a newly restored parterre. The Orangery, facing the parterre, is clad with *Wisteria* which is spectacular in early May. A small part of the garden has been set aside for cultivating plants typical of the eighteenth century. There is a grand terrace – with views over Bristol and the floating harbour – a yew-tree walk, and several mature trees, some planted by Goldney himself. Statues of Hercules and 'the Old Quaker', a waterpool (known by Goldney as the canal), a tower, and the famous Goldney Grotto are prominent features.

◆

Hill House, Wickwar
SALLY, DUCHESS OF WESTMINSTER

I moved here from Cheshire sixteen seasons ago. I fell in love with it really because of the obvious potentialities of the garden – neutral soil, a long length of Cotswold stone wall facing south-west, and the five acres furbished with mature eighteenth-century trees, including several cedars, and the tallest *Ailanthus* ever which throws out hordes of babies – pleasing my gardening friends. By a well-placed weeping birch I have put four eighteenth-century columns from Verona, thus dividing the lawns of the garden from the rough wild grass areas which have mown paths only. There is a large *Pinus ponderosa*, a beautiful spreading copper beech, a very tall holly of interesting variegation, and many other specimens – in fact a great inheritance forming the 'bones' of the garden.

The big drawback is that the whole area is completely flat and narrowish in length, so I have had to be rather crafty with block planting to enforce my friends to wander through jungles, round obstacles and emerge to find surprises in secret corners. A pleached red-twigged lime walk provides much-needed height, and this leads to a gold and silver planted 'promenade' – that is an area of gold and silver trees and shrubs and a certain amount of ground cover planted in strips of golden gravel. Here *Lonicera* × *tellmanniana* has obligingly climbed into a silver poplar and a fascinating dwarf *Cryptomeria japonica* which I had to battle for from a nursery in Devizes, shows itself off alongside. A golden bay which has survived some nasty winters, a silver weeping pear with a purple *Clematis viticella* running through its beautiful foliage, and a pine which glows in the winter months but turns green in the summer, with a carpet of chrysanthemums underneath, all help to fascinate throughout the year.

I have learned to be keen on the wild flowers of the countryside and have a varied collection of seed packets called 'The Farmer's Nightmare', among them tall flowering grasses, poppies, moon daisies and cornflowers, and I cheat a little by adding blue English *Iris* and a selection of cranesbills, *Linum* and the tall local *Campanula*. Love-in-a-mist thrives too.

Roses such as 'Rambling Rector', 'Mrs Henry Dyson', 'Francis E. Lester' and 'New Dawn' swarm up a couple of mulberries and old pear and apple trees. Perhaps my favourite trees are a *Ptelea trifoliata* 'Aurea', a good-sized *Sorbus* 'Mitchellii' alongside a variegated tulip tree, and a dancing *Cornus controversa* 'Variegata' with the grey form of *Buddleja alternifolia*. I have been careful to plant sweet-smelling *Philadelphus*, *Elaeagnus*

Box-edged beds and a formal pool at Goldney Hall, Bristol, in May.

umbellata, various lilies and that pretty *Dianthus*, 'Rainbow Loveliness' at corners where everyone has to pass. This again is a bit of a cheat because people get exaggerated ideas of how very specially the garden here is perfumed!

But what fun and interest it is, isn't it, to so many of us, those who work like peasants, and those who visit and admire?

◆

The Manor House, Walton-in-Gordano
MRS PHILIPPA WILLS

The present owners bought the property in 1976 and since then have planted a garden of interesting and unusual plants, ranging from trees and shrubs to the smallest alpines in troughs and raised beds. An old tennis court has been transformed into a fragrant garden which has four small, formal ponds, two of which have plants growing in them (one with fish), whilst the remaining two have been designed to take fountains.

This is a garden for the enthusiast, and as it is newly-planted with much still in the planning stage, there will be changes and developments for years to come. Despite the interest in the unusual, every attempt has been made to ensure that the whole is pleasing to the eye and careful colour schemes have been adhered to, such as pinks, blues and some white in the fragrant garden, which gives a cool and soothing atmosphere. Some of the most satisfactory planting has been achieved using shrubs and perennial plants in mixed borders. In June *Gleditsia triacanthos* 'Sunburst' with the emergent *Eremurus bungei* beneath the branches, and *Tradescantia* in the foreground is particularly attractive. There is a multitude of colour in the spring, with many bulbs. The summer is rich with the scent of *Philadelphus* and *Dianthus* and later the *Nicotiana* adds its fragrance to the evenings. Many *Clematis* and climbing roses have recently been added to grow up the large old yew trees and the established conifers. The bright autumn colour of *Parrotia persica*, *Liquidambar styraciflua*, acers and *Prunus* add much to the dying year, as do the leaves of a very large London plane which is now over a hundred feet tall, with a girth of twenty feet! Our visitors comment on the peace and tranquillity of this garden.

Orchard House, Claverton
REAR-ADMIRAL AND MRS HUGH TRACY

The garden at Orchard House can best be described as a combination of informal smaller gardens of differing character. It has evolved during the last twenty years from a need to provide a wide range of habitats, thus enabling many different kinds of plants to be accommodated, whilst remaining visually attractive. The plant collection is the result partly of that compulsion which so many gardeners feel when a plant new to them is on offer, partly of the wonderful generosity of other gardeners, and partly of plant collecting abroad.

The underlying idea in laying out the various beds has been to use foliage colour and contrast for restful and long-lasting effect, with flowers providing seasonal colour; autumn and winter borders near the house are a constant pleasure during the 'off' season.

Alpines and herbs are major constituents of

the plantings and these, with miniature and scented pelargoniums, are the main products of the small nursery (wholesale except when plants are sold in aid of charity on open days) which helps to meet garden expenses.

A large rock garden, with screes, peat beds and a small 'bog' is a main feature. Using rock in a fairly big way has shown how useful it is in modifying the soil 'climate'. Not only can it be used to protect plants and raise the soil temperature in winter, but it can also create that apparently anomalous situation, a well-drained soil that does not dry out! If you plant daphnes, for example, in a well-drained place and then arrange some flat rocks over the rooting area, you are likely to find that they survive both drought and winter wet.

Parsonage Farm, Publow
MR AND MRS ANDREW REID

This three-and-a-half-acre garden has been totally created since the thirties, and therefore has many interesting rare and mature trees and shrubs in it. It lies on a south-facing slope falling away from a Somerset farmhouse.

To the west of the house the soil is neutral to acid, and in this woodland area there are rhododendrons, azaleas, camellias, liquidambars and other acid-loving shrubs and plants, while to the east of the house, as is typical of the area, the soil is truly alkaline and includes one small area of special interest – a tufa rock garden.

A stream trickles down near a sheltered golden *Catalpa*, a mature *Metasequoia*, and Californian redwoods, near to which are planted ferns, hostas, Himalayan blue poppies, astilbes and hellebores. The paths zigzag down the slope and there are frequent changes of scene, from woodland to bog

garden, then shady stream with its banks covered with many varieties of *Primula*, then up through the birch wood area underplanted with spring bulbs to an open paddock area before arriving at the rockery and winter-flowering heather garden.

It is a plantsman's garden, at its best in spring, with many varieties of snowdrops, ferns, hellebores, and saxifrages including bergenias, and tiarellas. The garden is still developing, and people who return after previous visits are always interested in 'what next' is happening at Parsonage Farm. Inevitably while developing new areas we are always conscious of keeping maintenance down to a minimum by using interesting ground cover plants; in the acid woodland area *Montia sibirica* carries out this function while near the redwood we have used white foxgloves, and further on varieties of *Epimedium* and callunas.

Pear Tree House, Litton
MR AND MRS JOHN SOUTHWELL

Since 1964, we have been able to extend our original derelict quarter-acre garden by purchasing at different times small sections of the adjoining fields, so that now a garden of three acres showing varying stages of development can be seen. The site slopes gently to the west and is three hundred and fifty feet above sea level, on the foothills of the Mendips. The soil is neutral, and the main problems are waterlogged winter conditions, and late frosts flowing down the coombe.

Advantage has been taken of the length of the garden to provide a succession of small 'gardens' of contrasting character, ranging from woodland to large circular lawns, shrubbery gardens, a cottage flower garden, small orchard, a garden of giant grasses, and three ponds, one of which is eighty-foot long with a bridge. The principal feature of the garden is its display of several small collections of trees and shrubs: over fifty species of holly, twenty-five of *Acer*, several birches, and smaller collections of different nuts, chestnuts, walnuts, and a half-acre devoted to conifers. This 'pinetum' is, perhaps, the most unusual feature, as one seldom finds collected together such lovely specimens of *Pinus*, *Picea*, *Abies*, and so on – now well on their way to becoming mature trees – in small private gardens.

Severn View, Grovesend
MR AND MRS ERIC HILTON

This garden, an acre in extent, is devoted particularly to the growing of alpine and other dwarf plants, but there is also space given to herbaceous borders, shrubs and ornamental and fruit trees.

Situated on the edge of the Cotswolds with a limestone quarry only half a mile away, the

Orchard House, Claverton. A mixed border in May, with the contrasting colours and shapes of conifers and the red *Acer palmatum*, and a large *Viburnum* in the foreground.

pH of the native soil is 8.2 which favours the growing of a wide range of lime-loving plants. Provision is also made for those which prefer acid soil, and there are four areas where peat and lime-free loam have been extensively used to accommodate them. In addition there are raised beds, troughs and other types of containers which enable plants which demand special care to be grown.

Plants from the western American mountains feature prominently in the garden. A wide range of lewisias is grown, and in May the wonderful *Lewisia tweedyi* can be seen in various troughs which are later covered to simulate the dry summer conditions of its native habitat. Many species of *Penstemon, Erigeron, Townsendia, Aquilegia, Oenothera, Dodecatheon, Trillium, Erythronium* and *Brodiaea* are prominent in season, and the mat-forming phloxes create vivid splashes of colour. *Sanguinaria canadensis* is grown in both its single and double forms, and *Iris innominata, Smilacina racemosa, Viola pedata, Papaver kluanense, Hymenoxis grandiflora, Uvularia grandiflora, Primula ellisiae* and *P. rusbyi* are all well established.

The aim is to grow as wide a range of plants as possible, and every continent is well represented. There is a great assortment of saxifrages, and ramondas and haberlias enjoy the shadier positions. There are many types of *Genista, Cytisus, Daphne, Potentilla, Dianthus, Campanula, Gentiana* and *Primula*, and in spring and autumn there is a good display of dwarf bulbs.

Springfield Barn, Upton Cheyney
MR AND MRS H. JOSEPH WOODS

When the owners acquired this property in 1958, it consisted of a stable, drayshed, pigsty and yard, together with about one acre of ground, then being used as pasture for heifers and pigs. The only trees on the site were eight elms, six on the eastern and two on the southern boundaries (which have now all been felled as a result of elm disease), two sycamores by the turning space, and two 'Warner's King' apple trees. A further quarter-acre or so was acquired at the east side of what is now the house in about 1970; prior to this date it was rented and growth was kept down by a goat.

The lay-out of the garden now takes advantage of the small spring which enters the north of the garden; this was formerly piped roughly down the centre of the site, serving a tank used to supply water to the nearby Meadow Farm. The pipe was opened up to form cascades and a pool where moisture-loving and water plants thrive. Whilst there is a certain formality in the design close to the house and along the footpath to a small terrace, the general style and planting are quite informal, to give – as far as possible – a natural appearance. Primarily for labour-saving reasons (all planted areas are maintained solely by the owners), the main emphasis is on perennial plants and shrubs with those at

Purple-flowered *Ramonda nathaliae*, from gorges in southern Yugoslavia and northern Greece, flowering at Severn View in May. The four-petalled flowers are characteristic of this rare alpine.

their best during the winter months sited where they can be enjoyed most comfortably. Thus the garden is never a complete 'riot of colour', but the interest changes almost imperceptibly from one area to another, those areas without flower colour relying on form, texture or leaf colour for their interest.

The garden now contains some six hundred kinds of different species and genera without resorting to the truly exotic (and therefore more tender) species, a large number of which have been propagated from cuttings or seed obtained from the Royal Horticultural Society seed distribution, from the wild and from other sources. Some came from the Grange, Bitton, one of the gardens associated with Canon Ellacombe, the famous late nineteenth-century horticulturist; these include *Akebia quinata, Olearia virgata, Peltiphyllum peltatum, Rosa* 'Veilchenblau', *Crinum powellii* and *Miscanthus zebrinus*. Examples of propagation from seed include *Paulownia fargesii, Decaisnea fargesii, Gleditsia triacanthos, Callistemon rigidus, Hoheria lyallii, Cytisus battandieri, Indigofera gerardiana, Lysichitum americanum, Smilacina racemosa, Celastrus orbiculatus*, and several *Sorbus, Rosa, Helianthemum* and *Primula* species.

On the question of maintenance in the years to come, the owners, realizing the limitations that increasing age will bring, are already embarking on a gradual process of replanting, using those plants which will need less intensive labour, at the same time hopefully keeping it attractive in appearance.

University of Bristol Botanic Garden, Bracken Hill
CURATOR, DR D. GLEDHILL

Since the function of this garden is to encourage education and research in all aspects of plant life, the visitor should expect not only to find something new at each visit but also to be provided with new insights into plants – beyond the mere beauty of their flowers.

Formerly the home of Walter Melville Wills, and given to the University by his son, Capt. R. M. D. Wills in 1947, Bracken Hill became the third University Botanic Garden when the second site was relinquished in 1959. The grounds surrounding the Victorian house were landscaped at the end of the last century and have mature trees, various ponds and 'Pulhamite' rockeries. Recent planting has aimed at increasing the diversity of subjects, to show both botanical and horticultural themes.

The glasshouses contain collections of bromeliads, orchids, ferns and succulents, but also attempt to continue the theme of displaying plant diversity. The nursery area contains various ecological and systematic collections as well as changing displays of useful and ornamental plants.

Vine House, Henbury
PROFESSOR AND MRS T.F. HEWER

This two-acre garden within Bristol city boundary fortunately backs on to the woodland of the large Blaise estate landscaped by Repton. We, the present owners, have planted and developed it completely since 1946. We started by reducing almost the whole area to brown earth, thereby eliminating ground elder and worthless trees and shrubs. In planning the garden we marshalled sticks surmounted by caps of white paper as though they were the trees and shrubs that we then acquired. In part these produced a glade effect interplanted with bulbs and *Cyclamen* and other small plants, making the garden look as natural as possible with few flower beds and no bedding out. The soil is on the alkaline side of neutral.

To the north of the glade the ground falls steeply to Hazel Brook, and we built a pond near the top of the slope in a carefully constructed little valley supplied with water pumped up from a well which was then allowed to flow down a small artificial watercourse to a minute pond and a damp shallow valley.

There are rocky areas and a cliff of conglomerate facing north above a steep slope shaded by two large ancient yews.

By restricting our choice of subjects as far as possible to species (most of them labelled), we now have what amounts to a small arboretum and botanical collection; the result is in large part a wild garden. Some of the trees are rare and of interest, the age of all of them being known. The two varieties of *Davidia*, a sixty-foot *Metasequoia* and a pendulous *Picea omorika* are noteworthy. There is a collection of herbaceous and hybrid tree paeonies, and a plantation of large *Hydrangea sargentiana* with other lace-cap hydrangeas and an *Aesculus parviflora* are specially valuable in August.

Pear Tree House in October. The calm water of the pond reflects the autumn colour and contrasting shapes of *Cornus alba* 'Sibirica', the red dogwood, *Salix caprea* 'Pendula', the Kilmarnock willow, grey *Salix exigua* and grasses. For a description of this garden see page 16.

Wick Manor, Wick
MR AND MRS KENNETH BISHOP

An eighteenth-century folly is an unusual feature in our two acres of formal garden, where high stone walls enclose lawns and over two hundred feet of mixed borders. The views, across the long pond, beyond the old yew, and over the ha-ha, extend uninterruptedly to the hills on the edge of Bath. Beyond this garden we are creating a nine-acre park, by keeping mown the old pastureland surrounding our house. In 1983 we planted a hundred and ninety-one trees representing sixty species, and these are of continuing interest to our visitors. We are also proud of our avenue of pink chestnuts leading down to the River Boyd on the edge of our land.

Other specimen trees include wellingtonia (*Sequoiadendron gigantium*), Indian bean tree (*Catalpa*) and Swedish whitebeam (*Sorbus intermedia*). This means that there is colour and interest from March when the native trees bloom until the frosts of October when the various autumn coloured leaves fall. Greenhouses, cold frames and vegetable garden are worth a visit, and we are presently potting up daturas and miniature orange trees. A useful tip we can pass on is to try Duraglit on plastic plant labels for removing pencil labelling.

BEDFORDSHIRE
AND BUCKINGHAMSHIRE

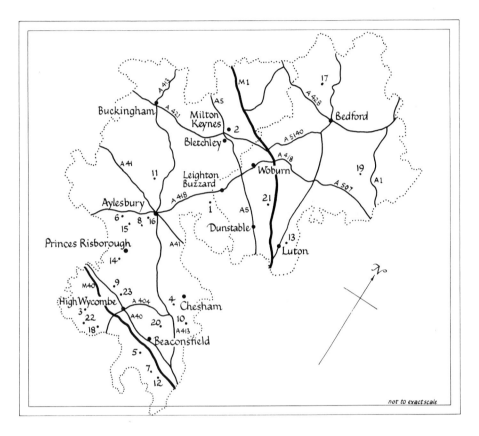

not to exact scale

Directions to Gardens

Ascott, Wing, 2 miles southwest of Leighton Buzzard, 8 miles northeast of Aylesbury, Bucks. [1]

Aspley Guise Gardens, Milton Keynes, 2 miles west of M1 (exit 13), towards Bletchley, Beds. [2]

Barnfield, Northend Common, 7 miles north of Henley-on-Thames, Bucks. [3]

Campden Cottage, 51 Clifton Road, Chesham Bois, north of Amersham, Bucks. [4]

Cliveden, 2 miles north of Taplow, Bucks. [5]

Commoners, Brill, 7 miles north of Thame, Bucks. [6]

Dorneywood Garden, 1½ miles north of Burnham village, Bucks. [7]

59 The Gables, Haddenham, 3 miles north of Thame, Bucks. [8]

Great Barfield, Bradenham, 4 miles northwest of High Wycombe, 4 miles south of Princes Risborough, Bucks. [9]

Harewood, Harewood Road, Chalfont St Giles, Bucks. [10]

26 High Street, Winslow, 10 miles north of Aylesbury, 6 miles south of Buckingham, Bucks. [11]

Little Paston, Common Road, Fulmer, north of Slough, Bucks. [12]

Luton Hoo Gardens, Luton, entrance at Park Street gates, Beds. [13]

The Manor House, Bledlow, near Princes Risborough, Bucks. [14]

Manor House, Long Crendon, 2 miles north of Thame, Bucks. [15]

Nether Winchendon House, Nether Winchendon, 5 miles southwest of Aylesbury, Bucks. [16]

Odell Castle, Odell, 10 miles northwest of Bedford. [17]

Quoitings, Oxford Road, Marlow, 7 miles east of Henley, 3 miles south of High Wycombe, Bucks. [18]

Southill Park, 5 miles southwest of Biggleswade, Beds. [19]

Spindrift, Jordans, 3 miles northeast of Beaconsfield, Bucks. [20]

Toddington Manor, 1 mile northwest of Toddington, 1 mile from M1 (exit 12), Beds [21].

Turn End, Townside, Haddenham, 3 miles northeast of Thame, Bucks. [8]

Turville Heath House, Turville Heath, 6 miles north of Henley-on-Thames, Bucks. [22]

West Wycombe Park, 3 miles west of High Wycombe, Bucks. [23]

◆

*Ascott, Wing

E. DE ROTHSCHILD, ESQ.; THE NATIONAL TRUST

This garden has formal and informal areas with many specimen trees and shrubs, an unusual topiary, a lily pond and fountains.

◆

Aspley Guise Gardens

Aspley House (MR AND MRS C.I. SKIPPER) is set in five acres in a formal design of lawns, part-terraced, with shrubs and trees.

The Rookery (C.R. RANDELL, ESQ.) consists of five acres of undulating land with a woodland containing various trees, shrubs and rhododendrons. Near the house are rose beds and herbaceous plants, as well as a vegetable garden.

Manor Close (SIR KENNETH AND LADY ALLEN) has a small garden of one and a half acres. The formal part is laid out with rose beds separated by a Lawson's Cypress hedge from the water garden and herbaceous border. On the other side of the house is a small orchard and a shrubbery.

◆

Barnfield, Northend Common

MR AND MRS JOHN ANNAN

In 1964, we were faced with a flat, west-facing field, seven hundred and fifty feet above sea level; the first thing we did was to plant trees and hedges to form vistas and break the site

19

up into different areas. The arrival of four cast iron decorative arches from the demolished Clock Tower Stand at Lord's Cricket Ground made an exciting focal point on which to grow roses and to lead one down a path. We decided that all paths cut through rough grass should be wide enough for at least two people to walk abreast. The house is modern with large sliding windows at ground floor level, so we felt that it was important to have wide borders with shrubs and herbaceous plants to create an interest even when looking out from inside.

Shrub roses mean a great deal to us so they have pride of place; favourites include a hedge of 'Frau Dagmar Hastrup', 'Blanc Double de Coubert' and 'Roseraie de l'Haÿ' which is a great success. We never hoe, so seedlings keep on appearing each year in unexpected places; birds also help us in this way. We never stop experimenting with ground-cover plants to suppress weeds, and an ivy bank and one of *Vinca* (periwinkle) mixed with *Hypericum* have been successful. Now, after twenty-one years, the bare bones are covered and it is a case of cutting back, renewing old friends and introducing new ones. There is always something to look forward to – cherry blossom, and daffodils in the spring, roses in the summer, and even in winter there is always something to pick.

Campden Cottage, Chesham Bois

MRS P. A. LIECHTI

This half-acre garden on heavy alkaline clay has been created, and is maintained entirely by me; although visitors admire the design, my main interest is in plants.

The front gate is flanked by two *Pyrus* 'Chanticleer', and in each front lawn is a huge Christmas pudding-shaped golden yew. The back garden is almost square, dominated centrally by a magnificent weeping ash. This is unfortunately too large for the garden and has caused difficulties in achieving a pleasing design.

I care particularly for good shape, attractive foliage and pleasing plant associations. Some successes include *Artemisia* 'Powis Castle' with *Anthemis tinctoria* 'E. C. Buxton', a purple *Berberis* and *Malva* 'Primley Blue' rambling through them; or a white flowered pea climbing through *Rosa glauca (rubrifolia)*. *Ceanothus impressus* 'Puget Blue' supports *Clematis macropetala* 'White Moth' with *Euphorbia wulfenii* 'Lambrook Gold', *Viburnum carlesii* and a purple sage sprawling over a York stone terrace; a lovely sight in May.

Helleborus atrorubens and *H. cyclophyllus* flower in December, followed by several other species, and later many *H. orientalis* hybrids including a yellow form given by Eric Smith. There are many *Narcissus*, particularly *cyclamineus* hybrids. Numerous daphnes include *D. burkwoodii* 'Somerset', *retusa*, *blagayana*, *bholua*, *neapolitana* and *collina*. I have many hybrid paeonies – bronze fennel looks good behind a double white – and a collection

of species including *P. cambessedesii*, *emodi* and *tenuifolia*. There is a large collection of autumn-flowering plants, many with blue flowers such as salvias, penstemons, and ceratostigmas.

Of the trees, the trunk of *Betula jacquemontii* glistens superbly white, while *Acer davidii* is always eye-catching, as also are a fine *Metasequoia glyptostroboides*, and *Cedrus deodara*, with alternate layers of branches removed. Finally, a well-shaped *Acer griseum* is, in my opinion, the finest tree in my garden.

Cliveden Gardens, Taplow

THE NATIONAL TRUST

The gravel hill top, now famous as the setting for Cliveden, was chosen in the 1660s for its views over the Thames valley. The planting of trees heralded the planning of the early eighteenth-century landscape which now forms the framework for examples of gardening styles as diverse as the huge parterre, on which the grey, clipped foliage of *Santolina incana* and *Senecio* 'Sunshine' contrast with the lawns and box hedges, and the herbaceous borders in the forecourt, on one side the 'hot' reds and yellows, on the other the 'cool' blues and pinks. The rose garden, with shrub roses in beds of a fluid pattern laid out by Sir Geoffrey Jellicoe in 1959, lies to the side of a lime avenue dating from the early 1700s. The long garden with topiary birds and spirals, hedges and beds of *Euonymus fortunei* 'Variegatus', with a wall sheltering *Calycanthus*, *Dipelta*, *Umbellularia*, viburnums etc. differs completely from the water garden, having rockwork, bridges, and plantings of acers, wisterias, magnolias, azaleas and cherries, magnificent in spring and autumn, while the beds contain ground-cover plants and spring bulbs. Enormous golden carp swim under waterlilies and dragonflies dart in the bog bean and iris.

All one hundred and eighty-two acres have variety and surprises, ranging from hanging woods above the river, garden temples, classical sculpture and fountains, to glades with snowdrops, daffodils and bluebells. Grand avenues vie with beautiful collections of wood anemones and lily-of-the-valley. One can enjoy the sombre simplicity of holm oaks informally planted in lawns, or the rich colours of delphiniums, *Phlox*, and *Rudbeckia*, in herbaceous borders arranged much as Gertrude Jekyll would have planted them. Ironically, influences from Italy, France, and Japan have been combined over nearly three centuries to make this an unique and magical English garden.

Commoners, Brill

MR AND MRS R. WICKENDEN

This small property has front and back gardens, with access to one another through the cottage. To one side are farm fields whilst on the other is the sheep-grazed grass of Brill

Common. Against the south wall of the cottage is a paved area with a garden seat. Up the white walls climb the redcurrant-red rose 'Parkdirektor Riggers' and a pinkish-red *Chaenomeles*. This, the front garden, is surrounded by low brick walls with an arched gate covered with clipped *Forsythia*. The garden slopes up from the house, stone steps leading to winding paths through a densely packed flower garden of shrubs, small trees, perennials, annuals and alpines. Near the end of the garden is another paved area where a crab apple (*Malus* 'John Downie') gives shade on summer days. In winter interest is provided by *Prunus Subhirtella* 'Autumnalis', witch hazel (*Hamamelis mollis*) and the red twigs of *Cornus alba* together with *Viburnum × bodnantense* and a *Pyracantha*. *Cyclamen coum*, *Helleborus niger* and heathers brighten the short days and bulbs, anemones and primroses abound in spring.

The back garden has a small lawn edged by a brick path and an old well where *Trollius* and kingcups grow. On the house walls are *Cotoneaster* and summer and winter jasmine. A planted bank leads down to the asparagus bed, which grows into a feathery hedge screening the vegetables – not many, and fewer as the nearby copper beech grows in stature! Finally, behind a bank of sweet briar and *Kerria*, is a small bog garden with *Mimulus*, *Crocosmia* and candelabra primulas.

Dorneywood Garden, Nr Burnham

THE NATIONAL TRUST

The garden here has many different features, including spring bulbs, flowering shrubs, roses, and herbaceous plants. There are many fine specimen trees from all over the world including acers, birches, oaks and *Nothofagus*.

59, The Gables, Haddenham

MRS M. A. JOHNSTONE

I took over the garden (a very dreary one!) in December 1982. Despite its small size (the back measures approximately thirty-five by sixty feet) it now contains a great variety of plants, including many bulbs, some of the more unusual perennials, and smaller varieties in keeping with the size of the garden. There are also shrubs and plenty of decorative foliage plants to provide interest when flowers are scarce. The herbaceous border, which is south-facing, features mainly pink and red colours and has a long season from the early *Paeonia officinalis* through to chrysanthemums, nerines and the pinky-purple berries of *Callicarpa giraldiana*. The fences surrounding the garden are gradually becoming covered with honeysuckles and *Clematis* which help to provide more colour above the level of the borders.

A narrow shady border accommodates a collection of hardy ferns and some cyclamen, and there is a small raised bed for alpines. There is a tiny herb patch, three espalier apples and a plum. Two grape vines grow on the south wall of the house and are joined by climbing French beans and tomatoes in the summer.

I have a large collection of bonsai trees and am experimenting with growing decorative trees and shrubs in pots that can be moved around for additional decoration and screening as required.

There is a small greenhouse and two cold frames for propagation and overwintering slightly tender plants.

A successful innovation in our garden has been to position the children's swing *across* the path where it passes through a fence. *Clematis* species are being trained up the posts to make an arch. The swing itself is hitched out of the way when not in use, and will be removed when outgrown.

Great Barfield, Bradenham
RICHARD NUTT, ESQ.

This one-and-a-half-acre garden, formerly a paddock, has been created, since 1976, on a gentle south-facing slope, on marl with chalk below. It is a plant collector's home. On one side there is a hazelnut hedge, on another a very old mixed hedge, which together with two flint walls help to make up the boundary. At the south end a small young wood has been extended and in it grow snowdrops, trilliums, and lilies, while foxgloves have become naturalized. There are mixed borders, one predominantly winter-flowering, one for species roses, another for old-fashioned roses, and one with herbaceous plants.

There is a wide range of smaller trees, planted for flowers, berry or autumn colour, and mostly numerous uncommon shrubs with a large selection of viburnums. For interest in winter there is a range of green-striped to silver barks, young red shoots, and yellow, red, orange and white-stemmed willows, and underneath a great range of hellebores and pulmonarias. Irises are in flower from October to July; crocuses are planted in drifts at the side of the lawn, and the reddish brown leaves of the bergenias light up in the winter sun.

The garden has matured quickly and parts are replanted as required; shrubs can be too big after five years and may need replacing. The borders of a garden are its framework, but even parts of that are altered, by cutting down trees and opening up new views. Just as the plants grow and leaves change colour so does the effect within the garden during the year.

Harewood Garden, Chalfont St Giles
MR AND MRS JOHN HEYWOOD

This is a one-acre garden which has been extensively replanted and developed by the

owners since 1980. The theme is one of informal planting within the formal structure provided by existing fine Edwardian yew and box hedges. Strident colours are avoided, and certain borders have been planted not so much to be of one colour but instead to achieve colour harmony by total exclusion of one particular colour, such as in one bed, from which yellow is excluded.

The garden has a wealth of climbers including many roses and *Clematis* as well as several substantial wisterias of both white and purple forms. Climbers are often used in combination, growing together to create interesting plant associations; one such successful group is a *Garrya elliptica* clothed with a *Jasminum officinale*, the double white *Clematis* 'Duchess of Edinburgh' and the flame-red-flowered

Chamaenerion angustifolium, rosebay willowherb. The white form of this common weed makes an attractive, if invasive, garden plant.

Tropaeolum speciosum, all of these happily growing on a north wall of the house. Another happy outcome is the blue-flowered *Clematis alpina* 'Frances Rivis' growing amongst a background of the silver leaved pear *Pyrus salicifolia* 'Pendula'.

We have a weakness for primulas and violas, and many varieties are grown, interbreeding enthusiastically to the benefit of variety but to the detriment of purity of line. Many old shrub roses are now becoming established as well as viburnums, daphnes, and other shrubs valued for their fragrance. The garden is framed by a variety of substantial conifers. All climbing and woody plants in the garden are labelled and catalogued with the plant list available to visitors.

26, High Street, Winslow
MR AND MRS DAVID DRAKARD

In shape and history the arrangement of this house and garden is typical of a mediaeval site

in the High Street of any small market town. The west-facing house fronts the street on a narrow but deep plot and on the south side reaches far back into the brick walled garden. In 1973 this garden was little more than a rubble cart track connecting the house and the service lane behind; formless, neglected and overgrown. To break the straight, hard look, the rubble track was replaced by a cobbled and brick path so arranged to disappear and re-appear in the long view of the garden after crossing a small lawn, itself shaped to give width and used as a contrast of surface and texture. In addition, to increase the choice of plants (restricted by light alkaline soil), a small bog area and raised peat bed were formed.

Our aim of never having to be without flower in a garden chiefly of climbers, shrubs and herbaceous plants was achieved by a mixture of deciduous and evergreen flowering shrubs. In the awkward months of late autumn and winter a *Prunus subhirtella* 'Autumnalis' forms a focal point, followed in flowering by the sweetly scented *Chimonanthus praecox*. In February and March come *Hamamelis mollis* and *Garrya elliptica*, this last being grown against the wall of a neighbouring building which forms a third part of the northern boundary. This wall is also used to support shrubs and climbers with flower and foliage held high above the border plants thus extending the limited growing area. In summer, annuals and perennials are allowed to seed on path edges, in cracks and odd corners as well as in borders, and thinned and hand-weeded rather than hoed, give the natural informal look, impossible to match by deliberate planting, of an English garden.

Little Paston, Fulmer
MR D.R. ALLEN

This pleasing garden comprising ten acres of woodland, gardens and lawns lies within the triangle formed by three major roads and is only some fifteen minutes by road from Heathrow Airport. The display of azaleas and rhododendrons in early summer provides a breathtaking blend of colour whilst the variety of conifers, shrubs and trees are of considerable botanical interest. A special feature is the picturesque water garden, several water lily pools linked by a running stream with attractive waterside plants.

Luton Hoo Gardens
THE WERNHER FAMILY

Luton Hoo stands amid a 'Capability' Brown landscape which gives the parkland an abundance of large cedars, oak, ash and beech trees. This in turn provides a mature backdrop for the gardens, which were originally designed at the beginning of the century by Romaine Walker.

Entering the formal gardens on the south side of the mansion, one finds the herbaceous borders, recently replanted with over two thousand new plants. A feature of this area is the pair of large *Magnolia × soulangiana* whose flowers herald the coming of spring. On the lower terrace lies the rose garden consisting of floribunda and hybrid tea varieties in eight large box-edged beds. On the walls are Himalayan musk roses, *Magnolia grandiflora*, *Garrya elliptica* and two fine specimens of *Wisteria sinensis*. Both terraces are surrounded by large yew hedges.

On leaving the rose garden one finds oneself on sweeping lawns which are carpeted with daffodils in the spring – a short walk takes you past a very large *Arbutus menziesii*, to the rock garden, built in the early part of the century by Sir Julius Wernher as a gift for his wife. This part of the garden has a feeling of peace and tranquillity; small ponds run through the centre of it, with water-lilies giving bright summer colours. Many of the dwarf conifers and maples are relics of the original planting, namely large specimens of *Juniperus horizontalis*, *Picea glauca* var. *albertiana* 'Conica' and different forms of *Acer palmatum*.

Extensive reshaping and replanting are now under way. Large scree beds have been planted with *Iris reticulata*, *Saxifraga*, *Sedum*, *Lewisia*, *Phlox*, *Dianthus*, *Delphinium* and *Thymus* to name but a few, and peat walls

with *Erica*, dwarf *Rhododendron*, *Abies*, *Picea* and *Pinus*. The whole garden provides an interesting and peaceful walk for the visitor.

The Manor House, Bledlow
THE LORD AND LADY CARRINGTON

The soil here is uncompromisingly alkaline and, apart from a five-hundred-year-old yew tree, some brick walls and an eighteenth-century granary, the garden had, when we arrived in 1948, no natural features. However, since then yew and beech have grown into magnificent hedges. The yew encloses three gardens: in the first, clipped box and yew within gravel and brick paths surround an astrolabe. A narrow opening leads to box-edged beds of lavender, *Santolina*, *Anaphalis* and dwarf hostas presided over by a statue of St Peter. The third garden is filled with lavender, irises, and white and yellow roses underplanted with *Cerastium*. Beyond there is a golden carpet of *Narcissi* in the old orchard in the spring. Shrubs, including old roses, *Dianthus* and silver-leaved plants, lead to an opening in the beech hedge and the lawn in front of the house. Paeonies and delphiniums thrive in abundance and so does lilac.

To the south of the house, at the end of a

wide gravel path between standard *Viburnum carlesii*, there is a sunken lily pond beneath the granary. On one side there are old roses intertwined in August with *Clematis viticella*. In spring there is a carpet of *Polyanthus* underneath the roses, and in June giant catmint spills on to the path to a white gazebo. On the other side a double row of pleached limes at a higher level lead from the granary through a circular spring garden of lilac, *Choisya*, broom, gentians and *Euphorbia* round to the front of the house.

Manor House, Long Crendon
W.J.M. SHELTON, ESQ.

The lawns of this seventeenth-century house sweep down to a small valley, which once comprised three fish ponds farmed by the monks of Notley Abbey until the dissolution of the monasteries. We started their reclamation and conversion in 1980, and today there are two small lakes, each with an island, while in what was the middle fish pond there is now a swimming pool and croquet lawn, with the changing-rooms hidden beneath another lawn. Many mature trees already grow in the valley and extensive planting has also taken place, including *Metasequoia glyptostroboides*, *Taxodium*, *Liriodendron tulipifera*, *Tilia petio-*

Part of the parterre at the Manor House, Bledlow, in August. The beds are bordered with dwarf box and contain *Hosta crispula*, *Festuca glauca* and *Hosta tokudama*. In the background beds green and golden thyme, *Ruta* 'Jackman's Blue' and *Anaphalis clypeolata* produce different tones and scents.

laris, *Robinia pseudoacacia* 'Frisia' and *Ligustrum lucidum* 'Excelsum superbum'.

Along the walk above the far side of the lower lake we have planted nearly a hundred willows and dogwoods, comprising more than twenty varieties.

The soil surrounding the house is sufficiently acid to support rhododendrons and azaleas, as well as roses and a variety of other shrubs. The soil varies greatly throughout the valley, ranging from rich loam taken from the bottom of the fish ponds to create the islands, to the clay which originally floored the fish ponds. We have planted a water garden at the head of the lower lake, which includes amongst others, *Iris pseudacorus, Caltha palustris* and *Butomus umbellatus*; we also have a small 'white' formal garden above the upper lake. A 'golden' border has been placed at the foot of the main lawn, which is dominated by a superb *Fagus sylvatica purpurea*. There are outstanding views towards the Chilterns.

Nether Winchendon House
MRS J. G. C. SPENCER BERNARD

This is a landscape garden with fairly large lawns and splendid trees, supplemented during the past thirty years by the planting of handsome and unusual trees; these set off the 'Strawberry Hill' gothic of the house and provide fine contrasts among themselves. Of particular interest are *Acer pseudoplatanus* 'Brilliantissimum' in front of a Leylandii hedge; copper beech and *Taxodium distichum* in front of *Salix alba*, and purple hazel against silver birches. Good hedges of green and copper beech, fastigiate beech, *Ilex* and yew define and divide areas of the garden. A limiting factor is the frequent flooding of the lower parts by the river. An avenue of ancient limes had to be removed in 1972 and we replanted with *Metasequoia glyptostroboides*, winning the Buckinghamshire County Council award for tree planting in 1973.

In spring, daffodils follow carpets of snowdrops and winter aconites. Near the house is a terrace with spring and summer bedding and roses specially selected to avoid yellow in their pedigree as a defence against black spot. In a walled area there are paeonies and old-fashioned roses, glorious autumn colours of leaves, hips and berries following the summer display. At all seasons the trees throw lovely shadows across the lawns, while in winter there are enough evergreens to give the garden framework and interest with fresh contrasts of colours, barks and lichens lit by the low sun.

Odell Castle Gardens, Odell
THE RT HON. LORD LUKE

This garden has been restored in the last twenty years, since its present owners, Lord and Lady Luke, have been there. It is really divided into three tiers – the upper terrace round the house, the middle below the wall

Toddington Manor in July. The pleached lime walk is underplanted with roses, bergenias, *Artemisia*, lavender and *Erigeron*. For a description of the garden see page 24.

which supports the terrace, and the long grassy sweep down to the river. Below the terrace facing the river is the rockery.

There are many old trees, such as those bordering the sweep down to the River Ouse and the ring of old chestnuts and beeches, but many like the Judas tree and a mulberry are more recent additions, together with the two *Prunus subhirtella* 'Autumnalis' on the terrace which flower between November and March.

The old kitchen garden now has a path with borders on either side, espalier apple and pear trees and more lawn studded with specimen trees. The old orchard below has a medlar of considerable age and various replacements have been made: a group of apple trees, two walnuts and a weeping lime, *Tilia petiolaris*, which has exquisitely scented blossom, several pink chestnuts, a *Metasequoia glyptostroboides* and a weeping willow.

There are roses all over the garden; round the terrace they are mostly hybrid teas with shrub roses below the wall and three rectangular beds of floribundas. There is a small pond below the terrace which is surrounded by a wooden arbour covered by climbing roses.

There is a mixture of flowering shrubs; viburnums, lilacs and buddlejas, and along the terrace walls are a number of wall plants; in particular two *Clematis montana* 'Elizabeth' with their lovely pink flowers, and a *Cytisus battandieri* whose yellow blooms open in June.

Quoitings, Marlow
MR AND MRS KENNETH BALFOUR

Quoitings is a well-established garden and many alterations in developing the garden's interests have taken place. The site is slightly sloping, facing roughly south-west and backed by a belt of tall mixed trees, some of which are superb limes. The soil is alkaline so does not suit plants of an ericaceous nature.

The four lawns are divided by steps and a ha-ha which give varied levels, and these contours add greatly to the general lay-out. Over recent years many conifers and other evergreens have been introduced adding variety of colour and shape. Near the house there is a magnificent *Liriodendron tulipifera* while on the house itself grows a very healthy pomegranate and a large *Magnolia grandiflora*; this perhaps dates the garden since it was the practice in the eighteenth century to grow magnolias against houses. In early spring a carpet of snowdrops appears, followed by daffodils naturalized in the lawns, colourful tulips and a bed of polyanthus. In summer the bedding plants include salvias, geraniums, fuchsias and heliotrope backed up with a fine selection of colourful shrubs including *Kolkwitzia, Elaeagnus, Philadelphus, Weigela* and various aucubas. Vistas, some furnished with stone ornaments, have been developed within the garden to give depth, and this, together with mature box hedges, all adds up to an interesting English garden.

◆

*Southill Park, Biggleswade
MR AND MRS S.C. WHITBREAD

Southill Park was landscaped for Samuel Whitbread II between 1800 and 1805 by Henry Holland who, by adding a lake and a temple to the north, must have greatly changed the landscape originally created on this side of the house by 'Capability' Brown for the Byng family in 1770.

The main part of the garden lies on the south side of the house, and the lawns stretch down to a ha-ha overlooking a cricket pitch and parkland on the west side. The main walk is lined with rhododendrons and classical statues bought at the closing-down sale at John Cheere's yard in London in 1812. On the right of the walk an old concrete tennis court has been turned into a garden with heathers, polyanthus, *Alchemilla mollis* and other rock-growing plants. Near the Orangery, built in about 1880, there are three herbaceous borders which lead down to a pergola made of round brick pillars and wooden crosspieces; these are covered with climbing and rambling roses. A border of shrubs, mostly coloured purple and grey, leads on the west side to a small kitchen garden and herb garden.

There are a number of magnificent trees in the garden, including two large cedars of Lebanon, three liquidambars and a beech tree which has been layered and has a circumference of a hundred and seventy yards.

◆

Spindrift, Jordans
MR AND MRS ERIC DESMOND

The one-and-a-half-acre garden was begun in 1933 when Spindrift was built. A third of the land slopes into a valley, and this has been terraced to accommodate the vegetable and soft fruit plots. Gravel had at one time been extracted from a seam, leaving a twelve-foot deep, irregular-shaped area which was landscaped with enormous rocks to form a sunken garden with a pear-shaped pond. Over one hundred mature trees, including a fine *Cedrus deodara*, and *Liquidambar styraciflua*, together with Japanese larches, spruce and other conifers, provide an interesting backdrop to the planting, while a large *Quercus borealis* stands by the gate. The herbaceous border is a joy during July and August when the many varieties of plants are seen to advantage against a good holly hedge. In summer fifty terrace pots introduce interesting colours to various parts of the garden. In addition, many unusual foliage plants and shrubs, some of them variegated, are used for their outdoor and indoor decorative value. During the growing season up to forty varieties of vegetable are cultivated and in the greenhouses vines, melons, peppers, aubergines and tomatoes can be seen.

Interest is provided during the winter and spring by winter-flowering shrubs and snowdrops, crocuses and daffodils.

◆

Toddington Manor, Toddington
SIR NEVILLE AND LADY BOWMAN-SHAW

We moved here in August 1979. The house had been to a large extent unlived-in for thirty years and the garden had been neglected for at least ten of them. Getting our priorities in order we completely rebuilt the derelict greenhouses! We inherited marvellous trees – limes, beeches and wellingtonias – a stream running through the garden, crumbling walled garden, ponds and lakes, plus a large jungle. With the help of bulldozers, loyal friends and willpower, we discovered a lovely old path running the length of the garden, now a pleached lime walk, two other smaller paths and very little else.

Now, six years later, we have a fully planted (and constantly added to), marvellously established-looking garden. The old rose garden has been reinstated with a yellow and white theme carried into the surrounding three large borders. The stream is a mixture of bluebells, Solomon's seal, snowdrops, primroses and primulas. Our 'friends bed', all gifts, includes the rose 'Nevada', white *Buddleja*, lavender and *Potentilla*. In the woods an area has been planted with rhododendrons and azaleas and on the islands is a mixture of shrub roses, *Gunnera*, *Forsythia*, *Viburnum*, *Amelanchier* and hydrangeas.

Because of massive costs we have not included many very rare or delicate plants – just a profusion of all the old favourites – but have planned the colour combination and long-term effect very carefully. In the greenhouses we do keep some rarer species and we have a house full of plants all the year round. The herb garden, nut walk and wild garden are new projects. In front of the house we have a cricket pitch which is used for many charity matches and we also have a Rare Breeds Centre for cattle, sheep and goats.

◆

Turn End, Townside
MR PETER ALDINGTON

This is an architect's garden, designed and made by its owners and their family.

It started with the award-winning house, one of a group of three which the owners designed and built for themselves in the 1960s. The first garden was an 'outdoor room', a courtyard enclosed on three sides by the house, and the fourth by an existing wall. It contains a paved area, an *Acacia* tree and a pool. After this a long grass glade was formed, curving diagonally across the site, its shape determined by the fine mature chestnut, walnut, holmoak and *Sequoia* trees.

Beneath these and some old apple trees are spring bulbs, shrub roses and shade-loving plants. The glade is linked to the house by stone paths and steps, near which the fine-barked birches, *Betula albo-sinensis* and *B. jacquemontii*, provide winter interest. We always plant trees with peeling bark so that they are predominantly seen against the light! The house wall on this side is smothered with a large honeysuckle, *Lonicera etrusca* 'Superba', the little seen *Prunus mume* 'Beni-shidon' and a yellow banksian rose.

As the garden has developed through the years, the glade has become a central element connecting a number of smaller, more formal gardens. Among these are the octagonal sunken 'daisy' garden backed by an old coach house; a small walled area with box-edged beds filled with annuals; a tiny court near the house with an old Pyrenean olive jar as its dominant feature, and the recently made raised bed area containing troughs of alpines, an alpine bed and a host of sun-loving plants, many with grey leaves and flowers of pastel colours.

This garden is little more than an acre in extent but, like the house it grew from, it feels much larger than it is.

◆

Turville Heath House, Henley-on-Thames
MRS T.A. BIRD

We took over this two-acre garden in 1975. It had the advantage of many fine trees on its border with the large estate next door and a number of big shrubs and high, ancient hedges, but in the main it was neglected and in serious decay. The improvements have taken years, and include replanting all the borders, mending the lily pool and putting many plants in and around it to make it a central feature; we have also added a fountain and a statue of a heron. New features we have introduced are a long rose trellis backing the main border, an azalea bed and, at the very end of the garden, groups of large specimen shrub roses, of *Hydrangea sargentiana* and of *Kalmia latifolia*. The soil is mildly acidic – azaleas flourish, but *Kalmia*, *Pieris*, *Pachysandra* and *Skimmia* need special treatment. We try to provide the borders with contrasting foliage (lime-green, sulphur-yellow, dark green, orange-gold and purple), which give a more permanent display of colour than flowers. The garden is in four separate sections divided by high hedges and old walls.

◆

West Wycombe Park, Nr High Wycombe
SIR FRANCIS DASHWOOD, BT; THE NATIONAL TRUST

This is a landscape garden boasting numerous eighteenth-century temples and follies, a cascade, and a swan-shaped lake.

BERKSHIRE

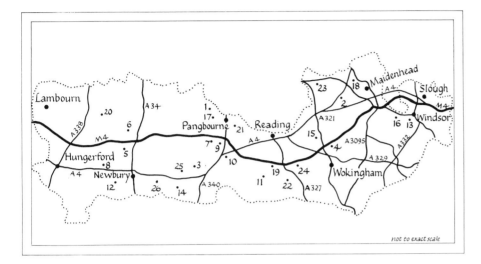

not to exact scale

Directions to Gardens

Basildon Park, Lower Basildon, near Pangbourne, 7 miles northwest of Reading. [1]

Bear Ash, Hare Hatch, 2 miles east of Wargrave. [2]

Beenham House, Beenham, halfway between Reading and Newbury. [3]

Binfield Court, 2½ miles north of Bracknell. [4]

Bussock Wood, Snelsmore Common, 3 miles north of Newbury. [5]

Chieveley Manor, 5 miles north of Newbury. [6]

The Coach House, Bradfield, Horse Leas, 7 miles west of Reading. [7]

Elcot Park Hotel, 5 miles west of Newbury. [8]

Englefield House, near Theale, west of Reading [9].

Folly Farm, Sulhamstead, 7 miles southwest of Reading, 2 miles west of M4 (exit 12). [10]

Foudry House, Mortimer, 6 miles southwest of Reading, 4 miles from M4 (exit 11). [11]

Foxgrove Farm, Enborne, 2½ miles southwest of Newbury. [12]

Frogmore Gardens, Windsor Castle, entrance via Park Street gate into Long Walk. [13]

Hazelby House, North End, 6 miles southeast of Newbury. [14]

Hurst Lodge, 7 miles east of Reading, leave M4 at exit 10. [15]

Jasmine House, Hatch Bridge, 3 miles west of Windsor. [16]

Little Bowden, 1½ miles west of Pangbourne. [17]

Oakfield, near Mortimer, 6 miles southwest of Reading. [11]

Odney Club, Cookham, near Maidenhead. [18]

The Old Rectory, Burghfield, 5 miles southwest of Reading. [19]

The Old Rectory, Farnborough, 4 miles southeast of Wantage. [20]

Old Rectory Cottage, Tidmarsh, ½ mile south of Pangbourne. [21]

Orchard Cottage, Sutton Road, Cookham, 3 miles north of Maidenhead. [18]

The Priory, Beech Hill, 9 miles south of Reading. [22]

Scotlands, Cockpole Green, midway between Henley-on-Thames and Wargrave. [23]

Shinfield Grange, Cutbush Lane, Shinfield, 3 miles southeast of Reading. [24]

Stone House, Brimpton, 6 miles east of Newbury. [25]

The Village House, Bradfield, 7 miles west of Reading, turn off M4 at exit 12. [7]

Wasing Place, Aldermaston, southeast of Newbury. [26]

◆

Basildon Park, Lower Basildon
LORD AND LADY ILIFFE; THE NATIONAL TRUST

A collection of colourful shrub roses and specimen trees in grass, with a lovely view across the Thames Valley. The private garden with its old-fashioned plants is open once a year.

◆

Bear Ash, Hare Hatch
LORD AND LADY REMNANT

Over the past six years this garden has been extended and replanted with the help of Mr Peter Coats. An upper part of the garden has made way for a swimming pool, which is screened from the field by a steep bank planted with *Genista aetnensis*, *Lavatera olbia* and *Hypericum* 'Hidcote' which is at its best in July. An old retaining wall has been embellished with a decorative willow-pattern fence, and the border below is full of shrubs with coloured leaves such as *Lonicera* 'Baggeson's Gold', *Cotinus coggygria* 'Royal Purple', blue-leaved rue, silver weed-smothering *Stachys lanata* and clumps of paeonies and perennial geraniums. The two herbaceous borders have been reshaped and replanted with shrub roses, interspersed with sun-loving *Cistus*, *Senecio*, dwarf lavender and *Artemisia*. From the terrace on the south-west of the house, steps lead down to a twin knot terrace of pink and grey gravel. The diamond pattern is outlined in rope-edged Victorian tiles, with big cushions of clipped hebes as centrepieces. More steps on one side of the terrace lead down to a silver garden paved with grey slates and with a sundial in the centre. The narrow beds below the walls are full of *Senecio*, *Artemisia* and *Lamium maculatum* 'Beacon Silver', whilst in the raised bed is a *Pyrus salicifolia* 'Pendula' and a *Buddleja* 'Lochinch' with its silvery foliage and violet-blue flowers, loved by the butterflies. The adjoining gold garden is bright with yellow roses, golden elder, *Philadelphus coronarius* 'Aureus' and *Spiraea × bumalda* 'Gold Flame' – a wonderful sight in the spring.

The soil is heavy clay. Though parts of the garden are exposed to cold winds, the many walls give protection to more tender plants, one of which is a red bottle-brush which miraculously survived the harsh winter of 1982.

Beenham House, Beenham
PROF. AND MRS GERALD BENNEY

Although the present manor house dates back only to the late eighteenth century, the site is an ancient one and there are many old and beautiful trees in the grounds, including majestic oaks, acacias, wellingtonias and cedars of Lebanon. The house sits in about twenty acres of lawns, shrubberies and woodland which were redesigned in 1964 to allow for modern gardening techniques using commercial machinery and only one gardener. There has been much new planting and one may walk between house and temple, from obelisk to summer house, finding interesting trees and shrubs at every turn. There are good views across the sloping parkland towards the Kennet.

◆

Binfield Court, Binfield
MR AND MRS CHARLES VAN BERGEN

Binfield Court is a well-established garden of about three acres which provides a setting for a Regency house. It is a place where a family of young people grew up, a much-loved garden where youth is still present in its plants without disturbing, indeed complementing, the underlay of maturity, a condition imposed upon it by the house and the elegance of that period. There has been a deliberate attempt, that began some twenty-five years ago, to make it sparkle as a place that understands fun, and to boast a bit about its youthful good health. Drabness was outlawed from the start when plants impersonating churchyard yews were taken out.

This has been done with the introduction of carefully chosen trees and shrubs with bloom or foliage or both, which will stand up with a touch of pride. Drabness was outlawed from the start when plants impersonating churchyard yews were taken out.

There is an emphasis on foliage which will provide prolonged interest, golds and silvers, and where possible, scents, as with *Catalpa*. The ponds have been made to conform both above and under water; ornamental ducks animate the surface while Japanese carp swim below. Much has been done using different species of *Acer*, from the Japanese dwarfs, such as 'Atropurpureum', blushing with a Victorian shyness in the sun, to *A. negundo* 'Variegatum', *A. platanoides* 'Drummondii' and, of course, *A. pseudoplatanus* 'Brilliantissimum'. The whole is presided over by an enormous swamp cypress, *Taxodium distichum*, with wellingtonias and the tongue-twisting *Metasequoia glyptostroboides* standing about in the wings.

Views from windows are important all round the house as one job the garden is expected to do is to cheer up the occupants. Daffodils turn an adjoining field into a mirror of the sun. Wall-trained *Forsythia* brings the bloom almost indoors and you step into the garden past concentrations of camellias.

The great thing about foliage and shapes is that, rain or shine, they go on delivering as they adapt their colours to the seasons. There

is no closing time for an *Acer*. If you watch a *Catalpa* it will tell you when the danger of frost is past. Plants are more than show-offs and they need a gardener's understanding before they will respond to the full. As with beautiful rooms, one does not over-furnish; it is not civilized either for people or plants.

◆

Bussock Wood, Snelsmore Common
MR AND MRS W.A. PALMER

Bussock Wood house and garden are situated in the centre of a large wood with a magnificent view over open farmland to the south. Within the wood is an iron-age camp, the fortification banks of which make an excellent *Rhododendron* backdrop to the formal garden; the latter is quite small, and mainly consists of a lily-pond and surrounding rose garden which is contained within a yew hedge. In the surrounding woodland bluebells vie with wild daffodils reinforced with large quantities of naturalized *Narcissus* varieties in the small park to the north of the house. Wild orchids and primroses are to be found throughout the wood, which is mainly deciduous and in the spring adds its own vital beauty.

There is a magnificent lime avenue leading down to the house which was built in 1907 by Mervyn Macartney, one of the great innovators of Edwardian architecture and editor at the time of the *Architectural Review*, the most influential of English architectural magazines. The house enhances the landscape in a position which would be anathema to present-day planning, and the surrounding garden has been designed so as to be economical of manpower. A garden to be enjoyed rather than worked in.

◆

Chieveley Manor, Chieveley
MR AND MRS C.J. SPENCE

Many gardens are as well laid out, but this one has the advantage of a marvellous view from the front of the house looking west across the lawn to a magnificent cedar tree and down a gentle slope, on which a variety of half-standard trees have been planted, to a wild pond. Beyond the pond lie paddocks with clumps of old chestnut and beech trees which provide shade for the mares and foals.

The principal garden, at the rear of the house, is enclosed by an old red brick wall that makes a fine backcloth for the climbing roses. The lean-to greenhouse contains a wide variety of beautiful houseplants, while on the south side is the rose garden, in the centre of which is a fine seventeenth-century millstone. In the north-east corner is the swimming pool and garden enclosed in what was originally the frameyard. The shrubs and roses throughout the garden are planned so as to flower in June and July.

A double herbaceous border is backed by weeping silver pears which show up the vivid blues of the delphiniums to perfection. These

borders are planned to flower from late May to late autumn and no bedding-out plants are used except *in extremis*. To save labour *Nepeta* is alternated with 'The Fairy' rose, which is most effective.

The kitchen garden, with additional greenhouses, is situated behind the principal walled garden and contains excellent examples of fruit and vegetables.

◆

The Coach House, Bradfield
MR AND MRS G.F. HARRISON

Ours is a small garden set on a north-facing slope amongst farmland, with a few mature trees on the periphery. From the back of the house we have lovely views over the Pang valley to the hills beyond. The front is almost all grass, so there is a happy unity between fields and garden and between garden and interior. The slope dictates terracing. My husband enjoys brick and stone-work, and we collected old bricks by the hundred for walls, steps and pavements, to form a number of linked enclosures which make for expectation and surprise. As a result, we have firm outlines within which we have planted in profusion, always two or three plants where one would do: 'China Pink' tulips and blue campanulas growing through *Berberis* 'Rose Glow', *Viola cornuta* scrambling over large hostas, sweet peas or *Clematis* through most of the shrubs, roses up old apple trees: the result is a carefully controlled jumble of mainly pale colours and a variety of form, scale, scent and texture. Our small wood is massed with spring bulbs, the pond is planted informally but, in contrast, our vegetable terraces nearby are decorative and formal, our 'mini Villandry'. Visitors are always puzzled by the large rock-climbing practice wall which my husband built nearby, from varied rocks which we have collected on our travels.

Recent successes are our 'footprint' bed, devoted to some thirty low-growing foliage plants, on a sloping lawn where neither a circle nor a rectangle seemed right; and a *Magnolia stellata* thickly underplanted with blue spring bulbs, followed by *Viola labradorica*, over which *Clematis* 'Nellie Moser' and then *Geranium wallichianum* 'Buxton's Blue' scramble.

All this growth is of course very greedy, so we feed with everything we can get, both organic and inorganic. Every month brings its joys, the garden is never out of season, and we are never out of work.

◆

Elcot Park Hotel, Nr Newbury
H.P. STERNE, ESQ.

Elcot Park is an elegant Georgian mansion, well sited on a south slope with distant views. The garden was carefully planned with respect to orientation and variety of effect. In 1945, after long neglect, it became an hotel and, since 1966, efforts have been made to improve the garden. Ten years of restoration

Englefield House, Theale, in June. *Rhododendron ponticum* and *Choisya ternata*, the mock orange from Mexico, frame part of the nineteenth-century parapet.

have resulted in a generally well-maintained appearance.

The entrance from the west is between banks planted thickly with daffodils. To the south the principal view is framed by hedges, and a terraced grass walk leads from the south front, past the west lawn (once a parterre of flower beds) to a dark grove of *Sequoiadendron giganteum*. To the east a larger horseshoe walk leads among large rhododendrons and bamboos with a more tortuous walk alongside it through the fringe of oaks.

To the north of the house the kitchen garden was once made a major feature with a shrub-lined walk to its main entrance. Against the shelter of its south wall a double walk retains something of its character with tile-edged gravel paths. A large multi-trunked *Cercidiphyllum* is the most noticeable remnant of the old planting. The kitchen garden within the walls has now been grassed over but the cross paths and central dipping pond are still evident and old fruit trees still cling to the walls. Over the last few years

considerable planting has taken place in the shrubbery and woodland walks have been restored.

◆

Englefield House, Theale
MR AND MRS W.R. BENYON

'If you help towards Englefield garden either in flowers or invention you shall be welcome thither' – so wrote the owner of Englefield to a friend in 1601. The grey stone steps, walls and parapets were added to this earlier garden in the mid-nineteenth century, and more recently alterations have again been made under the guidance of the late Lanning Roper.

In 1936 the woodland garden was laid out on the south-facing slope above the house, and many interesting small trees and shrubs have come to maturity among the oaks and sycamores. In May and June the *Davidia* is covered in 'handkerchiefs' while the rhododendrons, azaleas and camellias flower away from the magnolias reaching a wonderful height above them. The bluebells never

fail to provide the loveliest backdrop, and the water garden starts to come alive in early spring with primulas, ferns, irises, hostas, *Meconopsis*, *Rodgersia* and many other plants.

As the season progresses so the roses, *Clematis*, honeysuckle and other summer-flowering shrubs take over from the *Wisteria*, *Prunus*, *Malus*, *Viburnum* and others, and the wide variety of underplanting comes into its own.

For the last few years we have laid a heavy mulch of bracken on all the beds in mid-June which has proved a boon. It is high in nitrates, clean, not unsightly, rots down well and has cut down on weeding dramatically.

As autumn approaches the *Eucryphia* and blue hydrangeas flower among the woodland trees, and after the first frosts the *Acer*, *Cercidiphyllum* and *Nyssa* glow in their pinks, scarlets and crimsons. A *Euonymus* cheerfully carries its unlikely-looking orange and red fruits all winter, and no sooner is Christmas over than the *Hamamelis* is with us again and the ground comes alive with snowdrops and carpets of blue *Anemone blanda*.

◆

Folly Farm, Sulhamstead
THE HON. HUGH AND MRS ASTOR

Folly Farm is one of the most complex of the gardens designed by Sir Edwin Lutyens and Gertrude Jekyll. Lutyens also extended the house, and himself lived here for a summer; even Miss Jekyll was persuaded away from Munstead Wood to stay.

Folly Farm came to be the home of the present owners thirty-three years ago, and the garden is now moving into a new régime of simplification under Dennis Honour, the present head gardener, and his assistant.

In the entrance court, now paved, are a collection of hardy fuchsias and the bay trees are part of the original planting. The Barn Court is planted with silver-foliaged shrubs, white and pale pink roses, including 'Gruss an Aachen', and bold-leaved herbaceous plants such as hostas, bergenias and *Helleborus orientalis*, with beds of *Nepeta mussinii*. The lime walk, carpeted with snowdrops and aconites in early spring, leads to a white garden, made by the present owners, with the rose 'Iceberg', lilies, white foxgloves and *Wisteria sinensis* 'Alba'.

The canal was designed by Lutyens to reflect the Dutch character of the house, and is now framed with perfect lawns and stone paths. The flower parterre has been replanted in traditional Jekyll style, with paeonies, irises, delphiniums, lupins and day lilies, as well as traditional roses such as 'Madame Hardy' and 'Fantin-Latour', and the more modern 'Cerise Bouquet' with its arching sprays of pink flowers. The sunken garden is still surrounded by the original yew hedges. This is one of Lutyens' most elaborate garden rooms, with an octagonal central pool and four stepped platforms to hold seats of his own design. A complex pattern of beds is held together with swirling brick and stone paths and filled with the scents of lavender and roses.

After the intensity and brilliance of the formal gardens come the calm sweeps of the lawn, where the present owners have introduced spring flowers, small fields of white *Narcissus* and splashes of red tulips; nearby is a stream garden with irises, bog primulas, astilbes and drifts of *Anemone blanda* under the willows.

◆

Foudry House, Stratfield Mortimer
MR AND MRS J.G. STUDHOLME

The shape of our garden was principally formed by extensive replanning in 1962 when a swimming pool was built by our predecessor. He planted many interesting trees which are now approaching maturity – notably a fine *Populus alba* 'Richardii', *Catalpa bignonioides* and many varieties of *Acer* and *Eucalyptus*. The soil is acid, but there are awkward patches of gravel and Thames valley clay. Azaleas do well in spring – and later some lovely old shrub roses make a fine show with masses of *Philadelphus* as a backcloth. We have recently created a pond, planted a yew hedge, and built a terrace on the site of an old greenhouse. We are planting this with fragrant plants; lavender, lemon verbena, tobacco plants and *Cytisus battandieri* to make a pleasant place to sit in the evening. I hope our garden, which has grown from so many years' loving care, will continue to change and develop.

◆

Foxgrove Farm, Enbourne
MISS AUDREY VOCKINS

The garden at Foxgrove has been developing since 1958, so that *Liriodendron tulipifera* has now been flowering for the last three years. The site of just under one acre is flat, but interest has been improved by building a rockery and several raised beds for alpines and small bulbs. One-third of the garden is old orchard with fruit trees which give support to climbing roses. For three months at least this grass is carpeted with spring bulbs. There is a large collection of snowdrop species and hybrids, including the rare *Galanthus nivalis* 'John Grey' and *G. allenii*. *Eranthis hyemalis* has at last decided to colonize a large area under one of the two old horse chestnut trees, and there is a growing collection of *Cyclamen coum*, *Crocus tommasinianus*, *Scilla sibirica* and *Erythronium revolutum*. This grassy area is at last becoming colonized by cowslips and primroses among the drifts of *Narcissus*. In winter, the land is usually very wet, but clay over gravel gives good drainage and *Fritillaria meleagris* seems to love it and has become naturalized everywhere.

Around the lawns are beds for herbaceous plants and shrubs, planted to cover the soil all the year round with interesting colour and texture. *Clematis alpina*, *C. macropetala*, *C. orientalis* and *Eccremocarpus scaber* – orange, red and yellow forms – climb through the plants, and in summer the tender *Helichrysum petiolatum*, silver and yellow, surges through the contrasting foliage of *Viola labradorica*, while scented pelargoniums and tender herbs pour over the terrace area.

Autumn brings hosts of *Cyclamen hederifolium* which do not seem to mind the winter wet and force their huge corms up to the surface of the soil. Their seeds are carried all over the garden by ants and germinate in the most surprising corners to provide flowers, pink or white, followed by beautiful marbled leaves until spring returns again.

◆

Frogmore Gardens, Windsor Castle
BY GRACIOUS PERMISSION OF HER
MAJESTY THE QUEEN

For those interested in the Victorian era and in particular Victorian gardens, Frogmore will provide much of interest, development of the garden having followed the construction of the house in 1793.

The totally flat thirty-five-acre site was improved considerably by the use of the spoil from the extensive artificial waterway to provide large banks and several miniature hills. We know that the garden has changed since its inception, the major changes being the disappearance of the formal areas, and almost all of the original plants. There are, however, several large trees including beeches, oaks, a cedar of Lebanon and an excellent specimen of the swamp cypress still remaining. Many buildings are also still there. Frogmore House sits superbly at the centre of the garden, and the massive Mausoleum, the burial place of Queen Victoria and Prince Albert, takes pride of place on the other side of the garden. Nearby the graceful Mausoleum which provides a fitting resting place for the Duchess of Kent, Queen Victoria's mother, will be even more impressive for some. More typical Victorian garden buildings will be seen in the ruined Gothic summer house, a typical folly of the era, and the little tea house, both still very much in their original form.

The garden has always enjoyed Royal interest and involvement, an association which has never been more evident than today for Her Majesty The Queen spends many hours in the garden and is very much involved in its development. Indeed it was as a result of Her Majesty's involvement that a programme of rejuvenation was started in 1977. This was clearly necessary for, although good maintenance had been practised, over the years the garden had become stationary, particularly in the case of replanting.

This new work has now been carried out for nine years and the plantings are beginning to make a fine show. Soil conditions and climate always guide the gardener's arm and the soil at Frogmore is alkaline in the main with a few areas just suitable for rhododendrons. These areas have been made full use of and a wide range of hardy rhododendrons (the garden is also cold) have been planted. The season begins with masses of daffodils which are mostly naturalized in grass. A Spring Garden has also been planted; the aim is to provide a thin copse-like planting of trees and shrubs underplanted with drifts of primroses, bluebells, scillas, etc. Cherries grow well and a number of new trees are now well established. The alkaline soil suits lilacs and a large range of both species and hybrids are now flowering well. Viburnums, another quality genus, are also very much at home.

Early summer is heralded by deutzias, *Philadelphus* and shrub roses, both species and hybrids. A border has been devoted to old roses and eight large island beds have been bedded with hybrid musk roses, all helping to maintain the Victorian flavour in the garden. Lastly, the new Winter Garden deserves mention. This extensive area has been planted with a very great variety of trees, shrubs and herbaceous plants which provide interest during the winter months. Many of the plants for this area were part of a gift from the

National Gardens Scheme to commemorate Her Majesty The Queen's Silver Jubilee.

Hazelby House, North End

MR AND MRS M.J. LANE FOX

This garden has been planted entirely since 1974. It covers about four acres and takes advantage of a superb site facing the Downs, with a lake and beautifully wooded background. We started by making a strictly formal framework of brick walls and hedges of yew, beech, hornbeam and *Thuja* to create a number of compartments which were then connected and divided up by paths of brick, stone, gravel and grass. Statues, ornaments and a classical pavilion provide focal points for various 'views', and a rectangular canal and a smaller pond combine with the lake to introduce the peaceful effect of water.

Our planting is very generous, combining many varieties of trees, shrubs and herbaceous plants into different effects and contrasts in each compartment. Especially satisfactory is the rose garden where there are thick underplantings of herbaceous perennials and annuals which extend the flowering time and interest beyond the main rose season, and a small white garden where the glaucous foliage of hostas and rue combine with *Campanula burghaltii*, *Crambe cordifolia*, climbing rose 'Iceberg' and *Lilium candidum* to give a cool atmosphere throughout the summer. There are long double herbaceous borders backed by beech hedges with a central pergola of white trellis covered with the rose 'New Dawn'. Double shrub borders contain magnolias, abutilons, *Ceanothus* and drifts of *Lilium regale*, and the terrace round the house combines varied beds of herbaceous plants with clipped lavender, *Malus floribunda* and climbing roses, *Solanum*, *Clematis*, *Actinidia* and low growing alpines.

We keep the colours soft and avoid bright yellows and reds and the harsher variegations; don't forget that green in its many shades is the most important garden colour of all.

Hurst Lodge, Hurst

LADY INGRAM

I am very lucky to have marvellous trees in my garden – an enormous cedar, two very old yews, good copper beeches and scarlet oaks, a huge old oak with bulbs under it including some fritillaries, and a very well-sited great Scots pine which catches the evening light on its trunk. There are camellias and magnolias in the wooded areas, and a lot of Japanese maples, lovely in the spring and autumn, mixed with azaleas and rhododendrons.

Across the lawn is a bed of shrub roses, and a border with paeonies, delphiniums and irises. There is a little knot garden full of bedding plants and a walled garden with two large herbaceous borders. Here I have a lovely golden *Catalpa* which flowered

recently for the first time in twelve years.

In a large kitchen garden are some shabby greenhouses with my *Cymbidium* orchids and loads of tomatoes in summer.

Jasmine House, Hatch Bridge

MR AND MRS E.C.B. KNIGHT

We have about a third of an acre under cultivation but by design the garden appears much larger. At the front of the house *Betula costata* dominates a heather bed with a peat-block wall in which *Ramonda myconi* thrives. Nearby a fine mahogany-barked *Prunus serrula* guards the gate with *Rhododendron yakushimanum*.

The centre of the garden features irregular heather beds in which many species of conifers grow alongside trees chosen for their decorative bark. Here also mauve *Hosta* flowers rise through old roses such as velvety-crimson 'Tuscany Superb' – delicious! – and black-foliaged *Ophiopogon planiscapus nigrescens* spreads under a silver-blue spruce, *Picea pungens* 'Globosa'. Along the east, sheltered by *Ilex aquifolium* 'Handsworth New Silver' and *Rosa rugosa*, a grass walk a hundred and twenty feet long leads towards a statue of Venus (with apple!) and a graceful Serbian Spruce, *Picea omorika*, underplanted with *Rhododendron russatum*, a deep purple gem. The north border is host to many dwarf conifers and is adjoined by an expanse of crazy paving through which grows *Acer griseum*, another tree that is attractive throughout the year.

One great interest is our collection of bonsai, both on the display stand and on the terrace where three larches live in a turquoise Japanese bowl.

There are two pools, the smaller in the central area where a statue of Hebe stands by *Rosa* 'Penelope', a hybrid musk, and *Veronica teucrium* 'Shirley Blue' mingles with heavy-scented deep pink *Daphne cneorum*. The other pool, south of the bonsai display, is edged with the dwarf bamboo, *Shibatea kumasasa*, and cool lavender and grey-leaved *Senecio*.

Our list of hydrangeas all along the north wall of the house includes the wonderful blue 'Generale Vicomtesse de Vibraye'. There are many other attractions in our garden, from sink gardens to *Cyclamen*, from alpines to azaleas. We just keep adding!

Little Bowden, Pangbourne

MR AND MRS MICHAEL VEREY

Originally laid out in the early 1900s but much simplified by the present owners – in size about six acres – the garden is situated three hundred feet above Pangbourne village with views for miles across the Thames towards the Hartslock woods.

The garden comes to life early in the spring with its woodland full of bulbs, these being followed by a sea of bluebells with camellias, magnolias including *M. sinensis* and *M.*

sieboldii, and azaleas under the cherry trees. Two formal gardens paved with stone join each other around the house, one with a waterlily pond, roses and lilies, and the other with a sunk garden. Below the balustrade which is covered with roses, is a fine herbaceous border. The garden then slopes away to a walk through flowering trees and shrubs under a pergola draped with *Laburnum* to a swimming pool enclosed by yew hedges and red brick walls covered with roses, *Clematis*, *Vitis* 'Brant' and *Ceanothus*. The kitchen garden is a model of skill and neatness. A very special feature up on the edge of the wood is a bed of *Cardiocrinum giganteum* flowering in July against a dark background of Irish yews.

Oakfield, Nr Mortimer

SIR MICHAEL AND LADY MILNE-WATSON

When we arrived at Oakfield in 1952 the property had been empty for some years and the grounds seriously neglected. The grass was three feet high and the greenhouses in the kitchen garden were totally concealed by weeds and brambles, but the bones were good. There was a lime avenue leading to the east lodge, and to the west a drive lined with oaks, horse chestnuts, firs and rhododendrons. Opposite the front of the house, facing south, were two blue firs and on the house itself a beautiful *Wisteria*. On the west side there was, and is still, a large *Magnolia grandiflora* and there we have made a wide paved terrace and a long bed under the house. From there you cross a large lawn to the lake, passing a weeping *Prunus × yedoensis* so content with its habitat that it is now twenty feet or more across and is a superb sight when covered with white flowers in April. The eight-acre lake needed little done to bring it back to its former glory with reeds, irises, bulrushes and waterlilies. Where Lockram brook feeds into it there is sufficient seclusion to encourage the great crested grebe, teal and pochard and to provide more permanent accommodation for mallard, coot and moorhens. Hundreds of Canada geese visit each year and the heron and kingfisher are fond of the coarse fish to be found in the lake.

In the woods there are sheets of daffodils, followed by bluebells, wild white violets and orchids. In the garden behind the house there is little formality but a terraced rose bed and shrub borders under the walls on two sides of the garden, with free-standing magnolias, *Prunus*, *Malus*, azaleas and camellias (some brought from our old home in Dorset). We also have a 'memorial bank' with presents from friends; but wherever you walk there is usually something colourful to catch the eye. We have tried to preserve the 'wild' feeling of the garden and to encourage the birds and butterflies (though we are less keen on the rabbits, squirrels and now, occasionally, deer) and yet to provide a memorable place for people to wander and see lovely plants and trees.

Odney Club, Cookham
THE JOHN LEWIS PARTNERSHIP

Odney has been owned by the John Lewis Partnership since 1926 when John Lewis, the founder, bought it as a centre for relaxation and recreation for the Partners. In those first years charabanc parties of them travelled down from London for mammoth bulb-planting operations, and a hundred thousand bulbs were set out in the first year alone.

The front of the house is covered with an ancient *Wisteria*, possibly as old as the façade of the house itself which dates from the time of Waterloo. Large specimen trees in the main lawn, cedars, copper and weeping beech, tulip trees and many others have grown well in the rich silty soil of the Thames flood plain; long yew hedges enclose a pair of herbaceous borders, and an informal water garden has been made along the Cookham Mill stream, a carrier of the Thames.

Much of the garden is left as natural as possible to encourage butterflies, moths and birds, and the wild flowers typical of former hay meadows. One of these, known as 'the daffodil field', is the glory of Odney in the springtime. It was here that the thousands of bulbs were planted, at the instigation of the Founder, who wanted to have generous displays of spring flowers to delight the eye and also to allow his town-dwelling shop assistants to pick a bunch to take home.

The Old Rectory, Burghfield
MR AND MRS R.R. MERTON

In the garden at the Old Rectory, made from scratch since 1950, grow plants from all over the world, collected by a green-fingered lunatic! Whereas most people are cutting down on gardening, she is making new borders, planting new orchards and herb gardens and planning an arboretum. Unusual vegetables proliferate among rarer soft fruits, the whole being a frame for collections of hellebores, pinks, violas, paeonies, snow-drops, old roses; you mention them, she collects them.

There are drifts of daffodils and cowslips in the spring, and wild *Cyclamen* in the autumn. Giant asiatic roses climb every tree they can lay their grasping hands on, scenting the whole garden in July, and feeding the birds with their myriads of hips in the winter. We propagate *everything* and always have some treasure on the Old Rectory stall when the garden is open to the public – there are also other plantsman stall-holders, with tables full of goodies, so our 'Mini-Market' is well worth a visit.

The Old Rectory, Farnborough
MRS MICHAEL TODHUNTER

Perched on top of the Berkshire Downs at eight hundred feet with tall beeches and limes around it and a large lawn in front, stands the Rectory, which was built in 1749. A series of small gardens, protected by hedges and low walls, have become an obsession over the past twenty years. Collections of small-flowered *Clematis*, honeysuckles, old roses, daphnes, euphorbias, paeony species and violets are among our favourites. The use of colour is important; bright yellow and orange are banished to a bed of their own. The swimming pool door is flanked by beds filled with plants of warm reds – a contrast to the blues and cool yellows that grow round the pool. *Magnolia* × *loebneri* 'Leonard Messel' and 'Merrill', *stellata* and *wilsonii* are happy in the neutral soil, which was enriched with barrow loads of leafmould. The roses and shrubs

around the walls of the house support the *Clematis*. If planted together they grow hand in hand and defy the malevolent winds.

Old Rectory Cottage, Tidmarsh
MR AND MRS A.W.A. BAKER

At the end of a small lane, flanked with a hedge of *Rosa spinosissima altaica* and *Sorbus* of different kinds, you will find Old Rectory Cottage. The cottage is almost completely covered with climbers, and the garden looks like a typical cottage garden with winding grass paths and beds filled to overflowing with a wide variety of plants. Self-sown sweet rocket and variegated honesty intermingle with plants collected from many countries – but instead of dahlias and chrysanthemums, *Iris*, *Allium* and wild *Geranium* species take their place. Nine sinks provide homes for the less robust alpines, the rock garden being full of bulbs and smaller plants.

At the back of the cottage an old orchard has been converted into a wild garden; climbing into the old apple trees are vigorous *Clematis*, honeysuckle and roses while naturalized underneath are *Narcissus*, *Fritillaria* and *Cyclamen*. Beds raised up and edged with logs hold woodland plants and especially lilies; these last are favourites and most have been raised here.

A small lake fed by the river Pang is situated at the end of the wild garden and a local wild flower, the Loddon Lily, *Leucojum aestivum*, grows on the banks while candelabra primulas seed happily in the damper places. Water is a mixed blessing but where flooding occurs willows of many kinds are grown and are host to the beautiful blue parasite *Lathraea clandestina*.

Although some of the plant associations – such as putting a deep red Kordes rose through the weeping silver leaved pear – are contrived, it must be admitted that many are accidental. A good example is the blue *Phlox divaricata* surrounding the silver foliage of the Japanese painted fern *Athyrium georingianum* 'Pictum'. The overall effect is one of unrestrained abundance and naturalness, just as we like it, not out of control as it might appear.

Orchard Cottage, Cookham
MRS REGINALD SAMUEL

This garden, informal in design, surrounds the bungalow which was converted from an old stable; there are a number of different aspects in which to grow a variety of plants.

Fuchsias occupy a shady courtyard, begonias and heathers enjoy a north-facing situation, peaches and figs grow on a west wall and roses, dahlias, and fruit occupy sunny positions.

The rose garden consists of irregularly-shaped rectangular beds each containing a single variety divided by grass paths, and shows the large-flowered blooms to advan-

The Old Rectory, Farnborough, in July. A mixed border with rose 'Cerise Bouquet' (a *multibracteata* hybrid), delphiniums and the pale pink single-flowered *Dahlia merkii*.

tage; cluster roses and shrubs occupy larger beds, and ground-cover, roses and climbers are also grown.

The water garden has four informal ponds, with waterlilies and many kinds of water and bog plants, a waterfall and rocks, and occupies a prominent position in the garden. Much time has been spent on designing a method of deterring predatory herons without the use of unsightly netting.

There is insufficient space here to describe such features as the herb garden and the fruit garden, scree and shrub beds and perennials, but mention must be made of attempts to save labour.

Camomile and thyme have been used in place of grass for some lawns and paths (thus saving mowing) and a lot of use has been made of ground-cover plants; paving and shingle surfaces also save weeding.

A thirty-foot greenhouse is hard work, especially when, in addition to growing tomatoes, cucumbers and peppers and supplying all garden plants, the aim also is to have a colourful display of double busy lizzies, begonias, gloxinias and many other plants.

This garden was designed to give a pleasing view from every window and a collection of unusual plants to interest all who want to visit it; we hope we have succeeded!

❖

The Priory, Beech Hill
O. W. ROSKILL, ESQ.

This garden has the advantage of a stream, diverted from the river Loddon, which is said to have been made by the Benedictine monks who formerly lived in this house – originally a hermitage built by 'The Monk Goddard' in the twelfth century. The purpose of the diversion was to supply water to their Friday fishpond. The pond is surrounded by trees, including a fine but rather old *Catalpa*, and is planted on one side, in order not to spoil this view, with *Osmunda, Gunnera, Crambe* and *Acanthus*, and on the other with rock roses, a variety of irises and other dwarfer plants. A wild garden, also with many trees including bog cypress and weeping willow with shade-tolerant shrubs and ground-cover plants underneath, adjoins the pool.

On the side of the stream nearest the house is a large lawn which gives a feeling of spaciousness, with a fine copper beech in one corner; low yew hedges, cut with wavy rather than straight tops, are sited at the opposite end.

Behind these hedges is a kitchen garden (walled on the side away from the stream) run commercially, if not for profit, with asparagus (trenched) as the main crop. Down the centre of the kitchen garden, which was probably laid out in its present form in the seventeenth century, run long, old-fashioned herbaceous borders on either side of a gravel path.

Overlooking the big lawn is the stable, now a garage block, along the front of which runs a

Scotlands in July. A fine group of *Astilbe* hybrids by the pond and, in the background, a summer house, built to a Humphrey Repton design.

shrub border with particular emphasis on winter shrubs, including *Viburnum fragrans, Hamamelis mollis* and *Chimonanthus praecox*, but also a number of different *Cistus, Halesia carolina* and *Ceanothus*.

In front of the house is another lawn with a tall box hedge on one side to hide the 'yard' side of the stable block. On the far side of this lawn there is a blue cedar and a *Quercus ilex*, still huge despite the fact that at least half of it has fallen down during the last forty-five years. The acid leaf-drop from the ilex has permitted the planting of a variety of camellias (although the Loddon itself is a low-alkaline chalk stream). Close to the house, which has a *Magnolia grandiflora* in front and an old *Wisteria* next to a *Rosa banksiae* on the south wing, are a number of shrubs with attractive scents, including lemon verbena and red sage. Nearby is an *Abutilon vitifolium*. The small 'back pool' behind the house, from the bank of which Constable painted, is edged with wild kingcups with a bank of *Primula pulverulenta* and *P. sikkimensis* on one side.

❖

Scotlands, Cockpole Green
MR MICHAEL AND THE HON. MRS PAYNE

The garden covers about four acres, including a small area of woodland, and it is centred on the seventeenth-century chalk and flint farmhouse converted from a barn and overlooking the post and rail paddocks and beautiful parkland of the neighbouring stud.

To the west lies the formal part with lawns

and stepped yew hedges either side of an oval pool with stone surround. This features a lead statue flanked by stone tubs planted in the spring with wallflowers and tulips, and geraniums and grey foliage plants in the summer – round herbaceous borders each side are designed to give maximum summer colour. Behind the hedges are some good specimen trees including a fine *Cedrus atlantica glauca, Catalpa*, Spanish chestnut and copper beech.

To the east of the house, the land falls away sharply to a small valley. A large springfed pond was made here in 1979 from a boggy wilderness, the sides of which have been planted with groups of primulas, astilbes and other water-loving plants. *Gunnera* has grown spectacularly well and two fine *Taxodium distichum* (fortunately already there) add colour in spring and autumn. At the north end and backed by woodland, a summer house has been built to a Humphrey Repton design, complete with pine-cone finials and trellis work of nut branches! It is linked to the pond by a close mown lawn.

Three new small ponds are being made in the woodland, each connected to the others by a wide grassy path. When completed these should finalize what is essentially a small landscape garden made possible by the interesting contours of the land, springs and mature trees such as Scots pine, yew and oak in a very attractive natural setting.

❖

Shinfield Grange, Shinfield
UNIVERSITY OF READING

Shinfield Grange is a teaching garden, used for practical work by students reading Horticulture at Reading University. Because of this the garden is in a state of constant flux: borders become overgrown (by careful planning of course!) to provide areas in which enthusiastic first-year students can wreak havoc while second-year students learn the more refined aspects of garden management and third-years work on design schemes for improvement. Recent additions include the cherry-bowl (an ellipse of Japanese flowering cherries), a shrub rose border, and a border of local wild flowers.

The garden started from small beginnings in the 1950s, but the range and scale of planting has gradually increased to occupy the whole of the fifteen-acre site around the house. Near the house, the planting is formal with box- and yew-hedged enclosures for tender plants (on the south-facing terrace), seasonal bedding, and roses. The rose garden has been given a rest, using mixed hardy annuals – a great success – in place of roses, and replanned with a simple knot in the centre and a colour border changing through yellow, copper, peach, pink and white/grey around the edge. Sadly deer have discovered the roses and eat every bud, but the knot pattern and underplanting should continue to provide interest even if the rose garden has no roses.

Further away from the house the north garden has many heathers, some rhododendrons and many different small trees. A good specimen of *Sorbus cashmeriana* excites interest in the autumn when laden with large white berries, but the best tree in the garden is *Cornus nuttallii*, covered each spring with inflorescences whose petal-like bracts expand from green through cream to white and finally pink. Like the maples, amelanchiers, birches, parrotias and witch hazels in this area, the *Cornus* also has good autumn colour.

Southwards beyond the informal herbaceous borders the garden has two quite different aspects. To the east is a small lake, a newly-established wild flower meadow, a shade-garden (with many beautiful primulas), a rock garden and several interesting trees including a flourishing young pin oak, *Quercus palustris*. The willows, dogwoods, nettles, and meadow by the lake form a low-maintenance mini nature reserve.

To the west, near the visitors' entrance to the garden, is a border of shrub roses, and within the beech-hedged gardens north of this hardy and half-hardy annuals and other temporary plantings. The foliage border, with *Eucalyptus*, castor oil, beet, *Jacaranda* and many other plants, creates great interest – and disbelief that small plants set out in June can obscure the eight-foot-high hedges by September. Smaller beds accommodate a changing series of planting ideas such as ornamental vegetables, annual grasses, beeplants and annual climbers.

Lastly, although not especially attractive in the aesthetic sense, the north-east corner of the garden has our mowing trials and experimental plots where we are investigating the effects of different mowing regimes and especially techniques for the introduction of wild flowers into meadow grass. How to mow grass is a *very* popular talking point among gardeners!

Stone House, Brimpton
MR AND MRS NIGEL BINGHAM

There must have been some kind of garden here for perhaps three hundred years, which then developed as the house grew in size and stature. It acquired a fine walled kitchen garden using the farm buildings for the east wall. The old cow pond was turned into a miniature lake, with an island, which nowadays is ablaze with rhododendrons in May and June.

The soil is rather acid and thin, over gravel, and can dry out very quickly in a drought. The site is also windswept, perched as it is on the southern lip of the Kennet valley, but the views all round are very pleasing. The present owners, who came here in 1968, whilst striving to preserve the best of the earlier plantings have introduced many new ones both to extend the season and to widen the range of interesting plants, especially shrubs. Much emphasis has been placed on foliage plants.

House and garden are virtually surrounded

Wasing Place in June. Rhododendrons, azaleas and a young copper beech frame the view.

by a miniature park, with fine specimen trees, planted by a previous family. To quote a recent visitor 'a beautiful peaceful place'.

The Village House, Bradfield
MR AND MRS P. A. McN. BOYD

We have four acres of garden, the lawns sloping down to the river Pang with water meadows and a bird sanctuary on the other side. The garden is gradually being replanted after a severe attack of honey fungus, but we still retain mature trees all round the perimeter including *Robinia*, horse chestnut and plane. A magnificent and huge *Prunus subhirtella* 'Autumnalis' (probably grafted on plum) has pride of place on the main lawn. It is covered with palest pink blossom from December to April with a carpet of scillas beneath.

The soil is curious, being in patches solid gravel, chalk, clay and loam, so that choosing a position carefully means we can grow almost anything from maples and rhododendrons to all the wonderful chalk-loving shrubs. The garden is broken up into areas by hedges of laurel, *Pyracantha* and yew, a spring walk by the river, a sunken lawn surrounded by shrub roses and gold-leaved plants, a large mixed border on the main lawn, and a walled area massed with *Alstroemeria ligtu* hybrids. The kitchen garden has a fine old greenhouse, the last of a row of Victorian orchid houses. The garden ends at the top of the hill with a woodland walk and a view down to the Queen Anne house covered with climbing shrubs including *Wisteria*, *Ceanothus* and *Fremontodendron*.

Wasing Place, Aldermaston
SIR WILLIAM MOUNT, BT

The gardens are divided into two parts, the

pleasure grounds and the walled kitchen garden, each consisting of three acres. The former slopes north from the house with lovely views across the Kennet valley where the park is planted with copper beeches (in pairs), cedars, limes, oaks and poplars. The Victorian clumps of rhododendrons are interspersed with camellias, azaleas, kalmias, hydrangeas, lilies and tree paeonies, with a range of ground-cover plants. Species of *Halesia*, *Stuartia*, *Arbutus*, *Eucryphia* and *Magnolia* have all grown into tall trees. Beyond the pool is a Georgian Tea House with, as the story goes, Roman tiles from Silchester laid on the floor. The finest cedars stand between the fourteenth-century church and the house; we have records of seed being brought from Lebanon in 1684. The limes were planted in 1770.

The walled garden includes a formal paved garden with clipped hedges, fuchsias and roses; the vegetable plots are hidden by herbaceous borders. The central walk is edged with lavender and filled with paeonies, yellow roses and delphiniums, while *Lilium regale* seeds itself and spreads among them. Curved walls shelter the same roses, 'Else Poulsen', that have bloomed happily for forty years, and the cavity walls supporting the greenhouses show how the original heating system worked. Camellias of great age and size, including C. 'Adolphe Audusson', bloom from October to February, and many tender shrubs and plants provide stock plants for future use as well as winter pleasure. Outside the south wall is the American border with shrubs which include *Indigofera* and shrub roses. A gingko tree stands beside the ha-ha. A huge cut-leaved beech has sadly died, but its silver grey trunk and interlaced boughs make lovely statuary twenty feet high, while another grows in its place.

CAMBRIDGESHIRE

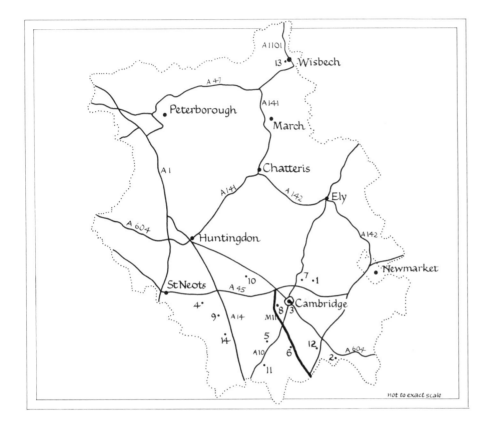

not to exact scale

Directions to Gardens

Anglesey Abbey, Stow-cum-Quy, 6 miles northeast of Cambridge. [1]

Bartlow Park, 1½ miles southeast of Linton, 6 miles northeast of Saffron Walden. [2]

The Bell School of Languages, Red Cross Lane, Hills Road, Cambridge. [3]

Berry Close Studio, Great Gransden, 15 miles west of Cambridge. [4]

Clare College, Fellows' Garden, Cambridge. [3]

The Crossing House, Meldreth Road, Shepreth, 8 miles southwest of Cambridge. [5]

Docwra's Manor, Shepreth, 8 miles southwest of Cambridge. [5]

Duxford Mill, 9 miles south of Cambridge. [6]

Emmanuel College Garden and Fellows' Garden, Cambridge. [3]

Hardwicke House, Fen Ditton, 3½ miles northeast of Cambridge. [7]

Home Grove, Grantchester, 2 miles southwest of Cambridge. [8]

King's College Fellows' Garden, Cambridge. [3]

Leckhampton, 37 Grange Road, Cambridge. [3]

Longstowe Hall, 10 miles west of Cambridge. [9]

The Manor House, Boxworth, 6½ miles west of Cambridge. [10]

Melbourn Bury, 2¼ miles north of Royston. [11]

Melbourn Lodge, Melbourn, 3 miles north of Royston. [11]

North End House, Grantchester, 2 miles southwest of Cambridge. [8]

The Old Vicarage, Grantchester, 2 miles southwest of Cambridge. [8]

The Old Vicarage, Pampisford, 8 miles south of Cambridge. [12]

Peckover House, in the centre of Wisbech town. [13]

The Rectory, Fen Ditton, 3½ miles northeast of Cambridge. [7]

Wimpole Hall, Arrington, 5 miles north of Royston. [14]

Anglesey Abbey, Nr Cambridge
THE NATIONAL TRUST

This garden, covering a hundred acres, surrounds an Elizabethan manor, and has been created during the last fifty years. There are avenues of beautiful trees, statuary, hedges enclosing small intimate gardens and spring bulbs, in addition to the magnificent herbaceous borders.

Bartlow Park, Nr Linton
BRIGADIER AND MRS ALAN BREITMEYER

The garden has been created over the last twenty years since a new house was built, close to the site of an old house which was burned down. The former garden, although it was in a sorry state of rack and ruin, has been incorporated into the new landscape. It was fortunate that we had some good mature trees in the small seventeen-acre park upon which to base the design. Every endeavour has been made to keep the garden simple and easy to maintain whilst making maximum use of the views across the park through which run the head waters of the river Granta.

We have recently reinstated the balustrading on the old terrace which makes a fine setting for a herbaceous border.

We have endeavoured to have colour, not only with spring bulbs followed by flowering shrubs and roses, but also through planting a variety of smaller garden trees, which provide the maximum contrast in foliage during the summer and the best autumn colour that we can devise with our chalk soil. To achieve these contrasts we have used *Acer platanoides* 'Drummondii' and 'Goldsworth Purple' and introduced silver-grey with *Pyrus salicifolia* and the shimmering silver poplar. In addition, the best of the golden trees, *Robinia pseudoacacia* 'Frisia' is outstanding, as are the autumn colours of *Acer ginnala* and *Amelanchier canadensis*. *Sambucus racemosa* 'Aurea' adds colour at lower levels throughout the year. Vistas have been created looking out of the windows from the centre of the house, leading the eye to focal points such as rough grass planted with a profusion of spring bulbs. This is very effective and we are indebted to that great amateur gardener, John Codrington, for the idea.

The Crossing House at Shepreth in early May. *Prunus tenella* and tulips, hellebores and a red-leaved Japanese maple grow happily together.

The Bell School of Languages, Cambridge

The garden, covering about twenty-five acres, occupies a level site on the edge of Cambridge, facing south with views across fields to the Gog Magog Hills. About six acres are under cultivation, with large greenhouses providing facilities for growing most of our own plants, both from seed and propagation, as well as flowering and foliage plants for indoor use in the school buildings. Large areas of naturalized bulbs of many varieties give a very colourful display in spring. The grounds are well provided with a great many mature and beautiful trees, while the profusion of shrubs gives a variety of leaf colour. The herbaceous borders, annuals and roses add to the general effect of a park-like garden.

Berry Close Studio, Gt Gransden
MR STANLEY ANDERSON

Berry Close Studio is an example of what can be done with a derelict piece of land. When this patch of three acres was taken over in 1964 it was waterlogged, boggy, and overgrown with waist-high weeds on very heavy clay soil.

A seven-year programme was planned in which the house would be built on piles, the land drained, moved and contoured, and over two hundred trees, numerous shrubs, and a beech hedge planted. The various levels that were created were deliberately arranged to add interest, and break the area up into pockets that gave the garden character.

The garden is based on shapes rather than flower beds; shrubs that vie with one another in colour or pattern are placed to give the maximum effect, and every opportunity has been taken to create a vista using views which are distant from the property.

There is a water garden on two levels created from local stone, and visited from time to time by mallard ducks.

The garden comes to life in the spring with a blaze of bulbs, and there is always colour or botanical interest as another facet of nature unfolds.

The aim of the creation of the garden was to supply the owner with first-hand material for his landscape paintings, which consist mainly of trees.

Clare College Fellows' Garden, Cambridge
THE MASTER AND FELLOWS

This garden in the Cambridge Backs occupies about two acres between the River Cam and Queens Road. It is bounded on the south by a raised causeway upon which stand five stately limes, all that remain of an avenue originally planted in the late seventeenth century. On the north side the garden is protected from the fenland winds by a line of yew trees. The soil is alluvial and the water-table high.

The garden was redesigned in 1946 in such a way as to provide a series of view-points and vistas and to satisfy the differing tastes of the members of the College, from bowls and play-acting to contemplation. A large lawn, edged by a mixed herbaceous border on its north side, provides a long vista from the windows of the College and an equally attractive view of the College from the garden.

The river bank itself is decorated by two weeping cherries, *Prunus subhirtella* 'Pendula', and between the bank and the lawn two 'red' borders produce flamboyant colour in the late summer. At one end is a venerable Judas tree, *Cercis siliquastrum*, and at the other a tall swamp cypress, *Taxodium distichum*. At the end near the latter a path runs westward between two wide 'blue and yellow' borders. One is backed by an old wall clothed with blue and yellow shrubs, the other by the evergreen bushes that also form the back-cloth to the mixed border and from which there now arises a stately Dawn Redwood *Metasequoia glyptostroboides*. The blue borders are at their best in July but turn to golden in the autumn. The path leads to a gateway in the yew hedge that encloses a sunk garden, in the centre of which is a pond with lilies and irises. This sunken lawn is bounded by a dry stone wall housing alpines, at their best in May. Behind the wall the Dean's Walk runs the whole length of the garden; between it and the yew trees is a 'white' border, interrupted at one point by a handkerchief tree *Davidia involucrata*. To the west of the sunk garden there is a small scented garden and also the nursery and propagating area.

The Crossing House, Shepreth
MR AND MRS DOUGLAS FULLER

Started in 1959, this garden has grown up beside the busy King's Cross to Cambridge railway line. In the main garden surrounding the house visitors may closely examine the smaller and choicer of the five thousand species and varieties grown. Roses and slow-growing shrubs are underplanted with old-fashioned cottage plants which mingle with uncommon varieties, ferns and subjects chosen for the variegated or otherwise interesting foliage, all confined in beds edged with low clipped box hedges. Although the soil is alkaline, camellias, rhododendrons and other calcifuges are included in sunken containers of acid compost.

Annuals and bulbs fill gaps, and climbing roses, *Clematis* and vines scramble up every possible wall and tree. Dwarf conifers and hellebores add interest during the quieter months until the *Hamamelis* blooms appear, red and gold above clumps of deep blue *Iris histrioides* 'Major' early in the spring.

Five raised beds overflow with alpines and small pools provide homes for aquatic flora and fauna; fountains and a waterfall delight the ear on hot still days. Three greenhouses shelter auriculas, tender bulbs and, during the winter, half-hardy shrubs.

Away on the far side of the railway (No Trespassing please!) can be seen the backcloth of the long border of plants bold enough to make an impact from a distance and of sufficient vigour to withstand the arid, stony soil of the trackside, draught from passing trains and splashes of diesel fuel and BR weed-killer.

The pink climbing rose 'Albertine' flourishes in these conditions and contrasts splendidly with the purple leaved hazel into which she has climbed.

Docwra's Manor, Shepreth
MRS JOHN RAVEN

The garden of Docwra's Manor surrounds a Queen Anne farmhouse on a flat site between road and railway. In 1954 we bought an acre and a half, subsequently expanded by another acre. In landscaping, we have used walls, farm buildings and internal hedging to subdivide the area into a series of enclosures of differing character; the walls give protection to plants typical of the Mediterranean garrigue. Collections of *Euphorbia* and *Clematis* species give interest from April to November. In late May, the pattern of perennial planting is diversified with gazanias, *Osteospermum* and *Chrysanthemum foeniculaceum* overwintered in the greenhouse. The main colours I use are greys as well as greens, blues, soft yellow and white with green. I like viridiflora tulips, *Ornithogalum nutans* and *Clematis viticella* 'Alba-luxurians'; the spiky biennial *Eryngium giganteum* contrasts in shape with *Lilium regale*. Yellow *Camassia leichtlinii* sows itself among groups of blue and brown *Iris germanica*.

I pay special attention to the beds I see from within the house. The bathroom window overlooks a succession of pink *Helleborus orientalis*, the near cerise of a large Judas tree underplanted with three shades of lily-flowered tulips and later by shrub roses.

Wherever *Rosa glauca (rubrifolia)* sows itself it enhances the colours of its neighbours. Self-sowing has always been encouraged, partly out of idleness and partly to give an unusual variety of height in each bed and a change of texture from year to year. Interference is limited to when the rampant plants threaten to exterminate the delicate, or the jungle to dislocate the overall plan.

◆

Duxford Mill
MR AND MRS ROBERT LEA

This garden extends to about five acres and was designed and made from wasteland alongside the river Cam, starting in 1948. As the land was flat, emphasis was placed on creating vistas from the beginning. The two most important examples are firstly, the view from the house looking down the river to a small Regency temple with a background of *Cupressus arizonica* and ×*C. leylandii* and, secondly, a large sculpture of angels by the noted Cambridge artist Wiles, which is also backed by various conifers covered with *Clematis montana* 'Elizabeth' and 'Tetratose', and flanked by two *Juniperus* 'Skyrocket' and two *Yucca filamentosa*.

Lawns running along the river and the rose borders, one of which is a hundred yards long, echo the river's curves. At the back of the borders the roses are some eight feet high graded to about two feet in the front and four roses deep; they make a splendid display in late June and July.

Groups of birches, *B. papyrifera*, *costata*, *jacquemontii* and *albo-sinensis* together with *Cornus* 'Westonbirt' light up in the winter sun to give a brilliant effect, and further on there is a series of small pools giving early spring interest with marsh marigolds, primulas and other aquatic plants.

A little later in the spring a group of trees and shrubs give a striking contrast of colour and shape. This group includes the *Acer pseudoplatanus* 'Brilliantissimum', purple hazel, Lawson's cypress 'Kilmacurragh', golden *Philadelphus*, weeping grey pear, and a purple weeping beech. Another spring delight is *Clematis alpina* 'Frances Rivis' scrambling over *Berberis stenophylla*, and later on in the same border a successful contrast is obtained by the proximity of *Clematis* 'Marie Boisselot' and *Cotinus coggygria* 'Foliis Purpureis'.

Lily-flowered tulips and grape hyacinths frame this view of Docwra's Manor, Shepreth, in early May. For a description of this garden see page 34.

Emmanuel College Garden and Fellows' Garden, Cambridge

There are many gardens of different kinds here, the oldest part surrounding a pool which probably goes back to the days of the monastery founded on the site in the thirteenth century. This, known as the Paddock, has many fine mature trees, dozens of ducks, moorhens and ornamental fowl, and one of the finest herbaceous borders to be seen. It is screened by a low wall from the Fellows' Garden (open to the public only under the National Gardens Scheme or by special arrangement), where there is a swimming-bath perhaps three centuries old and a magnificent oriental plane, as well as a superb copper beech. Within the College grounds there is a herb garden designed in about 1964 by John Codrington, who also designed the present layout of the Paddock. North Court contains a sunken oval with a *Paulownia tomentosa* and a manna ash, *Fraxinus ornus*, as well as hornbeams and a young cedar. But do not miss Chapman's garden, named after a Victorian Fellow who enjoyed the sole use of it. It has two tulip trees, and another pool overshadowed by a great weeping willow. The curious may seek for *Ehretia dicksonii* and *Celtis bungeana*, both of which can be traced with the help of a map obtainable at the Porter's Lodge.

Smaller gardens are the newly developed East Court, a model of adaptation to rather ugly backs of old houses, and the Roof Garden over the Junior Combination Room in South Court, meant to be 'self-maintaining',

Docwra's Manor in early May. An old sink, set under a scented *Viburnum*, contains the mutant form of grape hyacinth *Muscari armeniacum* 'Fairway Seedling' and the white *Muscari botryoides* var. *album*.

so far as that is possible. The really determined may also ask the Librarian's assistant to show them the Library Garden, tucked away in a sun-trap, and a great enticement to the non-studious student. After all that there remain only the floral strips with crabs and bird-cherries along St Andrew's street, and the barrier of colourful shrubs by the bus-stop in Emmanuel street. A Winter Garden in the Paddock is in preparation.

Hardwicke House, Fen Ditton

MR L. AND M.J. DRAKE

Situated amongst fields of wheat and barley, this exposed two-acre fenland garden is bordered by mature walnut trees that grow along Flem Dyke, a Saxon defence ditch. Hedges of beech, quickthorn, and hornbeam, pleached limes and silver birch avenues protect the planting which has been established within various enclosed spaces. Naturalized bulbs and wild violets welcome species tulips which grow amongst *Primula auricula* and perennial wallflowers such as 'Wenlock Beauty', 'Jacob's Jacket' and 'Old Bloody Warrior'. These scented varieties herald drifts of aquilegias (over eighty different varieties grow happily here) which are a feature of the garden in May. Above these and scrambling over sheds and into old fruit trees, roses flower profusely – *Rosa longicuspis* with its banana scent, *Rosa soulieana* with its delicate grey leaves and *Rosa moschata* with its ten thousand rose buds. All these and many more old-fashioned roses enjoy the rich brown loam, although one must check that new plants receive adequate water during the period of east winds which dry the soil in May.

Amongst the high hedge enclosures grow herbs, herbaceous plants and shrubs. Many of these were available to gardeners in this country before 1650. *Epilobium* and *Trifolium repens purpureum* are tucked under Good King Henry, whilst the feathery leaves of *Ferula communis* contrast with tough grey *Nepeta* foliage. Salvias, artemisias, origanums and lavenders bask in the baked August soil. These all respond to heavy mulching during the winter. By early summer the earth is covered with luxuriant foliage suppressing all weeds.

Hedges are trimmed with mechanized tools enabling the owners to relax and enjoy the fiery autumn shades of *Amelanchier*, *Euonymus alatus*, *Liriodendron tulipifera* and *Liquidambar* burning under harvest sunsets.

Home Grove, Grantchester

DR AND MRS C.B. GOODHART

Just over an acre of lawns and well-grown trees, with an orchard area over rough grass, are designed to provide vistas within a small space, and to encourage birds. A variety of shrubs, including roses of many types, flower throughout the summer and are easily main-tained without paid help. There is a 'Black Hamburg' vine in a small conservatory attached to the house, and a carefully planned kitchen garden with asparagus and seakale, as well as all the usual vegetables, a fruit cage and greenhouse.

King's College Fellows' Garden, Cambridge

As all local gardeners know, the chalky soils and relatively harsh, dry climate of Cambridge make their task unusually difficult. Nevertheless, the presence of the ancient University and its constituent Colleges means that the City possesses some fine gardens with mature specimens of unusual trees. The Fellows' Garden of King's College is a case in point. Laid out in the middle of the last century beyond the famous Backs with their superb view of the Chapel, it is a quiet, Victorian haven with a selection of interesting trees surrounding green lawns and a central, wooded island bed. Go there, if you can, in midsummer when the Pride of India or golden rain tree, *Koelreuteria paniculata*, is in flower: this unusually fine specimen is some eighty years old, and flowers and fruits regularly. Another tree well adapted to the Cambridge climate and soil is the Judas Tree, *Cercis siliquastrum*, of which the garden can boast two grand old specimens with gnarled and twisted branches, but still flowering freely in May every year. In the north-east corner of the main lawn is a magnificent specimen of the American black walnut, *Juglans nigra*, rarely seen in our gardens, and over on the west side a well-grown Chinese honey locust, *Gleditsia sinensis*, can be found. The garden can be dated by its wellingtonias, *Sequoiadendron giganteum*, of which there are two handsome trees overtopping the rest. This famous tree from the Californian coastal mountain ranges was not introduced into Britain until 1853, so that mature specimens date almost invariably from 1855 to 1870 – typical Victorian rectory garden trees!

When the garden is open to the public a small leaflet guide to the more interesting trees can be bought.

Leckhampton, Cambridge

CORPUS CHRISTI COLLEGE

Leckhampton House was built as a private house in 1880 by F. W. H. Myers, a prominent early member of the Society for Psychical Research, on land leased from the College. The long rectangular garden of seven acres, with the house at its northern end, was laid out by William Robinson. The house reverted to the College in 1961 and was used as the nucleus for a graduate residential community; a dining hall and residential block (Civic Trust Award 1965) have since been added, along with a further two acres of garden on the north side. Although altered in detail, the main garden has retained the principal features of Robinson's design, with lawn and herbaceous borders near the house changing into an extensive wild garden to the south. There are lime and chestnut avenues on the east and west sides, and fine specimen trees such as *Halesia* named after an old member of the College, Dr Stephen Hales (1671–1761), dating from the original planting. In the central waist of the garden are bulbs and spring flowers, cowslips and oxlips, and later lupins naturalized in the long grass. An old tennis court was replanted as a rose garden. There are many flowering cherries, including a fine *Prunus×hillieri* on the west side, and maples, *Parrotia* and autumn foliage on the east. The end of the garden is closed by a rockery bank, surmounted by a Grecian folly, originally formed from spoil from the adjacent lily pond, now converted into a swimming pool. The nearby wild garden under trees contains wild flowers, and other shrubs have been planted to encourage butterflies. The gardens added on the north side have fine lawns, with some heather beds.

Longstowe Hall, Longstowe

M.G.M. BEVAN, ESQ.

Laid out in 1910, the garden incorporates part of the park established in 1570 and retains some of the old park trees. It covers six acres, but is flanked by several acres of wild garden and a chain of three lakes, around which are a number of mown paths, offering attractive walks and vistas. This is all surrounded by woods and the park, giving a very secluded and peaceful atmosphere. The formal features include two long herbaceous borders between yew hedges, running down to the lakes and looking out over the park beyond, and a low-walled rose garden with twenty-five beds, each containing a single species enclosed by box hedging. Ornamental stonework plays a part through steps and balustrading at the bottom of the borders and a handsome bridge across the lakes. There is also elaborate balustrading with lead finials surmounting the rose garden walls but the stone is badly decayed, its replacement cost prohibitive, and a different solution will have to be found.

The floral display starts with big clumps of daffodils in the outlying areas which also produce a wide variety of wild flowers, and the woods are a natural home for oxlips followed by bluebells. The borders and rose gardens come into their own from June onwards. However, the principal glory of the garden is its extensive lawns and fine collection of specimen trees. The soil, being heavy clay with a strong lime content, imposes some restrictions, but the range of trees is impressive and the harmony of their various textures and colours very satisfying. In the main, big trees when mature fit the scale but need a lot of room; luckily the space is available and the sense of spaciousness is not lost.

Manor House, Boxworth
LT.-COL. E.B. THORNHILL

In 1882 this was a small farmhouse garden about one-eighth its present size. It was enlarged by taking in parts of adjoining fields and laid out by the head gardener of Diddington Hall, Huntingdon, with many trees, shrubs and flower beds and a long yew hedge. After about fifty years everything had grown so much that it was overcrowded and many trees and shrubs were removed making a much more attractive lawn. About the end of June the roses, herbaceous borders and bedding plants are at their best, and adjoining, in an old orchard, can be seen mistletoe, planted here in 1922.

◆

Melbourn Bury, Nr Royston
MR AND MRS ANTHONY HOPKINSON

The first impression of this garden is one of space. Large mature beeches frame a sweeping lawn which slopes gently down to a small lake with an island. Facing this is the house and a south-facing redbrick wall which shelters a long herbaceous border and forms a good backdrop for climbing roses such as 'New Dawn' and 'Albertine'. The lake and stream are fed by natural springs and this gives us scope to plant water and moisture-loving plants. The *Gunnera manicata* has done spectacularly well and so have the astilbes and *Scrophularia aquatica* 'Variegata'. The path by the herbaceous border leads on over a branch of the stream to the rose garden which is walled on two sides. Rose beds and box hedges surround a paved area with a stone sundial. The outer borders are filled with larger shrubs and more climbing roses which are also being trained up old apple trees. The most eye-catching shrub is *Buddleja alternifolia* with its cascade of mauve flowers in June.

Under the trees, and in the rough grass, there is a procession of spring flowers starting with snowdrops and finishing with a carpet of snakeshead fritillaries of chequered mauve and white.

As the house is largely late Victorian we plan to have many more climbing and shrub roses of that period. Every year we learn more and more and the garden is constantly developing. We know now that although the garden is sheltered it is also a frost pocket so we can only plant hardy plants. We are also hoping to have a herb garden and a white garden so we will be busy for many years to come.

◆

Melbourn Lodge, Melbourn
J.R.M. KEATLEY, ESQ.

The Grade Two listed house and garden were acquired in 1968 in a state of incipient dereliction. Since then there has been a policy of continuous improvement with a good deal of building work. Efforts have been made to create a private garden providing a multi-plicity of views, carefully interwoven, and some botanical interest. Views from the house are regarded as particularly important. Importance is also attached to ease of management and the aim is a two-acre garden capable of being maintained on less than twenty hours work per week in season. So far form has been given priority over content; but this is expected to change in the near future. There is a small collection of modern (post 1960) sculpture. Neither the soil nor the site is especially promising, the soil being alkaline with the chalk, in places, just below the surface. The site, while irregular, seems to possess a certain strength of design. One of the best specimens is *Cornus controversa* 'Variegata', planted in 1970, and now about twelve feet high. There is a large collection of bulbs and small collections of conifers, *Erica carnea*, *Iris*, *Clematis* and shrub roses, all of which flourish on the chalk. All seasons are catered for and plants which offer, or are capable of offering, more than one season of enjoyment are preferred. Thus *Prunus serrulata pubescens* supports *Clematis montana rubens* and an old but sturdy apple is burdened with *Rosa* 'Kiftsgate'.

◆

North End House, Grantchester
SIR MARTIN AND LADY NOURSE

This garden has been doubled in size by the acquisition of half an acre of derelict land which now consists mainly of lawns and shrub borders designed and planted under the guidance of Cdr. Charles Alington.

The boundary between the old and new land is formed by rose pergolas standing in twin herbaceous borders.

Other features are a water garden and rockery, old-fashioned roses and hornbeam and yew hedges. There is a small conservatory at the west end of the house.

◆

The Old Vicarage, Grantchester
MR AND MRS J.H. ARCHER

The present form of this garden owes much to Samuel Page Widnall, who bought the house in 1853 from Corpus Christi College, thus turning it from the Vicarage into the Old Vicarage. Widnall designed and built many features in the garden, notably the Castle Ruin (1857), the book sundial (1862) and the fountain (1865). The house is best known for its association with the poet Rupert Brooke, who lodged in it in 1911–12. Of Grantchester and the house, he wrote thus to Ka Cox: 'There is no wind and no sun, only a sort of warm haze, and through it the mingled country sounds of a bee, a mowing machine, a mill and a sparrow. Peace!' and to his cousin Erica Cotterill: 'This is a deserted, lonely, dank, ruined, overgrown, gloomy, lovely house with a garden to match.' Some of the garden still merits this judgement and the affectionate description later provided by Brooke in the poem *The Old Vicarage, Grant-chester* must be regarded as little less than an injunction to plant poppies and pinks. There is still abundant green gloom to be found at the foot of the garden by the river Granta although, sadly, the elm clumps no longer greatly stand; they were felled in 1980, victims of Dutch Elm disease. The present garden extends to nearly three acres with three main lawns, a wild garden and kitchen and herb gardens. There are many fine mature trees, including a cut-leaf beech, mulberry, walnut and *Catalpa* so that much of the garden is shady. There is a sunny herbaceous border and many parts of the garden have been newly planted with flowering shrubs, but these will not appear to advantage for several years.

◆

The Old Vicarage, Pampisford

Next to the well-kept church and churchyard, supported by the presence of mature trees, box and yew bushes, it is possible to get the atmosphere of a vicarage garden in the early part of this century.

A border under a north wall combines three different colour schemes; one end is blue and yellow; pink, white and red dominate the middle section, and the far end combines cream and green with a hint of pink. On the wall itself roses and *Clematis*, such as 'Comtesse de Bouchaud', 'Ville de Lyon' and 'Kathleen Harrop', flourish. An island border contains a pretty association of *Romneya × hybrida* and *Alstroemeria ligtu* hybrids backed by a large clump of *Aruncus dioicus*. Large areas of white predominate, using roses such as 'Iceberg' with white delphiniums, and ground cover plants such as *Lamium* are widely used.

A small conservatory, in keeping with the Victorian background of the house, demands much of our time but is a great joy in the cold winter months.

◆

Peckover, Wisbech
THE NATIONAL TRUST

This is a Victorian garden with broadleaved evergreens and exotic trees, full of interesting plants and worthy of exploration.

Around the eastern lawn near the house is the Wilderness Walk between the rich dark greens of hollies, laurels, box and yew, relieved by the spotted laurel, *Aucuba japonica*, and underplanted with hardy ferns. There are fine examples of *Gingko biloba*, tulip tree (*Liriodendron tulipifera*) and fernleaved beech (*Fagus sylvatica heterophylla*). On the western side are informal beds of evergreens and flowering shrubs with two specimens of the Californian redwood, the world's tallest recorded tree in its native habitat but a little tender for East Anglia, and a tall specimen of the hardy Chusan palm (*Trachycarpus fortunei*). The perimeter path passes the restored summer house, a nineteenth-century rustic Doric temple, shaded by a large evergreen oak (*Quercus*

Leckhampton House, Cambridge. Thousands of lupins are naturalized in the rough grass in this garden, laid out by William Robinson around 1880. For a description see page 36.

two glasshouses open to visitors. The first supplies tender plants for the garden and Orangery and the small lean-to glasshouse contains a collection of tender ferns. R. G. Peeling, the Trust's gardener-in-charge here, propagates all his own roses, climbers and ramblers, from hardwood cuttings. Throughout the garden the old walls carry many kinds of old-fashioned roses and other climbing plants.

The Rectory, Fen Ditton
REV. AND MRS L.A. MARSH

The garden of this late seventeenth-century house has been reduced to about one acre, but we are fortunate in retaining part of the original orchard and some lovely mature trees including a medlar, a fine beech, a large ash and limes. We have added to these by planting a mulberry, walnut, apricot, peach, fig, greengage, Morello cherries and several varieties of apple. The peach and the apricot are planted on a south wall and provide magnificent blossom early in the spring followed by some good fruit in the summer.

The kitchen garden consists of two large vegetable plots and a fruit cage – these produce sufficient vegetables for the year and about a hundred and fifty pounds of soft fruit. In 1984 we decided to become 'organic

gardeners' and the results have been most satisfactory. Most of the pests are controlled by homemade sprays, and we are lucky to have our own supply of poultry manure and plenty of leaves for the compost heap.

Winter ends with the arrival of many varieties of snowdrop and aconites. Spring is heralded by an abundance of bulbs including *Chionodoxa* and *Ornithogalum nutans* and is crowned by the magnificent sight of *Fritillaria imperialis*. Roses and herbaceous plants provide plenty of interest in the summer, and we have planted thirty-five varieties of old-fashioned and species roses and hope to add to these over the years. Our particular favourite is 'Rambling Rector' which we really feel belongs to the place! We have some interesting and rare plants in the mixed borders including the purple-flowered *Phlomis tuberosa* and an *Arisaema candidissimum*.

There is also a small herb garden conveniently placed under the kitchen window, and a very fine old grapevine reputed to be about two hundred years old.

Wimpole Hall, Arrington
THE NATIONAL TRUST

The grounds here form part of a three-hundred-and-fifty-acre park; there are many fine trees and a good display of daffodils in April.

ilex) and a small garden of roses edged with lavender that leads to the Orangery. East of this is a new border designed to give colour and form within a repetitive pattern of Victorian formality.

The Orangery contains traditional flowering plants in pots arranged for display and is dominated by some old orange trees which fruit regularly. Leading from the Orangery to the second summer house are double borders edged with pinks, one side being almost a mirror image of the other, with a variety of interesting and beautiful plants grouped according to colour. Iron cones support roses and *Clematis* and are backed by a short decorative hedge to divide each colour scheme from the next. Beyond the topiary peacocks is a pond surrounded by hydrangeas, paeonies and *Lilium henryi* edged with *Sedum spectabile*.

A right turn here leads into the third section, which until recently was mainly kitchen garden with a drive running through it. Here is a nursery border containing flowers for cutting, mixed borders of shrubs and herbaceous plants and specimen fruit trees, including a quince and a mulberry, recalling the original use of the area. Beyond the hedge are

Romneya × hybrida (R. coulteri × R. trichocalyx) thrives at the Old Vicarage, Pampisford, where it has formed a huge clump, covered in July with delicate white flowers. The name *R. coulteri* commemorates two Irishmen, the Rev. T. Romney Robinson (1792-1881) an astronomer, and his friend Dr. T. Coulter (1793–1843) who collected plants in California and Mexico.

CHESHIRE, THE WIRRAL, DERBYSHIRE AND STAFFORDSHIRE

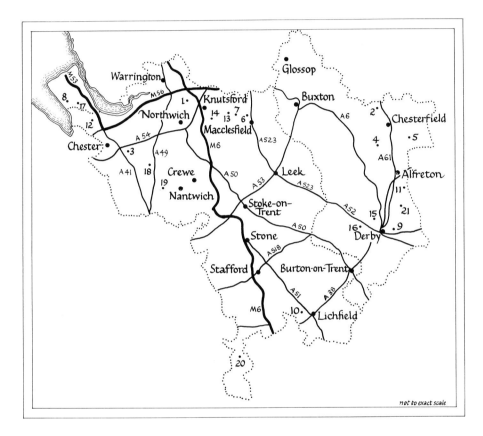

not to exact scale

Directions to Gardens

Arley Hall and Gardens, 6 miles west of Knutsford, Cheshire. [1]

Bramley Hall Cottage, Chapel Lane, Apperknowle, 5 miles north of Chesterfield, Derbyshire. [2]

Coomb Dale, Bickerton, Malpas, 10 miles southeast of Chester, Cheshire. [3]

Darley House, Darley Dale, 2 miles north of Matlock, Derbyshire. [4]

Hardwick Hall, Doe Lea, 8 miles southeast of Chesterfield, Derbyshire. [5]

Harebarrow, Chelford Road, Prestbury, 3 miles north of Macclesfield, Cheshire. [6]

Hare Hill, between Alderley Edge and Prestbury, 5 miles northwest of Macclesfield, Cheshire. [7]

Heathergate, Oldfield Road, Heswall, Wirral. [8]

Locko Park, Spondon, 6 miles northeast of Derby, Derbyshire. [9]

Moseley Old Hall, Fordhouses, 3¼ miles north of Wolverhampton, Staffordshire. [10]

210 Nottingham Road, Woodlinkin, Langley Mill, Derbyshire, 12 miles northwest of Nottingham. [11]

The Old Hall, Hadlow Road, Willaston, South Wirral, 8 miles northwest of Chester, Cheshire. [12]

Penn, Macclesfield Road, Alderley Edge, ¾ mile east of Alderley Edge village, Cheshire. [13]

Peover Hall, Over Peover, 3 miles south of Knutsford, Cheshire. [14]

Quarndon Hall, Church Road, Quarndon, northwest of Derby, Derbyshire. [15]

Radburne Hall, Kirk Langley, 5 miles west of Derby, Derbyshire. [16]

Thornton Manor, Thornton Hough, Wirral, from M53 exit 4 to Heswall, Cheshire. [17]

Tiresford, ½ mile south of Tarporley, Cheshire. [18]

Tushingham Hall, 3 miles north of Whitchurch, Cheshire. [19]

Wightwick Manor, Compton, 3 miles west of Wolverhampton, Staffordshire. [20]

5 Wood Lane, Horsley Woodhouse, 6 miles north of Derby, Derbyshire. [21]

Arley Hall, Nr Knutsford

THE HON. M.L.W. FLOWER

The greater part of these large gardens is enclosed by yew hedges and old brick walls, but on one side they overlook parkland seen from a long terrace laid out a hundred and fifty years ago by Rowland Egerton-Warburton and his wife; the gardens have been extended by four generations of his descendants. Their original and most noteworthy features are a pleached lime avenue and, virtually unchanged since its creation in 1846, a double herbaceous border flanked by a high yew hedge and a brick wall. An avenue of *Quercus ilex*, clipped into cylindrical shapes over twenty feet high, is also very unusual.

More recent additions include four enclosed formal gardens, a large collection of shrub roses, and an arboretum of rhododendrons, azaleas and ornamental trees. In addition, one of the two walled gardens (which in former years was a kitchen garden) has been converted to open lawns surrounded by shrubs with a pond and floribunda roses in the centre; and an alpine rock and water dell has been replanted with flowering shrubs and shade-loving plants. Here the blue poppy *Meconopsis grandis* thrives, looking magical among the pink, yellow and apricot azaleas.

The herbaceous border has two periods of colour; in early summer it is basically blue, mauve, acid yellow and white with delphiniums, cranesbills, *Campanula*, *Achillea* and *Verbascum*, whose colours are complemented by the light spring growth of the yew hedge. Later months bring stronger, more varied colours, turning to dark reds, golden-yellows and orange as autumn approaches.

Bramley Hall Cottage, Apperknowle
MR AND MRS G.G. NICHOLSON

This one-and-a-third-acre garden has been developed over twenty years on a south-facing slope looking over a valley to some of the hills of the beautiful Derbyshire countryside. We were fortunate that there were already some large conifers, a copper beech and many old apple trees, but we were faced with too many old privet hedges.

There is something of everything here; big shrub beds with ground cover, herbaceous beds, heather and conifer areas and a small amount of bedding. Some apple trees which we have cut down have been replaced by acers, *Sorbus*, *Cercis*, *Cercidiphyllum*, *Davidia*, *Nyssa*, *Embothrium*, *Halesia* and *Prunus*, including the magnificent snowwhite Japanese cherry 'Shimidsu Sakura', which looks so beautiful against an *Acer pseudoplatanus* 'Brilliantissimum'.

The shrub collection includes most of the common flowering shrubs but also many not so common including the striking *Viburnum plicatum* 'Lanarth' and the *Viburnum plicatum* (Japanese Snowball) which are at their best in June. Many kinds of *Cornus* are represented including the rare *C. alternifolia* 'Argentea'. All the beds of shrubs, heathers and perennials are of irregular shape and this, together with the slope of the garden and the height of shrubs and conifers, allows one to wander along the paths without at any time being able to see more than a small part of the garden, leaving the visitor wondering what delights are around the next bend.

Coomb Dale, Bickerton
MR AND MRS A.G. BARBOUR

The site, on a south-facing hillside, defies any attempt at formality in layout. This is essentially a garden of shrubs and trees together with an arboretum hidden in a natural valley, or comb, behind the house. This contains many rare conifers and deciduous trees as well as established hardy hybrid rhododendrons in many pretty shades of colour. Planting of the shrub borders is quite informal and follows the steep slopes of the garden. Rhododendrons are the chief spring attraction and many not completely hardy varieties have survived successive droughts and hard winters. Droughts have a particularly damaging effect on our light sandy soil, and a hard winter very often delivers the knock-out blow. We try and choose shrubs which will survive in these conditions and like poor soil. The successes include many varieties of *Cistus*, *Helianthemum* and broom. *Lithospermum* is a winner and shrub roses do well. Hydrangeas are risked for their essential late summer contribution and for foliage *Santolina neapolitana* is outstanding. We have tried to plan our planting so that there is something attractive to see from April to September.

Darley House, Darley Dale
MR AND MRS G.H. BRISCOE

Restoring a garden is one thing, but when that garden was originally owned by Sir Joseph Paxton, it becomes a daunting task. Extending to one and a quarter acres, well endowed with lawns, yews, copper beech, gingkos and a wellingtonia, all a hundred and fifty years old, the garden is on two levels separated by a stone balustrade and steps which are a replica of those at nearby Haddon Hall.

The garden comes to life in spring, with drifts of double snowdrops duly followed by a large variety of daffodils which cover a mound surmounted by an old copper beech giving a most pleasing effect.

Colour plays an important part with *Clematis viticella* dominating a tall conifer leading to *Abutilon vitifolium* growing through the *Cytisus battandieri* with *Rosa glauca (rubrifolia)* and *R.* 'Constance Spry' on either side.

The front of the house (which faces south) is covered with *Clematis*, *Wisteria* and a *Magnolia* with beds of scented plants beneath. Two large herbaceous borders below the balustrade contain perennials and shrubs such as *Tamarix pentandra*, *Geranium phaeum*, *Paeonia cambessedesii* and *Jasminum × stephanense*, to give a blending of form and texture without neglecting the charm of toning colours.

A newly restored alpine scree formed from several tons of tufa, 'found' some years ago in a corner of the garden, now holds an extensive range of alpines which complement the contents of the several Derbyshire stone troughs situated at strategic points.

In a shaded part of the garden, a complete bed is devoted to a wide range of hostas interspersed with *Acer japonicum* 'Aureum' *Smilacina*, *Polygonatum*, epimediums and *Digitalis* 'Apricot' and *D. lutea*.

To add a further dimension, a pond has now been constructed at the foot of a bank which has large gritstones interspersed with various acers and rhododendrons.

Hardwick Hall, Doe Lea
THE NATIONAL TRUST

This fine Elizabethan house is surrounded by grass walks between yew and hornbeam hedges, fine cedar trees, and a herb garden.

Harebarrow, Prestbury
MR AND MRS C.A. SAVAGE

When we moved to Prestbury from Switzerland in 1975 we decided to make some changes, setting out to create a low-maintenance garden with year-round colour using heathers supplemented by conifers and evergreen shrubs.

The one-acre garden, set on a hill and with distant views of the Pennines, has a water

garden, a pond where moorhens nest, formal rose beds and the more informal heather beds. In January *Erica carnea* and *E. × darleyensis* are already flowering, many continuing to provide colour until May. Pernettyas and *Viburnum tinus* are also attractive in winter, while in spring *Erica arborea* and *E. umbellata* flower and are joined by azaleas, *Berberis*, alpine phloxes, aubrietas, *Arabis* and *Iberis*. Naturalized daffodils and bluebells give drifts of colour, followed by mature rhododendrons, then *Erica cinerea*, *tetralix*, *terminalis* and *Daboecia cantabrica* flower for up to five months. In June *Kalmia angustifolia* and the hebes are attractive; in late summer *Erica vagans* and *ciliaris* bloom together with the callunas. The latter last until December, by which time the early *Erica carnea* is already out; the cycle is complete. Every month something is in bloom, and many conifers change the colour of their foliage three times during the year. At all times the garden looks tidy and attractive, with weeding a thing of the past. The vegetable garden was reorganized in 1980 around deep beds separated by slab paths. Yields improved – and slab paths mean that less soil is transferred from garden to house. A peach tree, ('Peregrine'), and a vine ('Black Hamburg') were planted in the greenhouse, and outside cordon redcurrants, gooseberries and apples were introduced in the autumn of 1984, together with an asparagus bed.

The adjoining two-acre paddock supports about eight, or with their lambs about twenty, black and white Jacob's sheep. Even they, and the pheasants which stroll across in winter, contribute to the colour in our garden.

Hare Hill, Prestbury
THE NATIONAL TRUST

The garden at Hare Hill was created by the late Colonel Brocklehurst. Around the walled garden he built on an existing framework of hardy hybrid rhododendrons and had not completed the work by the time of his death in 1981. The Trust is completing the development of the garden.

It is primarily a spring garden, consisting of woodland walks, dells, water and rustic bridges, with an extremely good collection of both species and hybrid rhododendrons, deciduous and evergreen azaleas, specimen trees and a number of holly cultivars. The woodland garden surrounds the walled garden in which there is a pretty gazebo, two modern sculptures and a formal pattern of *Pyrus salicifolia* and *Malus floribunda*. The walls are all clothed with climbing plants conforming to a blue, white and yellow colour scheme.

Heathergate, Heswall
DR ANNA SEAGER

The house is south-west facing, and the one-

and-a-half-acre garden slopes, at first gently and then more steeply, south-west towards the Heswall Dales and the estuary of the river Dee, three hundred feet below and about a mile away. Beyond the Dee there is a wide view of the North Wales coast, a scene of great natural beauty.

The view was the inspiration for the garden form. It had to be outward-looking, forming a framework for the landscape of the estuary and the hills beyond. The original soil was shallow peat over sandstone, so planting had to be mainly of *Ericaceae*, although we also grew roses, shrub and hybrid tea, in beds near the house, and lately a long island bed of grey, pink and red plants has worked well.

There is a main lawn of informal shape joining up with a smaller round lawn which is sheltered by a semi-circle of golden×*Cupressocyparis leylandii*. The lawn is surrounded by heathers, azaleas and rhododendrons, also *Myrtus*, *Pieris*, *Enkianthus* and *Genista*.

The trees, carefully placed, are *Sorbus*, *Eucalyptus*, *Eucryphia*, many *Acer* species and, of course, silver birch.

Paths zig-zag down the steeply sloping site, and smaller lawns were formed by building up walls on the river side and levelling the ground above, so that one lawn is semi-circular and forms a fine viewpoint with a seat set back between azaleas. A further small lawn stands as on a rampart above the Dales.

There is a small formal pool edged by primulas, hostas, *Arundinaria viridistriata* and a fine *Phormium* which makes a good architectural feature.

In planting the garden we gradually dug up most but not all of the original heather. The latter is still an important feature of the garden and by keeping it closely trimmed every winter it forms an unusual and effective edging to the paths.

◆

*Locko Park, Spondon
CAPT. P.J.B. DRURY-LOWE

A lovely park landscape which was mainly laid out in the late eighteenth century, with its large lake and many fine trees, provides a beautiful and tranquil setting for the house. Recent alterations on the immediate south side of the house have centred on the removal of various late Victorian additions to the garden and the restoration of the original ha-ha; this undoubtedly enhances the view across the park towards the lake. Newly-planted beds against the two wings of the house link it to the grass terrace lawn, while a large block of mixed hybrid rhododendrons in the south-west corner provides the necessary balance to the planting on this side.

The small formal Italian rose garden with its walls covered by many *Clematis* in summer, provides an ideal link between the house and the pleasure grounds which form the main part of the garden on the north side. Here is a wide collection of conifers and magnolias, together with many smaller trees. *Halesia*

carolina and *Robinia pseudoacacia* 'Frisia' are two examples amongst those carefully chosen trees which seem to set off the massiveness of the conifers so effectively. The area is widely planted with many different azaleas and rhododendrons. Last year, large parts of the pleasure grounds were cleared in order to create space for the planting of later flowering shrubs. This has mainly been achieved by block planting of hydrangeas; a large group of the white-flowering 'Madame Emile Mouillière' near some mature yews being particularly impressive.

◆

Moseley Old Hall, Fordhouses
THE NATIONAL TRUST

This is a small, modern reconstruction of a seventeenth-century garden with a formal box parterre, old roses, herbaceous plants, a small herb garden and an arbour.

◆

210 Nottingham Road, Woodlinkin
MR AND MRS R. BROWN

This is a garden of half an acre situated on a west-facing slope with clay soil that grows all kinds of shrub roses well. These range from 'Rosa Mundi' dating from the sixteenth century to the contemporary 'Golden Chersonese', and from the 'Miss Lowe' to the wall-covering 'Climbing Cécile Brunner'.

The idea of the garden is to give interest all the year round, to cover the ground with plants, and to encourage self-sown seedlings. An herbaceous layer of hellebores, geraniums, symphytums and similar plants give a framework for more seasonal herbaceous plants. A wide variety of deciduous and evergreen shrubs and trees ensures continuing interest of shape, colour and foliage.

The brick base of a disused greenhouse, with central 'walk-in' aisle, provides a good home for alpine plants.

◆

The Old Hall, Willaston
DR AND MRS WOOD

The Old Hall is a very fine seventeenth-century house, built as a farmhouse but now in the middle of the village. The garden is an irregular rectangle surrounded by a sandstone wall and also sheltered as far as possible from the wind and surrounding houses by trees and hedges. As there is no view outside, the aim has been to make it a garden of enclosures and vistas in a small space using yew hedges, sandstone walls and paving. We have mixed borders, shrub roses, fish ponds and terraces, kitchen garden and fruit. Nearly all the shrubs have been propagated from cuttings, and after eighteen years it is beginning to be difficult for many weeds to find a foothold.

Some shrubs give particular pleasure every year – *Cotinus coggygria* and *Lonicera*×*ameri-*

cana are so good they have been propagated for gardeners of greater repute in the south of England! In the winter come *Hamamelis mollis* 'Jelena' and *Viburnum* × *bodnantense* 'Dawn', and in spring, the reward of years of planting of daffodils and tulips in the orchard and polyanthus and primroses grown from Barnhaven seed. In the summer, roses, herbaceous plants and lilies, *Lonicera tragophylla* and *L.* × *tellmanniana* provide the highlights. There are always different colours of foliage, yellow conifers and shrubs, *Euonymus*, *Pyrus salicifolia*, species of *Rodgersia*, *Hosta*, *Euphorbia* and as many other grey-leaved plants and shrubs as I can find to give shape and colour when flowers are not around.

◆

Penn, Alderley Edge
MR AND MRS R.W. BALDWIN

Situated about five hundred feet up on the ridge of Alderley Edge, a spur of the Pennines, with a 15° slope westwards and acid sandy soil, this garden has been planted since 1949 with a wide variety of shrubs and trees but especially a notable collection of rhododendrons. The top backs on to the steep north-east slope of the Edge, so that the winter winds roar over our heads and we can grow species that fail in the plain below. In clear weather we see the Clwyd range by Denbigh, and the Berwyns in mid Wales.

The garden has two main parts, the first a large three-cornered lawn, overlooked by the house, surrounded by trees and shrubs, including camellias, and the second, the hill slope full of rhododendrons, deciduous and Japanese azaleas and other genera, but also including a secluded rectangular lawn which is the only level land on the site. This is bordered by shrubs chosen for leaf colour, especially gold, silver and grey.

The rhododendrons comprise about five hundred species and hybrids, from dwarfs to giants, flowering from January to August. Species include *R. mucronulatum, moupinense, ciliatum, impeditum, fargesii, fulvum, cinnabarinum, orbiculare, augustinii, yakushimanum, griersonianum, fortunei, thomsonii, wardii, macabeanum, rex, basilicum, calophytum, montroseanum, falconeri* etc., and the hybrids concentrate on the woodland sorts from *griersonianum, griffithianum, augustinii, cinnabarinum* and so forth. In spring there are masses of bluebells and euphorbias, some *Meconopsis*, an *Embothrium*, a *Davidia* and several species of *Magnolia*; and for later, *Eucryphia* 'Nymansay' plus the usual summer shrubs with *Cistus, Hebe, Hypericum, Potentilla* and *Hydrangea* in variety. Conifers include *Sequoia sempervirens, Taxodium, Gingko, Abies koreana*, cedars and many others.

◆

Peover Hall, Nr Knutsford
MR AND MRS RANDLE BROOKS

The garden of Peover was opened for the

The Old Hall, Willaston, Wirral, in June. Variegated foliage contrasts are provided here by *Acer negundo* 'Variegatum' and *Robinia pseudoacacia* 'Frisia'. For a description see previous page.

National Gardens Scheme for the first time in 1985. It is an old and established garden surrounded in parts by mellow brick walls. There is a large formal yew planting dating from early this century known as the Theatre Garden reached by a pleached lime walk. Beyond lies a woodland garden, the Wilderness, and a nineteenth-century Dell, with its rockery, old cedars and large rhododendrons and azaleas, which are a blaze of colour in late spring and early summer. The walled gardens near the house make a series of garden rooms; lily pond, rose, herb, white and pink gardens. They have been replanted since 1982 with many old-fashioned roses and other plants chosen for their scent and colour. The Elizabethan house has, on its walls, *Wisteria* and white roses intertwined with *Clematis*.

A blue and white border lies under one end of the house and opposite is the purple border. Over this is the Church Tower built in the mid-eighteenth century; the walk to the church has been planted to give a heady scent on the way to worship. Beyond the garden are the park and woods, laid out in the 1760s with a six-acre lake. On the other side lies the moat which surrounded the earlier house. Both these have been dredged recently to improve the setting of the house and garden.

After the war, all was deserted, ruinous and overgrown; it has taken many years to restore the whole. Perhaps the principal charms of our garden are its variety due to the many owners who have loved and extended it; its colours, sculptural yew hedging, and ornamentation.

Quarndon Hall, Quarndon
MR AND MRS PAUL BIRD

A one-acre lawn slopes down from the house to a small lake fed by a natural stream. There are mature oak, beech and yew trees in this very pleasant setting, and a *Taxodium distichum* which is at least sixty feet high.

Replanting started in 1980, and new borders are still being made with new plants introduced as fast as the available labour allows.

Rhododendrons, of which there are several hundred different species and hybrids, occupy the most favoured positions, but there are also many other unusual trees and shrubs.

The field which rises from the other side of the lake has been partly converted with the aid of fifty tons of local magnesium limestone and a waterfall, and tree planting is under way above this.

The terrace at the side of the house has been renewed and a conservatory and camellia house added bringing colour in spring and summer.

Radburne Hall, Kirk Langley
MAJ. AND MRS J.W. CHANDOS-POLE

Radburne Hall itself is a fine seven-bay Palladian mansion, built by William Smith of Warwick, circa 1735–40. The ground floor is of rusticated stone springing from which is red brick of a very pleasing quality and a fine entablature of stone with a segmental pediment containing fine stone carving. Around the house the garden is formal with a display of rhododendrons to the south, a sunken bowling green to the west and three rose terraces to the north. On the east side of the top terrace is a remarkable *Magnolia* planted by Erasmus Darwin between 1781 and 1783. There is also a fine display of roses of six different kinds.

The remainder of the garden is an extensive landscape garden with many lovely trees and shrubs and notably one magnificent *Cedrus libani* and a *Fagus sylvatica purpurea*.

The walled kitchen garden of about one and a half acres is now used for growing Christmas trees.

Thornton Manor, Thornton Hough
THE VISCOUNT LEVERHULME

The gardens at Thornton Manor were laid out by Thomas Mawson, working in close conjunction with the first Viscount Leverhulme. In front of the manor is lawn and a pattern of sandstone paths, looking down over some thirty acres of what are now horse pastures. The gardens extend either side of these pastures to give 'a garden for promenading and walking' as were Lord Leverhulme's instructions. There are long lime walks either side of the manor front. The Forum is the first feature, ablaze with roses and *Clematis* in midsummer. A fall in level leads to the tennis lawn flanked by a beautiful sandstone tea house which forms one wall of a large kitchen garden. The centre of this garden is now a paddock, but the original espaliers and patterns are retained over most of it.

Below the tennis lawn is the main garden centred around a sunken rose circle, with an Italian marble fountain in the middle. Around this circle are small gardens and paths with steps, mostly flanked by azaleas and rhododendrons and quite heavily wooded. The whole area is very beautiful and used to be considered a spring garden. Today, thanks to the late Lady Leverhulme's efforts, continued most ably by George Kenyon, head gardener, it remains just as fine throughout the summer. A number of new features have been made, including a lovely walk behind the sunny brick wall of the kitchen garden, which leads to a laburnum arch.

Beyond this a path leads round the horse pasture to join with the other side of the gardens, smaller in area, but containing a lovely small dell with ornamental pond and bridge. The dell leads back up to the manor through an area, in the spring, of crocuses, fritillaries and, later, daffodils. Mention should also be made of the beautiful lake with its wooded walks around the perimeter, approached over a bridge, which is an ancient 'look-out'.

Tiresford, Tarporley
MR AND MRS R.J. POSNETT

This garden was redesigned in 1938, having some lovely old trees to enhance and make good backgrounds. A huge oak tree stands on the lawn with wonderful views of Beeston Castle and the Peckforton Hills beyond.

There is a stone terrace on two sides of the house and there is a lily pond surrounded by water-loving plants and a bank of azaleas. As a background to the large herbaceous borders, there is a fine holly hedge in a semi-circular shape; beyond this is a pleasant kitchen garden.

Recently a new swimming pool has been skilfully placed in a sunken lawn without spoiling the old world charm of a real English garden.

◆

Tushingham Hall, Whitchurch
F. MOOR DUTTON, ESQ.

This medium-sized garden situated in beautiful countryside has interesting shrubs and trees including a very tall *Gingko biloba*.

It looks on to a pool measuring an acre and three quarters with a bluebell wood alongside, and an ancient oak twenty-five feet in girth. On the east side is part of the moat which originally surrounded the Manor House which was rebuilt in 1814.

◆

Wightwick Manor, Compton
THE NATIONAL TRUST

A seventeen-acre Victorian-style garden largely laid out by Alfred Parsons, famous for his illustrations of roses in *The Genus Rosa* by Ellen Willmott. Not surprisingly, there are roses in this garden, but there are also herbaceous plants, yew hedges and an arbour covered with *Clematis*. Also of interest to the garden visitor is the house, which contains many examples of the work of William Morris, the leading member of the pre-Raphaelites who derived so much inspiration from the colours and forms of flowers.

◆

5 Wood Lane, Horsley Woodhouse
MR AND MRS T.P. BOOTH

This three-quarter-acre garden, set in a pleasant rural position with good views over local farmland, has been created gradually by us since 1970. The soil is alkaline, suitable for the wide variety of trees, shrubs and perennials which we grow. The well-established Scots pines and ash trees blend well with the local gritstone used in the pergola, rockery and walls.

The perennial flower borders also contain shrubs to provide colour and change throughout the year, and the flower beds are packed with 'cottage garden' plants to provide a natural effect and reduce weeding. Plants such as poppies are allowed to seed themselves, where possible, and tend to grow in gay abandon within the borders.

The lawns are linked by paths, planned to provide interesting, colourful views and an element of surprise. Selected conifers, such as cedars and spruce, are planted in the lawns with space to grow to their natural shapes.

During spring the variegated maples provide a colourful background to the lawns, while in summer, the many shrubs and climbing roses give an attractive display, and their scent pervades the garden. *Clematis* climb naturally amongst the trees and roses.

Topiary, fine yew hedges and a design of beautiful paths in the rose garden at Peover Hall in early June. For a description of the garden see page 41.

43

CORNWALL

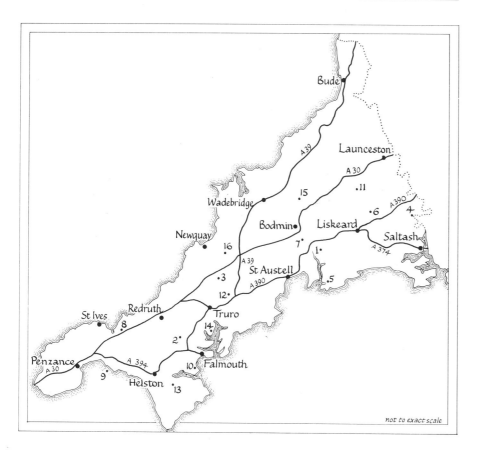

not to exact scale

Directions to Gardens

Boconnoc, Nr Lostwithiel

CAPT. J.D.G. FORTESCUE

The typically Cornish gardens of Boconnoc are situated in the centre of a well-wooded estate surrounded by deep, wooded valleys which were planted by members of the Pitt and Fortescue families. Now rich in lichens the trees are old, some oaks having witnessed civil war battles.

On arrival visitors first enter the 'Dorothy Garden' named after the present owner's grandmother. They should look back from the fountain and see the beautiful view of the wooded Lerryn river valley. Next is the shrubbery and here can be seen a fine example of a Japanese umbrella tree, a lily pond surrounded by Japanese azaleas, a cut-leaved beech, camellias, rhododendrons and many more acid-loving shrubs. Then on to the 'Stewardry Walk' where they will see more rhododendrons, azaleas and camellias and an unusual waterfall surrounded by palms, primulas and gunneras; from here there is a magnificent view of the 'Valley Crucis'. The cross which can be seen was placed there by G. M. Fortescue and stands in memory of his uncle Lord Grenville. Nearby is the fine fifteenth-century church where visitors will find pamphlets on the history of Boconnoc.

Carclew Gardens, Perran-Ar-Worthal, Truro

H.H. ROBERT CHOPE AND MRS CHOPE

Seen from the house, a lawn flanked by cherries and maples runs down to a low wall and granite steps. Beyond and below is a glimpse of another lawn and then in the bottom of the valley, large broadleaved trees underplanted with rhododendrons.

Not visible from the house, but close by for discovery, are five small walled gardens, all intercommunicating but at different levels and each with its own planting emphasis – roses, heather, dwarf rhododendrons – and at the lowest level the old croquet lawn where now, with little respect for the turf, the badgers too often play a nightly game.

Below their playground, but screened on all sides by rhododendrons and azaleas, there is a small lake with merman fountains and waterlilies.

The garden is very old and has been loved for centuries – the massed, and now massive, rhododendrons; the Lucombe oak dating from 1762, which has weathered more wild nights than its many owners; the golden larch, thought to be the largest in England; the round lily pond used by Howard Spring for a scene in *All the Day Long* and, in the walls on the top lawn, the mortar peppered with the rusting remains of nails from six generations of gardeners tying in or tying back.

Against one wall is a particularly happy young planting of golden yew, red maple and the plum-leaved *Berberis*. For those who can look ahead for two generations, the swamp cypress seen from above against the background of a copper beech is magic on summer days.

◆

Chyverton, Zelah
MR AND MRS NIGEL HOLMAN

This is a garden within a garden; the outer, a Georgian landscape developed from 1770 to 1825 by John Thomas, with lake, bridge, and fine trees, forms a splendid frame to the inner shrub garden started in 1925 by Treve Holman; the two form a successful partnership to which the house adds a handsome third dimension.

Over the past sixty years the collection of exotics has increased so that it now contains a wide range of genera originating from Asia, North and South America, and Australasia. With an acid soil, there are many rhododendrons and camellias, but it has become a policy to break up the plantings so that no one genus dominates. The pride of the collection is *Magnolia*, and big specimens of *M. campbellii, cylindrica, dawsoniana, sargentiana robusta*, and many more, are superb in March and April.

The great number of magnolias in the garden is due to honey fungus. Treve Holman found that magnolias seemed immune to the scourge which removed so many of his rhododendrons. Recently it has been found that copper carbonate, an easily applied powder, appears to be an answer; no rhododendrons have been lost since a handful of the powder has been mixed with the soil on planting.

With no outside help and twenty acres in hand, maintenance is a problem. Our solution: only grow plants that look after themselves, cut grass regularly (no need to pick up cuttings), minimal cultivation, and wild flowers are welcomed in what we aim to be the most natural and beautiful of gardens.

◆

Cotehele House, Nr St Dominick
THE NATIONAL TRUST

A terraced garden falling to a sheltered valley, with ponds, a stream, and unusual shrubs.

◆

Headland, Polruan-by-Fowey
MR AND MRS J.R. HILL

Headland is a cliff garden, rising from sea level to over a hundred feet, with the sea breaking on the rocks below on three sides. At the bottom of a flight of more than a hundred steps a gate opens on to a sandy beach which is safe for swimming; on the seaward side is a view along the south Cornwall coast to Gribben Head, Black Head and Dodman, with a glimpse of Lizard on a clear day. Whatever the wind direction there is shelter somewhere. Only one and a quarter acres on plan, the garden seems bigger because there are secret ways to find, with intimate seats in clefts in the cliff. Plants and trees must be able

to withstand salt-laden gales, but one corner facing south is frost-free and houses subtropical plants. Monterey pines tower over the 'North Col' and many *Lampranthus* blaze on the 'South Face'. In crevices aloes, *Sedum, Erigeron* and sempervivums thrive, while in 'Wattle Alley' there are gums and wattles. On the rock garden are junipers and cypresses, with red-hot pokers (*Kniphofia*) between them. Foxgloves, valerian, wallflowers, scabious and columbine grow wild everywhere. Torquay palms rustle in the breeze. When Laura, in the film 'Stolen Hours', of which part was shot at Headland, arrived, she dropped the onions and cried out, '*You didn't tell me it's so beautiful!*'

◆

Ken-Caro, Bicton
MR AND MRS K.R. WILLCOCK

This two-acre garden was designed, and planting begun, in 1970 – and we are still taking in more land to enlarge it. It is particularly noted for its variegated plants and everything is well labelled.

As flower arrangers, we have a large collection of hostas, as well as the lovely *Convallaria majalis* 'Variegata' and its pink form 'Rosea'. Our soil is acid, so we collect rhododendrons, notably the beautiful variegated 'President Roosevelt' and *R. ponticum* 'Variegatum', and camellias. Of particular interest in summer is the splendid *Aralia elata* 'Variegata'.

We also have a large collection of herbaceous plants, notably ten varieties of *Dicentra* which I find divides well in the spring. Conifers, featuring many dwarf varieties, are another speciality.

As our visitors say, the garden is full of surprises as we have not only many secret gardens, but also aviaries and a collection of water fowl, and we are developing a farm trail and woodland walk.

◆

*Lanhydrock, Bodmin
THE NATIONAL TRUST

A large garden, with a formal garden laid out in 1857 and a shrub garden with good specimens of rhododendrons and magnolias and fine views.

◆

Penpol House, Hayle
MAJ. AND MRS T.F. ELLIS

Penpol is in the extreme south-west of Cornwall, a hundred and twenty feet above sea level on a slight slope. The four-acre garden belongs to an old fifteenth-century house, until recently sheltered from salt sea winds by boundaries of elms. This shelter was removed when over three hundred trees had to be felled because of Dutch Elm disease.

However, old yew hedges – and more recently-planted trees and shrubs – are reshaping a garden well over a hundred years old. An alkaline soil makes it different from

many of the Cornish gardens, and mid-summer sees the glory of an infinite variety of flowers, especially lilies, roses and delphiniums, the latter (with unusual colours and spikes up to five and six feet) being grown from seed obtained from the Delphinium Society.

The garden leads from one colourful pocket to another with old walls, tall yew and *Fuchsia* hedges and low-growing box, edging the packed herbaceous borders. There is an old greenhouse with vines and a bright vermilion climbing *Geranium*, known to be over eighty years old, stretching along a ten-foot wall. The little grey garden has *Chaenomeles japonica, Ceanothus* and *Clematis* along the walls, *Lippia citriodora* contributing to the annual pot pourri, and *Cestrum parqui* with crinums adding a touch of strangeness. In the big main garden there are roses everywhere – beds of shrub roses, hybrid tea climbers and ramblers on granite and rustic pillars, while paeonies, lilies, and a mass of coloured flag *Iris* fill other beds.

A few of the old apple trees – varieties rare today – remain. A spreading walnut tree and a gnarled medlar are old friends to shelter beneath. Scattered around the garden are the granite troughs and presses from the old cider barn, hayrick toadstools stand sentinel along the paths and the old granite rollers lean back wearily, dreaming of tennis parties long ago. Throughout the year there is something to look forward to, from the daffodils, tulips, cherry, crabapple and *Magnolia* lasting through into summer until the last *Dahlia* or *Amaryllis*.

◆

St Michael's Mount, Nr Marazion
THE RT HON. LORD ST LEVAN; THE NATIONAL TRUST

The island provides a beautiful setting for this garden which contains flowering shrubs and rock plants, as well as having fine sea views.

◆

Trebah, Mawnan Smith
MAJ. AND MRS J.A. HIBBERT

The basic outlines of the garden at Trebah were laid out by Charles Fox in the middle years of the nineteenth century demonstrating admirably that remarkable eye for landscape that was so often characteristic of the period. Twenty-six acres in extent and breathtakingly beautiful, it remains privately owned and is of considerable historic and botanical interest.

A superb amphitheatre of giant trees encircles the lawns, with a break where the eye is led down through a dramatic two-hundred-foot ravine to the Helford river. The precipitous flanks are planted with a mixture of mature conifers and deciduous trees, many very rare. The floor and lower slopes of the valley are densely covered with those spring-flowering trees and shrubs common to the larger gardens of Cornwall. A small stream runs down the bottom of the valley to the sea via several large pools.

During the last few years this framework has been greatly enhanced by opening up vistas from the terraced paths winding their way through the woodland high above the stream and from which one can look down into the tops of the huge rhododendrons and magnolias, and outwards over the Helford river.

Another innovation has been to improve the flow of the stream and to introduce a long series of waterfalls, one having a direct fall of fourteen feet over huge granite boulders to the pool below. Along the stream-side moisture-loving plants have been massed; primulas of many kinds, *Zantedeschia, Lobelia cardinalis, Ligularia, Iris, Meconopsis,* astilbes in multi-coloured sheets and many others, increasing the garden's flowering season through May until July. The lower reaches of the stream wind through two acres of hydrangeas, extending the season still further to November.

On a number of south-facing, virtually frost-free rock-faces rare, sub-tropical exotics proliferate, complementing the great tree-ferns and temperate palms in ideal association. It is quite easy to imagine at times that one has strayed into a corner of an equatorial rain forest.

It is encouraging to see that Trebah – which once contained one of the major plant collections in Cornwall – is re-emerging as one of the most exciting gardens in the country.

Trebartha, North Hill
THE LATHAM FAMILY

After entering the gardens the visitor goes along part of the old carriage drive, by the river Lynher and past the pool where it is joined by the Withybrook, which comes down in a series of waterfalls from the moors above. Here are often to be seen dippers and the occasional kingfisher.

A footbridge of the Lynher leads to the 'Swan Pool' area – a large lake, now inhabited by ornamental ducks and geese. The lake is surrounded by azaleas and rhododendrons and is a blaze of colour in the early summer. At Eastertime the grassy banks on the far side of the lake are a mass of daffodils, followed by bluebells. There are a number of interesting trees round the lake, including an Oregon maple, *Acer macrophyllum,* picked out by Mr Alan Mitchell, the leading British authority on trees, as being particularly fine. There is a 'Camperdown' elm like an umbrella, Sawara cypress *Chamaecyparis pisifera,* and *Thujopsis dolabrata* from Japan, as well as common noble and silver firs. A small gate marked 'Cascade Walk' leads into the American gardens, a wooded area comprising some thirty acres, which rises steeply up to the edge of the moor below Hawkes Tor. This was planted up about a hundred years ago, at a time when it was fashionable to bring in trees from the west coast of America and there are a number

of Douglas firs, western red cedars, hemlocks, sequoias and the like. Many have passed their prime and much replanting is being done, introducing as great a variety of species as possible.

A path leads up by the Withybrook, where there are several views of the waterfalls, and a climb brings the visitor to the lower or upper terraces and back in a large circle, re-crossing the Lynher by another footbridge. Although these are in no way formal gardens, people return year after year to enjoy a lovely walk in beautiful surroundings.

Trehane, Nr Tresillian
MR AND MRS D.C. TREHANE AND MR SIMON TREHANE

The oldest planting in this five-acre garden dates from the late nineteenth century, and this has been renewed since 1963. A ruined Queen Anne mansion in the grounds provides a wonderful setting for many unusual plants, in particular a very fine specimen of *Holboellia,* which bears fruit here, and there is a large collection of camellias. In addition there is a wide range of old and uncommon bulbs and herbaceous plants.

Trelean, St Martin-in-Meneage
SQN/LDR G.T. AND MRS WITHERWICK

The garden is situated within a steep-sided valley, running north to south, and on the south side of the Helford, the least-spoilt river in Cornwall. Its design has an overall informality complementing the beauty of its natural surroundings; devoid of formal flower beds, pools or lawns, it contains well over a thousand plants set out around the valley paths, all well within sight and sound of the picturesque fern and tree-clad stream of fresh water from the Trelean springs.

There is a comprehensive collection of autumn-colour plants, especially of *Acer* – over fifty species with cultivars, – *Enkianthus, Euonymus, Cornus* and *Stuartia,* together with as many southern hemisphere plants as can be persuaded to grow. Other groups are rhododendrons, conifers and herbaceous plants.

The layout of the paths facilitates the viewing of the plants from above and below, and the large-leaved rhododendrons are enhanced by looking down upon their exotic foliage. Furthermore, the top valley paths are landscaped in such a way as to give the maximum advantage to the panoramic views over the valley to the river and the countryside beyond. Although the garden has only recently been created, it contains many large specimens of conifers, rhododendrons and ornamental trees, all brought from the owners' previous Surrey garden, thus giving a sense of maturity. In addition, the valley contains magnificent specimens of old oaks and hazels, festooned with ivy and moss, whilst ferns abound in massive quantities, together with primroses, bluebells and

wood anemones. There are, contained within the twenty acres, some exceptional viewpoints of the Helford, a riverside walk of a quarter of a mile, with access to the beach, a lovely Cornish lane beset with wild flowers, and a beech wood astride a hillside.

*Trelissick, Feock
THE NATIONAL TRUST

A large garden with a superb view over Falmouth harbour.

Tremeer Gardens, St Tudy
MR AND MRS HOPKINSON

Tremeer is primarily a spring garden and was created by Major-General Harrison between 1947 and 1978. The drive during March and April is lined with cherry trees in full bloom above a yellow sea of daffodils.

The main garden is situated below the house and at its lowest level is skirted by a pond. There is a very pleasant and natural progression about the whole garden starting with the house which is well clothed with plants, a very large variegated *Euonymus fortunei* among them.

Wide granite steps leads down to the main lawn, which is flanked by both evergreen and deciduous azaleas whose many colours form a spectacular scene during April and May. The far side of the lawn is dominated by a large oak tree at the foot of which *Cyclamen hederifolium* is naturalized. From this, wide grass paths force their way between even wider borders filled with shrubs of many kinds, rhododendrons and camellias predominating. Interspersed amongst these are *Hydrangea* and various trees including *Eucryphia cordifolia* and its offspring *Eucryphia × nymansensis* which flower in late summer long after the rest of the garden has lost its primary beauty. While the azaleas bloom near ground level, the many species of *Magnolia,* such as *M. fraseri, sargentiana robusta* and × *veitchii* dominate the skyline. Underneath grow some unique rhododendrons which were crossed and reared within the garden by the General, examples being 'Artist' which has brilliant white flowers and 'Achilles' ('Werei' × 'Barclayi') which has a fairly deep pink hue. Candelabra primulas, hostas and other moisture-lovers fringe the pond, converted from an old mill pool.

Above the house, facing north, is a large heather bank with dwarf rhododendrons intermixed, and above this feature select roses bloom against a curtain of evergreens. Also, in a particularly sheltered area camellias, including specimens of 'Brigadoon' and 'Inspiration', thrive.

Trerice, Newlyn
THE NATIONAL TRUST

A garden around a small manor house, rebuilt in 1571.

Trebah, Mawnan Smith, in May. The hardy palm tree from China, *Trachycarpus fortunei*,
and tree ferns give a tropical effect in this mild Cornish garden overlooking the Helford River.

47

CUMBRIA, DURHAM AND NORTHUMBERLAND

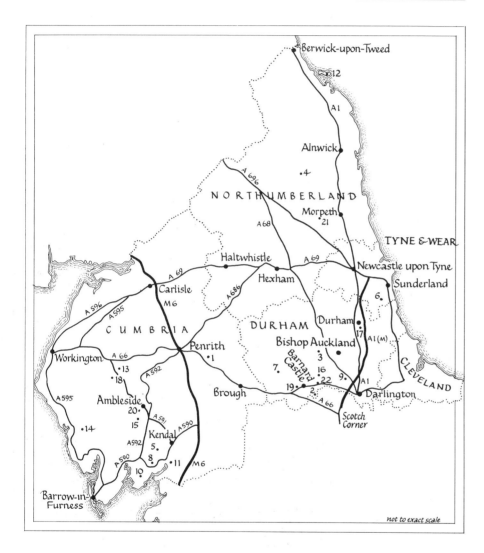

not to exact scale

Directions to Gardens

Acorn Bank, Temple Sowerby, 6 miles east of Penrith, Cumbria. [1]

Barningham Park, 10 miles northwest of Richmond, County Durham. [2]

Bedburn Hall, Hamsterley, 9 miles west of Bishop Auckland, County Durham. [3]

Cragside, Rothbury, 13 miles southwest of Alnwick, Northumberland. [4]

Crispin Cottage, Underbarrow, 4 miles west of Kendal, Cumbria. [5]

12 and 13 Durham Road, Middle Herrington, 3½ miles southwest of Sunderland, County Durham. [6]

Eggleston Hall Gardens, Eggleston, northwest of Barnard Castle, County Durham. [7]

Halecat, Witherslack, 10 miles southwest of Kendal, Cumbria. [8]

Headlam Hall, 2 miles north of Gainford, 5 miles west of Darlington, County Durham. [9]

Holker Hall and Park, Cark-in-Cartmel, 4 miles west of Grange-over-Sands, 12 miles west of M6 (exit 36). [10]

Levens Hall, 5 miles south of Kendal, exit 36 from M6, Cumbria. [11]

Lindisfarne Castle, Holy Island, 5 miles east of Beal, Northumberland. [12]

Lingholm, Keswick, 1 mile from Portinscale, 3 miles from Keswick, Cumbria. [13]

Muncaster Castle, 1 mile east of Ravenglass, 17 miles southeast of Whitehaven, Cumbria. [14]

Old Cottage, Outgate, 1 mile north of Hawkshead, south of Ambleside, Cumbria. [15]

Raby Castle, 1 mile north of Staindrop, northwest of Darlington, County Durham. [16]

St Aidan's College, Durham, 1 mile from the city centre, County Durham. [17]

Scarthwaite, Grange-in-Borrowdale, near Keswick, Cumbria. [18]

Spring Lodge, Barnard Castle, County Durham. [19]

Stagshaw, ½ mile south of Ambleside, Cumbria. [20]

University of Durham Botanic Garden, 1 mile from city centre, County Durham. [17]

Wallington, Cambo, 12 miles west of Morpeth, Northumberland. [21]

Westholme Hall, Winston, west of Darlington, County Durham. [22]

◆

Acorn Bank, Temple Sowerby
THE NATIONAL TRUST

A medium-sized garden with a good herb garden, set in parkland.

◆

Barningham Park, Nr Richmond
SIR ANTHONY AND LADY MILBANK

The surrounding woodland sets the scene for this garden with a view to the east for miles out across lower Teesdale to the Cleveland Hills. In the 1920s a large-scale rock garden was designed on the steep slope above the house, with a series of streams, waterfalls, and pools, flowing through banks of Mollis, Ghent and *luteum* azaleas; the fiery colours and wonderful scent are at their best in early June. In spring, multitudes of daffodils lead you up into the woods, which were landscaped with paths and flights of stone steps; all, hopefully, to be restored one day. A lot of felling and clearing has had to be done, but the bluebells and ferns will make a beautiful setting for the *Rhododendron*, *Acer*, *Sorbus* and *Betula* species in the new woodland plan.

New planting in the garden is still at an experimental stage, but the aim is for the garden to blend naturally into its surroundings. The challenge is to discover unusual plants which will flourish on a north-facing, windswept hillside all too often invaded by rabbits and deer. Inspiration comes from the high mountain regions of the world, and a collection of dwarf rhododendrons is growing well in the rocks, and, lower down, primulas and *Meconopsis* crowd together in half-shade by the waterside.

Around the house itself, the sloping lawns are bordered on the west side with large informal groups of shrubs and herbaceous perennials. These have been planted for contrasting foliage effects. Different colour schemes, all with predominantly grey and silver leaves to complement the stone background, give interest from mid-summer until the frosts. The autumn colours of the azaleas then take over, with bright splashes of flame from ×*Crocosmia* and *Potentilla* 'Red Ace'. The latter, if planted in half-shade rather than full sun, as recommended, will retain its brilliant colour and not fade to a washy orange.

Bedburn Hall, Hamsterley
IAN BONAS, ESQ.

This is an exciting garden, designed in 1900, with ten acres of woods, a lake, a millrace, streams, waterways and an arboretum.

Rhododendrons and azaleas grow abundantly and, apart from the formal terraced garden which runs down to the river, its great attractions are the wild flora and fauna such as roe deer, red squirrels and badgers. Towering bamboo and flag irises surround the well-stocked trout lake and hostas and day lilies thrive in the herbaceous borders.

The verandah is festooned with fuchsias and hanging baskets in mid-summer so there is scarcely any room left for the guests. Two new shrub beds planted in 1982 have taken years to establish themselves in the heavy clay soil, but should provide year-round colour from now on. There are two fine Japanese maples which are a wonderful sight in the autumn and unusual features include an old stag's horn sumach by the workshop. These are also monkey puzzle trees, maples, wellingtonias and other conifers planted when the house was built at the beginning of this century.

Cragside House, Rothbury
THE NATIONAL TRUST

The steep gables of this immense house, designed mainly by Richard Norman Shaw at the end of the nineteenth century, mirror the craggy hillside on which it is set. The garden and adjoining country park cover over nine hundred acres, and contain many interesting natural features such as streams and waterfalls, with the garden itself a kind of natural rock garden, using the endemic limestone.

There are many interesting shrubs, particularly rhododendrons and azaleas, and a large number of very large specimens of coniferous trees, particularly Douglas Fir, *Pseudotsuga menziesii*, Colorado Fir, *Abies concolor*, and the Red Fir, *Abies magnifica*.

Crispin Cottage, Underbarrow
MR AND MRS R.G. ROTHWELL

Natural rock formations and different levels divide the garden into five greatly varied sections. Facing south and at a height of only fifty feet above sea level, the soil is neutral though the valley is flanked by limestone scars. The garden, bordered on two sides by a road and a lane, merges with the surrounding hedges and wild cherries, giving distance to the view. As the soil is stony and light, in spite of making stony paths it is almost too well-drained to grow roses successfully, with the exception of *R. rugosa* and shrub roses. Naturalized spring bulbs, alpines, herbaceous plants, autumn crocus, colchicums, many wild flowers, and shrubs underplanted with winter aconites all flower in sequence so there is no particular peak time. Seed, divisions and cuttings are propagated, autumn semi-hardwood cuttings each in its own 'personal' greenhouse, an inverted jam jar, so that there are always plants for replacements, exchange or gifts. Troughs with alpines, tubs with camellias and *Hibiscus* decorate the paths and paved areas. Water has been introduced and an alpine house added in 1984. All trees are welcome: ash, silver birch, laburnum, willow, fruit trees, oak, larch, pine, Portugal laurel, and dwarf conifers all feature, but merge with the surroundings, encouraging birds to linger; over forty species have been recorded, some nesting successfully, and they provide constant song from dawn to dusk in spring and summer.

12 and 13 Durham Road, Middle Herrington
MR AND MRS R.F. HERON

This was originally two suburban gardens now combined and, with the addition of a church site in 1962, making in all rather more than an acre.

The garden is intensively cultivated, perhaps the main summer feature being seven beds of floribunda roses, fifty of a kind. There is an extensive shrub border to provide the backcloth for the roses and four perennial borders, most of the plants being grown from seed, particularly the delphiniums (with seed from New Zealand). There is a good collection of eryngiums – *E. giganteum*, Miss Willmott's Ghost, does particularly well. The seed, if collected, is very difficult to germinate, but, if the plant is shaken after the seed is set, there will be a heavy crop of seedlings in the spring, no matter how hard the winter. There is an old Elizabethan-style knot garden, with box hedging, and planted with annuals, and also

a large collection of hebes, some hardy and some not so hardy; we take cuttings of the latter in September. Some *Eucalyptus* (all grown from seed) are established in the borders, but many more are pot grown for summer and greenhouse decoration. In addition, about a hundred outdoor chrysanthemums are grown each year. Only one-third of the greenhouse is heated, and then only to 40°F. In summer, it houses many varieties of fuchsias, regal pelargoniums and begonias, followed by chrysanthemums from October to Christmas.

Eggleston Hall Gardens
MRS W.T. GRAY

Eggleston Hall lies beside the river Tees, six miles west of Barnard Castle, overlooking one of the most beautiful valleys in the north of England. The gardens have been built up and improved over the last fifteen years, but have a number of lovely mature trees to form a backcloth. Because of the different types of soil, the four acres are able to support many species of plants, especially those suitable for the flower arranger. The layout is informal, with many winding paths, along which are clumps of rare and sought-after herbaceous plants such as variegated Solomon's Seal and *Celmisia spectabilis*, as well as interesting shrubs, with emphasis on variegated varieties. A stream runs through the garden, and there are masses of naturalized bulbs in springtime. Running a cookery and flower school as we do, we need to have flowers, plants and foliage available for the students at all times of year, so plants are grown for their size, colour, shape and texture.

We have a large vegetable garden where we grow vegetables and soft fruit to cater for the needs of four teaching kitchens, and to supply our shops in Barnard Castle. There are three greenhouses; the first for stock plants such as *Delphinium zalil*, *D. brunonianum*, *Alstroemeria pelegrina* 'Alba', *Aeonium* 'Tête Noire' and *Campanula formanekiana*; the second for plant sales (these two using a minimum of heat in winter), and the third a cold greenhouse, used mainly for growing foliage to tide us over the winter months.

Halecat, Witherslack
MR AND MRS M.C. STANLEY

Creating a new garden at Halecat in 1952 was an adventure, the difficulties being limestone close to the surface, with thin alkaline soil, and the shape determined by a square lawn superimposed upon another square. Entering the garden by a white gate, the view towards Arnside Knott and beyond is channelled by the house and by fairly tall *Philadelphus* 'Beauclerk' underplanted with *Cytisus* × *praecox* and *C.* × *kewensis*. Round the corner terrace leads past the house to a mixed herbaceous border against a grey wall; this paving ends in a short slope of grass towards a hedge of *Prunus cerasifera* 'Pissardii' interplanted with whitebeam and fronted by azaleas, and a south-facing wall which gives shelter to delicate plants. A Gothic summer-house, designed by Francis Johnson, forms a long-stop. Turning to the right there are curved ironwork frames supporting the rose 'Fantin-Latour' underplanted with *Cotinus coggygria* 'Royal Purple'. This double border is terminated by a small *Rosa Mundi* hedge, and followed by a bank of junipers and rambling roses, and on the other side, a continuation of the beech hedge. Since gardens must change and improve, we are hoping to create an emphasis on pink and white in the section, with more *Philadelphus* 'Beauclerk' and some pink standard roses fronted by *Berberis thunbergii* 'Atropurpurea Nana' and rue.

Headlam Hall Gardens, Gainford
J. H. ROBINSON, ESQ.

These mainly formal gardens extend to almost four acres and were originally set out in the late eighteenth century though the house and certain features date back to Jacobean times. A high stone wall surrounds the gardens with stepped 'look-out' terraces at the southern corners. Inside, there is a small trout lake taken from a natural water course, and extensive lawns and walks bordered by high beech and yew hedges. Herbaceous borders give a blaze of colour from June onwards, after the spring flowers have played their part. There is also a small rose garden and an area devoted to soft fruits and vegetables.

After a recent period of neglect the gardens were restored in the late 1970s and now offer most of their original splendour. A belt of mainly beech trees shelter the gardens from the west and help to give them the tranquillity and privacy that is so apparent.

Holker Hall and Park, Cark-in-Cartmel
MR AND MRS HUGH CAVENDISH

This twenty-two-acre garden has associations with Joseph Paxton, and boasts a large number of exotic flowering trees, as well as azaleas, rhododendrons and magnolias. Also worth seeing are the daffodils, rose garden, cherry and woodland walks.

Levens Hall, Nr Kendal
C. H. BAGOT, ESQ.

The grounds here include the famous topiary garden and the first ha-ha laid out by M. Beaumont in 1692. Also of interest are the fine beech circle, herbaceous borders and formal bedding.

Lindisfarne Castle, Lindisfarne
THE NATIONAL TRUST

This small walled garden on Holy Island was originally designed by Gertrude Jekyll to accompany the castle, converted from a medieval fort into a country house by Sir Edwin Lutyens in 1903.

Lingholm, Keswick
THE VISCOUNT ROCHDALE

Lingholm gardens are situated close to the west shore of Derwentwater and command a wonderful view right up Borrowdale. The house was built to the design of the well-known architect Alfred Waterhouse for a Colonel J. F. Greenall in the 1870s. During the last years of the century the house was generally unoccupied, but it was sometimes let furnished during the summer. It was thus that Beatrix Potter and her family stayed here on various occasions, and it was at Lingholm that she wrote her well-known book *Squirrel Nutkin* – his descendants still come to visit us!

The gardens as they now appear began to be developed in the early 1900s by a new owner, Colonel George Kemp – later Lord Rochdale, and it was then that the terraces on the lake side of the house were built.

The main feature of the gardens, dating from the late 1920s, consists of a considerable collection of rhododendrons and azaleas, both large and miniature species and hybrids. These include a number of the fragrant *Rhododendron auriculatum* which flower in late July and August, and a fine planting of R. 'Shilsonii', with bluish leaves and smooth purplish-red bark. All these are to be found in an extensive woodland garden, where the conditions are ideal with largely peat soil and, as is to be expected in the Lake District, a high annual rainfall of sixty-five inches.

There are many other interesting and colourful shrubs and trees which play an important part throughout the season. They are all being constantly developed, providing important parent stock for our plant centre. There is an attractive small Memorial Garden and we also have formal gardens which in recent years have again been extended. Among other plants we specialize in are gentians, *Meconopsis*, begonias, heathers and primulas.

Muncaster Castle, Nr Ravenglass
MRS PATRICK GORDON-DUFF-PENNINGTON

The present owner's grandfather, Sir ?John Ramsden, laid out the grounds of the castle which extend to forty-five acres, with a famous collection of Rhododendron species, azaleas, camellias, eucryphias and acers. Many of the original plants and seedlings came from the expeditions of Ludlow and Sherriff and Kingdon Ward. There is currently in hand an extensive planting scheme, whilst many of the old hardwood trees, originally planted by the first Lord Muncaster in 1780, are being extracted. In addition, seventy-five new plants have been donated, derived from the seeds brought back from China in 1981 by Peter Cox and Sir Peter Hutchison.

Old Cottage, Outgate
MISS M. B. RUNDLE

Gardening in the Lake District is a matter of concentrating on those plants that like the

Barningham Park, near Richmond, in early June. The rock garden is imaginatively planted with dwarf rhododendrons and azaleas, *Meconopsis* and *Iris*. For a description of the garden see page 48.

climate and the poor soil, and forgetting about the others.

This small garden runs from north to south and is contained by stone walls. One-third consists of outcrops of rock facing south-east and rising, in some places steeply, from borders and a small lawn supported by a retaining wall from the field below to the level of the house from which it can be viewed. There is a very small fibre-glass pond near the house, fed by rainwater, which provides a constant source of interest and compensates for the lack of running water. It shelters frogs, snails, newts and a yellow-flowered waterlily among other aquatic plants. My twenty-five years here have been spent in learning by trial and error and in collecting plants, of which there are now approximately four hundred species and varieties in the garden. Those particularly at home here include rhododendrons, hydrangeas, hostas, *Meconopsis*, *Gentiana sino-ornata* and *G. asclepiadea*, hellebores, potentillas, astrantias and sedums. Curiosities include *Quercus coccifera*, the holly oak grown from acorns picked up at Epidauros; *Akebia quinata*, rampant on a south wall and covered with its brownish-purple flowers in June; and *Arisarum proboscideum*, the strange mouse-tail plant. A great favourite is *Geranium psilostemon* with its black-eyed magenta flowers, and a feature of the garden is a graceful weeping *Rosa glauca (rubrifolia)* planted twenty-one years ago. This strong grower is managed by cutting out several of the oldest stems from the base every five years or so and shaping the vigorous young shoots every year to the required angle by tying them down for a few months.

*Raby Castle, Staindrop
THE RT HON. THE LORD BARNARD

The large walled garden, laid out at the end of the eighteenth century by the Earl of Darlington, is sheltered by old brick walls, and fine yew hedges. The walls were originally heated by hot air channels for the benefit of fruit, especially apricots. Amongst the main features are the two massive yew hedges, several hundred years old, thought to have been planted when the Castle was first occupied.

The garden has changed considerably over the centuries. Originally it was devoted to the culture of fruit and vegetables to supply the Castle, but later flowers and parterres were introduced. Earlier this century large shrub and herbaceous borders were made by the Dowager Lady Barnard; then followed a period of market gardening, which ceased recently, and taking its place are a formal garden with lawns and yew hedges, and a heather garden interplanted with conifers and other shrubs, providing continuous colour. Two large lawns give scope for future planning. In July the borders with lovely old paeonies are at their best, as are the formal rose gardens near the central pond.

Plants of interest include *Veratrum album*, *Echinops ritro*, *Romneya coulteri*, *Baptisia tinctoria* and *Paeonia mlokosewitschii*. Near the south entrance, made in 1894, with its fine wrought-iron gates moved from the family church at Shipbourne in Kent, is the Raby Fig – a 'White Ischia', brought from Italy by William Harry, Viscount Barnard in about 1786. This colossal tree fills a house (no longer heated) sixty by eight feet, and twelve feet high – producing two crops annually but only the first ripening. Beside the new conservatory and pergola, two large raised beds growing scented and colourful plants make a pleasant place to sit. The gently sloping south-facing ground gives views of the Castle across the park.

Wallington, Cambo, one of the many National Trust gardens that open to the public on selected days for the benefit of the National Gardens Scheme. This ancient *Fuchsia* is one of the many interesting plants to be seen in the large conservatory. For a description of the garden see over.

St Aidan's College, Durham
THE PRINCIPAL, MRS I. HINDMARSH

The peace and tranquillity of St Aidan's gardens can be enjoyed all year long. The college (built to Sir Basil Spence's design in 1964) stands on a hill to the south of Durham City and the gardens, created by Professor Brian Hackett to be in harmony with the college buildings and surrounding landscape, were designed for minimum maintenance. Hardy species were chosen which were able to withstand the relatively exposed position. The bank by the drive approaching the college is planted as a rockery with brooms and heathers. There are superb views from the college entrance to the cathedral and to the observatory. Groups of trees and shrubs provide windbreaks – many are species found growing wild in the north-east, whilst nearer the buildings, garden shrubs appear – *Prunus*

lusitanica, *Viburnum fragrans* – as well as raised beds planted with a variety of spring flowers including fritillaries and dwarf irises. Banks of crocuses by the steps and drifts of daffodils and cowslips are a joy in the spring. The library wall has a fine display of *Pyracantha* and *Hydrangea petiolaris* in autumn.

The gardens continue right round the college buildings to a fine inner courtyard. A pond, rich with *Ranunculus lingua*, waterlilies and occasional visiting ducks and a stray heron, reflects the buildings. A series of oblique terraces with beds and hedges of sweet-smelling, old-fashioned rose species are at their best in July and August. A cedar of Lebanon was planted as a focal point at the base of the terraces, while a very attractive *Laburnum* walk leads to a series of small protected enclaves in the lawns by the tennis courts.

The same tradition of a marriage of architecture and landscape persists in the garden surrounding the new building. A feature is the use of unrestrained climbing roses to give ground cover and reduce maintenance.

Scarthwaite, Grange-in-Borrowdale
MR AND MRS E.C. HICKS

Situated on the edge of a Cumbrian village in the centre of a narrow valley facing north and south, the soil of which consists of stones left behind by an ancient glacier, this tiny cottage garden, planted to appear natural and uncontrived, looks vast, gay and abandoned, although its area does not exceed one quarter of an acre.

The main planting began in 1960 and the design has gradually evolved since then. Its sweet disorder blends beautifully with crags and mountains, dissolving into the surrounding scenery to become part of it.

It is thickly planted with alpines, bulbs, shrubs and trees, ferns, cottage garden flowers, herbs, old-fashioned roses, *Clematis* and English wildings. Plants from all over the world are to be found here; exotic species and local wild flowers grow in comfortable companionship. Red squirrels, birds, butterflies, moths and all manner of wild life enjoy its bosky lushness but, fortunately, rabbits are only occasional visitors. The garden is tranquil but never silent. Flowers spill over throughout spring, summer and autumn. Even in the steely grip of a Lakeland winter some plant can be discovered blooming bravely.

We enjoy opening the garden on special occasions and love to share the pleasure our garden gives. Almost without fail visitors exclaim 'Oh, this is just my kind of garden!'

Spring Lodge, Barnard Castle
COL. W.I. WATSON

The original grounds surrounding this Regency villa built in 1827 were typical of that age; a semi-walled garden containing herba-

Contrasting leaves of *Veratrum viride* and *Phalaris arundinacea* by the front door at Bedburn Hall (see page 49).

the main road which intersects the estate is the woodland garden where mature beech and oak trees provide a canopy to shade rhododendrons, *Hydrangea* and *Philadelphus* and enormous old yews and hollies provide shelter. Here are two ponds on different levels with a stream connecting them, and, above the lower pond, a great red-brick wall with a central Portico House. This was the northern boundary wall and gardener's house of the early eighteenth-century kitchen garden which was planted with trees to form an arboretum when a new walled kitchen garden was made in 1760. This 'new garden' is further to the east in a little curving valley mostly facing the sun, and since 1960 it has been landscaped and replanted as a flower and water garden. The *pièce de résistance* of this garden is the large conservatory where *Fuchsia*, *Plumbago* and *Abutilon* grow, while tender ferns, pelargoniums, *Begonia* and *Achimenes* are displayed on the benches.

The gardens as a whole have many features of interest – amongst them are the statuary and ornaments; fountain pool, ha-ha, ice house and folly; mixed borders, naturalized bulbs, notable shrubs, bog and water plants.

Westholme Hall, Winston
CAPT. AND MRS J.H. MCBAIN

This five-acre garden was originally laid out by the present owner's grandfather, and much of its interest stems from the way it has developed over the years – in the same family, but to meet the changing needs and tastes – round a much-loved Jacobean house.

In 1935 the garden was modified and softened to conform to the taste of the time – a rose garden was laid out and much interesting stonework incorporated from the break-up of nearby Streatlam Castle. The present owners have had to do a great deal to make the garden more labour-saving, and work it themselves without outside help.

There is interest at every season with drifts of snowdrops in a wood by the stream, followed by daffodils in the orchard while in late May white rhododendrons combine with a backdrop of blossom. The more colourful rhododendrons and azaleas give interest in June, when the species roses are out, and four enormous old Persian lilacs. July is the time for the old-fashioned rose garden, with a large collection of gallicas, albas, damasks, and bourbons, combined with a variety of interesting soft underplantings, and in August the mixed border along the terrace keeps the colour going, with more shrub roses, rugosas, floribundas and buddlejas. The garden is made secret by many mature trees and has a feeling of peace and tranquillity.

ceous borders and asparagus beds, all surrounded by yews, hollies, ivy and ferns, with a host of larger trees such as beech, oak and sycamore. Today the garden contains roses and herbaceous borders, with peach and other fruit trees on one wall and climbing roses and *Clematis* on the other, whilst many of the larger trees have been felled to enlarge the garden all round.

Wind and hard frosts dictate what can be grown; however, a number of shrub roses, such as 'Madame Hardy', 'Frau Dagmar Hastrup', 'Zigeuner Knabe', and the more modern one 'Alloa' all do well; other shrubs, such as hardy rhododendron hybrids do well too and even *Cytisus battandieri*, *Actinidia kolomikta* and *Abutilon vitifolium* all survive. The last is easy to propagate from cuttings or seeds – so is *Magnolia sieboldii* which also grows quite well in the garden. But were it not for the shelter of the ancient clipped yews there would be no garden at all. How tempting it is to enlarge one's garden! Recently a small paddock of daffodils has been added, in which individual snake-bark maples have been planted and in which an ancient elm already grows. Thus from snowdrops and aconites in the late winter to the autumn tints of the maples, there will always be colour.

Stagshaw, Nr Ambleside
THE NATIONAL TRUST

A woodland garden with a fine collection of rhododendrons, camellias, magnolias and embothriums.

University of Durham Botanic Garden, Durham

This botanic garden was founded in 1970, and its main purpose is to provide teaching and research material for the University. However, it also contains a number of trees and shrubs from European woodlands, North America, the Himalayas and China, while the greenhouses display arid-zone plants and plants from the tropics.

Wallington, Cambo
THE NATIONAL TRUST

I (Mr Moon) have been head gardener here for twenty-eight years, which is a big slice of my working lifetime, but for a very short span in relation to the garden's two hundred and fifty years of existence. I am a Northumbrian born and bred and served my time as a gardener in the county, working in a large private garden, and I consider myself very fortunate to have been involved in the restoration of the gardens at Wallington in recent years.

The gardens here are in three parts; around the Hall are spacious lawns with specimen trees and sheltering woodland, while across

DEVON (NORTH)

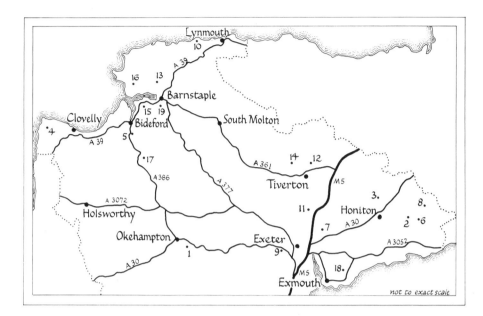

Directions to Gardens

Andrew's Corner, Belstone, 3 miles east of Okehampton. [1]

Burrow Farm Garden, Dalwood, 4 miles west of Axminster. [2]

Corydon, Luppitt, 5 miles north of Honiton. [3]

Docton Mill, Hartland, 14 miles north of Bude. [4]

The Downes, 3 miles northwest of Torrington, 4½ miles south of Bideford. [5]

Farrants, Kilmington, 2 miles west of Axminster. [6]

1 Feebers Cottages, Westwood, 2 miles northeast of Broadclyst. [7]

The Folly, Membury, 3 miles north of Axminster. [8]

The Glebe House, Whitestone, 4 miles west of Exeter. [9]

Heddon's Gate Hotel, Heddon's Mouth, 4 miles west of Lynton. [10]

Killerton Garden, 8 miles north of Exeter. [11]

Knightshayes Court, 2 miles north of Tiverton. [12]

Marwood Hill, Marwood, 4 miles north of Barnstaple. [13]

Middle Hill, Washfield, 4½ miles northwest of Tiverton. [14]

The Old Barn, Fremington, 3 miles west of Barnstaple. [15]

Putsborough Manor, Georgeham, northwest of Barnstaple. [16]

Rosemoor Garden Charitable Trust, 1 mile southeast of Great Torrington. [17]

Vicar's Mead, Hayes Lane, East Budleigh. [18]

Woodside, Higher Raleigh Road, Barnstaple. [19]

Andrew's Corner, Belstone

H.J. AND R.J. HILL

This garden, which has been created over the last twenty years, is situated on the northern side of Dartmoor at nine hundred feet above sea level. The garden, of about two-thirds of an acre, faces south and provides a contrast between the rugged grandeur of Dartmoor and the verdant serenity of a cultivated garden.

The garden – which contains a wide variety of trees, shrubs and perennials (several not often seen at this altitude) – is at its best in spring and early summer with bulbs, primroses, rhododendrons and *Meconopsis*

thriving in the damp acid conditions. Herbaceous plants, roses and lilies provide interest during the summer, with the brilliance of the maples and gentians extending the colour into autumn.

In our designing, we have used the different levels to create smaller gardens, with their own particular features and microclimates, separated by trees and rhododendrons, but still allowing glimpses of the Taw Valley and Dartmoor. Conifers and heathers on curving island beds give all-year colour, and an area of slow-growing conifers, surrounded by plastic sheet covered with stone chippings, provides an interesting and labour-saving area.

Dry stone walls, sink gardens and a paved area afford opportunities for growing lewisias and other unusual alpines, thus ensuring that every potential is exploited.

Burrow Farm Garden, Dalwood

MR AND MRS JOHN BENGER

I began to make the garden in 1966 by clearing the undergrowth (six to eight feet high!) and thinning out the overcrowded trees from a Roman clay pit in one of our fields. With more light getting in, the bluebells, primroses, wood anemones and foxgloves increased rapidly and the moist areas have proved ideal for primulas, astilbes, irises and the giant *Gunnera*, *Lysichitum* and *Heracleum*. Rhododendrons are a feature of these woodland slopes. The garden now covers about five acres in a beautiful setting with panoramic views over the Devon countryside. The soil is neutral so with the addition of copious amounts of humus to counteract the clay, we are able to grow ericaceous plants.

The use of variegated and yellow foliage forms of many shrubs on the open upper levels and round the swimming pool gives a sunny effect even on an overcast day. Groupings such as *Catalpa bignonioides* 'Aurea' and ×*Cupressocyparis leylandii* 'Castlewellan' underplanted with *Alchemilla mollis* and bronze fennel with the rose 'Apricot Silk' provide interest throughout the summer. Colour from foliage effects are the means by which I lead visitors from level to level, light to shade, from narrow pathway to open glades down to the primaeval stillness of the woodland garden.

Recently I have reclaimed a small paddock and this is now laid out with a long and wide pergola spanning a stone path. The design is formal with informal plantings of old-fashioned and modern shrub roses and grey foliage plants.

Corydon, Luppitt

PAUL CRUMP AND PETER WEBER

The garden has been created since 1972 on a derelict half-acre site with a slope to the south. It is over five hundred feet up in the

Blackdown Hills, with long views and their inevitable accompaniment – high winds!

The owners, before retirement, were professional growers concerned mainly with the intensive production of food and ornamental crops in heated glasshouses, so the new garden presented an entirely new interest and challenge.

The soil is a recalcitrant but fertile clay, waterlogged in winter and cracking badly in dry spells. These problems have been partly overcome by laying land and stone drains, and by converting the continuous slope into a series of levels, with raised borders, banks, walls, flights of steps, and lawns with trellises and hedges to create sheltered enclaves. The cracking of borders is reduced by applying liberal mulches of a mixture of sifted compost, peat and well-rotted manure. Most of the early donkey work was done with a hand barrow – one man on the handles, the other with a rope in front, all uphill!

Bulbs, annuals, biennials, herbaceous perennials, alpine plants and shrubs are used for continuity of colour. Trees and shrubs on the west boundary, planted to temper the winds, are heavily underplanted with a variety of *Narcissus*, quite content to disappear, after flowering, beneath a welter of foliage, as are hellebores and erythroniums. Barnhaven polyanthus and dwarf wallflowers, raised in separate colours, add to spring colour. A central feature is made of a rectangular border of annuals planted not in straight rows, but informally, with groups of five or seven plants of a kind. They blend perfectly with oval island beds of herbaceous plants, Bressingham style, and the rock garden on the uppermost slope. Plants displayed in containers are a feature too; ivy-leaf pelargoniums with foliage helichrysums scrambling through them and elsewhere, giant begonias, petunias, gazanias and *Verbena* 'Sissinghurst'.

Docton Mill, Nr Hartland

MR AND MRS N.S. PUGH

Docton Mill is a seventeenth-century watermill situated in a wooded valley designated as an area of outstanding natural beauty near Speke's Mill Mouth coastal waterfalls. Despite its proximity to the wild Atlantic coastline, the property nestles behind a north-facing hillside and the south-westerly gales roar harmlessly overhead. The hillside and trees together with a stream, numerous springs, the mill leat, pond, millrace and waterfalls are the predominant features of the landscape, and it is the ambition of the owners to develop a garden round them.

Work began in 1980. A small garden round the cottage had been neglected for many years. The woods and hillside were swampy and over-grown because centuries-old routines of ditching and coppicing had been neglected since the last miller died in 1914. Five years' work has changed all this: former bogs and open spaces are grassed and new

Docton Mill, near Hartland, in April. The water wheel makes an attractive focus for the *Narcissus* 'Ice Follies' and *Pulmonaria*.

trees, shrubs and perennials planted in areas throughout the garden which lend themselves naturally to cultivation.

The plan from the outset was to be conservative with natural beauty and cautious with development and this has brought rewards. Areas cleared of brambles and bracken in the woodland now produce a blaze of bluebells and campion followed by a profusion of foxgloves and gigantic male ferns – a show which no science of gardening could improve. At the same time nature has provided many clues which the owners have followed up; over five thousand bulbs have been added to the wild Tenby daffodils; a *Primula* collection to the primroses; and extensive planting of species and choice cultivars of *Prunus, Sorbus, Ilex* and *Acer* and wild cherries in the woodland. The moist acid soil also encourages rhododendrons and camellias. In the sunlit areas the interest extends into summer where there are more than a hundred shrub roses, mixed borders and also a rock garden.

The Downes, Nr Bideford
MR AND MRS R.C. STANLEY-BAKER

The garden covers about four acres below and around the late Georgian house with landscaped lawns descending steeply to the north-east, affording one of the finest views in North Devon over home farmland and woodlands in the Torridge valley, and intriguing vistas in the garden. It was first laid out soon after 1905 and, together with the small arboretum below the long drive, contains a considerable number of unusual trees and shrubs, the product of three generations of planting.

Many are now mature, for example, two *Davidia involucrata*, *Thujopsis dolabrata*, *Quercus* 'Lucombeana', *Halesia carolina*, *Eucryphia*, *Ailanthus altissima*, Indian and American chestnuts, American and Japanese maples and an exceptional *Acer palmatum* 'Dissectum'. In all the planting, colour and elegance of foliage and bark and compatibility with the incomparable surrounding landscape have been kept in mind, as much as the flowering potential of the plants. The silver and grey of *Cedrus atlantica* 'Glauca' and *Picea pungens* 'Koster' contrast with the gold of *Catalpa bignoioides* 'Aurea', *Acer cappadocicum* 'Aureum', *Acer japonicum* 'Aureum', and with the purple of *Acer palmatum* 'Atropurpureum', *Berberis* and *Cotinus coggygria*. The bark and leaves of several varieties of *Betula* and *Acer* and of *Eucalyptus niphophila*, in a spacious setting of lawn and flowerbeds, provide visual pleasure throughout the summer.

Flower colour emanates from great drifts of daffodils in spring, through many species and hybrid rhododendrons, evergreen and deciduous azaleas, and many varieties of *Clematis* clothing all the stone walls, to later flowering *Hibiscus*, hydrangeas, dahlias and herbaceous plants such as *Perovskia atriplicifolia*. There are woodland walks through the plantations of beech, oak, ash and sweet chestnut and finally, there is autumn colour in abundance.

Farrants, Kilmington
MR AND MRS M. RICHARDS

How can one put a garden into words? It is so different in every season. Set around a sixteenth-century cottage, our one-and-a-half-acre garden has been planted primarily for shapes and colours of foliage. Soft colours predominate – old shrub roses, lavender, rosemary, *Alchemilla mollis* and many other perfumed plants. A lovely boggy ditch runs down one side against a boundary hedge, and is planted with ferns, *Astilbe*, hostas, lilies, primulas and grasses. We are also lucky to have a brook, which is wonderfully cooling on a hot day, but which can become a raging torrent in a flash flood.

The house walls are planted with roses (pink and deep red), myrtle and many *Clematis*; *C. campaniflora* wanders through everything. At the base of the walls are mostly grey-foliaged aromatic shrubs: a favourite grouping comprises *Phormium tenax* Purpureum in the middle of a small bed filled with *Ballota*, *Artemisia splendens*, purple sage, grey santolina and lavender 'Hidcote'. Favourite trees are silver birch, maple and *Metasequoia*.

We hope we have created a garden of tranquillity, where it is easier to sit and enjoy the plants than to get on with the weeding.

1 Feebers Cottages, Westwood
MR AND MRS M.J. SQUIRES

Heavy clay, flat land, and late spring frosts; not a very good omen for a garden, but it came with the cottage in 1971. Combine this with two young children, and the inevitable pecuniary strain, and the result was that flower beds were dug with grass paths between; in fact this proved a bonus as, in places where mistakes were made, both paths and borders could be altered without too much trouble while the plants were still young. The garden is L-shaped, covers two-thirds of an acre and has been created from what was originally just rough meadow grass.

We now have a 'cottage' garden that is gradually attaining maturity with a varied selection of plants. It is still developing with the combination of new ideas and the acquisition of plants or other objects of interest – this year the gift of a large granite grinding ring. Our special interests include 'old' primroses and willows, but plants range from a large 'Kiftsgate' rose and young trees – including *Prunus serrula* and a variegated *Liriodendron* – through to alpines, herbaceous and half-hardy plants.

A drainage ditch enables us to grow 'bog' plants; sometimes in the winter it seems as if the whole garden is a bog when the stream the other side of the road overflows and comes through our front gate. This is the limiting factor when it comes to opening the garden; we can only do so when we are fairly sure that we are free from excess water and have had time to get on the ground to weed!

The Folly, Membury
SIR PETER AND LADY BRISTOW

One of the charms of this garden is the church tower which rises dramatically above it. The garden flanks two sides of the old house and each is quite different in character. To the north are two small lawns round which wind borders of shrubs and perennials, starting in spring with *Stachyurus praecox*, pink *Magnolia stellata*, *Chionodoxa* and tulips, soon followed by rampant *Clematis montana*, *Dicentra* and alpines. The borders then feature paeonies, alstroemerias, delphiniums and old roses, finishing with the rose 'The Fairy' and *Hibiscus*. Our greensand seems particularly to suit the alstroemerias which are best propagated by seed as they resent root disturbance. The orchard garden is landscaped with grass paths flanked by daffodils in spring and a good variety of shrub roses all summer long. Camellias and azaleas enjoy the shady stream and blend with a weeping willow and *Prunus×hillieri* 'Spire'. Many of the original pears, apples and cherries have been retained and support climbing roses. The house is also well furnished with roses and *Wisteria*, whilst *Clematis* and more roses have been planted along a new pergola.

Marwood Hill, near Barnstaple, in spring. A group of *Erythronium revolutum*, a native of western N. America, thrives in this damp corner of the garden. For a description of Marwood Hill see over.

The Glebe House, Whitestone
MR AND MRS JOHN WEST

The garden of The Glebe House, Whitestone (formerly the Rectory) comprising about two and a half acres adjoins Whitestone Church which stands at an altitude of six hundred and fifty feet some four miles north-west of Exeter. The garden slopes south on three levels including the broad terrace upon which the Georgian house stands facing due south, being flanked to the east by a fourteenth-century tithe barn, and to the west by domestic buildings. The soil is neutral, tending towards alkaline, and for this reason, the lower garden is laid out as a heather garden stocked mainly with the lime-tolerant varieties of *Erica carnea, arborea* and *vagans*.

If the heather garden is the first feature, the second is probably the full use made of the many old walls and buildings forming the middle level of the garden which are clothed with many varieties of climbing roses, *Clematis*, jasmine and honeysuckle. Most notable of any single plant in the garden is the enormously vigorous *Rosa filipes* 'Kiftsgate' which is trained along the barn and which in 1985 extended for over a hundred feet smothered with flowerheads. Derived from this *Rosa filipes* is an already sizeable and very interesting and vigorous seedling, which has a double flower with pink buds turning to white when fully out. The third, and upper level of the garden is given over to coniferous windbreaks providing protection from the predominately northerly and westerly winds. Behind these screens have been developed some walks flanked by old-fashioned roses representing most of the families together with a range of modern hybrid and species roses. From this high, south-facing garden views can be had covering the beautiful Devon countryside in an arc from Exeter to Dartmoor including the mouth of the Exe, the Haldon Hills, Teign valley and the northern slopes of Dartmoor.

◆

Heddon's Gate Hotel, Nr Lynton
MR AND MRS R. DE VILLE

Heddon's Gate faces south-west with some twenty acres of wooded ground, bordered all round by National Trust land within the Exmoor National Park. The main garden is a two-acre gorge with a gradient of one in four, banked, walled and terraced to form plateaux on three sides of the garden, leaving a steep, sheltered V-shape at the bottom, where steps lead directly on to the south-west peninsula footpath. The gardens had been laid out at the turn of the century, but neglected from the late 1950s until 1975, when the present owners, without any gardening experience or knowledge, undertook the restoration. Some fine specimens of trees and shrubs remained, and others were discovered and rejuvenated when cleared of the strangling undergrowth: one mature tree has so far resisted all attempts at identification. Working from old photo-

graphs and local knowledge, this fine and unusual site has lately been replanted with rhododendrons, notably *R. sino-grande, rex, hemsleyanum, cinnabarinum* and *hodgsonii* and species of *Eucalyptus, Acacia*, bamboos and tree ferns. A thicket of *Clerodendrum trichotomum* and *Eucalyptus gunnii* has been underplanted with white and purple honesty, Solomon's seal, wild ferns, *Euphorbia wulfenii*, mauve tulips, *Lilium regale, Crocosmia, Hosta sieboldiana* and *Clematis tangutica*, giving gentle colour and pleasing foliage for at least nine months of the year.

Heddon's Gate is a most informal garden, still untended in parts, and drifts of wild flowers are permitted to grow in the walls, and for the time being anyway, in the inevitable gaps between the younger shrubs and trees.

◆

Killerton Garden, Broadclyst
THE NATIONAL TRUST

Killerton Garden is beautifully situated on a south-facing slope amongst fine parkland and surrounded by some of Devon's most fertile soil – a deep, slightly acid loam which makes gardening a pleasure and ensures optimum growth when sufficient moisture is available. The terraced and mixed borders near the house are separated from the arboretum by a wide expanse of sweeping lawns which link the garden with the landscape and lead the eye up into the tapestry of mature trees. These form a magnificent backdrop to the garden and are the heart of the arboretum which was laid out during the first half of the nineteenth century and includes many original introductions such as notable *Fitzroya cupressoides, Saxegotha conspicua, Thuja plicata* and some fine redwoods. The flowering season starts in spring with rhododendrons, naturalized drifts of crocuses, *Cyclamen* and daffodils. Carpets of bluebells with groups of azaleas follow on into early summer, while colourful displays of hardy perennials in the mixed borders span the summer months. Fuchsias, dahlias, border chrysanthemums and asters herald the onset of autumn. More sheltered borders near or against the house accommodate a range of unusual shrubs and herbaceous perennials such as *Cassia corymbosa, Clianthus puniceus*, Mexican salvias, tender bulbs and various South African daisies, planted so that the colours harmonize and ensure a display from late May to early winter. Here can be seen the lovely deep maroon, almost black, *Cosmos atrosanguinea* aptly complemented by *Venidioarctotis* 'Champagne' reflecting the same colour towards the centre of each flower with the surrounding rayflorets of cream.

The generous gift of Killerton to the National Trust by Sir Richard Acland in 1946, coupled with the careful planning over the years, should ensure the future of the garden and maintain its own individual character and atmosphere with much to offer the interests of every garden visitor.

Knightshayes Court, Nr Tiverton
LADY AMORY; THE NATIONAL TRUST

This relatively modern garden was created by Sir John and Lady Heathcoat-Amory after the Second World War. There had previously been a garden on the site, which accounts for some of the old and magnificent trees to be seen, particularly the massive Douglas firs. There is a large woodland garden of exceptional quality with rhododendrons, azaleas, unusual shrubs and alpines. The formal gardens, with beautifully clipped hedges, cover a large area with an extensive range of trees and shrubs, spring bulbs and summer-flowering borders. Other features of interest include a willow garden, a conifer garden and a kitchen garden. This is one of the outstanding gardens of the south-west.

◆

Marwood Hill, Nr Barnstaple
DR J. A. SMART

The garden at Marwood Hill has been created over the last twenty-five years, although the formal rose garden and the walled garden are of a much earlier date. It has been built on either side of a sloping valley at the bottom of which a stream has been dammed in three places to make three small lakes. Where the stream runs between the lower two lakes a large area has been developed as a bog garden which comes into its own from early June onwards with big collections of candelabra primulas, *Hemerocallis*, astilbes and irises, with a particular emphasis on *Iris kaempferi*, as well as ligularias, *Senecio smithii* and many others. The garden covers some twelve acres and has been planted up with a varied collection of trees and shrubs, many of them very rare. There are collections of *Eucalyptus* which were brought back from the wild as seed and many of these are not grown elsewhere in the United Kingdom! One particular one, although still small in size, promises to be a great feature in the future: it is *Eucalyptus pauciflora pendula* which comes from a very limited area in New South Wales and has the white trunk and stems of *E. niphophila* but the habit of a weeping willow. Other trees from the Southern Hemisphere include a collection of eleven different species of *Nothofagus* and many shrubs from the same area, such as *Leptospermum, Callistemon* and *Ozothamnus*.

Amongst the young trees developing are collections of *Sorbus* and *Betula*, the latter being planted alongside the collection of *Eucalyptus* for the contrasting barks. *Magnolia* and *Cornus* are well represented in the garden and there are rhododendrons in flower from Christmas through until August. The *Camellia* collection is extensive, and with a large glass-house devoted to their culture, their flowering season starts early in February and carries on, in the open usually until June.

Thanks to the large walled garden with ten-foot-high walls, many *Ceanothus, Acacia pravissima, Cytisus battandieri* and *Abutilon megapotamicum* can be grown. A very large collection of *Clematis* claims pride of place here, with one particularly pleasing colour combination where *Clematis viticella* 'Etoile Violette' runs riot with *Eccremocarpus scaber* in its deep pink-red form. Other features are a comparatively new raised scree bed where alpines appear to thrive, and were more hardy here in the recent cold winter than anywhere else in the garden, thanks to the good drainage. Herbaceous and tree paeonies are at their best in May and June and later in the year a bed devoted to a very varied group of fuchsias adds colour before the *Cyclamen hederifolium*, which are planted around the shrubs in all parts of the garden, come on.

One feature of the garden which is always appreciated by visitors is the labelling, as much effort is devoted to keeping this up to date.

Middle Hill, Washfield

MR AND MRS E. BOUNDY

This small cottage-style garden was begun in 1964 and has developed since then. The site is windy and on clay soil. The first priority was to plant a windbreak and to erect chestnut paling to reduce the effects of the weather. Grit and compost of all kinds have been added to improve the texture of the soil, but inevitably mistakes have been made, for example, in attempting to grow plants which dislike the soil and the wind. A feature of the garden is colour and texture harmony. A planting enjoyed by many people consists of *Abies procera* 'Glauca Prostrata', *Sempervivum* 'Mahogany' and a dwarf *Hebe* with small bright green leaves, with pebbles as ground cover. Scented flowers and herbs surround the seats when the tour ends and 'garden talk' carries on longer than the paths! Visitors give us much pleasure and, indeed, information, even sometimes the answer to that endless question 'What is its name?' I do find that plants grown from seed and transplanted into their final position in a good compost when still young, establish themselves more vigorously on the clay soil than plants introduced when already old.

The Old Barn, Fremington

MR AND MRS A.H. VOUSDEN

Two acres of beauty are surrounded by nine-foot-high brick walls dating from the seventeenth century, all covered with climbing roses and *Clematis*, and intersected by a wide pergola planted with roses, *Clematis* and honeysuckle.

Standing near the centre of the garden is a fine mulberry tree, said to have been planted in the eighteenth century. This still dominates the garden, although the owners have planted forty-two other trees including *Gingko biloba*, *Gleditsia triacanthos* and *Koelreuteria paniculata*. This is a cottage garden, where

mass plantings have been made in the old-fashioned style, all interwoven with crazy paving.

A main feature of the garden is the collection of old shrub roses and *Clematis*, underplanted with pinks, pansies, and hardy geraniums of many varieties; herbs are also widely planted. The shell of an Edwardian vinery has been turned into an indoor garden where two fifteen-foot pillars of variegated ivy make a striking feature. A brick Georgian gazebo built in 1747 and restored in 1972, soon after the arrival of the present owners, overlooks the garden, which was described by a visiting London photographer as 'a garden that cuddles you; its colour, fragrance and peace envelop you completely'.

Variegated false oat grass, *Arrhenatherum elatius* '**Bulbosum variegatum**', contrasts with the sword-like leaves of *Phormium tenax var. purpureum* in the garden at Woodside. For description see over.

Putsborough Manor, Georgeham

MR AND MRS T.W. BIGGE

I have heard this described by visitors as being everyone's garden, and I find great pleasure in hearing that comment. Although it does not claim to be of classical design or particularly a specialist's garden, it is full of beauty – especially in June when the roses are out.

It also has the advantage of being set in lovely countryside which, although within half a mile of the sea, remains reasonably sheltered. The garden itself is in two parts. When we first came here the part to the front of the house was rather formal and divided by a driveway. In developing it we had the initial advantages of old walls, a stream running the entire length of one side of the garden, and a

very old mulberry tree which fell some sixty years ago but which, by keeping its feet in the ground and by re-rooting where it touched down, has produced a shape of its own of considerable architectural beauty. The other half of the garden which lies behind the house was originally all kitchen garden and is also walled. To save labour we have made the lower half into a grass walk flanked by shrub borders with cherry and other trees and bulbs behind. We like to think of the garden as being typically English in its setting, and in its content.

Rosemoor Garden Charitable Trust, Nr Great Torrington

THE LADY ANNE PALMER

Rosemoor displays plants of garden value, those collected or grown from seed from natural areas of the temperate world, collections of over a hundred holly species and cultivars, species and shrub roses and conifers great and small. A growing number of *Cornus* justify the garden being designated the National Cornus Collection by the National Council for the Conservation of Plants and Gardens (NCCPG), and many plants often ornamental, both woody, alpine and herbaceous, I personally value either for their beauty, or for sentimental reasons, as reminders of places and people, like a living diary throughout the garden.

The garden is to some degree educational, most plants being labelled with their botanical name, country of origin and year of planting; one hopes also that visitors find it pleasing aesthetically, although to collect worthwhile or rare plants rather than create an artistic whole, has perhaps been my main objective during the twenty-six or so years of its development. I like to feel that at least some endangered or threatened species are safely growing here in cultivation and can be propagated and distributed. The garden is the shop window for the nursery and the nursery is the life blood of the garden; since 1980 sales have increased sufficiently to support it and long may this situation continue for if it fails, so will the garden!

There are ten acres and three and a half thousand plants to see, and even in winter the coloured bark and tracery of twigs, together with the golden foliage of some conifers, are visually pleasing. So my message to those who read this book is to develop an interest in all plants, but in particular those which are rare, or endangered in their natural habitats, and thus to make a contribution towards the preservation of such species and cultivars by growing them in your own garden.

Vicar's Mead, East Budleigh

MR AND MRS M.F.J. READ

These three and a half acres of gardens really are different, containing many interesting features and unusual plants and providing a

57

Climbing roses and the beautiful broad grey leaves of *Hieracium lanatum*, are seen to advantage in the garden at Putsborough Manor, Georgeham. For a description see previous page.

thousands of snowdrops usher in the New Year and last Boxing Day a count showed sixty-seven different plants in flower.

Woodside, Barnstaple

MR AND MRS M.T. FEESEY

Woodside is a plantsman's garden, but one where flowers take second place; nevertheless it is a garden of great interest to the enthusiast, with the accent on shape, form and colour of foliage and on tender plants from around the world, including a collection of ornamental grasses, sedges and bamboos and other monocots such as the appealing *Astelia* species from New Zealand.

Little space is wasted in this two-acre south-sloping garden, with an intensity of planting ranging from dwarfs to trees, created over the past twenty-two years.

The owner has a most enthusiastic approach to gardening, with contacts world-wide, and is continually expanding the collection of unusual and rare plants in what is a mostly favoured climate under the influence of the Gulf Stream, as are many of the western coastal gardens.

Of especial interest are the New Zealand and other plants and alpines from the southern hemisphere, grown mostly in raised or sheltered beds with surface chippings to protect the foliage from winter dampness.

The soil is acid, which is ideal for the extensive ericaceous collection, although in the upper part of the garden so shallow that it needs copious dressings of mulch to prevent drying out during a hot summer.

In the early stages of the garden the wind-tolerant shelter trees had not only to be staked but also strutted, and still the wind would do its utmost to uproot the plantings. Now, after twenty years of growth, an ideal micro-climate has been created. For the windward side, an old nurseryman recommended *Thuja* as a suitable windbreak and these have proved invaluable with their fibrous root system and fragrance in wet weather.

Amongst the many variegated plants in the garden, there are oddities such as *Aquilegia vulgaris* with stunningly variegated foliage (and seeds germinating 90 per cent true) which first appeared in the garden about four years ago, and variegated forms of the common sycamore of which seedlings were recently discovered in a remote North Devon garden.

The owner, who is a practising architect, is the author of the Royal Horticultural Society's Wisley Handbook *Ornamental Grasses, Sedges and Bamboos*, in which his botanical paintings and photographs have been included. His enthusiasm extends to organizing the gardens of Devon for the National Gardens Scheme, and whilst these have their priority there is a special affection for the western coastal gardens of Scotland where the climate is similar.

unique setting for a five-hundred-year-old thatched historic former vicarage (where Sir Walter Ralegh was said to have had his early schooling) and bounded by an eight-foot-high thatched cob wall which gives shelter to many tender shrubs and plants. The house is sheltered from the south-west by the old red sandstone escarpment which rises high above the house and provides a spectacular back-drop of near vertical garden, displaying many coloured foliage trees and shrubs, as well as many thousands of spring bulbs. There are winding paths up and down the steep slopes with bridges and steps to ease the ascents.

Apart from two five-hundred-year-old yew and a hundred-foot ash tree of half their age, the garden is new and has been created by the present owners since 1977, and is, therefore, still developing and maturing.

Other special features include a *Hosta* garden with over sixty varieties, intermingled with the sword blades of phormiums, libertias and astelias; an ivy corner with some forty different types; rockery, pond, fernery, kitchen garden, propagating area, a gravel garden with a mainly blue theme, the old well of the house made into a giant Wardian Case and stone troughs in variety. Climbing and old-fashioned roses abound and nearly every tree of any size plays host to climbing roses, *Clematis* and other plants. Four NCCPG National Collections of *Liriope*, *Ophiopogon*, *Dianella* and *Libertia* are being established here, and already some fifty different species and cultivars have been collected.

There are many plantings for special effects – such as a drift of hundreds of pink-and-white-flowered autumn *Cyclamen* over-planted with *Ajuga* 'Burgundy Glow', and a large carpet of the black-leaved *Ophiopogon planiscapus* 'Nigrescens' underplanted with white crocuses, and many others. Tens of

DEVON (SOUTH)

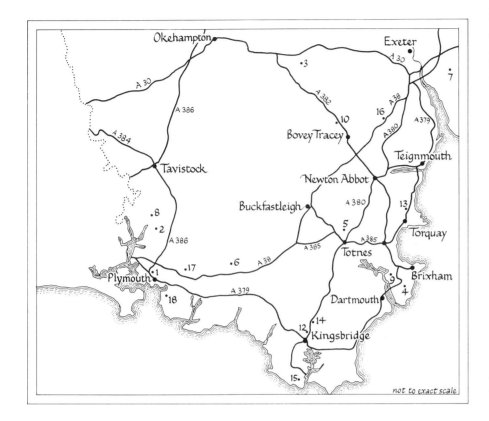

not to exact scale

Directions to Gardens

41 Beaumont Road, St Judes, Plymouth. [1]

Bickham House, Roborough, 8 miles north of Plymouth. [2]

Castle Drogo, Drewsteignton, 12 miles west of Exeter. [3]

Coleton Fishacre, 2 miles northeast of Kingswear. [4]

Dartington Hall Gardens, 2 miles northwest of Totnes. [5]

Fardel Manor, 1¼ miles northwest of Ivybridge, 2 miles southeast of Cornwood. [6].

Fernwood, Toadpit Lane, 1½ miles west of Ottery St Mary. [7]

The Garden House, Buckland Monachorum, Yelverton, 10 miles north of Plymouth. [8]

Greenway Gardens, Churston Ferrers, 4 miles west of Brixham. [9]

Higher Knowle, Lustleigh, 3 miles northwest of Bovey Tracey. [10]

Lower Coombe Royal, ½ mile north of Kingsbridge. [12]

Model Village, Babbacombe, 3 miles north of Torquay. [13]

The Old Rectory, Woodleigh, near Loddiswell, 3½ miles north of Kingsbridge. [14]

Overbecks, Sharpitor, 1½ miles southwest of Salcombe. [15]

1 The Parade, Chudleigh, 10 miles southwest of Exeter. [16]

51 Rockfield Avenue, Southway, Plymouth, 3 miles from the city centre. [1]

Saltram House, Plympton, 3 miles east of Plymouth. [17]

41 Springfield Close, Plymstock, 4 miles southeast of Plymouth. [18]

---

41 Beaumont Road, Plymouth
MR AND MRS A.J. PARSONS

We have tried to make an oasis of rest in the middle of a busy city, where bees, birds and butterflies can roam at will. The north-facing enclosed backyard and its narrow path (sixty feet long) are gardening conditions shared by many Victorian terraced houses, and our garden, though it breaks all the rules, may prove of interest to those with similar problems.

Intensive tub cultivation of climbing plants, roses, *Clematis*, *Ceanothus*, *Parthenocissus* and variegated ivies, provide privacy and clothe the arches that break up the length of the path. A focal point, at the far end, is formed by a figurine we call Aphrodite. The garden is crowded with *Pieris*, viburnums, camellias, conifers, roses and a succession of *Clematis*. Flowers of pale blue *Ceanothus* 'Gloire de Versailles' romp through billowing trusses of purple *Clematis* 'Etoile Violette' and the autumnal scarlet of *Parthenocissus henryana* provides a brilliant background for the silver seedheads and golden flowers of *Clematis tangutica*. On warm evenings it is pleasant to sit on the stone seat, listening to the fountain playing, the hum of the bees, the song of the blackbird or the bells of St Andrew's. At night the rustle of a gentle breeze may stir the leaves of the little trees or carry the perfume of *Daphne odora*, *Philadelphus*, *Viburnum farreri* or *Lilium regale* enclosed within this over-crowded secret garden. As Horace wrote:

'This was one of my prayers:
For a parcel of land, not so very large,
Which should have a garden,
And a spring of water near the house. . .'

Bickham House, Roborough
THE LORD AND LADY ROBOROUGH

Our garden consists of about sixteen acres running down a valley with spectacular views. We started it in 1954 and were encouraged by having many beautiful trees. We began very slowly but have increased the pace since.

It is principally a spring garden, with a mass of naturalized bulbs, and about a hundred varieties of camellias. There are many rhododendrons, magnolias and other interesting shrubs. Amongst our features are two walks, one of white semi-double cherries underplanted with blue *Rhododendron augustinii* (which all come out together if we are lucky!); the other of large single pink cherries, with bulbs. Lately we have been endeavouring to create a small arboretum, with the emphasis on maples. It was originally a small spinney, which we cut down, leaving a few important trees as a foundation; we have been rewarded by the area being carpeted with bluebells and campions. We also have two ponds, one large and one small, which enable us to grow aquatic plants; an interesting feature is the old cider press which has been incorporated within the small pond.

An old walled garden with a great many shrub roses is very attractive and enables us to keep open to the public through the month of June. There is an interesting old barn where we provide teas and it looks over the small pond and has extensive views.

Castle Drogo, Drewsteignton
THE NATIONAL TRUST

This twelve-acre garden was created from wild moorland and there are beautiful views of Dartmoor, framed by trees, shrubs and yew hedges. Indeed, Castle Drogo's architect, Edwin Lutyens, used clipped yew hedges to great effect in the garden, to add an architectural dimension to the castle, to enclose the huge circular croquet lawn and to act as the castle's sentinels.

It is really a series of gardens, the smallest being the chapel garden, recently replanted with miniature roses, lavender and box after the original plans were found. Below this is the rhododendron valley, a joy to behold in spring with its camellias, cherries and rhododendrons, both species and hybrids. The main garden consists of formal terraces and borders where, echoing the castle, Dartmoor granite has been used for steps and walls. The first terrace is planted as a rose garden, using modern cultivars chosen for their ability to withstand wind – one of the main problems in this garden, along with the light soil which needs constant feeding and mulching. At each corner are four weeping *Parrotia persica* which will eventually cover their supporting frames to form a cool umbrella of shade. Herbaceous borders full of old varieties of traditional plants such as monkshood, *Lychnis*, lupins and campanulas surround the rose terrace; a harmony of colours in June and July and, as with many National Trust gardens, planted to the original designs.

Coleton Fishacre, Kingswear
THE NATIONAL TRUST

The garden at Coleton Fishacre lies in a sheltered Devon combe, south-east facing and sloping down to high cliffs. Thanks to a mild maritime climate, with violent sea winds tempered by shelter belts of pine, and an acid soil, plants from every continent grow well, and the D'Oyly Cartes, who made the garden, exploited these advantages by planting many exotic trees and shrubs. In style the garden ranges from an Edwardian-derived architectural framework around the house, to almost subtropical woodland nearer the sea, with rhododendrons on the shadier slopes and a variety of Chilean, South African and Mediterranean plants on the banks facing the sun. Near the house the terrace walls provide shelter for such plants as watsonias, the subtropical *Impatiens tinctoria*, Mexican salvias, and the massive *Beschorneria yuccoides*.

Self-sowing annuals, such as *Calceolaria mexicana*, save much work in the garden, and we welcome *Nicotiana langsdorfii*, with weed-smothering foliage topped by elegant spires of small, lime-green, trumpet-shaped flowers enhanced by blue anthers – a plant of great character that fits in almost anywhere it chooses to put itself.

Dartington Hall Gardens, Nr Totnes
DARTINGTON HALL TRUST

Dartington is a garden where form has dominated design and where compositions have been attempted using the contours of the land to intensify the natural effects of height, depth and distance. Trees and shrubs are used to give structure to the compositions, and lawns to emphasize space. The great trees, planted long ago by the Champerowne family, have been cleared of undergrowth so that they stand out in all their grandeur, and vistas have been opened, to give greater sweep to distant views, and to link the garden with the surrounding countryside.

In the fourteenth century John Holland, Duke of Exeter, built Dartington Hall and, being himself a jouster of international fame planned, it may be assumed, his own tournament ground or tiltyard. Although altered and overlaid in later centuries, its original form has now been restored. The underlying rock structure of the garden is limestone. Superimposed are layers of slate and shale which, when broken up, are locally termed shillet. At the top of the garden is an extrusion of volcanic ash known as tuff or diabase, and it is this extrusion which has caused fissures. These tend to fill with water and account for the number of springs which break in and around the Dell. This geological structure provides a good growing soil with pockets of both acid and alkaline conditions.

No garden under active cultivation is likely to achieve a final form, and each year Dartington undergoes minor changes. Whether by overcrowding or damage wrought by gales, or by the natural process of decay, plants must often be rooted out and new varieties introduced. Experiments are continually being tried: in fact, so continual is the process of change that any description of the garden which aims to give an exact and permanent arrangement of plants would be deceptive. It might be well to bear in mind that this is not a garden of botanical specimens, it is a garden based on personal choice and discrimination, where only those plants will be found that seem to flourish and to fit into the total design.

Fardel Manor, Nr Ivybridge
DR A.G. STEVENS

A variety of secluded gardens, each with its own theme, covering an area of five acres, a formal fountain garden, herbaceous, bedding, shrubberies, and a working herb garden, surround the present sixteenth-century manor house which was originally listed in the Domesday Book and owned by the Raleigh family for three hundred years.

A south-facing wall with climbing roses, and, in late summer, the bright yellow flowers of the rambling canary creeper *Tropaeolum peregrinum* leads to the orangery, with its collection of plants including a productive vine, 'Black Hamburg', and *Citrus mitis* with its fragrant flowers and small fruits. Past recently planted hydrangeas and through an arch of holly, pillared roses lead through vegetable and fruit gardens to an orchard and small informal pond, surrounded by thistles, parsley, and wild irises mixed with astilbes, ligularias, day lilies and the giant rhubarb-like *Gunnera manicata*. From here a stream passes through a sloping south-facing paddock, newly planted with many varieties of trees and shrubs round a quarter-acre lake edged with beds of irises and primulas. Here wildfowl mix with resident Chinese geese. With conservation of wildlife and native flora in mind, it is planned to establish oaks, ash and beech with under-plantings of ornamentals in order to provide habitats for a large range of wildlife which will give the garden the added enchantment of natural movement and sound.

Fernwood, Ottery St Mary
MR AND MRS H. HOLLINRAKE

Maybe curiosity killed the cat! But to be curious about what lies around the corner makes a garden as surely as the plants that grace it. To hide most of the garden and yet indicate its scope requires some thought and a pencil and paper. Fernwood was planned this way, its main axis a clear and uncluttered lawn, bordered not by straight lines but curving borders, now widening, now narrowing, so its length is revealed, but with hidden interest glimpsed behind each curve, and through gaps in the borders.

A poor basic soil of sand and gravel, enriched by a hundred and fifty years of pine needle peat from a cover of Scots pine, forms the frame, within which planting began. Plants of fifty *Rhododendron* species were raised from seed. These, together with purchased hybrids, gave some five hundred plants, which form the main shrub planting. With a few exceptions, they were planted in groups of three or five and care was taken to consider colour grouping. On the whole this has been quite successful, but not without some mistakes.

Into this framework, filling-in followed, with a varied selection of other shrubs, some herbaceous plants, many lilies, shrub roses, and bulbs of all kinds, together with other deciduous small trees, such as *Acer*, *Cornus* and *Magnolia*, with some summer bedding. Things will grow, and as time goes on shadows lengthen, and the time comes when something has to come out – the most difficult decision the gardener has to take. So the process begins of slowly re-making the garden.

The Garden House, Buckland Monachorum
THE FORTESCUE GARDEN TRUST

An eight-acre garden, including a fine walled garden extending to two acres, and good collections of herbaceous and woody plants.

Greenway Gardens, Churston Ferrers
MR AND MRS A.A. HICKS

The garden at Greenway is situated on a steep slope on the banks of the river Dart – covering some thirty acres in all. It is basically a spring garden and there are some fine early magnolias – a magnificent *M. campbellii*, ×*veitchii*, *denudata* and a particularly good Raffill seedling, 'Kew's Surprise'. There are about thirty different magnolias altogether, including some fine *M. delavayi* growing in the woods. The trees have been wisely planted over some hundred and fifty years with much oak, beech and pine, and a tulip tree which even at the end of the last century was mentioned as exceptional. There is an old walled garden with camellias and a large cork oak. We grow many varieties of *Camellia* as well as other more tender trees and shrubs. Nature plays its part in making the garden beautiful with banks of primroses, bluebells and campions in the spring. The main walled gardens have plants such as *Caesalpinia japonica*, *Ceanothus papillosus*, mauve and white wisterias and a number of abutilons. In front of the house, which is Georgian and flanked by two huge *Magnolia grandiflora*, we have a number of other climbers, among them one of my favourites, *Mutisia oligodon*. For a long time we found this last hard to grow, until we placed it so that it grew up through something else, in this case *Akebia quinata*, after which it has never looked back.

Lastly, I should stress that Greenway is an old garden; there have been gardens here in various forms since the Gilbert family lived here in the sixteenth century.

Higher Knowle, Lustleigh
MR AND MRS D.R.A. QUICKE

Wisteria-clad walls integrate this granite house into the surrounding woodland garden, started in 1955 on a steep hillside with spectacular views over Dartmoor to the south-west. At the top of a shady drive winding under a high canopy of old beech, you emerge into bright sunlight. Rhododendrons

and magnolias can be seen on both sides rising from carpets of bluebells in the dappled shade of oak trees. An unusually tall *Embothrium coccineum*, with its profusion of brilliant orange-scarlet flowers in May and June, revels in full sun. Various ornamental cherries over a heather bank line the drive and, at the front of the house, grassy paddocks are seen falling to the Wray Brook (the route taken by early and late air frosts), and rising the other side to the moor itself. Passing through a beech hedge, you come to a well-tended enclosed lawn and the main display of deciduous and evergreen azaleas in May; these have merged together to form highly fragrant riots of bright and contrasting colours. In the woodland garden are large specimens of many choice *Rhododendron* species and hybrids, particularly *R. calophytum* 'Penjerrick' and a variety of different clones of *R.* ×*loderi*. A backcloth is provided by huge rounded boulders which appear poised to roll over the garden. The soil is thin, poor and acid, four hundred and fifty feet above sea level and with fifty inches annual rainfall.

Being old woodland the whole area is infested with honey fungus which weakens and kills many shrubs and trees. The application of thick mulches (stake peelings are ideal), frequent watering and foliar feeding, and layering to replace lost treasures, seem the best response.

Lower Coombe Royal, Kingsbridge
MR AND MRS H. SHARP

The garden lies sheltered from all but southerly gales in a deep but wide valley, with established beeches, chestnuts and sycamores along its skyline. Because of the natural shelter, the usually high rainfull and a measure of maritime influence, many older rhododendrons (notably *arboreum* forms and *thomsonii* hybrids) have avoided serious wind and frost damage and grown to spectacular heights. The older part of the garden, two acres lying along the valley bottom, was planted with calcifuge plants (mainly American and Asian) from 1840 onwards by John Luscombe, one of the early rhododendron hybridists. A surviving 'Coombe Royal' (1875) may be his original cross. Some decidedly old trees, for example *Magnolia denudata* planted in 1850, must be his original plantings; others may be offspring of his introductions. The effect of old trees keeling over and growing into each other, of self-sown seedlings developing in odd places during periods of neglect, and the deliberate policy of renovation during the last twenty-five years has been to create an informal jungle with the canopy at various levels, alternating with cleared glades and dells. The accumulation of leafmould over the decades, coupled with toleration of native wild plants and introduced ground-cover, has produced a garden largely free of undesirable weeds.

The remaining six acres of the grounds have been progressively developed over the

last twenty-five years in a semi-formal fashion, mostly with camellias, magnolias, eucryphias, hydrangeas, *Eucalyptus* and some more tender plants such as *Sophora* that need replacing after those bitter winters when the valley becomes a frost pocket. Current policy is to provide more colour from mid-summer to autumn, principally on the west-facing slopes, though without detracting from the fascinating contrasts in shade and texture that fresh growth on massed camellias and rhododendrons in particular provide at that time.

The Model Village, Babbacombe
T.F. DOBBINS, ESQ.

A four-and-a-half-acre steep Devon coombe was transformed during 1962 into a beautiful and unique coniferous garden with a lake, two waterfalls and many streams.

The gardens, situated in an east-facing valley, are primarily designed to display and complement the sealed habitat comprising a one-twelfth scale English scene of village and township, farmland and forest. Four hundred different conifers varying from dwarf and slow growing, to the larger and more vigorous types have been thoughtfully planted to give what was recently described as 'a masterpiece of miniature landscaping'.

Dwarf conifers, some rare, are used in profusion, while on the perimeter of the gardens larger conifers are used to form a background, the careful blending of shapes and colours being most attractive. Streams, crossed by rustic bridges, and waterfalls flow into a lake where varieties of goldfish are at home among the waterlilies.

The lawns are particularly fine, and during the spring and summer skilful positioning of bedding plants amongst the conifers creates a beautiful effect.

Many of the miniature conifers used are shaped to resemble deciduous trees and visitors often enquire how this is achieved, suspecting 'Bonsai' techniques. In fact, it is done by careful pruning during each stage of growth. The conifers are all numbered and a booklet is available giving the Latin and English names of each.

The Old Rectory, Woodleigh
MR AND MRS H.E. MORTON

This is a three-acre woodland garden with mature trees; and also a walled garden. The open woodland contains eight enclosures or glades, each one quite secluded but connected by paths. The underplanting consists mainly of rhododendrons, both species and hybrids, camellias, magnolias and hydrangeas, but there are other shrubs, and displays of spring bulbs, particularly crocuses and daffodils.

It is twenty-seven years since we came here, to find very neglected and overgrown conditions but also a few good mature rhododendrons, two large azaleas, *R. luteum*, a *Magnolia grandiflora* and a very large old *Wisteria*. Surprisingly there were no camellias and only a single *Hydrangea*. Over the intervening years we have been deeply grateful for gifts of interesting and beautiful trees and shrubs from generous gardening friends: these include especially rhododendrons and camellias but also some tender subjects.

Although the garden is at its most colourful in spring, an attempt has been made to retain interest and beauty throughout the year by planting evergreens and shrubs for scent and winter effect. Also, the walled garden has been developed with summer rather than spring in mind.

Attention to form has been the main consideration in all the planting, but over and above this has been an attempt to create an atmosphere of peace, tranquillity and harmony. This has been done by seeking to be fully aware of nature and natural forces, and no chemicals have ever been used. We like to think of the garden as a haven for as many varied animals and plants as possible, with us acting as sympathetic, and dare we hope, inspired, custodians.

◆

Overbecks, Sharpitor
THE NATIONAL TRUST

Situated high above the Salcombe estuary, Overbecks offers superb sea views and comes nearer to a garden on the Mediterranean Riviera than any other owned by the National Trust. The property was left by Mr Otto Overbeck to the Trust in 1937, but from the beginning of the century a succession of owners planted many exotic shrubs and trees. One of these, a *Magnolia campbellii* planted in 1901, is considered by many to be the crowning glory: spreading forty feet high and wide, it is an unforgettable sight in early March. Complementing the deep pink of the *Magnolia*, the creamy-white flowers of a nearby *Clematis armandii* provide a delightful combination, while sheltering at the bottom of the same wall are some good forms of *Helleborus orientalis*. But it is in summer when Overbecks really comes to life. In the herbaceous borders which surround a charming bronze statue of a young girl, cannas, *Agapanthus* and kniphofias combine with annuals to provide a symphony of colour and form, while above a large, sombre camphor tree, *Cinnamomum camphora*, is one of the garden's rarities. Tucked away in sheltered corners are some gems: *Datura sanguinea* thrives in one spot along with the Chatham Island forget-me-not, *Myosotidium hortensia*, while agaves are being encouraged to establish themselves. In recent years, several exotic plants such as *Echium, Beschorneria yuccoides* and *Fascicularia pitcairniifolia* have been planted, while an increasing collection of phormiums, with their variety of brightly-coloured leaves, provide much scope for colour association – such as *Phormium* 'Bronze Baby' with *Phormium* 'Cream Delight'.

41, Beaumont Road, Plymouth; *Clematis, Lilium regale* and foliage plants crowd around a cistern.

Everywhere there is something of interest. Adults and children alike enthuse over such sights as bananas (*Musa basjoo*) in fruit in the garden, and the abundance of oranges on trees in the conservatory. Indeed, although Overbecks is a plantsman's paradise everyone finds something of interest.

◆

1, The Parade, Chudleigh
DR AND MRS HAMILTON

A visitor leaving the garden said, almost accusingly, 'You don't have anything usual do you?' There are, of course, many usual plants but the ones which need endlessly digging up and dividing are, on the whole, avoided. The garden was originally gently sloping, long and narrow, but has recently been enlarged sideways and now covers about two-thirds of an acre. The mixed borders contain hostas, ferns, the smaller-growing kniphofias, and cimicifugas; the dark-leaved *Cimicifuga ramosa atropurpurea* is a striking plant and also enhances its near neighbours. *Cyclamen hederifolium* grows like a weed and often has to be removed to a place underneath three large holm oaks, where they, *Polygonatum multiflorum*, and *Anemone nemorosa* are the only plants which will survive the terrible summer dryness. There are very few true alpines, but there is an area for small plants, the tiny double *Erodium* and *Thalictrum kiusuanum*, small astilbes, *Geranium cinereum* 'Ballerina' and 'Apple Blossom', *Verbascum* 'Letitia' and many others. Not everything is small though, and there are shrubs and trees for flowers or foliage, some

of them tender which, sadly, can sometimes be lost. *Melianthus major* is well established and if cut down in a bad winter, soon recovers and shares a sheltered bed with *Alstroemeria pulchella* and *A. braziliensis, Hebe fairfieldii* and *Abutilon* 'Kentish Belle'. In their season, the old roses scramble about, possibly too much so, as managing them, despite help from Graham Stuart Thomas's books, has to be learnt by experience. As they are so lovely, they are forgiven everything, but resolutions are always made to do better next year. In one place the *Delphinium* 'Alice Artindale,' with small double flowers, rises serenely above them, and after the roses have gone, many of the bushes have *Clematis viticella* and other species climbing over them.

◆

51, Rockfield Avenue, Southway
MR AND MRS D.R. WATERFIELD

This is a very small town garden of just over a hundred square yards, but our aim in design is to give an impression of the country by using local Cornish stone for paths, covering the dividing walls with ivy and a variety of shrubs and roses, and by planting conifers and perennials to provide interest and colour. Corner planters of stone are used for spring bulbs and summer annuals. The arch dividing the lawn area from the greenhouse is covered in honeysuckle and the lovely *Clematis montana*; the blackbirds love it for nesting. We have four trees, all flowering at different times; a herb garden with a bay tree and various mints, sage, thyme and rosemary, all both pretty and useful; and even a tiny wild garden of primroses, violets and bluebells. For summer bedding we use fuchsias, geraniums and a wealth of annuals to give a profusion of colour until the frosts. As a backdrop we have the beautiful and fragrant rambler rose 'Bridal Wreath' and we make use of the ivy on the dividing walls to hold small pots of trailing geraniums and fuchsias.

◆

Saltram House, Plympton
THE NATIONAL TRUST

Despite its close proximity to the city of Plymouth, the garden of Saltram House still has an air of tranquillity about it. Surrounded by acres of park and woodland, the garden has many fine specimens of trees, plantations of shrubs and several small buildings to add to its interest. Careful planting has turned what was mainly a spring garden into one for all seasons. Late-flowering rhododendrons, hydrangeas, buddlejas and fuchsias have extended the flowering season into summer. Several unusual trees have been planted to give the garden autumn interest and colour, examples being *Nothofagus obliqua* which takes on a pinky red hue in autumn and *Fagus orientalis* which turns yellow. In winter the fine collection of pines throughout the garden comes into its own.

One of the garden's hidden delights is the

orange grove where orange and lemon trees are brought out of the Orangery in early summer to ripen the wood. At the centre of the grove is a pool surrounded by such water-loving plants as bogbean and marsh marigold. Camellias flower as early as January in this sheltered spot. The Orangery itself houses several ornamental trees in tubs, the cool grey leaves of *Acacia baileyana* contrasting with the green of the citrus trees, while the highly scented flowers of the climbing *Trachelospermum jasminoides* complement the orange trees.

Of particular beauty in spring is the lime avenue which is a blaze of yellow in early spring with old cultivars of *Narcissus*, while in autumn the pink flowers of *Cyclamen hederifolium* take over.

41, Springfield Close, Plymstock
MR AND MRS CLEM SPENCER

The basic design of the garden was arrived at on a drawing board some twenty years ago. The site was a gently sloping field with a natural hedge on the west side. Advantage was taken of the slope to create various levels combined with curves and banks. The natural hedge played an important part in determining the character of the garden which was intended to maintain a country atmosphere in fast-developing suburbia. The main features have been linked by winding paths to create the impression of space in a relatively small area (about five hundred square yards) and to provide subject matter for paintings. A bird-bath set in an area paved with natural stone is surrounded by ferns, grasses and ivy from which a path leads to a pond with a waterfall at one end and a statue at the other, partially concealed under a *Salix caprea* 'Pendula'. The curve of the pond merges into the curve of a herbaceous border containing some interesting plants, such as *Thalictrum dipterocarpum*. This border is backed by a path and a neatly clipped *Lonicera nitida* hedge leading to another naturally paved area with rockery and a small pergola and arbour attached to the studio.

Two *Thuja* 'Rheingold', neatly clipped in to domes, serve as pillars at the top of the steps leading from the lawn. There are also beds containing annuals, fuchsias, camellias and rhododendrons, and a rustic arch which leads to a small area where wild flowers are encouraged to grow.

Greenway Gardens, Churston Ferrers. A restful colour scheme provided by white *Iris laevigata*, foxgloves, herb robert, wall pennywort, ivy, hartstongue and male ferns. For description see page 61.

DORSET

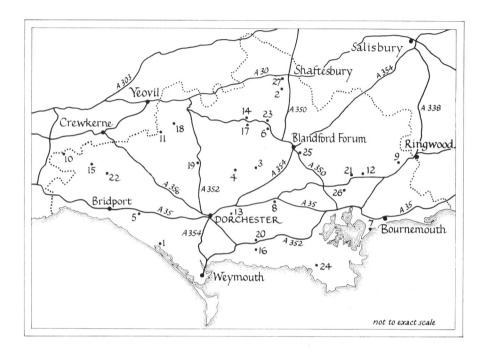

not to exact scale

Directions to Gardens

Abbotsbury Gardens, 9 miles northwest of Weymouth, 9 miles southwest of Dorchester. [1]

Acacia Cottage, 46 Twyford, 4 miles southwest of Shaftesbury. [2]

Aller Green, Ansty, 12 miles north of Dorchester. [4]

Catnap Cottage, Hilton, 10 miles south of Blandford. [3]

Chilcombe House, Chilcombe, 5 miles east of Bridport. [5]

The Cobbles, Shillingstone, 5 miles northwest of Blandford. [6]

Compton Acres Gardens, Canford Cliffs Road, Poole. [7]

Culeaze, 1½ miles south of Bere Regis. [8]

Dapple Grey, 40 Lions lane, Ashley Heath, west of Ringwood. [9]

Deans Court, in centre of Wimborne. [21]

Forde Abbey, 4 miles southeast of Chard, 7 miles west of Crewkerne. [10]

Frankham Farm, Ryme Intrinseca, 3 miles south of Yeovil. [11]

Highbury, Woodside Road, West Moors, 8 miles north of Bournemouth. [12]

Ivy Cottage, Ansty, 12 miles north of Dorchester. [4]

Kingston Maurward, Dorset College of Agriculture and Horticulture, 1 mile east of Dorchester. [13]

Lindens, Sturminster Newton, 11 miles northwest of Blandford Forum. [14]

The Manor Farm Garden, Littlewindsor, 4 miles northwest of Beaminster. [15]

The Manor House, Chaldon Herring, 9 miles east of Dorchester. [16]

May Cottage, Fiddleford, 1 mile west of Shillingstone. [17]

Melford House, High Street, Yetminster, 5 miles southeast of Yeovil. [18]

Minterne, Minterne Magna, 10 miles north of Dorchester. [19]

Moigne Combe, 6 miles east of Dorchester, 1½ miles north of Owermoigne. [20]

North Leigh House, Colehill, 1 mile northeast of Wimborne. [21]

Parnham, ¾ mile south of Beaminster, 5 miles north of Bridport. [22]

52 Rossmore Road, Parkstone, Poole. [7]

Russets, Rectory Lane, Child Okeford, 6 miles northwest of Blandford. [23]

Smedmore, Kimmeridge, 7 miles south of Wareham. [24]

Tarrant Rushton Gardens (Charlton Cottage, River House and Tarrant Rushton House), 3 miles southeast of Blandford Forum. [25]

Turnpike Cottage, 8 Leigh Road, Wimborne. [26]

14 Umbers Hill, Shaftesbury. [27]

◆

*Abbotsbury Gardens, Nr Weymouth
STRANGWAYS ESTATE

This twenty-acre garden is noted for its almost uniquely mild, Mediterranean-type climate, which enables a very fine collection of rhododendrons, azaleas, camellias, and many unusual and tender trees and shrubs to be grown. Planting started here in 1760 and was considerably extended during the nineteenth century. Much replanting has been carried out in recent years, and a special feature has been made of plants newly introduced from China.

◆

Acacia Cottage, Nr Shaftesbury
THE MISSES HASLAM AND MCTRUSTY

We moved to North Dorset on our retirement in 1977 with a great desire to create a garden and a minimum of experience. We had long been interested in, and admired, the results of gardening friends.

This garden, at its best in summer, covers two-thirds of an acre, is on greensand, almost level, and exposed to strong westerly winds. A lawn is bounded on the east side by a ×*Cupressocyparis leylandii* hedge, and on the west by two large herbaceous borders, with a well-grown beech hedge separating the kitchen garden.

As the garden is not large, we have avoided using plants with strong-coloured flowers. The larger border is planted with the paler shades of yellow and cream, through to varying shades of green at the cooler end. Shrubs and trees form a background, and these include *Betula jacquemontii*, *Gleditsia triacanthos* 'Sunburst' and *Rosa* 'Nevada'. The smaller border is planted with a mixture of blue, pink and white flowers, with a background of old roses and *Viburnum fragrans*, *Callistemon* and *Aesculus* 'Briotti', and some interesting ground cover plants.

On the west side of the house we built a patio surrounded by an old stone wall, with shallow steps leading to a lawn. The border here is sloping and planted with silver foliaged plants, lavenders, and *Salvia officinalis* Purpurascens', with *Rosa* 'Blanc Double de Coubert', *Rosa rugosa* and *Cotinus coggygria* to give contrast; silver birches form a background.

On the main lawn we planted *Morus nigra*, the black mulberry, for architectural interest and posterity.

We have made many mistakes and continue to do so, but we learn a great deal from visiting other gardens and exchanging ideas with their owners.

Aller Green, Ansty
A.J. THOMAS, ESQ.

This delightful one-acre informal cottage garden has changed little over the years; Boston Ivy, *Parthenocissus tricuspidata*, planted long ago covers the front of the cottage, and here birds such as flycatchers make their nests every year. The creeper-clad wall provides an ideal backcloth for the roses, geraniums, begonias and other interesting plants that grow in small beds near a little path that leads to the front door. At the back of the cottage the remains of an old orchard has been interplanted with trees and shrubs, with *Clematis* and rambling roses being trained to climb up the old apple trees. In spring this area is a mass of colour with daffodils and *Crocus* naturalized under the apples. Hedges surround the kitchen garden, which is entered through a small gateway, and surprises are in store as a great profusion of flowers border the grass paths that divide the vegetable plots. Here the borders of brightly coloured paeonies and oriental poppies blend well with the green foliage of the vegetables and, together with perennials like *Polygonum bistorta* 'Superbum', erigerons, euphorbias and ligularias show just how effective this kind of planting can be in the kitchen garden.

Catnap Cottage, Hilton
MRS M.J. PHILIPS

This is a plantsman's garden on a hillside with pleasant views, made from a medium-sized field since 1969. Designed and planted by the owner, it consists of several little gardens with grassy walks leading to the vistas, and includes a small pool, a rockery, patios, herbs and a wooded area with spring bulbs and wild flowers. Although there is a good range of conifers, trees and shrubs, the emphasis is on perennials and foliage plants, such as *Eucomis, Leptospermum, Helleborus orientalis* and *Epimedium* × *rubrum*.

Chilcombe, Nr Bridport
CARYL AND JOHN HUBBARD

Without doubt, the essential point of Chilcombe is its setting. The carved block of house, little church and farmyard sit halfway up the hillside facing south-east across the Bride Valley towards the sea. By 'garden' we include not only the walled enclosures but also the surrounding paddocks, pond and copses. We began rehabilitating the near-derelict site in 1969, although most of the serious planting began some ten years later. There is a small wild area, shaded with trees, and including a geranium bank and many hostas and hellebores; the front garden, with five beds of varying sizes surrounding a grass rectangle; and two simple courtyards, in one of which the planting is almost entirely of wild and herbaceous plants self-sown between the stones, while the other is divided into two beds designed to be seen from above as well as at ground level. The main walled garden slopes away from the house and is divided into quarters by a tapestry hedge and a double border. For the sake of privacy, mystery and shelter from the wind, there are further sub-divisions made from espalier fruit trees or small pergolas. One quarter consists of an apple orchard, with climbing roses such as 'Seagull' filling some of the trees – over-size cousins of the eighty-odd varieties of old roses in the garden. Another section, recently developed, is largely devoted to vegetables, its beds divided by iris-lined paths, the main feature being a potager, demarked by standard gooseberries, currant and raspberry bushes, with each small section outlined with lettuces, parsley or other herbs. A third quarter has a standard white *Wisteria* and a raised bank, the sides of which are covered with *Cistus* and a long bed of creeping thymes. The final quarter is bisected by a fifty-foot arbour covered with roses, honeysuckles, jasmine and *Clematis*. On one side, cobbled paths delineate eight small beds packed with herbaceous plants, including many salvias, penstemons and artemisias as well as scarcer plants. On the other side, guelder roses overhang vegetables and a tiny lawn. Everywhere, the planting is dense, conceived as a three-dimensional painting.

The Cobbles, Shillingstone
MR & MRS A.P. BAKER

This is a large cottage garden on chalk that was not designed but just developed over the years. Old stone has been collected during this time to make the terraces, and now gradually the stream is being turned into a feature. The mixed borders have shrubs, perennials, herbs, bulbs and annuals to provide a continuity of interest, many varieties of *Euphorbia, Geranium* and *Campanula* are used, and ground-cover plants help to cut down on weeding. There are plenty of foliage plants and groups of harmonizing colours; *Geranium sanguineum*, *Hebe* 'Carl Teschner' and the glaucous leaves of *Sedum hidakanum* are pleasing, as are the crimson burrs of *Acaena microphylla* running through the apple green bracts of *Origanum rotundifolium*, *Philadelphus* × *lemoinei* 'Erectus', the floribunda rose 'Iceberg', *Alchemilla mollis* and the vivid blue of *Veronica teucrium*. Two unplanned successes are blue *Nigella* mingling with Jackman's rue, and the golden Creeping Jenny cascading down a stone gulley into the pond. Each year we grow some unusual perennials from seed from the RHS and Hardy Plant Society's lists.

*Compton Acres Gardens, Poole

This garden overlooks Poole harbour and contains seven smaller gardens of differing styles, including Japanese, Italian, rock and water gardens, a sub-tropical glen and woodland.

Culeaze, Wareham
COL. AND MRS BARNE

Four acres of flat ground surrounding a new Victorian house was a challenge to any garden designer. However, my predecessor made sufficient features by careful planning, dug a large sunken garden in front of the house and, with the spoil, raised a mound inside the new walled garden (three-quarters of an acre) on which to grow roses. He also planted some ornamental trees, a shelter belt, and a screen of trees all round. After a century all this has come to a happy maturity.

I have extended the programme, reconstructed walled garden layout, and added an herbaceous border against the south wall – and I often wonder why the latter was not in the original plan.

The walled garden has two main crossing grassed paths, bordered with flower beds and flanked at one point with large old apple trees. These last give sufficient shade for two fine beds of mixed hostas, making an impressive sight for most of the summer. The beds in full light are interspersed with standard *Wisteria* and backed by high, clipped yew hedges. In the four squares behind all this are grown flowers and foliage for cutting and a self-sufficiency of vegetables and fruit.

I introduced rhododendrons in the main drive, and as they had never been grown before and the soil was 'neutral', I cosseted them annually with leafmould dug from my wood. After about ten years the rhododendrons became self-supporting, presumably on their own leaf droppings. They are now a magnificent sight in May, and, if not curbed, will soon close the front drive altogether.

Other successful introductions are *Juniperus rigida*, a wild, exciting-looking tree; *Nothofagus antarctica* and *N. procera*; *Metasequoia glyptostroboides* (1952); and a small attractive shrub, *Danäe racemosa* from the Elburz Mountains.

This short account may give an impression of lack of colour, but in fact there is, throughout most of the year, sufficient harmonious colouring to fill every available gap.

Dapple Grey, Ashley Heath
MR AND MRS D.C. COLE

In the heatwave summer of 1976, we took

over this half-acre plot which resembled a moonscape. The acid soil of almost pure sand was too dry and poor to support more than the native pine trees, heaths and weeds.

Once cleared, the whole oblong shape could be viewed at a glance, so we thought it important to create hidden areas of interest which could also provide the right conditions in which a wide variety of plants could grow happily. To this end we built a bog garden, two fish ponds, a frog pond, a rockery and sunken patio. The planting of many evergreen trees, shrubs and perennials helps to create interest, while the deciduous trees give lovely autumn colour and play host to many climbing plants. Rhododendrons, azaleas and many varieties of bulbs welcome the spring.

Form, texture and colour can be used to great effect in forming interesting plant groupings, one such group being the golden ground cover plant *Lysimachia nummularia* 'Aurea', with *Allium cernuum* and *Zygadenus elegans* bursting through. Overhanging this are the beautiful dark plum-coloured rounded leaves of *Ligularia dentata* 'Othello' with the contrasting form and colour of the spiky tall green leaves of *Crocosmia masonorum*.

Phormium tenax proved to be tender here and expensive to replace, so we have planted several varieties in large tubs; these we move into a cold greenhouse to overwinter and return to the garden in spring, when it is important to start a regular feeding and watering programme to maintain healthy plants.

◆

*Forde Abbey, Nr Chard
M. ROPER, ESQ.

This thirty-acre garden contains many fine shrubs and some magnificent specimen trees, in a post-war arboretum. Also of interest are the herbaceous borders, a rock garden and a bog garden, containing a large collection of Asiatic primulas.

◆

Frankham Farm, Ryme Intrinseca
MR AND MRS R.G. EARLE

This garden was started in 1960 and progressively made around the house, and the farm buildings, which are still used. The land being rather flat and windswept, it soon became apparent that shelter was needed and windbreaks, mainly conifer, were planted in the adjacent fields. These windbreaks have recently been thinned to allow hardwoods and more interesting conifers to develop and are underplanted with shrubs and bulbs, and wild flowers are being encouraged in places.

Rainfall averages thirty-two inches, and the soil is well-drained loam over flint and clay varying from alkaline to slightly acid. As the shelter increases more varieties of plants are tried including azaleas, rhododendrons and camellias. A wide range of plants may be seen to give year-round colour, including some

less usual varieties of trees and shrubs. Some less hardy plants are grown, not all of which survive hard winters, although *Fremontodendron californicum* and *Carpenteria californica* and *Mutisia oligodon* survived the winter of 1984–5. Plants on the walls, and on the stone farmhouse and buildings, are a feature here, and we are especially keen on *Clematis*, both the species (*C. alpina*, *viticella* 'Rubra' and *texensis*) and the large-flowered hybrids. There are also many shrub roses; *R.* 'Nevada' has reached a height of twelve feet and is splendid when in flower.

In the spring there are naturalized daffodils and many different early spring bulbs, including snowdrops, anemones and *Crocus* species which give colour around the fruit trees. These last produce fruit in abundance, as does the apricot 'Moorpark' which benefits from the shelter of a west wall.

The rambler *Rosa wichuraiana* 'Debutante' is one of the many interesting plants to be seen at Highbury, West Moors.

◆

Highbury, West Moors
MR AND MRS STANLEY CHERRY

This garden was begun in 1909, when the house was built, with some of the mature trees dating from that time. The garden was well known in the area but gradually deteriorated until a renovation and some replanting took place in 1956, although when the present owners took over in 1966 the overgrown state of lawns, paths and shrubberies again made restoration the first priority. Since then there has been a continuing planting programme of rare and unusual species until in 1983, Highbury was described in a broadcast as one of the most interesting small botanical

gardens in private ownership in the south of England.

A botanical garden, even with everything labelled, still need not be a museum, and a careful selection of plants provides a year-round pleasure garden. Amongst those to be found are *Illicium anisatum*, with its aniseed-scented leaves, +*Laburnocytisus adamii*, a chimera with yellow or pink flowers according to dominance, and *Trochodendron aralioides*, a flower arranger's delight. For history there are *Paliurus spina-christi*, the Christ thorn, and *Leycesteria crocothyrsos*, from seed collected by F. Kingdon Ward from the only known specimen found in habitat, in Assam in 1928. It will be a very knowledgeable plantsman who can find nothing that he has not seen before.

The garden is open for the National Gardens Scheme on Sundays and Bank Holidays each year from April until September. The owners pay for most of the printed publicity themselves, but are rewarded by the considerable pleasure they take in being part of the tourist scene and in the same league as the big boys, if somewhere near the bottom, and by the opportunity of exchanging advertising material and plants and pleasantries with them. If there has to be a goad for a gardener they believe they have found it in gardening for garden-opening.

◆

Ivy Cottage, Ansty
ANNE AND ALAN STEVENS

April arrives with a great flourish in this informal one-and-a-half-acre cottage garden when hundreds of daffodils begin to bloom. Many have naturalized themselves under mature trees and shrubs, along with other spring-flowering bulbs such as erythroniums, *Fritillaria meleagris*, triteleas and anemones. A delightful little stream runs through the middle of the garden, and this, together with several other very boggy areas, creates ideal conditions for moisture-loving plants such as *Trollius*, *Astilbe*, *Rodgersia* and *Gunnera*. Many varieties of Asiatic primulas are featured here and these look their best in late May and early June. Hostas, *Hemerocallis*, alliums and oriental poppies are just some of the large selection of perennials, many of which are unusual, that fill the herbaceous borders that sweep gently down from the front of the cottage. Here the plants are massed together so that hardly any soil shows between them; this does help to smother weeds. Young specimen trees, including *Liquidambar*, *Liriodendron* (the tulip tree) and *Metasequoia*, have been planted for their marvellous autumn colour. A well laid-out vegetable garden and a raised bed for alpines are two of many other features in this fascinating plantsman's garden that lies in the heart of rural Dorset.

*Kingston Maurward, Dorchester
DORSET COUNTY COUNCIL

As the horticultural department of a College of Agriculture the grounds at Kingston Maurward (originally laid out early this century by Sir Cecil and Lady Hanbury) are intended to be both educational and aesthetic. There are two distinct areas, the mainly formal garden around the Georgian house, and the demonstration/teaching area which is housed in the old walled garden.

The pleasure garden faces south and features terraces, balustrades, pools and clipped yew hedges linking the herbaceous borders, rose gardens and lawns, which slope down to a lake. There is an enclosed garden originally designed and planted in the Japanese style and a newly constructed rock garden. In the spring and autumn there is a good display of bulbs such as *Crocus speciosus*, *C. tommasinianus* and *Anemone blanda* on the large laurel bank to the west of the main lawn, and another point of interest is the National Collection of penstemons which was recently established here. The walled garden contains twenty-eight plots demonstrating plants for different purposes, and various horticultural techniques; there is also an area of fruit and hardy nursery stock. The glasshouses, which are used chiefly for plant production and display purposes, are always of interest.

◆

Lindens, Sturminster Newton
LADY MORSHEAD

When we came to this garden in 1958, we had the good fortune to find that it faced south, the ground was quick-draining gravel, that it had beautiful oak and lime trees, and an ancient mulberry. Otherwise there was nothing in the shape of a garden, so we had all the pleasure of making it from the beginning. Under the mulberry, *Cyclamen* flower for eight months of the year, to be followed in the spring by fritillaries. *Clematis* scramble over a spreading juniper as well as cypresses, the dark red *C.* 'Gravetye' lasting until the first frosts. A variegated *Trachelospermum* covering a large expanse of the house has survived the coldest winters and never fails to flower; while the nutmeg-like flowers of *Calycanthus fertilis* are an unfailing source of interest to visitors. A weeping pussywillow droops over cowslips grown from seed, and the copper colour of *Cotinus coggygria* makes a good background for a silver *Eucalyptus* and the golden leaves of a *Robinia*. A small weeping copper beech provides a lovely contrast to its neighbours – a large grey *Phormium tenax* and a bright variegated poplar always so late to show its variegation that one wonders if it has forgotten!

Snowdrops appear in January as well as *Iris unguicularis*, followed by daffodils and other spring bulbs and tulips which flower on into May, succeeded by alstroemerias and many lilies which carry on through August.

This garden has richly repaid all the care and affection lavished on it over the years.

◆

The Manor Farm Garden, Littlewindsor
MR AND MRS BIRCH

This garden was landscaped from a field by the present owner in 1968. The aim was to make a labour-saving garden that blended with the beautiful Dorset countryside, giving the impression there were no boundaries, and that it was not man-made.

At a height of five hundred feet on a north-facing slope exposed to strong winds, the task was a daunting one, and to filter the wind six thousand trees were planted in the adjoining fields.

With the aid of a bulldozer the garden began to take shape and a water garden was made with a pond and a stream which

A corner of the herbaceous border with *Campanula lactiflora*, *Monarda* and delphiniums at The Manor House, Chaldon Herring.
For a description of this garden in the Purbeck hills see over.

meanders through the garden, planted with primulas, hostas, and astilbes and bordered by many varieties of willows and other trees and shrubs.

By making use of the natural views, vistas have been created with grass glades winding round island beds and a picture painted with nature, using the subtle tones of foliage by mixing conifers and deciduous trees, species roses, the whole surrounded by ground-cover in drifts of blending restful colours.

The Manor House, Chaldon Herring
DALE AND ALICE FISHBURN

The Manor House, Chaldon Herring, lies in the last fold of the Purbecks, a mile inland from the south Dorset coast, to the west of Lulworth Cove. The Celtic origin of the name Chaldon meant 'safe hiding place' and the hamlet hides in a typically rolling alluvial valley with a thin soil over chalk. The advantages of such a location are the breadth of feel of the downs, different levels, and a genuinely rural setting. The disadvantages are exposure to wind and spray.

The garden has largely been laid out since 1976 and has been designed to display the maximum effect sustainable with only occasional help. It blends a predilection for large-scale plantings with a broad range of interesting and some unusual plants. The colouring is primarily muted, with old tapestry tones predominating, except in the deep herbaceous border and the two kitchen gardens, where flowers tend to outnumber vegetables.

The principal effects start with an early flush of spring bulbs in the orchard and beneath the pleached limes in the drive, and while rigid peasticking of the borders is still in progress, the first flowers of the rose 'Mme Alfred Carrière' open; seven of these roses smother the south and east walls of the house and stable. The main herbaceous border is at its best in mid to late July and many walls and tripods throughout the garden support numerous roses and *Clematis*. Amongst the varieties of *Clematis* are *C. nutans rehderana* (*nutans*), 'Alba Luxurians', 'Purpurea Plena Elegans' *jouiniana* × 'Praecox' and *fargesii*.

Perhaps one of the most interesting plantings is the chance effect of *Rosa glauca* (*rubrifolia*), which seeded itself on the north wall of the house. Although it is no rarity, now organized into a mass in the north border, underplanted with such perennials as *Pulmonaria*, *Tricyrtis*, violas, hostas and *Tiarella*, the foliage is wonderfully luxuriant, far more so than when grown in full sun. Although the roses are growing on solid rock, in a bare ten inches of topsoil, the effect of their foliage and flowers has 'made' the front of the house.

May Cottage, Fiddleford
MR AND MRS R.M. HALL

This three-quarter-acre garden, around a listed, thatched cottage, has been created since 1970 from an old orchard and an area of rough grass. Our plan was to build a garden which would blend with the pasture and woodland surrounding it, incorporating a variety of trees in contrast to the two mature walnuts and the few old fruit trees which we retained. Now, sixteen years later, we have substantial conifers, acers and other ornamental trees, including a *Catalpa bignonioides* 'Aurea', which flowers prolifically in July. With a flower arranger in the house, foliage plants and unusual perennials are a 'must', and these are housed in the shrubberies and herbaceous beds. Rockeries were constructed around two pools, which contain waterlilies and fish. Choice miniature conifers and alpines have found homes in the dozen or so sinks which are dotted around in odd corners.

One of the archways at Melford House, Yetminster. The elegant drooping sedge, *Carex pendula*, acts as a foil to the ferns in this peaceful garden.

With the recent conversion of the surrounding pasture land to arable farming, we decided to provide a small oasis for wildlife, and the result has been most rewarding. A small area was planted with wild flowers, and in this we made two tiny pools (no fish) in which frogs and toads could spawn. Wild vegetation is left near the hedges, which are trimmed only once a year.

Perhaps the most eye-catching feature of the garden in June/July is the collection of *Clematis* which run riot and produce enormous blooms in this alkaline soil. We find that by burying new plants horizontally, with only the top six inches above ground, the plants develop more substantial root systems and shoot from several points in the stems, thus being capable of supporting the enormous amount of top growth.

Melford House, Yetminster
RODNEY AND PAMELA RUSSELL

When we bought Melford the garden had been neglected for six years. As artists the challenge of creating a garden from a wilderness was something not to be missed. We had the frame; now all we needed was the picture.

We based our initial 'outline' on the idea that our garden must be a place where both pleasure and peace could be found and where nature could come into its own.

The joy of a garden on different levels immediately fired our imagination. Using existing stone, we created ponds, a waterfall, steps, arches and terraces and some graceful division of lawns with balustrades and urns.

Vistas are an important element in the design of every garden, punctuated occasionally by an element of surprise and with a pattern of walks moving through light and shade, from wider expanses to secluded areas which return one, eventually, to the starting point. Every corner of this garden has a point of interest. It is planted throughout with a variety of soft-coloured shrubs, roses, perennials and ferns which overflow into one another, creating harmony and contrast between shapes of plants and between colours and textures of leaves and flowers.

Each path urges the visitor towards some focal point, for example a vase or a piece of sculpture, and water is used to reflect the plants, the sculpture and the orangery. Contrasts abound between the stonework and the varied trees, including conifers and *Eucalyptus*.

Visitors seem to delight in the atmosphere of this garden, to which they readily relate because of its unspoilt but carefully designed natural beauty, where peace abides and where they are free also to wander into the artist's studio.

---

*Minterne, Dorchester
THE LORD DIGBY

Minterne, the home of the first Winston Churchill, was landscaped by Admiral Robert Digby in the eighteenth century after the manner of Capability Brown. A trout stream was transformed by a series of cascades into small lakes, from which rise steep banks of rhododendrons under a canopy of large beech, oak and rare trees, as well as species collected by Forrest, Rock and Kingdon Ward in the Himalayas. There are many of our own hybrids as well as those collected from other famous gardens. *Magnolia campbellii* and *M. mollicomata* tower over *Rhododendron sutchuenense* in March and April, followed by the big-leaved rhododendrons *falconeri* and *macabeanum* in May. In June the azaleas, particularly the flame-coloured hybrids, contrast with the many large specimens of *Davidia involucrata*, the 'Pocket handkerchief' tree. In July and August a magnificent specimen of *Rhododendron* 'Polar Bear' scents the whole bottom of the garden, and the reflections of hydrangeas (true blue in this acid soil) prove very effective, particularly in the evening sun. *Cercidiphyllum, Parrotia persica* and many forms of *Acer palmatum* provide sensational autumn colouring.

The charm of Minterne lies in the landscaped valley with hills and clumps sweeping down to the stream from which the ordered jungle of rhododendrons, magnolias, azaleas, Japanese cherries and maples rises in a steep bank protected by old beeches and specimen trees – all of which blends harmoniously with the mellow Ham Hill sandstone of the house.

Moigne Combe, Dorchester
MAJ.-GEN. H.M.G. BOND

This is a medium-sized wild garden best seen in May and June. It is sited on a steep south-facing slope with views across a wooded valley to the high coastal chalk ridge three miles away. Under mature specimen conifers and oaks, sweet chestnuts and limes, masses of rhododendrons, azaleas, *Pieris formosa forrestii* and heathers form vistas of colour to the south and to the west. A small lake surrounded by *Osmunda regalis, Laburnum, Taxodium distichum* and more rhododendrons is seen across a green field. The lake contains fine golden orfe and mirror carp, and a small heronry occupies the trees on the island. The prevalence of roe deer makes bedding-out impossible but the 'heart garden', an amazing Victorian conceit in the shape of a heart with lovers' knot above – is planted with herbs and lavender in the knot, and is surrounded by a clipped beech hedge and border of yellow *Genista*.

An avenue of *Laburnum, Wisteria* and *Clematis montana* hedged by *Pittosporum tenuifolium* leads to the heart garden which was laid out to commemorate the then owners' silver wedding in 1900. The *Pittosporum* grows freely and some are clipped to shapes in the more formal parts, while an eight-foot hedge of *Enkianthus campanulatus* makes another feature. To the east of the garden a woodland path leads under high Scots pines inhabited by many rooks and from here a thirty-year-old avenue of mixed azaleas opens another view to the lake below.

North Leigh House, Colehill
MR AND MRS STANLEY WALKER

Our garden of over three acres is rather different. We cannot claim the 'rooms' of Hidcote, or many of the exciting plants we have seen in numerous gardens also open under the National Gardens Scheme, but we do have rolling elevated mini-parkland with spacious views and fine trees, a fountain pool, water garden, and a very grand Victorian conservatory with lantern bay, slender ironwork, and a white marble floor. This leads to a gravelled and balustraded terrace, and to our lovely walled garden which has many homely

cottage-style herbaceous plants (and some rarer ones) in close boskage, and an attractive old outbuilding which we have converted to a charming little Tea Cottage. In springtime drifts of daffodils clothe the lawns, and in May the Early Purple and Green-winged orchids, reputed to be one of the largest colonies in east Dorset, appear. In August the specimen *Magnolia grandiflora* offers its large ivory flowers, and the enormous green 'Brunswick' fig, probably dating back to the days when the house was young, is laden with ripening fruit which visitors may, if they wish, sample in our Tea Cottage, lightly stewed and served with cream. After many years spent in the restoration of North Leigh House, a fine, but when we arrived dilapidated, Victorian mansion (1862), we have now turned our attention to the

Conservatories of all types are becoming increasingly popular in Britain, both for their attractiveness and for their practical uses. Seen here is the orangery at Melford House.

improvement and restoration of the grounds to some semblance of their former glory which we hope will delight visitors.

---

*Parnham, Nr Beaminster
MR AND MRS JOHN MAKEPEACE

The grounds here cover fourteen acres and were extensively reconstructed early this century; amongst the many features of interest are the Yew Terrace, with fifty clipped yews; the formal East Court; and the Italian garden. The house, which is a listed building dating from 1540 with additions by John Nash, is open to the public, as are the furniture workshops.

52, Rossmore Road, Poole
MR AND MRS W.E. NINNISS

This is a small town garden, a third of an acre

in size, with poor sandy, acid soil, but with the help of a little judicial feeding, we are constantly amazed at the amount of interesting and unusual plants that we are able to grow.

Although we have lived here since 1952, it is only ten years ago that we had the opportunity to buy a piece of adjoining land, and this gave us greater scope for carrying out some of our ideas in an attempt to turn it into a garden of surprises. As the visitor walks around he will come across perhaps *Cedrus atlantica* 'Pendula' or *Fagus sylvatica* 'Asplenifolia' (a twenty-year-old tree kept small by careful trimming) whilst around another corner there is a herb garden with a little statue representing one of the four seasons in the centre, this one being winter with his coat collar turned up against the cold. We also have a little knot garden and in one of the three greenhouses there is a vine. We keep one greenhouse for seed growing and the third is reserved for a plant collection and propagation.

The first thing we did with our new piece of land was to turf the whole area; we then placed the shrubs and trees in various experimental groups until we were satisfied with the effect, before cutting away the turf around them to make beds. We did a similar thing to a very poor lawn in the front of the bungalow, gradually cutting away the grass and planting alpine and rockery plants until there is only a token lawn left; this we have planted with *Crocus* and *Cyclamen* species.

I think our favourite bed is green and gold, the gold consisting of *Berberis*, golden yew and *Alchemilla mollis*, edged with *Hedera helix* 'Buttercup'.

One of the fine specimens of the handkerchief tree, *Davidia involucrata*, at Minterne, Dorchester. This tree was discovered by Père David in 1869. For a description of Minterne see page 68.

Russets, Child Okeford

MR AND MRS G.D. HARTHAN

This garden, designed and maintained by the owners, was made out of an old apple orchard and begun in 1972. It is just over half an acre in size and the soil is mostly neutral but with an alkaline tendency in parts. The subsoil is clay with small areas of greensand.

There are many varieties of trees, shrubs, perennials and alpines with much emphasis on foliage. Mixed borders predominate, one being mainly in gold and white colouring, though a purple *Berberis* is admitted to give contrast to the golden hop which clambers over it.

Early in the year there is a bank filled with *Helleborus orientalis*, the Lenten rose – an ideal way to grow these lovely plants so that one can look inside each flower without bending down.

One of the owners finds it difficult to see a plant without wanting to propagate it, and many hundreds of plants in the garden including large shrubs and conifers, were grown in this way, many being for sale when the garden is open during the summer.

The garden is at its best towards the end of June when the old shrub roses, *Clematis* and sweet peas are at their most attractive and fragrance fills the air. We try, whenever possible, to grow *Clematis* and sweet peas over shrubs as we feel that they look happier and more natural that way. At the moment we have thirty-three *Clematis* and the collection is growing steadily.

If you are offered cuttings of plants our advice is always to accept immediately, even though the time and conditions may seem totally wrong. You may be successful in propagating, you might not get another chance, and anyway it is always worth trying.

Smedmore, Kimmeridge

MAJ. AND MRS JOHN MANSELL

Smedmore House and its gardens lie a mile from the sea in a dramatic and unspoiled situation on the south slope of the Purbeck Hills.

The gardens are well protected by stone walls which act as shelter to various interesting and tender shrubs, such as *Fremontodendron californicum*, *Clianthus puniceus*, *Hoheria lyallii*, *Callistemon* and also many hydrangeas and fuchsias.

Visitors enter by way of an enclosed courtyard containing a variety of herbs, past three walled flower gardens beautifully kept by people living in flats within Smedmore House, and on to the main garden featuring a large herbaceous border and some interesting trees, including *Quercus ilex*, *Tilia cordata*, *Parrotia persica*, and *Eucryphia* 'Nymansay'.

From there they may proceed into a large walled kitchen garden where vegetables and fruit are produced for sale locally; plants and produce are usually available for sale on open afternoons. A section of the vegetable garden is devoted to everlasting flowers and grasses, bunches of which can also be purchased in season.

From Smedmore House the visitor can drive to Kimmeridge village and on to Kimmeridge Bay (via the private toll road) where the shore is exceptionally interesting and was given a European Heritage Award in 1984.

Tarrant Rushton Gardens, Blandford Forum

The three Tarrant Rushton gardens, situated in a quiet, unspoilt village, differ considerably in style. That of **Tarrant Rushton House** (DR B.K. BLOUNT) is an old garden with walls and outbuildings – the main features are trees and lawns by the River Tarrant (including a large *Metasequoia*) and a box-edged kitchen garden. There are herbaceous borders against walls facing both north and south, a long bed of bearded irises containing more than twenty varieties, and a planting of *Dictamnus albus* var. *purpureus*, the Burning Bush, which often attracts attention.

The **River House** (DRS A. AND P. SWAN) garden has been made round both sides of the Tarrant, and particularly suits damp-loving plants, such as primulas and willows (of which there are at least ten varieties). There are many shrub roses, but water is a main feature.

Charlton Cottage (THE HON. PENELOPE PIERCY) is four hundred yards to the south. The garden is in two parts; in front are two broad herbaceous borders, and beyond are fruit trees and vegetables. Beyond again a grass path leads through a conservatory in which a *Bougainvillea* is a main feature, to another garden. From this an admirable view across the Tarrant is obtained.

Turnpike Cottage, Wimborne Minster

LYS DE BRAY

This is the garden of a botanical artist and author; it is my 'living library' and some of the plants are grown especially to be painted. My working studio with paintings and books is also open to visitors.

It is a small walled town garden (one-sixth of an acre) on two levels, with a pond and cascades, a rockery of Purbeck stone with a dinosaur's footprint, and many interesting shrubs. The new paved garden provides a happy habitat for a wealth of tender plants, alpines, unusual annuals and many wild flowers, backed by roses and honeysuckle intertwined with morning glories (*Ipomoea*) climbing voluptuously up and over the street wall. Elsewhere, old-fashioned roses grow side by side with herbaceous plants. Foliage contrasts are pleasing for long periods and vistas lead the visitor ever onwards.

The raised bed in the paved garden is made from old bricks, with plenty of planting holes achieved by building in short lengths of plastic drainpipe at construction-time; these were afterwards pulled out, leaving a rough and porous surface more acceptable to plant roots. Alternatively, small-diameter clay drainpipes can be used and left *in situ*; this gives a pleasing 'finished' appearance. Planting is best done by wrapping the roots of small plants in a piece of thin, wet turf and rolling all into a tubular package slightly smaller than the diameter of the hole. The roots *must* be in contact with the soil behind the retaining wall. Larger plants can be inserted and any extra soil kept in place with a wedge of wet turf.

Parnham House, near Beaminster, a Tudor manor restored by Nash and surrounded by formal and informal gardens; the magnificent clipped yews are one of the features of this garden. For a description of Parnham see page 69.

14 Umbers Hill, Shaftesbury
MRS K. BELLARS

A small, gently sloping site facing south-west and with a lovely view, lent itself readily to a large rockery and the cultivation of alpines and rock plants, several stone sinks accommodating the rarer alpines. There are few lovelier flowers than the double form of *Sanguinaria canadensis* which occupies a shady place in the rockery; this large carpet of green-ruffed delicate white flowers often arouses great interest in our visitors during April. Sometimes called 'Bloodroot', because of the

red fluid bleeding from the roots, if broken, it was this red sap which was used by the Red Indians for decorating their faces and bodies.

Because they take up only a small root area *Clematis* are grown in various ways on trellis, walls, hedges and archways; up trees and through shrubs, on a tripod and as bedding plants.

A small collection of old chimneypots provides an added dimension in which to plant new varieties of bulbs for spring blooming, followed by colourful annuals.

With no space here for growing large trees,

there is an incentive to experiment with the nineteenth-century skill of 'pot culture'; so adorning the terrace is a brown turkey fig, *Lilium* 'Enchantment', strawberries, two apple trees (on dwarfing rootstocks) – an old variety, 'Ashmead's Kernel', and the recently introduced 'Greensleeves' – and a peach, 'Early Rivers'. A fan nectarine, 'Pitmaston', against a wall gives a good crop each year, as also do raspberries 'Malling Jewel', black-currants 'Boskoop Giant' and a vine 'Chasselas d'Or' – all fruits which are expensive to buy so are well worth growing.

ESSEX AND HERTFORDSHIRE

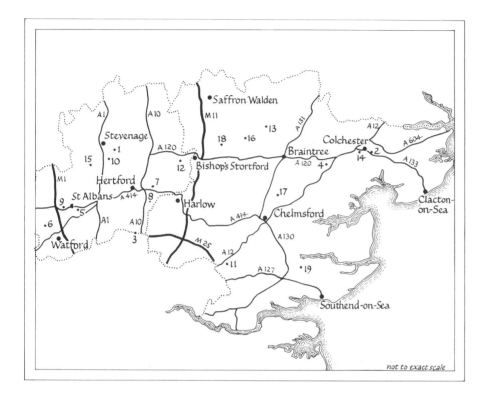

not to exact scale

Directions to Gardens

Benington Lordship, Benington, 5 miles east of Stevenage, Herts. [1]

Beth Chatto Gardens, ¼ mile east of Elmstead Market, Essex. [2]

Capel Manor Horticulture and Environmental Centre, Bullsmoor Lane, Waltham Cross, Herts. [3]

Feeringbury Manor, Coggeshall Road, Feering, 7 miles west of Colchester, Essex. [4]

The Gardens of the Rose (The Royal National Rose Society), Chiswell Green Lane, 2 miles south of St Albans, Herts. [5]

Great Sarratt Hall, Sarratt, north of Rickmansworth, Herts. [6]

Hill House, Stanstead Abbotts, near Ware, Herts. [7]

Hipkins, Broxbourne, Baas Lane, Herts. [8]

King Charles II Cottage, Westwick Row,

Leverstock Green, midway between Hemel Hempstead and St Albans, Herts. [9]

Knebworth House, Knebworth, 3 miles south of Stevenage, Herts. [10]

The Magnolias, 18 St John's Avenue, Brentwood, Essex. [11]

Moor Place, Much Hadham, Herts. [12]

The Old Rectory, Sible Hedingham, 4 miles northwest of Halstead, Essex. [13]

Olivers, Olivers Lane, 3 miles southwest of Colchester, Essex. [14]

St Paul's Walden Bury, Whitwell, 5 miles south of Hitchin, Herts. [15]

Saling Hall, Great Saling, 6 miles northwest of Braintree, Essex. [16]

Terling Place, Terling, 6 miles northeast of Chelmsford, Essex. [17]

Tilty Hill Farm, Duton Hill, 4 miles north of Dunmow, Essex. [18]

Volpaia, 54 Woodlands Road, Hockley, Essex. [19]

---

*Benington Lordship Gardens, Nr Stevenage

MR AND MRS C.H.A. BOTT

Fifteen years ago this seven-acre Edwardian garden was a sleeping beauty which I hope has not lost its magic while re-awakening. On the site of a Norman castle, the winter garden is in the ruined keep, a dry moat forms the southern boundary, and the inner bailey – with a neo-Norman gatehouse and summer house – make a sheltered courtyard which is a haven for sun-loving climbers.

The rest of the garden, three hundred feet above sea level on alkaline soil, stretches down a hill overlooking superb lakes and parkland. There appears to be only a spreading lawn, but tucked away are a rock garden and water garden, herbaceous borders backed by the kitchen garden wall, formal rose beds, a sunk garden with a lead statue of Shylock, a collection of old-fashioned roses, lots of shrubs, and a small nursery.

Helped and hindered by the birds, who are the real owners, we start the year with sheets of snowdrops followed by scillas, crocuses, cowslips and Welsh poppies. Suddenly by the middle of June, it gets too much and a battery of mowers move in. Tidy once more, *Philadelphus* scents the air and irises, roses, herbaceous borders, gold and silver borders unfold in succession, carefully tended by Ian Billot, the gardener.

Apart from making some of the beds smaller, we have changed the layout very little but we have built up a very varied collection of plants. My ideas for planting come from visiting other gardens and from books. However, so often the best combinations happen by mistake, like columbines amongst the irises or white foxgloves around a variegated *Cornus*. This leads to white tulips in the borders which look wonderful with the fresh greens in May.

Beth Chatto Gardens, Nr Elmstead Market

MRS BETH CHATTO

In 1960 the site lay as a neglected overgrown hollow between two farms, useless for crops because it was too soggy and boggy in the lowland, while even the native weeds curled up and died on the sandy south- and west-facing slopes. But with some knowledge of natural plant associations, and with much time and effort spent in ameliorating the extreme soil conditions, these problems have been turned to advantage.

Today, a walk through the matured gardens takes you from the southern-scented mediterranean garden, planted on dry gravel slopes, down to emerald green grass walks surrounding a series of large pools. These have been formed over the years by damming a spring-fed ditch. Exotic-looking plants, not normally associated with Essex droughts, flourish without irrigation, there being enough moisture provided by the underground springs. A boundary of ancient oaks, together with additional planting of trees and shrubs, has provided a long winding walk where shade-loving plants flourish on either side of the mown grass.

While overall the garden may appear large – some enthusiasts happily spend all day and say they need a week to take note of all the plants which fill the richly planted borders – there is also a feeling of intimacy. Little shady corners, paved courtyards filled with pot gardens, or individual groups of plants can provide inspiration for the smallest garden. Each month brings fresh colour and new ideas.

The overall use of mulching material together with the use of interesting groundcover plants shows that large gardens need not have a formidable weed problem.

Attached to the ornamental garden is the nursery and personal visitors will find many treasures produced in insufficient quantities to list in the catalogue.

Capel Manor Horticulture and Environmental Centre
BOROUGH OF ENFIELD

Although the primary role of the gardens is to service the wide range of courses the college offers, it has become a plantsman's garden with a difference. Building on the original woodland and parkland framework, various interesting ornamental features have been created since the college began seventeen years ago. The historic garden demonstrates a seventeenth-century knot garden, a collection of medicinal plants and a 'Garden of Delight' – a wrought iron arbour surrounded by the kind of plants found in gardens before 1700.

An extensive rock garden and pond were created from an old gravel pit. A hundred and twenty tons of Macclesfield sandstone were laid ten years ago, and today this rock garden has a mature appearance belying its relative youthfulness; extensive replanting is currently in progress. Plants on the borderline of hardiness for this region are being found a suitably sheltered niche to establish themselves. One recent introduction here is *Rhodochiton atrosanguineum*, a trailing seasonal climber with stunning dark purple-cupped sepals and a dark brown corolla. It has to be treated as an annual, but sets plentiful seed and is easy to germinate. The secret to growing it lies in making sure that it is potted on stage by stage, as a young plant, after it has germinated, from first a one-and-a-half-inch pot, then by half-inch stages, up to its eventual four-inch pot. It can be planted out by mid-May.

The enthusiasms of different staff members have led to many interesting collections of plants, including carnivorous species, scented pelargoniums, half-hardy salvias, plus many unusual and rare herbaceous plants. The garden has established a unified theme containing a developing collection of rare and interesting plants, grown in an attractive landscape representing a haven of plantsmanship away from the bustle of urban north London.

Feeringbury Manor, Feering
MR AND MRS GILES COODE-ADAMS

As I look through the kitchen windows draped with *Wisteria* blossom, I think that May is the most sensuous month in the year. The pink and white flowers of a 'D'Arcy Spice' apple are met by the burgeoning cow parsley in the meadow. In the new bed *Daphne* 'Somerset' is strongly scented and with *Veronica gentianoides* lighting the ground against the rich green all around, nature is at its best.

A mown path, edged in January with snowdrops and *Crocus tommasinianus*, and later with daffodils in rough grass, has a *Malus floribunda* avenue leading down to the stream. Here Solomon's seal, *Meconopsis betonicifolia* and *Ranunculus aconitifolius* 'Flore Pleno' contrast with giant yellow buttercups and primulas.

Along the nut walk, past the lower pond, the old kitchen garden, now grassed over, is planted with a weeping *Alnus incana* with long catkins in January, and the cut-leaved *Alnus glutinosa* 'Imperialis'. *Hamamelis, Magnolia, Cornus mas, Phillyrea* and various spindles also break up the grass area. In a bed by the top pond, planted with mainly pink and blue, candelabra primulas, *Polemonium*

caeruleum, rodgersias and a handsome crimson *Rheum* are backed by the large glaucous leaves of *Salix magnifica*. *Clematis texensis* and *Lonicera × americana* swathe the wooden posts of the terrace, scented in the summer with *Helichrysum* and pinks. A dark spot under a yew is highlighted with *Philadelphus coronarius* 'Aureus' and a golden elder. Scent saturates this well-protected garden from May till July with *Philadelphus* and lilies taking over from the lilacs and *Wisteria*.

The Gardens of the Rose, Chiswell Green
THE ROYAL NATIONAL ROSE SOCIETY

A twelve-acre display garden with some thirty thousand roses of every description.

Great Sarratt Hall, Sarratt
H.M. NEAL, ESQ.

The original garden has been extensively replanted with a varied collection of trees and shrubs, some rare, during the last twenty years. *Magnolia grandiflora* has just started to flower on the house, and some ginkgos are growing well.

The old farm pond, which is a central feature, has been planted at the margins with water-loving subjects, but it has proved impossible to grow plants actually in the water due to the numbers of carp. Junipers, *Gunnera* and weeping willows provide the main foil to the water.

There is a large, walled kitchen garden with a cold greenhouse which in the winter is used to house the pots from the terraces. There are two asparagus beds and a large soft fruit area. Espalier pears and stone fruits are trained on the south and west walls.

Laburnum at Feeringbury Manor, Essex. This tree, aptly called by some 'Golden Rain', is common, but beautiful and easy to grow. For a line drawing of this plant see page 112.

Hipkins, Broxbourne
STUART DOUGLAS HAMILTON, ESQ., AND
MICHAEL GOULDING, ESQ.

This three-and-a-half-acre informal garden has the benefit of a line of natural springs running through it, giving the opportunity not only of growing a wealth of water-loving plants, in particular a magnificent display of water crowsfoot and water forget-me-not, but also other garden plants which like plenty of moisture such as *Gunnera manicata* and bog primulas, together with many varieties of hostas and ferns such as *Osmunda*.

Colour in spring comes from a line of azaleas planted in the order in which they flower, and carrying on into a walk through mature rhododendrons, some of them established for more than fifty years. There is colour throughout the other seasons too; with each border planted to provide something of interest in its turn. Then there is a cool green and white area to offset all the colour elsewhere, which includes white foxgloves, hellebores and euphorbias.

As one would expect at the home of an eminent flower arranger, many plants are grown for their value in decoration. These include *Rosa glauca* (*rubrifolia*), the snowdrop tree *Halesia*, *Sedum spectabile*, golden and purple *Weigela*, *Elaeagnus* in variety, euphorbias, Solomon's seal, cotoneasters and sorbuses with yellow, pink and white berries for autumn use. Even dire necessity can become an ornament; the old air-raid shelter in the garden is now an apple-store with colourful foliage plants to cover it. The vegetable garden is extensive, and after years of care has reached a state of near-perfection in quality of crops and design; many herbs, brassicas and spinach, beans, tomatoes, melons, marrows and of course potatoes, thrive here. The house and garden no longer enjoy the isolation of the early 1930s, but with the careful planting of evergreens on the boundaries and the green expanse of gently sloping spring-fed lawn, the sense of privacy is complete.

The herbaceous border at Benington Lordship, near Stevenage. Amongst the plants are *Achillea ptarmica*, *A.* 'Gold Plate', delphiniums, lupins, *Lychnis* and *Lysimachia punctata*. For description see page 72.

The soil is acid, so there are a large number of shrubs in flower at the end of May, including a fine specimen of *Embothrium coccineum*, the Chilean Fire Bush, rhododendrons, azaleas, kalmias and magnolias. There are late bulbs, abutilons in variety, and a good specimen of *Poncirus trifoliata* on the terrace.

Hill House, Stanstead Abbotts
MR AND MRS RONNIE PILKINGTON

When we moved here in 1951 house and garden were derelict. Hip-baths caught the water pouring through the roof and the only sign of the rumoured five gardeners, pre-war, were dying vines and dead geraniums. Gradually, with the assistance of one gardener, we have created individual gardens to suit our eight acres of different levels which harbour small deposits of lime, clay and sand in the mainly stony subsoil. In the wild garden, rides have been cut through the white froth of Queen Anne's lace. 'Kiftsgate' and dog roses are scattered among the hawthorns, prolonging their flowering season. From a hillock we look down through *Prunus padus*, *Santolina* and many a plant from a Spanish hillside on to the aviary below, where

Fremontodendron vies with the golden pheasant's plumage. Another path leads out of the wood, where spring bulbs abound, into a water garden full of treasures. Shrubs, ferns and waterside plants thrive alongside native orchids.

Eremurus gives a sculptured line leading up to the house and main garden. Here the Victorian conservatory shelters *Acacia dealbata*, *Datura*, *Plumbago*, and that delight for a few days annually – *Rosa* 'Maréchal Niel'. But the view lures one out. Way below a rose- and foxglove-bordered lawn, Lea valley gravel pits have been transformed into shimmering lakes, beyond which stretches the remains of Charles I's hunting forest. A straight path leads through a wrought iron gate into a walled, quartered kitchen garden with wide main borders where shape and form play a major role. The addition of variegated *Weigela*, bronze *Spiraea*, purple *Prunus* and golden *Deutzia* have added months of interest to these borders. One quarter shelters a small rose garden full of perpetual flowering shrub roses. In another quarter a bed of 'Fantin-Latour' shows up well against a copper beech background, and elsewhere alstroemerias, strawberries and cabbages each have their place. Modern sculptures add another dimension, and scent is everywhere.

King Charles II Cottage, Leverstock Green
MR AND MRS F.S. CADMAN

Our one-acre garden, created from an old overgrown orchard, has evolved gradually over the past thirty years and a great gnarled apple tree near the yew hedge at the far end of the garden is a survivor from those days. Our friends and others who visit us here are kind enough to say that their first and, indeed, lasting impression is one of peace, harmony and tranquillity, and we would like to think that this is so. The pleasures of making a garden are so greatly increased by sharing it with others.

The roses have always been a special feature, planted in long beds following the curve of the drive from the main gate, and latterly we have been introducing some of the beautiful shrub roses which look so splendid

A harmonious combination of colours and form provided by *Euphorbia griffithii* planted under an old apple tree at Saling Hall, Great Saling. For a description of this garden see over.

in isolation. Our rock pool beneath one of the willows is another restful spot. So too is the terrace with its cushions of pinks and small bedding plants spilling from between the York stone paving. Here one can enjoy hanging baskets and various climbers on the black and white timbered cottage walls, roses entwining with *Clematis* and fragrant honeysuckles, as well as vistas across the lawns to the beech hedge with its unusual arch to a mixed border beyond.

Finally, the deep herbaceous border curving gently the length of the garden, contains many of the traditional old English flowers and herbaceous plants together with some unusual shrubs, providing changes of colour and form from the vivid beauty of the azaleas in late spring through the glory of a summer border to the glowing colours and mellow beauty of autumn.

Knebworth House

THE HON. DAVID LYTTON COBBOLD

The home of the Lytton family since 1492 has seen many changes, its gardens evolving from a simple orchard and green in Tudor times to Sir Edward Bulwer-Lytton's elabor-

ate design of the Victorian era. In 1908, following his marriage to Lady Emily Lytton, Edwin Lutyens undertook alterations to the gardens by simplifying the main central area of Bulwer-Lytton's garden. Since 1980 an active programme of restoration has been taking place with the aim of reinstating as much as possible of these former designs.

The main feature of the gardens is undoubtedly the twin pleached lime avenues planted by Lutyens, leading to the upper lawn of rose beds and herbaceous borders with their backdrop of tall yew hedges. These mixed borders make a tapestry of blue, pink, silver, mauve and white in a combination enhanced by the *Clematis* 'Perle d'Azur' and rose 'New Dawn' grown on the iron frames nearby. Through a kissing-gate one enters the 'wilderness' – a Victorian term for natural planting of trees, grass and flowers.

The 1891 edition of *Gardener's Chronicle* wrote 'The Knebworth wilderness is, in fact, one which ladies could pass through in their ordinary costume without being stung and torn . . .' In spring it is a sea of daffodils. Tree lovers will enjoy the magnificent three-hundred-year-old oak, the huge leaning wellingtonia and a small arboretum of exotic pines.

From the 'wilderness', the formal garden is

re-entered and offers an inviting view with *Clematis montana* and 'The Garland' rose climbing against the Lutyens-designed garden bothy. The quincux pattern of circular beds in the herb garden existed in this position as an arrangement of pink roses and lavender before Gertrude Jekyll used it as the basis of her planting plan of 1907; these beds now contain a delightful aroma of many unusual herbs.

The Magnolias, Brentwood

MR AND MRS ROGER A. HAMMOND

Perhaps the most frequent reaction of visitors to our garden is of surprise, when having walked through the small suburban front garden, they find that the back, by comparison, seems to go on and on. The basic idea of the layout of this half-acre garden is to have as much planting as possible, as little lawn (I don't enjoy mowing), and as long walks as possible, with surprises and features. The latter are a *Wisteria*-covered wooden bridge over a natural pond, and a vaguely oriental-style pagoda with a wooden verandah over another pond with stepping stones. There are also four concrete pools and koi carp.

We believe in filling up the ground with plants, preferring weeding around plants to empty ground, and in any case we think that many different plants make for greater interest. We like to get at least three layers and seasons of interest out of any area of ground. These might consist of a tree canopy, for example maple or *Magnolia* over shrubs often kept a yard back from the edge of the border, with climbers for extra interest. Large shrubs can support a *Clematis*, smaller ones a smaller climber such as the herbaceous *Tropaeolum speciosum* or *Codonopsis convolvulacea*. In the foreground, and extending under the shrubs, we use an herbaceous and bulb layer which greatly increases the season of interest.

Vigorous foliage plants such as *Hosta sieboldiana* or *Rodgersia pinnata* can be used with daffodils; after the latter have finished flowering, the foliage plants will grow over the dying bulb leaves. On a smaller scale crocuses or snowdrops can be planted with some of the dwarfer new hostas.

◆

Moor Place, Much Hadham
MR AND MRS B.M. NORMAN

There has been a substantial house here since Tudor times, for which the stables and walled kitchen gardens were built in about 1700. But the garden around the present house (1779) was created from about 1890 onwards and incorporates many old trees from earlier times, notably the old oak on the second lawn which is eight hundred years old and a relic from the great forest of Waltham.

Dividing the main lawns are two large yew hedges, making an excellent symmetrical framework for the circular rose garden and pergola with the stable block behind. Between the pergola and the walled gardens is a pond with many golden orfe.

The two walled kitchen gardens are about one acre each, and have vegetables, herbaceous borders, fruit trees, shrubs and other small trees outlined with old-fashioned low box hedges.

The soil here is medium to heavy loam (alkaline) so there are no azaleas, but we do have some wonderful autumn colour from the many maples, viburnums, liquidambars and so on and a superb *Vitis coignetiae* which never fails to turn.

◆

The Old Rectory, Sible Hedingham
MR AND MRS R.J. EDDIS

The re-creation of this garden started in earnest in about 1964, the original much larger garden having fallen into decay. Apart from the adverse climate and unhelpful soil, the main problem was the flat rectangular and narrow nature of the main part of the garden. To resolve this problem, the present owners sought the advice of John Codrington, and they are greatly indebted to him for the combination of vistas, mowing-lines and the care-

ful choice and siting of shrubs and trees which he suggested.

Shrubs and trees were chosen primarily to provide colour, variety and contrast for as long as possible, rather than spectacular, but short, bursts of flowering. The result is a garden with colour and interest somewhere from May until October, but which cannot be identified with any particular season. The house, which was built as a rectory in 1714, but has a late-Georgian façade added around 1800, is an integral part of the garden, its mellow red brick adding to the setting.

Much use has been made of variegated plants, especially maples, dogwoods and *Elaeagnus*, and colour contrasts are achieved by planting golden elder, *Cornus alba* 'Spaethii', *Robinia pseudoacacia* 'Frisia' and *Gleditsia* against purple *Prunus* 'Pissardii' and *Acer platanoides* 'Atropurpureum' against backgrounds of different shades of green. A stream, dammed to provide a mini-lake, allows plants that enjoy the waterside to thrive, and a heather garden adds colour throughout the year.

◆

Olivers, Nr Colchester
MR AND MRS DAVID EDWARDS

'A retired and agreeable place; with handsome gardens, canals and fishponds; and a wood adjoining cut out into pleasant walks.' This description of Olivers circa 1780, from Philip Morant's *History of Essex*, is as apt today.

The house, Georgian-fronted on an old timber frame, sits comfortably on what in Essex counts as a hillside. The soft red-brick walls and the stone-flagged terrace provide shelter for tender scented and sun-loving plants, and a viewpoint from which lawn, pools and woods lead down to the meadow and woodland bordering the Roman river.

In front, smooth-mown lawn, bordered with flowers, shrubs and yew hedges leads to a meadow, cut only so as to encourage wild flowers and grasses. To the east a Chinoiserie bridge crosses the top of the chain of pools which falls, through the comparative formality of junipers, *Wisteria* and roses, with carp plopping between the waterlilies, to the rush-fringed ancient monastic fishpond, overhung in summer with hogweed and cow parsley. From here the stream drops through a steep dell, gleaming with primroses, aconites and kingcups in spring, to the river.

The damp surrounds of the pools have enabled *Taxodium distichum*, *Metasequoia* and *Ginkgo* to flourish, but we were fortunate to inherit superb mature native trees in Walk Wood. Oak, ash, chestnut, hornbeam, beech, birch and wild cherry all thrive in the very varied soil (a glacial dump it has been called). Beneath them, bordering the rides and in the glades, flowering first above the daffodils and later above a haze of bluebells, are a wide variety of rhododendrons, species and hybrids, and later the deciduous azaleas and shrub roses, which are perhaps the greatest attraction to our visitors.

St Paul's Walden Bury
THE HON. LADY BOWES LYON AND
MR AND MRS SIMON BOWES LYON

St Paul's Walden Bury is one of the few remaining examples of a formal landscape garden which has survived since the early eighteenth century. It was designed when French influence was still dominant, with symmetrically-arranged patterns of avenues and rides leading to temples, statues and ponds. There are interesting collections of plants set in flower gardens of more recent date, and these additions have been linked to the original design without changing it. The whole garden covers about forty acres.

This was the childhood home of Queen Elizabeth the Queen Mother. Her brother David Bowes Lyon, President of the R.H.S., lived and gardened here for thirty years. He replanted the rides with beech hedges and created flower gardens with old-fashioned roses and other summer flowers.

Since 1960 an extensive area of woodland, with neutral soil, has been planted with rhododendrons and other shrubs. A number of these have been collected, as seedlings, by the present owner in the Himalayas.

St Paul's Walden Bury reflects the eighteenth-century English ideas on landscape gardening – that a garden should be in harmony with the surrounding countryside. Thus rides and avenues lead into the landscape, while features of the countryside, such as the church, are taken into the design. Trees are left to grow naturally and the boundary between garden and fields or woods is concealed wherever possible. The landscape is part of the garden and the garden is part of the landscape.

◆

Saling Hall, Great Saling
MR AND MRS HUGH JOHNSON

Saling Hall garden is essentially a garden for tree lovers. Hugh Johnson bought it in 1971, and when the huge elms surrounding the house died of Dutch Elm disease, he started turning the twelve acres of chalky boulder clay in Essex into an arboretum punctuated by features designed to evoke different moods.

The first sight of the garden is a noble row of mature Lombardy poplars leading up to the house, a seventeenth-century manor with Dutch gables. The walled garden, the walls of which are dated 1698, is entered by a door beside the house. Its lawns are punctuated by apple trees, pruned for many years into parasols. Clipped cypresses, Irish junipers and box hedges make a framework for the beds, planted with shrubs, bulbs and herbaceous plants.

A brick herringbone path leads to the vegetable garden, and thence to several enclosures, including a valley garden, a white border, a drying green, and rose glade. This contains mainly pink shrub roses, including *Rosa* 'Complicata', *Rosa soulieana*, and a great favourite in this garden, *Rosa glauca* (*rubri-*

folia). A bank of willows takes you to the Japanese garden and beyond, to another pond where the white trunks of *Betula jacquemontii* on the promontory are reflected in the water. All the trees in this area have been planted since 1975, and include collections of the genera that grow best on alkaline clay or gravel: *Pinus*, *Quercus*, *Sorbus*, *Aesculus*, *Robinia*, *Prunus*, *Salix*, *Betula*, *Juniperus* and certain *Acer* species.

The Long Walk, originally planted in 1959, is a dense tangle of shrubs, which brings you to the water garden, also of that date, but recently replanted with *Gunnera*, primulas, irises and other water-loving plants.

Each room or glade in the garden, and there are many, is intended to have a distinct atmosphere. This calls for self-discipline in planting. Often the best results come not from exuberance but through restraint.

◆

Terling Place, Nr Chelmsford
THE LORD RAYLEIGH

Terling Place garden reflects its history. In the middle ages a palace of the Bishops of Norwich stood in front of what is now the front door. Henry VIII appropriated it for his own use and visited it on several occasions. A few oaks survive from this period; pollarded for fuel many times, they have enormous trunks, the largest being twenty-six feet in circumference, and are marked as individual trees on a map of 1597. There is also a mulberry of Tudor date on the church terrace.

The present house was built in 1764, and the wings added in 1824; shortly afterwards a parterre with yew and box hedges, and borders with bedded-out plants, was made on the south front. This remains much like the original design, partly based on Carton's in Ireland.

Starting in the 1870s, Evelyn, Lady Rayleigh planted many ornamental trees and shrubs. These include the avenues of *Cupressus lawsoniana* to the north of the house, and other specimen trees then new to England, many given to her by her friend Asa Grey, and derived from the west coast of America. There are therefore some large examples of *Sequoiadendron giganteum* (wellingtonia), and the like. A magnificent cedar, now ruined by snowfalls, but formerly of perfect shape, dates from this period. She also enlarged the Swan Pond, a former mill pond, and landscaped the area around it.

In the 1920s and 30s Kathleen, Lady Rayleigh continued her work, introducing oriental species of trees, shrubs, and herbaceous plants. She placed many rhododendrons, azaleas and camellias, where conditions allowed; there are areas, especially near the river, which are lime-free. The size of the garden (some thirty acres) has made it impossible to maintain herbaceous subjects, except near the house.

The *Wisteria* on the west wing was about a hundred years old when, in 1930, the wing was burnt out; it paid no attention whatever.

The main trunk has long disappeared, but the plant survives, having layered itself repeatedly.

A useful tip, from our experience, is that if planting the easier lilies, such as *L. regale*, you can avoid having to stake them by growing them through a thicket of *Berberis thunbergii* 'Atropurpurea', clipped to a level of about two feet; which makes a good background.

◆

Tilty Hill Farm, Duton Hill
MR AND MRS F.E. COLLINSON

This garden on alkaline soil, situated on a windy hilltop facing south and open to sunshine from early morning till evening, presen-

Primula japonica, P. pulverulenta and *Lamium album* are set off by the foliage of *Alchemilla* and *Matteucia* at Saling Hall in June.

ted quite a challenge when we started it in 1957. A small farm garden, heavily cropped with bindweed, nettles and docks, to which was added an adjoining field, gave us two acres to start from scratch.

A copper beech, box, and some very fine old yew trees gave protection from the north, and under the yews stand the seventeenth-century beeboles. We understand that they are the only freestanding beeboles registered in England, as usually they were built into garden or house walls. After surveying the site very often from first floor windows, it has now developed into a series of separate gardens, some paved, some grassed, low stone or brick walls to alter the levels. A planting of blue flowers lends distance in many cases; forget-me-nots, irises, *Nigella*, delphiniums and *Polemonium*. The old farm pond has waterlilies, the small pools fish and waterlilies, surrounded by rose beds.

Conifers give colour for the winter, spring bulbs, alpines, flowering shrubs and herbaceous borders gradually build up the colour schemes, and finally there is the blaze of colour from over four hundred roses, which our son has made his hobby. Then autumn colour changes the scene.

The large vegetable garden is now a hard tennis court, whose wire walls support *Clematis*, honeysuckles and a peach tree. The fruit cage and a small kitchen garden grow ample for our needs and we have mechanized as far as possible – even to an electrically-driven wheelbarrow, which is a great help when carting compost or weeds.

For the last ten years we have gardened without any help, but gardening is a worthwhile hobby and there is always something to look forward to.

◆

Volpaia, Hockley
MR AND MRS DEREK FOX

Cutting the garden out of the natural deciduous woodland of hornbeam, oak and birch started almost thirty years ago. Just over an acre of acid loam slopes gently downhill to the west. Traditional lawns are set both to the front and the rear of the house, but they have been trimmed from time to time to provide little havens for choicer plants. This is a garden, perhaps, where the plants rather than the gardener takes priority, and is the home of Bullwood Nursery, specializing in lilies and woodland plants.

From the rear lawn, dominated by a mature five-stemmed silver birch, paths lead into the woodland. Rhododendrons, most of them species, fascinating in leaf, large and small, rough and smooth, as well as in flower, are interspersed wth camellias and magnolias, many of which grow with great vigour.

Ringing the changes there is a bog garden, or is it a pond? Here the *Gunnera* excels itself as does the equally mighty-leaved skunk cabbage, the yellow aroid of early spring. There are moisture-loving primulas around and many ferns and hostas.

Obviously this is a garden for a long-lasting spring because underneath the shrubs, themselves contending with a fairly heavy tree canopy, are choice woodlanders such as trilliums, uvularias, disporums, erythroniums, and many kinds of Solomon's seal. They take their stand against the native weeds. Sheets of wood anemones are followed by the misty bluebells and stately foxgloves.

Where space permits, lilies thrust up their strong stems for summer flowering and the willow gentian thrives like no other to give blue and white bells in autumn. At this time the *Eucryphia* is covered with beautiful white flowers, but then *Cornus* did it before in July and *Davidia*, the dove or handkerchief tree, before that in May. On a certain day it is easy to say, when birds sing, frogs leap, and the Speckled Wood butterflies flit between the bushes, that this is the garden at its best, and all is right with the world.

GLOUCESTERSHIRE

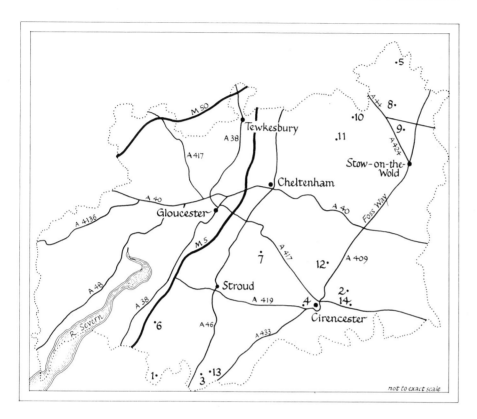

not to exact scale

Directions to Gardens

Alderley Grange, Alderley, 2 miles south of Wotton-under-Edge. [1]

Barnsley House, Barnsley, 4 miles northeast of Cirencester on A433. [2]

Beverston Castle, west of Tetbury on A4135. [3]

Cecily Hill House, 38 Cecily Hill and 42 Cecily Hill, on the west side of Cirencester, near gates into Park. [4]

Hidcote Manor Garden, 3 miles northeast of Chipping Campden. [5]

Hunts Court, North Nibley, Dursley, 2 miles northwest of Wotton-under-Edge. [6]

Kiftsgate Court, 3 miles northwest of Chipping Campden. [5]

Misarden Park, 7 miles northeast of Stroud. [7]

Paxton House, Blockley, northwest of Moreton-in-Marsh. [8]

Sezincote, 1½ miles southwest of Moreton-in-Marsh. [9]

Snowshill Manor, 3 miles south of Broadway. [10]

Stancombe Park, Dursley, midway between Dursley and Wotton-under-Edge. [6]

Stanway House, near Toddington, 5 miles south of Broadway. [11]

Stowell Park, 2 miles southwest of Northleach, off A429. [12]

Upton House, Tetbury Upton, 1 mile north of Tetbury. [13]

Yew Tree Cottage, Ampney St Mary, east of Cirencester. [14]

◆

Alderley Grange, Nr Wotton-under-Edge

MR GUY AND THE HON. MRS ACLOQUE

I had always wanted to create an aromatic garden since my first garden memories were those of the herb garden of a wartime neighbour Eleanor Sinclair Rhode, the famous herbalist. We came here twelve years ago and the wonderful garden that Alvilde Lees-Milne had created seemed a perfect setting in which to enlarge the collection of herbs and aromatic plants that she had started.

Having had little practical experience, my early efforts frequently turned out to be howling mistakes. However, with endless visits to nurseries and other gardens and the reading of old herbals, I gained the knowledge and confidence to adapt and replant where necessary.

The design of the garden is essentially as originally created, with the exception of the new herbary in part of the old vegetable garden. At the end of June, when it is open, this new garden looks like a mediaeval tapestry. It is densely planted with lavender, variegated sages and thymes, hyssops, rue, golden marjoram, santolinas and pinks. Bee plants include anise hyssop, mignonette and heliotrope which are planted annually. The whole is easily maintained provided bushy plants are cut hard back.

We inherited a splendid collection of old roses and further additions have been made. Many herbs with aromatic foliage blend well with the roses. Fennel and angelica make splendid backcloths, whilst lemon balm, lad's love and many of the mints all mix well.

Looking to larger planting, the aromatic garden would not be complete without balsam poplars, the incense rose, *Eucalyptus* and the allspice tree.

Less hardy plants such as lemon verbena, pineapple sage, myrtle and balm of Gilead are better grown in pots and kept in a frost-free place during the winter.

Don't be dismayed by your first mistakes when making an aromatic garden. The rewards for perseverance are well worth waiting for.

◆

Barnsley House, Nr Cirencester

MRS DAVID VEREY

When Barnsley became our home in 1951 we had a wonderful garden heritage; a Gothick summerhouse and Cotswold stone walls, built in 1770, which surround the garden on three sides, and tall trees planted a hundred years ago. Our four-acre garden, redesigned since 1960, has evolved slowly; we had no master plan, we learnt as we went along. First, David planted a lime walk and I chose trees for the 'Wilderness' – cherries and *Sorbus* for blossom, berries and autumn colour. My favourites are *Prunus* 'Tai Haku' and *Sorbus* 'Embley'.

Our aim has been to achieve a succession of interest starting with snowdrops, aconites, scented shrubs and small bulbs. The pattern of the herb garden with threads of clipped box is effective in winter when the herbs are low. The rock-rose path flowers in late May and June; the *Laburnum* walk made in 1964, underplanted with *Allium aflatunense*, is an early June feature. Four parterre beds in front of the house have many spring bulbs, then hardy perennials come through and hide the dying bulb leaves. The broad border leading to Simon Verity's fountain has a mixture of shrubs and herbaceous plants, the colour scheme predominantly yellow, white and blue.

But the most important feature is the Tuscan temple moved here twenty years ago; from this we created a vista ending in the fountain. Other works by Simon include the hunting lady and two stone gardeners guarding the way into the vegetable garden. Our idea in laying paths among the vegetables was to make it more manageable, but it has become quite decorative with trained fruit trees and roses mixed with lettuces and peas. Our garden is now a mixture of formal with informal, with patterns such as the knot garden, close planting in the borders and tubs around the house.

Beverston Castle, Nr Tetbury
MAJOR AND MRS L. ROOK

The main charm of the garden at Beverston is the mellow Cotswold stone of a thirteenth-century castle to which is attached a house built about 1700, after the castle had been damaged by the Cromwellian troops in the Civil War.

The terrace, which was laid down about twelve years ago, now melts into the base of the tower and house. Many of the plants are self-sown, which makes for a very informal effect. The moat border has gallica, bourbon, climbing and various other roses, together with various other plants such as *Clematis*, *Potentilla*, *Cistus* and *Dianthus* all in the same tones, with grey and blue plants to set off the rather bright pinks and purples.

In other parts of the garden we have tried to group plants in colour, some rather bright, others more peaceful, and through foliage and shrubs have tried to include a few plants of interest for most of the year.

There is a large lawn, surrounded by ancient beeches, some of which, sadly, have had to come down in recent years; these are underplanted with spring-flowering bulbs. Luckily the two very old walnut trees are still standing, which helps to emphasize the historic nature of the place.

Cecily Hill House
MR AND MRS RUPERT DE ZOETE

You enter by a courtyard, which has a small octagonal greenhouse, and is surrounded with quantities of tubs and pots, including two huge ones with *Hosta sieboldiana* 'Elegans', planted twenty-six years ago and still flourishing. We take seed from our hostas, and find that they germinate quite easily. There are masses of lilies too, which thrive undiscovered by slugs. These are given a light covering of bracken in winter.

In summer, there are many varieties of

unusual geraniums, some with scented leaves – a favourite is chocolate peppermint. In spring these are replaced with a variety of bulbs underplanted with blue, white and yellow pansies which flower in winter, even in snow.

At the entrance to the main garden, there is an architectural timber archway of unusual design, with climbing roses, *Clematis* and ivies. The main garden, on two levels, has borders of shrubs and perennials, chosen almost entirely for their form and foliage, which is harmonious and restful to the eye. Two of the many rare plants here are *Hydrangea quercifolia* and *Geranium pratense*

A view of the Indian Garden at Sezincote, near Moreton-in-Marsh (see page 81). A serpent climbs up a tree trunk on an island in the pool.

'Plenum Caeruleum', which has double blue flowers.

Visitors here seem to enjoy most of all the small ornamental kitchen garden, which is surrounded by a yew hedge. In the centre, there is a paved and pebbled area displaying a seventeenth-century geometric sculpture, which has a curiously modern feeling. At the far end, there is an eighteenth-century lead tank, above which a lion's mask gently gushes water.

The owner's ambition has been to create focal points, and also to endeavour to give an element of surprise, the latter so difficult to achieve in the restricted space of a town garden.

38, Cecily Hill
THE REVEREND AND MRS JOHN BECK

This is a garden of colour and contrasts. It is really two distinct gardens, small and large, on high and low levels (the latter sloping as well). They are seen primarily as a home for plants, many of them unusual, with at least five hundred different perennials, as well as roses and shrubs.

Informal flower beds characterize the upper garden, which contains a variety of cottage garden plants, while the lower one displays basically two long borders flanked by three paths for easy viewing. Named delphiniums are a feature of the borders in July. The overall aim is kaleidoscope – something of colour and interest for seven months of the year.

42, Cecily Hill
MR AND MRS ROBERT ITTMAN

This finely proportioned garden, with the castle as an interesting backdrop, has something to please everyone – roses, shrubs, a pond with waterfall, rock garden, and a colourful herbaceous border. The high walls accommodate a variety of climbers – rare and flourishing *Clematis* are very much a speciality.

Hidcote Manor Garden, Nr Chipping Campden
THE NATIONAL TRUST

Created from bare Cotswold upland, this garden now comprises a series of 'outdoor rooms' framed by hedges and mostly planted in an informal style within the formal framework.

The skill of the creator, Major Lawrence Johnston, shows in this mixture of shapes and textures, and in the contrast between the open nature of the Long Walk and in the intimate, closely planted areas of Mrs Winthrop's Garden, the Old Garden and the Pillar Garden. A huge variety of plants from far and wide was used in the original project which began eighty years ago, but today the outstanding features include old roses, paeonies (the National Collection is in the process of being assembled) and the miscellany of plants in the Red Border, where most shades in this portion of the spectrum can be seen. In addition there are the Hidcote varieties of lavender and *Hypericum*, rose 'Lawrence Johnston' and varieties of *Verbena*, *Penstemon* and other plants which can claim to have originated here.

Hunts Court, North Nibley
MR AND MRS T.K. MARSHALL

This garden happened – then it just 'growed'. Until 1976 the garden, bounded by walls, was large enough to grow vegetables and allow a busy farmer's wife a flower bed or two. Farmers are not usually gardeners. Then in 1976, overcome by old rose fever, I dug a patch of field outside the walls, just to grow old shrub and species roses. Sixty old roses packed in there is quite a sight in summer and is still interesting in winter with the different forms of growth and stem colour. I've forgotten how many times the fence has been moved since then, not to repeat a mass planting of roses, but using roses as shrubs mixed with other plants.

As the only trees were two ancient pears our plantings have ranged from an atlantic cedar, silver birches and a *Nyssa* down to many hardy geraniums and erodiums and several forms of *Acaena*. On the way are included *Acer palmatum* 'Senkaki', *Halesia*, *Aralia*, *Carpenteria*, many paeonies and dozens of hebes, cistuses and potentillas.

Now, nearly three hundred old roses form the connecting links in the garden, from the May flowering *R. primula* and *banksiae* 'Lutea' to 'Blush China' that gives us a bloom or two at Christmas; from the prostrate 'Dunwich Rose' or 'Max Graf' to 'La Mortola' or 'Paul's Himalayan Musk', with in between the albas, damasks, centifolias, gallicas, bourbons and hybrid perpetuals – a vast variety of form and colour complemented by the other shrubs and ground-cover.

The winter months are not forgotten with a heather bed, coloured-stemmed *Rubus* and *Cornus* and winter-flowering *Lonicera*, *Prunus* and *Viburnum*.

Our garden planning is laughable – a garden designer's nightmare – and consists of finding a home for a plant that we like. But we enjoy it and so it seems do a lot of visitors. Perhaps my first sentence was wrong – the garden is still happening.

Kiftsgate Court, Nr Chipping Campden
MR AND MRS A.H. CHAMBERS

Kiftsgate Court was built around a hundred years ago on a magnificent site surrounded on three sides by steep banks, with a lime avenue and Scots pines already in existence.

My grandparents bought it after the First World War, and for the next thirty-five years

my grandmother, Heather Muir, created the garden which by 1950 had been featured in the Royal Horticultural Society's *Journal*. My mother, Diany Binny, has continued her work, making a few alterations, but maintaining the original colour schemes of the existing borders.

In spring the white sunken garden is covered with bulbs – erythroniums, trilliums and scillas – as well as *Sanguinaria canadensis* 'Plena'. In front of the house there is the early *Magnolia denudata*, and along the drive daffodils abound. June and July are probably the peak months for colour and scent in the garden. Old-fashioned roses and species grow in profusion throughout, with *Rosa* 'Kiftsgate' outgrowing them all – a marvellous sight in mid-July when covered with its huge panicles of white flowers. The wide border is planted in tones of grey, lilac and pink, and here and there a splash of cerise crimson. It is dominated by a large Japanese maple intermingled with shrubs – indigoferas, roses and escallonias, and so on. There is also an exceptional collection of perennial geraniums, martagon lilies seven feet high, and clumps of purple-flowered *Dictamnus albus*.

Growing up the portico, a large *Wisteria* is complemented a little further along by *Actinidia kolomikta*, *Rosa banksiae* 'Lutea', and surprisingly, a *Rosa* 'Mutabilis' reaching to the top of the house.

Many species of *Hydrangea* provide interest in August and September, *Hydrangea villosa* growing up to fifteen feet high, and the beautiful *Hydrangea xanthoneura wilsonii* even higher. Japanese maples give splendid autumn colour in the beautiful bluebell wood.

Misarden Park, Nr Stroud
MAJ. AND MRS M.T.N.H. WILLS

This garden has the timeless quality of a typical English garden. The drive edged with Westmorland limestone, avenued with very tall horse chestnut and lime trees, affords spectacular views into the Golden Valley. A climbing *Hydrangea* and 'Albertine' rose cling to the walls of the Elizabethan manor house.

The south terrace is bounded by topiary

42, Cecily Hill

and the loggia is overhung with a magnificent *Wisteria* while a view to the east is framed by pines, cedars, and firs. Steps lead down to a small scented garden, and a double herbaceous border planted with the unusual white willow herb leads one to the main lawn. Following on there are a series of unique grass steps, an innovation of Sir Edward Lutyens. West of the main lawn is an extensive area of pleasure grounds with massed naturalized daffodils for spring colour, an Indian bean tree, *Catalpa*, and a fine copper beech. Below is the shrubbery bounded by some fine specimen trees – flowering cherries, *Cedrus atlantica glauca* and balsam-scented poplar – together with some more recent plantings of *Liriodendron tulipifera*, *Ginkgo biloba* and a Judas tree.

The terraced walled garden west of the house is flanked with two wide herbaceous borders and climbing roses on the south side. On the north side, divided by a very handsome and well-clipped double yew hedge, is a traditional rose garden. These borders are at their best in early June and in September when the yellow *Rudbeckia* and light blue *Aster acris* are flowering. There is much to be enjoyed in this beautiful Cotswold garden but not to be missed is the ancient sycamore, whose roots have become exposed clinging to the wall through the years, below which is a newly planted silver and grey border which blends so well with the natural stone.

Paxton House, Blockley
MR AND MRS PETER CATOR

Our small garden of half an acre is cut into a limestone hill and is on four different levels surrounded by walls. A favourite part is the yellow border set against a high mellow Cotswold stone wall, where the colours range from pale cream to deep yellow and bronze. *Clematis*, *Cytisus*, *Lonicera*, ivies and roses cover the wall and in front there are *Phlomis*, euphorbias, potentillas and various perennials to give a long flowering period. *Senecio* 'Sunshine' is trained on another wall and is a good foil for the rose 'Pink Perpetue', *Clematis* 'Perle d'Azur' and *Ceanothus* 'Gloire de Versailles'. Two facing beds between low walls have 'Iceberg' roses edged with *Stachys lanata* 'Silver Carpet'. Falling over one of the walls is the old rambler 'Adelaïde d'Orléans', whose creamy pink flowers hang gracefully down like cherry blossom. Nearby, climbing into an old pear tree is *Rosa soulieana* which looks a dream in late summer with its lovely white blooms, enhanced by greyish foliage. In the winter a dark corner is lightened by the white stems of *Rubus cockburnianus* underplanted with *Lamium* 'Beacon Silver'.

We have tried to create a feeling of abundance in a small area where foliage plants are much used and are allowed to spread over edges; purple sage and santolinas give a faded tapestry effect in a bed with brighter colours. A few good trees are planted which we hope in time will give pleasure and peace to us and future owners.

*Sezincote, Nr Moreton-in-Marsh
MR AND MRS DAVID PEAKE

Sezincote, the only Indian house in western Europe surmounted by copper dome and minarets, provides the exotic background for this water garden. The spring rises in a cave behind the Temple of Surya, the Hindu sun-god, and runs down a gently sloping and sheltered valley to the lake through a series of pools.

Thomas Daniell designed the temple and the bridge decorated with cast iron Brahmin Bulls (Nandi) and lotus buds. It is thought he may also have had a hand in the design of the garden together with Repton at the beginning of the nineteenth century. Some of the trees which appear in the pictures which he painted and exhibited at the Royal Academy in 1818 and 1819 are still growing here, many of unusual size now, including cedars of Lebanon and a weeping hornbeam said to be the largest of its kind in England.

Today the borders on either side of the stream are notable for the great variety of greens and of textures – massed groupings of hostas, rodgersias and peltiphyllums. To echo the eastern architecture, bamboos, palms and contorted specimens are grown together with the more usual flowering shrubs such as cherries, deutzias, viburnums and syringas. In late June a yew tree near the top pool shows off two rampant climbing roses, 'Paul's Himalayan Musk' and *R. filipes* 'Kiftsgate' which must have attained a height of about seventy-five feet. Soon after these fade, *Cornus kousa chinensis* stands out from a mass of primulas and *Campanula lactiflora* near the water. *Vitis coignetiae* and a *Rhus potaninii* on the bridge provide good autumn colour.

In front of the Orangery, which is at its best in May, containing several different abutilons and a yellow banksian rose, lies the Indian garden. This was laid out only in 1968; Irish yews, *Taxus baccata* 'Fastigiata', have been planted on either side of the canals whereas golden yews, *Taxus baccata* 'Dovastonii Aurea', are placed under the copper beech.

Snowshill Manor, Nr Broadway
THE NATIONAL TRUST

The garden was formed from 1919 by Charles Paget Wade as a setting for the Cotswold manor house in which he assembled his remarkable collection, ranging from Japanese armour to bicycles. Starting with a nettle-infested farmyard he created a terrace garden of great charm, in which his training in architecture reveals itself in the careful planning of relationships between shapes and levels. In an area of only two acres the eye is continually led on, from terrace to steps, walled enclosure to vista. Interest is further sustained by careful use of colour, by the placing of surprise features such as stone cisterns and by the presence of running water. The model village which once occupied parts of the garden has

Paxton House, Blockley, in June. The elegant doorway is framed by *Clematis montana* and white rugosa roses.

had to be removed to prevent further deterioration but some of the buildings are on view under cover.

Stancombe Park, Dursley
MR AND MRS B.S. BARLOW

Stancombe Park lies in an amphitheatre created by the Cotswolds which rise from the Severn basin.

There are two gardens, both of which are completely different. In the first, which surrounds the house, we have tried to create an area which blends into the magnificent scenery all around, so that the views may be fully enjoyed and for this reason there are no enclosures or hidden places. In the centre of the main lawn stands a large eighteenth-century Italian urn, surrounded by maples, a short pleached lime walk leads to an ornamental seat, and two long herbaceous borders cut transversely through the area.

The second garden is completely different. Here we found three lakes reached by an isthmus of green, where soldiers, returning from the Napoleonic wars and needing employment, had created a secret folly garden of grottoes, a temple, and mediterranean designs. Laurel had been plentifully planted but this is now giving way to shrubs of a more interesting nature. An *Acer* collection, *Gunnera manicata*, other bog plants and *Salix* species are taking their place. A new experiment has been to plant *Cornus* in a star pattern – all of different variety – this has yet to prove itself.

As there are over fifteen acres of garden it

would be impossible to mention more than a few outstanding specimens of trees which should be particularly noted: *Liquidambar*, *Paulownia*, *Fagus sylvatica* 'Heterophylla' and 'Dawyck Purple' to name but a few. *Euonymus radicans* 'Silver Queen' is a favourite little shrub.

*Stanway House, Cheltenham
LORD AND LADY NIEDPATH

Flowers are unnecessary in the beautiful English countryside; those who want to look at flowers should search the suburbs.

Although Stanway boasts old roses, *Clematis*, honeysuckle, magnolias, tree paeonies, hellebores, perennial peas, lilies and five acres of daffodils, these are not its claim to fame. Its true distinction lies in the integral relationship of the Jacobethan manor house, the massive tithe barn, the straggling village, the gate house – considered one of the gems of Gloucestershire architecture – the church and the planted parkland with its intersecting oak, chestnut and lime avenues set against the backdrop of the sheep-cropped Cotswold escarpment.

Within this framework are eighteenth-century terraced lawns planted with trees – including oriental planes, yews and tulip trees – leading by an infilled canal up through a nineteenth-century arboretum, including a collection of rare maples, the tallest cherry tree in Britain, wellingtonias, coast red-woods, noble firs and Corsican pines, Himalayan whitebeam, Antarctic beech and purple Dawyck beech, to a Palladian pyramid built in 1750 by Robert Tracy in memory of his father John Tracy. Dominating the skyline behind it is one of the largest cedar trees in the country (a hundred and fifteen feet by twenty-six feet eight inches). From here to the canal flowed a cascade, now dry, but efforts are being made to promote its restoration.

From the pyramid can be seen a fine prospect of Stanway House and village, and beyond it, of the vales of Evesham and Gloucester, the hills of Dumbleton, Alderton, Oxenton and Dixton, the Malverns and, in the furthest distance, the Black Mountains of Wales.

Tips from Stanway are: plant competitive perennials, buy a strimmer, use a Mountfield Triple M cylinder mower and kill all grey squirrels.

Stowell Park, Nr Northleach
THE LORD AND LADY VESTEY

Stowell Park stands on an escarpment of the Cotswolds with an unparalleled view across the Coln valley. An earlier house on the same site dated from the twelfth century, as does the existing church. The present house was started in the seventeenth century and has large nineteenth-century additions. During this period the balustrading, a major feature

The view towards the house from the garden at Stancombe Park, Dursley. Double herbaceous borders, backed by roses trained between posts, frame the view. For a description of this garden see previous page.

of the terraced gardens, was added and the walled gardens created.

The entrance is through two interesting gatehouses, built in the 1880s, with a newly-planted avenue of pleached limes leading up to the north side of the house. A series of steep terraces leads down from the south front of the house to adjoin the grass parkland planted with many fine trees including oaks. The terrace border has been planted with honeysuckles and *Clematis*.

Enthusiasts for old-fashioned roses will find examples of every class including a line of standard 'Canary Bird' along the herbaceous border. A beautiful seventeenth-century stone dovecote stands at one end of the terrace, whilst an avenue of *Malus* 'Golden Hornet' leads in another direction to the simple swimming pool and summer house. A knot garden, designed in 1982, has been laid out in a sunny corner of the garden. Further specimen trees, shrubs and herbaceous plantings are planned for the terraces.

The drive to the back of the house leads to the two old-fashioned walled gardens and greenhouses, the first being the cutflower garden where many of the old favourites are grown to supply flowers and pot plants for the house. Beyond is the fruit and vegetable garden, flanked by peach and vine houses. A recent addition is an ornamental orchard which is part of the present programme to re-develop the traditional kitchen garden.

◆

Upton House, Nr Tetbury
R. SEELIG, ESQ.

Upton House was built in 1752 by a local architect in the elegant style of its day. The front is of outstanding quality and elegance and a fine example of Georgian architecture, and nearby is an interesting ice house.

Many of the mature trees on the estate must have seen a good part of the house's two-hundred-year history. A cedar of Lebanon overlooks the large expanse of front lawn, whilst at the side a tulip tree, once amongst the largest in the country, towers above the fifteen-foot beech hedge. The tree has lost a few upper limbs now but is still an impressive specimen, and in favourable years has been covered in exotic yellow 'tulips'. Sadly a forty-year-old replacement has never flowered. The beech hedge shelters a long mixed border, which is ideally protected from behind by a wall of Cotswold stone; thus with judicious choice of plants little staking is necessary.

A recent project has been to lay out the one-acre kitchen garden to something of its former plan, with two herbaceous 'cutting' borders up the centre and four rectangular vegetable plots on each side. However, whereas in the past there was a separate acre of fruit (and also a dozen gardeners and lavish entertaining!), this kitchen garden is also our orchard. There are two lines of apple trees and wall-trained stone fruits. If the project has taught us anything, it is that the sight of an orderly mixture of flowers and healthy, compost-grown vegetables can be as pleasing in its way as the ornamental garden.

The abundance of fruit and vegetables from this garden is highlighted in autumn by bunches of 'Black Hamburg' grapes from the twenty-five-foot-long vine house, which is yet another reminder of Upton's luxurious past.

◆

Yew Tree Cottage, Ampney St Mary
MRS B. SHUKER, KIM AND PENNY POLLIT

This cottage garden of about one acre, enclosed by Cotswold stone walls and surrounded by farmland, has been made since 1962.

At the front, separated from the main garden, is a small lawn with well-stocked mixed borders of shrub roses ('Nevada', *glauca* (*rubrifolia*), *rugosa* and 'Golden Wings'), small shrubs (*Viburnum carlesii*, *Prunus*, tree paeony, *Potentilla* and dogwood) and herbaceous plants such as *Ballota*, *Aquilegia*, *Asphodelus*, *Veronica* and *Doronicum*. *Tropaeolum speciosum* grows happily among evergreen *Cotoneaster*. Two twenty-year-old lavender bushes are a haunt for butterflies and bees in the late summer. The yew trees, thought to be about two hundred years old, near the cottage were completely pollarded some years ago and now stand erect and fully clothed.

At the back of the house is another lawn with four old apple trees. The grass and borders around are carpeted with spring bulbs (daffodils, crocuses, snowdrops and aconites) and *Cyclamen* in the autumn. Some annuals – such as *Limnanthes*, *Lychnis* and white, variegated honesty – hellebores, lilies, foxgloves and *Clematis integrifolia* give colour after the bulbs. There is a small pond and moist area near the house with hostas, willows, kingcups and *Mimulus*. *Prunus tenella* runs happily near the pond.

A full and colourful rock garden with a number of troughs contains a variety of alpines and dwarf conifers with plants spilling on to the gravelled drive.

The vegetable garden is bordered by a *Potentilla* hedge and mature asparagus bed, with plum trees, fruit bushes and strawberries. Enough vegetables are grown to supply the family throughout the year.

Beyond the wall enclosing the garden is another area of vegetables, raspberry canes, more borders of flowers and shrubs, and an area of grass with chickens in a portable arc. There is also a small nursery where many of the plants seen in the garden can be purchased.

HAMPSHIRE (NORTH)

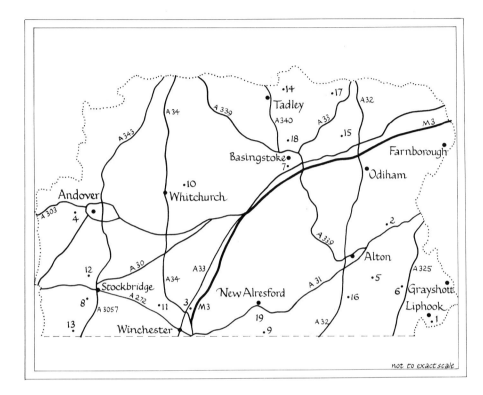

not to exact scale

Directions to Gardens

Bohunt Manor, Liphoook, west of Haslemere, Surrey. [1]

Bramdean House, Bramdean, midway between Winchester and Petersfield. [9]

Broadhatch House, Bentley, 4 miles northeast of Alton. [2]

Chilland, 4 miles northeast of Winchester, between Martyr Worthy and Itchen Abbas. [3]

Field House, Monxton, 3 miles west of Andover. [4]

The Gilbert White Museum, Selborne, 4 miles south of Alton. [5]

Greatham Mill, Greatham, near Liss, 5 miles north of Petersfield. [6]

Hackwood Park, 1 mile south of Basingstoke. [7]

Houghton Lodge, 1½ miles south of Stockbridge. [8]

Jenkyn Place, Bentley, 3 miles southwest of Farnham, Surrey. [2]

Laverstoke House, 2 miles east of Whitchurch, 10 miles west of Basingstoke. [10]

Little Court, Crawley, 5 miles northwest of Winchester. [11]

Longstock Park Gardens, 3 miles north of Stockbridge. [12]

Mottisfont Abbey, Mottisfont, 4½ miles northwest of Romsey. [13]

The Old House, Bramley Road, Silchester, southwest of Reading, Berks. [14]

The Ricks, Rotherwick, 2½ miles north of Hook. [15]

Rotherfield Park, East Tisted, 4 miles south of Alton. [16]

Stratfield Saye House, midway between Basingstoke and Reading, Berks. [17]

The Vyne, Sherborne St John, 4 miles north of Basingstoke. [18]

The Weir House, Alresford. [19]

Bohunt Manor, Liphook
LADY HOLMAN

Bohunt Manor garden was started by the present occupant and her husband thirty-four years ago, on his retirement from the Foreign Office. There were always magnificent specimen trees, such as a tulip tree, considered to be one of the tallest in the south of England, huge silver birches, oaks, cherries and chestnuts. We have planted a Judas tree, handkerchief tree, *Parrotia persica* and others which are all flourishing.

The three-and-a-half-acre lake was made by damming a river in the nineteenth century, and there is a charming walk around this to the *Rhododendron* wood. Its banks are massed with daffodils in the spring, followed by bluebells, other wild flowers and rhododendrons.

The finest feature in June is a large double herbaceous border leading from the house to the water, and planted so thickly that weeding is unnecessary, except at the edge. The phloxes in late June are a picture, and a clump of red delphiniums is planted in front of a white perennial everlasting pea that grows up the wall of the kitchen garden. A good specimen of *Rosa* 'Ramona' flowers somewhat earlier.

Visitors remark on the lovely vistas through the trees, and on the lake with its collection of ornamental waterfowl and crested crane walking freely.

Bramdean House, Nr Alresford
MR AND MRS H. WAKEFIELD

I imagine that Catherine Venables, who built Bramdean House in the mid eighteenth century, must have been both a keen and practical gardener. Her one-acre walled kitchen garden was built midway on a south-facing slope directly behind the house. Beyond there is an orchard, terminated by a pleasing contemporary apple house. In the spring the central grass path is bordered with daffodils, and there are more in clumps under the flowering cherries and apple trees.

Matching herbaceous borders now lead up from the house to attractive wrought iron gates opening into the walled garden. *Crambe cordifolia*, giant comfrey and onopordums are planted towards the centre of the borders, surrounded by a wide variety of perennial plants and bulbs. These are staked where necessary with pea-sticks and semi-circular iron supports which are invaluable.

On either side of the borders are extensive lawns with an encircling wall to the west, and fine beeches, limes and chestnuts to the east. There are aconites in profusion in the spring, and many varieties of snowdrop grow happily in the shallow chalky soil.

The walls are covered with *Clematis* and roses, honeysuckles, jasmines and other more tender plants which enjoy their protection. At their base are somewhat unruly masses of perennial plants, old roses and shrubs and varieties of bulbs, such as alliums and nerines. Plants that are new to us, and are perhaps more unusual, are planted in these borders so we can, hopefully, watch their progress.

White-flowered variegated honesty is invaluable for enlivening dark and sun-starved corners and *Lunaria rediviva* is a splendid spring-flowering perennial honesty with a delicious scent. Plant it near an outdoor seat if you ever find time to sit in your garden.

Broadhatch House, Bentley
MR AND MRS P. POWELL

This is a three-and-a-half-acre garden with a southern aspect and an unkind clay soil, constantly needing lightening with humus but with the great advantage of never drying out. Some rather unexpected plants seem to enjoy it though: *Acer palmatum* (there are mature specimens of the 'Atropurpureum Dissectum' type), *Exochorda* and *Magnolia*, and the little grey vetch *Dorycnium hirsutum* seeds freely on the terrace. The garden is roughly arranged in seasonal rooms partitioned by yew, beech and *Prunus* hedges, and the lawns planted with specimen trees such as *Nyssa sylvatica*, *Sorbus sargentiana* and *Acer* 'Osa-kazuki'.

With summer comes the peak of the year, a billowing profusion of roses, mainly shrub and old-fashioned types; from the tiny 'Nozomi' to tall 'William Lobb', and the low 'Comte de Chambord' to the exuberant *R. californica* 'Plena' and 'Countess of Munster'. In the old and new rose gardens the background is of dark yew, and the bushes are set off by grey foliage, *Cotinus* and *Abutilon viti-folium*, giving the eye a better chance to appreciate the soft brilliance of the roses.

The double herbaceous borders carry through from June to September; an autumn bed has recently been planted and is taking shape. The foliage beds perhaps give us more continual pleasure than anything; one can experiment with different forms and colours in a less transient way – a big-leaved *Hosta sieboldiana* set against a variegated *Festuca*, flanked by *Spiraea* 'Goldflame' and *Prunus* 'Cistena' backed by *Cotinus coggygria* and *Robinia* 'Frisia', for example. It is the challenge of growing botanically interesting plants and placing them to complement each other in the landscape, set in rolling Hampshire farmland, that we enjoy.

Chilland, Martyr Worthy
MR AND MRS L.A. IMPEY

The garden at Chilland has an attractive position on a gentle slope reaching down to a stream with river and water meadows beyond. A distant view of hill and woods is glimpsed under some fine trees, and the garden seems to extend its borders and merge with the countryside. This has been achieved

by an increasing informality away from the centre, with mown lawns, paved paths and mixed shrub and flower beds giving way to rough grass with many bulbs and wild flowers leading the eye onwards without check. Carefully massed shrubs and trees with mown paths winding behind them, also create an impression of space. Thoughtful planning has created a natural-looking garden and has achieved a variety of shape and colour by its use of trees and shrubs. One such combination uses spreading juniper, silver *Salix* with *Clematis*, *Rosa virginiana* and purple *Berberis* with *Rosa glauca* (*rubrifolia*).

Clever juxtaposition of colour, and unexpected contrasts of shapes and textures, provide a permanent backcloth and foil for the flowers that provide unexpected patches of colour. In the spring come drifts of fritillaries, *Erythronium revolutum* and chocolate lilies from Vancouver Island, *Fritillaria Camschat-censis*, the elegant *Tulipa sprengeri* and *Iris sintenisii* from Humphrey Waterfield at Broxted.

This is also a garden of interest to plantsmen. A hostile, stony soil has been induced to grow many rare and interesting plants, but these have all been integrated into the general concept, without being allowed undue dominance, to create an original and harmonious whole. There are some interesting associations of planting such as a huge *Clematis* 'Frances Rivis' sharing a wall up to the roof by the front door with a deep red summer rose and a small-berried *Pyracantha*. Mark Fenwick's *Alstroemeria ligtu* blends with a yellow hot poker, *Rosa* 'Iceberg' and *Philadel-phus* 'Beauclerk'. When the lilies are going over the superbly blue *Agapanthus* are starting, bred from ones given to us by Lewis Palmer for trial. There is always something of interest, and round the next corner another picture to please the eye, making Chilland a garden to linger in.

Field House, Monxton
DR AND MRS R.H. PRATT

When we bought Field House in 1952 it was a wilderness. We had it scythed and then put geese and cockerels to clear the ground. We started planting round the house with *Wisteria*, variegated ivy, *Clematis* 'Jackmanii' and *C. alpina* and roses up the walls; below are daffodils and *Scilla*, later on *Alstroemeria* and *Fuchsia* and finally nerines. The herbaceous border is the most time-consuming part of the garden but is very rewarding. Backed by a chalk wall many plants enjoy its sunny aspect. In the orchard there are mixed daffodils and bluebells, and climbing roses up some of the trees. A mulberry, planted by our daughter in memory of her grandparents, has just started to fruit.

When Dutch elm disease destroyed eighty elm trees, the old chalk pit was developed, a pond dug and our son built a flint wall and two flights of steps up the steep bank at the back. We have planted dwarf conifers and

junipers and groups of euphorbias, hostas, ferns, dwarf bulbs and *Cyclamen*. A *Cornus alba* and *Cotinus coggygria* make a nice contrast to the other shades of green and yellow. Ground-cover plants including *Tiarella*, *Ajuga*, *Saxifraga*, *Helianthemum* and many others, fill in corners.

In another corner of the garden there was a thatched privy with two seats! We have made it into a much-used summer house. We have a productive vegetable garden and the old greenhouse is used to overwinter less hardy plants, as we are in a frost pocket. After thirty years we have a mature garden, with trees that we planted now thirty to forty feet high, and many plants grown from cuttings or given by relations and friends are now well established.

The Gilbert White Museum, Selborne
OATES MEMORIAL TRUST

The Wakes, which is now a museum, is famous as the home of the Reverend Gilbert White, author of the classic *Natural History of Selborne*. However, less is generally known about White's great interest in gardening, which preceded his serious studies in natural history. Gilbert White lived at The Wakes for most of his life and kept regular diary entries on gardening activities from 1751 until he died in 1793. This is, therefore, one of the best-documented small gardens of the eighteenth century and in it are grown types of plants that White would have known. There are five acres of formal garden, including lawn and White's stone ha-ha and sundial, the remaining stretch of his fruit wall (dating from 1761) and brick path to the field alcove. Also in the garden are old-fashioned roses, eighteenth-century varieties of apples, a pond, herbaceous borders with annuals and perennials of the period, a herb garden, a fine *Laburnum* arch and specimen trees. Additional to the five-acre garden is the wild garden on Baker's Hill, which has drifts of snowdrops in March, followed by daffodils, fritillaries and wild tulips blooming from April to early May.

Greatham Mill, Nr Liss
MRS E.N. PUMPHREY

We came to live in this old mill house about thirty-five years ago and I set out to make a cottage-type garden which I felt would be in keeping. I had, and still have, two priceless assets; the able and intelligent assistance of my gardener, Jim Collins, and the river Rother and the old waterways of the mill. The soil is neutral alluvial clay, hard work but immensely rewarding, and improved immeasurably through the years by annual mulches of lovely cow manure, donated by our generous farmer son-in-law and his large herd of healthy cows.

In this garden of about two acres you will

find an enormous collection of plants, rare and everyday, all mixty-maxty – shrubs, roses, herbaceous plants and bulbs. There are two water gardens and what we call the outcrop. We can't grow proper alpines here, it is too damp in winter, so we compromise with less exacting subjects.

At the top end of the garden I am planting what I rather grandly call 'the arboretum'; I often garden above my station. Here we have some special trees such as *Prunus serrula*, *Gleditsia triacanthos* 'Sunburst' and *Acer griseum*. Do come and see for yourselves, you will be very welcome. You will also find a nursery garden with plants not easily obtainable elsewhere.

---

*Hackwood Park, The Spring Wood
THE VISCOUNT CAMROSE

Spring Wood is not a garden; it consists of eighty acres of semi-formal woodland planted originally by someone very much influenced by the French and/or the works of Le Nôtre. (It is known that Le Nôtre worked on the Italian garden at Bicton in Somerset.) The pavilions were designed by James Gibbs, the architect of St Martin-in-the-Fields and many other buildings and churches. He also created the house at the head of the menagerie pool which is full of lovely waterlilies.

The Great Avenue contains fine limes and leads to 'twelve-o'clock avenue', in the centre of the wood. The statue of Ceres was placed here by Lord Camrose. The cedar of Lebanon nearby is amongst the largest in the British Isles. Flowering cherries – *P. subhirtella* 'Autumnalis', *padus*, *avium*, *dulcis*, *serrulata*, *sargentii* and *cerasifera* ring the 'tea garden' whose pavilion is all that remains of a large conservatory.

Polly Peachum's garden is by legend attributed to Lavinia Fenton, who played the original Polly in Gay's 'The Beggar's Opera'; she subsequently became Duchess of Bolton and lived at Hackwood. The ruined temple heading the amphitheatre is supposed to have been restored by James Gibbs and the pillars are of foreign origin. The amphitheatre is perhaps the largest in England, though Bramham and Claremont would certainly compete! The pool temple was built by Lord Camrose, the design taken from a Vardy drawing in the muniment collection.

Lord Curzon carried out a good deal of planting in the 'wild' garden when he was a tenant at Hackwood. It had become impenetrably overgrown and is now being restored, together with adjoining 'The Dell'. The Chinese pavilion replaces a former one.

Spring is the best time to see the wood, when it is carpeted with snowdrops, followed by dwarf daffodils, including Lent lilies, and jonquils, fritillaries and then bluebells. *Malus*, *Crataegus*, *Magnolia stellata*, *Paulownia*, *Syringa* and *Philadelphus* and *Malus tschonoskii* flower at this time, as do many other young trees planted in the last twenty years.

Houghton Lodge, Nr Stockbridge
CAPT. AND MRS MARTIN BUSK

Houghton Lodge is a 'cottage orné' built towards the end of the eighteenth century by an unknown architect inspired by the contemporary passion for the Picturesque. It still looks out over a simple harmony of grass and trees which lead down to the River Test with unspoiled views over water meadows to the distant woods. Now listed Grade II* these landscaped pleasure grounds are a tranquil place to enjoy the natural life of the chalk stream and the wild flowers along its banks. This 'rustic simplicity' is enhanced in spring by a profusion of daffodils. Meadow flowers are sown among them so that in late spring their seed pods are sympathetically hidden till the area can be mown again in late summer.

A sheltering bank of *Philadelphus* and *Syringa* is topped by a serpentine path to the gothic postern gate with glimpses through the trees to the choicest views. Once restored it will be again a truly eighteenth-century shrubbery walk.

Under the guidance of David Jacques, author of *Georgian Gardens: The Reign of Nature*, new planting is taking shape to enhance the views to the north and to soften the impact of the rare high chalk cob walls of the produce garden. These walls absorb the heat of the sun for the earlier ripening of fan-trained fruit trees, and surround a traditional kitchen garden where old-fashioned greenhouses shelter orchids, carnations and jasmine. *Plumbago* and *Streptosolen* provide innumerable cuttings and the vines of 'Muscat of Alexandria' and 'Black Alicante' shade the new season's pot plants and bedding in early summer.

Jenkyn Place, Bentley
MR AND MRS G.E. COKE

The house, dating from 1687, faces almost

Jenkyn Place, Bentley.

due south. From the terrace a vista runs down to the 'sunk garden' some two hundred and fifty yards below, and there is a view over the trees and shrubs bordering the lawns to the distant ridge two miles away. To the west of this shallow valley lie a number of small gardens, each with its own characteristics. So the garden is both intimately related to the house for which it is the setting, and designed to show off a wide variety of plants.

The well-known herbaceous borders are perhaps the feature which most visitors remember but there are many other areas of varying size each with its own character. Two rose gardens contain a large number of species and old-fashioned roses; the 'leaf garden' has many plants interesting to the plantsman; the 'sundial garden' is filled with pots of pelargoniums as soon as the frosts are over; the 'lion walk', with its sleeping lion at the end of double hedges composed of mixed copper and green beech, is especially beautiful in spring; the 'lion garden', presided over by a pair of English stone lions, makes a less formal setting for some interesting shrubs and trees; and we are especially fond of the 'long walk', with a rock border on one side which has something in flower on virtually every day of the year.

We were fortunate in finding some beautiful trees whose presence we owe to a predecessor of a hundred or more years ago. The great cedar of Lebanon next to the house, planted in 1823, is one of the finest in the country; and there are also good specimens of tulip tree, oak, beech, lime, holly and several varieties of *Aesculus*, to say nothing of some large yews. These provide height and shade and form the background against which nearly all families of plants, except the *Ericaceae*, can be seen in all their variety and beauty.

Laverstoke House, Nr Whitchurch
MR AND MRS JULIAN SHEFFIELD

Laverstoke garden is enriched by a fine Palladian eighteenth-century house; surrounding house and garden is an exceptionally beautiful park. Until 1952 the only flower garden was a quarter of a mile from the house in a walled garden. The bones of the existing garden were laid down by my parents-in-law and their head gardener, Tom Brown, thirty-five years ago. Many rare shrubs, conifers and trees were planted. Colour in the garden commences in February with its white mantle of snowdrops and bows out in December with the last of the autumn tints.

Since moving here six years ago I have been able to add my personal touch. I have arranged the borders in colours, one such being a blue, white and yellow section. A rose garden is another addition, filled with pink modern and old-fashioned shrub roses. The beds are bordered with *Alchemilla mollis*, white lavender, *Geranium sanguineum* and *Geranium* 'Kashmir White'. In the centre of the rose garden stands a lead figure of Mercury.

Bramdean House in July (see page 83). *Thalictrum speciosissimum* with pale yellow flowers and glaucous leaves dominates this scene with catmint, delphiniums, pink *Centaurea* and *Clematis integrifolia*.

The bedding-out sections have been replaced with perennials. The only annuals we now have are in tubs and urns planted in the summer with ivy-leaved geraniums, petunias, fuchsias and *Helichrysum petiolatum*.

Beyond the rose garden is a grass tennis court which we reinstated after fifty years. Many a happy hour is spent on the court, surrounded by a myriad of plants, shrubs and trees. For the keen horticulturist it is often hard to concentrate on the ball!

Little Court, Crawley
MR AND MRS A.R. ELKINGTON

This two-acre garden on chalk dates from the early nineteenth century with cob and flint and brick walls dividing the different levels. In spring there are spectacular drifts of *Crocus tommasinianus* and the cream *Narcissus pallidiflorus* naturalized in the orchards. Thereafter the owners use foliage contrasts and subdued colours without planting annuals except those which seed themselves such as blue *Echium* and clary, *Salvia horminium*, which give an informal effect.

The beds are designed to be viewed from the house with a paved path of camomile and thyme leading from it. The old wall above has self-sown valerian, *Erigeron mucronatus*, with pinks and veronica in the crevices. On the upper lawn a small rectangular pond has *Acer palmatum* 'Dissectum Atropurpureum' as a focal point, and the surrounding paving is planted with small alpines in the crevices. The walled vegetable and fruit garden with grass paths is the ideal family size; this is hoed vigorously as the whole garden is maintained entirely by the owners. Geese at the end of the garden and free range bantams, often with chicks, provide additional interest and colour.

Longstock Park Gardens, Nr Stockbridge
LECKFORD ESTATE LTD., PART OF THE JOHN LEWIS PARTNERSHIP

The gardens are located in typical north Hampshire countryside with its flint over chalk downland. Here the finely balanced thin turf supports a wonderful variety of wild flowers and throughout the summer rockroses and birdsfoot trefoil can be seen amid great drifts of the foamy flowers of dropwort. Not far away the River Test rushes by, helping to provide the key to what lies behind the hornbeam hedge. Here a carrier from the river has been landscaped, and between 1946 and 1953 a fascinating and unique garden was developed.

This water garden is made up of a series of waterways and islands which are linked together by wooden bridges. In the water magnificent nymphaeas flower above lush foliage whilst all around the islands are drifts of *Iris laevigata*, *Scirpus*, *Primula* and the false skunk cabbage, *Lysichitum*. These grow exceptionally well and a hybrid between the yellow *L. americanum* and the white *L. camtschatcense* has appeared, bearing cream flowers and even larger foliage. *Taxodium distichum*, the swamp cypress, is amongst the trees and proves its contentment by having developed fine 'knees', which in spring are enhanced by *Fritillaria meleagris* naturalized amongst them.

Although basically alkaline, the valley has deposits of peat and leafmould which now support a delightful but uncharacteristic oak woodland where some trees must be two hundred and fifty years old; one of them supports a *Hydrangea petiolaris* which has reached twenty-five feet high. Within this area many calcifuge plants thrive, and include *Rhododendron*, *Pieris*, *Halesia* and *Stuartia*. One could almost imagine being far away in the

Sussex weald such is the contrast in vegetation. Even *Trillium* and *Erythronium* flower and seed well, and provide quite a feature during the spring and early summer.

Mottisfont Abbey, Mottisfont
THE NATIONAL TRUST

Thirty acres of landscaped grounds surround the house, which was originally a twelfth-century priory. The spacious lawns are bordered by the River Test, and there are many fine trees including an enormous plane, *Platanus acerifolia*, which is thought to date from about 1700, cedars, magnolias and an avenue of pleached limes. One of the most notable features of Mottisfont today is its very large collection of old-fashioned roses which includes almost every old European variety still in cultivation; these are housed in the walled garden, which is also planted with herbaceous borders to extend the season of interest.

The Old House, Silchester
MR AND MRS M. JURGENS

The Old House garden is primarily a spring one and is laid out on two levels and connected by a 'dell'. The upper section includes an oak-lined drive, bordered by daffodils in March and April, and this leads to extensive lawns, a formal rose garden, a pergola walk, terraces and other borders around the house.

Below the former Queen Anne rectory are two ponds from which a stream flows into an eight-acre wood which has good peaty soil ideal for camellias, rhododendrons and azaleas. In recent years the wood has been thinned to allow extensive additional plantings of *Rhododendron* species and modern hybrids, as well as a new *Camellia* walk. After extensive bramble clearance the wood once again has a carpet of bluebells in May.

The former bog gardens, rockeries and formal terraces have now been replanted with an extensive collection of old and modern shrub roses, large-flowering shrubs of all kinds and trailing ground-cover plants which extend the flowering season of the garden and reduce the maintenance requirement.

A striking feature of the garden is an avenue of cut-leaf silver birch *Betula pendula* 'Darlecarlica' planted above the Dell to give the illusion of greater depth. The garden is also endowed with a rich variety of maples; *Acer palmatum* 'Dissectum' and *A. palmatum*, *A. negundo* and *A. pseudoplatanus* 'Prinz Handjery' and these, by the constantly changing colour of their leaves, give us great pleasure for most of the year.

The Ricks, Rotherwick
MR AND MRS JAMES MORRIS

The garden at The Ricks is of medium size,

about one acre, on a neutral to acid loam over clay. Our aim is to have colour around the house all the year with the minimum of annual planting.

Golden and silver variegated foliage shrubs are used for winter and early spring effect together with naturalized daffodils. Camellias, rhododendrons and azaleas planted in island beds carry the colour forward. The herbaceous border then takes over together with hybrid lilies growing through the azaleas and other shrubs. In the autumn *Acer palmatum*, cherries, amelanchiers, *Liquidambar* and *Nyssa sylvatica* provide autumn colour together with the red twigs of a *Cornus*.

A small vegetable plot set out in six-foot-wide beds with grass paths, so that no deep digging is required, provides most of the vegetables needed in the house. All this is supported by a greenhouse and cold frames.

Herbaceous plants and roses grow in happy profusion in the garden at Greatham Mill, near Liss. For a description of this garden see page 84.

Rotherfield Park, East Tisted
SIR JAMES AND LADY SCOTT

This is a large garden on top of a windy hill five hundred feet up, and is glad of at least partial shelter from the south-west winds! There are spacious lawns with splendid old trees, especially sweet chestnut, while two fine *Cryptomeria japonica* and several wellingtonias represent the conifers, together with some swamp cypresses, *Taxodium distichum*; these flourish in well-drained soil and provide splendid autumn colour. A variety of young trees planted within the past fifteen years now take the place of old friends. There are fine views to the east across a well-planted landscape towards the village church, and beyond to Noar Hill, near the village of Selborne.

Features include a pond with banks planted with shrubs to provide interest and reduce a bad wind tunnel and a secluded rose garden with an ornamental pool, where on calm summer days it is so quiet that the snails can be heard munching away on the water lily leaves. The old walls of the kitchen garden provide shelter for many trained fruit trees and other plants; an attractive cross of grass paths is lined from east to west with espalier apples and from north to south by herbaceous borders. The entrance is through splendid wrought iron gates; a Georgian sundial stands astride the grass paths and there is an alcove, a fine example of Victorian brickwork, at the far end.

The glasshouses contain various climbers, two fan-trained apricots and a seasonal succession of pot plants. A mist-propagating unit is of great benefit in rooting cuttings and provides fast, even germination of many seeds. Near the house are more old roses; one rather gaunt hybrid musk has *Stephanandra tanakae* planted (by accident) in front of it. As they grow and bloom together each complements the other.

Stratfield Saye House
HOME OF THE DUKES OF WELLINGTON

American, rose and walled gardens, a pinetum, and a camellia house reputedly designed by Paxton are just some of the attractions here. In addition, the pleasure grounds are planted with fine trees.

The Vyne, Sherborne St John
THE NATIONAL TRUST

A beautiful garden in a riverside setting, with extensive lawns, a lake, fine trees and herbaceous borders. The walled garden contains many interesting plants, and the roses are especially good.

The Weir House, Alresford
MR AND MRS JOSEPH ADDISON

The Weir House garden consists of three and a half acres of lawns and flower beds bordered by the clean, fast-flowing waters of the River Arle and including a walled rose garden through which runs a carrier stream. Snowdrops and daffodils are a joy in the early part of the season.

Autumn in the Spring Wood at Hackwood Park. For a description of this garden see page 85.

HAMPSHIRE (SOUTH) AND THE ISLE OF WIGHT

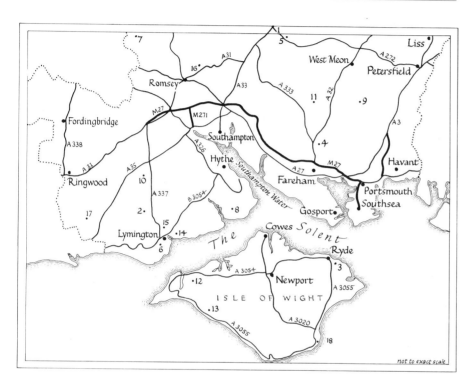

Directions to Gardens

Brockenhurst Park, Brockenhurst, New Forest. [2]

Cedar Lodge, Puckpool Hill, Ryde, Isle of Wight. [3]

Chantry, 11 Acres Road, 1 mile east of Wickham, 4 miles north of Fareham. [4]

Cheriton Cottage, Cheriton, 3 miles south of Alresford. [5]

Culverlea House, Pennington Common, 1 mile west of Lymington. [6]

The Drove, West Tytherley, 10 miles east of Salisbury, Wilts. [7]

Exbury Gardens, Exbury, 2½ miles southeast of Beaulieu, 15 miles southwest of Southampton. [8]

Fairfield House, Hambledon, 10 miles southwest of Petersfield. [9]

Furzey Gardens, Minstead, 8 miles southwest of Southampton. [10]

Holywell, Swanmore, midway between Wickham and Droxford. [11]

Kingsmead, Kingsgate Road, Winchester. [1]

Ningwood Manor, 3 miles east of Yarmouth, Isle of Wight. [12]

Owl Cottage, Hoxall Lane, Mottistone, 9 miles southwest of Newport, Isle of Wight. [13]

Pylewell Park, 2½ miles east of Lymington beyond Isle of Wight car ferry. [14]

Spinners, School Lane, Boldre, 1½ miles north of Lymington. [15]

28 Straight Mile, Ampfield, 2 miles east of Romsey. [16]

Withy Dell, Valley Lane, Thorney Hill, Bransgore, midway between Ringwood and Christchurch. [17]

Yaffles, Bonchurch, 1 mile east of Ventnor, Isle of Wight. [18]

Brockenhurst Park, Brockenhurst
THE HON. MRS DENIS BERRY AND MR AND MRS RICHARD BERRY

The garden was started in about 1777 when the Morant family came here. Some of the trees that they planted over the next hundred years have grown to an immense girth rather than height, possibly as this is the highest point around, though only a hundred and ten feet above sea level. Alan Mitchell's measurements in 1979 of the girths included *Cedrus libani* (16 ft 8 ins), *Ginkgo biloba* (6 ft 1 inch), *Pinus sylvestris* (15 ft), *Sequoia sempervirens* (16 ft), *Sequoiadendron giganteum* (17 ft 8 ins), *Magnolia acuminata* (9 ft 4 ins), *Tilia europaea* (14 ft 2 ins) and *Tilia platyphyllos* 'Laciniata' (4 ft 1 inch). There is also a very attractive many-trunked deodar cedar and a cork oak with five trunks.

In the 1860s the Morants made an Italian garden, some of the wonderful layout of which remains, including the long canal with a double flight of steps leading to another pool. There is yew topiary with some golden yew grafted on to the ordinary yew on either side of the canal and flanked by bay hedges. There are also many bay, *Quercus ilex*, oak, laurel, hornbeam and yew hedges, all forming different 'rooms' and 'corridors'.

We came here in 1960 when the garden had become completely overgrown. Sixteen woodmen, working for six weeks, cleared the garden, and two tree surgeons operated on sixty trees. The ponds were cleared out and repaired and most of the hedges had to be cut to the ground. A new lawn was laid in front of the new house, which was built on the same site as the old one. I extended the garden to about nine acres and have done a lot of planting of trees and shrubs every year. As it is acid soil on gravel, with a clay subsoil, rhododendrons and azaleas make the biggest impact, but I have planted so that there should be something in flower the whole year, as well as being easy to maintain.

It is a woodland garden, with some formal layout, within beautiful undulating old parkland. It is a great pleasure to me and I hope also to all our visitors who come to see it. The best garden tip, I think, is the old saying 'A shilling for the plant and a pound for the planting'.

Cedar Lodge, Ryde
MR AND MRS GEORGE HARRIS

The protective influence of many mature trees and the mild maritime climate has enabled a great variety of the more tender trees and shrubs to thrive in this four-acre garden. The luxuriant growth which is evident everywhere has helped to create a series of secluded but interconnecting areas flowing naturally from woodland to open aspect and then on to a water-garden. The terraced area with its fountains around the house is clothed in springtime with the lambent blue blooms of a massive *Wisteria sinensis*.

Of the mature trees the outstanding specimens are a giant cedar of Lebanon, a weeping beech, *Fagus sylvatica* 'Pendula', and a cork oak, *Quercus suber*. The most striking of all is possibly the unusually large free-standing *Magnolia grandiflora*. A variety of other mature and vigorously growing magnolias flourish here also, including *Magnolia campbellii*, *M.×veitchii*, *M. hypoleuca*, *M. wilsonii* and *M. sieboldii*, whilst the foxglove tree, *Paulownia tomentosa*, has reached a prodigious height and is quite spectacular in bloom.

Acacia dealbata in its vigour grows almost like a weed, whilst *A. armata*, *A. longifolia* and *A. pravissima* thrive here also in their more sheltered positions. The small butter-yellow flowers of a banksian rose positioned together with the clear blue of a *Ceanothus* on a south-facing boundary wall, burst into bloom prolifically in late spring in a most pleasing combination of colour and form. Within the garden are mature specimens of *Hoheria populnea*, *Hoheria sexstylosa*, *Drimys winteri*, *Pittosporum tobira*, the pink bottlebrush *Callistemon speciosum*, *Crinodendron hookerianum*, *Liquidambar styraciflua*, *Parrotia persica* and the aptly named golden rain tree *Koelreuteria paniculata*.

Although the garden represents a varied and extensive collection of plants, trees and shrubs from a great many parts of the world, careful siting and exuberant growth has enabled them all to blend together with charming and natural effect.

Chantry, Wickham
ADMIRAL SIR GEOFFREY AND LADY NORMAN

My husband and I started to convert the garden from a gorse and bracken hill-top in 1948. It has been a haphazard business without any overall plan but we have gradually learnt as we gained more experience, and our children helped us build the walls and patios.

Owing to our acid soil spring is our best time, with drifts of azaleas, camellias and rhododendrons but we also have a wonderful show of *Lilium tigrinum* and *Agapanthus* 'Headbourne' hybrids in August.

I find that men are better than women at juxtaposition of the contrasting colour and shapes of shrubs and women better at growing flowers – I have great fun growing plants from seeds and cuttings. I stratify the seeds in the winter and now have about fifty camellias flowering gaily which I have grown from seed. Owing to my husband's and my combined ages of one hundred and seventy years and no paid gardener, we try to keep down the work, but I still can't resist planting about fifty-four boxes of seedlings every year. We do have a friend who comes to help us most Saturday afternoons; he does any really heavy work and has greatly improved by his design a really dreary bit of land.

We have had great success lighting up a dark corner with a variegated poplar which I cut back savagely to about five feet high, and which is covered with white and pink leaves all the summer. We also have an extraordinary double *Camellia* which produces flowers of many different colours and is, I am told, a 'sport'; it came from Ireland, so perhaps that explains all!

Cheriton Cottage, Nr Alresford
MR AND MRS I. GARNETT-ORME

The garden of about four acres is situated on the edge of this beautiful village. The upper reaches of the Itchen run through the garden and the soil is light, overlaying chalk.

Some specimen trees, now mature, were planted on three sides of the garden by the steward of the Tichborne estate in the mid nineteenth century when he was living in the house. These include the weeping silver lime, the blue cedar and the weeping beech. Further trees have been planted during the last thirty-five years, including fern-leaved and Dawyck beech, sugar maple, fastigiate tulip tree and the lime *Tilia × euchlora*.

To the north the view across water-meadows and permanent pastures slopes upwards, and this combination forms a framework for the garden in which fine lawns link trees and shrub borders with the river.

Spring bulbs abound, amongst which are *Cyclamen coum*, *Eranthis × tubergeniana*, as well as *E. hyemalis*, *Scilla tubergeniana*, followed by *Scilla* 'Spring Beauty'. Drifts of snowdrops continue over a long flowering period ending with a group of *Galanthus plicatus* 'Warham'. *Narcissus* thrive, including some early miniature hybrids. Wherever possible all deciduous trees are underplanted with early-flowering bulbs.

Clematis flower from spring to autumn in association with other plants, for example *Rosa rugosa* 'Agnes' adjacent to yellow irises and *Clematis* 'Lasurstern'. Climbing roses, *Viburnum*, *Philadelphus*, *Alstroemeria ligtu* hybrids and lilies are prominent among the summer-flowering plants and bulbs.

The native flora is encouraged and the snake's head fritillary grows in moist areas. Whatever the season or weather this garden is a welcoming place, loved and cared for over the last hundred years.

Culverlea House, Nr Lymington
BRIG. AND MRS R.A. BLAKEWAY

Some twenty years ago we found this one-acre ex-vicarage garden on a sandy, acid site near the Solent. There was a framework of old trees and lawns and little else, a bare canvas on which to design layouts and plant a wide variety of trees, shrubs and perennials, and to build up a garden with emphasis on colour, variety and contrast.

For colour there are spring bulbs, many annual bedding plants, and roses. We have concentrated on garden merit – trees and shrubs with two or more seasons, or with individual beauty or rarity. Some favourites are *Ostrya carpinifolia* with spring catkins and summer hops; the snow gum *Eucalyptus niphophila*, and the snowdrop tree *Halesia monticola*, lovely against a blue sky; a little variegated oak *Quercus cerris* 'Variegata' and a copper beech 'Roseomarginata' with purple, pink-edged leaves.

For contrast we have rung the changes with colour, shape and size. *Pittosporum tenuifolium* 'Purpureum', hardy with us, is a most useful evergreen to contrast with the yellows.

Cheriton Cottage in July, with lavender, *Stachys lanata*, and *Geranium psilostemon* in the foreground, and a beautiful weeping silver lime *Tilia* 'Petiolaris', seen across the lawn.

Rhododendron lepidostylum nestling under a *R.×loderi* demonstrate extremes of size. In order to give a feeling of space in a small garden we have made long straight paths ending in focal points, to contrast with enclosed secret gardens.

We have planted hundreds of roses; for beauty, for scent, for sentiment (*R. gallica*, 'Albertine' and many more), for foliage, for picking – roses old and new, from 'Canary Bird' in early May to, with luck, a bunch on Christmas Day. Roses in formal beds are mixed with lilies and shrubs, and clamber up trees. We also have collections of maples, camellias, rhododendrons and magnolias; a small vegetable garden, *Cyclamen* and invasive bluebells and lilies-of-the-valley under the trees. Finally, a fish pond, sandpit, and see-saw for grandchildren, buddlejas for butterflies and *Umbellularia californica* for the Duchess who faints.

Ningwood Manor in July; *Galega officinalis, Artemisia, Lychnis* and *Holcus mollis* 'Variegata', backed by *Rosa filipes* 'Kiftsgate', jasmine and *Populus × candicans* 'Aurora', around a green glazed jar.

cedars of Lebanon and a fine spreading copper beech dominate the approach up the drive.

The owners came here in 1970 and have redesigned and planted the whole garden. Roses and other climbers clothe the house, canopy and verandah, while nearby borders provide other interest. On the east side of the house high walls with climbers and mixed borders enclose a small lawn and a Mount Etna broom screens a vine house producing two hundred bunches of grapes each season.

The main lawn on the south-west side sweeps up the slope beside a railed meadow to mown paths that wind their way through longer grass into the walled garden above the house. This contains a collection of large free-standing and shrub and species roses, interspersed with flowering trees, and contrasting mixed borders which include a variety of shrubs and plants. From the top there is a lovely view across the valley to the beech hanger. Below, a swimming pool and tennis court are designed to blend with the garden by use of old brick for paving and retaining walls combined with informal planting, a pergola and climbers on the netting between brick pillars. An excellent map and key identify all the roses in the garden – some sixty climbing and about a hundred shrub roses, which are at their best from mid-June to mid-July. A wonderful display of bulbs, with drifts of daffodils in all parts of the garden, is worth a spring visit.

The owners maintain the whole garden themselves with a helper for one day a week.

The Drove, West Tytherley
MR AND MRS T.H. FABER

When we moved house and garden in 1980, we were faced with a heavy clay soil, and a garden that had been cleverly designed, originally, but was sadly neglected. The problem of coping with the clay, and finding out which plants grow best, has been a question of trial and error, and one learns by one's mistakes!

Roses are the joy – a hedge of bourbon 'Honorine de Brabant' filled out to a height of five feet in three years; a bed of 'Evelyn Fison' with 'Iceberg' floribundas has a carpet of *Viola cornuta* spreading beneath, their little faces turned towards the sun. In the same bed *Rosa* 'Complicata' is climbing up a bullace tree.

The small lake, dug out of the clay, is a home for wildlife: goldfish and golden orfe breed prolifically, and grass carp are hopefully feeding on the pond weed, while avoiding the waterlilies! Toads and frogs migrate to breed in the spring, and the summer sun brings out dragonflies and damsel flies, hovering around the water like miniature helicopters; mallard nest on the island. The two smaller ponds lead to a boggy patch, planted with *Iris sibirica*, where the Spotted Orchid has naturalized itself. Besides roses, azaleas, potentillas, hydrangeas, *Weigela* and

Deutzia, many other shrubs and plants grow well. Though they seem to take two or three years to get well established, there is the advantage that the ground retains moisture in a period of drought. We dig in as much compost as we can lay hands on, as well as mulching beds with rotted-down grass mowings, leaves and other garden waste, to prevent the ground drying and cracking.

Exbury Gardens, Exbury
EDMUND DE ROTHSCHILD, ESQ.

Over two hundred acres of woodland garden incorporate the famous Rothschild collection of azaleas, rhododendrons, magnolias, camellias and maples. There are also many other interesting specimen trees, and a recently restored two-acre rock garden.

Fairfield House, Hambledon
MR AND MRS PETER WAKE

The Regency house is surrounded by four and a half acres of garden on a south-facing slope beneath a chalk down. Extensive walls, mature limes, beeches and yew afford protection from cold winds off the downland. Three

Furzey Gardens, Minstead

Furzey Gardens were planned in 1922 and laid out thereafter. Much of the soil was brought in by horse and cart, to enable the various trees and shrubs that are grown here to thrive.

This is an informal garden with meandering paths and many wild flowers, including anemones and orchids. In spring crocuses, snowdrops, bluebells and daffodils, including *Narcissus cyclamineus* which have happily seeded themselves into large drifts under the birch trees, are a delight. The heather, for which these gardens are well known, blooms all year round, including, in winter, our own *Erica* 'Furzey'. The rhododendrons and azaleas make a most spectacular show, with many interesting species and varieties from the large *R. macabeanum* to the fragrant deciduous azalea, *R. luteum*. Of special interest are the South American *Embothrium coccineum*, the six varieties of *Eucryphia* and the Australian *Callistemon* all of which appreciate our mild climate and sheltered aspect.

Holywell, Swanmore
THE LADY RHYL

Holywell garden covers about four acres and

was redesigned in 1964. Being on lime-free soil, it grows what we want, except for wall-flowers, which it rudely rejects! The herb garden is about thirty yards from the house, and can be reached dry-shod; it is surrounded by a circular hornbeam hedge. The scent of camphor reminds one of one's youth, while *Calycanthus*, the allspice, suggests roast beef. We also planted sweet briar and honeysuckle tucked away in the corners of this garden, so the scent is intoxicating in the summer months.

Nearby is an old red brick wall about ten foot high. Here the 'Albertine' roses gladly accept *Clematis*. It is pretty seeing 'Lasurstern' and 'Comtesse de Bouchaud' pushing their way through the roses but *C*. 'Henryi', the lovely white *Clematis*, has its special corner on the wall so as to avoid any interference. Close by is a double pergola, covered by vines, which are certainly over thirty years old. They still produce nasty little grapes, but are forgiven, because of the vine's lovely autumn colour. Nearby in a sheltered corner, grows *Nyssa sylvatica*, the lovely foliage of which turns orange, yellow and a rich scarlet in autumn. I believe the only way to propagate this tree is from seed.

We now approach the woodland garden which is guarded by a line of pine trees and oaks, and beech and sycamore are dotted about; amongst them we planted rhododendrons, camellias, azaleas, *Pieris forrestii* and magnolias. In May the wild bluebells take over and make a startling background. Near the house is a large old *Rhododendron*; after flowering is finished it looks rather dull, so we planted seeds of *Tropaeolum speciosum* and now after three years it covers the *Rhododendron* with scarlet flowers in mid-summer.

Kingsmead, Winchester
MR AND MRS HOPKINSON

We had the advantage of beginning our garden with a half-acre of bindweed and ground elder, as well as four sycamores, whose seeding propensities we have cursed ever since. One of our daughters, Lucy Huntington, a garden architect by calling, drew up a plan which we have gradually carried into effect over the last twelve years, modifying it as opportunity suggested – a peat bed, for instance, since our soil is river gravel over chalk, and a pool and marsh for the asiatic primulas.

A flint wall facing south provided suitably for the greenhouse, peaches, vines and melons, as well as for sun-loving plants from Australia, such as the delightful 'Paroo Lily' *Dianella tasmanica*, and the strange *Raoulia hookeri*. With a relatively small garden, one must aim at interesting (if sometimes difficult) individual plants rather than at massed effects, but by designing paths which twist and turn through shrub roses and in and out of the shade, it is possible to provide quite dramatic surprises – for instance *Cornus controversa*, shining as if lit by Christmas candles,

and miniature forests of the various hostas and euphorbias, together with five varieties of Solomon's seal.

We also have a bed where every plant has pink or red foliage, another where all the inmates have either white flowers or silver leaves, and a collection of oddities, amongst them the *Convallaria majalis* 'Variegata' and 'Rosea', a white celandine, and the green rose 'Viridiflora'.

We were lucky in that a sunk terrace round two sides of the house has made room for a rock garden where plants really can sprawl over each other, with such climbers as *Clematis texensis* and *Rosa banksiae* for company with a range of gentians and *Geranium* species. But perhaps our overall objective is that of the Chinese gardener – 'the immense within the minute, a mountain range from three stones, and the ocean in a pond'.

Ningwood Manor, Yarmouth
LT.-COL. AND MRS K.J. SHAPLAND

The gardens of Ningwood lie in two acres surrounded by magnificent views of the Island downs. Mellow brick walls and mature hedges of yew, bay and holly divide the gardens into rooms with the honey-coloured stone house forming the backdrop. The Georgian front is enhanced by an ancient pair of treasured *Magnolia grandiflora*. The clipped box hedges give the walled garden great character. One half is shaded by the feathery foliage of *Robinia pseudoacacia* and the other has two large fig trees growing against the walls. Here there is a selection of choice plants and a mass of bulbs to tempt us out in the early spring. Eventually the flowers of *Chimonanthus praecox*, opposite the french windows, will brighten a winter's day. Meanwhile we enjoy the purple berries of *Callicarpa giraldiana* and the vivid yellow splashes of *Hedera* 'Paddy's Pride'. The focal point of our new golden bed on the front lawn is the distinctive sundial, at whose foot, by happy chance, golden creeping jenny meanders through *Allium moly* and the yellow variegated forms of *Hosta* and *Iris*, creating a marvellous effect in May and June.

In the rose garden we have retained the traditional Victorian design of a circular bed surrounded by four crescent-shaped beds. The roses are interplanted with perennials and standing sentinel on the outskirts are twenty-seven climbing roses. The show-stopper of the white garden is an arbour fashioned by such climbing plants as white *Wisteria*, jasmine, *Clematis*, *Chaenomeles*, *Solanum*, *Rosa* 'Kiftsgate' and *Passiflora* 'Constance Elliott'. Underneath this canopy a green-glazed pot is planted with such tender treasures as white *Plumbago* and variegated *Coprosma*. Gravel paths line the garden which is home for a large variety of white-flowered and silver and variegated plants. Many old favourites mingle with rarities, they have all been selected to give continual interest, but September is the prettiest time.

Owl Cottage, Mottistone
MRS A.L. HUTCHINSON AND MISS S.L. LEANING

This seventeenth-century cottage was purchased from the National Trust, and it stands in an area of great natural beauty.

The garden is almost an acre in size and colour is the chief theme, though there is a great variety of interesting plants as one of the owners is a well-known flower arranger, who has a keen colour sense. There is one corner which is particularly lovely in summer; *Clematis* 'Madame Julia Correvon' intertwines with *Lonicera* 'Belgica', at the base of which is a large bed of *Alstroemeria ligtu* hybrids. At the ends of the bed are the very dainty *Campanula lactiflora* 'Prichard's Variety' flowers. We have outstanding views out to sea and up to the local forest. The garden is kept essentially as a cottage garden and this, I think, is one reason for its popularity with visitors. On two occasions we have had over four hundred visitors in one afternoon.

Other interesting plants include Japanese flowering cherries, among which is a wonderful specimen of *Prunus × yedoensis* 'Pendula'; I also have six or seven old-fashioned shrub roses.

*Pylewell Park, Nr Lymington
W. WHITAKER, ESQ.

The present garden is mostly the creation of my father, who inherited Pylewell as a young man in 1892. He started to take an interest in it immediately and continued to improve it until his death in 1936.

Owl Cottage, Mottistone, in July. The red *viticella* hybrid *Clematis* 'Mme Julia Correvon' combined with roses, *Alstroemeria ligtu* hybrids and *Campanula trachelium*, the nettle-leaved bell-flower.

Before his day there was, I think, only a rather elaborate parterre to the south of the house, now considerably simplified, and this was connected to the walled kitchen garden by a walk planted with a few shrubs. There was an herbaceous border outside the walled garden and that was about all that the garden consisted of except for the lake, constructed by a previous owner about the year 1820, which does not seem to have been connected with the garden in any way.

My father was mainly interested in flowering shrubs and particularly in rhododendrons. He started by planting up the area between the kitchen garden and the lake which had previously been a paddock used by the keeper for rearing pheasants. This was planted with shrubs of all sorts including some of the earliest Japanese cherries, which he brought back from a trip to Japan in about 1894. Unfortunately, there are none of these left, the last one having died off about seven years ago. There are also a number of other interesting shrubs; several varieties of *Cornus*, *Eucryphia* of all sorts, an exceptionally large *Photinia serrulata* (well over thirty feet high, I would guess) and many other rather tender plants, all of which are underplanted with daffodils.

He then started to plant up the woods each side of the lake with rhododendrons and azaleas and, in what must have been a boggy area above the existing lake, he made a lily-pond which flows into the large lake.

The area between the house and the walled garden was also improved by planting more shrubs and a great many bulbs and by building a wall facing south, along which tender shrubs were planted and where they still flourish.

The chief beauty of Pylewell lies in its situation, best seen from the house with the park sloping down to the Solent and vistas cut through the trees giving views to the Isle of Wight.

◆

Spinners, Boldre
MR AND MRS P.G.G. CHAPPELL

We bought a derelict stables in the New Forest in 1959 in an area of oak woodland. The top of the garden is on New Forest gravel which, after a drop of some thirty feet, gives over to solid clay often with very little topsoil. The latter area had to be drained – water lay in many of the depressions from October to May – and resoiled without making it too dry for moisture-loving plants. Clearing the woodland and planting with trees and shrubs took from 1961 to 1971 when the garden could be seen roughly in its present shape.

The aim was to create a garden in a wood rather than the typical English spring woodland garden. Early in the year rhododendrons, camellias, azaleas and magnolias do predominate but a large collection of lacecap hydrangeas provides interest during the summer and Japanese maples and other foliage

shrubs make a contribution right through the season. Between these shrubs are planted primulas, *Meconopsis*, hellebores, geraniums, irises, hostas and many other choice shade-loving plants. Of the bulbous plants perhaps erythroniums and trilliums should be singled out.

In the open area there is maquis-style planting of mixed shrubs and herbaceous beds and a small arboretum including a *Eucalyptus* grove. Visitors enjoy our primula dell. Here the yellow *P. helodoxa* and the pastel shades of the *P. bulleyana* hybrids are complemented by the blues of Himalayan poppies. Substance is given by rodgersias and ferns. A single plant of *Hosta sieboldiana* 'Elegans' eight feet across, lords it over all.

◆

28 Straight Mile, Ampfield
MRS D.C. ROWAN

We have made this garden since 1962 from a woodland of beech, oak and birch, which had been left untouched since it provided temporary cover for American troops awaiting D-day. Dense brambles and head-high bracken have been cleared, and birches thinned, to make woodland paths and to open a view across farmland to the south.

To our original planting of twelve rhododendrons and azaleas we have added many raised from cuttings, or grown from seed, some self-seeded. The soil is acid, with a pH of 6, so that maples, camellias and *Pieris* also flourish. The *japonica* camellias 'Adolphe Audusson' and 'Jupiter' have made fine specimens on the house walls and many of the × *williamsii* varieties are growing in the garden. Among the maples, *Acer pseudoplatanus* 'Brilliantissimum' is a splendid sight in spring with its shrimp-pink foliage. In late April, magnolias and amelanchiers complement the 'blue' rhododendrons and daffodils. Very fine specimens of *Rhododendron yakushimanum* and *Pieris* 'Wakehurst' always attract attention in May. Hostas grow particularly well in the damper parts and we divide these in early April, although larger varieties such as 'Frances Williams' can safely be split as late as July.

A rose bed was abandoned when deer persisted in invading from adjacent woodland to nip the young shoots; amongst the survivors are a few shrub roses.

Weed control is achieved by growing *Tiarella*, *Cornus canadensis*, *Vinca* and other ground-cover plants, and also by very gradual development – new areas are not opened up until plants which have outgrown their original positions need more space. We tame a little more each year and now cultivate about one and a half acres.

Although predominantly a spring garden, later interest comes from hardy perennials such as *Hemerocallis*, while sheets of *Cyclamen hederifolium* are in flower in September. Foliage plants, golden and variegated, play a great part and are always sought after.

Withy Dell, Bransgore
MRS MARY HOLMES

This garden, started twenty years ago as an escape from a busy working life in London, consisted of a third of an acre of slightly acid clay soil below a derelict thatched cottage. It was cleared of its jungle of briars and docks and planted for tranquillity and easy maintenance. The garden slopes southwards from the cottage to a green valley, all too often now hidden by the newly cultivated jungle, for we treasure some of our self-sown weeds. There is a backdrop of tall trees – the edge of the New Forest – and no other houses are visible from the terrace along the front of the cottage which backs on to a gravel lane. Shrubs and trees were planted, well away from the house, so that the sloping lawns give a sense of space and quietness, the plantings merging with the Forest beyond, giving an added sense of space. There are bulbs and ground-cover plants between the shrubs, and the stream that flows around two sides of the garden feeds a small pond and ensures that the garden is always green.

It is at its best in spring, with azaleas, rhododendrons and camellias interspersed with other shrubs and herbaceous plants designed to give a variety of shape and foliage, together with haunts for the many birds that frequent the garden.

Since the cottage became a permanent home, a greenhouse and three raised beds have been added making it possible to grow a few more delicate or demanding plants, but the emphasis is still on peacefulness and easy maintenance; a good place for a quiet cup of tea.

◆

Yaffles, Bonchurch
MRS J. WOLFENDEN

Yaffles garden has been wrested from a tumbledown cliff which lay at a precipitous 70° and was clothed in bindweed, sycamore saplings, sow thistle, sloe, hawthorn, stinging nettles and butterburr – this is not to mention some overgrown lowering Victorian shrubs.

The cliff was tackled with a mattock, toil and sweat, and terraced into a manageable set of glades with sheer drops. The loose earth and rocks were formed into a deep bed at the foot of the cliff, with a rough wall planted with creepers and alpines.

Chalky soil has limited the plants used to reclothe it and still the bindweed prospers. However, each year a little more chalk and ragstone is clad in beauty. The aim is to have at least one plant at its very best during each week of the year and to encourage outstanding wild flowers to thrive with their more exotic neighbours.

The best thing the garden offers is the spectacular view over the tips of a bowl of deciduous trees, seen below, and away to the English Channel.

HEREFORDSHIRE AND WORCESTERSHIRE

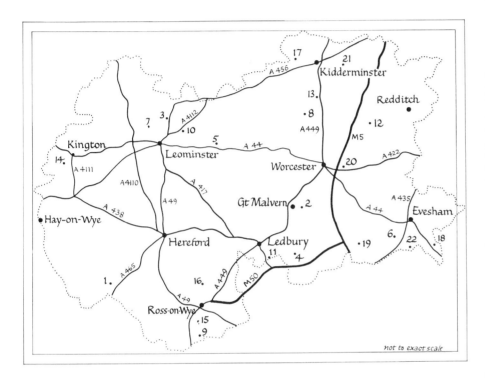

not to exact scale

Directions to Gardens

Abbey Dore Court, 11 miles southwest of Hereford. [1]

Barnard's Green House, 10 Poolbrook Road, Malvern. [2]

Berrington Hall, 4 miles north of Leominster. [3]

Birtsmorton Court, near Malvern, 7 miles east of Ledbury on A438. [4]

Bredenbury Court (St Richards), Bredenbury, 3 miles west of Bromyard on A44. [5]

Bredon Springs, Paris, Ashton-under-Hill, 6 miles southwest of Evesham. [6]

Croft Castle, 5 miles northwest of Leominster. [7]

Eastgrove Cottage Garden Nursery, Sankyns Green, near Little Witley, 4 miles southwest of Stourport. [8]

Glen Wye, Courtfield, 5 miles south of Ross-on-Wye. [9]

Grantsfield, near Kimbolton, 3 miles northeast of Leominster. [10]

Haffield, 3 miles south of Ledbury, off M50 at exit 2. [11]

Hanbury Hall, Hanbury, 3 miles northeast of Droitwich. [12]

Hartlebury Castle, Hartlebury, south of Kidderminster on A449. [13]

Hergest Croft Gardens, Kington, 20 miles northwest of Hereford. [14]

The Hill Court, 2¾ miles southwest of Ross-on-Wye. [15]

How Caple Court, How Caple, 5 miles north of Ross-on-Wye. [16]

Loen, Long Bank, 2 miles west of Bewdley. [17]

The Orchard Farm, Broadway on A44. [18]

Overbury Court, 5 miles northeast of Tewkesbury. [19]

The Priory, Kemerton, 4 miles northeast of Tewkesbury. [19]

Spetchley Park, 3 miles east of Worcester. [20]

Stone House Cottage Gardens, Stone, 2 miles southeast of Kidderminster. [21]

Witley Park House, Great Witley, 9 miles northwest of Worcester. [8]

Wormington Grange, 4 miles west of Broadway. [22]

◆

Abbey Dore Court, Hereford
MRS C.L. WARD

The four acres of Abbey Dore Court garden have evolved rather than been planned. When we came in 1967, there was so much to clear that we couldn't imagine that we would ever finish the work, let alone open the garden to visitors. We are fortunate in having a river, the Dore, and several mature trees, including two *Sequoiadendron giganteum* in the middle of a lawn. The river enabled us to make a pond and rock garden four years ago, in a field facing the house, and here a bank of over thirty different varieties of *Salix* flourish. Nearby are *Meconopsis betonicifolia*, *M. nepalensis*, *M. quintuplinervia* and *M. horridula*, and a large patch of *Digitalis × mertonensis* which looks well with the blue of the Himalayan poppies.

We have large clumps of *Eremurus himalaicus* and *E. robustus*, the latter growing through bronze fennel and white *Potentilla fruticosa*. Groups of *Camassia cusickii* have finished but were most welcome in a rather lean spell and there are great patches of *Thalictrum aquilegiifolium* with flowers ranging in shades from dark purple to white. These have seeded themselves freely and blend easily with various shrubs. The yellow and orange Welsh poppies, *Meconopsis cambrica*, are doing the same in an area full of ferns, and light up a shady place. Hardy geraniums in many different varieties and colours are scattered all over the garden. Plants frequently seed and often the result is better than anything I could have planned though the misfits do get removed. We have striven to produce a garden that radiates softness and harmony; I hope we have succeeded.

◆

Barnard's Green House, Malvern
MR AND MRS PHILIP NICHOLLS

This garden, set in three acres against the majestic backdrop of the Malvern hills, has evolved over many years. Its main feature is a magnificent cedar, though there is also a variety of unusual trees and shrubs. A riot of many different types of daffodil, with anemones and bluebells, fills the woodland and cedar border in spring, and the herbaceous border is colourful both in summer and autumn. There is a large heather bed, an area filled with mature trees, and a vegetable garden in which the owners grow flowers for

Birtsmorton Court in early July. The yew topiary garden is surrounded by ancient walls and mixed borders, newly planted with old roses, paeonies, *Phlox*, pinks and delphiniums. The modern wrought-iron gate at the end of this vista is an elegant surprise.

drying as well as vegetables. The garden, which is fairly level, is divided into several smaller gardens, each with its own character, so that everyone will surely find something of interest somewhere.

Berrington Hall, Nr Leominster
THE NATIONAL TRUST

Capability Brown set Berrington Hall in parkland of four hundred and fifty-five acres. The fourteen-acre lake, with a flourishing heronry, graces the near view, and in the distance, the clarity of the Black Mountains heralds the approaching weather. Successive generations of inspirational owners, and the eventual gift of the property in 1957 to the National Trust, have produced an interesting combination of the formal style, and personal favourites, among the plants thriving here.

In the early part of the year, snowdrops and *Cyclamen coum* lighten the woodland garden, where recent *Rhododendron* planting has taken place, and a later showing of the herbaceous plants *Geranium*, *Hosta*, *Pulmonaria*, *Meconopsis* and flowering shrubs can be enjoyed. On the sunny south wall we sport a wonderful specimen of the marrow-related *Thladiantha oliveri*, which at its height threatens the growth of more delicate climbers – *Buddleja colvilei* and *Solanum crispum* 'Glasnevin' – while further along, hundred-year-old wisterias are trained to form an archway of a

soft cloudy blue. Other climbers here of rarity and interest are *Abutilon × suntense*, and in October, the small yellow-flowering *Senecio scandens*. In the secluded walled drying ground our *Camellia* collection shelters and grows, and recent first blossomings of *Campsis*, and of *Davidia involucrata*, the handkerchief tree, have produced great excitement.

Birtsmorton Court, Nr Malvern
N.G.K. DAWES, ESQ.

The Court is completely surrounded by a large moat which immediately establishes the atmosphere of the place and, with the house, forms the focus of the garden. Each quarter of the garden is planned to come into its full glory in a different season. The east corner has drifts of spring bulbs, primroses, violets and cowslips growing in their natural habitat under the silver birch trees.

Summer belongs to the old-fashioned herbaceous borders behind which walls, dating from Elizabethan times, form a backdrop, and where shrub rose plantings have recently been added. The nineteenth-century topiary forms the other side of the herbaceous walk where the delicious smells of summer can be appreciated at their height. As the corn is harvested and one looks to the Malvern hills in the west, one sees the shadows of the trees across the water.

In winter when other parts of the garden

are bare, the specimen evergreens stand out majestically in the north, notably Lawson's cypress, *Thuja plicata*, *C. lawsoniana* 'Erecta' and the *C. nootkatensis* over the church wall. The prize of the garden is the five-hundred-year-old English yew whose spreading branches touch the ground on all sides.

Birtsmorton Court belongs to no single age in history and the character of the garden reflects this. Work in it, has I feel, to be aimed at continuing the mysteries of the past whilst planting for the future.

Bredenbury Court (St Richard's), Bredenbury
HEADMASTER: R.E.H. COGHLAN, ESQ.

The gardens and park were designed by John Adam in 1876 and incorporated thirty acres of formal, semi-formal and woodland areas, within the framework of an estate of several thousand acres. Other features include a deer park, hunt kennels, and many farms, now sold off.

The garden today is park-like in appearance with many fine and mature trees (mostly conifers) and the rose garden, which is now the only formal area, laid out geometrically with a mulberry tree in the centre, the second on the site. *Rosa banksiae* 'Lutea' is climbing the house wall, and *Garrya elliptica* grows well on an exposed corner showing that this shrub is hardier than is sometimes thought.

Bredon Springs, Paris

RONALD SIDWELL, ESQ.

This is the garden of two eighteenth-century cottages and it has been slowly evolving since 1948 at which time it was in a neglected and overgrown state. It is still rather wild and, in the opinion of many, overgrown. The one-and-a-half-acre site is on the lower slopes of Bredon Hill. It consists of steep slopes at top and bottom with a more level area between, and it is on this middle area that the springs emerge. Soils here are mainly calcareous and range from deep light loam to clay loam. We have a large plant collection and most countries in the world are represented. Some of the more tender things such as *Hebe*, *Olearia*, *Ceanothus* and *Myrtus* suffered severely in the 1981–2 winter. More surprising was the outright killing of cotoneasters, stransvaesias and escallonias.

At first glance there seems to be no design in this garden, and it is true that much of it has just happened, as the managed area has increased. There is, however, a fairly constant theme. All of the numerous paths lead somewhere – few paths are quite straight, yet there are no contrived twists or turns. All features are functional, and, it is hoped, appear natural; trees, shrubs and herbaceous plants merge. The natural characteristics of the site determine the planting. There are no herbaceous borders and no island beds.

Three large pear trees date from the beginning of the century, and an old 'Blenheim' apple heavily colonized by mistletoe is probably a hundred years old. These give maturity to the garden. No toxic sprays are used, although safe herbicides are used on paths and some odd corners. Insect pests are kept under control by birds, at least twenty-eight species of which have nested in the garden in recent years, twenty-two being regular breeders. Most forms of wild life are tolerated and even encouraged, but rabbits go too far on occasions and have to be dealt with. It will be seen that this is not just a garden of tidy flower beds and neatly edged lawns. It is a garden where the Schweitzer philosophy of Reverence for Life is never far away.

◆

Croft Castle, Nr Leominster

THE NATIONAL TRUST

A large garden with borders and a walled garden, specializing in eighteenth-century plants. Fine ancient trees remain in the park, especially avenues of oaks and sweet chestnuts, and there are walks in the fishpool valley.

◆

Eastgrove Cottage Garden Nursery, Sankyns Green

MR AND MRS J. MALCOLM SKINNER

Set down a quiet country lane in five acres of unspoiled meadow and woodland, Eastgrove Cottage, a seventeenth-century half-timbered yeoman's farmhouse, lies in the heart of rural Worcestershire.

The garden contains a collection of old-fashioned cottage plants which evoke childhood memories. How very personal plants are, reminding us of dear friends and loved ones – a continuous thread in life.

We have become aware how restful and pleasing pastel colours are, especially when laced with silver; how much more happily they blend with the surrounding countryside than the more strident tones.

An area which we have enjoyed creating was brought about through the inspirations arising from our various plant-hunting expeditions and the excitement from treasured plants that people have brought to us. The secret garden has a winding herringbone brick path and is packed with very largely pastel plantings and tiny, creeping thymes, and *Mentha requienii* amongst the bricks which give off heavenly scents when crushed underfoot. It is bounded by a small arc of copper beech on one side and an old *Lonicera nitida* hedge is being coaxed to thrive again to enclose the other. Entered by triple arches of climbing roses it promises well, given more time and loving care. We are working on a living, ever-moving picture! We look forward to winter evenings for gleaning more from the masters of our art – Jekyll, Fish and many others. One great concern and maxim will always be uppermost – we must not create more than we can happily look after. A garden should not be a burden, but a continuing joy.

Glen Wye, Courtfield, Nr Ross-on-Wye

MRS J. H. VAUGHAN

When we returned to live at Glen Wye in 1955, we found an overgrown wilderness with virtually no garden. Our first year was spent felling thirty-five sycamores – the only trees worth keeping were half a dozen Scots pines, elegant and lovely against the sky, and two fine old yews – and clearing, burning and digging out a swampy morass of sally bushes which later formed a water garden and swimming pool. The steep slopes lent themselves to walls, terraces and rockeries and we were lucky enough to find a German ex-prisoner of war, a genius with stone, who came to us for a few months every summer, so that over a period of twenty years, an architecturally satisfying garden evolved. In some ways it has become an extension of the house.

The landscape of the Wye valley all around is very green so we introduced many copper and golden trees and shrubs, a wide variety of silver and sun-loving greys, and made a variegated border. The soil is alkaline and being on a slope dries out quickly, so we constantly add peat and compost and only cultivate flowers that enjoy growing here – irises do particularly well, as do all spring bulbs. Evergreen bergenias hug our walls, and we grow a variety of foliage plants, hostas and euphorbias.

There are many different areas, not seen all at once, as a garden should unfold its beauties gradually as one wanders through it; we have terraces, rockeries, rosebeds, and a water

The Priory, Kemerton (for a description see page 98). This pre-Reformation house was on the pilgrim route to the abbeys of Pershore and Tewkesbury.

garden where primulas and bog plants thrive. The latest development is a wild garden leading down to the river; ferns, foxgloves, red campion, primroses, cranesbill, Solomon's seal, bluebells and snowdrops all make it inviting.

We were troubled by moles until a friend gave us the useful tip of sinking bottles in the ground, until gradually the moles disappear. It seems to work!

Grantsfield, Kimbolton
COL. AND MRS J.G.T. POLLEY

This garden needed total replanning when we purchased the property in 1975. It is sited at an elevation of about three hundred feet facing west, and we enjoy wonderful views across the Lugg and Arrow valleys into Wales and Radnor Forest. We had no overall plan and the garden has grown like 'Topsy'. There is something to delight the eye in every season; from *Prunus serrula* var. *tibetica* and other trees with coloured barks in winter, through drifts of spring bulbs and primulas, and the lushness of summer borders to autumn tints and flowering trees – *Prunus subhirtella* 'Autumnalis' amongst others.

The soil is heavy loam which is very productive but needs a lot of humus to lighten it. We have one acre around the house, half of which is given over to vegetables, grapes, soft and top fruit, and the other half to decorative gardens. We also have four acres of commercial fruit, and another four acres are rented to a sheep farmer. We have planted windbreaks around this field, experimenting with a diversity of trees and shrubs. Like most gardeners, we are inveterate collectors and are constantly having to enlarge existing beds or dig new ones to house the latest acquisitions. Two favourite plantings are a red *Chaenomeles* with white *Clematis armandii* against the pink sandstone back walls, and an area devoted to mauvy-pink colours – honesty, lilac, *Clematis montana rubens*, Japanese *Paeonia* 'Sitifukujin' and *Clematis* 'Proteus'. We do not have many bedding plants as they are too labour-intensive but we do have dahlias. Otherwise, the garden provides year-round colour with a minimum of upkeep.

Haffield, Ledbury
MR AND MRS ALAN CADBURY

The approach from the east is through semi-woodland, underplanted with azaleas, rhododendrons, daffodils and primroses, ending in the first glimpse of the pillar-faced house, designed by Sir Robert Smirke in 1815. To the west, in rough grass, are specimen trees, including cherries, magnolias, *Catalpa bignonioides* and a huge *Cryptomeria japonica*. Next to these is a double walled kitchen garden, a square within a square, well-stocked with vegetables, old fruit trees, flowers for cutting, climbing roses and a

beautiful *Wisteria*. In the venerable green-houses are four vines, accompanied by pelargoniums – 'Prince of Denmark', 'Lady Warwick' and 'De Gatta', to name but three – *Plumbago capensis*, *Campsis radicans* and red and orange *Mimulus*. On the way back to the house one walks between island borders, which contain herbaceous plants, such as *Phlox*, *Alstroemeria ligtu* hybrids and paeonies, as well as shrub roses. The south-west of the house is framed by a cedar of Lebanon planted in 1955, the ha-ha, and reputedly the tallest tulip tree in England (which never fails to flower). At first sight the quarry, east of the house, made my heart sink at the thought of taming this area of nettles and brambles. The stone, Haffield breccia, provides a lovely browny-pink background for roses, *Arbutus unedo*, acers, a cut-leaf beech and a magnificent *Vitis coignetiae*. Round the foot of the rock, in a continuous bed, grow rock plants, small shrubs, tulips, lilies and ivy-leaved geraniums, with a lily-pond and a water splash from twenty feet above. Three stone stairways are heavenly for children clambering up to 'Apple Tree Cottage' to play in. The quarry is a challenge, difficult and even hazardous to cultivate, but my chief joy.

Hanbury Hall, Nr Droitwich
THE NATIONAL TRUST

Extensive lawns and shrubberies, and a Victorian forecourt with detailed planting, are of interest in this garden. The beautiful brick orangery, thought to date from 1732, is clad with *Wisteria sinensis*.

Hartlebury Castle
THE RIGHT REV. THE LORD BISHOP OF WORCESTER

The gardens at Hartlebury Castle are much simplified today in comparison to years ago when a great number of staff were employed to keep up different areas. Nearly the same area of garden remains, but under the control of one gardener. The Castle has been the home of the Bishops of Worcester since 1237, and is now divided into the Bishop's private house, the State Rooms and the Hereford and Worcester County Museum.

To the front of the Castle is an impressive circular lawn bordered by roses and a new mixed planting of shrubs and herbaceous plants. Summer heralds a colourful display of mixed bedding. To the east of the chapel is a gravelled walk, known as the 'Elizabethan Walk', since the visit of Queen Elizabeth I in 1575, when she was known to have walked here with the then Bishop Bullingham. The walled border contains many of the species which could have been growing then. There are many herbs, comfrey, irises, poppies and crown imperials; thyme creeps across the walk and scents the air. The wall itself catches all the sun and is an ideal situation for fruit trees.

The orchard, containing mainly apple trees, as well as two very ancient mulberry trees, is alive with wild daffodils in the spring. This is then followed by a mass of colour from the bank of rhododendrons as the year progresses.

Hergest Croft Gardens, Nr Kington
W.L. BANKS, ESQ. AND R.A. BANKS, ESQ.

Hergest Croft is famous as a woodland garden with rhododendrons and azaleas in spring, as well as for its collection of trees. It always surprises me how few visitors come to see it at other times of year when, though less spectacular, the woodlands have much to offer. In summer there are many species roses, including the rampant *Rosa helenae*, thirty feet up a *Ginkgo* tree, and the delicate arching sprays of the Chinese *Rosa moyesii*. In autumn the many maples and birches provide splendid colour together with the brilliant fruits of different *Sorbus* species in a favourable year.

In some ways even more surprising is the scant attention paid to the bulbs and herbaceous plants which give me as much pleasure as the woodland garden. Two borders are particular favourites. The spring border which divides the nineteenth-century kitchen garden runs under an avenue of old apple trees; it starts in early April with daffodils, primroses and auriculas, which are succeeded by grape hyacinths, tulips and the old form of *Anemone fulgens* without the black annular ring, and finally, in early summer, by columbines, paeonies and penstemons. It is a pot pourri of plants, some common, some rare and a source of delight for three months. As the spring border fades into mid-summer sleep, so the parallel herbaceous borders beside it begin to awaken; the first fanfare is sounded by crimson oriental poppies standing proudly above the surrounding plants and looking at their best against a dark and stormy sky. As the summer progresses the shape and colour of the border changes from the varied silhouette of the blues of delphiniums and the frothy white of *Clematis recta* 'Purpurea' interspersed with *Eremurus* and *Allium* to the richer and more rounded shape and tapestry of August highlighted by the papery white of another poppy, the Californian *Romneya tricocalyx*.

There are roses too in the garden, in particular a hedge of the various forms of the Scotch briar *Rosa spinosissima*, beloved by Gertrude Jekyll, almost as lovely in hip as in flower. The garden, in the variety of its plants, reflect the taste and enthusiasms of three generations.

The Hill Court, Ross-on-Wye
CHRISTOPHER ROWLEY, ESQ.

The private gardens extend over two acres to the west and north of this early eighteenth-century red-brick mansion and are bounded by a ha-ha giving on to open parkland. The gardens are laid out on level ground but are exposed to the elements from this aspect, and woodland trees are therefore important in providing protection for a variety of borders.

The area is divided into formal lawns, gravel paths, trimmed yew hedges and herbaceous borders, while the woodland area is underplanted with shrubs. The soil is a sandy clay loam, slightly on the acidic side, and is suitable for rhododendrons and azaleas.

The garden is at its best in spring and early summer when colours and scent excel, and there is continued interest from the first daffodils and primroses in March until the azaleas fade in June. There are also several mature specimens of *Magnolia × soulangiana* and *M. stellata*, while a collection of border pinks has recently been planted along one of the principal walks. An enclosed fountain garden is notable for its symmetrical planting in shades of purple and silver. An unusual feature is the planting of standard *Wisteria sinensis* in the borders, where the mauve-blue flowers are accentuated against a background of *Laburnum vossii*. With the onset of autumn the woodland trees assume their vivid tints.

The walled gardens to the south of the house are now run as a garden centre and are open daily. Of particular interest here is the water garden and the yew walk with spectacular views over the ruins of Goodrich Castle.

A carved dish supported by four dolphins forms a fountain in the garden at Spetchley Park (see over). Behind, *Campanula lactiflora* is planted along the foot of the yew hedges.

How Caple Court, Ross-on-Wye
MR AND MRS PETER LEE

Fourteen years ago my husband inherited a lovely small estate on a bend in the Wye valley. There are two main buildings on the site, which has probably been inhabited since Roman times (there is still a Roman wall in the garden); one is the house, which was mainly rebuilt in the seventeenth century and added to considerably in the late Victorian times, whilst the other is a beautiful church, which is partially Norman and has also been added to over the years.

The original garden covered eleven acres, and my husband's grandfather employed thirteen gardeners to build and care for the gardens. Sadly nothing had been done since the beginning of the war, and only the formal terraces in front of the house still existed in their original state. Everything else seemed to be covered by Christmas trees.

Initially for the first eight years we could only hold the status quo, while the crippling death duties were paid off. We then started to expand outwards from the terraces, and this has been very exciting: we discovered a long terrace down one side of the house, which was covered in over a foot of earth and full of saplings pushing up between the steps and paving stones. The whole of the rest of the garden had become like a jungle. All the yew hedges had grown up and brambles and elders were covering everything. When we

started to clear it with two enthusiastic helpers, we discovered all sorts of exciting treasures: stone benches, water gardens, huge urns, and even some statues. When Alan Bloom came and saw what we had done, he got so carried away that he personally helped us replant some of the area.

We have now rebuilt many of the walls and the major circular pond holds water again! We have replanted about two-thirds of the garden and have cleared the jungle as far as the area which used to be known as 'The Sunken Florentine Gardens'. There is still a vast amount of work involved in the restoration of this garden but it will be surrounded by a covered walk, and its unique style and layout should be a fantastic surprise when it is finished. We have recently been joined by Tim Mowday and have decided to open the gardens to the public. We have also opened a nursery so that people will be able to purchase some of the interesting plants they will see on their way round.

Loen, Long Bank
MR AND MRS S.K. QUAYLE

The date was 1935 and we were planning to marry later that year. We searched in vain for a suitable house, so decided to start from scratch and bought ten acres of Wye Forest. It was a very rough patch and had been coppiced for many years, but there were some mature oaks and a lot of birches, on an acid soil. The first job was to clear enough ground for building a house and we soon found that removing the ancient stumps of oak was a daunting task (there were no bulldozers around then) but with the help of an ex-miner and a lot of gelignite, we cleared enough to start. From the beginning, we decided to keep

the natural undulations and retain a woodland character, so we left a lot of the trees and a screen belt around the perimeter.

It has taken the next fifty years to develop this area, and of course it is never finished. There is always some change to plan and both thinning and planting to do.

A central feature is a water garden with its string of pools and cascades between. In spring this area is aglow with primulas in variety and the pools with waterlilies and other water plants. The arching fronds of *Osmunda regalis* and the uncommon oak fern are to be found on the stream side.

The nature of the soil and site encouraged us to plant ericaceous subjects, so rhododendrons, azaleas, camellias and heathers are to be found in abundance and variety. Much of the area is lawn, which sets off many fine specimens of trees and shrubs. A *Cedrus atlantica* we planted as a sapling is now seventy feet high, while nearby a *Eucryphia* 'Nymansay' at forty feet gives us a fine display in late summer. In pride of place on the lawn is *Fagus sylvatica* 'Asplenifolia', while nearby a *Picea breweriana* looks well but needs another fifty years to develop its potential. There are many maples by the drive gate, notably *A. palmatum* 'Osakazuki', which gives a brilliant display in autumn.

In keeping with the nature of Wye Forest we have a growing collection of the genus *Quercus* and of special interest is a forty-foot specimen of *Sorbus domestica* – a scion of the famous and historic 'Witty Pear' of the Forest. There is a bluebell wood, and everywhere the lovely wood anemone carpets the ground in spring. In the wilder grass areas cowslips arrived of their own accord and are spreading well; there is also centaury and from time to time various orchids appear.

The Wye Forest is one of the few places in

Britain where the lily-of-the-valley is found naturally and this too has its place in the garden.

◆

The Orchard Farm, Broadway
THE MISSES S. AND M. BARRIE

This garden has been entirely redesigned and planted since 1974. The only things of interest were the old yews, and topiary, and with new yew hedges planted, these have made a background for an extensive lawn with shaped borders on either side, and an island bed in the centre. The borders have been carefully planned to make maintenance as simple as possible, and are planted with prostrate junipers, *Berberis*, maples, *Cotinus* and many other plants, to fill in the spaces.

A lot of grey foliage plants have been used in the foreground of the borders, which give a good colour combination with the purple-foliaged shrubs for most of the summer. The sunken garden is again composed of grey foliage plants, around a well-head, and *Erica carnea* is planted thickly round the edges.

The rest of the garden is made up of rough grass, which is planted with drifts of daffodils leading to a small lake, constructed in the course of the stream that flows down from the hill above.

The main idea, in the making of this garden, has been to create colour and interest, with labour reduced as far as possible.

◆

Overbury Court, Nr Tewkesbury
MRS E. MARTIN-HOLLAND

These gardens reflect the history of the house, built in 1740, and succeeding generations of the same family, living here since, who have left their stamp.

Entering by magnificent wrought iron gates, the path from the drive leads between a lawn with low spreading cherries and a border of mainly evergreen shrubs and conifers, created to give a patchwork of long-lasting colour. The garden then opens out to the south face of the house, standing above a terrace, paved with York stone, and looking down on a formal garden, mostly planned and created in the early 1920s, with a yew hedge surround and two rows of Irish yews, with symmetrical sunken areas either side, one a pool, the other a croquet lawn. An interesting west-facing border has recently been planned and planted against a lovely Cotswold stone wall, with buttresses to blend with the formal garden. The border, with its scalloped edge bounded by gravel, is filled with alternate gold and silver plants. Shrub roses form a colourful walkway to the road on the west side of this formal garden and the walled kitchen garden, now grassed down, forms a shelter for a hard tennis court.

In direct contrast to the south side, the garden on the west is informal in character – the long sweep of lawn is bounded by a stream connecting two large pools on dif-

Eremurus 'Cleopatra' at Spetchley Park in early July. In the background is a variegated ivy, one of the genera for which this historic garden is famous.

ferent levels, with waterfalls and towering plane trees and a large bank covered with a myriad of spring bulbs. This creates a gracious aspect in scale with the house. Emphasis on ground-cover and unusual coloured foliage has been paramount in helping to maintain the ease of upkeep, while still retaining interesting planting in this lovely garden.

◆

The Priory, Kemerton
MR AND THE HON. MRS PETER HEALING

The Priory may have housed some of the many pilgrims that visited the Abbeys of Tewkesbury and Pershore, but for many years it has been our good fortune to garden on the four acres of gently sloping land on Bredon Hill. It has been the home of plants and trees that have been collected from many countries.

To make a collection of interesting plants is one thing, but to arrange them to form a pleasing whole is another. The herbaceous borders are planted in colour groups and the main border, some twenty feet deep, is large by today's standards. It starts with greys and whites, leading into pale pinks and blues followed by the stronger yellows until a crescendo of scarlet and bronze is reached. Then the border returns in the same sequence to whites and greys but using different plants. Some borders are for lime greens and variegated foliage, whilst one is for reds and another for blues and purple. Then it is possible to fit in rare or unusual plants where they will be at home rather than having isolated specimens. One part of the garden, shielded

by yew hedges, concentrates on early summer. Shrub roses form a background to flowers in white, pink and mauve which predominate at this time of year, whilst the main borders have their heyday in high summer.

The Priory is fortunate in having a series of small gardens, some being walled and secluded where plant collections can be made; ferns and lilies with hostas and double primroses are concentrated in one, whilst tender plants in tubs, such as daturas and cassias, feature in another. The propagation of unusual plants takes up part of the kitchen gardens, but many tender plants have to take their chance on the walls, and orchids provide essential flowers for winter months.

◆

*Spetchley Park, Worcester
R.J. BERKELEY, ESQ.

The Spetchley estate was acquired by my family in 1605, and the parkland was landscaped in the second half of the seventeenth century. Sadly, the avenues of stately elms planted at that time succumbed to disease in the 1970s, but some of the great cedars remain, introduced in the 1660s by the diarist John Evelyn, a friend of the family. A visit to the Deer Park with its herds of red and fallow deer is well worth the short walk.

The garden, covering thirty acres, dates mainly from the late nineteenth century, when my grandmother, and her equally talented sister Ellen Willmott, created this lovely Victorian garden. Here you will find both formal and informal areas, woodland and herbaceous plants, at every turn a new vista, and all containing a large collection of trees, shrubs and plants. My father, a very knowledgeable gardener, continued to extend this large garden.

Being labour-intensive this garden creates problems of maintenance, but in such an extensive area there is always much of interest to satisfy the most ardent plantsman.

Spetchley is noted in spring for its bulbs – carpets of *Crocus tommasinianus* followed by masses of daffodils, succeeded in turn by fritillaries and naturalized lilies. May and June are particularly beautiful when a wealth of trees and shrubs are in flower, whilst the large collection of roses, old and new, hold sway in June and July. August is the month of the herbaceous borders, and September heralds the early autumn colour.

The Victorian custom of growing the stately *Agapanthus africanus* in large tubs is still practised at Spetchley, and what a sight they are in July and August! They are best left undisturbed, and except for feeding and watering they are of little trouble.

◆

Stone House Cottage Gardens, Stone
MAJ. AND THE HON. MRS ARBUTHNOT

A dilapidated and rather wild kitchen garden has, since 1974, been turned into a plantsman's walled garden, filled with rare plants, and into a nursery where most of the lesser-known plants are propagated.

The warmth and protection of the walls have enabled us to experiment with a whole range of supposedly tender plants. *Prostanthera cuneata, Ribes speciosum, Desmodium tiliifolium, Escallonia iveyi, Acacia pravissima, Fuchsia excorticata* and many others have become regular survivors and thrived.

Yew and box hedges have been used to create long vistas, hidden gardens and favourable micro-climates; eighteen inches to eight feet isn't bad progress for *Taxus baccata* in ten years! The garden is now somewhat

dominated by three towers built into the walls. Their extra height gives scope for growing that stunning evergreen rose 'Cooper's Burmese' and other mixtures like *Ceanothus* 'Southmead' with *Senecio leucostachys* intermingled.

We are fascinated by what will 'do' in shade and have made a north-east-facing raised peat garden. Nearby was an old greenhouse; we have pushed a path through the middle to make raised beds and made more with railway sleepers. *Convolvulus mauritanicus, Lithospermum* 'Cambridge Blue' and *Chrysanthemum haradjianii* mingle well, flopping over the edges towards the ground. Also from the

tower you can peep into the yellow and white, winter and spring gardens but no such pinnacle is needed to see the broad shrub rose and herbaceous border. We've evicted the last yellow and what a difference!

Witley Park House, Great Witley
MR AND MRS W. A. M. EDWARDS

This garden has been created from farmland since 1965 by the present owner, and includes Warford Pool which is the centrepiece of the garden, and occupies half the total area of eighteen acres. There is a pleasant walk around the pool and through woodland, with a fine view of Woodbury Hill. To minimize maintenance, many flowering shrubs and trees have been planted, and apart from the pool, these are the dominant feature of the garden.

In the early months daffodils are to be seen in profusion. Bulbs and wild flowers have been naturalized below the dam in the dell which is at its best in spring, or a little later when azaleas and rhododendrons are in flower.

Several hundred rose bushes, including rugosas, hybrid teas and floribundas, reach their peak in late June and early July. Along the pool walk there are numerous young oaks including *Quercus phellos, Q. × kewensis* and *Q. palustris*. Thanks to mechanization the whole garden is maintained by the equivalent of one full-time man (owner and part-time help); tools are stored in a shed known as the toy cupboard! Visitors find the garden full of beauty and colour whether they visit in spring, summer or autumn.

Wormington Grange, Nr Broadway
THE EVETTS FAMILY

These spacious gardens were landscaped by Sir Guy Dawber in 1920 for the present owners. He created a stunning framework of yew hedges and low Cotswold stone walls containing within them a number of smaller secluded gardens and a long herbaceous walk. We have a lovely display of roses in the summer months and of particular delight is the 'quiet garden'; a mass of old-fashioned roses, including 'Cécile Brunner', mixing with lavenders and *Clematis*. We plant a climbing rose and a *Clematis* in the same hole and when they are entwined, they produce a wonderful mix of colour and form. A recent addition is a herb garden with over sixty different plants, filling a network of small beds bordered by grass paths. Access to these gardens is gained through a marvellous collection of Cotswold Arts and Crafts gates made by Alfred Bucknall, a member of the Campden Guild. The overall feeling of the garden is one of expanse and beautiful views, particularly during the spring months when a myriad of daffodils and fritillaries carpet the long sweep to the lake.

An almost aerial view from one of the garden towers at Stone House Cottage Gardens; in the foreground are triangular raised beds supported by bricks.

KENT (EAST)

not to exact scale

Directions to Gardens

Bicknor Gardens, 5 miles south of Sittingbourne. [1]

Bog Farm, Brabourne Lees, 4 miles east of Ashford. [2]

185 Borden Lane, ½ mile south of Sittingbourne. [3]

Church Hill Cottage, Charing Heath, 10 miles northwest of Ashford. [4]

Cobham Court, Bekesbourne, 3 miles southeast of Canterbury. [5]

Coldham, Little Chart Forstal, 5 miles northwest of Ashford. [6]

Doddington Place, 6 miles southeast of Sittingbourne. [7]

Godinton Park, 1½ miles west of Ashford. [8]

Goodnestone Park, Near Wingham, Canterbury. [9]

Hales Place, Oaks Road, Tenterden. [24]

Longacre, Perry Wood, Selling, 5 miles southeast of Faversham. [10]

Luton House, Selling, 4 miles southeast of Faversham. [10]

Mount Ephraim, Hernhill, Faversham. [11]

Northbourne Court, west of Deal. [12]

Olantigh, Wye, 6 miles northeast of Ashford. [13]

Old Mill, Tonge, 1 mile east of Sittingbourne. [14]

Oswalds, Bishopsbourne, 4 miles south of Canterbury. [15]

The Pines Garden, Beach Road, Bay Hill, St Margaret's Bay, 4½ miles northeast of Dover. [16]

Sandling Park, northwest of Hythe. [17]

Sea Close, Canongate Road, Hythe. [18]

Street End Place, Street End, 3 miles south of Canterbury. [19]

Timbold Hill House, Frinsted, 4 miles south of Sittingbourne. [20]

Updown Farm, Betteshanger, 3 miles south of Sandwich. [21]

Weeks Farm, Egerton Forstal, 3½ miles east of Headcorn. [22]

Withersdane Hall, Wye, northeast of Ashford. [23]

Bicknor Gardens, Nr Sittingbourne

DR AND MRS R. HICKMAN, MR AND MRS A. TAYLOR AND MR AND MRS D.P. WAINMAN

Here are three quite different gardens situated in an area of outstanding natural beauty in the Kentish North Downs. They are all of fairly recent creation, even though the houses around which they are built date back many hundreds of years. The largest, **Placketts Hole**, has an interesting collection of herbs, out-of-the-ordinary shrubs and plants, and a formal rose garden with many old-fashioned varieties. It is about half a mile away from the smallest garden, **Deans Bottom Farm**, which in turn is situated next to the newest garden, **Deans Bank Farm**. All three gardens have splendid views across the lovely valleys in which they nestle. This is sheep and fruit-growing country, and from early spring when the first cherry blossom appears until December when the autumn colours finally fade, the gardens are enhanced by the surrounding natural beauty.

The North Down soil abounds with chalk, so few acid-loving plants are in evidence. However, their absence is more than made up for by those many lime-tolerant plants such as the numerous *Clematis* varieties which grow in abundance. As all three gardens are situated a few hundred feet above sea level the seasons arrive somewhat later than elsewhere. At the end of June most plants and shrubs still look young and fresh; the earlier-flowering roses like the pale yellow, saucer-shaped 'Frühlingsgold' at Placketts Hole cascades in torrents down an old hawthorn tree. The glorious white 'Duchesse de Nemours' paeonies at Deans Bottom have reached maturity and the annuals in the 'children's garden' at Deans Bank are in full bloom. All four children of the house (aged five upwards) have their own tiny garden plot in which they are encouraged to practise their skills. Whenever the garden is open, four very proud young gardeners are on hand to show off and explain their efforts.

Bog Farm, Brabourne Lees

We came to live here in 1958, and the garden has gradually evolved from an open space to one divided by walls, hedges and slopes forming different scenes and colour schemes.

As we prefer to have our flowers spread through the months, winter to summer, there is no peak period of bloom, so the play of green shades, textures, heights and outlines is an important part of the garden's character. Due to the sloping ground we have dry sunny places and very wet areas where the garden meets the bog wood. Therefore, by a happy chance, we are able to grow quite a wide variety of plants. Most of the plants are natural forms or species which seem to us to have a perfection which the hybrids often lack, though of course there are exceptions and one should never be too purist! The surrounding woods and fields make a natural peaceful setting and we attempt the same atmosphere within the garden, where although the design is formal, the planting is mainly informal.

185 Borden Lane, Sittingbourne

MR AND MRS P.A. BOYCE

Although not small, compared with the modern estate-house garden, this back garden of about one third of an acre has been altered by the present owners during the last nine years. It has two main seasons; in spring the magnolias, camellias, azaleas, rhododendrons and bulbs provide the first flush of colour, and from July through to the end of September the border comes alive with a riot of colour from over one hundred different varieties of fuchsia. Many of these fuchsias are not hardy and are planted out in May and returned to the heated greenhouse in October.

The main lawn is surrounded by borders containing shrubs such as *Viburnum rhytidophyllum*, *Berberis darwinii*, *Elaeagnus*, and *Mahonia* as well as the fuchsias and magnolias. The small lower lawn has a patio and small pond backed by a rockery planted with heathers and dwarf conifers. This leads to the upper lawn with its summer house and pergola from which are hung baskets of fuchsias. Beyond this area is the greenhouse and fruit and vegetable patch which makes the owner/hobby gardeners virtually self-sufficient.

Church Hill Cottage, Charing Heath

MR AND MRS MICHAEL METIANU

When we came to our garden in August 1981 we found a framework of mature trees, a few shrubs and cramped borders surrounded and intersected by overgrown hedges and poplar trees, while part of the lawn had been given over to sheep grazing. A small watercourse across the garden was completely obscured by high laurels and brambles. Since then the shape of the garden has been changed greatly and it has also been enlarged. The poplars and some antique ivy-clad relics of fruit trees have been removed and the laurels and brambles have disappeared. New borders and island beds have been established, and two circular gravelled beds, one for plants with scented foliage and one for old-fashioned pinks, occupy central positions in the lawns.

The soil, a light sandy loam with a pH of 6–6.5, allows a wide range of plants to flourish and though shallow-rooting subjects like hydrangeas are vulnerable to drought, the deeper rooters find moisture in even the driest spells.

One of the delights of the garden is that many plants seed freely; Miss Willmott's Ghost, *Eryngium giganteum*, appears by the dozen, and daphnes and hardy geraniums pop up in unexpected places.

Planting a wide variety of shrubs and herbaceous plants poses problems of association of colour and shape. This has been dealt with by grouping plants whose colours complement each other in separate borders and using shrubs and tall perennials to produce height.

Hardy geraniums, violas, campanulas and penstemons are all used to create borders where form and colour blend harmoniously. Grey and variegated forms are used to separate colours and to lighten the 'greenness', inevitable at some times.

With the wealth of plants we have now assembled the garden gives enjoyment throughout the year.

Cobham Court, Bekesbourne

MRS WALTER WHIGHAM

'I ran across the orchard and by the old acacia tree, the garden was around me. Cobham Court had no formal garden. Its flowers grew everywhere – in the orchard, the kitchen garden . . . Nothing was contrived or tidy, but year by year the pleasance was flushed with fragrance and colour. Although the house sprawled and had a high sounding name, its flowers were those to be seen round any cottage in Bekesbourne; china roses, hollyhocks, nasturtiums, moon daisies, sweet williams and love-in-the-mist. The paths were mossy and twisted enchantingly. Its orchard of plum, apple, cherry and pear stood right at the back and sloped down to a lane reached by crossing a brook. We had no marble "fancies" in the shape of statues, fountains and cunningly carved benches. The entire pleasance was girdled by tall quickset hedges and beyond it lay the fields farmed by my father.'

Strange as it may seem, this description is not of the present-day garden, but is an excerpt from the book *Life of Many Colours* by E. M. Almedingen, whose forebears lived here in 1766, and describes Cobham Court garden as it was then. It is not all that dissimilar today, two hundred years later.

The focal point of the garden is the age-old *Robinia pseudoacacia*, whose girth is over fifteen feet and which experts believe to be about three hundred years old. It has been suggested that it may have been planted by John Tradescant. The orchard has long gone and this area is full of wild flowers and interesting trees (many planted since the 1950s) which are a haven for butterflies, bees and birds. The old walls are now clothed with roses, *Wisteria*, *Solanum* and *Clematis*. They surround borders of herbaceous plants, old roses and many other plants, which are at their best during the summer months.

The front of the house is a spring garden, with hundreds of bulbs, flowering cherries and shrubs which give of their best on this Kentish chalk land.

Coldham, Little Chart Forstal

DR J.G. ELLIOTT

The garden has been developed over the last fourteen years in the setting of a sixteenth-century farmhouse with its outbuildings and old ragstone walls.

The walls are planted with many slightly tender climbers, and the raised beds beneath them with alpine plants, interspersed with dwarf bulbs. Around the house and drive, winter-flowering and scented plants are concentrated where they can best be appreciated; such plants as wintersweet, *Chimonanthus praecox*, *Daphne pontica*, scenting the air at night, and the more tender winter-flowering *Daphne bholua*, perhaps the most powerfully scented of the genus, with mahonias and sarcococcas. On the north sides of the walls are raised peat beds planted with small ericaceous plants, trilliums, erythroniums, and terrestrial orchids.

In the main part of the garden a few ancient apple trees from the original orchard have been retained to add height and character, and two old box hedges form a background for wide, rectangular herbaceous borders. Outside the confines of these hedges, informal mixed borders are planted with shrubs and perennials, including many usually confined to rock gardens, but quite happy elsewhere if the natural drainage is improved by incorporating coarse grit.

Many of the larger shrubs and trees around the boundary, especially *Sorbus* and *Acer* species, were grown from seed, but they are large enough to provide shade and shelter for plants liking woodland conditions, *Meconopsis* and *Primula* species, ericaceous shrubs and lilies. There are many thriving colonies of lilies, including *Cardiocrinum giganteum*, *Lilium auratum* and its hybrids, *L. martagon*, *L. szovitsianum*, *L. chalcedonicum* and others. All the lilies have been grown from seed in an attempt to avoid introduction of virus disease, with the result that many species have remained in good health over several years.

A fine specimen of *Aralia elata* in full flower catches the late summer sun, against a dark background of *Prunus lusitanica*, at Bog Farm, Brabourne Lees. For description see page 101.

Godinton Park, Nr Ashford
ALAN WYNDHAM GREEN, ESQ.

The gardens were originally laid out in the eighteenth century with the shrubbery covering about three acres, now underplanted with daffodils for a fine display in springtime.

The formal gardens were laid out in 1904 by Sir Reginald Blomfield and enclosed by a large yew hedge, within which is a topiary garden of box, as well as herbaceous borders and a lily pool, a long border and the Italian garden.

◆

Goodnestone Park, Nr Wingham
THE LORD AND LADY FITZWALTER

To many visitors Goodnestone possesses a peculiarly English air of romantic beauty. There is a nostalgic quality in the harmony between the old house and its surrounding trees and lawns, and the predominance of evocative, traditional plants of soft colour and heady scent.

Since the 1960s, Lady FitzWalter has revived the garden with plantings that have retained its old-fashioned character. On the lower terrace to the east of the house tall cypresses and *Pittosporum* form an evergreen shelter round *Daphne odora*, with auriculas in the spring and clumps of *Lilium regale* later. Above the retaining wall of this terrace are two enormous 'Nevada' roses framing the eastward view of the park from the house in line with fastigiate yews flanking the stone steps. In front of evergreen laurels, which mark the boundary between the garden and the woods around the carriage drive, more daphnes have been planted with *Magnolia stellata*, *Osmanthus delavayi* and reticulata irises beneath. The rockery contains dwarf maples and around the pond are arums and primulas, especially the yellow *P. florindae*.

The eighteenth-century walled garden at Goodnestone fulfils the ideal of an old-fashioned English garden. Filled with flowers, fruit and vegetables, it is hidden away beyond venerable cedars of Lebanon, now stripped of their tops and many limbs by gales and snow damage. Entrance to this secret place is gained through a gate set in an unusual flint arch. Old-fashioned roses, outstanding throughout the gardens, here spill out of borders where they mix with *Clematis* trained over wooden arbours, pinks, and small grey-leaved plants. On the mellow brick walls climbing roses and *Clematis* compete for space with a white jasmine and the more unusual *Jasminum × stephanense*, *Solanum jasminoides*, *S. crispum* and *Cytisus battandieri*. The far wall, beneath the church tower, is covered with a huge *Wisteria*; from this section of the garden the central path leads between borders of paeonies, hydrangeas, and more roses. To one side a grass path leads down to a decorative wrought-iron seat beneath a wooden arbour, again hung with roses. There is a remarkable free-standing *Magnolia grandiflora*, an *Ilex aquifolium* 'Ferox argentea' and, in a secluded corner, a pink border.

Doddington Place, Nr Sittingbourne
MR RICHARD AND THE HON. MRS OLDFIELD

Sweeping lawns bordered and divided by large yew hedges, fine mature trees and wide views over the valley characterize this ten-acre garden. Over the years the yews have assumed in part the shape and grandeur of a range of mountains. The main garden layout was executed in the first years of this century when Mrs Douglas Jeffreys, a member of the Oldfield family, came here. She had the advantage of some fine trees, including an avenue of wellingtonias, to plan around.

After the daffodils in spring the woodland garden, which is what Doddington Place is best known for, comes into its own. Here azaleas and rhododendrons prosper, fringed by Solomon's seal, *Smilacina*, hostas and many other woodland-loving plants. Each path reveals some fine trees and shrubs including *Styrax japonica*, *Halesia*, aralias, *Magnolia sieboldii*, and an unusually tall *Pieris formosa* 'Wakehurst'. With the abundance of growth it comes as a surprise to learn that this part of the garden was planned and planted as recently as the early sixties by Mr and Mrs John Oldfield with the help of their cousin, Stephen Stokes.

The exuberance of the woodland garden is succeeded by the more muted pleasures of the large rock garden with its butterfly ponds, and the roses in the formal sunk garden.

With the lawns, yews and woodland this garden is a peaceful spot.

Sheltered by the walls and the woods around the carriage drive, the garden in the summer is a medley of soft colours and intoxicating scent.

◆

Hales Place, Tenterden
MR AND MRS MICHAEL ROBSON

Classified as an historic minor Tudor mansion, Hales Place – amidst its apple orchards, chiefly Bramleys, and a joy to behold in blossom time – is approached through a fifteenth–sixteenth-century matching brick archway.

The north side of the house opens on to a large walled garden leading to a terrace flanked by two weathered pink gazebos. White *Wisteria* climbs the boundary wall; and alpines grow tumbling over the terrace edge. Below this a wide herbaceous border is a galaxy of colour in mid-summer.

On either side of central lawns with trimmed yew hedges, a variety of shrubs were planted for spring and late summer display. Thence, towards the house on the west side, is a long bed of hybrid tea and floribunda roses; and on the east, a dell with all manner of bulbs, such as snowdrops, and crocuses in late winter and early spring, followed by hybrid daffodils and bluebells.

Outside the walled garden stands a unique Tudor brick well house, tree embowered; together with rhododendrons and azaleas – needing much fertilization in this Kent Wealden clay soil – and shrub roses. Around the lily pond (a Crusader fish pond, it has been mooted) to the south of the house, shrubs and trees have been chosen for their colourful foliage.

◆

Longacre, Selling
DR AND MRS G. THOMAS

This one-acre garden has been developed since 1964. It is surrounded on two sides by woodland which protects it from the east wind and makes an ideal background for setting off the colours of foliage and flowers within the garden. The soil is predominantly acid so that a wide range of plants can be grown. The trees planted in 1964, such as *Liriodendron tulipifera* and *Acer davidii*, and mature shrubs such as a ten-foot high *Erica arborea*, screen one area from another giving an element of surprise. The island beds of mixed shrubs and herbaceous plants prolong the colour well into the summer.

Scree beds cut into the lawn and topped with pea gravel provide an ideal environment for alpines. The naturally well-drained soil gives excellent growth and the gravel sets off the plants, keeps in the moisture and makes weeding easy. An added bonus is that seeds easily germinate in it and treasures can be potted up or transplanted. Finally no rocks are needed, making this a cheap and effective way to grow a wide range of small plants.

Other rock plants are in a soil-filled one-and-a-half-foot purpose-built wall, which provides an interesting view from the kitchen window and in which small bulbs such as *Tulipa*, *Crocus* and *Narcissus* species can be seen more readily than at ground level.

A small woodland area has recently been developed where primulas, hostas, astilbes and lilies are becoming established amongst ferns and early-flowering ericaceous shrubs such as *Enkianthus* and *Corylopsis*.

Finally no garden is really complete without a vegetable section which provides the household with most of its needs during the year.

◆

Luton House Garden, Selling
MR AND MRS JOHN SWIRE

This garden has a mixture of trees planted many years ago, and shrubs planted mainly in the last twenty years. Situated on neutral soil, the carefully-sited shelter belts and hedges exist in an effort to mitigate the baleful effects of the strong east winds and frost which are such a prevalent feature of East Kent in spring. Shrub and rose species give colour and scent in mid-summer, but otherwise this is a spring and autumn garden with cherries, magnolias, viburnums, azaleas, witch hazels, parrotias, maples and Judas trees having a double season. October is a good month here and it is encouraging to look forward to this. During the summer fothergillas, eucryphias, lace-cap and other species hydrangeas are increasingly rewarding under giant tulip trees, chestnuts and oaks. Around them the daffodils and fritillaries are spreading year by year.

Roses – *R. longicuspis* and 'Wedding Day' – and *Clematis spooneri*, festooning hollies and yews, are a feature in late May and early June.

Beneath them we have made good use of *Sarcoccoca confusa*, so deliciously scented in February, as a most effective ground-cover through which, nevertheless, *Clematis* and lilies can force their way, and use as support; this has been an unexpected success which we intend to repeat. We are continuing our planting around the pond, the home of wild ducks and geese from many parts of the world.

◆

Mount Ephraim, Hernhill
MRS M.N. DAWES; MR AND MRS E.S. DAWES

My late husband inherited this garden in 1949, when two World Wars and the Depression had reduced it to a sorry state. However, it had splendid trees, and there remained the framework of the Edwardian garden. This we slowly rescued and modified, with dedicated, if inadequate, help. The complicated flower beds have gone; the 1914 topiary still remains, and the herbaceous border has been replanted. Yew hedges are still the backbone of the north-facing terraces which slope down to the lake and contain hybrid tea, old, species and shrub roses. Golden yews, clipped to a mushroom shape, are grafted into dark yew bases, and accent the glorious view over the Thames Estuary.

A beautifully curved Japanese rock garden, with its series of pools, leads also to the lake. It is planted with conifers, flowering cherries, dwarf azaleas, and other shrubs. There are alpines, silver plants, and interesting ground cover. Golden thyme and marjoram make a contrasting carpet for *Acer palmatum* 'Dissectum Atropurpureum' and the *Vinca minor* 'Variegata' spreads under purple *Berberis*.

A little wood of mature oaks rises steeply beyond the lake, giving shelter to the site,

Iris magnifica, a rare and difficult member of the Juno section, native of the mountains south of Samarkand, growing happily here at Coldham, Little Chart (see page 101).

with soil sufficiently acid to accommodate rhododendrons.

The colour combination of a purple beech and an Atlantic cedar (both mature trees) has given so much pleasure that we repeated it elsewhere.

A *Robinia pseudoacacia* 'Frisia' is spectacular against a dark background, and *Alchemilla mollis* is fun with *Sisyrinchium striatum* and yellow *Allium moly*.

The silver plants, severely cut back by the 1984–5 hard winter, are looking so well that I suspect I don't normally prune them hard enough in spring. As usual, I intend to do better next year.

◆

Northbourne Court, Nr Deal

THE LORD NORTHBOURNE

Once a formal Elizabethan garden, the soft orange brick terraces here have since 1925 been planted informally in a romantic style. An amphitheatre of terraces surrounds a rectangular lily pond. Wallflowers, rambler roses and box trees overgrow the ruins of an Elizabethan house burnt down in 1720.

The planting of this garden is skilfully designed to display the beauty of many chalk-loving plants, and grey foliage is used extensively. The planting emphasis is on carefully conceived, but casually presented, groupings designed to display the natural beauty of the plants rather than the expertise of the gardener.

The serenity of this garden may in part be due to its origins as a Priory of St Augustine's Abbey, Canterbury, but also in part derives from its designer, Walter Lord Northbourne, an amateur botanist and artist of distinction who loved and tended it for nearly sixty years.

◆

Olantigh, Nr Wye

J.R.H. LOUDON, ESQ.

The policies of Olantigh remain in general as laid out in, say, the 1830s with trees now in maturity. The Great Stour flows through the middle on its way to Canterbury. The garden is roughly divided into a formal plot, with an adjoining large rockery near the house, and a less formal or woodland area near the Great Stour. The formal part has Edwardian undertones as the present house, the fourth on the site, was only completed in 1910. The vault, on top of which much of the rockery stands, was probably the wine cellar of the Tudor house. Apart from the layout there are many plants of interest to be seen. The woodland area over the river is a place of tranquillity, a long valley bisected by a stream flowing out of the river. There are trees and shrubs of interest in the spring, and the adjoining wood is filled with snowdrops and daffodils, as is an avenue in front of the house. Apart from the valley which has alluvial deposits, having once been a lake, the policies and gardens are laid out on shallow soil over chalk.

Old Mill, Tonge

JACOBS AND THOMPSON PARTNERSHIP

The garden at Tonge has been set around the streams and old buildings of this ancient watermill which was recorded in the Domesday Book. Since 1877 the two-and-a-half-acre grounds have been transformed from neglected scrub and derelict orchard to a pleasantly informal garden.

Our aim has been to provide varied vistas and sitting areas from which to enjoy the special features of the site. These include a walled garden through which runs the mill pond leat; Rowena's walk, supposed site of an ancient local legend; a sheep dip, now serving as a splash pool for our children; terraces beside the 'milly'; and the orchard, containing old and new apple, pear and plum trees, among which an apiary has been established. Inevitably, we are in a frost pocket; however, this situation produces some extraordinary patterns of ghostly mist hovering about the plants of the stream-side, and very severe weather transforms the water plants into frost-flowers and icicles.

In keeping with the situation here, most of our flowers, shrubs and trees are familiar favourites and the exotics seem out of place. For an interesting contrast during July through to September, we have found the common *Fuchsia* planted behind *Potentilla* very attractive.

◆

Oswalds, Bishopsbourne

MR AND MRS J.C. DAVIDSON

Despite a thin alluvial soil over flint and gravel in a notorious frost pocket, the present owners were not deterred in the redesigning of this two-acre garden in its parkland setting in 1972, since when a wide range of trees and shrubs have been planted. Contrasting foliage colours and plant forms complement the Georgian house which was once the home of the author Joseph Conrad. Emphasis is on ease of maintenance as seen in the 'wild' shade garden with drifts of snowdrops, naturalized fritillaries and many species of hellebore, the mixed borders and the old rose bed.

Because the Nailbourne river runs only occasionally along its dry course between cowslip-studded banks, a permanent water feature has been created with a well-stocked pool including cascade and associated rockeries. A secluded courtyard garden planted in colours of blue, yellow and grey, a late summer herbaceous border, the herb garden and the silver and purple border with its rose arbour centrepiece, provide something of interest for all visitors. Bulbs feature prominently, with a wide range of dwarf species, many varieties naturalized in grass and a specialist collection in the large glasshouse.

Even the inner man is not forgotten, the kitchen garden supporting a family of four with year-round vegetables and fruit grown mostly inside a large cage due to the avarice of

the local bird population. Apple and pear trees grown as espaliers effectively screen the cage, with a blue carpet of scillas and chionodoxas beneath, providing a memorable picture in the early spring. Pruning in June and September keeps the trees shapely and cropping well.

June finds the most stunning plant association – a grouping of *Chamaecyparis lawsoniana* 'Stewartii', *Symphoricarpus orbiculatus variegatus*, *Ruta graveolens* 'Jackman's Blue', with *Potentilla fruticosa* 'Primrose Beauty' and *Philadelphus coronarius* 'Aureus' in flower.

◆

The Pines Garden, St Margaret's Bay

THE ST MARGARET'S BAY TRUST

This beautiful six-acre seaside garden, boasts a waterfall, lake with specimen fish, trees and shrubs.

◆

*Sandling Park, Hythe

THE HARDY FAMILY

No one would expect to find a garden like Sandling tucked in between the chalk of the North Downs and the Channel; the secret lies far back in Kent's history. Centuries of leaf-fall from the mediaeval forest of Westenhanger overlying a pocket of Hythe greensand provide an ideal environment for a collection of plants from all over the world, in spite of the often vicious winters and gales of east Kent.

The lawns, formal gardens and walled kitchen garden were designed for the eighteenth-century house, demolished after a direct hit by a bomb in 1942. Laurence Hardy, moving to Sandling in 1897, saw the potential of the grandly-timbered hillside and winding streams as a perfect setting for a woodland garden. He planted the first *Rhododendron*, 'Cynthia', in 1900 (still flourishing today) which began the large collection of rhododendrons, azaleas, magnolias, acers and other acid-soil-loving plants.

From the naturalized bulbs of early spring the garden reaches its peak of colour, splendour and scent in May. Particular favourites include *R. souliei*, the parent of so many of our home-raised hybrids; the spectacular long leaves and silvery young growth of *R. calophytum*; the collection of dwarf rhododendrons, especially the many forms of *R. campylogynum* with wax-like flowers, and *R. ludlowii*, so difficult to grow well. Several varieties of *Meconopsis*, a real challenge to grow in the south, give special pleasure, particularly *M.×sheldonii* 'Slieve Donard' for the brilliant blue of its flowers. Drifts of candelabra primulas and the uncommon *P. prolifera* also revel in the moist areas. Trilliums, epimediums, ferns and creeping *Cornus canadensis* combine with carpets of primroses, *Montia sibirica* and other wild flowers to keep this an essentially natural garden with lily-of-the-valley everywhere. There are many fine trees such as *Pinus insignis* planted in 1846, and *Abies bracteata*, but noteworthy for sheer size are *Nothofagus dombeyii* and the giant alder *Alnus glutinosa*, whose oak-like trunk foxes many, and which is said to be the largest in western Europe.

The garden has evolved in the love and care of four generations of the family. We treasure the gifts given to us by so many generous friends. Planted at any time of the year these survive even the driest spells, thanks to the advice of that great gardener, the late 'Cherry' Ingram, who taught us to water-in well and cover closely with a flowerpot for ten days or so: the results are magical. But then he called our leaf soil 'tonic' and he was right about that too.

Sea Close, Hythe

MAJ. AND MRS R.H. BLIZARD

Sea Close occupies a unique site on a steep south-facing hillside, a quarter of a mile from the sea. Although only just over an acre in size, it appears much larger.

Having taken over a neglected formal garden in 1966, primary attention was paid to the layout on the principle that the architecture must be interesting before a single plant is growing. Taking full advantage of the steep slope, a series of island beds and grass paths were fashioned around well-established trees and shrubs. The result is a series of mini-gardens and wild areas of independent character, which merge to give an overall harmonious effect. The hillside permits an unusually large number of viewpoints, each providing a quite different picture. Full advantage has been taken of foliage together with careful use of blending colours.

The owner and his wife have no assistance, but maximum use of ground-cover and close planting greatly reduce the amount of work. The most burdensome job is mowing the grass paths and lawns, and keeping the edges trim, but the owners insist that this contributes more to a pleasing end-result than any other single factor.

The soil varies throughout the garden, allowing rhododendrons and a *Daphne cneorum* to grow in fairly close proximity to one another. A particularly pleasing, though accidental, ground-cover effect has been achieved where London Pride and pinks have intermingled.

Street End Place, Nr Canterbury

LT.-COL. JOHN BAKER WHITE

There has been a garden of some sort at Street End Place for over two hundred years. Today it consists mainly of two walled gardens, surrounded by a shrub garden with mown walks and an extensive area of naturalized daffodils. This was created in 1909 and has been extended by the inclusion in 1962 of two former grass tennis courts, planted with daffodils and trees. The shrub garden includes a number of flowering cherries. This part of the

A small ruined courtyard at Northbourne Court, thickly planted with grey-leaved and scented plants such as pinks, *Artemisia*, purple sage and *Allium cristophii*.

garden, and the adjoining parkland, contains a number of fine cedars and two sweet chestnuts over three hundred years old.

Owing to rising costs one of the two walled gardens, which are about two hundred and fifty years old, is not kept up as a flower garden but used for chickens, vegetables et cetera. The other walled garden is notable for a large number of roses of different kinds

and for its delphiniums, including six which are pure primrose yellow. There are also heath and azalea beds, badly damaged in the winter of 1984–5, as was a row of bastard cypress, grown from seed brought from Cap d'Ail.

A feature of the walled garden is a two-hundred-year-old mulberry tree, still bearing a heavy crop of fruit, and a climbing rose over

Part of one of the double mixed borders at Northbourne Court in June, with centifolia roses, herbaceous paeonies and wild foxgloves. For description see page 104.

eighty years old. In general the garden and its surroundings reflect a policy of continuous tree planting that has been followed for more than a hundred and fifty years. Part of the park is the village cricket ground, and it is also the venue of the annual summer flower show.

◆

Timbold Hill House, Frinsted
MR AND MRS N.E. WINCH

When we moved into Timbold Hill's half-acre on retirement in August 1970 the long-term plan was to produce a cottage-type garden in which there was never likely to be any paid help. It had been neglected for so long that what to leave and what to take out presented no problem – everything had to go to make way for a completely fresh start.

Room was made to grow vegetables for two until this should become too demanding, when the area could be converted to shrubs and/or flowers. In fact, it became a rose garden in 1984–5 – the year of the first very hard winter. The soil is neutral to alkaline being derived from clay with flint over chalk, but drainage is bad in parts and at five hundred feet above sea level the garden suffers from north-east wind damage, though not from late frost. Approximately half the area is lawns and half shrubs and roses with one small herbaceous border adjacent to the house.

Minimum use is made of bedding plants, spring colour coming from bulbs, while self-sown *Myosotis*, red campion, *Nigella*, *Aquilegia*, foxgloves and marigolds provide the maximum colour with the minimum of effort.

Full use is made of ground-cover (*Ajuga*, *Alchemilla mollis*, *Lamium* and periwinkle) under the shrubs which have been chosen for flower (*Viburnum*, lilac and *Hebe*) as well as foliage (*Senecio*, *Berberis thunbergii*, *Corylus maxima* 'Purpurea', *Phlomis fruticosa*) and fruit (*Rosa rugosa*, *Malus*, *Crataegus*). The rather dull brick walls of the house support roses, including 'Cécile Brunner', *Hydrangea petiolaris*, winter jasmine, *Wisteria* and *Garrya elliptica*.

◆

Updown Farm, Betteshanger
MR AND THE HON. MRS WILLIS FLEMING

In 1976 we acquired our ancient brick and Kentish ragstone farmhouse, set on a terrace above a large derelict farmyard, and began the daunting task of creating a garden.

First we made a large central lawn by spreading nine inches of topsoil on the chalk of the farmyard, and added more soil to two large circular beds for herbaceous plants and shrubs. In a sheltered corner *Paulownia tomentosa* has grown magnificently, in almost pure chalk. With roofs removed and walls lowered, the farm buildings round the yard have provided warm courtyards, where grapes (and birds) flourish, and the bared timbers of a calf shed are hung with *Clematis*. A raised bed provides a home for camellias and other acid-loving plants. Around the house paving and stone sinks harbour small treasures.

One priority was planting trees for shelter and shade, the fast-growing species acting as 'nurses' to specimen trees for the future.

Hedges were important too, to draw together unrelated areas of the garden. A favourite tree, the decorative Italian alder, has grown well in poor chalky conditions.

The soil is mainly brick earth, and hundreds of shrub roses now flourish, climbing into old plum trees, tumbling on walls, and grouped both in beds and grass. Among them, to our delight, spires of white foxgloves seed themselves, while the air is scented with *Philadelphus*, *Lonicera*, *Buddleja*, *Syringa* and *Daphne*. Later in the season, varying shades of blue provided by *Salvia uliginosa*, *S. ambigens* and *S. concolor* shine among 'Iceberg' roses and white *Dimorphotheca*. As the garden diffuses into the landscape, lawns lead to mown paths among the long grass, with groups of ornamental trees and shrubs, bulbs, wild flowers – and wasps' nests . . . the mown areas cunningly shaped so that our ride-on mower can tackle the whole garden!

◆

Weeks Farm, Egerton
MRS PAMELA MILBURNE

I have progressed from mustard and cress in the nursery through one garden in Surrey, one in Kenya at 7,500 feet, and two in Kent. One was on a hill and this one is on a patch of very heavy Wealden clay, described as a badly-drained site. But, to everyone's surprise and my delight, it grows many things well. I have been at this garden for the last twenty-five years or more and have planted everything myself which makes me gasp when I look around it today.

Last winter opened up some views which I had forgotten in my admiration of the lovely blue of *Ceanothus* and the yellow bobbles of the *Buddleja*. I am replanting again in the spring but will block out different views. I appreciate things that seed themselves all over the place, resulting in muddles which I prefer to think of as interesting mixtures – a point open to argument.

I enjoy other gardens, they make me want to rush back to get to work on my own patch, then back home it might be a better bet to sit and look, and tell my mixed border how well it is doing – plants love admiration, it is a real tonic for them especially if the sun is shining, and that goes for the owners too!

◆

Withersdane Hall, Wye College
UNIVERSITY OF LONDON

The present gardens were largely laid out during the period 1948–55, and part of the design included the very successful transformation of the former kitchen gardens of the Victorian gothic house into a series of enclosures or garden rooms with a magnificent old mulberry tree as a central feature.

To the east, the backdrop to the gardens is a fine ridge of the North Downs, bracing and chalky and dominated by the great white crown cut in the hills in 1902 by energetic college students.

On exploring the different enclosures in the gardens, you will find many interesting plants and plant associations that like the chalky soil and the generally kind climate. Yew hedges have been used throughout, and we always pride ourselves on the standard of clipping. Here you will find a sundial garden of blue, golden and variegated plants, a traditional herb garden dominated by a weeping Kilmarnock willow; a pool garden, lovely in June with blue irises and yellow day lilies, campanulas and pinks, and a bold exotic Mediterranean border against a warm wall.

There are also the mixed borders which are at their best in late summer, and two rose gardens; one has a collection of roses of different species and hybrids, and the other a very new feature of modern ground-cover roses from France. The two young 'paper bark' birches are a feature here. The hostel wings added in 1951 enclose the Queen Mother's commemorative garden beneath the great holm oak, and the walls are clothed with magnolias and a superb white *Wisteria*, at its best in May.

A peat garden can be found as a demonstra- tion of methods of growing rhododendrons, azaleas, heathers and other lime-hating plants on calcareous soils.

Don't miss the *Paulownia* tree, said to be the largest in the south of England, smothered with large blue-purple foxglove flowers in early May.

There are many other features to discover at Withersdane. We try and label most plants, and we are making changes to update collections and demonstrate new ideas and techniques.

A plan and guide book or leaflets are usually available for visitors on open days.

Rhododendrons and azaleas in June at Sandling Park, near Hythe.
For a description of this garden see page 104.

KENT (WEST)

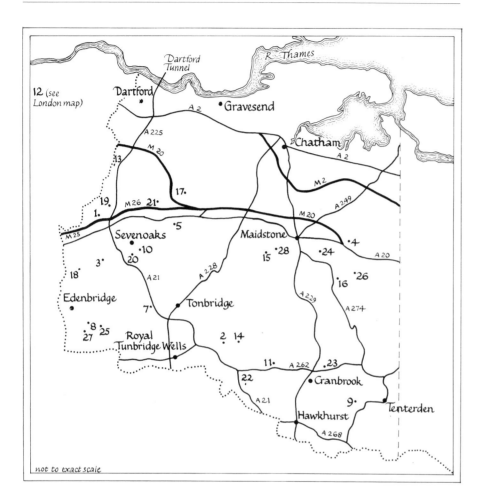

Directions to Gardens

Chevening Gardens and Park, 4 miles northwest of Sevenoaks. [1]

Crittenden House, Matfield, 6 miles southeast of Tonbridge. [2]

Emmetts Garden, Ide Hill, 5 miles southwest of Sevenoaks. [3]

Eyhorne Manor, Hollingbourne, 5 miles east of Maidstone. [4]

Great Comp Charitable Trust, 2 miles east of Borough Green. [5]

Hall Place Gardens, Leigh, 4 miles west of Tonbridge. [7]

Hever Castle, 3 miles southeast of Edenbridge. [8]

Hole Park, between Rolvenden and Cranbrook. [9]

Knole, Sevenoaks. [10]

Ladham House, Goudhurst, on northeast side of village [11].

43 Layhams Road, West Wickham, near Croydon. [12: N.B. on London map]

Lullingstone Castle, in the Darenth Valley, near Eynsford. [13]

Marle Place, Brenchley, 8 miles southeast of Tonbridge. [14]

Mere House, Mereworth, 7 miles west of Maidstone. [15]

The Old Parsonage, Sutton Valence, 6 miles southeast of Maidstone. [16]

The Rectory, Fairseat, 1½ miles north of Wrotham. [17]

The Red House, Crockham Hill, 3 miles north of Edenbridge. [18]

Ringfield, Knockholt, 5 miles northwest of Sevenoaks. [19]

Riverhill House, 2 miles south of Sevenoaks. [20]

St Clere, Kemsing, 6 miles northeast of Sevenoaks. [21]

Scotney Castle, 1¼ miles south of Lamberhurst. [22]

Sissinghurst Castle Garden, Sissinghurst, near Cranbrook, 14 miles from Maidstone. [23]

Stoneacre, Otham, 4 miles southeast of Maidstone. [24]

Stonewall Park, Chiddingstone Hoath, 5 miles southeast of Edenbridge. [25]

Ulcombe Place, Ulcombe, 8 miles southeast of Maidstone. [26]

Waystrode Manor, Cowden, 4½ miles south of Edenbridge. [27]

West Farleigh Hall, 4½ miles west of Maidstone. [28]

Chevening Gardens and Park, Chevening

The gardens to the south of the house were created by James, first Earl of Stanhope, in around 1720. The thermometer-shaped central canal was surrounded by extensive formal landscaped grounds, criss-crossed by a geometric pattern of rides or allées. Between these straight rides were wildernesses, labyrinths, mazes and flower gardens. This ornate pattern was not to last long, and by 1775, under the third Earl, the canal had been transformed into an informal lake surrounded by winding paths, and the complex hedging almost entirely removed; the rides on the west side remained, albeit in a softer form. The third Earl, an eccentric and inventor of some note, having altered the garden in his youth neglected it in his old age. His son, the fourth Earl, carefully tended it, restoring the allées on the west side and planting up the east side. He also planted the box-edged parterre and the park, while his son designed the maze.

In 1980 over a mile of hornbeam hedge was planted, thus restoring the west side to its eighteenth-century formality. Fastigiate hornbeam was also planted in 1980, forming a semi-circular frame for the lake. The parterre has been reconstructed, using colourful shrubs, and finally in 1986 Lady Stanhope's garden was replanted with shrubs and herbaceous plants.

The east side of the garden contains many magnificent trees, particularly some large oaks, and good specimens of *Nyssa sylvatica*,

Quercus coccinea and a huge *Liriodendron tulipifera*.

The park is one of the most beautiful eighteenth–nineteenth-century creations in this country, and it supports some enormous yews, including one or two thought to be over a thousand years old. There are also fine beeches and limes, and a 'keyhole', made of clipped beech, from which there are extensive views across the Darent Valley below.

◆

Crittenden House, Matfield
B.P. TOMPSETT, ESQ.

When I reunited the farmhouse and four and a half acres of land with the farm in 1955, I was faced with establishing a garden in unpropitious circumstances, for the area surrounding the house had all been worked for iron, centuries previously.

There was virtually no topsoil on the lower two acres, and this was put right by bringing in large quantities from building sites. There was, however, one valuable legacy from the iron-working activities, in the form of two large and beautiful ponds, whose margins were soon adapted for a host of plants suited to the situation. Some of my favourites are *Lysichitum americanum*, *L. camtschatcense*, *Phormium tenax*, *Gunnera manicata* and *G. chilensis*, *Peltiphyllum peltatum*, hostas, and of course bog primulas.

Among the jungle of trees and undergrowth which covered the pleasantly undulating land one could glimpse the framework of a beautiful garden. Clearing was done with great care to ensure that the best of the native trees and plants were kept.

The top end of the garden was slightly acid, lending itself to ericaceous plants, and perhaps I overdid the rhododendrons, not previously having had suitable soil for growing them, but I planted good species and varieties to provide a succession of bloom from *R. sutchuenense* through to *R. auriculatum*. The bays in among the rhododendrons lend themselves to choice bulbs, especially lilies. Those which have proved most successful are *L. regale*, *L. henryi*, *L. auratum*, 'Citronella', 'Destiny', 'Enchantment' and the Bellingham hybrids. With economy of maintenance in mind, hedges were eliminated except when shelter was needed, and planting was based on shrubs and trees in interestingly-shaped beds, with plenty of space between them. These are not dug but we maintain a cover of peat and 'litter'. To provide interest in the winter we have planted trees with attractive bark. Deciduous species include *Acer griseum*, *Prunus serrula* var. *tibetica*, *Cornus alba* 'Westonbirt' and *Arbutus menziesii*, while evergreens are represented by *Elaeagnus* 'Limelight', *Euonymus radicans* 'Silver Queen' and variegated holly. Willows are cut back each year to reveal their coloured bark. Drifts of *Crocus* and *Narcissus* species, *Cyclamen coum*, and winter aconites brighten the ground below early-flowering shrubs, such as *Corylopsis*.

During late summer *Ceratostigma*, *Abelia chinensis*, *Aesculus parviflora* and *Eucryphia* × *nymansensis* provide interest, and *Amelanchier*, *Fothergilla major* and various *Sorbus* show themselves to advantage in the autumn; *Malus* 'Crittenden' holds its bright red fruits until Easter.

This garden is basically naturalistic, attempting to merge and incorporate the exotic with the indigenous. We have attempted to keep the vistas 'alive' throughout spring and summer by ensuring that there are continuous areas of colour to lead the eye onwards.

◆

Emmetts Garden, Ide Hill
THE NATIONAL TRUST

Emmetts Garden lies just north of Ide Hill near Sevenoaks in Kent. The garden belongs to a large Victorian mansion and was bequeathed to the National Trust in 1965 by Mr Charles Boise. There are magnificent views and the wellingtonia, *Sequoiadendron giganteum*, of over a hundred feet, which is the country's highest treetop, can be seen from Crowborough Beacon. The northern half of this five-acre garden dates from 1860–70. The sandy loams which comprise the soil are shallow but excellent for acid-tolerant plants such as azaleas, ferns and heathers. Many of these and other smaller plants were introduced by Frederick Lubbock, who lived at Emmetts from the late 1880s until his death in 1926. He extended the garden from the northern area near the house across the road in about 1900 when the concept of exotics set in wild countryside was being advocated by William Robinson and Gertrude Jekyll. The planting was well done, giving space for the trees and shrubs to grow to good shapes in maturity.

The garden is particularly beautiful in springtime, with a mass of daffodils, especially *Narcissus* 'Angels' Tears' and erythroniums. A footpath leads to the bluebell wood, and autumn is also spectacular with the changing colours of the foliage.

The rose garden and rockery had been allowed to deteriorate but now a programme of restoration work has been put in hand and much clearing and replanting has taken place; the waterfall in the rock garden is also being restored. The statue of a little boy with a dolphin, found abandoned in the undergrowth, has recently returned home, to the centre of the rose garden.

◆

Eyhorne Manor, Hollingbourne
MR AND MRS DEREK SIMMONS

The garden, like the house, was in a sad state when we moved to Eyhorne in the spring of 1952: disused chicken runs, vegetable patches, old outside lavatories, rubbish tips and a tall hedge blown over; the well was between an apple tree and a *Laburnum*. All this reached by a deeply rutted lane and a

sagging five-bar gate. Old-fashioned plants revealed themselves: violets, purple honesty, double crimson paeonies, pheasant eye *Narcissus*, lilac, sweet rocket, lemon balm and feverfew as well as great bushes of the scented *Philadelphus coronarius* and the wild turk's cap lily. All these increased over the years and other cottage garden plants remembered from childhood have been added. Herbs grow well on the light soil and there are many, such as hyssop and burnet, that would have been strewn on mediaeval floors. There are over a hundred different roses, mostly old-fashioned.

Over the years the levels have been altered, rockeries made, paths and steps constructed, summer houses built, and the garden area enlarged; the original mixed hedge has been severely trained to contain the aromatic foliage. All this appears artless, perhaps rather wild, but it is loved, cherished and allowed to wield its own magic.

◆

Great Comp Charitable Trust, Nr Borough Green
MR AND MRS R. CAMERON

This seven-acre garden has been designed and constructed by the present owners since 1957, and is still being developed. The spacious setting, with well-maintained lawns and paths, shows off to advantage the plantsman's collection of trees, shrubs, heathers and herbaceous plants. There is also good autumn colour.

◆

Hall Place Gardens, Leigh
THE LORD HOLLENDEN

Samuel Morley, M.P., purchased the Hall Place estate in 1871, but the mansion did not meet his needs, was demolished, and the present Hall Place built. George Devey was the architect and undoubtedly fashioned the gardens. The present eleven-acre lake was constructed giving a total area within the gardens of twenty acres. In 1886 the eldest son, Samuel Hope Morley, 1st Baron Hollenden, succeeded his father. His notable contribution to the gardens was to build a rose pergola some two hundred and seventy feet long which still exists, and now supports numerous varieties of rambler and climbing roses.

Geoffrey Hope, the second Baron, was assigned the estate in 1925. He built the three bridges by the lake, the tea pavilion, nurtured the small arboretum and enlarged and planted the lakeside area. Some years ago, the late Lanning Roper redesigned parts of the gardens, adding much colour and interest. As the result of a fire in 1940, about a third of Hall Place became a ruin. The walls of this portion were lowered and within their confines a house garden was formed.

October in the woodland garden at Hole Park. Maples, birches (*Betula pendula*) and the flaming orange of the American *Cotinus obovatus*, with larger leaves than the familiar European 'smoke bush' (*Cotinus coggygria*) but equally good autumn colour.

Hever Castle, Edenbridge

BROADLAND PROPERTIES LTD

This formal Italian and landscaped garden with statuary, sculpture and topiary, and a large lake, surrounds the moated castle, the childhood home of Anne Boleyn.

Hole Park, Rolvenden

D.G.W. BARHAM, ESQ.

The gardens at Hole Park cover about fifteen acres and were largely laid out and planted in the years between the wars by the grandfather of the present owner, who has himself extended the planting in recent years. Much of their beauty is owed to the great variety which they offer, providing a succession of interest from the first flowers of *Chimonanthus praecox* in December to the last autumn colours in November, and a contrast between classic form on the one hand and a woodland setting on the other, against the lasting backdrop of lawns, hedges and trees.

Formal gardens surround the house which was reduced in 1960 to one-quarter of its former size, leaving a *Magnolia grandiflora* freestanding where once it stood against a wall. Close by a banksian rose reaches the roof providing a glorious display in May. Broad expanses of lawns are broken by walls and extensive yew hedges which are a particular feature of Hole Park and claimed to be unrivalled anywhere in the precision of their trimming. Fountain pools and ponds, roses, mixed borders and wrought ironwork all contribute to make a series of gardens within the whole, whilst outwards there are lovely views of the Weald over the surrounding parkland.

At the rear of the house beyond a huge beech hedge lies the policy massed with daffodils in April followed by heathers, flowering trees and shrubs, banks of rhododendrons and azaleas. On the old rockery can be seen a prized example of *Tsuga canadensis* 'Pendula' happily planted on a rocky outcrop to give additional fall to its branches.

Beyond again is the dell and the woodland garden where oaks predominate and autumn colours including varieties of *Cornus kousa*, *Cotinus obovatus*, *Nyssa sylvatica* and maples provide a special display in October. In early May when the bluebells are in flower, visitors may walk through a carpet of blue down into the wood beyond the garden boundary.

---

*Knole, Sevenoaks

THE LORD SACKVILLE: THE NATIONAL TRUST

A pleasaunce, deer park, landscape garden and herb garden are some of the features to be seen surrounding the ancient house at Knole. Also of interest are the *Wisteria*-covered walls, and a wild woodland area carpeted in spring with bluebells.

Ladham House, Goudhurst

BETTY, LADY JESSEL

The garden here covers ten acres with the house sitting in the middle. It is formal around the house with long mixed shrub borders backed by magnolias, including *Magnolia campbellii* 'Betty Jessel', a fine, deep rose-purple seedling from Darjeeling, camellias and *Cornus kousa*. Two years ago the rose garden next door was scrapped to cut down on labour and instead a fountain was erected in the middle, with low-growing shrubs put into the rose beds. In this garden there is also a good *Carpenteria californica* and *Azara serrata*.

To the north of the house are fine views to the Maidstone Downs and there is a walk through the heather garden down to the bog garden. On the way you pass azaleas, rhododendrons, trees and shrubs, *Embothrium* and a very tall *Metasequoia glyptostroboides* planted in 1950.

The bog garden is difficult to plant up as it is the only bit of clay in the garden and dries right out in summer, being partially under water at other times; but somehow it seems to have become one of the main features. I have to watch out for rabbits here, as it is quiet at the bottom of the garden, but I have learnt from experience that once my lawns have been fed, they will prefer my luscious grass to my plants. Slugs can also be a menace, but I put grit round plants they eat, as I have a theory that they do not like their stomachs tickled as they try to crawl across it. The garden has been in the family for a hundred years, so that the trees and shrubs are well established.

---

43 Layhams Road, West Wickham
MRS DOLLY ROBERTSON

This raised vegetable garden was built in 1974 and has been exclusively worked ever since by Dolly Robertson from her wheelchair.

The open-ended beds provide produce for her household all the year round, and have been used as a model for homes, hospitals and individual disabled gardeners.

No special tools are required because domestic items, such as a table fork for weeding and a paint scraper for hoeing, are used instead. Self-sufficiency is maintained by organic composting, intensive planting and judicious 'trading' with the neighbour next door.

Fruit and flowers are well represented in this much-loved garden and, although not part of the seventy-foot by twenty-four-foot vegetable plot, are largely accessible from a sitting position.

There is something to see throughout the growing season: early vegetable plantings, lots of spring flowers and a respectable rockery in March and April; well-behaved herbs and confident first crops in May and June. By July and August, the hop has rushed up to the roof, the grapes have zoomed off around the house and, even though we say we'll be brutal every year, the roses and Virginia creeper defy control. September brings signs of used blackbirds' nests, extremely fat ring doves and a rockery which has beaten us yet again.

Lullingstone Castle, Eynsford
MR AND MRS GUY HART DYKE

This is an ancient dwelling place in the lovely Darenth Valley where the same family have lived for over five hundred years. There is a church of Norman origin on the lawn close by the three-hundred-year-old cedar trees and a lake to the south. The earliest reference to the garden was in about 1560 when knot-gardens were found on small and large estates, notably Lullingstone and Penshurst in Kent where the gardeners exchanged plants and seeds. The hundred-and-twenty-foot-long mixed border set against an old wall facing east, was rescued from dereliction in 1976 and planned and planted by ourselves with some unusual plants and old roses in sweeps of varied colour; white, yellow, red, lavender and pink – however, it is difficult to keep these colours for all seasons; there is a new experiment in black and white and a small spring garden under an old cherry tree. Very few annuals are used except to help any disaster areas and accentuate colour; all plantings are chosen for alkaline soil and to keep the

feeling of the Tudor period. In the old walled garden a twenty-two-foot-square herb garden was planted in 1983, surrounded by roses and fruit, with a quince on the south side. There are also small features of interest made with labour-saving in view. Although the garden has suffered and survived many vicissitudes, it is still a quiet and peaceful place with twenty acres to wander in including woodlands.

Marle Place, Brenchley
MR AND MRS GERALD WILLIAMS

The site of the garden here was originally a farmyard with many outbuildings. These were demolished in Victorian times leaving banks and plateaux of brick rubble and heavy Wealden clay.

A grand plan, including a large rockery, a walled rose garden, and croquet lawn with gazebo, were all that remained – in a very dilapidated state – when we came here in 1950. We have been busy planting since then, and the rockery is now a herb and aromatic garden, open as part of a herb nursery business. The soil in the rose garden recently became 'rose sick' so we are filling the gaps as they appear with scented and aromatic plants to form a sweet-smelling jungle.

Our aim is to make the whole garden a series of 'rooms'; after twenty-odd years, and lots of hedge planting, this is beginning to take shape. Most of the borders contain shrubs, underplanted with herbaceous perennials and bulbs to give a continuation of colour after the springtime blossoming – the best time for us. One of our more successful plantings is *Eremurus* beneath an azalea bed. The foxtail lilies appear after the azaleas' glory, and are supported by their branches.

We have also recently made a scree bed for small alpines that would get lost in the exuberance of the other borders. The garden slopes away to a stream and ponds. We have planted many trees in the rough area which can be enjoyed by following a meandering woodland walk.

Mere House, Mereworth
SIR JOHN AND LADY WELLS

Here we are particularly keen on foliage contrast and are building up a collection of *Sambucus* which are useful for this purpose. Some of our main foliage plants are: *Rosa glauca* (*rubrifolia*), especially growing near the purple-leaved hazel; *Sambucus racemosa* 'Plumosa Aurea' contrasted with the ordinary copper beech; *Chamaecyparis lawsoniana* 'Stewartii' clothed right to the ground and surrounded by *Hebe pinguifolia* 'Pagei'. We find it helpful to cut the hazel to the ground every year and to coppice it. This gives larger, more lush foliage. We have a considerable area of daffodils which we leave uncut until mid-June; this gives a beautiful crop of moon daisies which can then be cut and raked off for autumn tidiness.

The Old Parsonage, Sutton Valence
DR AND MRS RICHARD PERKS

We were most fortunate in being able to buy this house twenty-eight years ago, with its large garden of about three acres containing the ruins of a Norman keep standing in an ancient nut plat, in the most spectacular position facing south with far-reaching views over the Low Weald towards the High Weald of Kent and Sussex.

Geranium psilostemon in July at The Rectory, Fairseat (see page 112). This striking species is a native of mountain woods and meadows in northern Turkey and the Caucasus.

Ragstone is the indigenous stone of this greensand ridge and it had been extensively used in terracing the steep slope to the south, but there had been very little planting, few trees, and thus little shelter from the strong prevailing south-west winds. Therefore we began planting in earnest, and this has continued up to the present day. Fortunately, the soil is fertile lower greensand, well drained and alkaline. Having the fine backdrop of the Weald we felt that the planting needed to frame this, but at the same time a series of enclosed and more intimate areas were created; this we achieved by using a mixture of hornbeam, beech and field maple hedges. Within these areas the choice of plants was adapted to the increasing shade given by the many growing trees. The planting is informal, consisting mainly of mixed borders, containing roses and herbaceous plants and other shrubs, particularly those with interesting foliage. Ground-cover has been vitally important to our design, and we have found that one of the most useful plants for this has been the cranesbill in all its many and colourful varieties. Owing to the recent work by The Department of the Environment in restoring and making safe the ruins of Sutton Valence Castle, which will soon be permanently open to the public, we have recently incorporated the Castle and its commanding site into the overall plan of the garden.

Cytisus laburnum

The Rectory, Fairseat
REV. AND MRS DAVID CLARK

This is a small garden of less than an acre which has been evolving over the last sixteen years, and still is. More recent developments include small colour association beds – silver and pink, predominantly yellow, purple, maroon and pink and the 'Gaudy Border'. A little yellow has been added to the white border to tone in with a *Robinia* 'Frisia'.

In mid-June viburnums are at their best, especially a large specimen of *V. tomentosum* 'Mariesii'. So are *Meconopsis betonicifolia*, and even if the pink *M. nepaulensis* is not in flower its foliage is fascinating. There are interesting irises – white *I. sibirica*, *I. bracteata*, *I. tenax*,

and in and around the small pond, *I. versicolor* 'Kermesina' and *I. laevigata*. *Morina longifolia* with tiers of white, pink-centred flowers is one of the *pièces de résistance* – an architectural plant that continues to catch the eye long after flowering. In late July the herbaceous border is coming into its own. Purple patches of *Iresine*, *Perilla*, *Atriplex* and *Dahlia* 'Bishop of Landaff' set off the hot colours at the centre. Elsewhere lilies make their presence felt, especially *L.* 'Red Lion', *L.* 'Clara Bow' and *L.* 'Festival'. Spikes of delphiniums are still making a show – the rectory garden is nearly seven hundred feet above sea level. At ground level there is plenty of colour on the island rockery, especially from campanulas, *C. waldensteiniana*, *C. raineri*, *C.* × *hallii* and *C. carpatica* 'Blue Chips', whose large saucers are known as the Fylingdales Early Warning System! Numerous shrubs and ground-cover plants with interesting foliage should make your visit worth while even it if rains heavily before or during Open Days!

The Red House, Crockham Hill
K.C.L. WEBB, ESQ.

Designed and laid out by Dr Black at the turn of the century, The Red House is a plantsman's garden as it contains many of the rarer trees and shrubs. The soil is calcifuge and shallow, and slopes down to the south overlooking the Weald of Kent and Sussex to Ashdown Forest. The garden is planted around the house situated in the higher part of Kent.

The most colourful time here is at the beginning of June when large banks of mature rhododendrons give a fine display of mixed blooms. Some of the earliest camellias were planted here along with specimens of *Cornus capitata* and *Cornus kousa*. At the lowest part of the garden a magnificent copper beech stands out against the distant panorama. On the left of the vista is a sweet chestnut which must be at least four hundred years old. Among many of the fine plants which should be mentioned are the Californian bay, *Umbellularia californica*, with attractive scented leaves, a large Judas tree, *Cercis siliquastrum*, *Fagus sylvatica heterophylla* and two blue cedars.

Oddities abound also, notably *Maclura pomifera*, Ossage orange, and *Diospyrus kaki*, Chinese persimmon; these fruit occasionally after a very hot summer. Before leaving the garden be sure to see a very beautiful mass of *Taxus baccata* 'Dovastoniana'; it is a superb specimen and how well it looks with its horizontal branches and lovely yellow weeping branchlets.

Ringfield, Knockholt
PROF. SIR DAVID SMITHERS

A record of the owners of this property goes back to 1780, but the garden was really made by Charles Hunter, who owned it from 1912 to 1927, and his gardener, H. Lockyer. Since

1944 it has been rescued, reconstructed and enlarged by the present owner and his gardener, R. Norgate. The garden was described and illustrated in its early form in *The Queen* in July 1926. The wall around the tennis court was built in 1912 with loving care in the placement of every brick and tile, some of curious shapes and sizes, with two summer-houses at the corners on one side, and a rondel on the other containing a beam carved in memory of W. Rupert Davison, the architect, who fell at Cambrai in November 1917.

Three fields were added in the 1940s and some one hundred and fifty trees of fifty different varieties planted, including what are now good specimens of *Paulownia tomentosa*, *Catalpa bignonioides* 'Aurea', *Fagus sylvatica* 'Pendula', *Liriodendron tulipifera* and a particularly pleasing *Betula ermanii*, together with many varieties of conifer including several cedars and a *Sequoiadendron giganteum*.

The new layout, extending the garden to seven acres, was based on a curved peripheral path, originally defined through the open fields using large balls of string. Hedges of *Carpinus betulus* enclose a paved octagonal garden, a round garden with ten clipped *Chamaecyparis lawsoniana* 'Triomf van Boskoop' and a low-walled rose garden, a spring garden, a drift of daffodils, rhododendron dell, curved summer border, maple plantation and a fish pond provide a succession of interesting features.

---

*Riverhill House, Sevenoaks
MAJ. AND MRS DAVID ROGERS

Family hearsay has it that John Rogers coveted Riverhill when still a very young man and he certainly wasted no time in acquiring the property when it came on the market in 1840. Horticulture was his great preoccupation and he was hoping to establish new plant introductions. The very favourable situation and acid soil commended this small estate which seemed to offer ideal growing conditions. He started planting straight away and continued until his early death in 1867, and most of the big trees in the grounds today date from this period. Of particular interest are the first deodar cedars in England, early monkey puzzles, Austrian pines, a *wellingtonia* and huge specimens of *Magnolia* × *soulangiana*; there is also a Monterey cypress which makes a laughing stock of docile, docked macrocarpas. John Rogers' gardening notebook tells of plants received from Robert Fortune in China, and a particular *Spiraea* mentioned still flowers each May. He initiated a family tradition for growing fine trees and shrubs with a special emphasis on rhododendrons.

Gone are the days of eight gardeners, and first-class machinery must now play a large part in maintenance. High on the list at Riverhill is an invaluable winch which takes all the strain from righting victims of heavy snow or uprooting elders and other unwanted horrors. Our greatest pest is rabbits, but our greatest joy is the success of a young grandson's vegetable garden, and the certainty that flair and interest have been inherited by a further generation.

St Clere, Kemsing
MR AND MRS RONNIE NORMAN

This is an old garden on alkaline soil and with terraces laid out in the last century. In a biography of a previous owner, born at St Clere in 1730, it is described as having 'the fairest view in Kent'. There are fine trees, including *Ginkgo, Metasequoia, Cedrus atlantica glauca*, copper and cut-leaf beeches. The old fish pond with a temple at Lower St Clere adds to the view. The garden has obviously changed with each owner from the bedding-out days to the present. Shrub and herbaceous borders, climbing roses and plants tumbling over walls and a pergola add to the colour. Much planting is going on at present to replace elms and very old trees. The old mansion of coral Tudor brick, but Georgian appearance, adds to the beauty and colour of the garden.

Scotney Castle, Lamberhurst
MRS CHRISTOPHER HUSSEY: THE NATIONAL TRUST

Scotney Castle garden must surely be one of the most perfect examples of the romantic and the picturesque one could find anywhere. Standing on the bastion which overlooks the whole valley below, one has one's first view of the old, half-ruined fourteenth-century castle lying in its moat, with meadows and woods rising to the horizon beyond.

Directly beneath the bastion lies the quarry, from where the stone for the new house (1837) was taken which is now, amidst its rocks, the home of many flowering shrubs throughout the season, beginning with a big clump of *Magnolia stellata*, followed by a blaze of azaleas and maples.

In early spring, daffodils drift down the slope past the magnificent limes which, with the ancient oaks and other big trees, are one of the glories of the garden. Successive flowerings of rhododendrons clothe the hill and moat side, followed by splendid groups of *Kalmia latifolia*. The inner garden surrounding the old castle comes into its own in summer, with herbs, sweet-smelling old-fashioned flowers, many species of roses, paeonies, irises, and a wonderful white *Wisteria* climbing the castle wall.

Autumn has a special charm of its own. When the waterlilies sink into the dark waters of the moat, the huge *Osmunda* ferns on its bank become a rich, deep bronze, and all the trees and shrubs turn into muted shades of gold and brown; it has a softer, but very appealing beauty.

Scotney is a large garden – one to explore at leisure, to wander in and enjoy its own particular magic.

Sissinghurst Castle Garden, Nr Cranbrook
NIGEL NICOLSON, ESQ.: THE NATIONAL TRUST

This garden created by the late Vita Sackville-West is still one of the most famous in the country. It is made up of numerous separate gardens or features; a spring garden, with pleached limes, carpeted with dwarf bulbs; a nut grove with woodland plants including fine epimediums; a garden of old-fashioned roses underplanted with cranesbills; an old orchard planted with daffodils; the original 'white garden', and one of the best collections of unusual herbaceous plants in the world. The castle is Tudor, with brick towers and other buildings.

Stoneacre, Otham
MR AND MRS CECIL THYER-TURNER: THE NATIONAL TRUST

The present garden was started in the spring of 1977 when the new tenants Marta and Cecil Thyer-Turner came to this National Trust property and set about the work of creating a garden out of the lawns that surrounded the house. Although largely on a north-facing slope with difficult soil conditions (the name Stoneacre provides a clue!) a number of interesting features have been established. There is a well-stocked herb garden surrounded by a yew hedge and stone walls, comprising some seventy-two herbs and various plants mentioned in the sonnets of Shakespeare. Adjacent is a small white garden inspired by Sissinghurst. Passing two wide borders with a selection of herbaceous plants one approaches a small rosebed with largely ancient roses. Beneath the retaining stone wall is an outstanding border which from spring onwards has a magnificent display of hellebores and, in the height of summer, a variety of hostas. In late June/early July a 'Rambling Rector' (white) climbing rose offers a profusion of blossom outside the main gate, competing with a 'Himalayan Musk' on the east-facing wall outside the drawing-room window. In the west border a rare *Staphylea*

Waystrode Manor, Cowden.

fills the garden with its wonderful fragrance in May.

Stonewall Park, Chiddingstone Hoath
MR AND MRS V.P. FLEMING

This woodland garden was formed by the Meade-Waldo family between the wars. It consists of some fifteen acres comprising a well-sheltered and watered woodland valley leading to a small lake with a man-made dam. The trees are oak with some chestnut, and the rhododendrons and azaleas represent a mix of the traditional species and hybrids, the former including good forms of *R. augustinii, campylocarpum, falconeri, hodgsoni, lacteum, lutescens, fulvum, sutchuenense* and *thomsonii*, mostly grown from the original collector's seed. At the top end of the valley the main bluebell glade is bordered by a tall outcrop of sandstone rock. The present owners arrived in 1966 to find the structure of the garden in good shape with paths visible but the plants relatively untended. Since then we have removed a few trees and many brambles and conducted a steady programme of opening up small glades in the winter and then filling the glades with either layered species or, in some instances, purchased rhododendrons. Our mistakes include the failure, until recently, to increase the selection of magnolias, to introduce primulas and to make more use of different foliage colours to complement the basic green of the existing plants. The plan also is to make more use of the stream and, if possible, to accentuate its noise by the introduction of modest dams throughout its length. The introduction of a ride-on tractor has greatly facilitated the maintenance of the glades, but otherwise the work is done with a turk scythe, longarmed pruners and a bow saw, and essentially the owners' own efforts each and every weekend.

Ulcombe Place, Nr Maidstone
MR AND MRS H.H. VILLIERS

I shall never forget the first time we saw the garden at Ulcombe. It was a day of high summer in late June 1965, and the impression was of vegetation run riot. The drive was a dark leafy tunnel, the grass was a foot high, and through a gap at the bottom of the lawn the Weald of Kent, like a huge park, stretched away to a shimmering horizon.

Since then much clearing has been done and many aged shrubs, long past their best, are no longer with us. In the walled garden, completely overgrown, we discovered many old rambler roses, such as 'Sanders White', 'Goldfinch' and a number still unidentified. On the walls there are now new climbers such as 'Maigold', 'Veilchenblau' and 'Schoolgirl' and we have planted a group of conifers including *Pinus radiata* and *Cedrus atlantica* – both rapid growers.

The house has a Victorian verandah, under which we found some considerable rarities.

Chief amongst these are *Cestrum elegans*, with clusters of brilliant scarlet trumpet-shaped flowers, and *Fendlera wrightii*, the arching branches wreathed in dainty white flowers during early summer. Both are surprisingly hardy and survived the frosts of January 1985. We have added *Solanum crispum* and *Jasminum fruticans* to these.

Scent is an important feature – first the lilacs, then masses of *Philadelphus* in June and July, almost overpowering at times, and in August *Clerodendron trichotomum*. Planted some fifty yards from the front door the fragrance on a warm evening is delicious and much to be recommended.

Waystrode Manor, Cowden
MR AND MRS PETER WRIGHT

Our garden covers eight acres, although we actually work six and a half, the balance being woodland. The aim is to produce an informal English garden with surprises around corners, vistas through trees, and coloured borders. In springtime thousands of mixed daffodils bloom everywhere, and massed primroses and cowslips provide a yellow carpet to the north of the drive. The soil is heavy clay, but it has been worked well over the years. Specimen trees have been planted to provide a wide variety of coloured foliage. These, with a great many shrubs, have been planted since 1963 to blend in with the already existing North American oaks which turn vivid red in the autumn.

There are various handsome chestnut trees in the garden and the approach drive is lined with chestnuts, *Aesculus* × *carnea* 'Briotti', planted in 1937 to commemorate the coronation of Their Majesties King George VI and Queen Elizabeth. There are four interlinking hammer-ponds, providing a tranquil setting

Cestrum elegans, **a tender native of Mexico, growing under the verandah at Ulcombe Place (see page 113). The flowers are sometimes followed by deep red-purple berries.**

which enhances the fourteenth-century buildings and house.

Old-fashioned roses predominate in the flower beds, including *Rosa filipes* 'Kiftsgate' *R. longicuspis*, *R. banksiae* 'Lutea', 'Penelope', 'Fantin-Latour', 'Queen of Denmark', 'Mme Grégoire Staechelin', 'Nevada', 'Cerise Bouquet', *Rosa glauca* (*rubrifolia*), *Rosa moyesii*, 'Cornelia', 'Celestial', Scots briar and *Rosa ecae*. Several old trees have roses growing

through them, for example 'François Juranville', 'Seagull' and 'Paul's Himalayan Musk'. Many consider this to be a plantsman's garden because of the wide variety of interesting and unusual plants, and all trees and plants are clearly labelled. Large expanses of lawn, divided by yew hedges, break the garden into various sections and arches and statuary create further interest.

West Farleigh Hall, Nr Maidstone
MRS CHARLES NORMAN

This is a walled garden scarcely changed in design since 1719. Badeslade's contemporary drawing shows newly-planted yews, looking like little bottle brushes; these now form a mature hedge enclosing a rose garden of modern hybrid teas. Beyond is a lawn, still known as 'The Bowling Green' (though a bowls player would shudder at the idea of using it as such). On its east side there is a double border of the old-fashioned shrub roses, whose soft pinks and purples do not blend with modern roses. At the south end full-grown yew trees form an archway leading to a very long wide double herbaceous border. This is divided into four sections in colour groups, and although this has become a cliché, it seems the only satisfactory way to deal with a large variety of different species of flowers. Coloured foliage such as *Prunus* 'Pissardii', purple *Corylus*, golden privet, and *Cotinus coggygria* is used in the appropriate sections, and grey and silver foliage in all. An intersecting path is bordered by a large variety of bearded irises, behind which is a deep belt of tall modern shrub roses – 'Maigold', 'Scarlet Fire', 'Nevada', 'Golden Wings' and many others. These screen the most important part of the garden – the vegetables, organically grown, and the compost heaps.

LANCASHIRE AND YORKSHIRE

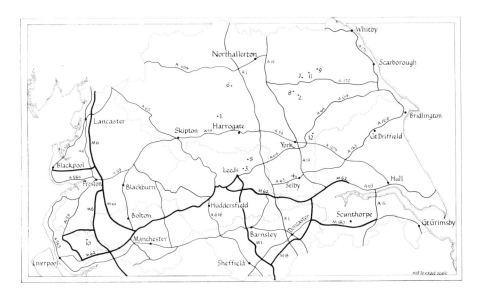

Directions to Gardens

Bewerley House, Bewerley, ½ mile south of Pateley Bridge, northwest of Harrogate. [1]

Gilling Castle, Gilling East, 18 miles north of York. [2]

30 Latchmere Road, Leeds, 16. [3]

78 Leeds Road, 1 mile west of Selby. [4]

Ling Beeches, Ling Lane, Scarcroft, 7 miles northeast of Leeds. [5]

Old Sleningford, Mickley, 5 miles west of Ripon. [6]

Ryedale House, 41 Bridge Street, Helmsley, east of Thirsk. [7]

Shandy Hall, Coxwold, north of York. [8]

Silver Birches, Ling Lane, Scarcroft, 7 miles northeast of Leeds. [5]

Sleightholme Dale Lodge, 1 mile from Fadmoor, 3 miles north of Kirkbymoorside. [9]

Wass Gardens, ¼ mile from Byland Abbey, 6 miles southwest of Helmsley. [8]

Windle Hall, St Helens, 5 miles west of M6, Lancs. [10]

Wytherstone House, Pockley, 3 miles northeast of Helmsley. [11]

York Gate, Back Church Lane, Adel, Leeds 16. [3]

York House, Claxton, 8 miles east of York. [12]

Bewerley House, Bewerley, Nr Pateley Bridge

MR AND MRS A. SIGSTON THOMPSON

The garden, now covering six acres set on a hillside, consisted, when the present owners came nearly forty years ago, of two flower borders, an impenetrable Victorian shrubbery and the remains of a rock garden planted in the 1930s by the once famous nurserymen Backhouses of York, and one or two good parkland trees. The owner describes himself as a plantsman rather than a gardener, which, he says, explains why the garden has little organized plan, trees and shrubs keeping what lies around the next corner secret to the last moment. The chief interest here lies in the flowering trees and shrubs, particularly rhododendrons, shrub roses and rose species, many of the latter scrambling into and

through trees. Among other flowering shrubs which thrive here are the Chilean fire bush, *Embothrium coccineum lanceolatum*, the Japanese *Cornus kousa* and its Chinese form *Cornus kousa* var. *chinensis*, witch hazels, magnolias, *Philadelphus* and lilac species. Lilies, both species and hybrids, are another feature of the garden.

The 1930 rock garden now consists solely of 'dwarf' conifers showing the height to which they can grow if given time – for example, Young's golden juniper is now a golden column fifteen feet tall and *Picea* 'conica' has formed a perfect cone ten feet or more high.

The further and later parts of the garden, bounded by the Fosse Beck, are sheltered from the west by a double screen of *Thuja plicata* and on the east by a belt of Scots and Austrian pines. Here in July a free-standing bush of *Rosa* 'Kiftsgate' some twenty feet across makes a wonderful sight with its mantle of white, golden-anthered flowers.

Gilling Castle, Gilling East

THE RT REV. THE ABBOT OF AMPLEFORTH

Gilling Castle stands on the eastern shoulder of a hill, and the garden slopes away on the south side in a series of terraces to a small valley in which a golf course slopes up southwards to a long wood of deciduous trees.

The main garden is bounded by trees to the east, and on the west side by trees and shrubberies containing rhododendrons, azaleas, portugal laurel and holly. It covers about two acres, and each terrace is reached at the western end by a flight of stone steps.

The first terrace below the general level of the house has peach trees on the south-facing brick wall, and a herbaceous border in which the main features are hollyhocks and dahlias. A rose bed divides the broad gravel walk along the centre between narrow stretches of lawn. The next terrace is narrower, with a long strip of lawn between pear trees on the south-facing wall and a full-length bed of 'Evelyn Fison' roses.

Below lies the main herbaceous garden with three long borders and a shorter one against the south-facing wall. In the early summer there are many paeonies, irises and oriental poppies, followed later by many dahlias, summer and autumn perennials, and annual bedding plants. This area slopes gradually down to a vegetable garden, ending at a six-foot stone wall drop to the golf course. There are also two small rock gardens and, on a higher level a small sunken garden.

---

30 Latchmere Road, Moor Grange, Leeds

MR AND MRS JOE BROWN

This very small garden on a housing estate over five hundred feet above sea level, with a north-west prevailing wind, has gained an international reputation as a garden well worth seeing. It has been designed by its owners (with no previous garden experience) in such a fashion that all the overwhelming disadvantages of dark corners, odd angles, and lack of space have been turned to advantage by the welding together of local sandstone, water features, different levels and a great variety of climbing plants, and although a plantsman's garden it is the placing and grouping that bears the hallmark of an artist at work.

The cool green lace of the choice and rare ferns enjoys the shade of the north-facing house wall and the calm water of the sunken pool reflecting the sky. In the herbaceous borders old favourites grow in harmony with the choice and rarer plants, and beyond the ornamental iron arch the alpine garden, the camomile lawn and the small wild garden lie open to the sun through the day. Stone troughs, ornamental urns, tubs, pots, statuary and seats are all part of the integral design, and soaring above it all is a living curtain of the collection of forty-five *Clematis* growing and scrambling through the climbing honeysuckle, roses, jasmine, *Ceanothus*, and tree branches.

---

78 Leeds Road, Selby
MR AND MRS R. MARSHALL

Our long and narrow garden, designed by my husband, consists of five different planting areas. An alpine section near the house, where we also grow climbing plants, leads to a curved lawned garden. In this garden are two small borders where many lovely plants grow. A 'Bramley' seedling apple, a 'Williams' pear and a few small shrubs are also included.

There is lovely planting here of *Euphorbia niciciana*, and the early foliage of *Spiraea* 'Gold Flame', *Saxifraga fortunei*, *Carex elata* 'Bowles Golden' and *Viola* 'Irish Molly' light up a shady corner.

Through a narrow path we come to another alpine garden with troughs, a small pool and rockery. There are massed plantings of astilbes where a soakaway gives us a wet area. This leads to another curved lawn and borders where we grow roses, old violas, tall campanulas, aconitums, tall grasses and many things which do well in the moist soil.

A hardy perennial garden, the full width of our plot, now takes over and in high summer is a blaze of colour, including a double row of *Phlox* of many colours which do well there. At the end of the garden is a small slope or flood barrier, which overlooks 'Selby Dam', an artificial tributary of the river Ouse. Grazing cattle in the meadow across the water give a feeling of peace and tranquillity on a summer's day when all seems well with the world and it feels good to be a gardener.

Ling Beeches, Ling Lane, Scarcroft
MRS ARNOLD RAKUSEN

This two-acre garden, carved out from mixed woodland, has been designed for year-round interest and also to be enjoyed from the house-windows during inclement weather. Focal points change as different trees and shrubs in flower lend their particular emphasis but contrasting foliage and form play their part at all times. I enjoy 'layer-cake' planting; spring bulbs precede early-flowering shrubs which, in turn, give way to interspersed herbaceous perennials, autumn colours giving way to winter skeletons, barks and stems. Scent, too, plays a large part here and many native plants attract a varied wildlife population; forty-five bird species have been sighted and their singing is much appreciated.

Compost-making is necessary to provide the nourishment required by intensive planting. Soft woody material is included in the heap of garden and household waste, the latter including carpet sweepings, rags from natural fibres and bones, often wrapped in newspaper, to keep it all 'open' for the worms to do their work – especially necessary when grass-mowings are added otherwise putrefaction, not decomposition, takes place.

Close planting gives the weeds little chance and much of my 'gardening' is the removal of over-enthusiastic growth. Constant deadheading conserves plant-energy – unless seed-heads are required; careful cutting-back of shrubs conserves their shape and form. I enjoy light-coloured flowers, also pale and variegated foliage, for this is a shady garden and such colours show up more than darker ones; even variegated ground-elder has a place – but only in poor ground and under strict surveillance.

Hollies and laurels, planted for protection from ground-draughts, allow shrubs such as

78, Leeds Road, Selby; a series of steps lead up from the water's edge, between dense plantings of flowering and foliage plants.

Eucryphia 'Nymansay', *E.* × *intermedia* and some camellias to flourish – plants not usually associated with this area where rainfall is a mere twenty-eight inches; at five hundred feet above sea level the garden is at the mercy of all winds and one of our problems is lack of autumn sun to ripen the previous year's growth – not only because winter comes early in Yorkshire but also because our trees partially obscure the weak sun when it is low in the sky. Sheer weight of snow can be a problem too but problems and challenges are what makes gardening so fascinating and provide the ever-changing interest that constantly enchants and surprises us.

◆

Old Sleningford Hall, Nr Ripon

THE RT HON. JAMES AND MRS RAMSDEN

This garden is on two levels: there are extensive lawns, views and interesting trees around the house, in particular an old copper beech which has rooted in a circle round the trunk. Near the house (c. 1810) there is an older stable yard with two towers, a clock and dovecote. A mown path leads down through an old beech wood to the water garden, where there is an old millpond with four variously planted islands and an ornamental duck-house. The mill is covered in *Wisteria* and a high brick wall encloses the kitchen garden on two sides. A long herbaceous border is backed by a yew hedge, which is covered in *Tropaeolum* in the summer, while a tall old beech-hedge screens the tennis-court. Besides fruit and vegetables, and a tree nursery, flowers and grasses are grown for drying. An alternative walk to the garden takes you past a Victorian fernery stocked by the Northern Horticultural Fern Society. In spring there are daffodils everywhere.

A garden tip: honesty picked when the pods are green dries equally well as when the seed heads are silver, and also stops it seeding itself where it is not wanted.

◆

Ryedale House, 41 Bridge Street, Helmsley

DR AND MRS J.A. STORROW

Here is a small walled garden in the middle of Helmsley; people say 'I never imagined there was a garden like this behind the houses'. When we came thirteen years ago it was a desert: a rectangle of lawn with stone path round and bare rotavated beds, and of course the lovely old stone walls. In planning it we had three equally important aims: firstly, to do away with the flat rectilinear aspect by raising some parts and lowering others, edging beds with walls to give the illusion of height, and cutting curved beds out of the lawn. Now that bushes have grown up a different view waits round every corner. Secondly, the garden had to be easy to maintain – annuals were out, shrubs and perennials in, ground-cover encouraged. Thirdly, there had to be colour and something blooming all year round: by a careful choice of plants (e.g. hellebores, periwinkle), varied conifers and evergreens, this has been achieved and a walk round is a pleasure even on the dreariest winter day. Contrast of colour, shape, texture is important: the *Sambucus racemosa* 'Plumosa aurea' is set off by the weeping copper beech behind; the 'Hidcote Blue' lavender hedge along the broad walk is punctuated by *Cupressus*; the old yew tree sets off the irises. A balsam poplar bought as *Populus candicans* 'Aurora' gives colour, shade and scent to the lawn. The walls support *Clematis* in various forms, *Wisteria*, *Ribes speciosum* (always a feature of interest to visitors), a fig tree (many figs but few ripen), *Hibiscus*, *Solanum* and others. As the bushes have grown, so has the number of birds; an old stone sink from a moorland inn makes a splendid bath for them. They add life to the quiet of the garden to create its special atmosphere.

◆

Shandy Hall, Coxwold

THE LAURENCE STERNE TRUST

A drystone wall encircles nearly an acre of land here. The area within has been gardened (on and off) since the eighteenth century. In its neglected, late 1960s state it still included an ancient yew, variegated hollies, box-edged beds, lilacs and old apple-trees. These have been preserved and enhanced by a mixed planting of cottage-garden perennials, old shrub roses and herbs so that the garden is at its most 'floriferous' in mid-July. It looks full and interesting all the year round due to close planting, and the use of contrasting foliage.

A very striking feature in late May is a stark dead chestnut festooned in a flowing cloak of *Clematis montana rubens* – its roots buried in *Vinca major* 'Variegata'. Later *Rosa* 'Paul's Scarlet' peeps through the bronze foliage of the *Clematis*. It is rather a romantic garden with roses, honeysuckle and a Japanese vine growing through the old apple-trees. A planting of *Alchemilla mollis* and *Brunnera macrophylla* at the foot of the wall round the orchard has proved pretty and practical as the grass can be mowed right up to the plants. They are both good weed-smotherers and cannot become invasive in a situation like this.

The boundary walls are edged with raised beds retained by eighteen inches of drystone so that climbers, erect, horizontal and creeping plants grow together in happy juxtaposition. There is a magic moment in July when a frothing pink mound of blossom from *Rosa* 'Paul's Himalayan Musk', flows over the wall.

◆

Silver Birches, Scarcroft

MR AND MRS S.C. THOMSON

This two-and-a-half-acre garden is cut out of an old spinney of bracken and birch, facing south over farmland. A feature of the design has been to merge the garden into the surrounding countryside.

A woodland pool, flanked by plants and shrubs which are mirrored in its surface, forms the focal point. From there the eye is carried through a gap in the trees to the farm on the distant hillside.

The woodland of beech, birch, pine and other conifers is underplanted with many rhododendrons, azaleas and shade-loving shrubs and plants, whilst hydrangeas and fuchsias provide colour in the late summer and autumn.

The English cottage-type house is clothed in *Wisteria*, *Clematis* and climbing roses, whilst two fine cedars, *Cedrus deodara* and *Cedrus atlantica glauca* frame it from either side of the lawn. Tree trunks are used to good effect in hosting *Clematis*, variegated ivies, honeysuckle and climbing roses, which scramble to great heights, and there is also an interesting collection of shrub and bedding roses. Lilies and bulbous plants, interplanted amongst the shrubs, bring colour throughout the season.

Particular care has been taken in choosing plant forms and locations, such as the positioning of the deep purple of *Campanula superba* around the shrub rose 'Lavender Lassie', a fine *Robinia pseudoacacia* 'Frisia' against the background of copper beech, *Acer japonicum* 'Aureum', *A.* 'Dissectum' and others in front of dark backgrounds, whilst *Elaeagnus* is used to liven up dark areas.

Good examples of *Magnolia* × *soulangiana*, camellias, *Enkianthus campanulatus*, *Embothrium coccineum lanceolatum* (the Chilean flame tree) *Euonymus europaeus* and *Leycesteria formosa* can be seen.

This is a garden of spring flowers and bulbs, summer fragrance and rich autumn colours blending in with the year-round moods of the countryside.

◆

Sleightholme Dale Lodge, Fadmoor

MRS GORDON FOSTER; DR AND MRS M.B. JAMES

This garden is on the slopes of a hillside, in a valley facing south-west. The oldest part (begun in 1910) is protected from the north by a high, L-shaped wall, and behind this a double avenue of flowering cherries, *Prunus avium*.

Inside this wall are stone paths, oak fences and arches – the whole divided by a double herbaceous border running up the hill, in which the delphiniums in July are a special feature. On the fences are roses, honeysuckle and *Clematis*. What were once rose beds of hybrid teas are now filled with many other plants, including the older roses, especially the hybrid musks. Alongside is an orchard of apple trees and two more mixed borders (with many paeonies). Some special favourites include the *Clematis* 'Royal Velours'; *Clematis macropetala* – and *C. orientalis*, climbing roses 'Golden Emblem', rambler rose 'Minnehaha', *Lonicera* × *americana* as well as *Linum*, geraniums, *Kniphofia*, *Centaurea*, *Campanula*, and *Lychnis*.

During the war and 1950s – in a spirit of

Old Sleningford Hall (see page 117). The old millpond and herbaceous border in June, backed by yew hedges which are covered later in summer by *Tropaeolum speciosum*.

optimism, with a wonderful gardener and two dry wallers – the garden was much enlarged. A paddock beyond the high wall is planted with flowering cherries and crabs, azaleas, species roses (such as *R. spinosissima altaica, hispida, webbiana*) and many wild daffodils.

On the steep banks below the house, are steps and dry walls, with a pond at the lowest level, all divided from the field by a grass walk above a dry wall, and ha-ha.

This bank above the pond has been a favourite spot – there are two stone seats (in the walls) and shrubs, and smaller plants include *Philadelphus* 'Avalanche', *Philadelphus* 'Belle Etoile', *Acer palmatum, Rosa macrantha, Rosa* 'Raubritter', *Hebe cupressoides* – these high up – while lower down are *Daphne cneorum, Lithospermum, Magnolia stellata*, and near the water *Iris sibirica*.

Wass Gardens, Wass, Nr Helmsley

To explain the beauty of the four Wass gardens one really has to describe the village of Wass, in particular its situation in the Vale of Mowbray. The parish is called Byland-with-Wass, the remnants of Byland Abbey being about a quarter of a mile away. Looking northwards from the Abbey, visitors have their first glimpse of the village of Wass tucked away in a broad cleft at the foot of the steep and well-wooded Hambleton hills beyond which the rolling moorlands of north Yorkshire extend to the sea. A good road leads up from Wass through thickly wooded slopes to the moorlands above.

The residents of Wass, whose houses are mainly built of the local stone, endeavour to match their gardens with the wild beauty which surrounds their village. The steep and well-wooded Hambleton hills form a natural backcloth of unbelievable colours which appear to change every day of the year, and also provide a form of sanctuary for the wild bird life and a few deer. In order to compete against all this surrounding day-to-day beauty, the 'Wass gardeners' have to surpass themselves in order to take a poor second place. This they have done, mainly by making full use of foliage plants, along with a wide variety of trees, spring flowers and bulbs, many varieties of roses and *Clematis* and various rockery plants and all-year heathers.

One could continue with many, many more descriptive words about the grace and beauty of the Wass gardens, so in conclusion one can only say 'seeing is believing'.

Windle Hall, St Helens
THE LADY PILKINGTON

My late husband used to say that his house and garden, part of which dated back to 1750, came under new management when we married twenty-five years ago and that the new broom made a very clean sweep! I certainly enjoyed myself enormously. We had first met at five a.m. as rivals at the London Rose Show, and when we later joined forces, we decided that many of the one and a half-thousand roses at Windle Hall needed replanting. Some have been changed a few times since when they did not live up to their catalogue promises.

The main garden is about four acres, with a grass tennis court and several other lawns surrounded on three sides by a wood. Here are some beautiful old beech trees but most of it has had to be replanted with a variety of young trees owing to the sad loss of over four hundred elms. There is an old walled garden whose walls used to be heated but the

espaliered pears, peaches and cherries still flourish. Within this area are three traditional herbaceous borders which we thin and replant as necessary. Recently we added a pergola made from the stones of our old church. It is now covered by *Laburnum* and I call it my baby Bodnant.

We gradually introduced water into the garden. First, an oval goldfish pond with a boy and fish fountain. Then a rockery and stream beside a tufa stone grotto. Then a large pool with a mermaid statue and, a new interest, Mandarin ducks, which at the moment are rather too full of wanderlust for peace of mind. I have a number of ornamental pheasants, including the rare white-eared pheasant, in cages down one side of the wood.

The most recent additions are beds of Japanese azaleas and cherry trees and some alpine rockeries. I like to keep the garden and greenhouses colourful from the first spring flowers to the last November roses and they give me a great deal of pleasure.

Wytherstone House, Pockley
LADY CLARISSA COLLIN

This garden has been created out of a field and rubbish tip during the past twenty years. There was virtually no top soil, so both alkaline soil and peat were imported. This enabled us to make an attractive and colourful spring garden with acid-loving plants such as rhododendrons and azaleas.

We have planted a number of ornamental trees in the lawns. In order to keep labour to a minimum, circular beds surround the trees and these are filled with daffodils, followed by *Geranium rectum album, Geranium renardii* and so on, giving colour for the majority of the summer months and at the same time smothering weeds. Beech hedges have been planted to provide shelter, making smaller gardens within the garden and adding greater interest to the layout. Roses grow particularly well here and we have a number of well-established old-fashioned varieties; we have also successfully covered unwanted tree stumps and other eyesores with *Rosa* 'Max Graf' and *Rosa* 'Paulii'. Possibly one of the most rewarding plants, especially as this garden is on the edge of the North York Moors, is the *Abutilon vitifolium* which flowers for about six weeks in June and July, and grows eight to ten feet within a year. Although it appears to live for only about three years, it is extremely easy to take cuttings from the *Abutilon*.

We have another rewarding feature – a *Pyrus salicifolia* 'Pendula' with three different *Clematis* growing amongst the grey leaves, providing an excellent contrast of colour.

York Gate, Back Church Lane, Adel
MRS SYBIL B. SPENCER

The garden at York Gate, extending to an

acre, has been created and maintained by the owners since 1951, and is renowned for the variety of its plants and miniature gardens all within this small area.

Original features include paving in many colours, associations of materials and patterns – including a maze; and garden ornaments primarily made for use such as stone troughs, sinks, millstones, grinding wheels, old boilers, pump heads and even large old kitchen pans which all help to maintain the cottage garden atmosphere and act as focal points for many eye-catching vistas – inspiration for the latter coming from a lovely photograph of Rosemary Verey's *Laburnum* tunnel.

It is designed to be an 'all-the-year-round garden' – with colour at either end of the season and two, or even three, successions of blooms from the same patch, and this aim is usually achieved.

A profusion of bulbs (which mostly revel in the sandy but hungry soil), grasses, arums and aciphyllas act as a foil for the herbaceous plants. There is also the silver and white garden, herb garden with box topiary, beautiful *Iris* border leading to the so-called folly, paeony bed, nutwalk, a raised canal, orchard with pool and even space for a vegetable garden! Lastly, there is my special garden called after me – Sybil's.

Indeed there seems to be nothing missing in this garden, which many visitors kindly describe as beautiful, unusual and very interesting.

◆

York House, Claxton
MR AND MRS W.H. PRIDMORE

This garden lies on the glacial terminal moraine east of York, the soil varying from light loam to almost clay with a pH measurement of 5 overall. It covers an acre, rising behind the house to the hundred-foot contour, and over half is intensively gardened. Seventeen fruit trees grow on the perimeter; shrubs and small trees are in very large 'island beds' full of herbaceous plants which in summer grow into each other covering the soil (but various willowherbs blow in and root beneath till autumn). There is a token 'scree' garden for some alpines, but many are scattered through the beds. *Lithospermum* 'Heavenly Blue' grows in a mass about two yards square and even climbs into a *Prunus laurocerasus* 'Otto Luyken'. The acid soil also favours *Styrax japonica*, *Halesia carolina*, azaleas and hardy hybrid rhododendrons (the species sulk, finding twenty-four inches of annual rainfall too low), and both Asiatic and European gentians. About forty shrub roses, old and new, flower towards the end of June. There is a vegetable plot which provides nearly all our wants. My husband and I retired here in 1974, and had to plough up the half acre till it was a lifeless desert – to eliminate couch and other invasive grasses. We planned the layout with wide grass paths and small lawns and in 1975 began to plant. Two

York Gate, Leeds, in June. A fine tree paeony and unusual paving in this small but very interesting garden.

years later we added × *Cupressocyparis leylandii* on our eastern boundary, to filter the killing early May winds; and various shrubs are sited to 'stop the wind' (a theme-song here), whether from east or south-westerly gales. Ground-cover plants were encouraged, to ease handweeding problems – but some became problems in their own right and needed restraining.

Though May, June and July see the garden at its most floriferous, there is nearly always some colour, including spring and summer bulbs and seed-grown lilies. Some shrubs are grown for their foliage, as well as various evergreen and conifers. *Eucalyptus gunnii* survives as a pollarded shrub. It is a plantsman's garden, but also full in season of common colourful things like lupins and delphiniums; also of ligularias and Siberian *Iris* in the 'bog'.

LEICESTERSHIRE, RUTLAND, LINCOLNSHIRE AND NOTTINGHAMSHIRE

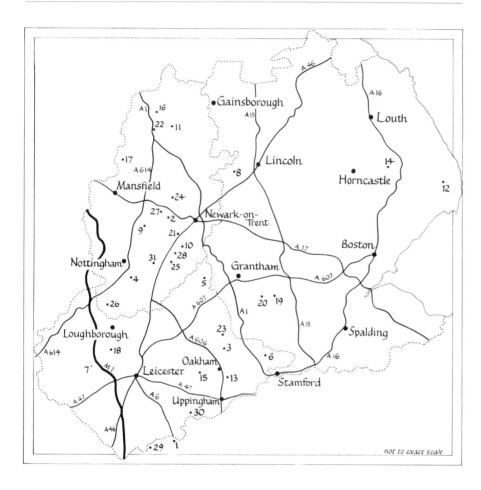

not to exact scale

Directions to Gardens

Arthingworth Manor, Arthingworth, 5 miles south of Market Harborough, Leics. [1]

Arum Croft, 22 Halloughton Road, Southwell, west of Newark-on-Trent, Notts. [2]

Ashwell House, 3 miles north of Oakham, Rutland. [3]

7 Barratt Lane, Attenborough, Beeston, 6 miles southwest of Nottingham, Notts. [4]

Belvoir Lodge, near Belvoir Castle, 7 miles west of Grantham, Lincs. [5]

Careby Manor Gardens, Careby, 6 miles north of Stamford, Lincs. [6]

Clyde House, Westgate, Southwell, west of Newark-on-Trent, Notts. [2]

Derwen, 68a Greenhill Road, Coalville, northwest of Leicester, Leics. [7]

Doddington Hall, 5 miles southwest of Lincoln, Lincs. [8]

Epperstone House, Epperstone, 7 miles northeast of Nottingham, 5 miles southwest of Southwell, Notts. [9]

Flintham Hall, 6 miles southwest of Newark-on-Trent, Notts. [10]

Green Mile, Babworth, 2½ miles west of Retford, northeast of Worksop, Notts. [11]

Gunby Hall, 2½ miles northwest of Burgh-le-Marsh, Lincs. [12]

Gunthorpe, 2 miles south of Oakham, Rutland. [13]

Harrington Hall, 6 miles northwest of Spilsby, Lincs. [14]

Hill Close, Owston, 6 miles west of Oakham, 3 miles south of Somerby, Leics. [15]

Hill House, Epperstone, 5 miles southwest of Southwell, Notts. [9]

Hodsock Priory, Blyth, northeast of Worksop, Notts. [16]

Langwith Mill House, Nether Langwith, north of Mansfield, Notts. [17]

Long Close, Main Street, Woodhouse Eaves, south of Loughborough, Leics. [18]

Manor Farm, Keisby, 9 miles northwest of Bourne, 10 miles east of Grantham, Lincs. [19]

The Manor House, Bitchfield, 6 miles southeast of Grantham, Lincs. [20]

Manor House, Owston, 6 miles west of Oakham, 3 miles south of Somerby, Leics. [15]

Mill Hill House, Elston Lane, East Stoke, 5 miles south of Newark-on-Trent, Notts. [21]

Morton Hall, Ranby, 4 miles west of Retford, northeast of Worksop, Notts. [22]

The Old Rectory, Teigh, 5 miles north of Oakham, Rutland. [23]

The Old Vicarage, Maplebeck, 7 miles northwest of Newark-on-Trent, Notts. [24]

Paddock House, Scarrington, near Bingham, east of Nottingham, Notts. [25]

Rose Cottage, Owston, 6 miles west of Oakham, 3 miles south of Somerby, Leics. [15]

St Anne's Manor, Sutton Bonington, 5 miles northwest of Loughborough, Notts. [26]

St Helen's Croft, Halam, 2 miles west of Southwell, Notts. [27]

Skreton Cottage, Screveton, 8 miles southwest of Newark-on-Trent, Notts. [28]

Stoke Albany House, 4 miles west of Market Harborough, Leics. [29]

Stone House, Blaston, northeast of Market Harborough, Leics. [30]

Sutton Bonington Hall, Sutton Bonington, 5 miles northwest of Loughborough, Notts. [26]

The Willows, 5 Rockley Avenue, Radcliffe-on-Trent, Notts. [31]

Arthingworth Manor, Market Harborough

MR AND MRS W. GUINNESS

Arthingworth was begun in the middle sixties by landscape gardener John Codrington; wherever you see effective planting that is he, and wherever chaos reigns that is me. Advance planning has sometimes gone by the board when I have fallen in love with plants and then had to find somewhere to put them! All ericaceous stuff is out and not much is safe from the east wind.

The garden is rolling, lending itself nicely to curves and corners, although a skeleton has been created of yew, hornbeam and leyland cypress to provide necessary screens. The borders are combinations of small trees, shrubs and perennials.

There is a secluded white-and-green garden which manages to be pretty well white, although we do get odd colours planting themselves. I can't bear to pull these out until they've finished flowering which rather defeats the object. This has its hey-day in July, but snowdrops, crocuses, anemones, grape hyacinths and double white primroses start us off. Wisteria, lilac, Philadelphus, irises, Clematis, poppies and delphiniums produce a profusion of white to carry us through.

The rose garden is a tangled mass of old roses, the lay-out continuing the established pattern: curving grass paths wandering through great big beds of gallicas, bourbons and species roses. Double-height standards planted in groups in the grass are beginning to make small trees, and the scent on a warm July evening is enough to send you silly.

The woodland garden looks best in spring when the bulbs get going, in particular the baby Cyclamen which is planted alongside violets, primroses and a variety of spring things. A sea of cow parsley takes over in the summer.

The herbaceous borders are meant to be a balanced pair; identical plantings have been made on either side of a gravel path. The general effect is pleasing, although needless to say a plant on one side will flourish and its partner on the other side will look definitely seedy.

Nothing happens in the winter here.

◆

Arum Croft, 22 Halloughton Road, Southwell

MR AND MRS R.C. CRIPPS

A quarter-acre garden with a diagonal slope surrounds a U-shaped bungalow and provides the opportunity for a new aspect at each corner. There is a formal rose bed in front, and a rock garden where spring bulbs grow up through a prostrate juniper and heathers; a south-facing patio with pool and fountain forms a suntrap, and a dry stone wall retains the rising land with a bed of off-beat coloured roses interplanted with hostas, catmint and foxgloves. On the bungalow walls grow Pyracantha and Clematis, the roses, 'Mermaid' and 'Handel', Ceanothus and Chaenomeles.

The garden is that of a flower arranger and therefore has to provide foliage which is both interesting and varied in shape and colour. Hostas contrast with Alchemilla mollis and the golden raspberry, euphorbias with hellebores and Stachys lanata. Amongst the trees are five varieties of willow including Salix 'Setsuka' and Salix melanostachys; the bare branches of Salix matsudana 'Tortuosa' and Corylus avellana 'Contorta' provide interest in the winter; in the spring the brilliant foliage of Elaeagnus pungens 'Maculata', Acer pseudoplatanus 'Brilliantissimum' and Amelanchier add impact. French lilac, Weigela and Cotinus coggygria 'Royal Purple' are amongst the shrubs that combine with the trees to contribute to the variety of colour not only in blossom but also in the shades of foliage from gold through greens to deep purple and brown.

◆

Ashwell House, Nr Oakham

MR AND MRS S.E. PETTIFER

In 1975 we inherited a flat vicarage garden around a house built in 1812.

The main garden is square and faces west. To the south there is an attractive but rather narrow walled vegetable garden whose box-lined paths were probably laid out in the early nineteenth century. This remains wonderfully productive in the care of our superb gardener who has tended it for the past thirty-five years. He always aims to get the soil turned over well before Christmas and never sows seeds in the spring until conditions are right and the soil has warmed up.

At the west end of the vegetable garden we dug a swimming pool and pushed the spoil into the main garden to give it a much-needed change of gradient. The drive was altered to put car-parking on the north side of the house and the old drive, carriageways and island beds were grassed down and vistas opened up to the windows of the house.

All-year-round colour has been achieved by planting various shrubs and roses against a background of old yews and hollies in rough grass, the edge of which is sculpted weekly by the mower.

On the north side of walls we have found the great leaves and shapes of Rheum and butter burr invaluable and, if one can control it, the great giant hogweed adds architectural form.

◆

7 Barratt Lane, Attenborough

MR AND MRS D.J. LUCKING AND MR AND MRS S.J. HODKINSON

Hidden behind a high wall and mature specimens of yew and Parrotia persica lies the half-acre garden of a dedicated plantswoman. Over thirty years she has gradually replaced the original Edwardian planting dominated by laurel, holly and privet with about a thousand varieties of shrubs, border plants, alpines and fruit. Early introductions, now mature, include Viburnum×burkwoodii 'Park

Farm Hybrid' whose shiny leaves turn deep red in autumn and the pink garlands of Deutzia × elegantissima 'Fasciculata'. Many Clematis have been added to this framework of shrubs, the association of Hibiscus syriacus 'Woodbridge' and Clematis macropetala being especially successful. The Clematis flowers in May while the Hibiscus branches are still bare, leaving fluffy seed heads which last until the deep pink Hibiscus flowers appear in late summer.

The verandah of the brick-built house, dating from 1910, overlooks the former croquet lawn, now dissected by several island beds. In the sunniest corner lies 'E. B. Anderson's Pavement', where wide spaces between uncemented flat stones provide an ideal habitat for alpines such as Aquilegia pyrenaica and Globularia nudicaulis grown from seed collected in the Pyrenees. The lawn is backed by former rose beds now containing a wide range of plants and a low stone retaining wall. Here, imported acidic soil supports rhododendrons and azaleas, including the soft pink bells of Rhododendron williamsianum and the bright orange Ghent azalea 'Coccinea Speciosa'.

Passing through an old apple orchard one reaches the soft fruit garden, now surrounded by flowering shrubs. Nearby, colourful displays of tall bearded irises reflect a new interest in breeding improved pink and apricot forms of remontant irises, which should flower in both summer and autumn. Part of a neighbouring garden has recently been added to provide vegetables and a play area for the grandchildren as this much-loved garden continues to evolve.

◆

Belvoir Lodge Garden, Nr Grantham

THE DOWAGER DUCHESS OF RUTLAND

Situated almost in the shadow of Belvoir Castle, and on the edge of the rolling Vale of Belvoir, this garden of approximately three-quarters of an acre has several appealing features. Partitioned into smaller areas by yew hedges, it gives one a sense of greater size.

One such area is the 'white garden' where subjects both tall and dwarf merge to give a very pleasing effect. Pride of place goes to a large Buddleja davidii 'White Cloud' with white roses and arums, white geraniums, Clematis and white Agapanthus, providing blooms throughout the summer months. The small rose garden and patio have a mixed variety of colour; delphiniums give a little height and paeonies flower during the early summer.

Herbaceous borders take pride of place in the bottom section of the garden. Every endeavour has been made to retain many of the older types and varieties of plants here, and age-old Phlox are religiously divided with care every three years to retain their vigour. Here are the most superb views of the rolling countryside. The mound, once a rubbish tip, has been cleared in recent years and planted with shrub roses and ground-cover plants. To all this add two small fountains, beautiful lawns throughout and countless well-matured trees and shrubs (amongst them *Escallonia*, *Laburnum* and several different *Acer* varieties), and you have an extremely attractive garden which still retains the atmosphere of peace and tranquillity of the old Priory which once stood here.

◆

Careby Manor Gardens, Nr Stamford
MR AND MRS NIGEL COLBORN

When we came here in 1976 there was little to call a garden and a great deal of planning and planting has been done in the last decade. We inherited some fine old limestone walls which help to divide the land into a series of individual gardens.

We made a rose garden with old species and varieties, and a spring garden containing bulbs and our collection of ancient primroses. We planted hedges to subdivide the area further creating more compartments – with hornbeam to back a red border, and copper beech to accentuate the coolness of the white border. Our 'Elizabethan garden' houses various treasures in series of little beds.

The newest area has been laid out in five more separate gardens: there is an old carriage drive, a bog garden leading to a traditional cottage garden with random planting, and a small 'town' garden which has a handkerchief-sized lawn and a lot of wall space for climbers.

We like growing things in gravel. Many plants which would otherwise be considered to be tender in Lincolnshire thrive in beds mulched with pea-sized grit. The 'scree' effect is easy on the eye and the plants like it too.

We have resisted the temptation of planting to save labour. We have a large collection of rare plants (we started a plantsman's nursery in 1983) and as many of them must be allowed to seed freely in the borders, most of the weeding is done by hand. One has to be something of a fanatic to go this far, but provided the weeds can be kept at bay, a very natural effect is achieved. Wild flowers play a very important role and we have a border devoted to them as well as a fair number growing 'wildly' under trees and in odd corners.

◆

Clyde House, Southwell
MR AND MRS G.H. EDWARDS

You leave the street opposite the butcher's, walk through the house and enter a walled garden of two-thirds of an acre. A mown path at the far end between shrub roses leads to a green gate and beyond to open country. The town is Southwell, cathedral city of Nottinghamshire. The spires of the Norman Minster are seen over a wall which is covered all summer with blooms of *Rosa* 'Dortmund'. There is evidence of ancient ecclesiastical buildings in the garden in the shape of an arch made from stone mullions, now covered with

Clematis and *Lonicera* 'Fuchsioides'. In winter the wall shelters tender plants; *Ceanothus*, hebes and *Cytisus battandieri* survive well and it provides support for roses, honeysuckle, variegated jasmine, *Passiflora caerulea*, *Solanum crispum*, peaches and figs.

There is a small but productive vegetable plot of eight hundred square feet, worked in small square beds to facilitate crop rotation. The bottom of the garden is wild with daffodils, bluebells, primroses, honesty, foxgloves and whatever wild flowers take root, the grass being mown first in late June. The large centre bed is dominated by the eight-foot stump of a weeping wych elm, which forms a sculpture of contorted shapes. This bed, as do all the borders, contains *Geranium* species.

Nearer the house *Zantedeschia aethiopica* and *Lobelia cardinalis* grow in a pond, set in an area paved in natural stone surrounded by a rock border containing *Lewisia*, *Calceolaria falklandii*, gentians and *Zauschneria inter alia*. *Nerine* and *Agapanthus* thrive under the house, which is covered with roses 'Handel' and 'Compassion' grown from cuttings, summer jasmine and *Wisteria*. The border nearest the house contains plants for winter interest, *Lonicera fragrantissima*, *Prunus subhirtella* 'Autumnalis', *Pulmonaria rubra*, early bulbs and hellebores. A rose bed is planted with the giant chive 'Frühlau', which appears to keep black spot in check, and gives colour before the roses bloom.

◆

Derwen, 68a Greenhill Road, Coalville
DR AND MRS M.W. WENHAM

This garden, made since 1974 on the site of an old orchard, is on heavy clay soil made worse by building operations. Winters tend to be very cold, late spring frosts are frequent and the winter water-table is high, which guided us after many errors and failures to concentrate on foliage rather than flowers.

Because the garden is small (the whole site is slightly under a quarter of an acre) we have not attempted to give areas a strong individual character but have rather aimed at variations on the theme of beautiful leaves, following Vita Sackville-West's principle of the maximum of formality in design (all rectangles in our case) coupled with the maximum of informality in planting. The density of planting is very high, which leaves little room for weeds and creates the effect of a lush and friendly jungle, but does call for careful control.

Even in dry summers we manage to keep a fairly lush effect through the lavish use of surface mulching, applied annually in early spring. This not only keeps moisture-lovers such as *Primula florindae* and *Rodgersia podophylla* happy in full sun, but over the years has resulted in very significant improvement in the soil, especially the heaviest clay. Having a generous source we use leafmould, but composted bark works just as well.

Our basic principle of plant grouping is

simple: to place groups of plants with broad simple leaves, sword-shaped leaves and compound leaves next to each other, for example *Hosta glauca*, *Iris sibirica* and large native ferns. The most effective colour grouping in the garden, which lasts for months, is however *Rosa glauca* (*rubrifolia*) alongside *Sambucus racemosa* 'Plumosa Aurea' (cut back hard each spring) with *Hosta glauca* in front.

◆

Doddington Hall, Nr Lincoln
ANTHONY JARVIS, ESQ.

The gardens at Doddington Hall provide a romantic and sheltered setting for the beautiful Elizabethan mansion in the flat Lincolnshire landscape. The original brick-walled gardens, gatehouse and outbuildings provide a series of formal enclosures, while beyond them stretch five acres of wild garden culminating in a stone Temple of the Winds. The Hall is approached from the east through a walled courtyard guarded by a Dutch gabled gatehouse. The courtyard contains a simple and formal pattern of gravel, lawns and plant tubs designed to set off the dramatic architecture of the Hall.

The west garden on the far side of the house is in total contrast to this severity. The whole space is full of colour and scent. A broad border on all sides contains old-fashioned shrub roses, flag irises, border pinks and a wide range of other herbaceous plants chosen as much for scent and for leaf form as for their flowers.

Within these broad borders the box-edged parterres of a knot-garden are planted with patterns of scented bedding roses and flag irises, while the bank below the house contains a large collection of pinks, dwarf and intermediate *Iris* and spring bulbs, together with the few *Cistus* that can be coaxed into accepting our harsh climate.

Beyond the formal setting for the house, the wild garden contains drifts of spring bulbs among mature trees, and these are followed by a succession of flowering shrubs and bold herbaceous plants. In high summer the picture is completed by magnificent rambling roses and *Clematis*.

Irises, with their stately flowers and handsome foliage, form an important part of the west garden display. We ensure regular flowering by doing all our transplanting immediately after the *Iris* have flowered in June or early July. This gives the plants time to re-establish and make a good flower set in the autumn. Overcrowded clumps or beds are not lifted wholesale, but rather a sharp spade is used to remove a half or a third of the total plants leaving gaps for further expansion. Again this technique encourages regular flowering.

◆

Epperstone House, Epperstone
COL. AND MRS J. GUNN

This is an old and mature garden of two acres,

which is being rejuvenated. Some large trees and a magnificent yew hedge provide a central frame for lawns, a rose garden, shrubbery and formal borders.

Surrounding the main garden are smaller areas including a herb garden, vegetables and fruit, and a fine old *Wisteria* on the tennis court.

An adjoining wild garden is full of primroses, violets and bluebells in the spring, and includes an area of old and species roses.

The main feature of the garden is its roses which thrive in clay soil and are usually at their best at the end of June.

Flintham Hall, Nr Newark

MYLES THOROTON-HILDYARD, ESQ.

Flintham Hall was purchased in 1789 by Colonel Thoroton with the intention of creating a grander layout than was possible at his previous home, near Screveton Hall. From .newly-enclosed fields he made a two-hundred-acre park south of the modernized mansion. The view over the lake and woodland, now mature, to the Belvoir hills is Flintham's greatest beauty. Within a ha-ha to the west are fine trees, Lucombe oaks, Turkey oaks, beeches and cedars, which shelter a great display of snowdrops, daffodils and, latest of all, species and hybrid rhododendrons. This is the beginning of the Long Walk, which ends up back at the house again.

The gardens proper are east of the house, where a border along the old kitchen garden wall leads to the pheasantry and a vista over the lake. Both here and elsewhere there are statues. The Regency pheasantry is hidden among roses, shrubs and trees, which support climbers. Within the old kitchen garden the owner has introduced fine double borders and, in the further half, a romantic half-wild shrub garden. The vinery is hung with passion flowers, sweetpeas, morning glory and other creepers, as well as vines. But Flintham is most famous for its magnificent Victorian conservatory – part of the house, very high, and built for palms. Its beds are filled with daturas, abutilons, tree ferns, camellias and hedychiums, while the walls are hung with *Plumbago*, jasmine, *cobaea* and other creepers.

Green Mile, Babworth

MR AND MRS R.C.M.B. SCOTT

In 1952 a start was made on converting eight acres of derelict woodland and old pasture into five interconnected gardens, the emphasis being on trees, shrubs and roses. Many dying trees were felled and prostrate junipers and blue spruce used to hide their roots. The main feature is a vista of golden Irish yews which lead you first to the hybrid tea rose garden and then to the floribunda roses, both framed by yew hedges and merging into the silver birch (*Betula platyphylla szechuanica*) avenue, which is bordered by

A riot of perennial poppies (*Papaver orientale*) and bearded irises in the box-edged herbaceous borders at Flintham Hall in June.

shrub roses growing in an area of grass with naturalized daffodils.

The woodland garden with rhododendron, azaleas, camellias, mahonias and *Pieris* growing under oak, Spanish chestnut and various maples leads to the pond, recently dug out of a patch of clay fed by a spring, and now supporting fish, wildfowl and wild flowers on its banks. The winter garden contains many unusual trees and a large bed of dogwoods and brambles for winter interest. It leads to the heather garden with five random-shaped beds and various coniferous trees and shrubs.

Colour contrasts are a feature; for instance blue cedars, golden limes, purple beech, silver pear, golden acacia, *Cotinus coggygria* and many others have been used to form spectacular colour groups and, in the winter sun, the silver stems of the birch avenue show up brilliantly against the yew and beech hedges. The whole garden is protected from the gales which, in these parts, commonly blow the light top soil into the next parish, by a ten-foot beech hedge – a fine sight at any time of year.

The walled garden, surrounded by eighteenth-century barns until recently housing a large and smelly herd of pigs, produces fruit and vegetables in abundance enlivened by climbing roses, *Clematis* and honeysuckle.

◆

Gunby Hall, Spilsby

MR AND MRS J.D. WRISDALE; THE
NATIONAL TRUST

Unpretentious, a poet's garden, Tennyson's 'haunt of ancient peace', the garden here was created by generations of the Massingberd family who gave the Hall and estate to the National Trust in 1944. Its present appearance owes much to the skill and sensitivity of Mr Graham Thomas who was for many years the National Trust's Gardens' adviser. Seven acres of loam on chalk, protected from easterly winds by old brick walls, the kitchen and pergola gardens, house a homely mixture of flowers and vegetables beneath old fruit trees. There is a fine collection of old roses and a notable herb garden.

◆

Gunthorpe, Nr Oakham

A.T.C. HAYWOOD, ESQ.

It is said 'fools build houses for wise men to live in' but it would be unfair to apply this to Gunthorpe. Harvey Dixon and his wife built this house and laid out the garden over the years 1905–8. A farmhouse and buildings were previously on the site. Everything was demolished except for some magnificent trees and the stone from the original buildings which was incorporated in the new house so successfully that many newcomers today gain an impression that it was built in the eighteenth century. The Dixon family lived here for thirteen years to enjoy their creation. Since then Gunthorpe has had two owners who have benefited from the maturing of trees, from oaks to *Prunus* and Scots pine to *Sorbus*. In fact specimens of most home-grown trees and shrubs are to be found somewhere around the policies.

The Watt family who lived here from 1921–39 were keen gardeners and cherished the place, as I like to think that we, the present owners, do. However, before the war there were five gardeners where now there is only one, although machinery and modern science have compensated somewhat for the reduction in staff. Sadly we have had to reduce the extent of the garden but the lovely house and the superlative setting of course remain, and I would like to think we have made a contribution to the whole complex. We have however, had to repair the ravages of Dutch Elm disease but miraculously (touch wood) two magnificent elms remain. Principally we have concentrated on creating foliage effects and

flowering shrubs, but perhaps the area of bulbs and wild flowers gives us the greatest pleasure.

◆

Harrington Hall, Nr Spilsby

LADY MAITLAND

The ancient mellow brick walls in the garden at Harrington form the perfect background for many old-fashioned varieties of plants. The narrow borders on two sides of the forecourt contain blue, pink and mauve plants; outstanding are *Agapanthus*, various *Geranium*, *Iris* and the striking *Eryngium alpinum*. The walls are covered with *Ceanothus* 'Cascade', roses and *Clematis*.

In the south walled garden surrounding the croquet lawn is the raised Jacobean terrace, the high hall garden of Tennyson's Maud. Both sides of the herringbone brick path were totally replanted in 1980 with aromatic plants, dwarf shrubs, *Cistus* and alpines. From the top of the terrace steps (built in 1722) it is possible to see across the garden and through the arch in the Irish yew hedge leading to the white borders with hedges of *Prunus* 'Pissardii'.

The east-facing border below the terrace is mainly yellow and cream, including a good collection of day lilies and *Cimicifuga racemosa*. A pair of old *Ilex aquifolium* 'Ferox Argentea' stand at each end of this border.

The plantings on the narrow south end of the house include the early *Rosa banksiae* 'Lutea' and *R.* 'Charles de Mills'. Red, pink and mauve dominate the west-facing border with herbaceous plants, roses and *Clematis*. A 'Wedding Day' rose scrambles through the pear tree by the arched summer house. The garden beyond was developed by the Maitlands and their head gardener since 1959, Mr Knights. The long spring-flowering borders are filled with lilacs, flowering prunus, *R.* × *cantabrigiensis*, hebes, potentillas and hellebores. The recess garden, next to the garden centre, is at its best in late summer. The soil suits lime-tolerant plants. As this garden is flat, the importance of walls and hedges is immediately apparent.

◆

Hill Close, Owston

MR AND MRS S.T. HAMMOND

This cottage garden of an eighteenth-century former alehouse/farmhouse is made very sheltered by the backdrop of hundred-year-old horse chestnuts and beeches in the adjacent churchyard of a twelfth-century abbey. From grass, an overgrown vegetable patch, banks of laurel and holly, has evolved the present garden design – in spite of children and animals! I have tried to enlarge the square quarter-acre into differing areas.

A sagging *Laburnum* was chopped down to leave a curved support up which a *Clematis* 'Perle d'Azur' climbs and is central to a shaded area, in which hellebores and unusual polyanthus, followed by ferns, *Meconopsis*

and astrantias intermingle. From a stone seat in their midst one looks at my favourite and newest area, a carefree but organized stone terrace, where I am trying hard to grow my collection of hostas – anything to try and beat the slugs, which plague this three-walled courtyard garden! *Acer palmatum* 'Dissectum Atropurpureum' and *Acer* 'Senkaki' are two more favourites, which enhance this area.

After the initial clearing, I constructed an elongated L-shaped rockery around the square piece of grass and made curved areas on the opposite side to begin the gentle effect of a cottage garden. Another predominant 'area' is a paved herb garden surrounding the barbecue. Although chiefly handy for flavouring food, the differing foliage of the herbs also makes a pleasing tapestry. From the herb garden one is led to the kitchen door through a pergola, which is now, after two years, becoming more established with various honeysuckles, pink jasmine, *Clematis* 'Vyvyan Pennell', *C. montana rubens* and *Eccremocarpus scaber*. Under the kitchen window are alpines and little 'specials' in various containers. My dream of a double herbaceous border is scaled down to a single south-facing curved one backed by a red-brick wall. *Actinidia kolomikta*, *Humulus lupulus* 'Aureus' and two *Ceanothus* provide a background to this slowly developing view.

◆

Hill House, Epperstone

MRS T.H. SKETCHLEY

The interest in this garden may lie in the fact that it has grown from 1947 when the initial trees and shrubs were planted in a bare and windswept two-acre field. The only features were thorn hedges on the boundaries.

The soil is heavy red clay – hard work at all times. It is like concrete in dry weather and very heavy and sticky when wet. Lessons have gradually been learnt, for example that ericaceous plants will not survive, but roses are happy.

Progress at first was very slow, but by adding large amounts of compost, coal and wood ash, we have gradually improved the soil. Trees, and of course all plants, take time to get going in these conditions and so we always plant them in compost and/or peat. Once established, however, they grow well and are far less susceptible to drought than plants on light soil.

The original plans have evolved and changed over the years, planting has continued steadily and it is hard to believe now that the garden is under forty years old. We now have well-grown trees and flowering shrubs, a good yew hedge backing the wide herbaceous borders, a rose garden, a collection of shrub roses and a formal herb garden.

◆

Hodsock Priory, Blyth

SIR ANDREW AND LADY BUCHANAN

This five-acre garden is on a site occupied

through the Bronze Age, Roman and Saxon times, and recorded in the Domesday Book. It is ringed by earthworks, the remains of a moat, and a fine Tudor gatehouse. The pleasure grounds are mentioned in old books. The terraces, dating from 1829, and originally in the Italian style with cypresses, bedding-out and urns, are now planted simply with roses.

Despite the vicissitudes of fortune, resulting in a period of neglect, with little fresh planting, the garden has never been completely abandoned. Starting from the centre and moving outwards we have removed or pollarded etiolated and oppressive evergreens, and since 1982 have been replanting with interesting trees and refilling the borders with mixed planting to provide continuous effect. It is a joy to clothe the bones of this romantic place with colour, texture and scent. Shrubs and trees are underplanted with bulbs, hellebores, pulmonarias, geraniums, hostas, *Alchemilla mollis*, catmint, pinks and rock roses. Tree stumps are surrounded by roses, and we have planted ramblers to scramble up through the trees. The moat banks are bright with bulbs, and the grass there is not cut until the wild flowers have seeded themselves. The large pond is stocked with trout, and we have found that railway sleepers are effective in retaining water plants. Also of interest here are the giant beeches, an immense *Catalpa* (terrific scent in August) and a long clipped hedge of *Quercus ilex*. Irish yew, swamp cypress (*Taxodium distichum*) *Cornus mas*, *Rhododendron ponticum*, *Acer* 'Brilliantissimum', and the rose 'Nevada' thrive here, and a favourite sight in the autumn is a tulip tree backed by a dark cedar. We are lucky to follow so many who have loved this place and much is planned for the future!

Langwith Mill House, Nether Langwith
MR AND MRS PETER GELDART

The mill-race of a now disused, but scheduled and still attractive, cotton mill forms the natural centre of this garden. Since the garden had been derelict for some years, and the aspect is north to north-west, planting was at first confined to well-tried varieties, and it is only now, after eight years, that we have begun to extend our choice to more unusual types. The garden follows the contours of the land, and graduates from semi-formal through meadow to wild marsh, with fine views of this softer part of Nottinghamshire. The herb garden, although small, is planted with over eighty varieties, and stresses colour combinations – golden marjoram, interplanted with the red-leaved sage and *Rosa gallica* 'Officinalis' underplanted with *Santolina*, for example. Island beds divide the garden, and old roses and species, such as *R. hugonis*, 'Complicata', moyesii, and 'Roseraie de l'Haÿ' are encouraged to form specimen bushes, while others form borders. *Rosa filipes* 'Kiftsgate' is flourishing after only a year by

being allowed to tumble through ivy on a brick wall over water.

◆

Long Close, Woodhouse Eaves
MRS GEORGE JOHNSON

The Long Close garden of five acres has been called a secret garden and fairyland. Situated in the centre of Woodhouse Eaves, it lies behind a high wall and an old three-gabled house. One enters the garden by a forecourt surrounded by high stone walls, Victorian stables, loose-box, garage and the house. Here many tender shrubs are grown on the walls, amongst them *Sophora tetraptera*, *Crinum* × *powellii*, *Schisandra rubriflora*, *Schizophragma integrifolium*, *Crinodendron hookeranum*, *Campsis radicans*, *Magnolia grandiflora* 'Exmouth' and *Clematis armandii*.

The whole garden is surrounded by mature trees, and the ground slopes away from the house towards the east; here are a series of lawns, terraces, steps, a fish-pond and fountain, and a beech hedge twenty feet high, all surrounded by beds containing dwarf species of rhododendrons, azaleas and other plants.

Lower down are two more ponds, surrounded by a yew hedge twenty-five feet high and five feet across the top. Here are water-lilies, frogs, toads, tadpoles and dragonflies. From there is the wild garden where the grass is full of wild flowers and bulbs, and many trees and shrubs grow, all enhanced by a beautiful oak.

Amongst others are magnolias *salicifolia*, *kobus*, *obovata*, × *soulangiana*, 'Highdownensis', *stellata*, *conspicua* 'Picture', *sprengeri diva*, *wilsonii*, × *thompsoniana*, camellias and many varieties of *Rhododendron*; *Halesia carolina*, *Cercis siliquastrum*, *Catalpa bignonioides*, *Ponciris trifoliata*, *Paulownia tomentosa*, *Parrotia persica*, *Gunnera manicata*, *Dipelta floribunda*, *Cornus kousa*, *Actinidia chinensis*, *Carpenteria californica*, *Chusquea couleou* and old varieties and species roses.

In the centre of the wild garden is a gravestone to a favourite horse – 'The Countryman' which died in 1874. There are many garden ornaments, including lead figures of the four seasons, stone urns, putti, a lead dancing girl and a fruit gatherer.

◆

Manor Farm, Keisby
MR AND MRS C.A. RICHARDSON

Our garden is about half an acre – developed since 1972 – and is richly planted with unusual herbaceous perennials. Trees, shrubs and old-fashioned roses provide a backcloth, and many bulbs give early colour.

The large lawn is surrounded by several borders. At the back of the largest of these is a pergola supporting several rambler roses – 'Seagull' which flowers abundantly every year, 'Goldfinch', 'Félicité et Perpetue' – with various scented honeysuckles. Steps lead down to a shady border under an old apple

tree filled with *Helleborus orientalis* hybrids and *Smyrnium perfoliatum* all flowering at the same time.

Further on, a stream bank is planted up with moisture-loving plants. A bold summer planting here is *Ligularia przewalskii* 'The Rocket', *Inula magnifica*, a purple-leaved elder, *Sambucus nigra* 'Purpurea' cut hard back each year, *Monarda didyma* 'Cambridge Scarlet', a purple-leaved *Lychnis* × *arkwrightii* with bronze-leaved fennel *Foeniculum vulgare* 'Purpureum', and a lily hybrid 'Honeydew' to tone down the hotter colours.

In springtime the main border is a pleasing sight with *Robinia pseudoacacia* 'Frisia' underplanted with *Brunnera macrophylla* 'Hadspen Cream', *Iris sibirica* with rich purple flowers and the blue foliage of *Thalictrum speciosissimum*. Later *Rosa glauca* (*rubrifolia*) foliage shows off the flowers of the pink cow parsley *Chaerophyllum hirsutum* 'Roseum', *Thalictrum aquilegifolium* fronted by a small pink-flowered foxtail lily, and *Eremurus* 'Romance'; *Eremurus* 'Cleopatra' is also splendid with glowing orange spikes.

In early autumn *Lonicera nitida* 'Baggesen's Gold' is host to *Clematis viticella* 'Purpurea Plena Elegans'. Nearby, a blue-leaved *Hosta tardiana* 'Halcyon' sets off *Origanum laevigatum* 'Hopleys' and one of the few annuals grown, the pink corncockle *Agrostemma githago* with *Gaura lindheimeri* backed by a pale mauve *Geranium pratense* hybrid which keeps on flowering if all its seed heads are removed.

Astrantias, hardy geraniums, the newer-named hostas, pulmonarias and small named violas are some of our favourites.

◆

The Manor House, Bitchfield
JOHN RICHARDSON, ESQ.

Our garden, covering some one and a half acres, was recreated fourteen years ago and improvements continue to be made.

The owner who is also the Head (and only) Gardener has worked on the principle that only plants that like to grow in the limy soil are invited to do so. The garden slopes somewhat to the west and this has permitted three themes – some formality, different levels and water – to be followed.

A simple topiary garden of box and variegated *Vinca minor* is established on a small flat piece of lawn on to which opens a door from the drawing room. Two main rose and shrub borders flank the garden; there is a kidney-shaped bed backed by a yew hedge between them, and also the recently installed pond of some forty by twenty feet to which two irregularly-shaped beds are adjacent and round most of which damp and water-loving plants are being established.

The spring bulbs are good in March and April, the roses, of which there are some eighty varieties, take over in June and most of July, followed by numerous later-flowering *Clematis*. Ground-cover is mainly supplied by rampaging *Viola cornuta* of every shade of blue and white, and many different herbaceous

Long Close, Woodhouse Eaves (see previous page) in June. A beautiful effect is produced by the different colours of young foliage in this woodland glade, with *Rhododendron* 'Sappho' in the foreground.

apples after a shower of rain and in autumn their hips glisten, attracting blackbirds and thrushes. Viburnums, pheasant-eye narcissi, jonquils and cowslips release their scent in the warm spring sun. The smell of eau-de-cologne mint planted by gates and pathways catches you by surprise when you touch it in passing. *Philadelphus* 'Belle Etoile' is beautiful and evocative in June, and the muted lavenders have delightfully aromatic foliage. The shrub roses 'Blanc Double de Coubert', 'Maiden's Blush', 'Celestial', *Rosa moyesii* and 'Frühlingsgold' share their ground with clusters of foxgloves and very handsome they look together.

The wildlife of the garden is something to be cherished. One of the few pleasures of weeding is finding frogs, newts and toads in their secret places under damp, dark foliage. One spring afternoon a pair of elegant partridges came foraging amongst the borders and some moorhens have done us the honour of nesting on the pond. Windfall apples are always left upon the ground, as winter gets underway, for hungry birds.

It is not only the constant change, from dawn to dusk, from winter to summer, that makes the garden such a satisfying environment but also that one is part of it.

◆

Mill Hill House, East Stoke
MR AND MRS R.J. GREGORY

The garden, once the site of a windmill, and adjacent to the location of the Battle of East Stoke (1487) has been redesigned and almost totally planted since January 1983. Re-development continues and the aim is to provide year-round ornamental variety and interests; soft fruit and vegetables are also grown. The half-acre, well-drained, alkaline site slopes gently to the north and lies among arable fields with little protection from wind save that of its own thorn boundary hedges. New plantings of hedges and shrubs within the garden create added shelter. Twin hedges of *Berberis* × *ottawensis* 'Superba' enclose borders of mixed hardy plants and some shrubs. Planting is arranged for both flower and foliage effect with silver foliage to enhance the colour. A *Robinia pseudoacacia* 'Frisia' forms a focal point at the end of the borders and gives height to a yellow border complemented by some purple foliage.

An alpine scree provides interest and colour, particularly in June, as does a 'dry' ditch which offers a change in levels and allows for an additional range of plants which appreciate shade around their roots. Here *Ligularia clivorum* 'Desdemona' and *Scrophularia aquatica* 'Variegata' give a prolonged and much-enjoyed harmony of colour. A collection of *Allium*, *Dianthus* and *Penstemon* has become an obsession, and a group of old fruit trees provide ideal conditions for spring bulbs, pulmonarias, hellebores, foxgloves, among others. Five hundred years on from that historic battle, the garden now offers a much more tranquil scene.

geraniums. A newly built ha-ha separates the garden from rolling pasture land.

◆

Manor House, Owston
MR AND MRS R.H. HARVEY

I see this garden, which is approximately a quarter of an acre and surrounds the house on three sides, as a lightly-controlled and informal environment where favourite plants can be introduced amongst those that happily seed themselves. Dominating the garden is a mature copper beech tree which is the perfect foil for summer greenery. Scent rather than colour has influenced my choice of plants. Honeysuckles tumble from the walls of an adjoining barn and vie for space with the old shrub roses 'Mme Hardy' and 'Mme Plantier'. Sweet briars fill the air with the smell of

Morton Hall, Ranby

LADY MASON

Morton Hall has a park and gardens land-scaped in the 1870s with the emphasis on trees and shrubs that flourish on acid sand. The Pinetum, damaged by the gales of 1976, still has a good collection of conifers. The glade of monkey puzzles grows larger and eerier. The shrubberies near the house, filled with early rhododendrons grown under a canopy of conifers, predominantly Corsican pine, have specimen trees on the perimeters: a wellingtonia, a weeping blue cedar, golden yew and golden *Cupressus macrocarpa*. Amongst the rhododendrons are a tulip tree, magnolias, azaleas, cornels, *Prunus, Philadelphus, Exochorda racemosa* and *Eucryphia glutinosa* grown not only for their flowers but for their autumn colour too.

Although we have added modern rhododendrons and deciduous trees with interesting foliage, such as *Robinia pseudoacacia* 'Frisia', a golden-leaved *Sorbus, Liquidambar, Parrotia persica, Cotinus obovatus*, the planting is still as originally planned; a woodland area in which rhododendrons grow as they do in the wild. Other parts of the garden have changed considerably. The rock garden, once the pride of its botanically-minded creators, is now a sunken area with good rocks, lovely surroundings, some water, dwarf shrubs and alpines. It can be captivating in its season but the true 'alpinist' would be disappointed.

The kitchen garden is a nursery complete with greenhouses, standing-out and growing-on beds. It has plants galore, large and small, in the ground and in all kinds of containers. It is interesting and sometimes lovely; more important it has made the maintenance of the rest of the gardens almost possible.

Our season begins with snowdrops in Kaye's wood in February. In March, daffodils everywhere, culminating in an entrancing display around the trees on Chestnut Hill. Bluebells take over, sheeting the ground from the rock garden to the Pinetum. In Kaye's wood pink and white lily-of-the-valley scent the air, followed by the climax of our year, mid-May to mid-June, the flowering of the azaleas and the rhododendrons.

◆

The Old Rectory, Teigh

MR AND MRS D.B. OWEN

This garden was originally designed and planted by Raymond and Kathleen Gibbs in the early 1950s. They spent the next twenty years working on it and it was quite a responsibility taking it over in 1973 when we moved here. However, it was so well laid out, with beautiful curved beds, never letting the eye lose interest, that our enthusiasm was fired. We have strived to maintain their high standards while trying to keep our workload to a manageable level.

The advantages of having a walled garden are infinite, and almost every inch is covered, either with *Clematis* or roses or other slightly tender shrubs. An *Akebia quinata* is particularly rampant. At the foot of one wall and in front of the house *Alstroemeria ligtu* hybrids have taken charge and are an exotic sight through July – golden hop is a spectacular newcomer too: there is always beautiful colour here.

The beds in the walled garden contain mixed shrubs and herbaceous with bulbs too. This can lead to gaps later, but I don't have time to deal with a lot of bedding out, nor do I think it is in keeping with the garden. The autumn tints of *Acer griseum, Liquidambar*, and *Amelanchier* are superb and the scent of our old and large *Viburnum farreri* is a bonus in November.

Manor Farm, Keisby (see page 125). Strong shapes and colours in the herbaceous border in July. Seen here is a white *Lychnis*, deep red-purple *Cirsium rivulare* var. *atropurpureum*, orange *Papaver* 'Nanum Flore Pleno' and red double potentillas.

The Old Vicarage Garden, Maplebeck
MR AND MRS D. KNIGHT-JONES

The garden lies around a Victorian vicarage on rising ground overlooking the twelfth-century Church of St Radegund. Mature horse-chestnuts, yews and a tulip tree surround the church, and between the churchyard and garden proper is a semi-wild garden of ornamental trees and an orchard.

From the church one ascends into the front garden passing between a large *Rosa rugosa* hedge of 'Blanc Double de Coubert' and 'Rosaraie de l'Haÿ' mixed with silver weeping pear trees, and up a path dividing a double border of herbaceous plants, backed by shrub roses on to the main lawn. This is the basic pattern of the garden; a large variety of herbaceous flowering plants with shrub roses at the back to give height.

The roses grow to enormous dimensions on the rich heavy clay soil. 'Félicité Parmentier', 'Fantin-Latour', 'White Wings' and 'Camaieux' are just some of my current favourites; there are approximately one hundred and fifty different varieties of mainly old-fashioned shrub roses in the garden. The borders are very deep, and divided into rooms by hedges, and the four sides of the house and stables, forming several small flower gardens.

Foliage and moisture-loving plants also thrive in our soil and hostas, variegated comfrey, *Veratrum nigrum*, *Ligularia*, massive ornamental rhubarb, and globe artichokes provide areas of visual calm amongst the flowers of the geraniums, campanulas, valerian, violas, gillenias and shrub roses.

A feature of note is a pergola of old apple trees with *Clematis* growing on them which extends up the centre of a double border. First and foremost this is a flower garden and in high summer the effect is extravagant.

Paddock House, The Saucers, Scarrington
MR AND MRS H.J. DAVIES

Designing and planting this garden of nearly two acres commenced in September 1978. It has been developed as a series of interesting small gardens, tempting the visitor to walk on and see what is around the corner. A formal terrace leads to a fairly traditional garden of individually planted beds with selected trees, including *Acer laxiflorum* (a snake bark) and *Robinia pseudoacacia* 'Frisia'; shrubs, heathers and herbaceous plants, plus a large pond and waterfalls with primulas, *Iris* and *Arum italicum* 'Pictum'.

Beyond the pond with its background of golden leylandii cypresses lies a small private cobbled courtyard shaded by two *Acer pseudoplatanus* 'Simon-Louis Frères', a variegated *Philadelphus* and toning sempervivums – a pleasing gold and pinky brown colour combination. There then opens a grassy area for specimen trees including *Fagus sylvatica* 'Tricolor', *Pinus wallichiana* and naturalized

daffodil drifts beyond an indoor garden into a large greenhouse. Along the western perimeter are two large pebbled areas surrounding the original field water trough, with a collection of unusual conifers including *Taxodium distichum*, *Metasequoia glyptostroboides* and *Sequoiadendron giganteum*. Across the southern end a path leads through two wide beds with flowering trees and rhododendrons, underplanted with hostas, euphorbias, hellebores, naturalized cowslips and bluebells, followed by oriental poppies for summer colour.

This path leads to a *Rosa rugosa* circle designed to emphasize one of the remaining ancient dewponds from which 'The Saucers' name derives. Here too is a quiet sheltered garden made within a raised brick bed in a south-facing horseshoe shape – a secret garden planted with alpines including *Saponaria ocymoides* 'Rubra compacta', gentians, dwarf *Iris* and miniature bulbs.

Rose Cottage, Owston
MR AND MRS J.D. BUCHANAN

Situated at a height of five hundred feet on the clay uplands of rural East Leicestershire, much of our one-and-a-half-acre garden, although exposed to the prevailing westerlies, enjoys panoramic views across the open arable fields of the Cottesmore hunt. The garden itself is undulating, the lower part being originally a sand quarry which, by the time we took over in 1977, had become a rough field. This has encouraged split-level techniques in the overall design, involving lawns, shrub and flower borders, specimen trees and, at the lowest point, a pond.

The site is dominated by a fine specimen ash which stands at the point where the upper garden descends to the lower. From there the eye is drawn to the contrasting colours of *Berberis thunbergii atropurpurea*, golden privet, broom and the silver underside of the white poplar leaves. In spring naturalized daffodils provide a fine display, together with pansies and a variety of smaller bulbs in the border. The upper garden is the chief interest in midsummer with roses leading the way, notably 'Margaret Hilling' and 'Fritz Nobis'. A bank of wild flowers, alpines planted in sinks, heathers by the pond, herbaceous and shrub borders, and a variety of conifers in island beds, ensure a continuous interest through most of the year.

St Anne's Manor, Sutton Bonington

As one enters St Anne's Manor both house and garden have an atmosphere of complete tranquillity, following architectural principles of an earlier period. Essentially it is a collection of gardens within a garden, contrasting the formality of terrace, pool and rosebeds with natural woodland glades planted with hardy geraniums, of which Sir Charles Buchanan was an avid collector.

St Anne's Manor has historical connections, in that one can find many rare and unusual plants introduced by E. A. Bowles and Lady Buchanan's mother, Lady Beatrix Stanley, both noted plant collectors in the 1920s. In June the flowers of *Salvia buchananii*, introduced by Sir Charles from Mexico and still comparatively rare, shine like red plush velvet. The Buchanans also brought many rare and interesting plants from Sibbertoft Manor, Lady Beatrix's home in Northamptonshire. At St Anne's Manor, there are a wealth of old red brick walls, a kitchen garden, and crinkle-crankle walls designed to provide varied angles for sheltered planting for many tender climbing shrubs. Other interesting features include a wide double border leading to a clairvoyée, a sunken garden, and many sculptured animals. The garden has notable collections of tree and herbaceous paeonies dating back to the years between the wars, and old shrub roses of a much earlier period. True gardeners will marvel how, in somewhat adverse conditions of elevation and hostile soil, tender plants flourish here, notably a huge plant of *Paeonia cambessedesii*, which has been growing outside, without protection, for many years, and the extremely rare tree paeony 'Joseph Rock', which regularly produces fifty or more blooms at the height of summer. Another feature is the collection of camassias in a range of colours rarely seen today, and the two magnificent magnolias M. × *soulangiana* and M. × *veitchii* underplanted with *Paeonia peregrina*.

Lady Buchanan is always keen to try new plants and to introduce new features. In April 1985, in conjunction with the East Midlands NCCPG conservation group, an area of the long double border was cleared and replanted with a wide variety of penstemons, a somewhat neglected group of plants, which produce a mass of colour in ranges of red, pink, white, blue and purple throughout the summer.

St Helen's Croft, Halam
MRS E. NINNIS

Situated as it is in a lovely part of the county amidst fields and hills, I have attempted to blend the garden into the countryside. The north lawn has a gentle curved border planted with silver and soft colours; plants include *Crambe cordifolia*, *Gillenia* and white delphiniums with *Lilium candidum*. *Clematis* 'Perle d'Azur' climbs through *Rosa glauca* (*rubrifolia*) and R. 'Boule de Neige' with more delphiniums, *Perovskia*, *Penstemon*, various campanulas and phloxes.

On the south side another cultivated border contains *Magnolia*, *Eucryphia*, *Romneya*, apricot roses, violas, white lavender and yellow lilies; *Nepeta govaniana*, *Curtonus*, *Weigela* 'Looymansii Aurea', *Ribes Sanguineum* 'Brocklebankii', geums, yellow and white tulips and *Narcissus* 'Dove Wings' and N. 'Thalia' in spring.

Great use has been made of local stone troughs, steddle stones, millstones and querns while a path of blue stable bricks has been planted on either side with winter heathers. Elsewhere the *Rosa banksiae* cascades over *Carpenteria*, and *Hebe hulkeana*. The main feature here is a path of York stone running to the brick and pantile summerhouse, which is backed on either side by mixed borders of old roses, honeysuckle, *Viburnum, Indigofera, Dahlia* 'Bishop Llandaff', pinks and violas. Almost every crevice in the path contains some treasure, such as saxifrages, sedums and alpine *Phlox*, and by midsummer the growth is so profuse that the flagstones look like stepping stones in a stream of flowers.

Skreton Cottage, Screveton
MR AND MRS J.S. TAYLOR

A walk through this medium-sized garden begins by passing the drive flanked by trees underplanted with spring bulbs. At the front of the house is the winter-flowering garden which includes hellebores, *Viburnum, Hamamelis mollis* and *Corylus* 'Contorta' and is designed to be viewed from the house. Walk past the formal fish pool through a *Clematis*- and rose-covered arch to the walled and paved garden. Here, unusual silver foliage plants and pink and white colours predominate. *Lilium formosanum, Cyclamen neapolitanum* and *Primula* 'wanda' surround the base of *Prunus subhirtella* 'Autumnalis'.

Pass under the arch in the yew hedge to the next level noticing *Sorbus aria* and purple hazel underplanted with blue violets and up to the swimming pool area where architectural *Yucca* has *Clematis* twining among it and *Eccromocarpus scaber* clambers through a *Potentilla*.

On the right are beds of *Rosa* 'Silver Jubilee' and a mixed shrub border. A bed on the left contains contrasting *Berberis thunbergii atropurpurea* and *Physocarpus opulifolius* 'luteus' and perennials with red and pink colours predominating. Cross the spacious main lawn containing other mixed beds and pass between two sentinel *Pyrus salicifolia* underplanted with violas through further shrub beds which include *Kolkwitzia, Weigela* and old-fashioned roses with *Hosta sieboldii* and *Euphorbia wulfenii*.

The orchard, which is reached via a rose-covered pergola, is a carpet of gold in spring, and at the end of the garden, there is a summerhouse from which can be seen a lovely view of the church and unspoilt countryside.

Returning along a path towards the main entrance the visitor passes the rockery which contains some unusual and colourful alpines. Another interesting spot is the south-facing border by the wall of the vegetable garden; here *Fremontodendron, Solanum* and *Choisya* flourish.

Our aim over the past twenty-three years has been to divide a rather long thin plot into many smaller gardens each with its own character, colour and form.

The Old Rectory, Teigh, in June. Sunlight falls on the glowing golden leaves of *Sambucus nigra* 'Aurea' and catches the double herbaceous paeonies and flowers of *Rosa* 'Nevada'. (For a description see page 127).

Stoke Albany House, Nr Market Harborough
MR AND MRS A.M. VINTON

I inherited a large garden with wonderful mature trees and shrubs, but unfortunately it had been allowed to run downhill for a few years and was full of ground elder; hence the chance to replant the herbaceous border. This is backed partly by a yew hedge, partly by a brick wall; pink is therefore impossible for this border and its colour schemes run through yellow and oranges against the hedges, into reds and purple, finishing with blues and lilacs. White, grey, and wine-red flowers and foliage are dotted throughout.

There is also a large walled garden, part of which is still a vegetable garden, and a tennis court. Next to this I have laid out a grey garden; it was formerly a square piece of lawn, with a brick wall on one side and yew hedges on the other side, so I planted five

Flagstone paving and stone sinks make an appropriate setting for a collection of alpines and dwarf conifers at St Helen's Croft in June (see page 128).

circular beds of grey perennials, a large one in the centre, with four small ones set around which have identical planting. These are very effective and easy to maintain.

Against the brick wall is a long bed, again containing grey flowering and foliage plants, but only white flowers are allowed, including white shrub roses, climbing roses and miniature roses.

The rest of the garden is the 'wild' part, full of mature trees and shrubs, with paths mown through the long grass.

Stone House, Blaston
MRS PEN LLOYD

The tiny hamlet of Blaston is in a valley with lovely views from the surrounding hills, making a gorgeous setting for this three-acre garden. Stone House was built during the reign of Henry VIII for a member of the Cromwell family, and was originally known as Cromwell's Manor; its present name refers to the building material used. The garden has

several interesting features, including a Japanese cherry walk, a lily pond and a small lake, as well as rose and herbaceous borders.

Sutton Bonington Hall, Loughborough
ANNE, LADY ELTON

The gardens here are at their best from June to September, when the roses and herbaceous borders are at their peak and can be enjoyed along with the variegated borders and beautiful trees. The gardens nearer to the house are formally laid out and are all in white. The herbaceous borders back on to the rose beds and these are surrounded with low walls and yew hedges. There is also a conservatory in this area, and the gorgeous scents it exudes pervade the house during warmer weather when the doors are left open.

Further from the house the gardens are more open and informal, and here the emphasis is on trees, although the borders, of plants with variegated foliage remain a

feature throughout the year; these are laid out with a colour theme to each bed, and a strong sense of design.

The Willows, Radcliffe-on-Trent
MR AND MRS R.A. GROUT

The Willows is a place of ideas for those who are contemplating their first garden in a modern suburban 'semi', or for the experienced gardener who is searching for plant associations or unusual plants. The owners have had many years' experience in larger gardens, and here they have achieved the seemingly impossible – in their own words 'a quart in a pint pot'. Although only fifteen by sixty yards, the garden follows the principles of flowing vistas, focal points, island beds and complete informality.

One approaches The Willows through a quiet residential backwater leading to an enchanting Memorial Park, which provides a backcloth of mature blue cedars and copper beeches. The front garden is a formal courtyard area, with beds of dwarf conifers, hollies and ivies to give contrasting foliage effects of blue, silver and gold around a central bed of dwarf willows from which the house derives its name. An effect of tranquillity is obtained from pinks, thymes, alliums, dwarf *Phlox* and penstemons.

From a teak seat on a patio of crazy paving, amongst a collection of planted urns, one's view of the garden consists of a series of grass or paved paths vanishing into banks of flowers; a mass of hellebores and variegated hostas on one side, and opposite a flowing border of geraniums, astrantias and paeonies ends with a slate-grey chimney pot planted with *Malva* 'Primley Blue' and the double *Lobelia* 'Katherine Mallard'. A winding path leads between a white and purple bed, and a blue and gold border to a terracotta sundial. Another, between a lemon and apricot island bed, and opposite a pale pink and lilac bed, leads to a paved area of alpine troughs and a pool. Other interesting features include shady and bog areas, a scree bed, a raised peat bed, old apple trees draped with *Clematis* and old climbing roses and many plants worthy of conservation, such as pink lily-of-the-valley, *Delphinium* 'Alice Artingale', rare pinks and wallflowers, hellebores and pulmonarias in profusion. The large collection of plants with variegated foliage provides interest throughout the seasons.

LONDON (GREATER)

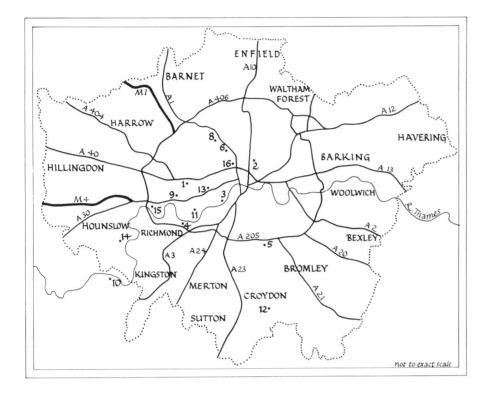

not to exact scale

Directions to Gardens

29 Addison Avenue, Holland Park, London W11. [1]

Canonbury House, Canonbury Place, Canonbury, London N1. [2]

46 Canonbury Square, Canonbury, London N1. [2]

Chelsea Physic Garden, 66 Royal Hospital Road, Chelsea. [3]

53 Cloudesley Road, Islington, London N1. [2]

29 Deodar Road, Putney, London SW15. [4]

The Grange, Grange Lane, Dulwich. [5]

7 The Grove, Highgate Village, London N6. [6]

37 Heath Drive, London NW3. [16]

82 Highgate West Hill, Highgate Village, London N6. [6]

Highwood Ash, Highwood Hill, Mill Hill, London NW7. [8]

4 Holland Villas Road, West Kensington, London W14. [9]

Kenwood Gate, 40 Hampstead Lane, Highgate, London N6. [6]

43 Layhams Road, West Wickham, near Croydon. [12] (For description see under Kent (West).)

Little Lodge, Watts Road, Thames Ditton. [10]

338 Liverpool Road, Islington, London N7. [2]

35 Perrymead Street, Fulham, London SW6. [11]

7 St Albans Grove, Kensington, London W8. [13]

7 St George's Road, St Margaret's, Twickenham. [14]

Strawberry House, Chiswick Mall, London W4. [15]

10 Wildwood Road, Hampstead, London NW11. [16]

---

29 Addison Avenue, W11
MR AND MRS D.B. NICHOLSON

Imagine my delight when, having lived for twenty years in central London with a garden fourteen foot square, we moved to a house with a garden more than twice as big – thirty by forty feet. It is wonderful how much can be done with a plot this size. We have a paved area and a lawn, two big pear trees and all sorts of shrubs, climbers and perennials, with bulbs and bedding plants to fill the gaps. Like most gardens, ours is at its best in June and July, but there is enough evergreen and variegated foliage to keep it looking well-furnished all the winter. In fact winter is almost my favourite season, as I love planning ahead for summer. As I can see the whole garden from my kitchen window, inspiration often comes while stirring the soup. No sooner planned than done – a quick foray out into the cold and two plants swap places. Everything here is quite used to being moved, and hardly ever sulks. Our five-foot *Camellia* has been moved twice, and this admittedly is quite an effort, but I feel sorry for people who are afraid to dig anything up even when it has grown too big or makes an unhappy clash of colour.

A small garden is better with a limited colour scheme, so we restrict ourselves to pink, white and blue. My favourite plants, the 'real' geraniums, come in this colour range. Everyone knows 'Johnson's Blue' and 'Wargrave' but we have many other sorts, including the lovely 'Wisley Blue', 'Kashmir White', and the early 'Mayflower'. These trouble-free plants grow so well in London, giving the feel of a country garden.

Canonbury House, N1
JOHN ADDEY, ESQ.

This comfortable garden, replanted seven years ago after some years of neglect, is overshadowed by two fine old chestnuts and a large plane tree. Camellias of different varieties are successful as are – for London – rhododendrons. Despite the shade (which allows cover for ducks to breed) the lawn is good, and large enough to allow croquet for visitors on open days.

One bed has a happy association of white hydrangeas and tall blue *Campanula* – both against a background of ivy and *Hydrangea petiolaris*. In the contiguous garden is the famous mulberry tree planted by Sir Francis Bacon, who lived by the property. In between is a long bed of roses, primarily 'Iceberg', densely underplanted with fragrant flowers. The garden, being newish, is under constant review. The most spectacular season for it is the spring, with mostly white daffodils and tulips in apricot, white and 'Queen of the Night'.

---

46 Canonbury Square, N1
MISS PEGGY CARTER

This was originally two gardens. The end house of the terrace had been demolished and its garden added to mine, giving a scope denied to owners of most terraced houses. Part of the dividing wall remains at the far end, making a small enclosure round a sundial, with a sheltered sitting-out place in front of a shell and pebble wall. The lawn on the other side leads to a figure of Hebe guarded by lions and backed by shrubs. The formality of this focal point is welcome even in winter; I am fond of statuary if used with discretion. Another stone group stands under a *Prunus subhirtella* – the first of the trees which flower in dazzling succession in spring and which, with many bulbs, make this one of the garden's best times. The trees here do throw some shade, so planting has to be careful, nevertheless the general aspect is open and sunny.

The site is flat, but different levels have been created: digging a small pool supplied soil for a sunny bank, while raised or sunken beds give plants the conditions they like. The surrounding brick walls are clothed by climbers: an astonishing *Hydrangea petiolaris* grows from a tiny pocket. It almost covers two basement walls and is starting on a third: the roots must have found the London water level which is near the surface here. When I began the garden in 1953 there was nothing except some *Iris*, two roses and a proliferation of golden rod. The soil was powder-fine, but has been altered by continual dressings of compost. I suggest to other gardeners in towns, where burning is taboo, that they make a pit for dead leaves and add these, half-rotted, to the compost heap as they build it.

◆

Chelsea Physic Garden, SW3
TRUSTEES OF THE GARDEN

The second oldest botanic garden in England,

A large and free-flowering *Camellia japonica* 'Konron Koku' in the garden at 29, Deodar Road, which runs down to the Thames.

of nearly four acres, with a collection of over three thousand plants. There are family order beds, and collections of *Cistus* and *Salvia*. The garden has many historic associations, and large unusual trees, including an olive which fruits regularly, and other tender plants.

The Grange, Dulwich, in June. The path pushes between banks which support a riot of colour, with lupins and columbines set off by the glaucous leaves of opium poppies.

53 Cloudesley Road, N1
DR AND MRS N. MILWARD

In 1970 we were able to enlarge our typical London patio garden by purchasing an area behind it of about forty by forty-five feet, covered at the time in concrete and granite setts. After a season's hard labour removing the former and re-laying the latter around what was to be the lawn, we brought in good topsoil – an excellent investment. We were helped in our planning by having a natural change in levels and an irregular shape. We have tried to capitalize on this by strategic placing of trees and hornbeam hedges to 'frame' the view of the garden from the house, and prevent the whole garden from being seen at a glance.

Our idea in planting was to obtain good varieties of plants in order to get maximum value in terms of shape, texture and colour. To maximize space, we have often trained large shrubs, such as *Viburnum × burkwoodii* and *Bupleurum fruticosum* as climbers. A happy combination on a north wall with the former is *Euonymus* 'Emerald Gaiety'. Many well-trained shrubs such as *Carpenteria californica* and *Cytisus battandieri* act as hosts to small-flowered *Clematis* once their own flowering season is over. Being in a sheltered location we are able to grow the fragrant, evergreen *Trachelospermum* and the lovely white *Solanum jasminoides* which flowers from July until November.

People sometimes say that yellow-leaved plants are difficult to place in a garden, but by grouping several different leaf-shapes together interspersed with green-leaved, yellow- or white-flowered plants we are beginning to achieve an attractive sunny border. One of the main tasks in a small garden is pruning, and by being fairly rigorous about this we have managed to fit a large variety of plants into a relatively small area.

◆

29 Deodar Road, Putney SW15
PETER AND MARIGOLD ASSINDER

Twenty-eight years of this garden – narrow, running down northwards to the Thames and in the winter very much in the shadow of the house – have constituted a hard lesson on what can and what cannot abide the conditions; so many alpines and azaleas have turned up their toes. However, successful early plantings were a black mulberry, fruiting only seven years after planting, a fastigiate *Magnolia mollicomata* from Caerhays, a whitebeam and above all a wonderful dark red *Camellia japonica* called 'Konron Koku' from Lionel Fortescue: these are now dominating features in the garden. There are two huge plants of *Rosa* 'Nevada'; five camellias flourish under their arching branches – space is very precious – and there are seventy *Camellia* cultivars in the garden. Camellias are one of the three serious obsessions in evidence! The others are hardy *Geranium* (cranesbills) and 'good' wild

7, The Grove, Highgate, in late October. Deciduous maples, cherries and willows contrast with evergreen conifers and variegated ivies; the pink flowers of the creeping *Polygonum vaccinifolium* provide welcome colour in late autumn.

flowers, some of which the uninitiated consider weeds – symphytums, pulmonarias, bugles, lamiums, bladder campion, blue gromwell, green alkanet, several *Lychnis* including ragged robin, red and white campion, *Lychnis alpina* and *L. chalcedonica*, soapworts and primroses.

Three *rugosa* roses, 'Blanc Double de Coubert', 'Roseraie de l'Haÿ' and 'Frau Dagmar Hastrup', combine very well with the whites, blues, mauves, greys and pinks of the geraniums. Two *Mahonia japonica* scent the air in the winter and *Osmanthus decorus* and *Viburnum carlesii* are outstanding in the spring. Buddlejas have been planted to encourage butterflies (and there is a small patch of nettles) but so far without much success.

A happy association is the white form of the ivy-leaved toadflax running about under *Lithospermum diffusum*; another is the magnificent hardy perennial *Macleaya cordata* (why is this not more often grown?) with *Lonicera japonica* var. *chinensis* by the river wall overhung by *Salix matsudana* 'Tortuosa'; and *Clematis montana* 'Elizabeth' grows through *Senecio* 'Sunshine'. Another lovely combination is *Dicentra spectabilis* with red valerian and *Camellia* 'Donation'. It is all a bit crowded and the lawn gets a little smaller every year. Perhaps later in the year a tiny pool and bog garden . . .?

The Grange, Dulwich, SE21
G. FAIRLIE, ESQ.

The Grange is a country house, dating from 1823, on a unique one-and-a-third-acre site, surrounded by fine old trees, but within six miles of Charing Cross. Though a London house now, it is still enclosed by open land, a golf course and playing fields.

The eastern half of this site is virtually the original Victorian garden, with a woodland strip on the north, planted with camellias, rhododendrons and azaleas thirty years ago. The western half was originally occupied by even older farmyard buildings, for whose farmer The Grange was built. The buildings of this farm were entirely destroyed in 1940, by the Blitz. The old cottage and two barns have been replaced, leaving a fragmented site which has been developed as a natural informal garden, landscaped to give in parts in the spring an alpine meadow effect, now linking the water garden to an earlier rock garden. This enables many alpines to be grown, blended with a wide selection of herbaceous plants, shrubs, and a few trees. Many are uncommon, having been collected or bred over the last fifty years by the present owner.

Three-dimensional landscaping can give more dramatic effect to taller items, planted on high spots, while leaving scope for growing miniatures in the lower areas, to show off their charm.

The trees in this garden include two paulownias – thirty years old – a fine old weeping ash, a mulberry, possibly a hundred years old, and a magnificent pear tree at the north of the house, probably planted when that was first built.

◆

7 The Grove, Highgate Village N6
THE HON. MRS JUDITH LYTTELTON

The lawn, which had been planted with vegetables during the war, was replanted with two beds of floribunda roses and an herbaceous border against the fence.

All this was soon abolished, as was the rose garden, which lasted for two years, but was then discarded as being labour-intensive; it is now an ivy garden. I had promised my husband that I could manage the half-acre garden without a gardener, he and my sons doing the mowing and looking after the paths. I planted many shrubs – yew, both gold and green, golden privet, five varieties of box, *Cotinus coggygria* and so on, and the result is a gold, green and red garden, with lasting interest and minimum upkeep.

37 Heath Drive, Hampstead NW3

MR AND MRS C. CAPLIN

This is a town garden of about one-fifth of an acre, with a lawn, paved areas and pergolas supporting climbing plants. Dry walls run along two sides of the garden. A pond carried too many fish until the herons from Regent's Park cleared the lot, but a duck and a drake now visit twice daily. Beyond the small cascade is a large rockery built from the spoil excavated from the pond and there is a small fernery in the most shaded part of the garden.

The beds are devoted largely to shrubs. The garden is seldom out of flower, although of course the shrubs are mostly at their best in the spring. Amongst other magnolias are a large *M. grandiflora*, and there are also tree paeonies, both species and hybrids, and a considerable output of bedding and indoor plants from the greenhouse and cold house. A conservatory contains tender subjects which spend most of the summer in the garden. Trained fruit trees provide an arbour and point of interest with one goblet-shaped pear tree and one trained in candelabra style.

◆

82 Highgate West Hill, Highgate Village, N6

MRS T. KINGSLEY CURTIS

The only noteworthy thing about this garden is its site. It is basically an old garden because there was an Elizabethan house here which was replaced in about 1780 by a Regency house incorporating numbers 81, 82 and 83 Highgate West Hill. Number 81 was cut off in early Victorian days, and 82 and 83 were separated after the Second World War.

We bought the central part and the longer garden section in 1946 when the garden was a completely neglected wilderness. My husband and my superb two-days-a-week gardener have created the garden as it stands. It is a homely, peaceful, good-to-live-in garden, but there is nothing unusual growing here, no special colour plans nor conspicuous design. The upper garden provides us with flowers to enjoy and to cut, the lower garden more or less keeps us with vegetables and gives us quite a lot of fruit, and I think there is colour somewhere in the garden all the year.

This is a personal garden because the plants in it have largely been grown from seeds – mementoes of holidays spent abroad or seeds brought to us by friends. We have umbrella pines grown from cones we brought from Elba and Corsica, bittersweet and thorn apple brought from America, and oleander from seeds brought from South Africa.

I think it was possibly best summed up by an elderly gardener who visited us on an open day a year or two ago. He said to me as he left 'I have never seen so much in so small a place so beautifully kept'. This is a just and worthy tribute to the genius of my gardener who has worked in this garden for nearly forty years; he comes from five generations of gardeners and has it in his blood.

Highwood Ash, NW7

MR AND MRS ROY GLUCKSTEIN

This is a three-and-a-quarter-acre garden, a mixture of formal and informal, on a sloping site in the green belt to the north-west of London.

When we arrived here in 1960 we inherited one and a half acres of elm suckers and a stagnant pond. We cleared the suckers, filled the pond, and planted Exbury hybrid rhododendrons and azaleas. The remaining one and a half acres to the rear of the house was completely redesigned by Percy Cane and includes a paved rose garden, a formal garden, sweeping shrub borders and an herbaceous border. His idea was to give a series of surprises each time a corner was turned.

In 1970 Peter Rogers redesigned the front garden to create a courtyard effect for the Grade II listed four-hundred-year-old house. Future plans include a water garden and a new terrace. We have recently planted a silver border, given to us to celebrate our silver wedding and have newly planted a 'Kiftsgate' rose which will ramble through our holly tree.

◆

4 Holland Villas Road, W14

THE MARQUIS AND MARCHIONESS OF DUFFERIN AND AVA

Most London gardens are conventional in shape and ours was no exception, a flat oblong surrounded by walls and other people's plots. We have created interest by dividing it three-quarters of the way up with a beech hedge that has a five-foot entrance guarded by Venetian statuary. The area nearest to the house is dominated by a large *Magnolia* and a pear tree, and has a substantial lawn cut with the mower set high to keep it green even during a drought and to protect it from trampling feet. Planting here is formal and bright, and contrasts with the far area treated as secluded woodland space containing forest trees that are remnants of the old Holland Park. Our garden is a pleasant place to entertain guests but a primary consideration is to have created a stimulating environment in which to paint. It may be individual plants that fascinate or a mass of colours and shapes that intermix into abstract patterns.

A *Ceanothus arboreus* 'Trewithen Blue' has been successfully established as a standard specimen. It needs a strong stake and careful pruning after the mass of flowers in early summer to retain the rounded 'tree' shape. Many exotic-looking but hardy grasses are used, and the black-leaved *Ophiopogon nigrescens*, which in spring forms a beautiful background for the white fritillaries planted amongst it.

To save major bedding-out work, the plants are mainly perennial, but a few annuals – such as candytuft – seed themselves, and the biennial Canterbury bells are raised from seed each year to ensure a permanent display. Plants used in perhaps unexpected ways include the common *Acanthus* in two large

pots standing on the paved entrance to the garden. These add to the architectural interest and act as a foil to the softer, more colourful effect beyond.

◆

Kenwood Gate, 40 Hampstead Lane, Highgate

MR AND MRS K.D. BROUGH

The garden is just over half an acre, one-third of it in front of the house, two-thirds at the rear.

To obtain relative seclusion, three sides of the plot have a laurel hedge rising to nine feet on the boundary; the other side has a privet hedge of similar height. The front garden is mainly planted with azaleas and rhododendrons, as well as a rose bed. Down one side of the garden there is an old-fashioned herbaceous border culminating in two ponds with a fountain and small interlocking waterfall.

The main garden to the rear of the house is largely lawn with two beds of 'Orange Sensation' roses in the centre leading to steps to the lower lawn which is bounded by raised beds. One side is backed by flowering shrubs in front of which are dahlias and chrysanthemums. The far end has a long hedge of sweet peas in summer and the other side on a higher ledge has rhododendrons and azaleas below which is a bed of begonias and standard fuchsias. The garden is maintained entirely by my wife and myself. There is a greenhouse where all the bedding plants are raised and a large stock of pelargoniums are maintained. There is also a conservatory for begonias and pelargoniums.

We have found that one of the most useful tools is a small two-pronged stainless steel hand fork. The prongs are four inches long, and it has proved over the years to be invaluable for general weeding; unfortunately its maker and supplier are unknown.

◆

Little Lodge, Watts Road, Thames Ditton

MR AND MRS P. HICKMAN

Our one-third-of-an-acre garden at Little Lodge has been developed over the past fifteen years, the idea being to create a cottage garden in suburbia. The garden surrounds the house on three sides, and is enclosed by a high wall on one side and mature deciduous trees at the front. The high wall enables us to grow climbing plants that provide a backdrop to a border of shrubs, old roses and perennials, all selected to give a profusion of colour and fragrance. We grow many cottage garden plants, and we are increasing the use of wild plants in the border – ragged robin, *Lychnis flos-cuculi*, bladder campion, *Silene vulgaris*, corn cockle, *Agrostemma githago*, evening primrose, *Oenothera erythrosepala*, and sweet rocket, *Hesperis matronalis*, together with foxgloves. All of this helps to give a natural look which creates a feeling of peace and informality. Many of the shrubs give fragrance and colour throughout the year – the winter-flowering honeysuckle, *Lonicera fragrantissima*, and *Viburnum farreri* in winter, whilst various *Philadelphus* or honeysuckles provide the fragrance in early summer. Other shrubs are used for colour, the spindle tree *Euonymus planipes* being spectacular in autumn.

A small pond is set to create a small damp area in this dry sandy garden. Around it are grown kingcups, *Iris foetidissima* and Solomon's seal. The house walls are covered with rambling roses, *Wisteria*, *Lonicera × americana* and *Solanum crispum*. An area of the garden has been devoted to a well-organized productive kitchen garden, designed with pathways of old bricks to give interest to the rows of vegetables and fruit.

◆

338 Liverpool Road, N7
MR AND MRS SIMON RELPH

We are fortunate in having three quite distinctive gardens; the smallest, a basement area at the front of the house, is devoted to ivies and ferns, all self-sufficient and requiring little maintenance. This has been our aim in all three gardens as gardening time is limited. The front garden is paved and planted principally with silver-leaved and aromatic plants; again foliage is the main feature. Finally, the garden in which we spend most time is at the back of the house. Shrubs predominate, chosen for their foliage and seasonal variation – *Daphne mezereum*, *Amelanchier*, *Cornus kousa*, *Mahonia aquifolium*, *Piptanthus*, *Senecio greyii* and *Viburnum davidii* amongst others.

A glass-roofed garden room full of plants opens on to a terrace, then water, then a lawn with shrubby borders either side. At the end of the garden stands an ancient pear tree, sadly dying but playing host to a vigorous 'Mermaid' rose and a *Wisteria*. Around the walls are *Hydrangea petiolaris*, 'Climbing Iceberg' rose, more ivy, *Ceanothus* and a wonderful unnamed small-leaved evergreen *Clematis* inherited from another garden.

◆

35 Perrymead Street, SW6
MR AND MRS RICHARD CHILTON

Our garden is narrow, well-shaded and measures eighty-four square metres. We have tried to avoid the over-square and flat appearance of many town gardens by ensuring that as you enter it from the house not all the garden can be seen at once. Here there is a narrow paved path with shrubs and flowers in pots, including a fragrant *Pelargonium* with tiny white flowers and a shrubby mallow *Lavatera olbia* 'Rosea'. This blends with the lavender flowers of *Clematis* 'Comtesse de Bouchaud' growing above it and entwined with a *Wisteria* growing up the wall of the house.

Before reaching a wider paved area, the path winds round a raised bed on the left. Here we have many contrasts in the leaves of

the plants and the predominant colours of the garden are yellows, many greens, white and silver with splashes of pink and lavender. Flowers and foliage are again arranged in layers, leading the eye up to the boundary trees, some of which are very tall. To bring all into focus an architectural feature has been provided in the far corner of the garden in the form of a raised arbour with an arch in white wood flanked with white trellis. In this way the mystery of the narrow path leads to a surprise. We are often asked for hints on labour-saving methods, although these have mostly eluded us. There are twenty separate pots or containers in the garden. Their contents have to be disturbed and the soil partially changed twice a year, the stones of the paving have to be swept and also carefully washed for open days and for competitions. On one such day our neighbours were startled to see us at eight o'clock in the morning, drying the stones with a hairdryer after a downpour.

◆

7 St Alban's Grove, Kensington W8
MRS EDWARD NORMAN-BUTLER

This garden is the size of a tennis court with a paved run-back at either end. By the house three octagonal pillars support a wide balcony facing south, up and over which grow *Clematis armandii* and *C. macropetala*, *Jasminum × stephanense*, *Rosa* 'Albertine', *Hedera* 'Goldheart' and *Eccremocarpus scaber*. A *Magnolia × soulangiana* grows alongside, laced with *Clematis montana* 'Rubra' and *Rosa* 'The Doctor'. An elongated oval lawn below leads to an arch covered with 'Madame Butterfly' and 'Alberic Barbier' roses, *Clematis spooneri* and *C.* 'Lady Betty Balfour'. This is the entrance to a paved space surrounded by azaleas, hellebores, foxgloves, hollyhocks and London pride. Beyond this again, raised by a stone semi-circle to a higher level, there is a lion-mouth fountain set in the boundary wall. On either side, various camellias planted in October 1946 as rooted cuttings have grown to a great height and make a beautiful backdrop to the whole garden.

Rosa filipes 'Kiftsgate' and *Hedera colchica* 'Paddy's Pride' climb up a red may, matched by a *Ceanothus arboreus* 'Trewithen Blue' which has grown into a notable tree. Under the may, the scented *Jasminum mesnyi* and the evergreen *J. revolutum* cover the walls while *Rhododendron luteum*, *Iris japonica*, and various salvias fill the beds. *Fatsia japonica* 'Variegata', *Pieris formosa forrestii* and *Viburnum* 'Lanarth' flourish on the other side. One grey corner consists of *Teucrium fruticosum*, *Halimium halimifolium*, *Artemisia* 'Lambrook Silver', *Lamium* 'Beacon Silver' and various lavenders.

Cestrum elegans flowers all year round in a small greenhouse, which also shelters *Jasminum polyanthum*, *Plumbago capensis*, verbenas and scented geraniums. The garden is designed for one pair of elderly hands, with youthful help in the autumn when leafmould,

which has rotted all year under the camellias, peat and bone meal are dug into the beds. A spring cocktail for everything, and several doses of mosskill for the lawn are essential.

◆

7 St George's Road, St Margaret's, Twickenham
MR AND MRS RICHARD RAWORTH

The garden was redesigned and replanted in 1974 with hedged areas to create the effect of rooms, long views and surprises. Planting is informal with old shrub roses intermingled with herbaceous plants and rambling *Clematis*. On the north wall of the house is a large conservatory, constructed out of conventional materials. Its unusual aspect creates an ideal environment for cool conservatory plants. Ferns, ivies, jasmine, *Trachelospermum*, *Clematis florida*, *Plumbago* and climbing geranium thrive. Pots of pelargoniums, fuchsias and *Schizanthus* add summer colour. The house itself is clothed by *Vitis coignetiae*, *Hydrangea petiolaris*, *Wisteria*, *Clematis* and climbing roses, which soften its Victorian outline. At the far end of the garden stand two beehives in a recently created knot-garden. Its four beds are divided by formal gravel paths and edged in miniature box. Carpets of thyme, woodruff, sage, camomile, marjoram and hyssop are punctuated by tall *Lilium regale*. Beyond the bee garden, on the edge of the communal grounds, it is a wild garden, frothy with white and pink cow parsley in early summer.

◆

Strawberry House, Chiswick Mall W4
BERYL, COUNTESS OF ROTHES

The front of the house faces south-east and overlooks Chiswick Mall, and a lawn leading down to the Thames. This is flanked by shrubs such as *Cotinus coggygria*, *Buddleja* 'Dartmoor', *Salix* and *Cornus*. The rectangular walled garden at the back of the house is only one-third of an acre in size, but owing to being well mulched, acid- and alkaline-loving plants prosper. Although the garden predates Kew the present layout was planned in the early 1920s. The shape is not inspiring, but has the advantage of three large trees, an *Ailanthus*, a mulberry and a wild cherry. Next to the house is a paved courtyard, surrounded by flourishing camellias, a *Hydrangea petiolaris* and large terracotta pots filled with hostas. A flight of steps leads up to a small pond, beyond which is a lawn and extending from this a pergola covered with roses, *Wisteria* and *Clematis*.

Being fond of bog plants, particularly candelabra primulas, my late husband and I were delighted to find a sunken ditch between two ponds where these could be grown. Also round one of the ponds grow *Iris kaempferi* and *Arum* 'Green Goddess' and in the water *Iris laevigata*, *Pontederia* and waterlilies. Beyond the pond is the wild garden with many shrubs, more camellias, *Viburnum*

Little Lodge, Thames Ditton, in July (see page 134). *Campanula persicifolia* 'Alba' and *Rosa glauca (rubrifolia)* dominate the scene.

tains plants selected over thirty years and includes *Achillea filipendulina* 'Gold Plate', *A. millefolium* 'Cerise Queen', *Anchusa* 'Loddon Royalist', *Anemone japonica*, *Astrantia major*, *Coreopsis verticillata*, *Salvia* 'Superba', *Helenium autumnale*, *Solidago* 'Goldenmosa' and *Rudbeckia fulgida* var. *deamii*.

Delphiniums are grown to exhibition standard with up to thirty in the main border. These are replaced every third year with fresh plants from cuttings taken in the spring. Some old plants survive, but vigour can only be maintained by propagation, which also reduces black rot and slug problems. Our favourites are 'Daily Express', 'Loch Maree', 'Blue Nile' and 'Purple Ruffles'. Only one spike is allowed to flower in the first year and a maximum of four in the second and third years. We find that over-generous feeding tends to increase gappiness in the florets and only a general fertilizer is given in the spring with a dressing of hop manure or mushroom compost. Abundant water is essential in dry periods if exhibition spikes are to be grown. Staking and tying must allow the plants to move in the wind. Further dressing and fertilizer are given after flowering, and in dry spells in the autumn it is essential to continue watering if the plant is to build up new flower spikes for the next year. Liberal use is then made of slug bait and kept going through the winter during mild spells. If this programme is followed carefully, delphiniums do not just disappear over winter as many people complain. Fundamentally you need to maintain young, vigorous plants.

Lilies at Strawberry House, Chiswick Mall, in July. For a description of this garden see page 135.

'Fulbrook', *Escallonia iveyi* and tree paeonies. Underneath are hellebores, hardy geraniums and euphorbias. On the north-east side of the lawn are magnolias and on the south-west side a mixed border of low-growing shrubs, herbaceous plants and lilies. Here an *Abeliophyllum distichum* survived the 1985 winter. Against the walls are *Stachyurus*, *Clematis*, *Rubus* 'Tridel', *Chaenomeles* 'Apple Blossom' and much else. Under the mulberry, to the surprise of experts, grows a large *Ceanothus*, and *Stephanandra* with a ground-cover of woodruff, wild strawberries and self-sown violets.

◆

10 Wildwood Road, Hampstead NW11
DR AND MRS J.W. MCLEAN

The background of the garden is set in Hampstead Heath so that the view from the house merges into the Heath. This was deliberately planned with a sloping serpentine lawn leading down to the trees and rhododendrons and providing a focal point at the bottom of the garden. Since delphiniums are our speciality, the main feature is a large herbaceous border approximately fourteen feet deep. *Clematis* are allowed to ramble up the conifers at the back of the border and include the spring-flowering 'Nelly Moser' and summer-flowering 'The President' and 'Ernest Markham'.

Herbaceous plants are carefully selected for their long flowering season and minimum staking. At the back the six-foot *Helianthus* 'Monarch' is interplanted with *Hibiscus* 'Woodbridge' and 'Blue Bird'; *Macleaya cordata* and *Aruncus sylvester* are excellent plants of architectural interest. The main border con-

NORFOLK AND SUFFOLK

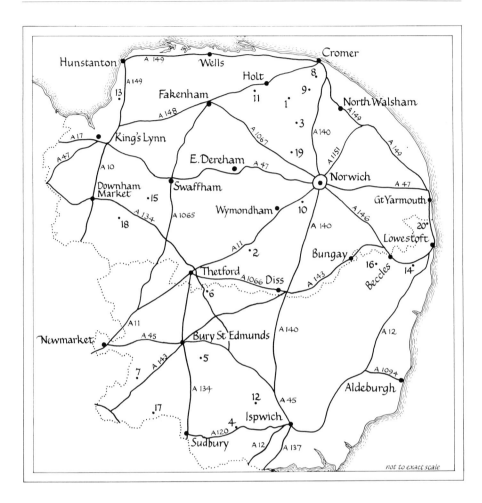

not to exact scale

Directions to Gardens

Barningham Hall, Matlaske

SIR CHARLES AND LADY MOTT-RADCLYFFE

Barningham Hall, built by the Pastons in 1612, owes its scenic value to the skills of Humphrey Repton, who in 1807 designed the gardens and made a lake by building a dam across a small stream lying between the field below the house and the woodlands immediately beyond. Repton also added a wing on to the south-east side of the house, and built a large walled garden, which to this day is still kept up as originally designed, with espalier apple trees (a few of which undoubtedly were planted approximately a hundred and fifty years ago, and still bear fruit) along most of the paths. His work was carried out under the instruction of John Thruston Mott (1784–1847) the great-grandfather of the present owner. The extensive gardens planned and made by Repton are today curtailed and inevitably made more manageable.

The main feature of the gardens round the house are the extensive lawns, with a long herbaceous border, which leads to an enormous beech hedge with yew buttresses, beside which is a rose garden. Beyond the rose garden is a green garden with cedar trees, and a circular path surrounded on one side by rhododendrons, and on the other by Irish yews. The twenty yews lining the walk were planted in about 1850.

Besthorpe Hall, Nr Attleborough

JOHN ALSTON, ESQ.

This is a formal garden within Tudor enclosures and includes an old tilting ground. There is colour and interest for every season; daffodils, hellebores and flowering shrubs for the spring, roses and a double herbaceous border for the summer, with poppies, foxgloves and hollyhocks growing at will. The hydrangeas and colchicums are notable in the autumn, with a collection of birches and maples providing winter interest.

The old walls provide a home for a collection of *Clematis* and climbing shrubs: the kitchen garden is especially fine and the winter garden provides a refuge for camellias.

Barningham Hall in September (see page 137). A scene in the walled kitchen garden, built by Humphrey Repton, with cabbages and a row of early chrysanthemums.

month of the year, from the earliest snow-drops and *Cyclamen*, through the blues of anemones and grape hyacinths and scillas to the sophisticated lines of fritillaries and the onion family, lilies in summer and the final vinous delights of *Colchicum*. I think perhaps the garden is at its best in early summer, when marsh marigolds glint along the stream and the scent of cow-parsley drifts in from the field to mingle with that of honeysuckle and the tall yellow lilies under the trees.

Elm Green Farmhouse, Bradfield St Clare

DR J.W. LITCHFIELD

In 1965 my wife and I started remaking the derelict garden of our thatched seventeenth-century farmhouse, on about an acre of slightly alkaline boulder clay surrounded by open farmland.

We aimed to plant a great variety of form and colour in flower and foliage. Trees and shrubs grow in mixed borders with roses and herbaceous perennials; lilies are grown with enthusiasm despite heavy clay; aconites, *Anemone blanda*, *Scilla*, *Muscari* and *Crocus* have had time to seed widely, and in summer osteospermums and other half-hardy plants provide reinforcements.

The main plantings are around the two lawns each partly shaded by an ancient apple tree. A succession of partly secluded areas leads from these to provide homes for different types of plant and an element of surprise. A shady glade bordered by a large *Magnolia*, *Parrotia persica* and other trees is a setting for drifts of aconites, anemones and erythroniums in spring and willow gentians in summer, while along a sunken path, flanked by a dry wall, there is moisture enough for candelabra primulas, globe flowers and ferns. *Dactylorhiza fuchsii* rescued from a wood clearance has naturalized itself here. Between the main plantings are many rare plants whose recognition gives visitors something of the pleasure of botanizing on a country walk.

Another special feature is a gravelled courtyard, within a hornbeam hedge – here are troughs of alpines and a raised bed backed by a weather-boarded barn, supporting climbers in variety and flanked by an open byre where various irises and ferns flourish. Other areas of interest include an old horse-pond with marsh marigolds, irises and primulas around it but still invaded by willow herbs and an area of rough grass where cowslips and ox-eye daisies grow in profusion. We like to think the garden provides interest for all sorts of gardeners who are warmly welcome.

Euston Hall, Nr Thetford

HIS GRACE THE DUKE OF GRAFTON

This garden has been entirely created within the past twelve years by the present Duke of Grafton – not an easy task, as much of it encompasses the area of the large portion of

*Blickling Hall, Nr Aylsham

THE NATIONAL TRUST

A large garden, with a parterre, herbaceous borders, a crescent lake, azaleas and rhododendrons, surrounds the magnificent house, built in 1628.

Caley Mill, Heacham

NORFOLK LAVENDER LTD

The red sandstone of our early nineteenth-century watermill is an ideal centrepiece for the largest display of lavender in England. Most of the lavenders that we grow are ones that have been developed by us, and the more popular ones are available to the general public. Not only can the visitor see lavender being used in its commercial sense, but we have also laid out the gardens to show different sorts of lavender being used as hedges around our rose garden. There is also an extensive herb garden planted on the old monastic basis showing the plants to which lavender is allied as a natural cure.

A small riverside garden runs beside the old mill-stream which is well sheltered if the wind is in the south-west. Here visitors can take their tea and watch the trout rising.

Chequers, Boxford

MISS J. ROBINSON

This two-acre garden, full of plant varieties though it is, is very dependent on its setting. Old walls, one of them a Suffolk speciality, a 'crinkle-crankle' wall, give it shelter, the church tower dominates the skyline, and a stream carries one's eye up the valley to the fields beyond.

It is very much a do-it-yourself garden. I have only had the minimum of help since I started making it from scratch in 1958 and I have raised many of the plants in it here from seed or cuttings.

Despite all this, sometimes bitter, experience I have no particular tips to pass on, except to say that I treat every plant as an individual with its own likes and dislikes. The majority here are species and I try and find out the conditions they grow in in the wild and imitate this as best I can. After giving them a good start they must stand on their own feet. I have no time for coddling and for this reason never try to grow plants (anything ericaceous, for example) which are totally alien to the conditions prevailing here.

Bulbs are perhaps my speciality because they like the perfectly drained soil and our (usually) dry summers. They flower in every the house demolished by his father thirty-five years ago. In fact, one garden is laid out on the site of the demolished wing. The first thing to do was to remove a disued tennis court, to grass over the courtyard of the original house, which meant excavating and bringing in a large amount of topsoil, to make a York stone terrace on the south front, and to create five new borders and a small walled garden on the site of a Victorian greenhouse.

The idea is to have colour all through the summer and for this some annuals are essential. One long border is purely herbaceous, the others are mixed shrubs, roses, irises and many fuchsias. There is a fountain surrounded by four beds of the rose 'Ballerina' and the lavender 'Hidcote'. The soil is poor and very light, and in a hot summer is apt to burn up. Beyond the stables is a large lawn and another border with climbing roses, many of which do very well here. The garden has a handsome William Kent seat with lions' claw feet and one of Kent's 'Bowling Green' seats similar to those at Rousham. On the south front are four fine lead urns, dated 1671, and bearing the cypher of Lord Arlington, the builder of the house. He was responsible, with the help of John Evelyn, for laying out the Pleasure Grounds which immediately adjoin the gardens.

Felbrigg Hall, Roughton
THE NATIONAL TRUST

These large pleasure gardens, consist mainly of lawns and shrubs; other features of interest include an orangery with camellias, a large walled garden recently restocked with fruit, vegetables and flowers; a vine house, dovecote, and a superb display of colchicums.

Great Thurlow Hall, Nr Haverhill
R.A. VESTEY, ESQ.

The house and garden were bought by Mr Vestey in 1942 and the garden, which then consisted of a walled vegetable garden and a small rose garden, has since been considerably extended to its present twenty acres. With the help of Major Daniels of Dalham, it was landscaped with flowering trees and shrubs, herbaceous borders and roses. Since then a goldfish pond and swimming pool have been added.

A feature of the garden is the grassed walks which extend both sides of a natural river which runs through the grounds. In spring these walks and other parts of the garden are carpeted, first with aconites and snowdrops, then with daffodils of all varieties and later with tulips, bluebells and forget-me-nots. More recently a trout lake has been added and this is also fringed with daffodils in spring and has islands planted with shrubs to make cover for the birds which populate the lake.

Hanworth Hall, Nr Cromer
H.M. BARCLAY, ESQ.

We have a Spanish chestnut tree on the way down from the house to the walled garden. The girth of this tree is twenty-nine foot-seven inches, and in spite of being about seven hundred years old it is still healthy. The walled garden was made at the same time as the house, which was built circa 1695; the walls are fifteen feet high and have survived so long because they stand on a seven-foot brick angular base below ground. They enclose an acre and a half of garden, which used to contain vegetables, herbaceous borders, fruit trees and so on.

In 1968 we decided to change this garden into shrubs and mown grass, with a circular centre of heather and dwarf trees. Round the walls inside and out grow many kinds of *Clematis* and climbing roses, and we have dozens of sweet-smelling shrubs, such as *Philadelphus* of all sorts and old-fashioned roses and potentillas. Camellias do very well, and there are clumps of hybrid musk roses such as 'Buff Beauty', 'Cornelia' and 'Felicia'.

Intwood Hall, Nr Norwich
MRS M.B. UNTHANK

The visitor approaches the gardens through the rhododendrons and yew trees, and will see first the two magnificent cedars, planted between the years 1760–75, and the expanse of grass that stretches to the park, separated from the garden by a fine example of a ha-ha.

Behind us is the terrace garden, with three Tudor walls still standing, where there was a bowling alley when Queen Bess was entertained by Sir Thomas Gresham in 1578; the wall seats for the bowlers are still there, as is the Tudor archway nearby, set into a Victorian wall. Also in the garden, on the terrace, is a good example of Victorian work in a plant urn. Outside the terrace garden is a sprawling mulberry, planted just before the turn of the century from a truncheon (a stake from a mulberry).

Through the archway is the rose garden, with its high walls which make for very good acoustics, and in recent years open-air concerts have been held from time to time on summer evenings. In another part of the garden, the so-called wild garden, shrub roses and various older roses, labelled for the rose-lover, are scattered about and it is hoped that they will become a feature of the area set aside for wild flowers as well.

In the spring the two walks bordering the park, the church walk and the lilac walk, are richly adorned with snowdrops, aconites, daffodils, primroses and bluebells in their seasons. The woods and walls provide shelter and nesting places for a great variety of birds. It is a tranquil spot with its old-world charm, its box hedges, its many nooks and corners and its summer-houses.

Letheringsett Gardens, Nr Holt:

The Glebe (THE HON. BERYL COZENS-HARDY)

Hall Cottage (MR DAVID MAYES)

Letheringsett Hall (MR AND MRS MITCHELL)

Old Rectory (MRS M.E.B. SPARKE)

Water is the focal point for all four gardens at Letheringsett, with the River Glaven providing waterfalls, cascades, fountains and other features. Many visitors will be interested to see the various pumps and hydraulic systems which were installed at the turn of the century

Immaculate paths, lawns, and yew hedges set off the flights of steps and stone urns in the garden at Blickling Hall in September.

to provide power for the local brewery and to drive a turbine for operating farm machinery.

The Hall garden contains many features of interest, in particular a natural area designed to attract wildlife. Hall Cottage garden contains two fish pools with waterlilies, water hawthorn and moisture-loving plants including orchids, while the garden of the Old Rectory is particularly noted for its abundance of daffodils. The lawns of The Glebe run down to the river and in spring the area near the bank is colourful with crocuses, snowdrops, primroses, bluebells and wood anemones. A variety of trees and shrubs, including many *Clematis*, are also to be found here. A fishpond features marginal plants such as primulas, hostas, irises and *Trollius*.

Nedging Hall, Nr Hadleigh
MR AND MRS R. MACAIRE

The garden at Nedging Hall has evolved over many centuries. There are numerous fine old trees including a magnificent oak, which is reputed to be eight hundred years old. The site slopes gradually down to a very attractive lake below which is a large rock garden. The garden has a very spacious atmosphere with large areas of grass, which in spring are a mass of bulbs. There are numerous interesting shrubs, some many years old, some planted more recently, and situated near the house are more formal rose beds. The old kitchen garden was redesigned recently and is now half vegetable garden and half an extremely attractive swimming pool area with planting which gives a wonderful show during the summer months. The different areas are divided by gravel paths and yew hedges.

The garden is approached by a long drive bordered by shrubs and trees, which is particularly impressive in the spring when the flowering cherries are out and the grass is carpeted with cowslips. Although the garden is large it has been planned for easy maintenance with only parts of the grass cut as formal lawns and all the beds planted with permanent planting. Other features are a fine old box hedge and a large herbaceous border which is a mass of colour throughout the summer. The tennis court is surrounded by a *Prunus* hedge and, although quite close to the house, is completely screened from it by shrubs and trees.

North Cove Hall, Beccles
MR AND MRS BEN BLOWER

The five-acre garden was originally laid out around 1760, and the park and garden retain many of the oaks, limes, beech and holm oaks planted at that time, with a large, more recently planted cedar of Lebanon. The garden, which formerly depended on herbaceous borders with numerous small beds planted out annually, has recently been transformed to reduce costs.

It is unusual that the vegetable garden – enclosed on three sides by tall garden walls – merges into the pleasure garden. The paths, bordered by dwarf box hedges, lead to a west-facing shrub border edged with stone paving, which enables the smaller plants to tumble forward without interfering with the mowing of the broad grass path between it and the large lily-pond. The pond contains five different varieties of waterlilies.

A statuesque *Gunnera manicata* is bordered on one side by a slender *Taxodium ascendens* 'Nutans', and on the other by a group of *Betula jacquemontii* surmounting *Viburnum tomentosum* 'Lanarth', all of which reflect most effectively in the water. Nearby is a fine *Alnus glutinosa* 'Imperialis' growing out of a clump of *Osmunda regalis*. Recently a large collection

of shrub roses has been introduced round the croquet lawn, and roses climb the house and pergolas together with many varieties of *Clematis*.

Through the west border a wooded area is being developed as a winter garden, and elsewhere is a collection of dwarf conifers with *Erica carnea* and other lime-tolerant heathers to add interest in late winter and spring.

Oxburgh Hall Garden, Nr Swaffham
THE NATIONAL TRUST

The Hall and moat are surrounded by lawns, fine trees, colourful borders, and a charming parterre garden of French design.

The garden at Chequers, Boxford. The garden is described on page 138.

Redisham Hall, Nr Beccles
MR PALGRAVE BROWN

This estate had been taken over by the army and the Ministry of Agriculture during the war, so in 1945 the garden was a wilderness and the park strewn with Nissen huts.

Our policy from the outset was to restore the gardens and park for simplicity and minimum maintenance and this policy remains.

With the Georgian house set in the middle of the two-hundred-acre park it was clear that the garden, about five acres, should merge with the park, which in itself has been treated as an extension of the garden. Thus the emphasis has been on planting specimen trees giving a variety of colour throughout the year but inevitably the colours, particularly of the oaks, are seen at their best in October and November. Colour is added in summer by traditional flower beds mainly as borders to the lawn. The green of the lawn flows into the green of the park where the grazing cattle also form part of the picture.

Much of the activity centres round the kitchen garden. This is large by any standard and is enclosed by an old brick wall and a twenty-foot-high beech hedge. The produce is sold to the estate and any surplus to the local community. It is the kitchen garden that seems to invite the greatest interest for our visitors during the open day, enhanced by the enthusiasm of the estate staff.

Riverside House, Clare
MR AND MRS A.C.W. BONE

The garden is about one acre in area, and lies between the Elizabethan house on the northern boundary and the River Stour to the south. Its particular features are its long herbaceous beds, backed by shrubs or old brick walls and its delightful riverside setting. For a relatively small garden there are no less than seventy trees at one stage of growth or another, set off by immaculate lawns which are perhaps the central theme of the garden.

The garden can in no way be described as grand, being not much more than a large cottage garden, but enthusiasts will find many interesting plants growing if they look carefully enough. As each year passes the shape of the garden will mature as the trees grow and changes are made to the planting schemes to accommodate the increasing areas of shade.

Ryston Hall, Downham Market
MR AND MRS E.R.M. PRATT

The layout of the gardens dates from the latter part of 'the eighteenth century when the house and formal gardens were redesigned by Sir John Soane. The garden consists of lawns and herbaceous borders, with shrubberies and a rock garden, and is mostly on one level with wide vistas of open parkland.

The lily hybrid 'Limelight' at Elm Green Farmhouse in July. For a description of this garden see page 138.

There are some particularly fine examples of rhododendrons and azaleas encouraged by the natural acidity of the soil, and there is a rock garden around a small ornamental pond. The garden has many very fine long-established trees including three large London planes, wellingtonias, swamp cypresses and cedars.

Swanington Manor, Nr Norwich
MR AND MRS RICHARD WINCH

Swanington Manor, a seventeenth-century red brick house, has a large old-established garden, framed within a three-hundred-year-old yew and box topiary hedge, which provides a wonderful backcloth for herbaceous borders and other plantings. Visitors over the past few years have described it as romantic and peaceful, and it is within this description that we have tried to improve it with more plantings of herbaceous borders which contain many unusual plants, all fully labelled.

The garden includes a pretty flowing stream along which are planted ferns and other moisture-loving plants, and a woodland walk, with sheets of spring bulbs, winds amongst fine limes, a superb copper beech and new plantings of unusual trees. A herb garden and well-maintained greenhouses, including a large *Cymbidium* house, provide interest in the winter months. Some of our favourite plantings include a large weeping pear, *Pyrus salicifolia* 'Pendula', underplanted with *Hosta sieboldiana* 'Elegans' and white foxgloves, appearing through the leaves; the blue *Viola cornuta* twining through the base of a pyramid of lavender sweet peas and the white *Campanula alliarifolia* with its pretty heart-shaped leaves beside them; the huge heads of *Allium cristophii* underplanted with *Gypsophila* 'Rosy Veil' and *Campanula glomerata*, and a large terracotta vase filled with *Aster capensis* and its variegated form, flowering with their lovely blue daisies for weeks on end, surrounded by *Lotus berthelotii* trailing to the ground.

107 University Crescent, Gorleston
MR J. BARTRAM AND FAMILY

This is a town garden, at the end of a terrace, about three-quarters of a mile from the sea. Wind is a problem in winter although a conifer hedge offers some protection. The garden slopes from the house, so a series of raised walled flower beds were built. Originally there were five lawns but gradually they were removed, and a combination of crazy paving and shingle paths make access to all the garden possible even in wet weather. Not being a lover of bare soil in winter I have designed the garden with herbaceous plants mixed with dwarf conifers, heathers, alpines and dwarf shrubs. One hedge is north-facing and under it a variety of shade-loving plants thrive including *Cyclamen*, rhododendrons, azaleas, hostas and astilbes along with other dwarf shrubs. Bulbs have been naturalized in many parts of the garden.

May to June is a good time to see the garden awake, with a burst of new growth from heathers and conifers trying to outdo the rhododendrons and azaleas for attention. The blue of *Rhododendron impeditum* is set against the red of *Azalea* 'Nico' with a carpet of *Erica carnea* 'Springwood White' underneath. Summer sees a change, as many heathers and conifers take on their new colours along with bedding plants such as petunias, antirrhinums and marigolds, 'Naughty Manta' being a favourite. Many heathers show their colours until late autumn, along with a number of bulbs, including *Nerine bowdenii* and *Cyclamen hederifolium*. One shrub that attracts attention is *Pieris* 'Forest Flame' with its red new growth followed by lily-of-the-valley-type flowers, the red leaves turning to cream then green as spring gives way to summer.

NORTHAMPTONSHIRE

Turweston Gardens, 1 mile east of Brackley. [15]

Spring Valley; Turweston Barn; Turweston Glebe; Turweston Lodge; Turweston Mill

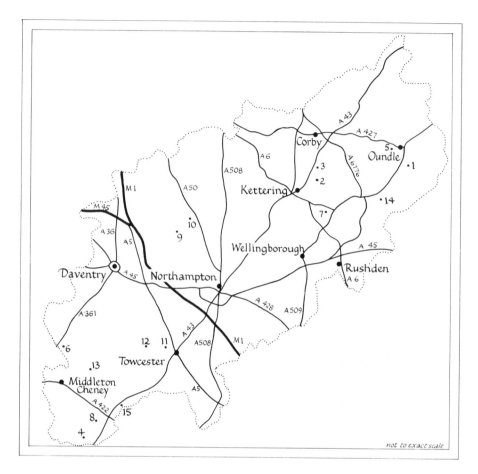

not to exact scale

Barnwell Manor, Nr Peterborough
T.R.H. PRINCESS ALICE DUCHESS OF GLOUCESTER AND THE DUKE AND DUCHESS OF GLOUCESTER

An unusual feature of Barnwell Manor garden is that most of it surrounds the ruins of a fourteenth-century castle enclosing a hard tennis court. From out of these ancient walls grow a vast quantity of aubrieta, wallflowers and bunches of small pinks of old varieties, and growing on the outside walls are some pear trees over four hundred years old, still bearing very delicious round pears.

Unfortunately trees and shrubs have also embedded their roots amongst the stones, and far too many pigeons make their homes there, not to mention one or two families of wild duck in the spring. In other parts of the garden extensive lawns and yew hedges need much time in the mowing and cutting thereof.

A small round garden of white and silver plants surrounds an ancient stone well. This garden was a silver-wedding present from our staff in 1960. Another welcome gift was a line of flowering cherries from the Royal Air Force.

The garden is open to the public at least twice a year, and on other special occasions. Coachloads of organizations such as the Women's Institute, Red Cross, etc. are also welcome on request and turn up at intervals, usually after 6.30 p.m., and are shown around by the Head Gardener.

Directions to Gardens

Barnwell Manor, 2 miles south of Oundle, 4½ miles east of Thrapston   [1]

Boughton House, 3 miles north of Kettering. [2]

Bowood Cottage, Queen Street, Geddington, 3 miles northeast of Kettering   [3]

9 The Butts, Aynho, 6 miles southeast of Banbury, Oxon.   [4]

Cherry Orchard Yard, 17 Benefield Road, Oundle.   [5]

Chipping Warden Manor, Chipping Warden, 7 miles northeast of Banbury, Oxon. [6]

26 Church Lane, Cranford, 4½ miles east of Kettering.   [7]

The Coach House, Hinton-in-the-Hedges, just south of Brackley.   [8]

Coton Manor, 10 miles north of Northampton near Ravensthorpe Reservoir.   [9]

Cottesbrooke Hall, 10 miles north of Northampton.   [10]

The Dower House, Boughton House, 3 miles north of Kettering.   [2]

Easton Neston, Towcester.   [11]

Old Rectory, Bradden, 5 miles west of Towcester.   [12]

The Spring House, Chipping Warden, 7 miles northeast of Banbury, Oxon.   [6]

Steane Grounds, just south of Brackley.   [8]

Thorpe Mandeville Court, 4 miles northeast of Banbury, Oxon   [13].

Titchmarsh House, Titchmarsh, 2 miles northeast of Thrapston.   [14]

Boughton House, Kettering
THE DUKE AND DUCHESS OF BUCCLEUCH AND QUEENSBERRY

The great eighteenth-century garden at Boughton has long since disappeared except for the restoration by my husband of the lake, canals and star pond which give us beautiful long-distance views and reflected light.

The garden is, therefore, in each generation very much the design or the whim of its owner. In my case I garden for colour, and am no plantswoman, as our visitors can see! The pedigree of the plant, or its rarity, matters not at all if it is the perfect shade of blue for my blue and yellow border. This is five years old now, and comes into flower in two waves. First the large, blue *Iris* 'Jane Phillips' and the smaller *Iris pallida* 'Variegata' and a dense cover of forget-me-nots are contrasted with our earliest rose, 'Canary Bird' a lovely old creamy-yellow *Iris* 'Starshine', the acid yellow of *Alyssum saxatile* var. *citrinum* and clumps of variegated sage. In the next wave come a spectrum of yellows, from the very pales, through the tree paeony 'Kinshi' to the subtlety of the roses 'Buff Beauty' and 'Penelope', together with *Digitalis* 'Sutton's Apricot'. The delphiniums are planted in large clumps in four shades which include 'Loch Nevis' and 'Cream Cracker' which lives up to its name. The wall behind is planted with roses 'Paul's Lemon Pillar' and 'William Allen Richardson' and *Clematis tangutica*.

My favourite combination, which does not, alas, always come out simultaneously, but has done this year, is a large group of *Verbascum* 'Broussa' against the exquisite violet-blue *Clematis* 'Ada, Countess of Lovelace'. The wall ends with a *Cytisus battandieri* and a double marbled sweetbriar, both of which scent the entire border. The whole is underplanted with grey and silver foliage and with occasional splashes of white *Dianthus* and cream paeonies. Not everyone's idea of gardening, you may say, but one which can give great pleasure and satisfaction.

Bowood Cottage, Geddington
MR AND MRS JOHN AMBERY

We and the 1976 Great Drought arrived here simultaneously. In anguish we contemplated first the copper sky, then the baked dust of our future garden and gave up virtually all planting intentions until the following year. Many established features date from then, but in 1980 extra land enabled us to extend our range of planting and to contrive our present third-of-an-acre layout.

Basically this is a circuit, the visitor following a more or less well-defined route through areas of differing character, each merging into the next except where the occasional abrupt change provides an element of surprise. Inevitably the scale is pretty small, but one way of enlarging apparent size is to locate one's paths along the perimeter in order to maximize the distance traversed, a small deceit we have adopted here. Plant densities vary: mostly thick to conceal what happens next, now and then sparse to allow glimpses through to other parts. We wanted an atmosphere suggestive of a world apart, enclosed and remote, so external influences have largely been planted out, the exception being where a slightly lowered boundary leads the eye out to a sweeping panorama over the Ise Valley, towards Boughton Park and distant woods.

Elements used within this framework vary from calm gravel and clipped hedges to rough grass and wild serpentine walks. Everywhere planting has been allowed to rip simply because when it comes to plants we cannot say no. To this add climbers, *Clematis*, over-filled borders and contrasts of form, foliage and berry and the result is a garden that is busy indeed for three seasons. But the fourth season brings a quiescence to all gardens and then, as from inside we view the openwork of branches against a winter sky, the contrast with the beginning could not be greater.

Bradden Old Rectory, Towcester
COL. AND MRS K.C. GOLDIE-MORRISON

In 1962 we moved into a four-acre wilderness that had once been a Victorian rectory garden. This lime-soil garden, complete with walled kitchen garden, orchard and quarter-acre pond inhabited by Cayuga and Muscovy ducks, is now tamed, but not too much. In spring, large areas are carpeted with winter aconites, snowdrops and *Scilla sibirica*. Crocuses and *Anemone blanda* in white and blue flank the drive.

Come early summer, my ground-cover comes into its own to help me combat the weeds. Silver grey *Stachys lanata* (secret pruning of the flower spikes is essential) makes a beautiful cover, likewise *Ajuga* – orange-cream and purple-cream, alpine *Polygonum*, *Epimedium* and geraniums, both pink and blue. *Hypericum* can run riot around the pond,

and *Lamium argentatum* invades the rough ground, once strongholds of ground elder, thistles and stinging nettles. We like these too, with some reservation, as ours is a wild garden. Wild flowers, encouraged but not successful in the lush grass, are for the insects and our bees, a recent acquisition, which have greatly improved the performance of our fruit trees.

In June the tall white paeonies in circular beds are spectacular, especially in the dusk of a summer's evening. At this time too, there are the flowering shrubs and trees: *Syringa*, *Laburnum*, *Cytisus*, *Weigela*, *Philadelphus* and *Potentilla*.

A resounding success is the north-facing wall to the orchard. It is underplanted with all the hellebores, and ivies 'Goldheart' and 'Buttercup' climb the wall that never sees the sun. *Alchemilla mollis* is another life-saver. It foams out from its base, and elsewhere looks par-

Coton Manor in July (see over). This shady herbaceous border is filled with white meadow cranesbill, *Geranium pratense*, and Dame's Violet, *Hesperis matronalis*; *Clematis montana* scrambles over the old wall.

ticularly good circling a large copper container, removed from the old washhouse.

Ours is not especially an autumn garden, but at this time we rejoice in the *Anemone hupehensis* at the front of the house, just outside the windows, and a large bed of *Physalis franchetii* is very colourful until destroyed by wind and rain.

Dictamnus albus, the burning bush, flowering at Coton Manor. The plant is covered with glands and gives off a volatile oil which can be ignited, with spectacular effect, on warm still evenings.

9 The Butts, Aynho
MR AND MRS R. CHENEY

Our garden is flat and rectangular, equally divided between front and back of a long bungalow. From our south-facing sitting room window at the back we look on to a small rock garden fronted with winter flowering heathers dominated by 'Foxhollow' with its lovely golden summer foliage. Miniature conifers and summer-flowering alpines surround two birdbaths and a tiny pool, behind which stands a small statue of a boy with a dolphin. This feature provides year-round interest a few feet from the window.

To the left is a path which curves round the lawn and disappears behind a row of conifers to the back gate. Along the rose border to the left are groups of floribunda roses, those nearest the window being 'Sea Pearl' – in constant bloom from June to December. The border is underplanted with *Aubrieta*, campanulas and heather. A nearby new bed of old shrub roses is underplanted with ground-cover plants with grey and silver foliage.

Across the lawn is a stone-edged pond with an interesting selection of water plants and goldfish backed by a rockery with small conifers and alpines. The wide and curved back border is planted for foliage effect; *Philadelphus coronarius* 'Aureus', *Spiraea* 'Goldflame', purple beech with *Clematis* 'Nelly Moser' climbing through, for example. At the end is a large *Cotinus coggygria* which contrasts beautifully with a fine *Robinia pseudoacacia* 'Frisia' planted in the lawn.

The kitchen and dining room in the front look on to a large border planted with polyanthus, primulas, and tulips in the spring, followed by potentillas, *Ceratostigma willmotianum*, fuchsias, sweet williams, purple and yellow sage. A border of lavender edges the lawn, planted with trees and shrubs, notably a fine silver birch and *Amelanchier*. Thus we always have something of interest to see from our most used rooms.

Cherry Orchard Yard, 17 Benefield Road, Oundle
MR RICHARD WARWICK

Although this could not be described as a large garden, its varying levels and contrastingly-planted areas give an impression of a greater size than is really the case. Rather than one long vista, the layout forms several rooms

contained in part by hornbeam hedging and for architectural interest, several species of conifer of differing shapes. A disused old duck pond, now filled with peaty soil, makes a luxurious area of moisture-loving plants, while at the end of the garden a wooded area contains a stretch of wild flowers including both spring and autumn-flowering *Cyclamen*, *C. hederifolium* and *C. coum*, along with *Anemone blanda*. In summer shrub roses and shrubs give colour. Plants of botanical interest include *Tropaeolum polyphyllum* which makes a bank of gold.

Chipping Warden Manor
MR T. AND THE HON. MRS SERGISON-BROOKE

This is an unusual manor house garden, no larger than three acres, with unexpected surprises round each corner.

At the side of the house there is a formal garden of flower beds surrounded by yew hedges, with an old sundial and rock garden in the middle. A ha-ha separates this from the adjoining field and gives a sweeping view of Edgcote Park.

A large herbaceous border, backed by an old wall of Hornton stone, faces the lawn on another side of the house. The east side of the house is another contrast with an orchard of old apple trees leading down to a pond surrounded by romantically wild and overgrown shrubs.

In spring this area explodes with colour; the floor of the orchard is a daffodil carpet of yellow and white.

There is a large kitchen garden which is a joy to vegetable growers and a small greenhouse bursting at the seams. It could be thought to be rather Heath Robinson as the smart mist propagator has been replaced by

coffee jars over the cuttings. It works amazingly well, and does not get furred up by hard water!

26 Church Lane, Cranford
MR AND MRS RICHARD LOAKE

This is a garden which is constantly evolving. It was begun in 1975 on a quarter-acre site but has since grown in three directions both by accident and design. The intention is to provide interest all year round with two heated greenhouses to help out through the winter. There are several peak times when special emphasis is given by concentrated planting of such flowers as hellebores in variety, and snowdrops and snowflakes, of which we grow more than fifty named kinds for spring display, assisted by primroses, *Cyclamen* and *Iris*. The main speciality of the garden, however, blooms in mid-June and July; these are the delphiniums which dominate the herbaceous borders when the many roses are in bloom. Pansies are also a favourite.

In the autumn the garden is still in bloom, and we enjoy the display of white, pink, orange, scarlet and crimson nerines filling one of the greenhouses. The other greenhouse is given over to a permanent collection of cacti and other succulent plants, particularly *Echeveria* in a great many varieties.

The Coachhouse Garden, Hinton-in-the-Hedges
MRS W.M. GRAY DEBROS

This garden of one and a half acres was designed as a miniature landscape. Woodlands and lawns slope down to the stone courtyard house – formerly coachhouse and stables – nestling in one corner. On the garden side the house looks south and east with broad paved terraces edged with low limestone walls where pink saxifrage, white *Arabis*, *Aubrieta*, stonecrop and violets, purple and white, give spring colour and ground-cover all year round.

To the north an old stone wall, flanking a picturesque Early English church, shelters a broad perennial border and there are glimpses of spreading farmlands through the trees.

Planning was for minimum maintenance. Overhanging trees were cleared and slopes levelled and regraded to focus on a few features – a magnificent old copper beech partnered by a gnarled old 'Beauty of Bath' apple on the south lawn, with a small copse beyond leading to another lawn with more limestone walls and grass terraces above, bordering woodland. To the west stone steps and a beech walk lead to an old glass hexagonal building, now an attractive summerhouse, with more woodland beyond.

The soil is hostile and planting has been by trial and error to give ground-cover, varied with seasonal colour. The woodland is wild, with enchanting drifts of daffodils, clumps of bamboo and *Philadelphus* and magnificent autumn colouring. An unusual feature is a plantation of giant *Polygonum sachalinense* which shoots to ten feet in summer and, with massive spreading leaves, gives the illusion of a tropical jungle.

Lilac, broom, rambler roses and *Acanthus* form the background in the perennial borders. Extensive use has been made of *Euphorbia robbiae*, the sturdy *Stachys lanata*, sage, purple and golden thyme, and the dwarf hebes. *Geranium himalayense* and *dalmaticum*, columbine, yellow and white daisies and Lady's mantle bloom freely and *Ajuga*, *Lamium maculatum* and *Cerastium biebersteinii* (snow-in-summer) clothe the limestone walls.

◆

Coton Manor Gardens
CDR AND MRS H. PASLEY-TYLER

'This is like spending an afternoon in paradise' is one of the many enthusiastic comments made by a visitor to Coton Manor Gardens during the last sixteen years.

The attractive old English manor house, constructed in mellow Northamptonshire stone, stands in a commanding position overlooking the thirty-acre reservoir, with views across the rolling Northamptonshire countryside.

Abundant and running spring water fills the main pond – a central feature of the gardens – whose overflow supplies the water gardens and numerous ponds and waterfalls. The introduction of colourful and free-ranging water-fowl, flamingoes and cranes has brought a new dimension to an unusually enchanting scene, which appeals to nature- and garden-lovers alike.

Coton Manor Gardens is not just a beauty spot; it is also a garden of exceptional quality. Against a background of mature trees and hedges, the planting of unusual and interesting shrubs and herbaceous borders has been carried out with consummate skill, giving exciting and ever-changing patterns of growth and colour.

Titchmarsh House in July (see page 147). *Philadelphus coronarius* 'Aureus' dominates and scents this shrub border. In the foreground are hostas and the yellow buds of *Phlomis fruticosa* and behind the red flowers of *Rosa moysii* appear above the purple *Cotinus*.

Cottesbrooke Hall, Nr Northampton
THE HON. LADY
MACDONALD-BUCHANAN

The garden surrounding the Hall (not open to the public) has both formal and wild areas, herbaceous borders and statues originating from Stowe, in Buckinghamshire.

There are several fine old cedars on the front lawn, which are believed to have been planted when the house was built in 1704. Other features include a pool garden and the Dutch garden, which is at its best in spring.

Good examples of wall-trained fruit – peaches, vines and figs – can be seen in the kitchen garden; and there is also an extensive selection of soft fruit. Vegetables, both common and unusual, are also grown, some of them in a large polythene tunnel. The greenhouses are used to produce pot plants and flowers for cutting.

The Dower House, Boughton House
SIR DAVID AND LADY SCOTT

This is a most unusual garden, for it is really two gardens, joined to make an harmonious whole, and it reflects faithfully the differing but complementary interests of the two owners. More than half is a shrub garden, on a very heavy clay soil and a north-facing slope where, in these seemingly inauspicious conditions, a large and choice collection of about eight hundred hardy trees and shrubs flourish. Here grow viburnums, shrub roses, *Euonymus*, maples and willows in grass or in island beds, underplanted with an extensive range of woodland plants and bulbs. Although designed primarily for the welfare of the plants and not to a strict plan, it is nevertheless a place of natural and seductive beauty.

Below this garden, separated from it by a limestone wall, and reached through a fine wrought-iron gate, is an enclosed area, some seventy by twelve yards, of kitchen garden and orchard, with, round the walls on all sides, raised beds of small hardy plants. The ones facing north are filled with acid soil (the pH of the soil is very alkaline), so that a collection of calcifuges – alpine rhododendrons, cassiopes, ledums, andromedas and lithospermums – may thrive.

Further down still and across the drive is the house, which supports numerous interesting climbers, among them *Buddleja colvillei* and *Clematis orientalis* 'Bill Mackenzie'. Close by are a number of planted stone troughs. In this garden grow plants, raised by Valerie Finnis, which have gone out from here to other gardens, amongst them *Hebe* 'Boughton Beauty', *Dianthus* 'Constance Finnis', *Helleborus* 'Boughton Beauty', *Hepatica transsilvannica* 'Ada Scott' and the Constance Finnis strain of Iceland poppy. There is a small nursery where these and other plants are propagated.

Kneeling pads are found most useful for hand-weeding this large and varied garden,

and the handles of garden tools are painted white so that no time is wasted looking for them.

Easton Neston, Nr Towcester
THE LORD HESKETH

The house at Easton Neston stands supreme, built by Nicholas Hawksmoor and completed in 1702. It enjoys marvellous vistas to the east and west, flanked by avenues, many replanted due to Dutch elm disease. The eye is drawn, on the west and forecourt side of the house, to a pair of stone gateposts and, beyond, to the spire of Greens Norton church. To the east and garden side lies a formal canal with a newly-planted double avenue as far as the eye can see. Hawksmoor's incomplete plans were later taken up by Sir Thomas Fermor-Hesketh who laid out the present garden with its large formal oval pond, clipped hedges and topiary. Much of the statuary came from Stowe when it was sold by the Duke of Buckingham prior to becoming a school in 1923. Fermor-Hesketh also laid out the arboretum which lies beyond the pedimented garden house or temple dated 1641. There is a variety of trees (mainly conifers) and shrubs including many Californian redwoods and *Acer palmatum* 'Dissectum' underplanted with spring bulbs.

A large walled garden lies to the north of the house with a central avenue of espaliered apple trees. A new border now hugs the west-facing wall, while planted in a tumbling array are climbing roses (mainly old-fashioned varieties) which seem to do well in the very heavy clay soil. Other climbing roses adorn the wall between the house and the oval pond.

The Spring House, Chipping Warden
MR AND MRS C. SHEPLEY-CUTHBERT

Having always dreamed of having a bog garden, imagine the luck of finding a derelict one. Two Irish yews flank steps leading down to a considerable hollow with a backcloth of closely planted limes, now some sixty feet high, and dominated by a vast willow *Salix alba* 'Sericea' over the water. The bog, now mainly restored, with the addition of extra pools and the accompanying sounds (so soothing to work in) ends with a drop into a shining verdant watercress bed. Elsewhere *Tulipa greigii* and *kaufmanniana* hybrids give the first signal of spring, followed by bluebells of several hues. Later ribbons of *Primula* species, *P. rosea*, *japonica*, *beesiana*, *bulleyana* and *pulverulenta* flower in succession, whilst forget-me-nots show off tiny and ancient rhododendrons and a recent planting of azaleas, under a *Liquidambar* and hornbeams. *Lonicera maackii*, the honeysuckle tree, provides dappled shade, meanwhile hostas, irises, zantedeschias, rodgersias, peltiphyllums and the gunneras begin their foliage display which culminates in riotous colour in

the autumn with large-leaved American red oaks giving support. Banks are clad in ivies, geraniums, especially *G. macrorrhizum*, *ibericum* and *sanguineum*, as well as pockets of small ferns, and under the willow, though for all too short a time, is *Meconopsis betonicifolia*.

The main garden, which is not a plantsman's garden, is entered through a high and wide tapestry hedge of mixed beeches and limes and leads on to a lawn with views across the Cherwell Valley with vistas all round. It was laid out in farmland in the twenties by Miss Kitty Lloyd Jones, a pupil of Gertrude Jekyll. There is a collection of interesting trees, augmented by ourselves, but with a basis of ancient beeches, oaks, chestnuts and glorious cherries with sheets of daffodils, though there are plenty of more recherché bulbs in abundance. These are emphasized by mown paths. Of further interest are several stone ornaments, old and new, a special one being a recent commission in the guise of a Solomonic column.

Steane Grounds, Nr Brackley
MR AND MRS R.G. ELLIS

From an established garden out of control, one acre was cleared, dug, coerced and coaxed into a young garden now beginning to show stature and flesh. Paths were reborn, a bank reclaimed, lawns planted, rockery, herbaceous, shrub borders, tennis lawn and patio made. Colour, form, perfume, textures and impact are all very important. From a neglected boggy spot, a pond was created, and bog plants are now becoming established including the majesty of *Gunnera*. A lovely willow oversees all.

Different levels, hedges and trees are beginning to show in the shape of things to come. A terrace leads to a shrub border where *Cotinus coggygria* (Notcutt's Variety) rubs shoulders with *Cornus alba* 'Elegantissima'; *Philadelphus coronarius* 'Aureus' overlooks *Hosta sieboldiana* 'Elegans' and 'Thomas Hogg'; on a dappled bank under sixty-foot-high pines nestles *Acer palmatum* 'Dissectum' flanked by *Hosta fortunei* 'Albopicta' and *Lamium* 'Beacon Silver'; this area is particularly delightful in mid-June. Nearby, what began as a four-foot ditch emerged as a stream with three steps, giving glorious movement and sound to clear water, spring fed. The banks were duly planted – *Rodgersia tabularis* is a favourite. A *Berberis × ottawensis* 'Purpurea' hedge is fronted by 'Iceberg' roses. We find all the variegated, yellow and cream foliages of great 'lift' and surprise value in beds and dark corners.

Thorpe Mandeville Court
COL. AND MRS E.T. SMYTH-OSBOURNE

This is an old garden which was redesigned by Waterers in 1947. They varied the levels of the lawns with sunk walls and divided up the four acres with screens of bamboos, banks of shrubs, and what are now enormous bushes of yellow yew. The result is that whilst walking round you are continually coming upon another little garden with its own character. There is the lower pond with waterlilies and a rockery behind, and the top pond which is wilder, with shady trees and small paved paths winding through hostas, primulas, astilbes and ferns. Then there is the sundial garden – square and formal – and a path, flanked by lavender and *Nepeta*, leading back to the summerhouse.

The view east from the house, looking across a ha-ha, is framed by half-moon beds of old-fashioned roses, while on the south side the formal rose garden leads down to a goldfish pond and fountain. The lawn in front of the house is sunk and bordered on two sides by retaining walls. These have narrow borders along the top which provide an ideal situation for alpines and other small treasures, also the more tender grey-leaved plants which seem to enjoy the good drainage and have survived several severe winters here when they have succumbed in other, more sheltered, spots. We have made an island bed on the left side of the lawn, and, with emphasis on coloured foliage, have planted purple nut and *Berberis × ottawensis* 'Purpurea'. The lovely bright yellow of *Sambucus racemosa* 'Plumosa Aurea' is echoed further along by *Robinia pseudoacacia* 'Frisia', and in front *Salix lanata*, *Berberis thunbergii* 'Aurea' and *Juniperus* 'Grey Owl'. The tall spires of white foxgloves followed by self-sown *Campanula lactiflora* and the apricot plumes of *Stipa gigantea* all combine to give a marvellous colour effect that lasts from spring until leaf-fall.

———————◆———————

Titchmarsh House, Nr Wellingborough
MR AND MRS EWAN HARPER

When we bought the house it stood in an acre of land, over a third of it a walled kitchen garden. A tribe of young children meant that we wanted a garden that would be fun to play in. The need for space led us to acquire two further acres, and it was then that we had room for thoughtful planning as well as play areas for cricket and tennis.

The site is exposed to the north from where we get both our view and a devastating winter wind. We were able to convert a sheep dip into a south-facing border backed by a stone wall. Here foliage effects have been sought as well as the protection for one or two rarer shrubs. *Poncirus trifoliata* flowered for the first time in 1985 and *Buddleja farreri*, with its charming silver foliage, has survived the harsh winters of 1982 and 1984. *Clematis*, *Caryopteris* and *Hibiscus* extend the flowering season into the autumn. Cherries do well with us and have provided some quick height and a splash of spring colour. One of the problems with planting up fields is a lack of mature trees except in the hedgerows; so the architecture is slow to develop. But we have taken a long-term view with our yew hedges, cedars, oak and limes.

Shrub roses like our alkaline soil and survive the winds to give a glorious display in June. The border by the path that looks up to the outstanding church tower of St Mary's, Titchmarsh, is planted with well-scented varieties in pink, white and deep crimson. 'Fantin-Latour', 'Comte de Chambord' and 'Madame Hardy' are particular favourites.

Through the wrought-iron gate one enters a quiet garden. Designed on the formal side, it is bounded to the west by an ancient yew hedge, to the east and south by young yews and to the north by two tender borders set into a bowed and protective stone wall built in 1976. Here are *Ceanothus*, *Hebe*, *Eucalyptus*, *Hypericum* 'Rowallane' and much-loved *Abutilon vitifolium* and *A. × suntense*. Our bottle-brush flowered for the first time in 1984 as did the *Campsis radicans* 'Mme Galen'. In the lawn facing them the large leaves of *Paulownia tomentosa* contrast with the yews but in a quiet and restful way. Similarly the gentle splash of the fountain emphasizes the stillness, especially on a fine summer's afternoon, when the cry is not for tennis!

———————◆———————

Turweston Gardens:
Spring Valley (MR AND MRS A. WILDISH).

Turweston Barn (MR AND MRS A.J.M. KIRKLAND)

Turweston Glebe (MR AND MRS HEDLEY)

Turweston Lodge (MR AND MRS T.R. SERMON)

Turweston Mill (MR AND MRS HARRY LEVENTIS)

This lovely village of greystone houses lies beside the Great Ouse on the borders of Oxfordshire, Northamptonshire and Buckinghamshire. There are usually six gardens open in the spring – each with a completely different character and five of which have the added attraction of water or springs.

Spring Valley has terraced lawns and herbaceous borders leading to ornamental ponds with fountains and a bog garden.

Turweston Barn is in a lovely setting with wall vines creeping up old grey walls and a lovely herbaceous border. The water here is represented by a spring running beside an old stone wall.

Turweston Glebe has a mature garden with herbaceous borders, mature trees and shrubs and drifts of daffodils in the spring.

Turweston Lodge has a walled garden with a paeony walk and a variety of features including a herb garden and grape vines. The water here is a dark, spring-fed pool.

Turweston Mill is mentioned in the Domesday Book and has the mill stream racing under the house. The garden has recently been replanted with water-loving plants and has a paved rose garden.

OXFORDSHIRE (NORTH)

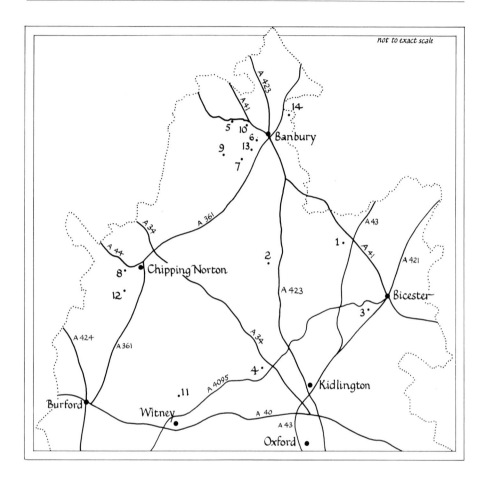

not to exact scale

Directions to Gardens

The Barn, Souldern, midway between Banbury and Bicester. [1]

Barton Abbey, 1 mile from Middle Barton. [2]

Bignell House, 2 miles southwest of Bicester. [3]

Blenheim Palace, Woodstock, 8 miles north of Oxford. [4]

Brook Cottage, Alkerton, 6 miles west of Banbury. [5]

Broughton Castle, 2½ miles west of Banbury. [6]

Buddleia Cottage, Wigginton, 6 miles southwest of Banbury. [7]

Cornwell Manor, 3 miles from Kingham, 2 miles west of Chipping Norton. [8]

Epwell Mill, Epwell, 7 miles west of Banbury, between Shutford and Epwell. [9]

Laurels Farm, Wroxton, 3 miles northwest of Banbury. [10]

Mount Skippet, Ramsden, 4 miles north of Witney. [11]

The Old Forge, Souldern, between Banbury and Bicester. [1]

Sarsden Glebe, Churchill, 3 miles southwest of Chipping Norton. [12]

Tadmarton Manor, Tadmarton, 5 miles southwest of Banbury. [13]

Wardington Manor, 5 miles northeast of Banbury. [14]

Wroxton Abbey (Wroxton College of Fairleigh Dickinson University), west of Banbury. [10]

Yeomans, Tadmarton, 5 miles southwest of Banbury. [13]

The Barn, Souldern
MR AND MRS J. TALBOT

The Barn has a medium-sized walled garden with a thin calcareous soil. This burns up humus very rapidly, so that drought soon becomes a serious problem.

The chief features are the wide mixed borders which contain a good range of shrubs and herbaceous perennials, with annuals to fill gaps. A formal pond has been allowed to go wild in order to provide a habitat for frogs, toads and newts, in an attempt to reintroduce these into an area from which modern farm practices have eliminated them. To this end, no pesticides whatever are used in this garden, nor in the adjoining vegetable plot, with the happy result that there has been a marked increase in the number of birds in the vicinity.

Near the pond, a simply-constructed bog garden has been a success, allowing moisture-loving plants such as *Ligularia*, *Astilbe*, and *Thalictrum* to flourish. Among the shrubs there is a good specimen of bladder senna, a Judas tree, and an *Indigofera*. Climbers include several *Clematis*, *Actinidia kolomikta*, pineapple-scented broom, and a 'Kiftsgate' rose.

◆

Barton Abbey, Middle Barton
MRS P. FLEMING

This is an old informal garden consisting of herbaceous borders, flowering shrubs, and many fine specimen trees. Approximately three acres slope down to a large lake containing trout and several species of wild fowl. In spring the banks around the lake are well furnished with daffodils, which with the flowering shrubs make a fine show. The rock garden has become very overgrown and is now more of a wild garden, but still interesting.

The walled kitchen garden contains soft fruit and a large variety of vegetables. Flowering plants, peaches, nectarines, and grapes are grown under glass. An interesting feature at the entrance to Barton Abbey is an avenue of *Sequoiadendron giganteum* (wellingtonias), which are believed to be some of the finest in the country, and are around two hundred years old.

◆

Bignell House, Chesterton
MR AND MRS P.J. GORDON

These gardens were designed and established in the 1860s, when the house was built. Originally there was an arboretum containing mature trees from many countries; a circular rose garden, laid out with stone archways and a central pagoda; a croquet lawn; four yew trees cut as foxes in full flight and numerous other features. At this time the gardens were tended by thirteen gardeners but during the war years the grounds fell into disrepair and became very overgrown, and later the larger part of the house was also pulled down.

The present owners have, since 1979, been endeavouring to restore the gardens to something resembling their past glory. It is still not a garden for perfectionists or plant enthusiasts, but more for those who wish to wander at leisure and appreciate the fine mature trees, the wild plants and animals, and the abundant daffodils and fritillaries in the woodland.

The gardens now take the form of lawns sweeping down to a lake system fed by several springs. There are three islands (one with a pet graveyard) reached by bridges; a rock pool and stone archways. The formal gardens are now mainly roses and herbs and the circular area is an orchard paddock for rare sheep.

---◆---

*Blenheim Palace, Woodstock
HIS GRACE THE DUKE OF MARLBOROUGH

The gardens, at their finest in the spring and summer, are set within the beautiful landscape of Blenheim Park. The present appearance of the gardens reflects many influences over the years; from the great walled garden begun by Henry Wise in 1705; to the arboretum completed in 1984.

Two formal gardens designed by Achille Duchesse for the ninth Duke lie adjacent to the Palace. To the east of the Italian Garden, a sunken garden of patterned box and golden yews is interspersed with white tulips and yellow daffodils in spring, whilst in summer it is edged with groups of fuchsias, dahlias and geraniums. To the west the water terraces are reminiscent of the Parterre d'Eau at Versailles, comprising clipped box scrolls surrounding the fountains on the upper terrace, whilst the lower terrace features a Bernini fountain and a magnificent summer display of cannas planted in the jardinières. The visitor may walk through the terraces to the west of the gardens, where continuing westwards beyond drifts of daffodils the rose garden is the last echo of formality before the more natural area of the arboretum, which contains many specimen trees together with more recent plantings.

Crossing the vast south lawn, site of Wise's parterre, grassed over by 'Capability' Brown, one passes through a magnificent grove of cedars and on towards the walled garden, past shrubberies of laurel and an Exedra of box and yew, the whole exemplifying the Victorian 'pleasure grounds'.

Brook Cottage, Alkerton
MR AND MRS DAVID HODGES

This is a garden for all seasons – designed and planted since 1964 on a four-acre steeply-sloping, west-facing site. We aimed to use its natural features to make an interesting layout on differing levels, defined by enclosures of stone walls and hedges of beech and yew. Within this framework we have planted a wide variety of trees, shrubs and perennials providing something of special interest from spring to autumn, and have designated areas of individual character such as one-colour borders and a newly-formed alpine scree.

Drifts of naturalized bulbs are a joy in spring which is brightened by the catkins of many types of willow and the coloured stems of *Cornus*.

The avenue of double white cherries can be spectacular, birds and weather permitting, for three weeks in May. In June the water garden, made where cattle used to drink, is at its best when *Iris laevigata*, *I. sibirica* and candelabra primulas are all in flower. July is the month for roses here, especially the large species, old-fashioned and modern shrub roses grown in grass, and they in turn are

Brook Cottage in July. A restrained planting of *Primula florindae* and flowering rush, *Butomus umbellatus*, by an elegant and unusually-shaped pool. The glowing crimson young growth of a copper beech hedge reflects in the water.

succeeded by late-flowering *Clematis* and herbaceous plants.

Among the latter a special favourite is *Convolvulus althaeoides* – an exuberant plant and therefore difficult to keep in bounds. However, planted in a strawberry pot we can allow its silvery foliage and pink flowers to cascade freely over its container to great effect.

But whatever the season, the beauty of a garden is not just in its flowers. We enjoy especially one harmony of colour – the purple leaves of a *Cotinus coggygria* and the silvery-green foliage of *Elaeagnus × ebbingei* seen against a yellow curtain of climbing golden hop – and, later on, the rose hips, the autumn foliage and the berries of *Sorbus* and *Viburnum*.

---

*Broughton Castle

LORD SAYE AND SELE

In 1900 there were fourteen gardeners caring for elaborate beds and borders planted with fussy annuals together with a three-acre kitchen garden. Now there is one gardener, well able to manage a garden redesigned in 1969 with the inspiring help of Lanning Roper.

The garden, surrounded by the moat, starts with the benefit of stone walls and water. It is based on borders of mixed shrubs and roses together with perennial border plants.

The west-facing border, backed by the battlement wall, has a colour scheme of blues and yellows, greys and whites – roses 'Golden Wings', 'Buff Beauty', 'Maigold' and *rugosa* hybrids intermingled with *Philadelphus*, *Hypericum*, lots of shrubby *Potentilla*, *Anthemis*, *Penstemon*, *Geranium* and many *Campanula* species; any gaps are occupied by *Viola cornuta*.

On the south side of the Castle is the walled 'ladies' garden' admired by Gertrude Jekyll, with fleur-de-lys beds of the floribunda roses 'Chanelle' and 'Pink Parfait'; in the borders old-fashioned roses 'Belle Poitevine', 'Celestial', 'Trier', 'Mme Hardy', 'Roseraie de l'Haÿ', together with blocks of the invaluable rose 'The Fairy'; on the walls, *Clematis* 'Comtesse de Bouchaud', 'Marie Boisselot' and in the autumn, *C. × jouiniana*, *Solanum*, *Hydrangea petiolaris* and various *Ceanothus*. Also, a half-moon-shaped bed with white tulips in the spring and a great bank of roses 'Felicia' and 'Ballerina' to follow, edged by catmint. Favourite roses in other borders are 'Fantin-Latour' and 'Fritz Nobis'; on the walls, the incomparable rose 'New Dawn', the splendid white rose 'Purity', creamy 'Leverkusen' and the striking red 'Dortmund'.

We try to stick to big blocks of plants; to allow the frontal plants to spill and flow over the edges; not to mix red or pink with strong yellows; to use lots of *rugosa* roses and plenty of grey artemisias and helichrysums. We also plan in future to try much harder to do better!

Buddleia Cottage, Wigginton

MISS M. J. BARTLETT

This is a small garden made on rising ground on the north side of the house. There is no grass but a winding path, paved and punctuated by upright conifers leading to a paved area surrounded by rockery and overlooked by a summer house. It is planted with flowering and coloured shrubs and the rose 'Seagull' has covered an old plum tree. Ground-cover is used with perennials, *Clematis*, and many bulbs in spring. Self-sown poppies, spurges, salvias and golden feverfew are selectively weeded out and everywhere scent is rather important.

Cornwell Manor, Kingham

THE HON. MRS PETER WARD

A fine nine-acre Cotswold manor house garden, set in rolling countryside, possesses qualities of great contrast and unexpectedness. The house walls are covered with many climbers, including the yellow *Rosa banksiae*. A south terrace has roses clambering over the balustrading, and grass sweeps down to a croquet lawn. Natural fast-flowing water is carried through the tiny village and into the gardens by a series of formal canals, eventually cascading down through the rock garden and on through the bog garden.

Spring sees the woodland walks and banks clothed with aconites, snowdrops and many thousands of daffodils. Facing east, the spring garden is dominated by a huge beech tree, home for a carpet of *Chionodoxa* and *Scilla*. A relaxed formal garden on three levels gives way to a riot of flower, foliage and ornamental grasses. To the west, an enclosed secret garden is full of interesting shrubs and herbaceous plants, a small tranquil haven.

Over half a mile of hedging, mainly yew, gives a perfect backcloth to secluded corners and informal beds. Late summer colour is enhanced by *Alstroemeria*, *Perovskia*, *Potentilla* and the lovely slender-stemmed *Agapanthus campanulatus* 'Albus'.

The kitchen garden is organically cultivated, and maintained in the traditional

Cornwell Manor, Kingham

---

manner, now rarely seen. Trained trees are in abundance, and a central path leads to the upper pool garden where a border is devoted to paeonies backed by climbing and rambler roses. The lower garden is a series of small island beds where lavender, *Achillea* and *Lilium regale* merge together. Cherry and *Robinia* trees feature prominently; outstanding autumn colour is headed by *Acer griseum*. Despite the age and maturity of the garden, there has been much recent planting, providing interest for the plantsman and gardener alike.

Epwell Mill, Nr Banbury

R. WITHERS, ESQ.

This garden was designed about twenty years ago, around the original water requirements of an ancient mill (mentioned in the archives of Bruern Abbey *c.* 1250). It has two highlights in the gardening year; the first is in late April when the drive is lined with several thousand daffodils. The second is in early June for its show of azaleas, rarely seen in north Oxfordshire, but cosseted and coaxed here into a fine annual display. Use has been made of the abundant supply of water to form a descending series of terrace pools and a round pond (with unsentimental central nymph), all fed by gravity from the former mill pool which, well above the house, has itself been formed into a water garden in which thrive a splendid *Gunnera manicata*, numerous annually crossbreeding primulas, and *Meconopsis betonicifolia*.

Below the house which is, as it were, on a shelf, is the only formal part of the garden with two largish beds backed by tall yew hedges and a box-edged parterre giving successive displays of bulbs and annuals. Between is a pear-shaped lawn into which obtrudes a roughly grassed spur, with a low dry stone containing wall planted at its apex with a tall weeping willow under whose foliage is a life-size bronze, 'Girl on Swing' by Sydney Harpley R.A. She has been positioned to appear to gaze to the distant Long Hill. Nearer the house is a large round feature, once a fountain fed by the outlet from the millstream, but now a central bed of conifers encircled by an interestingly planted border and scree.

The garden has been inconspicuously lit so that, with the accompanying sound of abundant water, it has a nocturnal atmosphere much appreciated by NGS supporters in the neighbourhood who have attended the annual Midsummer Night Wine and Cheese party.

Laurels Farm, Wroxton

MR AND MRS ROBERT FOX

This is essentially a summer garden, crammed full of flowers in June, July and August, when it is at its peak. It faces southeast, catching a chill wind in winter and full sun in summer. It is on limestone, so we miss the massed rhododendrons and azaleas in May, but are amply compensated by the many other plants that grow happily here. All the old cottage garden favourites grow in abundance, mingling with old roses, honeysuckles and sweet williams.

Originally the garden was a square lawn surrounded by narrow borders, backed by greedy laurels. The wall into the field was removed, as were the laurels, and now the lawn tumbles down a gentle slope to an old lawn at the bottom. We dug our small oval pool and in the bed around planted the large-leaved *Crambe cordifolia* and *Rheum palmatum* which lend a feeling of lushness. There is a twisted willow, *Salix matsudana* 'Tortuosa' and a small bog garden.

During the summer months we rarely use a hoe as everything is planted so closely, We do our weeding using an old kitchen knife, taking care not to chop roots as we go, and in this way have found hundreds of healthy seedlings from the plants and sometimes shrubs that have layered themselves – a welcome bonus for friends. Some of our best colour combinations have come from seedlings that missed being removed, such as dark blue campanulas under apricot roses, and many more.

Mount Skippet, Ramsden
DR AND MRS M.A.T. ROGERS

Three factors make this a worthwhile garden: as background an old Cotswold stone house (once three cottages); a superb setting, with long views southwards towards the Wiltshire Downs; and a wealth of interesting plants. About half of the two acres is intensively cultivated, the rock gardens and raised beds housing many alpines as well as herbaceous plants and shrubs. *Abutilon × suntense* and *A. vitifolium* 'Alba' overwinter quite well on the south wall. *Adlumia fungosa* rambles through a *Daphne* 'Somerset' and a six-foot *D. mezereum* 'Album'. *Cuphea cyanea* has survived eight winters out of doors and *Phygelius aequalis* has come through a hard one. *P.* 'Yellow Trumpet' will be tried outside when we have enough to risk. *Alstroemeria ligtu* flourishes, as does the splendid candelabra *Primula aurantiaca* 'Candy Pink' with its wide range of colours, and *Lilium pardalinum* enjoys the same conditions.

Several old kitchen sinks have been covered with hypertufa, and lumps of this have been successfully used as a growing medium. A small alpine house displays a regularly renewed series of alpines in flower, and in the working greenhouse, where propagation by seed and cuttings is carried out, there may be seen tomatoes grown by the straw bale method. During most of the year the conservatory is stocked with plants in season.

Wroxton Abbey in September (see page 153). The canal and a cascade seen from the Viewing Mount, part of this Renaissance garden which is now being restored.

The Old Forge, Souldern
MR AND MRS D. DUTHIE

This is a two-hundred-year-old small and typical cottage garden containing many old-fashioned plants and flowers, with many interesting features, and fine stone walling.

It is resourcefully and densely planted to give a colourful display during spring, summer and autumn. Herbaceous borders and shrubs are planted to complement the background of Cotswold stone walls.

Sarsden Glebe, Churchill
MISS JUDY HUTCHINSON

This garden was laid out in 1819 by George Repton, who was also the architect of the house. The garden faces south and looks on to a small park with good trees. There are three terraces, a wild garden and small pool. It is at its most beautiful in the spring when there is a carpet first of snowdrops and later of blue anemones and daffodils under the old oak trees, with vistas to the Cotswolds across the countryside. The flowers are secondary to the lay-out of the garden, but there is an herbaceous border and a collection of old roses.

◆

Tadmarton Manor, Nr Banbury
MR AND MRS R.K. ASSER

Ancient stone house, dove-cote and thatched barn provide a peaceful setting for this two-and-a-half-acre garden. The spacious tranquillity is enhanced by the view over park and farmland, reminiscent of a Stubbs painting.

There are lawns and slopes, hedges, fine trees with shade-loving plants beneath, a kitchen garden and mixed borders in which grow herbaceous plants, shrubs, bulbs, plants with good form or foliage and annuals to give changing colour effects. Plant associations are arrived at, such as *Phlomis fruticosa* with *Campanula* 'Hidcote' and *Thymus nitidus* at its foot and the pink of the rose 'La Reine Victoria' behind. During the summer notes

Wroxton Abbey near Banbury. The lake in September.

are made on the effect desired and bamboo canes are placed so that plants can be moved to the right position at the right season.

The mixed borders have a framework of shrubs such as *Viburnum davidii*. These are appreciated in spring as a background for bulbs; they help to support less robust neighbours and give a luxuriant quality to the borders in summer; in autumn they remain firm when all around are going to pieces; and in winter they hold the stage.

One of the satisfactions in gardening is achieving a good grouping of plants no matter how uninviting the position. Under the dense shade of a beech tree, in poor soil, we have *Hosta sieboldiana, Helleborus orientalis, Tellima grandiflora, Lysimachia punctata, Phlomis samia* and *Campanula trachelium*. Some peat was added in the original planting and the plants have flourished ever since.

Top prize for a plant that has self-seeded and made a success of itself goes to *Eccremocarpus scaber*, growing high up out of the wall of the barn and cascading down over a stone archway.

◆

Wardington Manor, Nr Banbury
LORD WARDINGTON

The gardens are a series of surprises. Looking in from the road, through the wrought-iron gates and high topiaried yew hedges, you see a lawn with wide herbaceous borders and banks of hydrangeas, against the *Wisteria*-clad walls of the Carolean house. There is no hint of a much larger lawn bounded on one side by two long beds of roses, which in the spring are blue carpets of scillas and chionodoxas, a lily-pond surrounded by box-edged rose beds, a long border edged with rock plants and backed with a rose pergola, and more ancient yew hedges.

Behind a holly hedge the black swimming pool is a surprise to some, particularly the dramatic effect of the 'Zéphirine Drouhin' roses climbing the tennis court netting, and reflected in the pool.

The most exciting climber on the house is *Actinidia kolomikta* with its green, white and pink leaves in June.

Across the orchard, a mass of daffodils in the spring, a high yew hedge contains a small formal garden around a sundial. This leads – surprise again – to a hundred-and-fifty-yard grass walk enclosed between wide shrub borders. Among the profusion of shrubs are *Magnolia stellata* and *M. × soulangiana*, rhododendrons and azaleas, roses, deutzias, golden and variegated privet, viburnums, mahonias and *Weigela florida* 'Variegata'. These are underplanted with a most successful selection of ground-cover perennials such as *Tellima, Tiarella, Hypericum, Pulmonaria, Polygonum affine, P. amplexicaule*, and *P. bistorta* 'Superbum', *Geranium, Brunnera* and *Alchemilla*. There are always splashes of colour and contrasts of shade and texture.

This walk leads to a tiny walled garden containing many varieties of *Hosta* and a large

Yeomans, Tadmarton, in July. Day lilies and hybrid lilies such as 'Enchantment' dominate the foreground, with *Chrysanthemum maximum*, *Lilium regale* and the sulphur-yellow *Anthemis tinctoria* 'E. C. Buxton' underneath *Rosa glauca* (*rubrifolia*). Background purple foliage is of *Berberis* and *Cotinus*.

armillary sphere. Around a bend there is a pond, full of carp, with willows, water irises and the giant *Rheum officinale* at its edge, and a rockery with primulas, heathers and *Osmunda* ferns, sheltered by bamboos.

Wroxton Abbey, Nr Banbury
WROXTON COLLEGE OF FARLEIGH DICKINSON UNIVERSITY

Historically the gardens are of much interest. In 1727 Tilleman Bobart was commissioned to construct a renaissance-style garden comprising a long canal with terrace walls, but by the late 1730s this garden had been grassed over in favour of an early example of the newly-emerging landscape style. From about 1740 Sanderson Miller designed some of the garden buildings.

Much of this early landscape garden, consisting of a serpentine river, lake, grand cascade, viewing mount, Chinese bridge, Gothic dovecote, obelisk, ruined arch, trees and lawns, has recently been rescued and restored from a very overgrown and derelict state. Further restoration has included the formal flower garden laid out in the 1840s, when W. A. Nesfield was consulted, the Doric temple, and the fine eighteenth-century entrance gate.

The new planting has been carried out to continue the succession of specimen and woodland trees, notably cedars, and to keep the flower beds supplied with low-upkeep shrubs and roses; the restored Victorian knot garden is planted with dwarf box and herbs.

Yeomans, Tadmarton
MR AND MRS A.E. PEDDER

Yeomans, a sixteenth-century thatched cottage of Cotswold stone, has approximately three-quarters of an acre of garden. It is made up of four small gardens with stone walls, each with its carpet of lawn. It is exposed at the front to the north-east winds; though protected somewhat by four enormous beech trees across the road.

In winter there are heathers and conifers, our favourite being *Juniperus communis* 'Hibernica' and *Chamaecyparis lawsoniana* 'Wisselii', while in spring aconites and white daffodils fade as the 'Bramley' apple blooms profusely.

Early summer sees the stone walls clad with climbing roses, honeysuckles, *Clematis* and later *C.* 'Perle d'Azur' and *C. tangutica* ramble through the light green leaves of the *Wisteria* and the cool greens of hostas enjoy the dappled shade of the fastigiate hornbeams. Soon the air is scented by the tall bearded irises, *Rosa* 'Albertine', *R.* 'Fritz Nobis' and a variety of lilies, some liking our alkaline soil better than others.

OXFORDSHIRE (SOUTH)

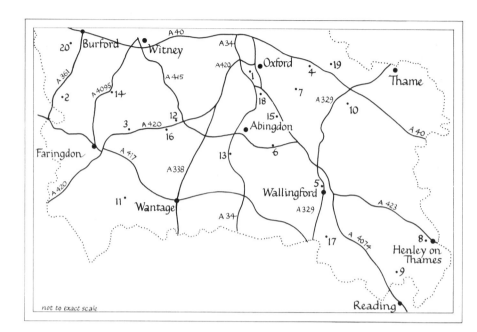

not to exact scale

Directions to Gardens

23 Beech Croft Road, Oxford. [1]

Broughton Hall, Broughton Poggs, between Burford and Lechlade. [2]

Buckland Mead, 4 miles northeast of Faringdon. [3]

Chestnuts, Park Hill, Wheatley, 6 miles east of Oxford. [4]

The Coach House, Castle Street, Wallingford. [5]

The Court House, Broughton Poggs, between Burford and Lechlade. [2]

Evelegh's, High Street, Long Wittenham, 4 miles northeast of Didcot. [6]

Garsington Manor, southeast of Oxford. [7]

Greys Court, Rotherfield Greys, 3 miles northwest of Henley-on-Thames. [8]

Greystone Cottage, Colmore Lane, Kingwood Common. [9]

Haseley Court, Little Haseley, southeast of Oxford. [10]

High Croft, Wheatley, 6 miles east of Oxford. [4]

High Tilt, Wheatley, 6 miles east of Oxford. [4]

Kencot Cottage, Kencot, 5 miles northeast of Lechlade. [2]

Kencot House, Kencot, 5 miles northeast of Lechlade. [2]

Kingstone Lisle Park, 5 miles west of Wantage. [11]

Lime Close, Henley's Lane, Drayton, 2 miles south of Abingdon. [13]

Little Place, Clifton Hampden, 5 miles east of Abingdon. [6]

The Malt House, 59 Market Place, Henley-on-Thames. [8]

The Manor House, Bampton, between Faringdon and Witney. [14]

Martens Hall Farm, Longworth, 8 miles west of Abingdon. [12]

Nuneham Park, 7 miles southeast of Oxford, 1 mile from centre of Nuneham Courtenay village. [15]

The Old Manor, Broadwell, 5 miles northeast of Lechlade. [2]

The Old Rectory, Broughton Poggs, between Burford and Lechlade. [2]

Oxford College Gardens. [1]
   Christ Church, entrance through Christ Church meadow off St Aldate's;
   Corpus Christi, entrance through Christ Church meadow off St Aldate's;
   Lady Margaret Hall, Norham Gardens, 1 mile north of Carfax;
   Merton College, entrance through Christ Church Meadow off St Aldate's;
   New College, New College Lane;
   Queen's College, High Street;
   Wadham College, Parks Road.

Pusey House, 5 miles east of Faringdon. [16]

Querns, Goring Heath, 3 miles northeast of Pangbourne. [17]

Silver Trees, Bagley Wood Road, Kennington, southwest of Oxford. [18]

Waterperry Gardens, 8 miles east of Oxford. [19]

Weald Manor, Bampton, between Witney and Faringdon. [14]

Westwell Manor, 2 miles southwest of Burford. [20]

Wood Croft, Foxcombe Lane, Boar's Hill, south of Oxford. [1]

---

23 Beech Croft Road, Oxford
MRS ANNE DEXTER

My garden is twenty-three yards long and seven yards wide, enclosed by five-foot-high walls and a fence at the end. A paved path winds down towards an oak door in the fence giving an illusion that the garden goes beyond it through the trees to the adjoining ground. In this shady and moist spot are trilliums, hostas, primulas, *Kirengeshoma*, many bulbs and a collection of ferns.

The brick walls have been extended by poles and trellis, and the shrubs all around the garden are now twelve or more feet high; these are pruned several times a year, if necessary, to keep them within bounds. Thirty *Clematis* grow amongst them, from *alpina* to *viticella*. *Clematis texensis* 'Etoile Rose' twines through *Prunus* 'Cistena', and *C. × durandii* falls over *Lonicera nitida* 'Baggesen's Gold'.

In the middle of the garden divided by the path are herbaceous borders packed with perennials, pillar roses and flowering shrubs. Near the house are rock beds on each side of a sunken path; the alpines grow amongst dwarf conifers and shrubs, while stone troughs stand round the edges of the paved area by the french windows.

Broughton Hall, Broughton Poggs
MR AND MRS C.B.S. DOBSON

The house dates back to Tudor times and the entire grounds now cover only a little over five acres. But in them, there is something from every century. The fifteenth-century carp lake, recently restored; the sixteenth-century 'ladies' walk', which Anne of Cleves is said to haunt; the seventeenth century was represented by a large knot-garden, now, alas, destroyed save for a few of the outer box hedges; the eighteenth century gives us the topiary work, the ha-ha and the pretty gazebo, and the nineteenth century adds some specimen trees, a grass tennis court and more. The twentieth century saw the garden derelict and the present owners, over the last ten years, have been replanting to fight the ravages of disease and neglect and to prepare for another century only thirteen years away.

Buckland Mead, Nr Faringdon
MRS RICHARD WELLESLEY

This is a woodland walk, not a garden, and was laid out by a disciple of Capability Brown. It starts near the Manor House, descends through the woods and past a very well preserved eighteenth-century ice house. Coming to the small lake, there is a large old horse chestnut under which are masses of daffodils and bluebells. Then over a bridge, along the side of the lake, and past trees and shrubs.

At the end of the lake is a rustic-style thatched boat house and tool shed. The large lake flows into the small lake over steps which form a small waterfall. Walking alongside this lake, again past masses of daffodils, one looks over the park to Buckland House. This house was built by the Younger Wood of Bath in 1749. There are fallow deer in the park as well as many fine old oak trees and a copper beech. By the lake are *Platanus × hispanica*, *Parrotia persica*, and a *Liriodendron tulipifera*. The lakes were artificially made to look like a river, when viewed from the house. At their end is a stone arch rebuilt by my husband in the 1970s, in the style of the eighteenth century, and this is the source of the springs which feed the lakes.

Walking up the park one passes an eighteenth-century temple, similar to one at Stowe, and finally past Buckland House, where there are some very old sweet chestnuts. As my late husband said, you take away from here a feeling for the English countryside with its great quiet and beauty.

Chestnuts, Wheatley
MRS D.E.W. MORGAN

A strip of old orchard approximately eighty by thirty yards was our garden twenty-four years ago. Fortunately there were quite a number of established trees, such as walnuts, silver birch, firs and some very old apple trees. The orchard grass is now a lawn with a curved stone path laid between the trees making the lawn look wider than it is.

The main feature of the garden is two raised alpine beds built across the south side of the house with a small patio between house and raised beds. Large patches of daffodils bring colour in spring, leaves of autumn-flowering *Cyclamen* making excellent ground cover.

There is a variety of shrubs flowering during the year and an herbaceous border consisting mostly of perennials with some roses.

The Coach House, Wallingford
LADY HEDGES

This small town garden was made in 1978. Part was an old Victorian drive, so we had the advantage of mature trees. We have concentrated on plants that will grow in this limy soil with minimum maintenance, and have achieved a variety of colour from flowers, foliage and shrubs, very few annuals, and plenty of ground-cover. Some of the more interesting plants are *Cytisus battandieri* with its lovely yellow flowers smelling of pineapple, silver-leaved and flowering in the spring, *Caragana arborescens*, also flowering in the spring, and *Koelreuteria* the lovely flowering tree in August. The old tree stumps are covered with *Clematis* and climbing roses and there is a small walled paved area, with plants in the paving and surrounding beds. Extra colour is given by planted urns, containing flowers from spring to late autumn.

The Court House, Broughton Poggs
RICHARD BURLS, ESQ.

It was the towering copper beech in the autumn sunshine which sealed my fate some years ago, and I bought the land and a glorious jumble of Cotswold stone buildings. The first priority after making a home out of the buildings was to construct the 'bones' of the garden with stone walls and tapestry hedges dividing the one and a half acres into four smaller areas to which we gave rather grand names. The garden had to be planned for ease of maintenance for it would only receive attention at weekends; grass, trees, shrubs and naturalized bulbs were the obvious answer. It had been my intention to keep 'the grove' as a wild garden, but Nature had other ideas, and the character changed when Dutch Elm disease meant the felling of sixty-nine trees. It did, however, give me the opportunity to replant a selection of interesting trees for their foliage. A *Catalpa bignonioides* stands out in its fresh green against the copper beech, and a group of maples changes colour magnificently in the autumn.

In spring thousands of naturalized bulbs carpet the grove and a vivid pool of *Anemone blanda* is wonderful in the sunshine. The 'secret garden' is my resting place from toil, preferably under the vine with its voluptuous bunches of sadly inedible grapes. I have a delight in garden statuary and urns and there are the results of several Continental trips; pots from Greece, Tuscany, and Paestum; baroque limestone *putti* from Florence and a St Francis also carved in Italy.

The centrepiece of the 'terrace' is a large oil storage jar from Corfu planted with trailing geraniums in summer. A wonderful specimen of *Rosa webbiana* with lovely bottle-

shaped hips dominates one end whilst two Lawson cypresses provide support for *Rosa filipes* 'Kiftsgate' which has romped thirty feet and in July is a cascade of white blossom which perfumes the whole garden.

Evelegh's, Long Wittenham
MR AND MRS JOHN H. ROSE

An acre of land runs for nearly three hundred yards in a narrowing strip from the village street north-west down to a backwater of the River Thames. Such length gives scope for gardening in many different aspects, and for experiment; the garden has been developed over the past ten years, and is in a constant process of renewal.

The soil is alkaline on the higher ground which lies over gravel; it is very light and thirsty but compensatingly easy to work, even in wintertime. On the low-lying land by the river the soil is heavier from centuries of flooding and silting, and the pH is lower – about pH 6.5.

The south-east face of the house gives shelter for abutilons and a *Fremontodendron*; the opposite side gives shade for hydrangeas and ferns. A long stone wall backs the herbaceous border. Nearby an old and many-stemmed yew protects a few square yards of gravelly 'garrigue' where mediterranean plants mingle with alpines and some British natives. In seven years a patch of *Raoulia hookeri* has spread over two feet in diameter.

Further from the house, mature limes and chestnuts make a windbreak for a border of shrub and old-fashioned roses, with compatible plants amongst them.

Down by the river the habitat is right for willows, *Cornus*, hostas, *Kirengeshoma*, *Abeliophyllum*, *Strachyurus praecox* and other shade- and shelter-loving plants.

When conditions are right it is a garden conducive to self-seeding of plants; a reminder that eyes should always be open for findings in a gravel path. *Euphorbia stricta*, *Commelina coelestis*, hellebores and eryngiums can all be relied on to scatter new plants there; while under the trees *Cyclamen* – *C. coum*, *repandum*, *cilicium*, and *hederifolium* – overflow with seedlings easily transplanted to new colonies.

Garsington Manor, Nr Oxford
MR AND MRS L. INGRAMS

The garden was mainly laid out by Philip and Lady Ottoline Morrell, members of, and hosts to, the Bloomsbury group. The ground slopes away steeply below the Elizabethan manor giving fine views south between descending rows of ilex oaks over the Italian garden and the orchard, as far as the Berkshire and Wiltshire downs. The garden is arranged in different compartments which combine the natural and the formal in a way which preserves its beauty in all seasons.

From the stone terrace in front of the loggia

to the east of the house one steps down to the Elizabethan-style parterre of twenty-four box-bordered beds with pencil-trained Irish yews in the corners of each bed. A grass path between long, low yew hedges leads to a bench from which there is a handsome view of house and parterre. Below, lies a large croquet lawn overlooked by a seventeenth-century dovecote, shaded by a mulberry tree and bordered by stone terraces with banks of lavender, pinks and roses. A display of species tulips and *Aubrieta* brighten these terraces in spring.

To one side of the croquet lawn a *Laburnum*-shaded walk leads by descending stages to the orchard. Halfway down a gate opens on to the Italian garden where tall yew hedges and stone statues are placed round a large square pool. A private yew walk behind the pool with clairvoyées cut out at intervals on the south side leads to an upper pool surrounded by willows. Naturalized bulbs in this wilder part of the garden make a fine show in spring. A water garden has been started in the dell where the spring runs. The newly made *potager* by the kitchen has been enclosed by free-standing wisterias. The north front of the house is framed by what are claimed to be the tallest pair of yew hedges in the kingdom.

Greys Court, Rotherfield Greys
LADY BRUNNER; THE NATIONAL TRUST

The gardens have been made among the ruins of the original thirteenth-century house. To the east of the Bachelors Hall is a superb ancient tulip tree and a weeping ash, both of which can be seen in a print in Skelton's *Antiquities of Oxfordshire* published in 1823. The late Humphrey Waterfield became interested in the possibilities of the gardens at Greys Court in 1950 and much of the planting was undertaken on his advice. It was his suggestion that the walls of the old tithe barn should enclose a garden of Japanese cherries.

In the small courtyard framed by the stables and the Bachelors Hall is a mediaeval archway incorporating what may well be Roman tiles. This leads into a rose garden, in which were planted many of the old-fashioned varieties, and this in turn opens into a circular walled area in which are a number of very old wisterias.

In 1980 the old kitchen garden was laid out in such a way as to preserve its character and traditional use. As there are traces of Roman occupation before the de Greys came, it is fitting that there should be a reminder of this early presence. Frances Pollen designed the octagonal tank that is a focal point, approached by two paths, one through an avenue of standard 'Morello' cherries, the other from a stone-paved pathway, flanked by espalier apples and a border of paeonies.

The 'tower garden' is full of white flowers and shrubs that are reflected in a lily pond. The surrounding walls with their window openings and variety of design and materials provide a charming diversity of background. Facing the house, banks of *Cistus*, rosemary and lavender cover the ground under venerable Scots pines.

The larch tree to the north-west of the house, the branches of which touch the ground, must be one of the oldest in the country. A Chinese bridge and moon-gate lead over the ha-ha to fields and woodlands. Beyond the kitchen garden, crossing the nut avenue, another bridge leads to the brick-paved maze, which was laid out by Adrian Fisher in 1980. Its plan follows the Christian symbolism of the pavement mazes to be found in the cathedrals of Northern France which in turn stem from the Greek legend of the Labyrinth. At the epicentre an inscribed pillar supports an armillary sundial.

◆

Greystone Cottage, Kingwood Common
MR AND MRS W. ROXBURGH

The two-acre garden lies three hundred feet up in the Chilterns and is sheltered by beech woods. It has been developed since 1970 from an Edwardian kitchen garden which was a mass of weeds, and brambles, well browsed by Muntjac deer.

The sixty-year-old trained pear trees form a feature and a delight in spring, and they are preceded by *Prunus subhirtella* 'Autumnalis Rosea' and *P.* 'Myrobalan'. Close by are *Eucryphia* 'Nymansay' and *E. × intermedia* 'Rostrevor' with their simple scented white flowers, filled with delicate gold stamens. Our damp soil suits the *Primula* family, the early flowering bright pink *P. rosea*, followed

Steps at Little Place, (see page 158), Clifton Hampden, in September. Pink hydrangeas and geraniums with yellow *Antirrhinum* are set off by white petunias and sweet *Alyssum*.

by the double primroses, 'Jack-in-the-Green', 'Hose-in-Hose', gold and silver laced, and lastly the various candelabra primulas; we now have our own self-sown double primroses.

What was once a mass of coal waste and rubble is now a new border planted with *Meconopsis*, gentians, primulas, dwarf rhododendrons, bog myrtle, and even cranberries! In another shaded border are royal and hardy maidenhair ferns and meadowsweet and white ragged robin. A white *Viola cornuta* seeded itself here and makes excellent ground-cover. Behind, the bright red *Tropaeolum speciosum* scrambles up a white wall. The wood edge provides useful shelter for azaleas, camellias, and other woodland plants.

At the front of the house is a small woodland garden, facing west. It offers a sunny well-drained corner for my mediterranean shrubs, including *Cistus*, *Myrtus* and various yuccas.

◆

Haseley Court Coach House, Little Haseley
MRS C.G. LANCASTER

On a sunny afternoon in July 1965, I came upon Haseley Court at the end of its small hamlet. It was deserted, overlooking a wide view of fields stretching to the Chiltern Hills. In front of the house, some garden flowers had escaped cultivation and seeded themselves in the uncut grass. Rabbits and hedgehogs reigned undisturbed. The romance of its neglected state made me vow to leave it so, but if one necessary weed is pulled alas the magic disappears. On the south side of Haseley sitting in a sea of nettles was a topiary garden over a hundred years old, and planted like a chess game in box and yew. Its care was due to the love and interest of Mr Shepherd who bicycled from Great Haseley and kept it clipped during the war, thereby saving it.

The west courtyard was full of army debris, but it had two high old stone walls surrounding two sides of a field and this is where I made my garden. The first thing I did was to enclose the two bare sides with tall wide iron hoops, like giant croquet wickets to which I could tie three-foot-high hornbeam to grow and make a tunnel – inside the tunnel I had a wide path with narrow beds each side for early spring bulbs and anemones – these bloomed before the leaves unfurled! On the unwanted side of the field I planted an orchard. Between the hornbeam arbour and the stone walls I divided the area into four with gravel walks, which had beds of old roses each side; these beds were bordered on both sides with boxwood. Unfortunately instead of buying rooted clean boxwood I planted old material given to me, and I have the largest crop of ground elder in the country. In these borders I planted some apple trees to give height and old-fashioned flowers such as *Salvia turkestanica* and *S. haematodes* which go well with old roses.

The walls were planted with climbers and had a broad border for herbaceous plants with shrubs. At the intersection of the four gravel paths I built a lattice summer house planted with *Rosa* 'Adelaide Arteaus'. Two of the grass squares had designs – one was for hedges and one for fruit and vegetables. The remaining two had grass centres surrounded with flower borders.

I like the garden planting to be like a cottage garden. I am not partial to large groups and colour combinations, and I like a feeling of mystery and informal planting in a formal design.

◆

Haseley Court, Nr Oxford
MR AND MRS DESMOND HEYWARD

John Leland, the Tudor antiquary, who was also Rector of Haseley, writes in 1540 of the 'marvellous fair walks topiari operis and orchards and pooles' at Little Haseley. The present topiary was planted in 1850 and consists of thirty-two chessmen in box and yew. Low beds of *Santolina* and lavender planted between make a haze of silver-grey at their base. The topiary is surrounded on three sides by yew and standard Portugal laurel. On the fourth side steps lead up to the fence through a white border with lilies, paeonies, galtonias, *Phlox* and tobacco plants against a background of *Rosa alba* 'Maxima'.

This leads to a small courtyard with more topiary, box hedges and large pots with *Agapanthus*, geraniums and *Helichrysum*. From here a path continues down to the canal (possibly an old fishpond or the remains of an ancient moat) past a compartmented herbaceous border on the left and woodland densely planted with spring bulbs on the right. Willows surround the canal, with *Hemerocallis* and primulas lining the edge. A nutwood underplanted with *Helleborus orientalis*, opens into a clearing at the north end of the canal with a long box walk drawing the eye to a large urn in the distance. Silver and grey plants predominate throughout the garden and link it all together.

◆

High Croft, Wheatley

Established twenty-seven years ago from a cabbage field, the garden is mainly on the south-facing slope of an ironstone ridge.

The soil is light and sandy, but fairly acid. With generous additions of peat, ericas, camellias, azaleas and rhododendrons are doing quite well. The aim was to make it labour-saving, but attractive to look at every day of the year, by planting a number of evergreen plants, including some golden and grey varieties, bulbs, a lawn of fine grasses and a succession of other plants, mainly flowering shrubs. The largest tree is a specimen of *Cedrus atlantica glauca*. Brooms do especially well, the last to flower being *Genista*

An autumn scene at Nuneham Park in late October (for a description of this garden see page 159).

aetnensis, the tall and graceful Mount Etna broom.

In June the combination of *Laburnum* 'Vossii', *Rhododendron* 'Mrs T. H. Lowinsky' (pale cyclamen) and *Rhododendron* 'Purple Splendour' (black centres, yellow anthers) is rather pleasing. A number of plants, such as columbines, evening primroses, honesty and foxgloves are allowed to seed fairly freely, to reduce weeding and to give a feeling of informality.

Blue and white flowers, such as campanulas, are encouraged, to leaven what might, otherwise, be a preponderance of yellows, reds and pinks. *Campanula portenschlagiana* is rampant (usefully!) under the deciduous hedge of *Prunus* 'Myrobalan', smothering most weeds, and is covered in flowers in June and July.

◆

High Tilt, Wheatley
MR AND MRS P. FREEBORN

Evergreen and deciduous shrubs and trees form the most important features of the garden to the south of the house; individually beautiful, they complement each other and give form and balance, and create an illusion of greater space.

Some are old friends (acers, camellias, magnolias, rhododendrons, *Malus*, *Prunus* and *Pieris*), others are more recent additions (*Exochorda*, *Styrax japonica*, *Pyrus salicifolia*, *Cornus kousa* and the wonderful *Rhododendron yakushimanum*); they blend happily with roses, *Clematis* and herbaceous plants. A wide terrace against the house has wall plants, hostas and an ornamental pond.

Below the terrace a good lawn, with more trees, enhances the wide meandering mixed borders. Here is scope to satisfy an irresistible

urge to move plants around. Long experience convinces one that almost anything will transplant – certainly in this garden few plants find a permanent home at first planting! The expense of new purchases is not necessarily involved; just give existing ones new companions, and see if they are compatible.

A grassed area contains hundreds of spring bulbs, plum and nut trees, and there is a cage of soft fruits – all splendidly prolific. This is well screened by wide planting. The garden is small enough to know intimately and to manage without undue effort, but large enough to provide continual interest. Perhaps the greatest success may be claimed for what began as a happy accident, and is now always borne in mind when planting, long views, in all directions, reward those who seek them out.

◆

Kencot Cottage, Kencot
MRS MOLLY FOSTER

In late winter a succession of flowering bulbs provides a welcome splash of colour, followed by spring bedding plants. In the front of the house by the roadside, rock plants brighten the scene. Before the summer bedding plants come into full bloom, various perennials, honeysuckle and roses attract the eye.

Autumn frosts finally finish the show of chrysanthemums. Other items of interest are a large espalier 'Conference' pear tree, a collection of bonsai trees, mostly raised from seeds or cuttings, and young plants being grown in the greenhouses for sale in aid of the local hospital.

Kencot House, Nr Lechlade
MR AND MRS ANDREW PATRICK

Nature itself has forced the greatest changes on our garden. First we lost three aged elm trees from the northern boundary, which gave more access to the cold winds, and then the bitter winter of 1981/2 killed two one-hundred-year-old cedars on the eastern side, nearly breaking our hearts. However, now that they have been removed there is so much more light in that part of the garden that we have made a large irregular island bed in the middle of the lawn. This is filled with a mixture of shrubs, perennials and bulbs in shades of pink, yellow and white, dominated by the beautiful *Acer* 'Flamingo', which keeps its pink growth all through its leafy season – a bright and happy colour scheme. I derive great pleasure from combinations of colour, such as a shady border planted with primroses 'Bluejeans' and 'Coral Island', soft but flowing, also *Lilium* 'Enchantment' growing through large clumps of *Alchemilla mollis*, in a sunny position.

We have two triangular beds at one end of a big lawn containing bearded irises in bright colours which are only of interest in May and June, so they are underplanted with Iceland poppies of orange, yellow, white and pink which flower from April until October. Our aim is to look forward to something blooming during every month of the year.

◆

Kingstone Lisle Park, Nr Wantage
MRS T.L. LONSDALE

Kingstone Lisle Park is a large, open-plan garden, using lawns, trees and shrubs to blend into the surrounding Berkshire Downs.

In 1945 it was an old Victorian garden full of Irish yews, box and closed in with elms. The box has been taken out, leaving very old yews which have been clipped, making a feature around the house. Avenues of limes have been replanted and realigned to replace the elms. One feature is a pleached undulating lime screen which is not often seen in Britain. Old-fashioned and species roses give colour all summer backed up by a large rose garden, laid out in the same way as the Queen Mary's rose garden of Regent's Park.

Bulbs give colour in spring, massed under cherries and lilacs, and summer colour is obtained from a large herbaceous border. The cedar of Lebanon must be one of the oldest and biggest in the country, and a small arboretum includes a collection of *Cupressus* in yellow, blue and grey.

◆

Lime Close, Drayton
MISS C. CHRISTIE-MILLER

I started planting shrubs in this garden during the winter of 1972–73. Over an acre was cleared of scrub and rubbish by a JCB and then put down to grass. I began by planting the shrub borders, mostly with very small plants grown from seed and cuttings taken from my father's garden. He usually managed to grow the best form of any tree or shrub he planted. A good example of this is *Kolkwitzia*. Cuttings from his form are a far better colour than ones I bought.

The garden is at its best in spring as I have a big collection of bulbs, snowdrops, *Crocus*, dwarf and large *Narcissus* and fritillaries. *Tulipa sprengeri* is one of the features in late May and is now naturalizing itself all over the garden. The spring shrubs make a lovely setting for the big daffodils, and several viburnums are now big bushes.

Magnolias seem unreliable. I lost five *M. wilsonii* one hard winter just as they had reached flowering size. A planting which has proved very pleasing is *Rosa glauca* (*rubrifolia*) growing out of silver-foliaged ivy; the rose shows up well both when in flower and hips. I inherited several different variegated hollies when I bought the property, and these I moved to form a hedge of alternating yew and holly.

Near the house are three raised beds growing rock plants and bulbs, an alpine house with a big collection of small bulbs, and a bulb frame which has a collection of fritillaries as well as *Crocus* and *Narcissus* and so on.

I use *Verbascum olympicum* for weed control. It's a great help in keeping down bindweed and couch; usually it stands up to wind but this year's gales have been exceptional.

◆

Little Place, Clifton Hampden
HIS HONOUR JUDGE MEDD AND MRS MEDD

This one-and-a-half-acre garden in the river-side village of Clifton Hampden is on a south-facing slope, but has presented many problems of design. This is because the house is at the bottom, near a road, and backs into a steep bank. Little of the garden is visible from the house. Our aim has therefore been to make it a garden for walking around. By using some terracing that remained from an old bit of a former garden, possibly laid out by Gertrude Jekyll for Lady Ottoline Morrell, who lived in the house before moving to Garsington, we have tried to create a series of interestingly varied spaces which increase in size as one ascends from the side of the house.

At the top is a croquet lawn, bounded by old walls and hornbeam hedges, with a septagonal gazebo in an angle of the wall. An herbaceous border runs along the northern side. Beyond the old wall and a small orchard was the disused village rubbish tip. This we have now laid out as a woodland walk and small water garden. Most of the garden is alkaline but the site of the rubbish tip, probably because much ash was tipped there, is acid, so rhododendrons and azaleas underplanted with bulbs border the paths. Through the young trees – beech, chestnut, cherry, rowan, and whitebeam – glimpses are obtained of the Berkshire Downs and the Chilterns. Returning down the hill, one passes through the smaller hedge-framed sections of the garden, showing off paeonies, roses and shrubs. Half way down, by a small formal pool and fountain, one looks out across a water meadow to shimmering silver-leaved willows and alders bordering the Thames.

◆

The Malt House, Henley-on-Thames
MR AND MRS D.F.K. WELSH

This is a town garden, and one's first impression is how imaginatively a most unpromising shape has been used. A long thin strip of ground, barely five yards wide, has been broken up into rooms by conifers, bamboos and shrubs. In each is a little pond, and between them a York stone path weaves from side to side. Along each border the original brick and flint wall has been heightened by fencing, from which *Clematis* and honeysuckle, magnolia and *Buddleja alternifolia* cascade.

Interesting use has been made of contrasting foliage in this predominantly green garden: a yew provides a background for the lush leaves of *Veratrum album*, the grey-leaved *Rosa glauca* (*rubrifolia*) arches out among the purple *Cotinus coggygria*, *Iris foetidissima* 'Variegata' provides a spiky background for the soft *Dicentra spectabilis* 'Alba'. *Trillium sessile*, *Sanguinaria canadensis* and *Hacquetia epipactis* provide less usual flowers and leaf forms at your feet.

At the end of the path is a sixteenth-century brick and flint Malt House covered in *Wisteria*, and just when you think you have finished your tour, the path turns a sharp corner, and below you is another secret and unsuspected area. From an open terrace, a few stone steps lead to a round lawn, its circumference paved and surrounded by beds of perennials, shrubs and small trees, punctuated by sudden exclamation marks, like the huge-leaved *Rheum palmatum*. Old apple trees are smothered in the rose 'Kiftsgate' and *Clematis*: a bank of the dwarf *Iris* 'Green Spot', leads the eye to tree paeonies. A *Carpenteria californica*, associated with *Lonicera tragophylla*, is not only a rare delight to the eye, but fills its corner with overpowering scent in June. One bed is hot and predominantly yellow, with various *Oenothera*, *Dictamnus albus* and *Sisyrinchium striatum*; another cool, with mauves and powder blues of *Veronica*, bluebells, *Geranium phaeum* and *Thalictrum aquilegifolium*. A tiny woodland area is carpeted with wild strawberries and in another corner, spiky Scotch thistles, *Galactites tomentosa* and *Astrantia major* are menaced by a giant hogweed.

◆

The Manor House, Bampton
THE EARL AND COUNTESS OF DONOUGHMORE

The garden was designed by Countess Munster when she came to Bampton in 1948. There are really several small gardens, each complete in itself with surrounding walls or hedges and each with its own character and atmosphere. The whole is set against a background of fine mature trees.

There is a white garden enclosed within a high yew hedge, where all the flowers and foliage are white, grey or green. This peaceful little garden was built as a memorial to a small child who was drowned. There is also a small rose garden where the roses are intermixed with other plants including lavender and herbs.

In front of the house are the famous twin herbaceous borders, which, like many other parts of the garden, we have had to largely replant as so many plants died in the exceptionally cold winter before we came to Bampton in 1982. On the west side of the house, the summerhouse and swimming pool are surrounded by high walls, on which there is a profusion of climbing plants, mainly roses and *Clematis*.

In springtime the gardens are a delight with successive carpets of colour as the aconites are followed by pale mauve sheets of *Crocus tommasinianus* and many interesting varieties of daffodils which we inherited. We have continued to add new varieties – including miniature daffodils and tulips – of which we are completing a collection under the avenue of lime trees.

◆

Marten's Hall Farm, Longworth
MR AND MRS JOHN PARKER-JERVIS

An old farmhouse, mellow stone walls and huge weeping willow are the bones of our garden. Listing some of the plants reads like a horticultural *Who's Who* and reminds one of many generous and knowledgeable gardeners.

Early spring brings the snowdrops. *Galanthus* 'Sam Arnott' is sweetly scented, *G.* 'Lady Elphinstone' has yellow in her double skirts and *G.* 'Lady Beatrix Stanley' is a stately double. *Helleborus* 'Miss Jekyll' and *Anemone* 'Lady Doneraille', a blowsy wood anemone keep company with the deep blue *Pulmonaria* 'Lewis Palmer'. *Saxifraga* 'Ruth McConnell', a compact red 'mossy', and *Thymus* 'E. B. Anderson', a prostrate golden form, are in a corner near *Primula* 'Linda Pope' whose mealy leaves complement the soft lavender flowers. *Astrantia* 'Shaggy' reminds us of Margery Fish and a charming small-leaved willow, *Salix* 'Nancy Saunders', was probably found on a holiday abroad. *Dianthus* 'Charles Musgrave' and *D.* 'Mrs Sinkins', two delightfully scented members of that family, here mix well with the silver white of *Artemisia* 'Valerie Finnis' and *Hebe* 'James Platt' with pewter foliage. *Agapanthus* 'Lady Moore' with neat white flowers and *Myrtus* 'Jenny Reitenbach', a compact bush covered in cream flowers, are followed by the late-flowering *Colchicum* 'E. A. Bowles' and 'Dick Trotter' which stay with us till late autumn.

Try growing snowdrops around clumps of hostas; as one finishes, the other takes over.

◆

Nuneham Park, Nuneham Courtenay
NUNEHAM PARK CONFERENCE CENTRE

Nuneham is an outstanding example of eighteenth-century taste and feeling in a landscaped garden. The terraces on the garden front, with fine views on to the 'Capability' Brown parkland to the south, are nineteenth and twentieth century. The house, sited as a Palladian villa to enjoy the river landscape and distant views of Oxford, originally sprang out of the lawns. A walk leads up to Athenian Stuart's temple (1764) the first church to be remodelled as a garden ornament. The mediaeval church it replaced was part of the old village transplanted to the turnpike in the making of Lord Harcourt's landscaped garden, the inspiration of Goldsmith's *Deserted Village*. As in the poem, one old widowed lady was allowed to remain and her memorial may be found on a tree on the walk leading round the bowl of the hill, which was itself a road of the old village.

The second Earl Harcourt was the patron of William Gilpin and the picturesque, and many carefully composed pictures can be seen from different parts of the garden; one particularly picturesque station is from the viewpoint beyond the old lady's tree across to the temple-church. At this point is a statue of Dr Fell sent from Christ Church by Dean Liddell, Alice's father. Lewis Carroll was a friend of Vernon Harcourt and used to bring the children for picnics in the Nuneham woods which feature in the White Knight's farewell in *Through the Looking Glass*.

The Carfax Conduit was removed from Oxford in 1787 in a road-widening scheme and featured on Brown's hill. Mason's garden with its Temple of Flora hidden between the house and the church is a rare example of an eighteenth-century informal flower garden, using flowers in the landscape. The flower beds are now being reinstated by the Garden History Society according to Mason's plan and Sandby's famous painting using flowers of the period mentioned in letters to Harcourt's friends and relations, including Marvel of Peru, Venus' Looking Glass, tuberoses, pink yarrow, hollyhocks and *Nigella*. The Nuneham flower garden shows what flower gardening was like in the forgotten stage between parterres and carpet bedding.

◆

The Old Manor, Broadwell
MR AND MRS MICHAEL CHINNERY

This beautiful old garden is made up of a series of small gardens, including a walled courtyard with thymes and acid-loving shrubs in pots and lemon tubs with tulips, and a topiary garden with two enormous yew Noah's Ark birds and some cones, with a centrepiece of a Florentine trough sur-

rounded with grey-leaved plants and a box hedge.

A wrought iron gate leads into the main garden with mixed herbaceous borders in quiet colours and a mulberry, yews and walnut trees. Next is a garden for sitting in on windy days, hedged with yew and with a white rose climbing through an old apple tree.

The soil is very workable and slightly alkaline, but because we 'overplant', it is given quantities of food, compost and shredded bark. Yellow looks warm against the stone walls and a successful combination is a *Humulus lupulus* 'Aureus' growing through *Solanum crispum*, white foxgloves and golden privet with *Alchemilla mollis*, *Ruta* 'Jackman's Blue' and *Viola labradorica* associate well with *Carex elata* 'Aurea', Mr Bowles' golden sedge, which shines in the sun even in winter.

A line of pleached lime trees is growing to hide the garage and the house walls are clothed with old roses and *Clematis*, fairly young, but fast-growing *Magnolia grandiflora* and *Vitis coignetiae*. The vegetable plots are kept as formal as possible with borders of chives, tree onions and parsley and supply most of our needs. We tried wild strawberries, but the dog ate them before they could be picked!

◆

The Old Rectory, Broughton Poggs
MRS E. WANSBROUGH

There is a tradition in the neighbourhood that this house and garden are the originals for Anthony Trollope's *The Small House at Allington*, and this may very possibly be so. The garden is a charming, old-fashioned typical Rectory garden surrounding a delightful seventeenth-century Cotswold stone house. Its chief features are a magnificent beech tree and two fine well-matured lawns, one having been the Rectory tennis-court and the other its croquet lawn. Both lawns are bordered by flowering shrubs – magnolias, hydrangeas, roses and paeonies, the whole being enclosed by a Cotswold dry-stone wall.

◆

Oxford College Gardens:

Christ Church (THE DEAN AND STUDENTS) The Master's garden was created in 1926, with fine views of the Cathedral and college. The Priory House has Pocock's Plane, an oriental plane planted in 1636, while in the Deanery garden, where Alice played, is the Cheshire Cat's chestnut tree.

Corpus Christi College (THE PRESIDENT AND SCHOLARS) The Fellows' garden has herbaceous borders and views over Christ Church and meadows.

Lady Margaret Hall (THE PRINCIPAL AND FELLOWS) Eight acres of formal and informal gardens, with daffodils, and water meadows by the River Cherwell.

Merton College (THE WARDEN AND FELLOWS) Features include an early eighteenth-century lime avenue, and an ancient mulberry.

New College: Warden's garden. A small old garden enclosed among college buildings.

Queen's College: Fellows' garden. Half an acre with a large *Quercus ilex* and splendid herbaceous borders seen against high old stone walls.

Wadham College: Fellows' private garden and Warden's garden. Good herbaceous borders and ancient trees; in the Fellows' private garden is a Civil War embankment with period fruit tree cultivars.

Pusey House, Nr Faringdon

MR AND MRS MICHAEL HORNBY

The garden at Pusey was started in 1934. It is a modern garden in an eighteenth-century setting, with large sweeps of lawn and a two-acre lake, crossed by an eighteenth-century Chinese Chippendale bridge, with a simple stone temple at one end.

The house is set off by terraces designed in 1934 by Geoffrey Jellicoe, these terraces facing south and containing many tender plants.

The herbaceous borders are the main feature of Pusey: one long border stretches from the house to the temple and the other double border, which comes into its best in August, flanks the entrance path to the garden through the kitchen garden. Round the lake there are large shrub beds underplanted with water-loving primulas and astilbes. One of the features of the garden is the fullness of all the beds, with ground-cover under shrubs and roses, and borders packed full. One of the best reasons for doing this, apart from the fact that flowers are prettier than earth, is that if you have a full garden you reduce the amount of weeding.

Pusey looks good all through the year, but has three main seasons – the spring, early July and the autumn, when the colours are really beautiful, reflecting in the dark waters of the lake.

Querns, Goring Heath

MR MICHAEL AND THE HON. MRS WHITFELD

Our garden lies on high ground and can easily suffer from harsh winds, so we have divided it into smaller areas using the yew and beech hedges as strong, natural divisions. In front of the east side of the house, we have large mixed borders of shrubs and herbaceous plants. Yew hedges cross the centre of the garden and, looking down to the end, we have a large lawn, dominated by the tall statue of a Roman warrior and surrounded by rough ground which is a mass of daffodils in spring. To the side, and behind a new beech hedge, lies the long walk, a surprise to find as you walk through, but it is a quiet corner with

the flower bed at one end designed around an elegant bird bath.

The rose garden faces south, with a background of yew and the flint walls which surround it, giving a brilliant display of the various colours from June to September. By the entrance to the house, there is a paved courtyard containing small flower beds filled with plants predominantly coloured silver-grey, white and blue with a touch of pink from the *Rosa willmottiae* and the climbing rose 'Compassion'.

Silver Trees, Kennington

DR AND MRS P.F. BARWOOD

Silver Trees is surrounded by Bagley Wood, and when we came here twenty-five years ago we determined to respect and enjoy our native oak, of which a superb specimen with trunk and curving branches can be seen across the grass twenty-five yards south of our verandah. We soon dispatched the hybrid teas and creeping thistle which bordered the lawn, and these were replaced with shady borders for hellebores, hostas and a variety of other plants. To the south-west of the lawn is a tall copper beech, fronted by an old *Prunus* 'Pissardii' and the purple cut-leaved maple – a study in brown; to the south-east a space was filled with delicate sub-shrubs, including *Magnolia*, *Cornus nuttallii*, with *Prunus sargentii*, allspice and witch hazel, not forgetting the *Viburnum* × *burkwoodii* with its scent in spring. The camellias and the *Eucryphia* seedling were much daunted by the great frost.

South of the house the garden is sunnier, and here alpines flourish, with four old sinks and a collection of thymes. To the east is a shaded bed full of spring bulbs, foliage plants, and hellebores, white *Phlox* in variety, lilacs and daphnes, even *Paeonia cambessedesii*. This August the yew hedge celebrates the conjunction of the scarlet *Tropaeolum* and the purple climbing aconitum. There is so much – the ivies, the × *Fatshedera*, the willows – that this truly informal part of the garden seems at last mature.

The garden moves on, however, as to the west of the house we have recently lost four large birches, which allows us more light for the shrubs in the north-west and for the old roses.

By taking a short path into the wood, one can admire the wood anemones, the primroses, the moist areas, or the grassy bed. The wood is almost a greater pleasure in winter when the rather misplaced wellingtonias stand out, and the gold and silver privets come into prominence. In early November, when the sun is in the west, to lighten the trunks, the autumn colours are wonderful – *Amelanchier*, maple, *Cercidiphyllum* and even Norway maple – and a sheet of autumn *Crocus*, never forgotten.

Waterperry Gardens and Horticultural Centre

Waterperry, place of water and pears, lies on rich silt loam between a sleepy River Thame and the low hills of Shotover to the west.

The main summer feature is the long herbaceous border backed by a mellow brick wall. From June to September the contrasting colours and shapes make a moving picture, reaching its climax in July and August. The pathway flanking this border links the parkland with its specimen trees, including massive sycamore and copper beech, to the meander of the riverside where mature box trees abound in a wilder setting and the banks are carpeted with daffodils and fritillaries.

Beyond the herbaceous border and the small rock garden are shrubs, rose and foliage borders, and the herbaceous stock beds, where the flamboyant summer colours of *Rudbeckia*, *Penstemon* and *Phlox* varieties are clearly named. Here too, are soft fruit plantations and apple and pear trees in a broad range of varieties. Within the walled garden are the glasshouses, one containing a mature Seville orange tree, and a wide range of alpines including the National Collection of Kabschia saxifrages.

Weald Manor, Bampton

MAJ. AND MRS R.A. COLVILE

Apart from the mixed daffodils and crocuses that we have planted, there are many winter aconites, *Anemone blanda* and scillas, and some *Ornithogalum nutans* and *Fritillaria meleagris*. Although these derive from planting many years ago, it is nature which provides the flowers when the garden is at its best.

Westwell Manor, Nr Burford

MR AND MRS T.H. GIBSON

Westwell is in spirit an enclosed inward-looking Tudor garden made up of a series of rooms divided by stone walls, box and yew hedges. There are no long views; it is rather a haven secluded from the outside world. The seven acres include a double thirty-foot herbaceous border, avenues of pleached limes, *Pyrus* 'Chanticleer' and hornbeams, a pergola underplanted with *Lilium regale*, *Galtonia candicans* and *Gladiolus callianthus*, a white and mauve garden, a lavender border interplanted with irises, a knot garden, a nut and primrose walk and two orchards.

At the lowest boundary of the garden the fish pond is planted with water-loving *Iris*, grasses and primulas. The island has large-leaved *Hosta sieboldiana* to reflect in the dark water and a recent delight is *Meconopsis betonicifolia* grown from seed in a peat pocket dug out of the extremely alkaline soil. Diamond-shaped beds marked roughly by stepping stones echo the diamond hedges of *Teucrium* which form the main outline of the nearby knot garden.

The rose garden consists of eight beds, each planted with a different old-fashioned rose. We have added a pergola on either side of the dividing path planted with climbing 'Iceberg', 'Kathleen Harrop' and others to give a longer flowering season, but have kept to the pink and white theme. The feet of the pergola are clothed with alternate clumps of pink and mauve lavender.

We are experimenting with a meadow garden trying to coax poppies, campions and cornflowers to follow the narcissi in the small orchard planted with a symmetrical arrangement of *Malus* 'John Downie'. A new combination that gives pleasure in October is a *Cotinus coggygria* 'Notcutts Variety', whose purple leaves set off the late-flowering pink rose 'New Dawn' and the fading *Hydrangea paniculata* 'Grandiflora' which grows pink as it ages.

Wood Croft, Boars Hill
MRS GEOFFREY BLACKMAN

My husband was an avid collector of rhododendrons, from the early thirties, and a great admirer of Kingdon-Ward, many of whose introductions still flourish in our garden – the yellow *Rhododendron wardii, R. macabeanum,* and *R. venator* as well as *Primula floribunda* from Tibet. When Geoffrey retired I found him the opportunity to make his third small woodland garden.

It lies along the edge of Bagley Wood where ancient oaks spread their boughs to provide the dappled shade which suits rhododendrons so well. Bagley Wood belongs to St John's College as did my husband, a Fellow and Keeper of the Groves, so he had an unlimited supply of leafmould into which he moved over a hundred rhododendrons. The site is unusual because, across the lawn, steps lead down into a cavern of dark green where a path now circles a chain of ponds.

In early spring kingcups, then daffodils and anemones, reflect in the ponds and behind them glows the brilliant mauve of *Rhododendron* 'Praecox'. A little later sheets of candelabra primulas, wine-red, then pink and yellow, cover the marshy ground, seeding themselves even in the gravel path. On drier soil and up to the edge of the forest many rhododendron species and hybrids flower in succession up to the August blooming of *R. auriculatum.* Beyond the ponds through a grove of silver birch you look up to a bank of brilliant azaleas and dwarf rhododendrons.

A corner of the garden at Westwell Manor in July. Hostas, delphiniums, *Lilium regale* and *Chrysanthemum frutescens* stand out against a yew hedge; behind are standard 'Iceberg' roses.

I must leave you to imagine summer with *Hydrangea* 'Preziosa' surrounded by astilbes, a bank of *Hydrangea* 'Blue Wave' the arching fronds of willow gentian, lilies standing up among the smaller rhododendrons, and at the last a giant *Eucryphia*.

SHROPSHIRE

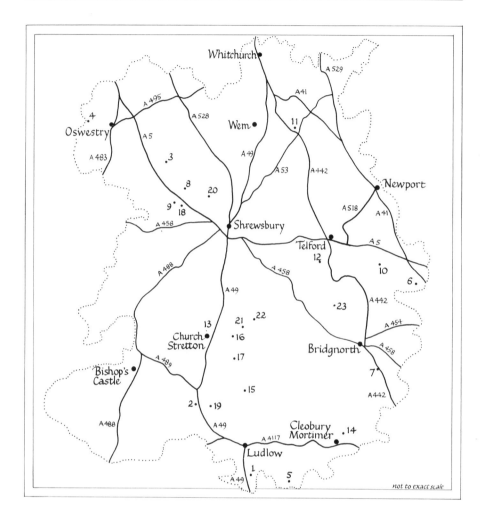

not to exact scale

Directions to Gardens

Ashford Manor, Ashford Carbonel, 2¾ miles south of Ludlow. [1]

Broncroft Castle, Craven Arms, 14 miles southwest of Bridgnorth. [2]

Brownhill House, Ruyton XI Towns, 10 miles northwest of Shrewsbury. [3]

Brynhyfryd, Rhydycroesau, 4 miles west of Oswestry. [4]

Burford House Gardens, 1 mile west of Tenbury Wells. [5]

David Austin Roses, Bowling Green Lane, Albrighton, 7 miles northwest of Wolverhampton. [6]

Dudmaston, 4 miles southeast of Bridgnorth. [7]

Greystones, Little Ness, Baschurch, 8 miles northwest of Shrewsbury. [8]

The Grove, Kinton, near Nesscliff, 10 miles northwest of Shrewsbury. [9]

Hatton Grange, 2 miles south of Shifnal. [10]

Hodnet Hall, 5 miles southwest of Market Drayton. [11]

Limeburners, Lincoln Hill, on outskirts of Ironbridge, Telford. [12]

Mallards Keep, 13 Alison Road, Church Stretton, south of Shrewsbury. [13]

Mawley Hall, 2 miles northeast of Cleobury Mortimer. [14]

Millichope Park, Munslow, 8 miles northeast of Craven Arms. [15]

The Morleys, Wall Bank, 3½ miles east of Church Stretton. [16]

New Hall, Eaton-under-Heywood, 4 miles southeast of Church Stretton. [17]

Oak Cottage Herb Garden, Nesscliff, 7 miles northwest of Shrewsbury. [18]

Oldfield, near Long Meadow End, near Craven Arms. [19]

The Old Rectory, Fitz, near Shrewsbury. [20]

The Old Vicarage, Cardington, 3 miles east of Church Stretton. [21]

Preen Manor, Church Preen, near Church Stretton. [22]

Swallow Hayes, Rectory Road, Albrighton, 7 miles northwest of Wolverhampton. [6]

Willey Park, Broseley, 5 miles northwest of Bridgnorth. [23]

Ashford Manor, Ashford Carbonel
KIT HALL, ESQ.

I have been fortunate enough to have had control of this garden since 1928. Since 1945 it has been designed and maintained to be both decorative and also to supply plant material for flower arrangements, of which I have had a certain amount of experience – both lecturing and showing. The garden still keeps up a small commercial weekly supply to a leading flower shop.

A visitor to the garden (a complete stranger) said 'I think I like this garden better than Hidcote' – I thought I must have misunderstood, but a friend said, 'Oh no, what he enjoyed was that it is so uncontrived – a completely natural garden.'

Broncroft Castle, Craven Arms
MR AND MRS C.T.C. BRINTON

This garden is an interesting one, with a number of mature trees planted at about the turn of the century by a very knowledgeable man. Many of the shrubs too are a rare version of a common type. There is also a magnificent yew hedge some ten foot tall and sixty yards long which is castellated and divides the garden in the front of the house from the kitchen garden.

The soil is clay and therefore roses, particularly climbing roses, grow extremely well and are a major feature of the garden.

The Tug brook flows through part of the garden, and in 1960 a water garden was made along its banks. The water garden is at its best in spring, along with plantings of daffodils and *Anemone blanda*. The kitchen garden is interesting as the present owners, one of whom is slightly handicapped, decided to plant low-growing vegetables such as beans, strawberries, carrots, asparagus and herbs in raised beds (twenty-five feet long by six feet wide) which were constructed with wooden railway sleepers as a retaining wall. The purpose of this was to make both the planting and the harvesting easier, and the beds were filled with good soil to enable vegetables such as carrots to be grown. As the beds are never walked on the earth does not suffer from compaction and the vegetables grow well.

Brownhill House, Ruyton XI Towns
ROGER AND YOLAND BROWN

Take one and a half acres of north-west-facing 45° slope with light soil over sandstone, previously used as a scrapyard, and make a garden; the result is labour-intensive but definitely very unusual. The compensation of a slope is that it naturally provides interest, especially when as at Brownhill House it descends to a river and affords fine views across the valley.

The garden has been developed since 1973 to give the maximum of variety from a formal paved walk with pond and gazebo to wild woodland. Using terracing with stone retaining walls, we have formed a series of beds and features with a connecting system of paths and steps linked by grass banks planted with shrubs and trees. Spring is welcomed with a drift of daffodils, early-flowering plants in the rockery and the catkins of hazel and willows along the river. In early June many trees and shrubs are in flower, notably a *Laburnum* walk and specimens of *Crataegus*, lilac, rhododendrons and the rose 'Frühlingsgold'.

Cultivars and wild species are blended so that there is an abundance of campion among the trees, and foxgloves border the lawn in association with shrubs and modern perennials. In summer there are notable specimens of *Gunnera* near the water whilst a formal parterre is bright with bedding plants and small shrubs. The garden is also productive with four vegetable plots and two glasshouses. Some sixteen types of fruit and nuts are grown including a fine specimen apricot and wall-trained peaches. There is no need to separate food from flowers; in a walled border next to the vegetables we have peaches and sweet peas behind vines with *Aquilegia* at the front.

Brynhyfryd, Rhydycroesau
MR AND MRS M. RUANE

In 1973 a Welsh hillside, a thousand feet above sea level, was transformed into an alpine garden of two acres. Two-thirds of it is covered in heathers, mostly with coloured foliage. These great patches of colour – yellows, golds, oranges, bronzes, pinks and reds, change in hue through the seasons, the winter colours being just as pleasing, if not more so, than those of summer. The flowers are but an added bonus, and throughout the year it is a riot of colour. This multi-coloured patchwork quilt is given architectural form by conifers of different shape, colour and size.

The extensive rockery is filled with hundreds of alpine plants, many of them rare in this country. Of particular interest are hundreds of lewisias, grown both in stone walls and on the flat. These include several species and some unique interspecific hybrids. A special feature is a collection of more than thirty stone troughs stocked with beautiful alpines.

A natural spring feeds the ponds stocked with mirror and koi carp.

Burford House Gardens, Tenbury Wells
JOHN TREASURE, ESQ.

Two very large lawns, a magnificent copper beech, two huge London planes and a towering wellingtonia – these were the only garden features in existence when the present owners acquired the property in 1954. Now, some thirty-one years later, the four-acre garden, completely redesigned, is approaching maturity.

The lawns have been extended, huge island beds have been formed, and two streams introduced where an interesting collection of moisture-loving plants are thriving. Many rare and unusual trees, shrubs and herbaceous subjects are planted. Old roses – species and climbers – are prominent in June and July, and there is a large collection of interesting hardy ferns.

Some hundred and fifty *Clematis*, both species and hybrids, scramble through shrubs on walls and in the open border as well as being trained prostrate at ground level where they mingle with herbaceous plantings. *Clematis* 'Ascotiensis', a dark blue, growing into the brilliant scarlet climbing rose 'Parkdirektor Riggers' is a startling sight. *Clematis* 'Niobe' (a deep red) trained through *Cornus alba* 'Variegata' makes a pleasing effect as does *Clematis* 'Daniel Deronda' growing through the pink *Wisteria*-like flowers of *Robinia kelseyi*.

The gardens lie in a frost-hollow and some winters can be intensely cold. The soil pH is 7.9 but, somewhat surprisingly, ericaceous plants thrive here. The 'Old Moat' on the north side is a home for ornamental ducks and also on the north side the fountain pool provides a display of colourful waterlilies in summer.

In the stable block (under the clock) is the museum which tells the story of the gardens and exhibits relics of past days; here also is a fine set of pictures portraying the genus *Clematis* and its history.

David Austin Roses, Albrighton
MR AND MRS DAVID AUSTIN

This nursery stocks some seven hundred varieties of old roses, shrub, species and climbing roses. In addition there are gardens displaying mature roses in two-hundred-foot-long beds; English roses (old and modern roses crossed); and an area devoted entirely to irises and paeonies.

Adjoining the nursery are two acres of gardens surrounding a fine Queen Anne house. There is a formal garden, with beds containing small plants and bulbs, two large mixed borders containing a variety of shrubs and hardy plants, and a 'canal garden' with a wide grass walk between the water and a hornbeam hedge. There are many fine trees and a number of sculptures by Pat Austin.

Dudmaston, Bridgnorth
SIR GEORGE AND LADY LABOUCHERE:
THE NATIONAL TRUST

The garden slopes steeply westward to the 'big pool', a large sheet of water over which there is a distant view of the Clee Hills. Wild cherry and snowy mespilus, *Amelanchier*, give a shimmering beauty in spring when the daffodils are at their best.

An interesting feature is the ornamental boathouse dating from 1840, and situated next to the Dingle. Walter Wood, the poet Shenstone's gardener, created this romantic valley in the last quarter of the eighteenth century inspired by the first Mrs Whitmore to live at Dudmaston.

In the garden is a 'Ladies' bath' planted with primulas and by the 'big pool' is a water garden where a giant cuckoo flower, *Cardamine raphanifolia*, flowers freely each year.

The garden terraces and the rock garden were made in the mid-nineteenth century, the latter against red sandstone rock and planted with many heathers, rock roses, lavenders, thymes, *Cytisus* and escallonias. Under the top terraces by the house are a variety of old-fashioned roses and the Spanish climbing roses 'Gava' and 'Lorenzo Pahissa'.

To the south-east is the American border, created in about 1850, where a few of the original rhododendrons and azaleas remain. The planting has been augmented with magnolias, halesias, kalmias, ornamental cherries and many other trees and shrubs, with an underplanting of hostas and lily-of-the-valley and a variety of ground-cover plants.

Greystones, Little Ness
MR AND MRS A.A. PALMER

Greystones is a country garden in a rural setting with 'borrowed' scenery of rounded hills, fields and trees. The gently sloping south-westerly aspect is open to strong winds at certain times of the year, but the sandy soil is easy to work, and, provided that you can supply ample manure and compost as well as retain moisture by mulching, gives early colour and deliciously precocious vegetables. In the garden proper, wide borders are stocked with a mixture of herbaceous plants and shrubs, including many unusual varieties, with particular emphasis on good foliage for

The alpine garden at Brynhyfryd (see page 163) relies for its colour on the foliage of dwarf conifers and heathers as much as on flowers, such as the red and pink mossy saxifrages and auriculas seen here in May.

long-term effect. We are very attracted to variegated foliage and the double forms of common plants such as primroses and buttercups.

A feature of the garden is the old shrub roses, at their best in the latter part of June and early July. Also good around this time are the numerous *Clematis*, both species and hybrids, which not only decorate walls and fences but also scramble through many of the taller shrubs and trees.

Of interest to visitors whose gardens are too small to include a lawn, or who find the chore of cutting one too much, is the gravel garden. This is an area of about thirty by twenty feet, with shallow soil on a stony foundation mulched with a four-inch layer of small gravel and grit. Though not special enough to be dignified with the name 'scree', it does have similarities and makes a wonderful home for many of those difficult plants like *Convolvulus cneorum* who do not enjoy winter wet round their feet, as well as being an excellent device for cutting down weeding. Finally I must mention the alpine house which early in the year is home to a selection of show auriculas and later in the summer a comprehensive collection of succulents.

The Grove, Kinton
MR AND MRS PHILIP RADCLIFFE EVANS

This garden faces south, sloping towards the Severn plain, with fine views to the Breiddens and the Shropshire hills. The aim, over the past twelve years, has been to create as many interesting and surprising viewpoints as possible within a small area, the boundaries never being continuously visible. Domestic features, such as the old orchard, vegetable and soft fruit areas, remain. As the garden is entirely maintained by the owners, consideration has been given to future reduction in labour, and the design ensures that the 'bones' of a good general garden will remain.

From the mainly silver and grey border against the red-brick Regency house, one sees contrasting masses of shape and colour throughout the year. Thought has been given to the use of less common hardy plants and shrubs, many with variegated foliage. This is a detailed garden which repays close inspection since many of its plants have been carefully collected from gardens of the past, and are less strident and showy than their modern counterparts. It is their quieter colours and their association which help to create the

atmosphere. The collections of old-fashioned roses and the many cranesbills are at their best in June, and it is then that the garden is at its most colourful. But obviously one season cannot show the visitor what every good gardener works for – continual interest from a combination of trees, shrubs and herbaceous plants as attractive when fading as in full bloom, interplanted with bulbs and tuberous subjects giving constant renewal as new life emerges through the old.

Separate from the garden is an acre and a half conservation area, planted over the last twelve years with native trees including such comparative rarities as quince and medlar.

Hatton Grange, Shifnal
MRS PETER AFIA

The gardens at Hatton Grange comprise various differing mysterious areas incorporating about thirty acres in all. The oldest part is a valley of red sandstone rock containing four monks' fishponds and surrounded by sloping banks of azaleas and rhododendrons. Often the light – enhanced by water reflections – produces a most magical atmosphere.

The shrubbery area nearer to the house has an ageing mulberry tree and an attractive water garden surrounding the blue pool. There are flowers here from February to November; primroses, polyanthus, primulas, day-lilies, *Iris* and anemones.

The rose garden has been recently renovated and is now full of beautiful old-fashioned shrub roses. The garden is entered by two rose arches covered with the climbers 'Madame Alfred Carrière' and 'Sombreuil'. Adjacent to the roses is the lily-pond garden with four circular beds edged in old rock stones, each centred with *Pyrus salicifolia* 'Pendula', the attractive grey/green tree more commonly known as the weeping pear. There are rambling dwarf plants in carefully chosen colours tumbling through the rock stones. As you walk you discover large areas of wilderness with long grass showing *Crocus*, orchids, woodbine and snowdrops which luxuriate until cut in July – a huge copper beech stands majestically viewing the stretches of this beautiful garden hidden from many who do not choose to visit us.

---

*Hodnet Hall Gardens, Nr Market Drayton
MR AND THE HON. MRS HEBER-PERCY

A sixty-acre landscape garden with a series of lakes and pools, magnificent forest trees, and a great variety of shrubs and other plants.

Limeburners, Ironbridge
MR AND MRS J.E. DERRY

When, in 1970, the present owners purchased this nine-and-a-half-acre site, it consisted

Oak Cottage, Nesscliff, in June (see page 167). Lime-green *Alchemilla mollis* contrasts with the glaucous foliage of pinks, and the last flowers of the orange form of Welsh poppy, *Meconopsis cambrica*.

Paeonies and catmint at Greystones, Little Ness, in June (see page 163). These anemone-flowered 'Imperial' paeonies have their stamens replaced by flattened staminodes.

mainly of a disused refuse tip. Its setting was beautiful – south-facing with fine views of the wooded slopes of the Severn Gorge – but the 'soil' was a black amalgam of compacted foundry sand and other waste materials; nothing would grow there.

Having spent five years clearing the site of all loose items and scrap (including abandoned cars), the owners then collected huge quantities of top-soil which they spread over the tip. A house was built on the site and the main planting of the area was carried out in 1975, with the aid of two strong sons using pickaxes for every major plant-hole and even hammers and chisels on occasions.

The aim throughout has been to attract and protect wildlife, particularly butterflies and moths; the main feature of the garden is therefore a combination of wild and cultivated plants surrounding a large lawn and pool, with extensive areas of rough grass adjoining.

Wild flowers abound (including bird's-foot trefoil, horseshoe and kidney vetch, rock-rose, dog and wood violets, thyme, honeysuckle, devil's-bit scabious, wood sorrel, ragwort, knapweed, cowslip and primrose) and there is also a wide selection of buddlejas, hebes, sedums and geraniums.

Many trees have been planted with wildlife in mind along with holly, broom, blackthorn, alder-buckthorn, gorse, privet and dogwood. Also encouraged to grow are scabious, honesty, sweet-rocket and valerian.

This is an all-the-year-round garden with a wide selection of climbers, shrubs and other plants (some rare) and with an emphasis on foliage-colour associations, but visitors are invariably attracted by the *Gunnera* which dominates the poolside and by an old Scots pine which one night 'walked' seventy feet!

Mallards Keep, 13 Alison Road, Church Stretton
MR AND MRS FRANKLIN BARRETT

The garden, started in 1966, is situated in a small estate surrounded by the Church Stretton hills on the lower slopes of wooded Helmeth hill. The area on the south front of the house is screened from the road by trees and shrubs including a Judas tree that flowers freely in May/June. There are roses, old and new, a rock garden with choice alpines, a *Magnolia* × *soulangiana* 'Alba', and some rather tender plants which are grown against the wall of the house where the double yellow *Rosa banksiae* blooms well in early June. The garden at the rear is dominated in spring by a deep bank of rhododendrons and other shrubs and trees, effectively disguising the north-eastern boundary of the garden; among them are *Rhododendron* 'Hawk Crest' and *R.* × *loderi* 'Venus', *Amelanchier*, camellias and *Magnolia* 'Leonard Messel'. The garden also contains a collection of dwarf rhododendrons and other ericaceous subjects. Along the western boundary is a twenty-foot orchid house holding a collection of some three hundred tropical and sub-tropical orchids that flower mainly between autumn and the early spring. Outside a curving border facing south, along a broad grass way, is the home of a variety of herbaceous plants with a background of shrubs interesting for their leaf colour and flowers, whilst a damp area in front of the orchid house accommodates primulas and other moisture-loving plants.

In this small garden in which shrubs are the main feature, we endeavour, by careful pinching and pruning, to maintain an open and airy feeling in a garden which otherwise might become claustrophobic; in this way we are able to enjoy the individual shrubs and trees yet are also able to lift our eyes to the beauty of the hills around us.

Mawley Hall, Cleobury Mortimer
MR AND MRS ANTHONY GALLIERS-PRATT

Perhaps the most interesting point about the garden at Mawley is that it has just been slowly growing in a slightly haphazard way since a major restoration of the house in the early 1960s. First of all the rubble collected from the building helped to create a terrace which now makes an attractive formal parterre. Then the vast machines on site easily dug out a sunken area in front of the old stables; this was a natural place for a rose garden. Later another clearing programme made a place available for the herb garden, where there is a large and varied collection, many of which are used in the kitchen. Finally in an old yard in front of the ancient barn it was possible to make a swimming pool; this is painted black which gives mirror-like reflections to the plants at either end.

The rest of the garden just meanders off in different directions amongst the beautiful old trees; the idea is that not too much help will be required to keep it together in the future, and there are extensive plantings of young trees and shrubs, roses and bulbs, with a lucky return of many wild flowers.

Plants that are of special interest in their own seasons include *Prunus* × *yedoensis*, *Rhododendron* 'Mrs A. T. de la Mare', *Cornus kousa*, *Sorbus* 'Mitchellii', *Clematis armandii*, *Rosa filipes* 'Kiftsgate' and many more which improve annually.

Oak Cottage in June. *Agave americana* in an old jar is seen across a mass of moon daisies, *Chrysanthemum leucanthemum.*

Millichope Park, Munslow
MR AND MRS L. BURY

Millichope stands on the southern slopes of Wenlock Edge looking across the Corvedale to the Brown Clee Hill. It is essentially a landscape garden, laid out in the early nineteenth century to complement the neo-classical house. The outstanding feature of the garden is the sweep of lawn descending from the house to a large lake on the opposite bank of which a temple stands on a cliff. It is this combination of landscaped garden in the foreground and the 2,000-foot Brown Clee Hill in the background which gives the garden its special character.

The ground behind the house is wooded, with a grass glade leading up to an obelisk. In spring the woods are carpeted first with daffodils and then with bluebells. Below these woods, and level with the house, is a formal lawned terrace. Steps lead down from the terrace to the big lawn and on this level is a series of small gardens surrounded by yew hedges and the old garden wall. Here there are lily ponds, herbaceous borders and a swimming pool surrounded by old roses. The walls are well clothed with climbing shrubs and roses.

The trees on the big lawn and around the lake were mostly planted at the end of the last century, although some of the hardwoods may date from the time of the earlier house on the site. Amongst the most notable are a 140-foot *Abies procera*, a 130-foot *Sequoia*, a 110-foot Lawson cypress and a 125-foot cedar of Lebanon. The latter stands poised over the temple, an interesting building which pre-dates the house and was designed by George

Stuart in 1785 to commemorate the deaths of two members of the More family, the then owners, who were killed in colonial wars.

The main lake, which is artificial, is fed by an existing stream which subsequently runs into the River Corve. A series of silting pools or small lakes fill the valley above the lake, and are punctuated by dams and a cascade. Rhododendrons have been planted in the woods above one of these pools and should provide colour in the spring. The lower lake is almost entirely surrounded by trees, but where the path runs along its bank a water garden is being made. Below the main lake the garden is informal with long grass, bulbs, spring-flowering shrubs and wild flowers.

Millichope is a garden for all seasons. In the spring the wild flowers are its main feature with cowslips, primroses, violets and later bluebells, lady's smock and campion carpeting the woods and banks. Daffodils are also in profusion at this time of year with spring-flowering shrubs. Summer is the time for the herbaceous borders and roses, and in the autumn the trees are at their most spectacular. The consolation for a garden with water in the winter is the arrival of migrant ducks and geese who chance their luck with the very territorial resident swans. From 1939 until the early sixties the house was a school and the garden was either given over to cricket nets or neglected. Over the last twenty years the wilderness has been partially tamed and a lot of planting has taken place. It is a question of recreating a garden designed in the nineteenth century in a way which is practical for the twentieth.

The Morleys, Wallsbank
MR AND MRS J. KNIGHT

This is a three-and-a-half-acre garden, made and maintained by my wife and myself, comprising three-quarters of an acre of fifteen-year-old mixed tree planting with wild daffodils and shrubs. There are herbaceous borders, rockeries and damp areas allowing planting of moisture-loving subjects. There is also a sloping site with a mixture of trees, conifers and shrubs together with some suitable herbaceous plants, the beds being bordered by grass paths.

We have a vegetable and soft fruit area and a small orchard, and in addition to this there is one acre of old meadowland kept for wild flowers and grasses, partly planted five years ago with shrubs and trees, ornamental and native, in order to conserve the wild plants and to provide interest throughout the year.

Spring bulbs, such as early-flowering *Crocus* species followed by daffodils, are naturalized in grass.

New Hall, Eaton-under-Heywood
MRS R.H. TREASURE

This is a wild-flower garden, at its best in April, May and June. There are drifts of naturalized primroses, violets and bluebells as well as marigolds and smaller quantities of orchids, herb paris and many other varieties. We have planted a few shrubs, many trees and many daffodils but, in our opinion, the beauty of these is small compared to the natural beauty of a wild fritillary, an oxlip or even a cowslip.

We have planted no wild flowers; they come naturally, but the grass through which they appear must be kept short, so that in late April and early May one can see the ground turn white with wood anemones and as May progresses the blue of the bluebells takes over.

Our woodland garden has its natural population of wild animals – they watch us come and go and do us little harm; this is a garden for animals as well as human beings.

We use no insecticides, or fertilizers, and, as a result, there are countless butterflies, damsel flies, and dragonflies. Frogs and toads are here in thousands (there are pools to help them) while kingfishers speed up and down the brook.

Oak Cottage, Nesscliff
MR AND MRS J. THOMPSON

Described by the Cottage Garden Society as a 'cottage garden *par excellence*', this plot is a delightful medley of 'cottage' plants and herbs. The herbs are one of the main features and are planted or self-sown everywhere, mingling with old roses, violets, pinks and other old-fashioned plants in rich and fragrant profusion. A network of paths links a series of yew-hedged terraces and other 'rooms', with rose-covered arches inviting the visitor to taste the magic beyond. Raised stone sinks and troughs provide homes for smaller and more delicate plants that would otherwise be lost amongst the mass of taller things. Thymes, musk and pennyroyal nestle in corners, spilling over on to paths and trailing over the old blocks of red sandstone that were brought here to form the terraces and walls. In the lowest part of the garden is a rustic summer-house beside a natural-looking pool where dragonflies rest in summer on the leaves of yellow *Iris*, mingling with ragged robin, bog bean and a host of others. In spring there are snowdrops, daffodils and other bulbs; wild primroses and cowslips abound. These are followed by woad, sweet cicely, columbines and the violets. But the garden is perhaps at its best in June, when the old roses fill the air with their scent and the intimate magic of this half-acre garden is most intense.

Oldfield, Long Meadow End
MR AND MRS PAUL HOUSDEN

In 1978 when my wife and I purchased Oldfield it was nothing but a derelict collection of empty buildings. Earlier, much earlier, it had been a hamlet, sheltered in the south-facing valley but without road access of any kind.

Nowadays it is difficult to recall just how awful the weeds and the scrub and the brambles all were.

The initial gardening problem was that of drainage: what to do about the copious water sweeping down from the sheltering but steep hills to the north. The solution was found in terracing. When the slope had been cut into, the sub-strata of heavy clay so exposed had to be removed and replaced with imported soil. Pipes had to be laid in trenches and finally moisture-greedy plants, such as *Cornus* and willow, planted freely. The area which once was farmyard is now mainly lawns and flower beds, with roses predominating. Where once, long ago, cattle watered there is now an ornamental pond. The garden of a cottage now dismantled is today an orchard containing twenty-seven half-standard fruit trees. In another area the vegetables and soft fruits grow inside three fruit cages, for this is a place where rabbits, pheasants and pigeons are numerous.

Heathers, both spring and autumn flowering, are grown not only for their own beauty but also to help feed bees of which we have six colonies. They help with the pollination of apples, pears, plums, currants, gooseberries, raspberries, strawberries and also damsons growing wild. It is a quiet garden, a long way from road or railway, and also it has variety. There are no acid-loving plants, but there are plenty of plants for dry soils, for wetlands, and ornamental shrubs. There is woodland too, planted in 1979 with spruce, alder, oak, beech, holly and chestnut.

An arch and steps at Swallow Hayes, Albrighton (see page 168), surrounded by the weeping branches of an old specimen of the weeping cherry *Prunus × yedoensis* 'Ivensii'.

The Old Rectory, Fitz

MRS J.H.M. STAFFORD

We took over this house and a quarter-acre garden in 1977 which, though more or less neglected, had some very good features. The best of these were the house itself, built in mellow brick in 1720, a hundred-and-twenty-year-old Deodar cedar, and other mature trees which gave interest to an otherwise rather flat site. The garden had been laid out with paths edged with sandstone curbs and these we kept as they made a convenient and well-designed shape on which to work.

The cedar was unfortunately killed in the great frost of 1981/2, but as a result there is now a wide view to the south Shropshire hills and much more light and air giving scope for new planting.

On the south-west boundary of the garden was a swampy and scrubby wilderness which we opened out. We dug a pool, keeping a belt of shelter, both to lessen the cold from the prevailing wind and to provide a nesting place for warblers – mainly blackcap and chiff-chaff. I enjoy the vegetable garden which is in the sunniest part of the garden, bordered by flower beds so that it does not appear too clinical.

The planting generally is governed by my inclination to plant species. Plants which seed themselves are often allowed to remain regardless of suitability. *Clematis tangutica* is a particular favourite, and plants that I grow for my botanical education but do not incline to are weeded out regardless. This obviously makes for a rather haphazard scheme which is forever changing as the mood takes me or as plants grow too large or are too rampant to be tolerated. Trees are very important and as these will outlive me they remain as a basic structure for my whims in between. My maxim is – never tolerate anything you do not like: throw it out!

The Old Vicarage, Cardington

W.B. HUTCHINSON, ESQ.

This old garden, covering two and a half acres, was rescued from complete dereliction by the owner in 1970/71. Since then a redesigned garden has been evolved with two objectives in mind: easy maintenance, and blending with the surrounding rural landscape over which it has extensive views from a south-west-facing slope. Achieving this has involved sacrificing year-round colour through herbaceous plantings or bedding-out, and concentrating instead on an informal layout of interesting trees, shrubs, roses, heathers and alpines against a background of some fine hundred-and-seventy-year-old beeches and indigenous daffodils, bluebells, snowdrops and *Crocus*; hostas have been used extensively for ground-cover especially under the larger shrub roses. An existing source of water has also been used to create a 'wild' water garden with a varied collection of moisture-loving primulas, irises and large marginal plants such as *Gunnera*, *Lysichitum* and *Peltiphyllum*. An exercise of this sort has produced some useful lessons, for the amateur at least, the most important of which is not to attempt to design a complete garden in detail all at once. We have found it better to take time and give nature time to express her inclinations, especially where conditions within the garden, as here, are very variable.

Although there is spring colour from rhododendrons, azaleas and bulbs, the garden is generally at its best in June/July.

Preen Manor, Church Preen

MR AND MRS P. TREVOR-JONES

Our garden, which we have completely restored during the last seven years, is approached through a small park with many specimen trees. It is on the site of a Cluniac priory with a yew tree reputedly planted in AD 457. A stone archway divides the formal planting on the drive from the vestry garden which borders the thirteenth-century church with roses climbing through *Cotoneaster* on the ruined vestry wall. From the main lawn the view of Wenlock Edge is framed by a low herbaceous border with a great cedar of Lebanon on one side and a remarkable specimen of red cedar on the other.

A shaded path with low walls leads through an archway into a secret garden in part of a derelict fifteenth-century barn and then up steps to winding paths bordered by mixed plantings which lead to a yew hedge and a rose garden with 'Escapade' roses and mixed borders of paeonies and *Iris*. There is a pot garden which allows semi-hardy plants to be grown in an otherwise hardy situation, and a miniature garden pool.

Beyond is the kitchen garden, with flowers bordering the vegetables and leading to the orchard. Steps go down to a long lawn which shows to advantage the garden wall, all that remains of the Victorian house built by Norman Shaw. We have planted varieties of *Prunus* between the buttresses.

Leaving the upper gardens, it is interesting to walk on and explore the Victorian water and bog garden which we are reclaiming and replanting as the final stage of our planned restoration. There is a further pleasant walk through the old laurels and woodland which still bear traces of their mediaeval history.

Swallow Hayes, Rectory Road, Albrighton

MRS MICHAEL EDWARDS

The garden here was started in 1968 in a one-and-a-half-acre site sloping to the west with sandy, slightly acid loam soil.

Firstly, it is a family garden, which has developed with the family, so it includes putting, badminton and an area developed from the children's 'camp'.

Secondly, it reflects our interests in plants; there are over two thousand different species and varieties, most of them labelled. Considerable thought has been put into the design, which basically shows the visitor how plants can be used to give effect, delight and surprises. It includes a number of rare shrubs and beds, herbs and vegetables. Each section displays different associations of plants; many are suitable to give ideas for small gardens. Amongst the trees of interest are *Cercidiphyllum*, *Paulownia*, *Davidia involucrata*, *Pinus strobus* and *Metasequoia glyptostroboides*.

Lastly it provides cuttings for our nursery and garden centre and acts as a trial ground for new plants we have discovered, before we offer them to the public. We think that it is a good example of low-maintenance design, as we reckon it takes the housewife of the family an average of eight hours per week through the year to keep up. We provide a leaflet for visitors, which explains the main points of interest. We are currently extending the garden, eventually to about four acres.

Willey Park, Broseley

THE LORD AND LADY FORESTER

Willey Park, a Wyatt-designed mansion built prior to 1825, is finely placed in its extensive park with woods and lakes. Around the mansion are the formal gardens of borders, lawns and terraces: to the south and west a ha-ha gives uninterrupted views over the parkland. The azalea garden is notable, having been set out at the turn of the century.

Falling eastwards towards the church and village is a quarter-mile gravelled walk through ancient woodland planted around 1885 with rhododendrons and azaleas. Since then many interesting shrubs and trees have been introduced in the continuous process of renewal and regeneration as age takes its toll.

SOMERSET

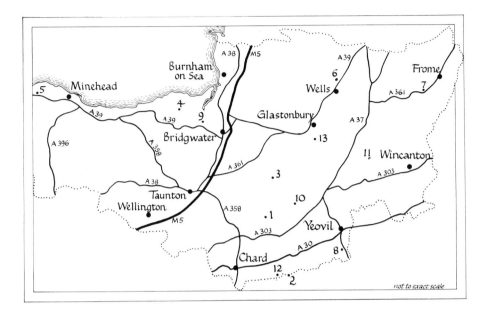

not to exact scale

Directions to Gardens

Barrington Court, northeast of Ilminster. [1]

Clapton Court, 3 miles south of Crewkerne. [2]

East End Farm, Pitney, 3 miles northeast of Langport. [3]

Fairfield, Stogursey, 11 miles northwest of Bridgwater. [4]

Greencombe, ½ mile west of Porlock. [5]

Milton Lodge, ½ mile north of Wells. [6]

Nunney Court, Nunney, 3½ miles west of Frome. [7]

The Old Rectory, Closworth, 4 miles south of Yeovil. [8]

Somerset College of Agriculture and Horticulture, Cannington, 3 miles northwest of Bridgwater. [9]

Tintinhull House, northwest of Yeovil. [10]

Wason House, Upper High Street, Castle Cary. [11]

Wayford Manor, southwest of Crewkerne. [12]

Wootton House, Butleigh Wootton, 3 miles south of Glastonbury. [13]

Barrington Court, Nr Ilminster
A.I.A. LYLE, ESQ.: THE NATIONAL TRUST

This garden was constructed in 1920 by Col. Arthur Lyle from derelict farmland, and its design and lay-out were approved of by Gertrude Jekyll, with attractive paved paths and walled *Iris*, rose and lily gardens.

Clapton Court, Nr Crewkerne
CAPT. S.J. LODER

One of Somerset's most colourful and immaculate gardens, with its formal terraces, spacious lawns, rockery, water and rose gardens, in a lovely setting. In addition, there is a woodland garden, with natural streams and banks of rhododendrons and azaleas. There are many unusual trees and shrubs of botanical interest, amongst them the biggest ash tree in Britain, with a girth of twenty-three feet, and a fine *Metasequoia glyptostroboides* over sixty feet tall, planted in 1950 with seed from the Arnold Arboretum in America.

The season opens with a display of daffodils and other spring bulbs while the many camellias and magnolias provide vivid splashes of colour to complement them. The varied collection of *Prunus*, with blossoms eventually falling and lying like snowdrifts, heralds the start of the main flowering season of the large collection of rhododendrons and azaleas from April to June.

With high summer, the numerous herbaceous plants, roses, fuchsias and geraniums fill the garden with their colours and sweet scent. The eucryphias are white with flowers and the hostas show their purple caps above luxuriant foliage. The lilies nod majestically and the hydrangeas emerge in their many shades of blue and pink and creamy panicles.

As summer fades to autumn, the maples flame and huge clusters of scarlet and orange berries hang from the *Sorbus*. The wonderful shades of red, yellow, pink and orange seem to be the garden's final blaze of triumph before winter.

East End Farm, Pitney
MRS A.M. WRAY

The garden here is set among seventeenth-century stone farm buildings and my chief aim has been to preserve old roses.

The visitor walks up the short drive bordered by a hedge of *Rosa spinosissima altaica* and through tightly clipped *Lonicera nitida* for a first view of an avenue of pollarded *Cotinus coggygria* with a stone water basin half-way along. Flanking this walk are broad herbaceous borders planted in muted colours – blue, pink, lavender, apricot and pale yellow dominated by the old shrub roses, carefully supported as they luxuriate in their natural abundance, their perfume joined by six different *Philadelphus* set around the garden.

The shady walk leads on to a rose pergola and two more massive ancient stone barns (one thatched) each supporting various climbers. Between their walls a tangled mass of *Clematis* almost hides a small entrance. Stepping down is a further secret formal garden which is a contrast of sunlight and shade, and steps lead up the small cobbled yard now supporting a sundial. The centre of the square lawn holds a small pool. Steps on the western side lead up to a wooden seat with views over neighbouring farmland.

One border in the garden is made over to winter-flowering shrubs and is a mass of hyacinths in spring. In this border 'May Queen' has climbed twenty-five feet up into a tree – five other trees about the garden support more *Clematis* and roses.

The garden was a rick yard, and the formal part a stockyard but, when we came in 1946, we had to start by scything through seven-foot brambles and nettles!

Fairfield, Stogursey
LADY GASS

This is an informal garden of great variety surrounding a house dating from the twelfth century but largely rebuilt in Elizabethan

An arch leading into the rose garden at Clapton Court, Crewkerne (see page 169).

The garden would not suit those who like perfect tidiness, but its atmosphere is refreshing and it is an ideal place to unwind.

Greencombe, Porlock
MISS JOAN LORAINE: GARDEN TRUST

Perched between the curlews' territory and the woodpeckers' overlooking Porlock Bay and the Severn Sea, this strip of three and a half acres is a well-loved forty-year-old garden. Its magic may lie in looking northwards, in the angle of light off the Exmoor hills, or in the sixty-foot-high trees whose grey trunks make Far Wood a natural cathedral. The site is steep and acid, with virtually no soil except the leafmould of generations, to which home-made compost is added yearly. Camellias and rhododendrons (mainly species) flourish, along with many other shrubs and an abundance of herbaceous plants, sedges and special ferns.

The aim has been to garden from the moss-covered ground to the canopy overhead, and to include every height of plant. If all goes well, the brilliance of spring reaches its climax towards the end of May, with the sizzling colours of azaleas. At midsummer the lawns, on different levels around the house, are drenched in the fragrance of roses. Then *Clematis*, leptospermums, honeysuckles and hydrangeas take over the pageant of bloom. There is always a rich pattern of frond and foliage.

Autumn is brilliant with maples, oak and the late gold of sweet chestnuts. In winter the tall fastigiate Lawson's cypress come into their own. These evergreen columns would lose their shape in a snowstorm or gale, but they were tied when young and for the last twelve years have been comfortably corseted in polyurethane salt-dump netting, which soon became invisible as the foliage grew. The spaces in this netting are six inches square, so birds in need of warmth and shelter can get through.

*Milton Lodge, Wells
D.C. TUDWAY QUILTER, ESQ.

A few years ago Lanning Roper attributed the glory of this garden to its position on the slopes of the Mendip Hills and its panoramic view across the meadows to Wells Cathedral and the Vale of Avalon. Fascinating glimpses can be seen from various vantage points on the four terraces, a framework built by my grandfather during the first decade of the century. The replanting reflects the needs of an alkaline soil and the family's interest in mixed borders of shrubs and herbaceous plants underlaid with different forms of ground-cover. These borders contrast well with the mown grass on each of the terraces which are divided by yew hedges and stone walls covered with climbers, among them *Magnolia grandiflora*, a variegated *Euonymus* and *Feijoa sellowiana* – all over fifty years old.

Shrub roses form the basis of one border, in

times. The eighteenth-century park has fine beech, oak, sweet chestnut and evergreen oak trees, and views of the Quantock Hills and of the sea a mile and a half away. The light soil is neutral, and although some trees and shrubs are affected by the prevailing west wind and by salt, in sheltered places frost-tender plants like mimosa, *Acacia dealbata*, usually survive the winter.

The walled former kitchen garden is now mainly grass and small trees, with a rose garden and herbaceous border; a few dwarf

box hedges have been maintained. In the woodland part of the garden are shrubs and many naturalized bulbs, especially fritillaries, *Crocus tommasianus*, blue and red anemones, and of course daffodils, snowdrops and bluebells, while the *Cyclamen* under the trees are an encouraging sight for months.

Trees include a handerkerchief tree, *Davidia involucrata*, a *Parrotia*, several Judas trees, a *Wisteria* grown as a free-standing tree, and a sixty-year-old *Magnolia grandiflora* as high as the house.

particular the hybrid musks which give an autumn flowering if they are pruned slightly after the summer bloom has faded; a group of *Felicia* underplanted with the blue *Geranium magnificum* makes a charming sight in a sunny corner. The stone paths and steps linking the terraces are softened with pockets of *Aubrieta*, pinks, *Anthemis cupaniana*, campanulas and the green froth of *Alchemilla mollis*, a beauty in any garden if it is contained. *Abutilon vitifolium*, both white and mauve forms, are a feature in late May, and the white flowers of *Clerodendrum trichotomum* scent the air in September. Nearby is a seven-acre arboretum developed by generations of the family which forms a pleasant contrast to the more formal terraces of the garden.

◆

Nunney Court, Frome
MR AND MRS R.R.C. WALKER

Nunney Court garden is essentially a green garden, bisected by a small river, its depth changing from one to nine feet over a distance. There is a sluice at the deep end, and there was a water wheel, given for scrap in the war, that originally ran the famous eighteenth-century garden tool works started by the Fussell family – now a ruin. The far side of the river is left wild as a bird sanctuary with large alders, beeches and a marshy pond. The house and lawn, with magnificent cedar tree, are built up on a terrace high above the river, and look down on the fourteenth-century towers of moated Nunney Castle.

The garden is surrounded by huge local stone walls and has little walled gardens inside, with many wrens. It is an alkaline soil. Yellow Welsh poppies abound, and *Crambe cordifolia* has to be ruthlessly controlled, though the cloud of white flowers and the scent of honey are lovely in June. There are natural outcrops of rock lining part of the lower terrace, and ferns, especially in a wet season, grow everywhere.

◆

The Old Rectory, Closworth
MR AND MRS MALCOLM SHENNAN

The house, which was built in 1606, is set on high ground with particularly fine views to the north and east. It has a small garden with many planted areas, containing a mixture of shrubs, perennials and the occasional rose. Hardy geraniums, being a particular favourite of the owners and in their opinion second only to grass as a ground-cover plant, are to be found everywhere. Another point of interest for the lover of herbaceous perennials is the wide choice of plants which do not require staking, despite the problems encountered by wind. It is policy not to stake anything in the garden other than young trees.

An old, unusual right of way leading from the village to a neighbouring hamlet has been cleared and planted with an unusual range of willows, a diverse genus with something to offer at most times of the year. Of note, too, are many different ferns and their surprising

Milton Lodge, Wells, in June. A mixed border with hostas and cranesbills, and large clumps of *Alchemilla mollis* in the paving.

tolerance of dry shade, perhaps a point which should be borne in mind more often.

◆

Somerset College of Agriculture and Horticulture, Cannington

This is an old college and Benedictine priory dating from 1138, with a fine Elizabethan west front. Seven old sandstone walled gardens protect a wide range of tender plants, including *Ceanothus*, *Fremontodendron* and *Wisteria*. Ten very large new greenhouses contain a variety of ornamental and tropical food plants. Many demonstration gardens, and collections.

◆

Tintinhull House, Nr Yeovil
THE NATIONAL TRUST

This famous two-acre garden divided into compartments, was developed between 1900 and 1960 and influenced by Gertrude Jekyll and the garden at Hidcote.

Wason House, Castle Cary
MR AND MRS B.J.R. MORETON

This is a long, narrow garden, saved from rectangularity only by a hint of dog-leg and a fine brick wall which twice changes direction. Happily, the lines of the perimeter are masked by our neighbours' trees, notably a splendid copper beech which dominates the garden. A flow of grass, now widening into lawn, now dwindling to a path, shapes our half-acre into islands and peninsulas of shrubs and smaller plants, while short cross hedges help to disguise the garden's disproportionate length.

Though not botanists enough to claim plantsmanship, we do perhaps meet the definition of a plantsman as one who wants to grow what he can't where it won't. Turnover is therefore rapid, and to list the plants we grow is to invite nemesis. But in their seasons we hope to enjoy the double bloodroot, *Acer pseudoplatanus* 'Brilliantissimum', eighty square yards of *Wisteria sinensis*, an immense *Kolkwitzia*, *Buddleja alternifolia* grown in standard form, *Arisaema candidissimum*, many bulbs and a few alpines. We grow few roses except as shrubs. They, like other shrubs, are expected to muck in with lilies, *Meconopsis* (when we are in luck), day lilies, sea-hollies, crocosmias and *Clematis*, fending off the hardy geraniums which, with the grass, provide a measure of continuity.

Our liking for bulbs is shared by the local badgers, which make it increasingly difficult to grow crocuses or tulips in the open garden. Daffodils and fritillaries are so far spared; and in the shade of the copper beech we grow aconites, *Cyclamen*, erythroniums and others. Weeding a large area of small bulbs is not easy: separating the clumps by narrow 'paths' kept weed-free with simazine does at least comfort the gardener with the illusion that he is in control.

Nunney Court, Frome, in June (for a description of this garden see page 171). Single paeonies, *Paeonia arietina*, grow alongside a mossy path.

*Wayford Manor, Nr Crewkerne
ROBIN L. GOFFE, ESQ.

This is a terraced garden and an informal woodland garden of about three acres on a favourable southerly slope with views into Dorset. It was redesigned by Harold Peto on a site which in Elizabethan times was noted for its 'fair garden'. The mainly Elizabethan house, originally a thirteenth-century mediaeval hall, is fronted by a paved court, flanked by clipped yew hedging, which is also U-shaped round a copy of a Byzantine font and enclosing an iris and fig garden with a statue of Mercury. The east court between the house and the church contains a well-head and a large weeping ash, and the upper terrace a lily pond, topiary and a summer house. The lower terrace has a balustrade, based on fragments found on the site, with a conservatory and loggia attached to the house at

one end and a pair of fine horse chestnut trees at the other.

Steps lead down on to the main terrace which has a path flanked by rose beds and herbaceous and shrub beds against the surrounding walls; further on a small pond is dominated by a vast specimen of *Magnolia × soulangiana*. Through an archway or down steps from the terrace is an enclosed secret water garden with maples, irises, hostas, paeonies and dwarf rhododendrons. A rock garden with a pool, conifers, maples and Japanese stone ornaments leads to a two-acre wild area. This predominantly spring garden contains a fine collection of trees and shrubs including many varieties of *Magnolia*, maple, *Rhododendron*, cherry, and *Camellia*. Notable trees include *Magnolia denudata*, *M. salicifolia*, *Betula maximowicziana*, *Ginkgo biloba*, *Malus baccata* and a collection of mature maples.

Wootton House, Butleigh Wootton
THE HON. MRS JOHN ACLAND-HOOD

This is a garden of about five acres around a seventeenth-century house set in parkland and farmland with views of woods, the Hood Monument, and vistas to Glastonbury Tor and West Pennard Church and hill. The soil is heavy clay and lime, and the stone walls are blue lias. It was redesigned in the early twentieth century with the help of Auray Tipping and contains many shrubs and trees, with herbaceous borders, a rose garden, a woodland garden and a kitchen garden with two greenhouses – one for vines and the other for propagation. The woodland garden has many *Cyclamen*, *Anemone blanda*, *A. appenina* and *A. fulgens*, masses of fritillaries and bluebells, as well as daffodils, cowslips, primulas, lilies, pulmonarias and violets. The orchard (known as Chapelhay) is the site of an ancient chapel.

SURREY

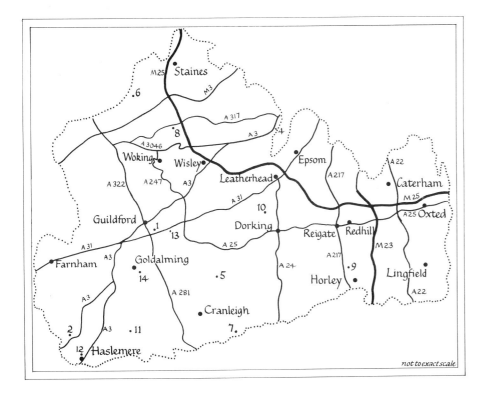

not to exact scale

Directions to Gardens

Bradstone Brook, Shalford, 3 miles south of Guildford. [1]

Calluna, Whitmoor Vale Road, Hindhead, 5 miles north of Haslemere. [2]

Chilworth Manor, 3½ miles southeast of Guildford. [13]

Claremont Landscape Garden, ½ mile southeast of Esher. [4]

Coverwood Lakes, Peaslake Road, Ewhurst. [5]

Gorse Hill Manor, Gorse Hill Road, Virginia Water. [6]

Hogspudding Farm, Baynards, near Rudgwick, 3 miles southeast of Cranleigh. [7]

Lime Tree Cottage, 25 Ellesmere Road, 1½ miles from Weybridge. [8]

The Moorings, Russells Crescent, Horley. [9]

Polesden Lacey, 1½ miles south of Great Bookham, near Dorking. [10]

Ramster, 1½ miles south of Chiddingfold. [11]

Surrey End Cottage, Tennyson's Lane, near Haslemere. [12]

Vale End, Albury, 4½ miles southeast of Guildford. [13]

Winkworth Arboretum, Hascombe Road, near Godalming. [14]

Bradstone Brook, Shalford
SCOTT BROWNRIGG AND TURNER

A walk around the newly-discovered gardens at Bradstone Brook brings many diverse delights and is a charming example of an Edwardian garden which has been refreshed and revived for enjoyment in the eighties.

When the current gardeners started work, most of the garden was derelict. The water garden in particular revealed much of the original plan devised by Gertrude Jekyll – at one stage a series of stepping stones were discovered quite by chance whilst planting. They now provide a leafy walk through the wild garden toward the *Acer pseudoplatanus* 'Brilliantissimum' whose foliage is most colourful, particularly in the spring. The tall stems of foxglove lead the visitor into the shady cherry-tree walks, through which one has a view of the spacious lawns in front of the house, and the azalea border which is set against the backdrop of the Surrey hills.

Within the shelter of the house is an ornamental rose garden which was found in an unruly state. It has now been brought back to its former condition with lavender and box hedges, and the roses 'Fragrant Cloud', 'Whisky Mac', 'Grandpa Dixon', 'Southampton' and 'Mischief'. The brilliance of the rose garden contrasts with the subtle grey foliage around the newly-planted lily-tank, and a recently uncovered alpine garden and extensive woodland walks are set against the backdrop of the splendid house.

Calluna, Hindhead
MR AND MRS PHIL KNOX

Calluna is a garden in the west Surrey hills five hundred feet up on a site slightly sloping to the north. Therefore it has a cool situation where cassiopes, gentians, *Meconopsis* and *Nomocharis* flourish. The half-acre plot has evolved over the last twenty-five years from a somewhat unpromising sweet chestnut coppice of overgrown giants some seventy feet tall. As we cleared the land, we planted new trees including *Pyrus salicifolia* 'Pendula', *Cercidiphyllum japonicum*, *Chamaecyparis pisifera* 'Filifera Aurea', *Juniperus squamata* 'Meyeri' and *Arbutus unedo*.

From these beginnings, beds, borders and paths have been sited giving the effect of many small vistas and individual plantings. Emphasis is on foliage and interest all the year round from the rugged beauty of *Mahonia lomariifolia* in November, as the herald for many winter-flowering shrubs, until spring when the peat beds come into their own with dwarf rhododendrons and other ericaceae combining with primulas and bulbs to make a carpet of colour. This rivals the rock garden with its own appeal of colourful sun-lovers and tiny treasures.

Summer brings shrub roses, lilies, *Hemerocallis*, *Agapanthus* and other perennials in colourful display in the central island beds contrasting with the cooler, shadier aspects of the garden where hostas, ferns, *Veratrum* and willow gentian flourish. All grow well in our poor sandy soil enriched with deep mulches of leafmould, which is also the gardener's way of suppressing weeds. A further labour-saving device is the use of pine-needle peat paths (needing neither mowing nor edging) where plants can overlap gracefully standing out against the rich brown of the peat.

So to the early autumn with a carpet of *Gentiana sino-ornata*, the blue blending with the tints of autumn leaves; colchicums, too, add colour at this time of year.

Chilworth Manor, Nr Guildford
LADY HEALD

I sometimes wonder what gives me the greatest pleasure in my garden; a little plant like a *Dimorphotheca* or a tulip species that is loved and cherished in the rock garden, or the effect of the border with delphiniums, lupins, shrub roses and a *Rubus* 'Tridel'. My feelings about the garden are that it must always have some treasures to be shared with visitors. First aconites then scillas and all the heavenly little anemones come peeping through the cold ground; then come the fine spring daffodils and blossoms in all their glory, followed by primulas, bluebells and, on the right soil, rhododendrons and azaleas and then to roses and herbaceous plants.

As the summer passes into autumn there are sedums, michaelmas daisies, *Cyclamen*, autumn crocuses and all the lovely colouring from vines and other shrubs, not to mention ground-cover provided by such pleasing plants as the various cranesbills, ivies and epimediums.

Winter brings with it the beauty of the naked trees and silhouetted branches on those such as the snowdrop tree, *Halesia*, *Catalpa*, the Judas tree and cherry trees. My garden is on seven different levels, which provides the joy of sunny and shady spots and allows me to grow almost anything.

◆

Claremont Landscape Garden, Nr Esher
THE NATIONAL TRUST

This is believed to be the earliest surviving English landscape garden, and it has recently been restored. Begun by Vanbrugh and Bridgeman before 1720, it was extended and 'naturalized' by William Kent during the early 1730s. He it was who altered what had been a small formal lake to the irregular design we see today, with an island and pavilion. Probably the best-known feature of the garden at Claremont is the turf amphitheatre which was designed by Bridgeman, and which was restored to its former state after much hard work clearing the mass of laurels and *Rhododendron ponticum* which covered almost the entire area.

◆

Coverwood Lakes, Ewhurst
C.G. METSON, ESQ.

This beautiful garden, covering approximately twelve acres, is made up of a cottage garden and the bog and water garden. In the cottage garden against a backdrop of a blue *Cedrus atlantica*, *Aesculus indica*, the Indian horse chestnut and a tall *Liriodendron tulipifera*, the garden slopes to the south. A small arboretum contains *Prunus subhirtella* 'Autumnalis', *Cornus florida*, *Malus* 'Golden Hornet', *Laburnum* 'Vossii', *Ginkgo biloba* and a number of *Crataegus*. Roses and daphnes share their borders with paeonies, viburnums and *Cotinus coggygria*, and climbing roses reach the cottage bedroom windows.

As you enter the bog and water garden, a line of *Taxodium distichum* confirms the constant dampness of this area, and to the right is the first of four lakes which are fed by natural springs. A thirty-foot-tall *Rhododendron* merges with its own reflection in the water. Golden orfe swim in and out of the waterlilies and a creeper-clad stone arbour provides a shady spot. Opposite the third lake a cyclone some years ago blew down large numbers of mature trees and the area has been replanted with specimens of *Sorbus*, sweet chestnut, *Nothofagus*, *Prunus* and many varieties of oak. A path leads through to the azalea wood which in springtime is a breathtaking mass of colour.

The garden abounds with interesting trees – *Sequoiadendron giganteum*, *Stuartia sinensis*, *Davidia involucrata*, *Oxydendrum arboreum* – as well as many fine rhododendrons. The natural springs and streams provide the necessary damp conditions for lysichitums, both white and yellow, and *Gunnera manicata* to thrive. Bordering the paths are a great many varieties of *Hosta*, *Trillium* and candelabra primulas, whilst lily-of-the-valley forms a natural carpet.

◆

Gorse Hill Manor, Virginia Water
MRS E. BARBOUR PATON

Gorse Hill Manor is situated on the northern corner of Wentworth Estates, a property of about eighteen acres, which includes six acres of forestry and three of garden, the rest being pastures for summer cattle, grazing and permanent residence for two donkeys and one retired pony. The soil is clay at the top half and acid sand elsewhere.

The house was built in 1938, in Tudor style, but with great care and old materials, giving thought to brickwork and roofing.

In spring the highlights of the garden are the azaleas surrounding two standard wisterias, *Prunus subhirtella* 'Autumnalis' and a magnificent *Pieris formosa forrestii* with scarlet young leaves followed by large terminal drooping panicles of waxy white flowers, various magnolias, camellias and viburnums. There is also a group of *Cedrus atlantica glauca*, five *Picea omorika*, Siberian spruce, and a magnificent *Abies homolepis*.

Chilworth Manor, Nr Guildford

Roses become the next attraction, particularly in front of the porch where they are planted up a bank of brickwork. *Kalmia latifolia*, *Romneya*, *Potentilla* and *Photinia* × *fraseri* 'Red Robin' are all worth a place. For the autumn showing there is an *Acer palmatum* 'Atropurpureum' and a small dome-shaped *A*. 'Dissectum'. The evergreen bed opposite the house gives a good show throughout the winter with *Elaeagnus pungens* 'Maculata', hebes and *Robinia pseudoacacia* 'Frisia' against a background of Lawson's cypress.

◆

Hogspudding Farm, Nr Rudgwick
MR AND MRS FRANCIS RITCHIE

This two-acre garden around a converted farmhouse has been carved out of sticky Wealden clay since 1981. Wide open to all the winds that blow, the first rule of providing hedge shelter was deliberately ignored as surrounding hedges would have interfered with the views of farmland and nearby woods on all sides. Instead, there are many island beds with a wide variety of shrubs and young trees, terraces with alpines and smaller shrubs, and an embryonic wild flower meadow with close-cut paths fringed with shrub roses. The latter are evident everywhere, and at the last count there were ninety-nine varieties.

Stocking a new garden can be expensive, so wide use has been made of plants easy to propagate and reasonably happy when windswept, such as *Cistus* and *Escallonia* – both much hardier with us than their reputation. We have had *Escallonia* in variety for thirty years, on greensand in a frost pocket and now on clay, and have hardly lost a plant. Also doing well in the wind is the sea buckthorn *Hippophaë rhamnoides* with attractive grey foliage and orange berries – a splendid background.

There are no hybrid teas, no bedding out, no traditional herbaceous border, but a number of unusual plants (such as the dwarf *Clematis scottii* 'Rosea' and *Hebe diosmifolia*). We use a lot of the hardier penstemons, such as 'Garnet' and 'Firebird' daylilies, and geraniums in groups and drifts, quick to grow and, again, easy to propagate! *Rosa* 'Moonlight' with *Geranium psilostemon* makes a great show.

◆

Lime Tree Cottage, Ellesmere Road, Weybridge
MR AND MRS P. SINCLAIR

'A garden should look good all the year round.' I believe I have achieved this in my tiny cottage garden by the use of structural evergreen plants such as yew, box, laurel, ivy and *Bergenia*, planted in bold clumps, thereby making the garden appear larger than it really is. Statues, stonework, architecture and trees give interest when there are no flowers. However, even in the dead of winter, hellebores flower prolifically and *Pyracantha* berries cover the walls, making it a haven for the birds.

This is a mature cottage garden divided into three compartments, connected to one another by complementary plants, yet each retaining its own character. A white picket gate in a clipped yew hedge leads you to a sunny garden of herbs, cottage flowers, shrub roses and foliage plants, all surrounded by box edging. From here a path goes to a more informal area with an old farm gate, and a seat under a spreading cherry tree, underplanted with euphorbias and forget-me-nots, hostas, bergenias and wild strawberries, overlooking a golden privet, set in a lawn, backed by a dark green yew hedge. A gravel drive flanked by herbaceous plants such as achilleas, delphiniums, daylilies and *Agapanthus*, blue rue and more box takes you to the third section of the garden, with yellow tree paeonies, shrub roses, mounds of *Senecio monroi* and purple sage, golden bay, *Hebe rakaiensis*, *Phlox*, euphorbias and blue hostas in large terracotta pots. Statues are half-hidden by ivy and other foliage plants. Another seat invites you to rest awhile.

The whole garden is furnished prolifically yet, with bold clumps of green planting giving a backcloth to the flowers, tranquillity prevails all the year round.

◆

The Moorings, Horley
DR AND MRS C.F.L. WILLIAMSON

This town garden is just one acre of flat, undrained clay, less than a mile from the terminals of Gatwick. Nevertheless, the impression is of peace and seclusion, an oasis of quiet and calm. The heavy clay is now a rich soil supporting a huge range of plants, from fine trees and shrubs to many alpines in the York stone rock garden.

The garden is really in two halves; the first, a formal one, surrounds the Edwardian house. On the south side of the house are tender Californian shrubs, a vigorous palm and many cheerful pots on the terrace. A large lawn leads to the beds filled with modern and old-fashioned roses, and a pergola that divides the view.

From the house it appears that only woodland exists beyond, but in fact the second garden begins there. The path behind the rose garden lies across the main axis, and from it secret paths run to the end of the property. Here is the herbaceous border, followed by mixed beds, where every plant must justify its inclusion by interesting leaf form or colour. Annuals are essential.

One small path runs down to the bog garden, and over a small bridge, before entering the vegetable section through a brick arch. Another path runs beside a border containing large architectural plants. Under the old oaks to the west is a smaller lawn, effectively an arboretum where *Nothofagus solandri*, *Davidia* and a fastigiate Atlas cedar are among the trees. Narrow upright conifers are placed all over the garden to add height and interest, and yellow-leaved gives trees light and col-

Calluna, Hindhead, in June (see page 173). A dark red mound of *Berberis thunbergii* 'Atropurpureum Nana' in the foreground, contrasts with the horizontal branches of *Viburnum plicatum* 'Mariesii'.

our. The land rises slightly at the end past a pond to a seat among the rocks, where the view back is a gentle antidote to a modern life and environment.

◆

Polesden Lacey, Bookham
THE NATIONAL TRUST

The grounds here cover thirty acres and include many different features of interest, notable among which are the long walk with woodland on one side and a yew hedge on the other, and the open-air theatre in which events are staged during the summer (for details contact The National Trust). One area of the garden contains bedding plants during the summer, and there are walled gardens with many different varieties of roses. There is also an herbaceous border and a winter garden containing many interesting shrubs. Throughout the garden there are urns, vases and statues which were arranged by the former owner of the house, the Hon. Mrs Ronald Greville, a well-known Edwardian society hostess.

At the entrance gates and round the pond *R.* 'Cynthia' makes a brilliant splash of pink, while *Davidia involucrata* drops its pocket-handkerchiefs on the moss. Around the beds of Exbury and Mollis azaleas grow a few clumps of *Rhododendron luteum* providing the scent that these beautiful hybrids lack.

We are lucky to have many fine species rhododendrons as well as hybrids old and new which flourish under their canopy of oaks and larches, giving us flower from January to November, but any plants, however precious, whose growth threatens to close up a view or overshadow a path is cut back. The open spaces and views are so vital in this type of garden. Except on the paths, the grass is never cut until the end of July, so that when the garden starts to fade we have the pleasure of acres of wild flowers and their attendant wildlife.

Surrey End Cottage, Haslemere
DR AND MRS W.R. TROTTER

The greatest asset of our one-and-a-half-acre garden is its situation. Perched high above a densely wooded valley, we look out on as tranquil a scene as can be found anywhere. Facing south-west, we get the gales, but escape the north-easterly winds. The soil is an atrocious mixture of sand and stones, covered by a thin layer of peat, and very acid. Yet trees flourish here astonishingly well, and so of course do rhododendrons and heathers. In the surrounding woods deer abound, and have to be excluded by a high fence.

In this situation, a conventional garden was out of the question, so our aim has been to build up an interesting and decorative collection of trees and shrubs, always bearing in mind the aesthetic value of form and foliage, as well as flower. One problem which soon

A Judas tree, *Cercis siliquastrum*, frames this view of the garden at Chilworth Manor in June; for a description of the garden see page 174.

*Ramster, Chiddingfold
MR AND MRS PAUL GUNN

Ramster garden was originally laid out in the early 1900s by Gauntlett Nurseries of Chiddingfold. It is now a mature flowering shrub and woodland garden covering nearly twenty acres, on Wealden clay with pockets of sandy soil. We owe the slightly Japanese style of the garden to Mr Gauntlett, who introduced the stone ornaments, the many different varieties of bamboo, the avenue of *Acer palmatum* 'Dissectum' and the huge plants of *Gunnera manicata* which make the bog garden such a mysterious place in the summer.

In early spring the ground is carpeted with naturalized daffodils, the *Camellia* garden fills the middle-distance with rosy pinks and reds, while overhead *Magnolia* × *soulangiana* 'Lennei' makes a spectacular display against a blue sky. In May the garden reaches its peak. Bluebells take over the ground-cover, the glade is filled with the pinks and whites of the Loderi rhododendrons, and the azalea garden becomes a patchwork quilt of colour, under the shade of the Atlantic cedar, the Californian redwoods and the wellingtonias.

Coverwood Lakes, near Ewhurst, in June; the young leaves of *Vitis coignetiae* cover the pergola. For a description of this garden see page 174.

became apparent on our steeply sloping site was how to cover the numerous banks left bare by the construction of access paths. Much experience has taught us that the best ground-coverers for this type of situation are *Gaultheria procumbens*, *Polygonum vaccinifolium*, *Vaccinium myrtillus* and *Vinca minor*. On our one patch of level ground we have recently made an informal herb garden, traversed by a winding path of camomile.

Our year starts with winter-flowering heathers and early rhododendrons, followed in May and June by the main body of azaleas and rhododendrons (some of them raised from seed). After that come a variety of flowering shrubs, including the more vigorous of the shrub roses. In late summer, a collection of *Sorbus* species provides a variety of berries, and a spectacular bank of heathers lights up the steep slope above a pond. Our best autumn colourers are *Fothergilla*, *Aronia*, a *Stuartia* and a good *Liquidambar*.

Vale End, Albury

MR AND MRS JOHN FOULSHAM

We came as novices to this charming and essentially cottage garden and are still coming to terms with our acre. In a rural setting on a

Ramster, near Chiddingfold, in June. Azaleas are reflected in the still water of the lake.

Autumn colour, berries and contrasting conifers at Gorse Hill Manor, Virginia Water, in late October. For a description of the garden see page 174.

Surrey End Cottage, Haslemere, in May. Dwarf conifers and heathers and the foliage of *Lonicera nitida* 'Baggesen's Gold' provide year-round colour. For a description of this garden see page 176.

steep south-westerly slope, the garden runs down to a large mill pond with woodlands beyond. The soil is a light, slightly acid loam, and in places is kept moist by springs and several wells. Within its surrounding walls, terraces and a bank of trees create enclosures of widely differing character. A lawn sweeps down to the mill pond, of more moss and bugle than grass, but we made it from subsoil obtained from local roadworks.

The garden is at its best in early summer with beds overflowing with the old familiar favourites, growing happily together in profusion with here and there a little gem. A very old *Magnolia*, with a spread of forty feet, is a wonderful sight when spared by our all too frequent frosts. A few less common plants such as *Diascia* and *Tovara* blend with traditional cottage flowers of Canterbury bells, delphiniums, foxgloves and roses whilst annuals such as love-in-a-mist are allowed to seed freely. This makes weeding more of a task but adds informality particularly round a small formal pond.

Behind a bank of trees, and at bedroom window level, lies our fruit and vegetable garden. From these windows we have been known to make eye-ball contact with pigeons sitting on our brussels sprouts! Squirrels have forced us to net our fruit cage completely, but contrary to some advice, overhead wire netting does not seem to cause any damage to the yield, whilst shade from a group of sycamores only prolongs the picking season.

◆

Winkworth Arboretum, Nr Godalming
THE NATIONAL TRUST

The arboretum, which covers nearly a hundred acres, is maintained by the local councils of Surrey and Waverley. It is situated in a valley, through which flows a stream which has been dammed to make a series of lakes. The majority of trees in the arboretum were planted to provide autumn colour, and it is at this time of year that a visit is particularly worthwhile. Dr Wilfrid Fox, who bequeathed a large amount of the land to the Trust, was particularly fond of autumn tints and acquired many trees to add to his collection.

SUSSEX (EAST)

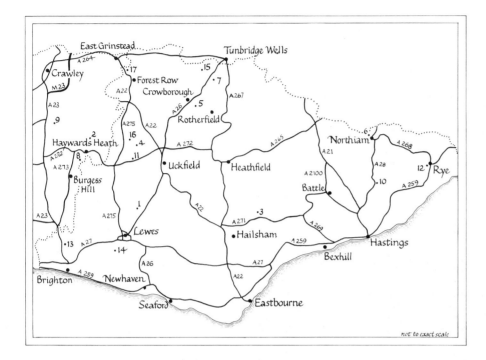

not to exact scale

Directions to Gardens

Banks Farm, Barcombe, 4 miles north of Lewes. [1]

Borde Hill Garden, 1½ miles north of Haywards Heath. [2]

Chilsham House, Herstmonceux, 5 miles northeast of Hailsham. [3]

Clinton Lodge, Fletching, 4 miles northwest of Uckfield. [4]

Cobblers, Mount Pleasant, Jarvis Brook, Crowborough. [5]

Coplands, Dixter Lane, Northiam, 8 miles northwest of Rye. [6]

Crown House, Eridge, 3 miles southwest of Tunbridge Wells. [7]

Great Dixter, Northiam, 8 miles northwest of Rye. [6]

Heaselands, 1 mile southwest of Haywards Heath. [8]

The High Beeches, 1 mile east of Handcross. [9]

Hornbeams, Brede, 5½ miles west of Rye. [10]

Ketches, Newick, 5 miles west of Uckfield. [11]

Lamb House, West Street, Rye. [12]

Newtimber Place, Newtimber, 1 mile north of Pyecombe, 7 miles north of Brighton. [13]

Nightingales, The Avenue, Kingston, 2½ miles southwest of Lewes. [14]

Nymans, just southeast of Handcross. [9]

Penns in the Rocks, Groombridge, 7 miles southwest of Tunbridge Wells. [15]

Ridge House, Kingston Ridge, Kingston, 2½ miles southwest of Lewes. [14]

Sheffield Park Garden, 5 miles northwest of Uckfield. [16]

Standen, 1½ miles southeast of East Grinstead. [17]

◆

Banks Farm, Barcombe

MICHAEL WARREN, ESQ.

In 1957 the area of the present garden comprised a very rough old grass 'tennis court' (young trees and brambles), a derelict orchard, and a pond half full of tin and old bicycles. Below that was a two-acre gravel pit, and beyond was a corn field.

The first area was laid out with informal beds on an approximate circle, to echo the wide expanse of sky and Downs. The bicycles have become waterlilies, with varied planting on the banks, and the view remains predominant. As experience bred ideas and courage, the pit was replanned a few years later; a small lake now reflects the glow of *Rhododendron* flowers and colourful trees and shrubs.

Part of the field was hedged into the garden in 1972, and a small arboretum stands among further beds and blocks of shrubs.

Wide use of shrub roses, *Cotoneaster*, *Escallonia* and *Berberis* provides the architectural forms as well as scent and colour, many other plants being complementary, while flowering trees reach into a wide sky. An exciting discovery was a small group of young wild service trees (*Sorbus torminalis*) which were growing in the line of an old hedge. As poor natural propagators, they are seldom found where landscape changes have occurred; further plantings have been made to embolden this rare find.

A few of the plant associations have given particular pleasure, such as the golden rain of *Genista aetnensis* falling upon the gentle blue of *Agapanthus campanulatus* in August. The blue of *Ceanothus* 'Gloire de Versailles' spreading harmoniously through *Hebe* 'Waikiki', a riot of colour in large drifts of shrub roses – such as 'Complicata', 'Scabrosa', 'Margaret Hilling', 'Anthony Waterer', 'Agnes' and 'Nevada' – and the curious marriage of the great blue spruce attended by the scented pink elegance of *Syringa microphylla*. Another successful combination is *Rosa* 'Paddy McGredy', *Fuchsia* 'Mrs Popple' and *Geranium* 'A. T. Johnson', all backed by the beguiling scent of *Philadelphus* 'Belle Etoile'.

Thirty years have sadly seen the loss of key elm trees but fortunately other trees have taken their place. A garden lives, and as it takes its own course surprises and pleasures give every month of the year its own flavour.

◆

*Borde Hill, Nr Haywards Heath
R.N.S. CLARKE, ESQ.

Since taking over as head gardener, the thing which has struck me most about Borde Hill is not only the great variety of plants but the variety of species. We have for example sixty-four different species of *Quercus* (oak), seventy-two maples and forty-two magnolias.

Borde Hill is most famous for its azaleas and rhododendrons and the area called the 'azalea ring' is a delight of colour and perfume in May and June.

Adjacent to the garden are Warren and Little Bently woods which provide splendid woodland walks; in spring bluebells make a haze of colour here. The woods contain many interesting trees and shrubs including *Prunus*, *Robinia* and two fine examples of the 'Handkerchief tree', *Davidia involucrata* var. *vilmoriniana*.

Cobblers, near Crowborough; a rocky bank with massed perennials and biennials is dominated in July by *Genista aetnensis*, a beautiful and hardy broom from Mt Etna in Sicily, and from Sardinia, which is long-lived and can make a small tree.

There is also an outlying area, Gores wood, about one mile from the garden which can be seen by prior permission. It is an established wood but since 1977 has been developed into a natural setting for rhododendrons. Each year protected areas within the wood are cleared and subsequently planted out with rhododendrons (mainly species). We also have seedling rhododendrons in our nursery from many parts of the world and have just received seeds from an expedition to Bhutan in October, 1985. This means that we have the exciting possibility of adding new collectors' numbers or different forms of species to our already large collection.

Borde Hill is set in the beautiful Sussex Weald with marvellous views and offers a diversity of plants and surroundings which can be enjoyed by the serious botanist and amateur gardener alike.

Chilsham House, Herstmonceux

MR AND MRS P. CUTLER

The garden of Chilsham House has been created since 1973 and, like most gardens, is still being altered and expanded. In the white bed, which is first seen when entering by the garden gate, there is a fine group of hybrid musk roses ('Moonlight') behind which there

are white delphiniums and other white flowers. A lot of annuals are grown, different each year; a special tip is to avoid sowing half-hardy annuals until the end of March in the greenhouse. Then no heat is required, and they very soon catch up with the earlier-sown seeds.

Next there is the blue bed; in one corner a *Pyrus salicifolia*, lavender, *Phlox*, blue *Agapanthus* Headbourne hybrids, hybrid musk rose 'Lavender Lassie', and hybrid perpetual 'Reine des Violettes' (1860) with its soft, velvety-violet flowers. On the house we are trying to grow rarer climbers and shrubs such as *Actinidia kolomikta* from China with heart-shaped leaves marked with pink or white, the New Zealand tea tree, *Leptospermum*, and *Magnolia grandiflora* 'Goliath'; on one side of a short avenue with a statue at the end there is the yellow garden, where yellow roses 'Arthur Bell', 'Apricot Nectar', 'Jan Spek', hybrid musk 'Buff Beauty' and 'Nevada' with branches covered with large, creamy-white blooms are a magnificent sight in June. On the other side is the pink and red garden and some grey plants, a formal pool with pink waterlilies; there is also a herbaceous garden. Behind the house is the natural garden, with a large pond and an abundance of primulas, hostas and astilbes and the giant-leaved *Gunnera*. Lastly, there is the little garden stuffed

with old roses – the damask 'Celsiana', 'Fritz Nobis' and the beautiful gallica 'Charles de Mills' with its blooms of purples and deep red, to name but a few.

Clinton Lodge, Fletching

MR AND MRS H. COLLUM

Clinton Lodge has a formal Georgian garden front and we have tried to set this in an eighteenth-century landscape with grass, a ha-ha and nothing but the Sussex landscape with trees and pasture for interest.

However, the house has a seventeenth-century front, so we have tried to echo this in a recently-planted scented herb garden following seventeenth-century ideas. This is an enclosed garden with brick and camomile paths, pleached lime walls, gargoyles and seats set formally in a bower or at the end of a path. I have planned this myself with inspiration from Hatfield House as well as garden history books.

To the side of the house we have planned a series of small gardens which probably have a twentieth-century aura. We have a wide double herbaceous border, enclosed in yew with colours restricted to white and yellow or blue, depending on the season. An enclosed rose garden is unfortunately set in 1980 beds, but is planted with old roses so that at mid-summer it is overpoweringly ebullient with arching six-foot-high roses. In the spring a walk of white cherries leads to a stone muse, and is underplanted with white bulbs. A walled swimming pool garden is heavily planted to come to life in late summer. A small orchard and a peaceful area of grass and exotic trees give restful moments.

This is all planned and maintained by an amateur gardener and myself and I hope reflects romantic and enthusiastic research rather than perfection.

Cobblers, Jarvis Brook

MR AND MRS MARTIN FURNISS

This garden in Crowborough is of two acres, on a sloping site overlooking Ashdown Forest, round a seventeenth-century house and barn. In spite of its size, it retains the character of a cottage garden.

The two features which strike any visitor are the design and the fact that from May until September all parts of the garden glow with colour and, in addition, a high standard of

Heaselands in June (for a description of the garden see page 182). Tulips underplanted with forget-me-nots form a perfect combination.

maintenance is shown for such an informal garden.

The design is in some ways unique, in that the whole area, which includes some fifteen herbaceous borders and two water gardens, is welded together in one complete involved pattern and by imaginative brick and stone features and paths.

The long span of colour over nearly six months is obtained by the great diversity of plants and shrubs, including many rare and unusual specimens. The main groups of interest are the rhododendrons and azaleas, Asiatic primulas and *Iris* of many species including some very recent introductions of *Iris sibirica* and tall bearded. Alpines are planted on drystone walls, and later in the season there are unusual tall moisture-loving lobelias and lastly a collection of the almost extinct large-flowered Victorian montbretias.

Items of special interest are the water gardens, which unusually again follow the long period of colour, and the use of special garden seats, which are designed to fit into the pattern of the brick paths and which are manufactured by the owner.

Some indication of the universal appeal of this garden may be gained by the fact that it is represented in ceramics, embroidery, water and oil paints, almost every horticultural journal in Britain and a number of publications in Europe and the U.S.A.; horticultural groups visit annually from almost all over the world.

Coplands House, Dixter Lane, Northiam

MR AND MRS HUGH SAUNDERS

This is a sheltered garden of just under an acre surrounding a sixteenth-century farmhouse.

The High Beeches in May (see page 182). *Rhododendron caloxanthum* from Burma and Yunnan is one of the many wild species grown in this beautiful woodland garden.

The house is clothed with *Wisteria*, yellow *Rosa banksiae*, *R.* 'Albertine' and *R.* 'Mme Alfred Carrière', various *Clematis* and *Chaenomeles*.

There are some fine yew trees, a *Liquidambar*, *Arbutus unedo* and several lilacs, but presiding over all from the south-east corner is a majestic oak, keeping the wind away and providing summer shade and coolness for resting bulbs. Along the south-east side is a bank of rhododendrons backed by flowering cherries, crabs and rambling roses. Many spring bulbs – snowdrops, aconites, *Crocus* and daffodils – combine with spring-flowering shrubs to keep the garden bright from early April.

Recent plantings include golden-leaved shrubs and ground-covering plants, and a collection of *Sorbus* provides filtered shade in summer and good autumn colour. Shade is also cast by an arbour on the patio, over which scramble vines, *Clematis* and climbing roses. The patio itself is decked with urns out of which cascade geraniums and *Helichrysum*, while various flowering plants grow between the paving stones. The walls are decked with *Clematis*, honeysuckle and a *Carpenteria*, and all are set off by Italian cypress trees.

At the end of the patio a large *Prunus sargentii* shades a group of *Camellia × williamsii* and various honeysuckles. Leading on past the summer house there is a bush *Magnolia grandiflora* guarding the way to a new planting of azaleas and lilies. All about the garden are hostas, periwinkle and the invasive *Alchemilla mollis*. There are always interesting things to be seen as the garden has been planned for successive colour leading to a final display in the autumn.

Crown House, Eridge
MAJ. AND MRS L. CAVE

This garden is situated in one of the most lovely parts of Sussex; the views are quite outstanding, whichever way you look, and as the house faces south, we benefit from the sun all day long. We moved to Crown House sixteen years ago and found the whole two acres of land covered with old bottles, bed springs and endless rubbish. Therefore we had to start from scratch, as apart from the yew hedges and a very attractive beech hedge, there was nothing to design around. However, we were fortunate enough to find two extremely talented landscape gardeners, and since they arrived they have completely transformed the garden.

We now have a beautiful herbaceous border, ending with two brick pillars, which hold a wrought iron gate leading to the croquet lawn. At the opposite end of the border are the alpine water gardens, with their wide selection of colourful plants giving pleasure all year round. The rose garden, surrounded by trellis work, and covered by *Clematis montana*, contains over a hundred roses; the sundial built on an old millstone provides the centrepiece.

The garden is interlinked by the most pleasing feature of all, old brick paths which harbour many varieties of small creeping plants.

Great Dixter, Northiam
THE LLOYD FAMILY

This garden is a remarkable combination of historical design and contemporary adventurous planting based on a deep knowledge and love of good plants.

The half-timbered house was built around 1460 and was restored and enlarged for Nathaniel Lloyd, himself an architect, by Sir Edwin Lutyens. A garden with walls, stone steps and paths, topiary and a sunk garden with a pond (this last designed by Nathaniel Lloyd) was also laid out.

The present planting is the work of Christopher Lloyd. *Clematis* and herbaceous plants of many kinds are the specialities of the garden, and the borders are famous for their exciting combinations of colourful flowers and shapely foliage.

The rough grass has been developed, over many years, into a series of meadow gardens and has accumulated a great number of different native flowers; some of these, such as the green-winged orchid, *Orchis morio*, are now almost extinct in the surrounding district because of changing land usage, so the meadows also act as conservation areas.

Heaselands, Haywards Heath
MRS ERNEST KLEINWORT

The garden at Heaselands, begun in 1934 on completion of the building of the house, has now developed into an area of some thirty acres. East of the house the entrance forecourt is bounded on one side by a rock bank of Sussex sandstone, planted with dwarf conifers, heathers and evergreen azaleas. Leading from this, and the main lawn, a walled garden of azaleas and rhododendrons has a fine specimen of *Cornus kousa chinensis* which is magnificent both in flower and autumn colour. Lower down are the rose garden, and paved garden of roses and paeonies, for summer colour – the whole surrounded by yew hedges.

Below the house terrace, with its view over woodland to the South Downs, a sunken garden, dominated by a *Cedrus atlantica glauca* is planted with seasonal bedding. Lawns with heather, roses and azalea beds fall away to longer grass with trees and shrub groups. Below is the water garden running east–west, with ponds and streams edged with primulas, irises and other water-loving plants. Beyond, the ground rises again to trees and woodland and here there is a collection of over three hundred and fifty hybrid rhododendrons and azaleas which produce a riot of colour in late spring.

Whilst May and June is the most colourful period, the garden is attractive at all times. Roses and heathers brighten the summer months, followed by shrubs and trees which produce magnificent autumn colour. This is followed by more colour and, throughout the winter, the evergreens and conifers come into their own.

Heaselands may not have a very wide range of plant species, but those it has are arranged to give pleasant views and prospects in all directions, making it a place of pilgrimage for many of our visitors who return year after year.

The High Beeches, Handcross
THE HON H.E. BOSCAWEN

Oaks and beeches provide a fitting backdrop for one of the finest woodland gardens in the south of England. Planted on a south-facing slope broken by ghylls down which streams flow into a central pool, the garden now covers about twenty-eight acres.

At the beginning of the century a start was made by clearing the undergrowth and thinning the oaks. Planting began with trees and shrubs, some of which came from the collections made by E. H. Wilson in China. Between the wars, plants collected by both Forrest and Kingdon Ward in Asia were added, as were plants from other sources in North and South America. Good hybrid rhododendrons and crosses made from species in the garden, have also been planted.

Now in their maturity can be seen davidias, magnolias, styraxes, and the National Collections of *Stuartia* and *Pieris*. *Euphorbia griffithi* and primulas grow in masses in the stream beds, and the willow gentian spreads throughout the wood. In autumn the nyssas, maples and fothergillas show their brilliant colours of red and gold.

Hornbeams, Brede
MR AND MRS D.J. CATER

The site is of one and a half acres sloping to the north, on heavy acid clay, with fine views over the Tillingham valley furnished with a number of mature forest trees, mainly oak, but with other species forming the line of an ancient hedgerow.

This is a young garden still in the process of development by a husband and wife team. We have a woodland area with hundreds of narcissi under apple blossom and *Magnolia*, where we have encouraged wild flowers in an area of uncut grass. Under a canopy of oak trees, we have planted rhododendrons and camellias, while nearby massed ericas, including the yellow foliage of 'Valerie Proudley', contrast with *Acer palmatum* 'Dissectum Atropurpureum' which is at its best in early summer. A young yew hedge partly encircles a rose garden, against a backdrop of *Clematis* of various species carpeted with *Viola cornuta* 'Alba'. A minute vineyard of 'Müller Thurgau' provides us with sufficient grapes to produce a few bottles of white wine each season.

Rabbits have decimated our rose bushes in previous years, and after many experiments we now circle the beds with twine soaked in 'Renardine'; it really seems to work. We hope that an increasing collection of unusual ground-cover plants combined with annual mulchings of leafmould and compost (to improve soil structure and discourage weeds) will enable us to continue to develop and maintain the garden without outside help.

Ketches, Newick

DAVID MANWARING ROBERTSON, ESQ.

The setting of this garden is, I suppose, its best feature, with mature oaks, beeches and a Spanish chestnut, as well as two giant cedars planted in the fields to the south and west. Parts of the two-and-a-half-acre garden were established before the Second World War, but most of its present form was started about fifteen years ago. The emphasis is upon labour-saving planting using shrubs, mostly those which produce double dividends – flowers and autumn colour. Shrub roses are another feature, particularly those which produce good scent. The view to the south from the terrace is pleasant, and dominated by a three-hundred-year-old oak beyond the croquet lawn and by the equally old Spanish chestnut to the west. There is a large *Magnolia grandiflora* hard by the house, protecting a myrtle which only just survived the harsh frosts of winter 1985. To the west are three small borders with strong specimens of rose 'Apricot Nectar'. Beyond the hedge backing this border lies the wild garden with several species of *Acer* including *A. negundo* 'Variegatum' and *A. palmatum* 'Osakazuki' – the latter looks particularly good in autumn. There are also big plantings of old-fashioned well-scented shrub roses and a large specimen of *Robinia pseudoacacia* 'Frisia'.

We are fortunate in living on greensand which means that nearly everything thrives. I like dogwoods and have been able to establish plantings of *Cornus alba* 'Elegantissima', *C. alba* 'Sibirica' and also a nice specimen of *C. kousa chinensis*. Trees with interesting bark are another feature, including *Acer griseum, A. hersii* and *A. capillipes*, gum trees and *Arbutus × andrachnoides*. I feel the garden is now beginning to mature, although, as with all gardens, new planting continues each year.

Lamb House, Rye

SIR BRIAN AND LADY BATSFORD; THE NATIONAL TRUST

The garden of Lamb House comes as a surprise to most visitors as it is an acre in extent and yet right in the centre of the historic town of Rye.

Surrounded on all sides by ten-foot brick walls, it provided a haven of peace and quiet for the American novelist Henry James whose home it was from 1898 to 1916, and later for the brothers and authors A. C. and E. F. Benson.

The garden itself is predominantly formal in keeping with the early eighteenth-century house. Special features are the climbing roses in June and July, the spacious lawns and a shrub border. The present tenants have redesigned the garden during the last four years – within the inevitable limits imposed on a National Trust property and the need to keep down the growing costs of maintenance.

Newtimber Place, Pyecombe

HIS HONOUR JUDGE CLAY AND MRS CLAY

A trout of 1¾ lbs has been caught from our library window! That was possible because water in the moat laps against the west wall of the house. On the other side the water is further away and encloses lawns, the herbaceous border, and beds of 'Queen Elizabeth', 'Frensham' and yellow roses of different varieties including the splendidly prolific 'Maigold'.

Here, also, we have a small vegetable garden with a weeping mulberry in its centre and a hedge of 'Roseraie de l'Haÿ' on two sides to screen it from the kitchen windows. Also conveniently close to the kitchen is an excellent tulip tree giving shade for meals out of doors. Other trees at Newtimber include a fine evergreen oak, *Quercus × hispanica* 'Lucombeana', and two lovely cedars. Young successors have been planted for the enjoyment of future generations.

Beyond the water is the Moat Walk with beds of roses including 'Vanity' and 'Buff Beauty' and shrubs leading to the wild garden which in the spring has masses of daffodils of many varieties with an unusual profusion of fritillaries and a drift of *Anemone blanda* under the trees near the wood. In the summer a large variety of wild flowers takes over. At the back of this part of the garden are beech hedges and another rose hedge of *Rosa rugosa* 'Scabrosa', with the park and Newtimber Hill beyond them. Our third rose hedge, 'Blanc Double de Coubert', surrounds the small garden of Stables Cottage.

The moat itself has many waterlilies, including the lovely red 'Escarboucle', and reeds and flag irises forming cover for the ducks, coots and moorhens. In the shallower water are *Pontederia* and *Zantedeschia*. Crossing the water are our three bridges from which can be seen the golden orfe and trout. All round are reflections of the weathered brick and flint buildings. Here then are scenes of unusual beauty and blessed peace.

Nightingales, Kingston

MR AND MRS GEOFFREY HUDSON

This is a half-acre slope of poor alkaline soil which we have improved by the addition of horse manure. We have aimed to make a peaceful, informal garden keeping old trees such as a rowan and a 'Bramley' apple and

growing species roses, herbaceous and Mediterranean plants and wild flowers. The centrepiece is a paper birch; other trees are *Robinia pseudoacacia* 'Frisia', *Prunus sargentii*, *Prunus* 'Tai-Haku' and *serrula*, lime-tolerating magnolias, *Amelanchier* and *Cotoneaster* 'Cornubia'. Behind the birch are the roses 'Frühlingsgold', 'Nevada', 'Marguerite Hilling', 'Canary Bird', *R. glauca* (*rubrifolia*) and *R. rugosa* 'Alba' and 'Roseraie de l'Haÿ'. In between the roses is a pool with a golden *Carex*, surrounded by primulas and alchemillas. A stone terrace is enclosed by a brick wall on which grow the dessert vine 'Siegerrebe', *Jasminum revolutum*, *Campsis radicans* and *Carpenteria californica*. Brick steps lead to a flagstone path edged with lavender, *Iris* and pinks, passing through an arch with rose 'Schoolgirl' and *Romneya coulteri* to a fuchsia border. On the terrace are Spanish pots with *Agave*, *Hibiscus*, *Bougainvillea*, *Phormium* and lilies. Do try pots; you can bring tender plants indoors in winter and grow acid-lovers even if you have a limy soil, provided you use rain water and an ericaceous compost.

Nymans, Handcross

ANNE, COUNTESS OF ROSSE; THE NATIONAL TRUST

This garden, originally created by Lt. Col. Leonard Messel and his wife, is a treasure-house of interesting plants, in particular old-fashioned roses. Many good plants have been raised here, notably *Camellia* 'Leonard Messel', *Eucryphia × nymansensis*, and *Magnolia × loebneri* 'Leonard Messel'.

Penns in the Rocks, Nr Groombridge

LORD AND LADY GIBSON

The property takes its name from the distinguished American Quaker, William Penn and his descendants, who owned Penns in the Rocks from 1672 to 1762, and from the impressive rock formations of Tunbridge Wells sandstone in the garden.

From the front of the house with its Georgian façade, there is a fine view over a gently sloping lawn and up the glade, formed by the huge rocks, to a brick temple, surrounded by masses of ferns and yellow azaleas. On a stone slab in the temple floor are carved six names of 'The poets who loved Penns', among them W. B. Yeats, Walter de la Mare and Vita Sackville-West. This wild, romantic area contrasts with neatly clipped hedges, flights of steps flanked by Irish yews and the rectangular walled garden. A very big *Salix elaeagnos* near the garden wall is worth noting for its long silvery leaves.

In the lawn a few specimen trees have been planted including *Cercis siliquastrum*, *Styrax japonica* and the August-flowering *Koelreuteria paniculata*. Old shrub roses are freely used, and some of David Austin's more recent introductions including 'The Friar' and 'The Prioress' have proved excellent, as they have

Newtimber Place in July (for description see page 183) with roses, meadow sweet and codlins and cream, *Epilobium hirsitum*, on the edge of the moat.

the quality of the old roses, yet bloom throughout the summer.

From the west lawn, with its enormous cedar, there is a fine view to the lake which the Gibsons made at the bottom of the valley, and to the classical Ionic temple which they erected beyond it. A few trees including *Nyssa sylvatica* and *N. sinensis*, *Taxodium distichum* and a cut-leaved alder have been planted near the margins of the lake. A huge *Rosa filipes* 'Kiftsgate' growing through a yew is spectacular in summer.

The walled garden and its adjacent areas, the azalea glade with its spectacular rock formations and the lake in its sylvan setting are certainly a study in contrasts and underline the difference between gardening and landscape gardening.

Ridge House, Kingston
MR AND MRS K. BLOOMFIELD

Our special feature is a superb view to the coast. We have a greenhouse with many rare plants including *Salvia neurepia* and *S. patens* and a number of abutilons. The herbaceous bed has a path on both sides, so it is raised, with *Salvia haematodes*, *Echinops* and the graceful *Buddleja alternifolia*. Shorter plants are *Echinacea purpurea*, *Linum narbonense* and *Asperula orientalis* which seeds so well. At Ridge House we believe in growing plants near together thus avoiding weeds, in leaving seedlings where they grow and in mixing wild plants such as campion, violets and primroses with cultivated varieties.

Sheffield Park Garden, Uckfield
THE NATIONAL TRUST

This is a magnificent landscape garden covering a hundred acres and incorporating four lakes, two of which were designed by Capability Brown. In addition to the satisfactory design of the whole, the component elements are individually pleasing – some of the trees are extremely old and many have reached fine proportions.

Standen, East Grinstead
THE NATIONAL TRUST

This ten-acre garden slopes downhill and across a valley to rising ground beyond, making a beautiful site. There are many interesting trees and shrubs, as well as daffodils and wild flowers.

SUSSEX (WEST)

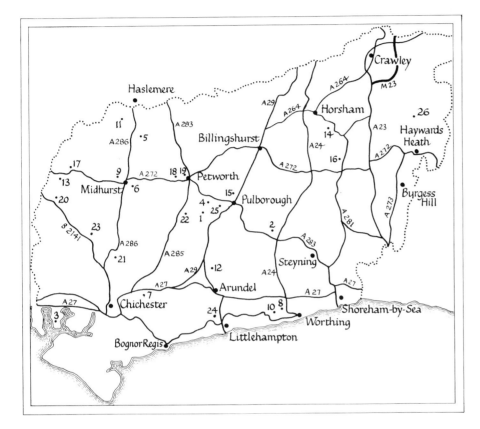

Directions to Gardens

Bignor Park, Pulborough, 5 miles south of Petworth. [1]

Cedar Tree Cottage, Rock Road, Washington, 7 miles north of Worthing. [2]

Chidmere, Chidham, 6 miles west of Chichester. [3]

Coates Manor, ½ mile south of Fittleworth, between Petworth and Pulborough. [4]

Cooksbridge, Fernhurst, between Haslemere and Midhurst. [5]

Cowdray Park Gardens, Midhurst. [6]

Denmans, Denmans Lane, Fontwell, near Chichester. [7]

Floraldene, Findon Road, 2½ miles north of Worthing. [8]

Hammerwood House, Iping, 2½ miles west of Midhurst. [9]

The Hazels, Fittleworth, between Petworth and Pulborough. [4]

Highdown, Goring-by-Sea, Littlehampton Road, 3 miles west of Worthing. [10]

Hollycombe, Liphook, near Haslemere. [11]

Houghton Farm, Houghton, north of Arundel. [12]

Hunters Lodge, Rogate, 5 miles east of Petersfield, 5 miles west of Midhurst. [13]

Lane End, Sheep Lane, Midhurst. [6]

Leonardslee, 4½ miles southeast of Horsham. [14]

Littlehill, Hill Farm Lane, Pulborough. [15]

Long House, Cowfold, ¾ mile north of A272, Cowfold-Bolney. [16]

Malt House, Chithurst, 2 miles east of Rogate. [17]

The Manor of Dean, Tillington, 2 miles west of Petworth. [18]

Norman Place, East Street, Petworth. [19]

Pyramids, South Harting, 4 miles southeast of Petersfield. [20]

St Roche's Arboretum, Singleton Hill, West Dean, 6 miles north of Chichester. [21]

South Corner House, Duncton, 3½ miles south of Petworth. [22]

Telegraph House, North Marden, 9 miles northwest of Chichester. [23]

Toddington House, Toddington Lane, 2 miles north of Littlehampton. [24]

The Upper Lodge, Stopham, 1 mile west of Pulborough. [25]

West Dean Gardens, Singleton, 5 miles north of Chichester. [21]

Whitehouse Cottage, Staplefield Lane, 5 miles north of Haywards Heath. [26]

Bignor Park, Pulborough
THE MERSEY FAMILY

This garden is Victorian in design, and in 1958 when we came here, was large and unmanageable. We have gradually reduced its size. Two sections contain patterns of box hedging, and in one of these we now grow vegetables, surrounded by roses, *Macleaya*, *Iris sibirica*, paeonies, and other herbaceous plants.

Spring is our best season, as perhaps it is in most gardens, before dead-heading and weeding set in. The ground is full of promise from snowdrops onwards, and a succession of bulbs come into flower from February to May, followed by irises. *Rhododendron arboreum* flowers early, and later varieties continue until June. We are pleased with our *Carpenteria californica*, which hardly grew, and never flowered, for about five years. Now it is a large shrub and covered with bloom every year. It is next to a *Ceanothus* and they go well together.

We have grown a kind of tunnel of *Laburnum* 'Vossii', trained over the skeleton of a greenhouse, from which the glass was removed. The basic beauty of this garden is its position, facing south across a dip in the land to the Downs and Bignor Hill. Also there are wonderful trees, including a grove of *Ilex*, which is at least a hundred years old.

Cedar Tree Cottage, Rock Road, Washington
MR AND MRS G.H. GOATCHER

This small garden – just over half an acre – has been built up largely over the past twenty-five years, although based on an older garden evidenced by a hundred-foot *Sequoiadendron* (with *Hydrangea petiolaris* swarming up it) and a group of *Rhododendron arboreum*, both dating from the 1850s.

The idea has been to create 'hidden' areas and vistas in this limited site, and also to give colour and interest throughout the year.

These two aims are being achieved by a series of island beds planted with a blend of trees and shrubs, underplanted with low shrubs and perennials.

Examples of colour combinations include *Acer palmatum* 'Shindesojo' blending with *Pittosporum* 'Garnetti' and *Artemisia* 'Powis Castle'; elsewhere are *Acer palmatum* 'Senkaki' with *Berberis* 'Rose Glow' and *Cotinus* 'Foliis Purpureis' flanked by *Cornus* 'Elegantissima' and *C.* 'Spaethii'.

Two survivors from the older garden are a superb *Acer palmatum* 'Dissectum Atropurpureum' providing magnificent autumn colour as a bonus, and a *Viburnum carlesii* which is thought to be one of the oldest specimens in the country and which scents the whole garden in May.

Among other interesting trees are the whitest of birches, *Betula jacquemontii*, *Styrax japonica* with its delightful bell-like white flowers, and the little-known *Photinia villosa* which has fine autumn tints; whilst among the shrubs and perennials can be found *Cleyera fortunei*, *Rubus thibetanus*, a particularly good form of *Euphorbia polychroma* and the charming 'Fair Maids of France', *Ranunculus aconitifolius* 'Flore Pleno'.

One lesson learnt: unless your idea of pleasure is raking up leaves every week of the year, do not plant *Eucalyptus*!

Chidmere House, Chidham

THOMAS BAXENDALE, ESQ.

This five-acre garden was created between 1930 and 1935 by the late Hugo Lloyd Baxendale on the site of a decayed farmyard, orchard and field surrounding the attractive Tudor house which Mr Baxendale acquired in 1930 in a very forlorn state and restored sympathetically. To the south the area is bounded by the five-acre expanse of Chidmere Pond which, with the mellow brick walls of the house, gatehouse and former stables, provide the setting for these imaginatively laid-out grounds.

The main features are long vistas giving access to a number of separate formal gardens enclosed by hornbeam hedges or old walls, and ornamented by urns and a set of statues brought back by Mr Baxendale's great-grandfather from the Paris Exhibition of 1867. A fine display of daffodils in the old orchard, and also under the plantation of hardwoods made in 1936, and a handsome herbaceous border in late summer, provide the principal sources of colour. There are also good specimens (now mature) of various flowering shrubs and trees such as *Davidia involucrata*, *Halesia carolina*, *Cornus kousa chinensis* and *Ginkgo biloba*, as well as of the more common but spectacular *Magnolia × soulangiana* and Japanese cherries.

A feature much admired by visitors is the conservatory on the edge of the lake with its colourful display of plants including cymbidiums, a *Callistemon* and geraniums trained to cover a fifteen-foot-high wall.

A wide variety of plants and shrubs are to be found in this garden which, only half a mile from Chichester Harbour, receives as much sun as almost anywhere in England, although by no means free of severe frosts and coastal gales. Due to the high lime content of the soil, rhododendrons, azaleas and camellias are absent but *Berberis* and viburnums thrive.

Coates Manor, Nr Fittleworth

MRS G.H. THORP

Since 1960, when the Elizabethan house was neglected and surrounded by fields, the objective for the garden has been to create a setting for the house.

In order to include the peaceful countryside within the atmosphere of the garden, a lawn surrounded by a low mixed shrub border together with ground-cover was made in front of the house. The remainder of the garden is approached through an archway in a long stone wall which adjoins the house.

Here the outline of trees, such as a Japanese cherry with its umbrella shape, underplanted with *Juniperus × media* 'Pfitzeriana Aurea', the stark white trunk with peeling bark of *Betula jacquemontii × papyrifera* and the pyramidal shape of *Liquidambar styraciflua* 'Worplesden' give form to the garden in winter, as do the strategic placing of horizontal conifers and clipped yews.

In order to emphasize the view over unspoilt countryside to the north, a clairvoyée has been made in the clipped conifer hedge with low stone wall and paving, also creating a seating area overlooking the lawn. In a shaped bed curving into the lawn is a predominantly blue and yellow theme with golden foliage, underplanted with *Agapanthus* Headbourne hybrids and including *Genista aetnensis* flowering above *Picea pungens glauca*.

Leading from the open lawn through an archway is a small walled garden, and here the emphasis is on scent and on marginally tender plants. The clipped pillar shape of *Taxus baccata* 'Standishii' provides a focal point at the end of the central paved walk, ground-hugging evergreens breaking the hard edges.

Throughout, the emphasis has been on foliage and a search for successful plant associations, this combination giving interest during the summer, followed by autumn colour and continuing into winter, with shapes of trees and conifers – all so necessary in a comparatively small garden.

Cooksbridge, Fernhurst

MR AND MRS N. TONKIN

Once a working farm and now a mellow stone house, Cooksbridge nestles in a fold of the Sussex Downs, the walls providing a home for jasmine, *Clematis*, honeysuckle and *Akebia*. The six-acre garden entered through a wrought-iron gate from the courtyard has great variety, but only gradually does it reveal its secrets.

A favourite corner is the secluded lily pond and fountain surrounded by low-walled beds of *Osmanthus*, *Cornus kousa*, *Buddleja* and many more to maintain interest throughout the year.

The main lawn sweeps down to the lake, bounded by splendid mature oaks silhouetted against the sky. Summer colour abounds in the traditionally planted herbaceous border where bold groups of *Allium cristophii* yield marvellous seed heads to delight the flower arranger.

Around another corner is a rock garden with trickling stream and small stone bridge, a home for a collection of primulas, hostas, ferns, astilbes and other shade-loving plants.

Wide York stone steps, planted on either side with conifers, lead down to the lake where marginal plants including dramatic *Gunnera manicata*, huge clumps of *Phalaris arundinacea*, reeds, water *Iris* and – in spring – the *Viburnum plicatum* 'Mariesii', are a sight to be seen. A weeping willow keeps the island cool. The ornamental water fowl add another dimension to the lake and are very efficient at consuming the vast amounts of water weed which grow in these conditions.

The orchard, greenhouses and kitchen garden are planned to provide fresh produce for the family throughout the year – of particular interest are the black Hamburg vine and the established asparagus bed.

The garden is designed to take advantage of the natural fall of the land from the house to the banks of the little river Lod and is enhanced by distant views of Blackdown to the north and Bexley Hill to the south.

Cowdray Park, Midhurst

THE VISCOUNT COWDRAY

This is a garden which has been largely constructed from an old woodland site since about 1870 and extends to approximately twenty-two acres. The area is divided by a valley running approximately north to south, the banks on each side rising steeply before levelling out on both sides of the garden; on the eastern side stands Cowdray House. At the north end of the valley several springs flow into a small stream which has been used to feed a pear-shaped fish pond. The overflow is then piped to another pond, a fountain, and on to the top of a rock garden where the water flows freely through the rock garden.

A feature of the garden is the use of conifers which make a very pleasing skyline seen from the lawn to the west of the house looking north. Notable specimens planted in about 1870 include an avenue of wellingtonia, now a hundred and twenty feet tall, *Abies grandis*, *A. procera*, *A. nordmanniana* in the valley (all over a hundred and thirty feet in height), while on the lawns are *Chamaecyparis lawsoniana* 'Erecta' and *C. pisifera*, and a very tall *Thuja plicata*.

Also of interest are beds of hybrid rhododendrons planted in early 1900, and beds of azaleas which in ideal weather conditions provide some striking colour in May and early June. Another noteworthy shrub planted in clumps is *Kalmia* which gives especially fine colour in June.

Denmans, Fontwell
MRS J.H. ROBINSON

The converted gardener's cottage, and an eighteenth-century stable block with its clock tower within the old walls, is the setting for the three-acre garden at Denmans.

Designed and planted by the owner since 1946, always keeping a vista to the fields beyond, it was planned to form quiet areas of lawn broken with large plantings of trees, shrubs and perennials. Wide paths and clearings of gravel wander through the masses in which the good garden plants they contain are allowed to self-seed. They are then carefully weeded to form colonies of shape and colour to make a fascinating ground-cover under dappled foliage. Winter-flowering subjects and a mass of spring bulbs are part of the profusion.

Clothing the old walls and mixing the flower and herb plantings within the walled garden has perhaps been our greatest joy. Old-fashioned species roses combine with pomegranate, *Wisteria, Fremontodendron, Magnolia, Trachelospermum, Solanum,* honeysuckle and all types of *Clematis,* forming a rich backdrop to the wide plantings in their foreground, making the areas enclosed by walls and buildings another garden in themselves. Wide mown rides are cut through the longer grass of the orchard adjoining a dry watercourse of gravel and water-worn stone to the water garden.

The cold house shelters a collection of New Zealand and other half-hardy plants and climbers. Gardens are not usually made for a generation, or even for a known time, so the planting and caring goes on.

Floraldene, Findon
MR J.R. TUCKER

Work on this garden started in 1952, and at that time it was part of a nursery on the South Downs. I started planting heathers here from the beginning, and some of the original plants are still flowering; there are now about two hundred varieties. Azaleas are also to be seen here, and as the soil is loam over chalk I have given them liberal amounts of peat. Evergreen shrubs provide a background for the heathers, and these include *Pittosporum* 'Warnham Gold', *P.* 'Irene Patterson' and *P.* 'Garnettii'. In the winter *Erica lusitanica* and *Hamamelis mollis* look well together, while *Cornus* 'Westonbirt' and *Rhamnus alaterna* 'Argenteovariegata' – the latter over ten feet high – also provide good colour.

Hammerwood, Iping
MR AND MRS JOHN LAKIN

The garden at Hammerwood House is at its best in the second half of May when azaleas, rhododendrons, *Prunus* and magnolias make a great show of colour. With the South Downs in the far background, it creates a beautiful scene, especially when the sun shines and throws shadows among the trees and shrubs. Again in the autumn the colouring of *Parrotia persica, Photinia,* acers, azaleas and hydrangeas give much pleasure.

There are some fine trees, in particular a cedar about a hundred and seventy years old, a very tall lime, and a lovely copper beech. There are also very good chestnuts, oaks, some scented limes and *Robinia pseudoacacia* 'Frisia'. Perhaps the most interesting shrub is a persimmon brought from Warwickshire about twenty-five years ago; it was very slow-growing but has put on a lot of growth in the last few years.

The wild garden was reclaimed from a pig unit and has some beautiful trees and many daffodils, bluebells and wild flowers in the

Cedar Tree Cottage, Washington, in August (see page 185). *Picea breweriana,* **from the Siskiyou mountains, was planted here in 1970 and has already made a striking specimen on a lawn.**

Coates Manor, Fittleworth, in July (see page 186). A glade is subtly planted with blue *Agapanthus*, silver-leaved *Artemisia*, purple *Berberis thunbergii* and various golden-leaved shrubs dominated by a small *Catalpa bignonioides* 'Aurea'.

spring. With the Hammer stream wandering through the garden, it makes a very pleasant walk about a quarter of a mile from here.

◆

The Hazels, Lower Street, Fittleworth
M.C. PRATT, ESQ.

This garden of about one acre, planted since 1970, is designed to resemble a British deciduous woodland, with its tree-layer, shrub-layer and herb-layer.

The tree-layer includes a collection of magnolias and flowering cherries with some unusual chestnuts such as *Aesculus neglecta* 'Erythroblastos'. Trees for foliage effect include the weeping silver pear, *Pyrus salicifolia* 'Pendula', Sutner's plane and Richard's poplar, *Populus alba* 'Richardii'.

The shrub-layer is dominated by deciduous azaleas which I have been hybridizing for many years. The widest possible range is grown, including many species and my own late-flowering hybrids which extend the season by about six weeks. The azalea flowering season here is from late April until early August. A number of hybrid camellias are grown, their flowers being protected from spring frost by the trees overhead.

Tree and shrub groupings which are admired by visitors include *Laburnum* 'Vossii', *Syringa reflexa* with pink flowers, and *Wisteria sinensis* growing into them, the Judas tree, *Cercis siliquastrum*, and the cream yellow *Rosa* × *cantabrigiensis*. Among the rarer shrubs are *Aesculus mutabilis* 'Induta', a lovely dwarf chestnut, and *Cornus alternifolia* 'Argentea' planted in 1970 and now over ten feet high.

The herb-layer contains the well-known bulbous plants flowering from February until late May; bluebells and cowslips have naturalized all over the garden.

◆

Highdown
WORTHING CORPORATION

This famous garden was created in a disused chalk pit by Sir Frederick Stern and was left by him to the people of Worthing. The south-facing slope enables a number of interesting trees, shrubs, herbaceous plants and bulbs to be grown, and there are fine views over the sea.

◆

Hollycombe House, Liphook
MR AND MRS JOHN BALDOCK

When John Nash started to build Hollycombe for Sir Charles Taylor, friend of the Prince of Wales in 1800, there were no buildings on the site of the house and perhaps there had been none since the camps of the Middle Stone Age, twelve thousand years ago, which had left many of their worked flints along the banks above the springs. There is a strong possibility that Humphrey Repton had a say in the site, with the house's axis exactly along the Rother/Thames watershed and its remarkable views to the Goodwood racecourse on the South Downs. It is a site that would be hard to improve upon and certainly Repton's son, John, did some of the drawings of the house for Nash. In the middle of the last century the view was further improved by planting a fine clump of beeches on Dunner Hill about two miles away in the middle ground.

Subsequent generations have steadily increased the planting which reached a crescendo about a century ago when the Hawkshaws were owners. Over a million trees were planted on the estate, including many rare species in the wild garden. Some of the survivors (for example *Pterocarya stenoptera, Quercus variabilis, Cunninghamia lanceolata*) are now the largest, or among the largest, in this country. This area has been described as one of the finest small arboreta in

England. The soil is very light sand and because of the sheltering woodland and the steep slopes to drain away cold air, it has proved possible to grow quite tender varieties, such as *Raphiolepis, Abutilon, Crinodendron, Sophora* and *Feijoa*, in spite of an altitude of about five hundred feet. Architectural features include stone walls and terraces and an ice pit.

Other points of interest include an azalea walk nearly a quarter of a mile long, a hanger planted with late rhododendrons, a *Laburnum* tunnel and chain of lakes. Some spectacular subjects include *Eucryphia glutinosa, Aesculus parviflora, Pieris formosa* and fine *Calocedrus decurrens*.

Houghton Farm, Arundel
MR AND MRS MICHAEL LOCK

When we moved to Houghton Farm house in the autumn of 1956, we found a garden which had been sadly neglected over a period of many years. Unfortunately, we were unable to do much to rectify this sad state of affairs until the middle sixties.

I always think of our garden as having evolved, rather than having been meticulously planned. It was a mammoth task removing all the ivy from the lovely Sussex flint walls which surround the garden, clearing away brambles, old chicken runs, rabbit netting and so on, which abounded. It is difficult now to remember just how awful it really was but with the encouragement of my husband and the willing hands of our late gardener, George Taylor, we made slow but sure progress.

The garden overlooks Arundel Park and surrounding downland, sloping down towards the river Arun, which runs beyond the field below. We have tried to create an informal garden of unusual trees, shrubs and herbaceous plants, in which climbing roses entwined with *Clematis* and paeonies make a wonderful sight during June.

A few years ago we built a conservatory off the kitchen; this extension of the garden gives me endless hours of pleasure just pottering about especially during the winter months when everything outside has come to a standstill but why oh why didn't someone warn me about the bugs – scale, thrip, red spider mite etc!!

To me the most exciting time in this garden is from late winter to early spring when plants such as winter aconites, *Galanthus, Anemone blanda, Crocus, Helleborus atrorubens, Prunus subhirtella, Viburnum × bodnantense* and *Viburnum × burkwoodii*, struggle against the unpredictable winter weather; the pleasure of seeing the spring flowers is something to look forward to.

We have managed to cut down on some of the weeding in the garden by using gravel around some of the shrubs which surround the drive.

Hunters Lodge, Rogate
MR AND MRS S. RIMMER

Our garden of approximately half an acre is on a gentle slope facing south, overlooking farmland towards the Rother valley, with views of the South Downs providing an ever-changing background.

This is essentially a shrub garden with a variety of plants used to give added interest and provide ground-cover. The soil is free-draining acid sand, so a wet summer suits it very well!

The shrub borders follow the semi-circular contour of the garden, with some individual beds in the lawn. These borders are in shade for part of the day, while below the house terrace are south-facing borders.

The season starts with welcome colour from a border of winter-flowering heathers, complemented by a small collection of dwarf conifers. In the shade of a large beech tree are camellias, azaleas and rhododendrons under-planted with bulbs, hellebores and several varieties of snowdrops. In the lawn are two *Magnolia × soulangiana* underplanted with *Geranium macrorrhizum*, and a pair of *Viburnum plicatum* 'Mariesii' give a magnificent display of flower in May. In late spring the shrub borders take over. The colour theme here is gold, purple and silver; variegated shrubs contrast with conifers to give height and change of texture. Ground-cover is provided by a variety of shade-tolerant plants, such as hostas, *Epimedium, Tiarella cordifolia* and many similar plants.

The south-facing beds contain sun-loving plants, in complete contrast to the shrub and foliage borders. The colour is now the silver and grey of foliage, with varying shades of pink and blue flowers, provided by small flowering shrubs and herbaceous plants. The walls of the house give shelter to the more tender flowering shrubs.

Lane End, Sheep Lane, Midhurst
MRS C.J. EPRIL

This two-acre garden stands on the crown of a hill on the eastern edge of the old town. It was once part of the grounds of a nearby eighteenth-century house and, although when we came here on retirement in 1972 much of it had been bulldozed, there remained many old walls and fine mature trees. My husband designed a new garden against the background of the old, and used the natural divisions of the site to form a series of plantings, each with its own characteristics, to merge harmoniously. The soil is acid, and massed rhododendrons, azaleas, and heathers provide colour in the spring. There are two rock gardens (one with pools), roses in a wide variety of colour, shape and habit, alpines, fruit, including old espalier apples, and vegetables.

It is a garden of surprises, both in the planting and in unexpected vistas. The first part, with three walls and on different levels, closely planted for colour and texture at all seasons, contrasts with the next area which commands a spectacular view over the Cowdray ruins and the parkland beyond, while the path along the northern ridge where the ground falls steeply away affords a pleasing and colourful roofscape.

An old flight of steps down the buttressed

Littlehill, Pulborough, in July (see page 190). The hot colours of day lilies, antirrhinums, and purple-leaved *Heuchera* in this summer border are set off by the grey foliage of a clump of pinks.

wall leads to a dell where wild flowers grow in profusion, together with spring bulbs, under lilacs, hawthorns, rhododendrons, tree paeonies, ancient quinces and sweet chestnuts, while towards the western end a magnificent lime and horse chestnuts have their flowers and foliage level with the main garden for which they provide an impressive background.

The variety of planting is such that in every part enthusiasts, including alpinists, find choice plants and striking juxtapositions, as for instance *Meconopsis* against dark red rhododendrons, and a well-grown *Choisya* lighting up a corner.

One of our aims was the maintenance of the garden with the minimum of labour. In the three years since my husband died, it has continued to mature with the aid of one enthusiastic gardener once a week.

---

*Leonardslee, Nr Horsham
THE LODER FAMILY

This large garden contains an extensive collection of spring-flowering shrubs, notably azaleas, rhododendrons, camellias, and magnolias. Much of the garden is sited in a valley with lakes, and these reflect the colour of the trees in the autumn.

Littlehill, Hill Farm Lane, Pulborough
MR AND MRS TIMOTHY SANDEMAN

It was the garden more than the house that attracted us to West Sussex in 1975. Mature yew hedges divided the formal layout of sunken rose garden with fish pond, formal paved hybrid tea rose garden, and a wild garden with mulberry tree, all sadly neglected. Some mature ornamental trees and a large lawn completed the three and a half acres. We have since made new herbaceous and shrub borders, a rockery and an area of old-fashioned roses in box hedges, with a rose-clad pergola down the middle leading to a herb garden. What was a stone quarry is now a pond and bog garden. One of our favourite plant associations is the pink *Clematis* 'Comtesse de Bouchaud' growing through *Cotinus coggygria* 'Royal Purple'. In front of this are *Elaeagnus commutata*, *Ribes sanguineum* 'Brocklebankii' and white, scented lilies. As we are on top of a hill with fine views, wind is our greatest problem, but to compensate the frost drains away well. The soil is poor quality greensand which drains out quickly.

To walk in the garden and enjoy all the scented blooms on a warm summer evening is one of our joys, and there is always a flower to be picked, even on the coldest day. We particularly enjoy visiting the lovely gardens open around the country, and it is there that we see the unusual plants that we try to collect to place in our garden.

Long House, Cowfold
MR AND MRS MICHAEL RICHARDSON

Long House is an Elizabethan Sussex house set in a fold in the ground facing east–west. It has a particularly attractive Horsham slab roof and its name describes the nature of the house, long and in places only one room thick.

The house is surrounded by a walled garden which separates it from the park. Inside the wall on three sides of the square are herbaceous borders and the walls are covered with roses and fruit trees. The house was originally that of an ironmaster, and there are ponds surrounding it where the iron was tempered. The main walk up to the front door is set in old Sussex paving stones and on either side there are standard roses set above bush roses. Against the house there are beds which are set out with summer and winter bedding plants on an annual basis. The main walk to the house is cut in half by yew hedges each with beds on the house side. From the back of the house, two further herbaceous borders lead away to an ancient iron gate into a further garden with a long bed full of lilies and shrubs around a tennis court.

There are small features such as a tufa rock garden and a long bed on one of the cross walls with particularly attractive paeonies. The garden is not large, but it is sheltered from all sides and over the years this has enabled it to become particularly well established.

The Malt House, Chithurst
MR AND MRS GRAHAM FERGUSON

This garden of over six acres is on a west-facing hillside with distant views of the South Downs towards the Rother valley. A beautiful house, dating in part from about 1560, fits perfectly into the woodland setting. The soil is of peaty sand and ideal for rhododendrons and azaleas, though many other interesting trees and shrubs are to be found, forming the principal features in April, May and early June. Most of the original rhododendrons are Exbury hybrids though the present owners have extended the range considerably and specimens can now be seen in flower at most times between February and September.

Other features are two magnificent *Cornus nuttallii* and a fine display of *Wisteria*. Yellow and blue are beautifully set together in *Rosa banksiae* 'Lutea' and *Ceanothus* 'Blue Boy' and on a smaller scale, the same theme is repeated several times by *Lithospermum* 'Grace Ward' and *Genista pilosa*. Some spectacular tree paeonies demand attention and there is a cliff covered with 'Kiftsgate' roses and *Clematis montana*.

The garden gradually dissolves into the dappled shade of a fifty-acre wood where giant redwoods, western hemlocks and an incense cedar can all be seen growing well over a hundred feet high on a spectacular woodland walk. A small nursery offers for sale several hundred of the plants found in the garden.

The Manor of Dean, Tillington
MISS S.M. MITFORD

The garden at The Manor of Dean has been open to the public since 1946 and was begun by William Slade Mitford in 1943, shortly after he inherited Pittshill estate. Much of the garden owes its character to his influence, and amongst other features of interest are beautiful stone vases, an old sundial, coppers and grinding wheels brought from his old home. He was a member of the North American lily and *Iris* Societies, and a subscriber to Kingdon Ward's plant collecting expeditions.

The gardens cover several acres; borders and lawns surround the Manor House (parts of which date from 1411), and there is also an area of mature woodland; rhododendrons, azaleas, camellias and other trees and shrubs flourish here, with carpets of snowdrops, crocuses, daffodils and bluebells in spring. The walled garden, covering about an acre, is planted with soft fruit, vines and vegetables, and one of the greenhouses contains an orange tree which produces fruit for marmalade. Another greenhouse shelters a yellow rose which is over a hundred years old, having decorated the Hon. Mrs Mitford's wedding breakfast table in 1853.

Norman Place, East Street, Petworth
MRS M. PARRY

Moving from a large garden to a very small one is like moving from a mansion to a two-room flat. One has to disregard all the experts' advice about planting in threes, fives or sevens. Every single plant must be selected with infinite care – mistakes show up much more in a confined space. There were very few flowers in this garden when I took over four years ago. There were lots of rocks and a fountain which switched on – perhaps a man's garden? Now it is a flower garden, situated surprisingly in the middle of a very busy little town.

Being L-shaped and on two levels makes it more interesting. The blending of colours is all-important – one part is planted with pale pinks and blues and many white lilies, while the other, longer border is given over to stronger colours, with silver and foliage plants acting as a foil throughout. The two arms of the L curve away from the house. One has a paved path and the other an area of grass with roses at the end, giving in both directions a suggestion of distance. No matter that the path finishes up at my neighbour's fence and the grass at the compost heap!

This postage-stamp sized garden, appropriately situated behind the Post Office, taxes one's ingenuity more than the three-acre site, but is much easier to weed. One can take time to sit and look and plan a little change here and there.

Pyramids, South Harting

GILLIAN JACOMB-HOOD

The six pyramid roofs of the house, harmonizing with the Sussex Downs, dominate this informal half-acre garden. Terraces and paved areas link the garden to the house; the white terrace, with white flowers and grey foliage, looks on to the magnificent sweep of the Downs; the vine pergola terrace provides dappled shade, with geraniums and lilies for colour; and the pool terrace, with its weeping peach arching over the water. Near the house are scented *Cistus*, lavender, rosemary, lemon verbena, and wallflowers and tobacco plants (the only concession to bedding out).

Urns and figures discreetly placed provide focal points. Golden yews provide essential shelter. The tiny orchard is also the wild garden, with its fine old Bramleys opened up to show their dramatic architectural shapes and underplanted with hellebores; a shady contrast to the exposed area round the house. In the spring it is a mass of delicate daffodils, followed by Queen Anne's lace and then old-fashioned roses. At one end is a Victorian fern seat, with ferns, hostas, foxgloves and shade-loving plants on either side of it; at the other end steps lead through the 'Penelope' roses which are the chief feature seen from the pergola terrace. A rose-clad pergola leads into the orchard, and this, together with other old-fashioned roses, is the glory of the summer flowering.

Against one wall of the house is the Bourbon rose 'Zéphirine Drouhin', underplanted with valerian and wild strawberries; by another wall, the carpet of *Euonymus* 'Emerald 'n' Gold' provides a lovely foil for the tulips and *Rosa* 'Roseraie de l'Haÿ'.

Amongst the winter-scented shrubs, *Iris unguicularis*, snowdrops and *Crocus* give immense pleasure; the joy of the garden is that it offers mystery and surprise at any time of the year.

St Roches Arboretum, West Dean

THE EDWARD JAMES FOUNDATION

The arboretum, which forms part of West Dean Estate, extends to some forty-two acres, situated in and on either side of a dry valley on the slopes of the Downs. The soils are chalky with some clay and flints. Planting in the arboretum was begun in the early nineteenth century and takes the form of woodland richly interplanted with exotic species, particularly conifers which have reached a surprising size on the thin soil. Specimen trees include redwood, cedar, Douglas fir, western red cedar, incense cedar, Turkey oak, red oak and Lucombe oak. At the turn of the century trainloads of peat were transported to the arboretum to allow rhododendrons to be grown; this has since been supplemented by the litter from the conifers, which has allowed many acid-loving plants to be grown. *Rhododendron ponticum* thrives and some of the trees are over-mature, but a continuing

policy of clearing and replanting is under way.

South Corner House, Duncton

MAJ. AND MRS SHANE BLEWITT

This one-acre garden lies under the rising beechwoods of the South Downs which form an attractive backdrop in all seasons. The ground, which is undulating, is laid out and planted in such a way that all is not seen at once. This, particularly in a small garden, creates an air of mystery and intimacy.

The garden was landscaped in the 1920s, and includes a miniature stone-walled rose garden, from which steps lead down to shrubberies on the lower slopes; there is also a small circular rosary which provides a break between the more formal aspects of the garden and a further group of shrubberies to the south.

Apart from a number of old fruit trees through some of which roses and *Clematis* clamber, most of the planting is the work of the present owner. The herbaceous border, which is entirely traditional with no shrubs or non-herbaceous plants, is a major feature, and considerable care is taken over choice of plants to achieve continuity of flowering throughout the summer and harmonious contrasts of foliage and colour.

Similar care has been taken over the selection of trees and shrubs. These include *Pyrus salicifolia*, maples, tulip tree, copper beech, and a wide variety of viburnums and shrub roses. Two old Irish yews and a large topiary acorn-shaped yew are statuesque in their effect. Darker corners of the garden are lightened by the judicious planting of shrubs such as variegated cornuses, golden *Philadelphus*, *Fatsia* and *Elaeagnus*. The soil is alkaline, which acts as a challenge and not as a barrier to possibilities.

The owner does much of his own propagating in his small greenhouses, which contain many interesting and rare plants and shrubs to use in the house during the winter. Two greenhouses display during the summer a colourful collection of scented and single pelargoniums. There are many climbing roses and shrubs on the house, and around it are pots of fuchsias and tender abutilons.

Telegraph House, North Marden

MR AND MRS DAVID GAULT

At seven hundred feet above sea level with long views south-west to the Solent, we have tried to make a sheltered garden on our high downland site which offers minimal topsoil overlying virgin chalk rock. The garden was started about fifteen to twenty years ago.

Predecessors left us high beech and yew hedges within which to furnish our garden rooms amounting to about one and a half acres. Outside the enclosed part is a hundred and fifty acres of ancient yew woods sprinkled with whitebeam, oak, ash and

beech, also a long avenue of copper beeches which are spectacular in May and June.

We have found that site preparation and breaking up of the substructure is the key to gardening on chalk, and a number of shrubs and ornamental trees have reached good sizes and now flower well. Examples are *Hoheria lyallii*, *Parrotia persica*, the rowan and Canadian lilacs and the invaluable *Syringa microphylla* 'Superba'. *Abutilon* loves the sharp drainage and in the late summer large clumps of *Hydrangea villosa* are superb.

Many shrub roses are happy here, particularly hybrid musks, other modern shrub and rose species but not bourbons, hybrid teas and other more fastidious examples. A bed of *Rosa* 'Ballerina', interplanted with *Penstemon* 'Garnet' has been admired, as has a group of *Rosa glauca* (*rubrifolia*) growth with *Clematis viticella* 'Rubra'. We have also made beds where herbaceous plants dominate, and others which feature evergreen and aromatic shrubs.

Toddington House, Littlehampton

MR AND MRS P.F. HOLLAND

Our garden of approximately one acre has been developing since 1981 when we called in John Brookes, the landscape architect/designer. The courtyard approach was completed in the spring of 1985, and here a stone wall was removed to allow the house to be appreciated on entering from the road. In the middle of the gravelled courtyard is a raised octagonal pond and fountain.

The planting leading to the front door is as cottagey as possible to blend in with the ancient house. Through the garden wall gate, the land ascends in different levels, culminating in a swimming pool and an adjacent pool house; the lowest level is a gravelled area at the base of a rockery. In the curve of the dividing wall a fountain splashes via a lead cistern into a reflecting pool. A mixed perennial and shrub border in bright colours lies to one side of the pool. Through the pool house arch a lead 'piping boy' on plinth with golden yew hedging behind closes the vista, whilst to the right is our young son's garden planted with miniature red roses and with begonias surrounded by box hedging. To the left a pergola covers a wide brick walk, and off this is a small garden planted entirely with red flowers and foliage. At the bottom end of the pergola is a square pool with fountains balanced by a bed of blue plants on the other side of the grass walk which is edged with white and grey plants.

The garden is designed as a series of rooms so that the visitor passes from one to another and in time we hope this effect will be heightened as the hedge grows up.

The Upper Lodge, Stopham

J.W. HARRINGTON, ESQ.

This is a small cottage garden which is packed

The pergola at West Dean in July. Rambler roses, *Wisteria*, and ornamental vines are trained up the classical columns leading to a summerhouse floored with horses' molars.

House, rebuilt in 1804 and now a college of arts and crafts, are informal, extensive, nineteenth-century in atmosphere and planting and very much reflect the style and scale of the flint mansion. The outstanding features are the specimen trees including cedar of Lebanon planted in 1746, ginkgos, fern-leaf beeches, Atlantic cedars, tulip trees, limes, horse chestnut and many rare and unusual species. A frost pocket and thin alkaline soil restrict the range of plants that can be grown here, but it is a useful indication for gardeners who have similar problems. Additional features of the garden include a three-hundred-foot pergola, rustic summerhouses, a wild garden and the walled garden currently undergoing restoration. A nursery is established here specializing in old-fashioned roses and unusual plants.

Whitehouse Cottage, Staplefield Lane
BARRY GRAY, ESQ.

The cottage is timber-framed, probably late sixteenth century, with modern additions designed by the architect Patrick Lichfield. The garden, which now exceeds four acres, has been created over the past twenty-five years in one of those long, narrow, wooded valleys which in these parts of Sussex link the fields and carry small streams to the river Ouse; in consequence there are hardly any parts of it on the level. In the first years a lot of clearing was necessary, but all mature trees, of which there were many, including a fine old yew, were kept.

The area nearest the cottage was planted with small unusual trees, shrubs and old roses; the furthest part is still woodland, and wild anemones, primroses, and bluebells are steadily increasing there. The stream, which runs the length of the garden, dividing it, has been dammed in three places to make a small pond near the house and two larger ones in the wood.

Fifteen years ago a bordering strip of field on the south side was acquired, and this has been designed more formally, with yew hedges surrounding a croquet lawn, and beds of shrubs, old roses and various quiet perennials. In this part there is a plantation of twenty-two standard *Amelanchier* which in the spring are remarkable for their massed blossom and in the autumn for their coloured foliage.

Another feature is a large planting of 'Penelope' roses under a band of tall weeping birches. Between these and the wood is an area of wild meadow divided by an alley of pleached limes where there is a succession of species *Crocus*, snowdrops, daffodils, anemones, fritillaries, buttercups, camassias, the occasional marsh orchid, and in high summer masses of ox-eye daisies. Two years ago another acre of adjoining land to the north was bought. This has been planted with young oaks, hazels, hawthorns, wild cherries and so on, to compensate a little for the other woodlands destroyed hereabouts.

with interesting and unusual plants, especially those suitable for acid soil conditions. Some of the more tender shrubs, including *Ceanothus* and *Fremontodendron*, are trained up the house walls, while a large number of rhododendrons and camellias are planted on terraces behind the house. In spring primulas, polyanthus, lily-of-the-valley, crocuses, snowdrops and daffodils provide a wealth of colour in this plantsman's garden.

West Dean Gardens, Nr Chichester
THE EDWARD JAMES FOUNDATION

The gardens are situated in a scenic valley setting at the foot of the South Downs, in the valley of the River Lavant, an intermittent chalk stream or 'winterborne'.

There has been a garden here certainly since 1623. The present gardens of some thirty-five acres which surround West Dean

WALES (NORTH)

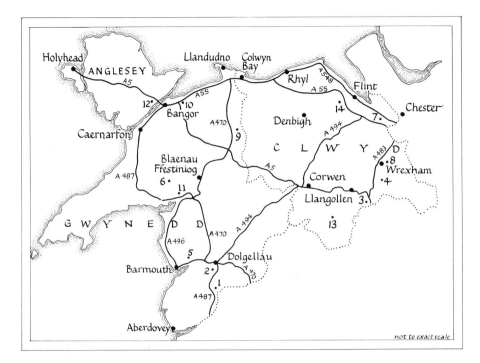

not to exact scale

Directions to Gardens

Brynhyfryd, Corris, 6 miles north of Machynlleth, 10 miles south of Dolgellau. [1]

Cefn Bere, Cae Deintur, Dolgellau. [2]

Chirk Castle, Chirk, 7 miles southeast of Llangollen. [3]

Erddig Park, 2 miles south of Wrexham. [4]

Farchynys Cottage, Bontddu, 4 miles west of Dolgellau. [5]

Hafod Garregog, Nantmor, 5 miles north of Penrhyndeudraeth. [6]

Hawarden Castle, just east of Hawarden village, 6 miles west of Chester. [7]

Langlands, Maesydre Road, Wrexham. [8]

Maenan Hall, 2 miles north of Llanrwst. [9]

Penrhyn Castle, 3 miles east of Bangor. [10]

Plas Brondanw, Llanfrothen, 3 miles east of Porthmadog. [11]

Plas Newydd, 1 mile south of Llanfairpwll on the Isle of Anglesey. [12]

Tynant, Moelfre, 8 miles west of Oswestry. [13]

Welsh College of Horticulture, midway between Mold and Flint, ¼ mile west of Northop. [14]

◆

Brynhyfryd Garden, Corris
MRS DAVID PAISH

This garden was started in October 1961 on a steep mountainside with beautiful outcrops of large rocks and a cliff. This is all above the house; below is a more formal garden of shrubs, rhododendrons and some perennial plants. The mountainside is planted with rhododendrons and azaleas, mostly species, but some hybrids. *Rhododendron moupinense* will start flowering at the end of January or beginning of February and given suitable weather conditions other species follow on until the end of July, with some repeat-flowering after that. The soil is very acid, so the choice of plants is rather limited. Shrubs that do well are *Viburnum*, *Halesia*, *Styrax*, *Hydrangea*, cherries, magnolias and rose species and, of course, heathers in variety. There

is also some water – a small pool fed by a steady trickle from a slate pipe driven into a rock where primulas do well. There are many attractive wild plants growing here, heathers and, of course, ferns which have to be controlled, and many others including blue milkwort, yellow pimpernel and the dwarf, creeping *Hypericum humifusum*.

◆

Cefn Bere, Cae Deintur
MR AND MRS MALDWYN THOMAS

This is a quarter-acre garden, on a steep southerly slope facing over the small stone town of Dolgellau to the spectacular Cader Idris range of mountains. Tall beech hedges protect it from the prevailing south-westerlies and inside a very wide range of plants is grown. There is a backbone of small mountain rhododendrons, which can sometimes suffer from late spring frosts, but these are supplemented by daphnes, vacciniums, kalmias, *Cistus*, brooms and some species and old-fashioned roses. The fringes are planted with alpines, the shrubs are underplanted with woodlanders and small herbaceous plants, hostas, ferns, and grasses. Bulbs show colour nearly the whole year round and small climbers are also used. There are troughs, an alpine house and a bulb frame. In spite of being very much a plantsman's garden, we do aim at a feeling of naturalness and wildness. A feature towards the end of summer is the flame flower, *Tropaeolum speciosum*, draping the shrubs – a plant which many find difficult to establish. Plant the long macaroni-like roots horizontally at the bottom of a foot-deep hole and lightly cover with, preferably, leafmould. When the shoots emerge, top dress them gradually as they grow up to the original ground level. We were fortunate to read this in an old Wallace and Barr catalogue in our salad days and had no trouble. Of course our climate helps.

◆

Chirk Castle
THE NATIONAL TRUST

The garden at Chirk Castle, which has existed for at least two hundred and fifty years, has undergone many alterations according to the tastes and fashions of the day. The entrance to it is through beautiful wrought-iron gates which once formed a part of the wings of the famous gates by the brothers Robert and John Davies, now at the main lodge, originally made for a forecourt to the castle. A wide gravel path, flanked by clipped yews, leads to the rose garden and a small herbaceous border, augmented by bulbs and a little bedding. The lawns are surrounded by yew hedges and a gap in these leads to the lower lawns and less formal parts of the garden. The daffodil lawn to the right is studded with ornamental trees for which the huge yew hedge makes a splendid background.

Further down to the right is the shrub

garden, largely redesigned since 1946 because neglect during the war years left it a jungle. Here may be seen two spectacular *Cornus nuttallii* in happy association with magnolias and *Pyrus salicifolia*, and later on there are eucryphias and many varieties of *Hydrangea*. In the middle of the shrub garden is the recently extended pool.

To the left is the Hawk House converted in 1912 into a mews for falcons. Now it is surrounded by a flowery rock bank and has vines and camellias growing upon it. Embothriums do well but are difficult to place because of their brilliant colour; they seem happy enough alongside most azaleas.

The terrace at the bottom of the garden leads to a neo-classical pavilion designed by Emes and, from the terrace, the magnificent view extends across many counties.

◆

Erddig Park, Nr Wrexham
THE NATIONAL TRUST

This eight-acre garden has been restored to its eighteenth-century formal design and includes summer bedding, roses, herbaceous beds and climbing plants as well as formal orchards and espalier-trained apples, pears and peaches. Victorian fountains, a parterre, canal and pool can also be admired, and the seventeenth-century house is open to the public.

◆

Farchynys Cottage, Bontddu
MRS G. TOWNSEND

Farchynys Cottage is a former gardener's dwelling with grounds of four acres. Part of this area is a well-established garden and the remainder is woodland, in which we are planting many attractive and unusual shrubs and trees.

Being situated on the unsurpassable Mawddach estuary we are fortunate in having a comparatively equable climate and a south-easterly aspect. These factors, and our acid soil, lead us to believe that, over the years, we can create a beautiful garden, and towards this goal we made our first extensive planting in the autumn of 1982, followed by major landscaping and further planting in 1984 and 1985.

The layout of the garden is dictated by the natural outcrops of pink shale rock which provides a superb contrast for the blooms of azaleas, *Syringa* and *Clematis* and a perfect harmony to magnolias, rhododendrons and maples. Behind the cottage on a steep slope is a natural oak and conifer wood rising to the 'top pool' – a rain-water filled reservoir which forms the catchment for our 'mountain stream'. This tumbles through a valley down which we are constructing falls, pools and bridges to link several terraces of azaleas, rhododendrons and junipers. At the bottom is our 'bog garden' with its massive *Abies grandis*, bamboos and willows.

The terrace at the front of the house is

Rhododendron orbiculare at Brynhyfryd, see page 193. This hardy species from Sichuan, central China, is very special, with its almost round leaves and bell-shaped deep pink flowers.

dominated by an eighty-year-old *Liriodendron tulipifera* and contains a beautiful *Kalmia latifolia* which is at its best in late June. On the west side is a landscaped area where we have constructed a pergola covered by several varieties of *Clematis* and climbing roses, and the upper terrace, which is bounded by *Magnolia liliiflora* 'Nigra', *M. stellata* and *M.* × *soulangiana*. We believe that a moderate pruning twice a year gives us the best results and increases the number of blooms significantly.

◆

Hafod Garregog, Nantmor
MR AND MRS HUGH MASON

Although Hafod Garregog has been known to be occupied since 1400 when the Bard, Rhys Goch Eryri, had his home there, the gardens had long since disappeared and have been entirely re-made since 1971 when the present owners restored the property.

Hafod Garregog means 'stony place' and the gardens are certainly stony with a minimum of soil, a pH of 4.5, and being five miles south of Snowdon there is a rainfall of over seventy inches per year. Although surrounded by mountains, the garden is only a few feet above sea level and the River Hafod, and is on the edge of oak and silver birch woodland which is now a two-hundred-acre National Nature Reserve.

Behind the house there are lawns of well-tended grass dividing up beds of azaleas, roses, herbaceous plants and shrubs. Maples and viburnums flourish in this climate. The

lower garden, on a slope to the river, has water running through in a series of pools and has been terraced to make beds for heathers, dwarf conifers, shrubs and small trees. Both in this garden and above there has been a concentration on achieving foliage colour.

There is an extensive kitchen garden where most vegetables will flourish and soft fruits enjoy the wet conditions. The plots are reasonably free of pests and little spraying is done but clubroot in brassicas has become troublesome. There are three greenhouses nursing young plants and also used for growing tomatoes, cucumbers and chrysanthemums.

The main appeal of the garden must be its backdrop of trees and mountains, and it is interesting that ground that was just sheep grazing fifteen years ago and is now covered by shrubs and trees has become a nesting haven for many varieties of small birds.

◆

Hawarden Castle
SIR WILLIAM AND LADY GLADSTONE

A massive stone keep erected by the agents of King Edward I on the site of a prehistoric hill fort is the dominant feature of a garden in which Nature has been tamed but not subdued. The keep's great day of glory, after which it required substantial repair, was Palm Sunday, 1282. It suffered two sieges during the Civil War (1642–44) and lay a ruin for more than two hundred years until it was restored by William Ewart Gladstone, four times Prime Minister. The rubbish of centuries having been removed, snowdrops, daffodils, cowslips, blue anemones, bluebells, forget-me-nots and even the humble primrose (Mr Disraeli's favourite flower) have been encouraged to take pride of place.

For the connoisseur of the early eighteenth century, there are an earth amphitheatre, a no-longer-pristine belt of lime trees and a few stupendous beeches. Many specimen forest trees survived the legendary Gladstonian axe, and the garden enjoyed a liberal planting of late Victorian and Edwardian *Rhododendron* favourites. In spite of some tasteful and expensive masonry of the 1920s, it can be confidently stated that formality is not obtrusive. Even the elaborate flower beds on the formal terrace were first modified for reasons of economy in 1897. In the rock garden and the bog garden, wild plants appear to be more successful than tame ones, yet the general effect from February to June is not of a jungle but of a paradise.

The particular aim of the postwar incumbents, apart from encouraging wild flowers, has been to contrive mixtures of colours throughout the spring and early summer, counter to the one-colour or single 'theme' fashion of the last half-century. The garden is, however, a garden not of plants, nor of colours, but of compositions.

Langlands, Wrexham

MR AND MRS C.L. LACEY

We have planted this garden densely and extravagantly, for we are in the centre of a busy town and want to feel that the moment we walk through the gates we are stepping into our own green and fertile world, a complete contrast to the man-made environment around us. We exercise no restraint and cram every border with shrubs, climbing plants, herbaceous perennials, roses, herbs and bulbs in typical cottage garden informality and profusion, so that by midsummer not a square inch of bare soil is visible. This means, unfortunately, that we cannot open the garden later than July for visitors would soon lose themselves in the undergrowth and would probably not be discovered by us until the first frosts in late autumn! In May and June there is still some semblance of order.

We have tried to give each area of the garden a different mood and flavour through the use of colour and scent, and the choice of plants. There is a path lined with pink and white geraniums, dicentras and old shrub roses; a border devoted to silver foliage, white, blue and yellow flowers, punctuated by deep red *Cosmos*, potentillas and smoke bushes; a paved garden complete with lily pond, bamboos and grasses, decorated with pots of apricot *Mimulus*, silver senecios and damson black pelargoniums; and there is a rock garden submerged in Welsh poppies, bluebells and alpine aquilegias. Luckily the garden is large and protected by trees and walls on all sides; these not only give us privacy but enable us to grow a range of plants not reliably hardy this far north – we can boast a large specimen of evergreen *Ceanothus* 'Puget Blue', for example, healthy clumps of silvery *Convolvulus cneorum*, and generous stands of kniphofias including, appropriately, the stately yellow variety 'Wrexham Buttercup'.

Maenan Hall, Nr Llanrwst

THE HON. CHRISTOPHER MCLAREN

Ornamental trees and shrubs, backed by mature woodland trees and mountain views, are the essence of Maenan. The garden is at its peak in spring and autumn with roses and eucryphias outstanding in summer, and *Prunus subhirtella* 'Autumnalis' in winter. It lies on the slopes of the Conway Valley with slightly acid soil and sixty inches of rain in an average year.

The main garden, surrounding the Elizabethan and Queen Anne house, dates from 1956, with formal features adjoining the less formal areas. A rectangular lawn before the house is flanked by formal yew hedges from the front of which a pair of sphinxes descends from the lawn to an avenue of magnolias and cherries. A blue cedar and a copper beech stand each side of the lower end of the avenue and produce fine colour con-

A smooth-barked birch and evergreen azalea at Cefn Bere in May; for a description of the garden see page 193.

trasts with each other and with the prevailing greens of summer.

An avenue of *Laburnum* 'Vossii' continues the line of the left hand yew hedge down to a statue of Bacchus standing within a semi-circle of *Cotoneaster* 'Cornubia'. The laburnums grow upright, rather than being trained over arches as at Bodnant, because the external view of this avenue is even more important than the internal. The heavy clay soil here makes a comprehensive drainage system obligatory.

Behind the house a walled garden contains magnolias and maples, cherries and *Cotinus*, eucryphias, amelanchiers and roses; beside the house is an ancient circular fish pond.

The woodland dell with cliffs, streams and

Plas Brondanw, Llanfrothen

a canopy of ash, oak and sycamore complements the main garden. The first rhododendrons date from 1949 and there has been continual development since 1958. The highlights are the camellias under the cliff amongst the rocks, the bluebell carpet and the concave slope of deciduous azaleas.

Penrhyn Castle, Nr Bangor

THE NATIONAL TRUST

These are large gardens, with fine trees and shrubs, a wild garden and a well laid-out walled garden. There are superb views across the surrounding countryside, including the Menai Strait and the coast of Anglesey.

Plas Brondanw, Llanfrothen

PORTMEIRION FOUNDATION

The gardens at Plas Brondanw were made by Sir Clough Williams-Ellis, the creator of Portmeirion, and are a fine example of his talent for creative landscape design. The main features date from the early part of this century, before he began Portmeirion, but work continued on and off until the 1960s.

Sir Clough was given Plas Brondanw by his father in 1902, when it had long been abandoned by the family, and only the big trees remained of its earlier grandeur. His main objective in landscaping was to provide a series of dramatic and romantic prospects. Inspired by the Renaissance gardens of Italy, the design of the Plas gardens is strongly architectural, relying on stone walls, topiary

The large-flowered tree heather *Erica australis*, with *Aquilegia alpina* and a grey-leaved *Artemisia* at Cefn Bere in May (for description see page 193).

and avenues to form vistas which lead the eye to distant mountain tops. Sir Clough used carefully trained Irish yews to give the effect of Italian cypresses which were tender in this climate. There is a fine specimen holm oak, and by the orangery, a mulberry tree and a fig. In late August, the big standard *Hydrangea paniculata*, flowering in the forecourt, is spectacular. The horse-chestnut avenue leading to the folly castle or watch tower, which provides a wonderful view of the mountains of Snowdonia, was planted with trees from the nursery started by John Evelyn.

Plas Newydd, Isle of Anglesey
THE MARQUESS OF ANGLESEY: THE NATIONAL TRUST

Backed by marvellous views towards Snowdonia, the garden here has lawns sloping down to the Menai Strait, massed shrubs – including a good collection of azaleas and rhododendrons – and fine trees. Much of the design and recent planting has been carried out by the present Lord Anglesey.

Tynant, Moelfre
MR AND MRS DAVID WILLIAMS

Tynant used to be an old smithy and mill, sitting at the foot of a mountain by the side of

the main stream leaving Moelfre Lake. The property was ideal for developing into a garden, with five acres of land made up of a small level stretch for vegetables and lawns, deciduous woodland (the Dingle), a rough field, artificial pools fed from an underground water source and a conifer wood (now being developed into a series of gardens). The setting is enhanced by beautiful drystone walls which together with the house were rebuilt by a craft stonemason from Oswestry.

My wife and I plunged our plants willy-nilly and with enthusiasm into all the areas available, and soon started clearing bits of the conifer wood to continue the bombardment. Lately we have come to realize that we don't want a museum of plants and so are placing groups of plants that harmonize with each other.

The wet areas by the stream and pools allow us to grow many varieties of *Primula, Hosta, Astilbe* and other plants liking damp spots. The other areas are usually very dry, the soil being typical of Wales, very slaty and well-drained. Many of the small herbaceous plants, shrubs and trees are grown for not only flowers but foliage too – for example, red or purple leaves of *Cotinus* 'Royal Purple', *Prunus* varieties and *Lobelia cardinalis*; silver blue leaves of *Eucalyptus, Elaeagnus, Pyrus salicifolia, Salix* and numerous small plants like *Artemisia* and *Euryops*; yellow or variegated leaves of *Euonymus, Cornus, Sambucus, Robinia*; and various conifers.

We try to offer our visitors something to suit all interests, i.e. alpines, camellias, rhododendrons, azaleas, clematis, various herbaceous plants, a wide variety of *Sorbus* species, acers and *Berberis*.

Welsh College of Horticulture, Northop

The College grounds extend to two hundred and twenty-five acres of which twelve are laid out with ornamental features including lawns, a rhododendron and heather garden, island beds of mixed shrubs and herbaceous plants, a pinetum, seasonal bedding areas and many established specimen trees on a lawn. At present it is being extended to include a bog garden and other ornamental features. There is also a decorative display glasshouse containing a varied collection of plants of botanical and economic importance from various regions of the world. In addition to this there are a further two acres of land covered by a variety of glasshouses, one section consisting of small individual houses of different designs containing a wide range of flowers for cutting and pot plants grown for amenity and interior landscaping. The remainder of the area consists of a fully automated block, where the major edible crops, cut flowers, flowering and foliage pot plants are produced. Tomatoes are grown by nutrient film technique and cucumbers on rockwool slabs. A further large glasshouse contains a variety of experiments and projects demonstrating the latest developments in horticultural techniques. There is a tree, shrub and hardy plant nursery of two and a half acres and a small propagating house to service this unit. Container-grown trees and shrubs occupy an area close by.

Seventy-five acres are devoted to the production of commercial vegetables and there is a small orchard of 'Bramley' apples, together with five acres of raspberries, blackcurrants and gooseberries.

Tynant in May. The largest-flowered Japanese cherry 'Tai Haku' and *Acer pseudoplatanus* 'Brilliantissimum' are both striking features of this garden in spring.

WALES (SOUTH)

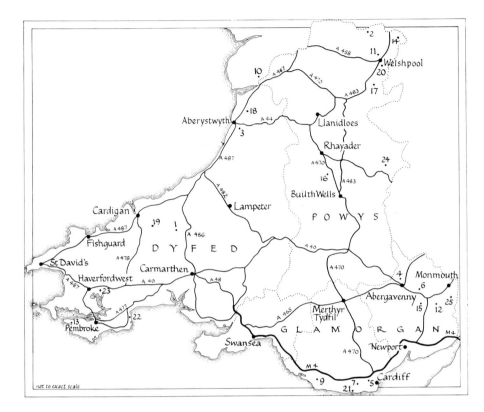

Rhoose Farm House, Rhoose, Barry, Glamorgan. [21]

Saundersfoot Bay Leisure Park, Broadfield, Saundersfoot, Dyfed. [22]

Slebech Hall, 6 miles east of Haverfordwest, Dyfed. [23]

Trawscoed Hall, 3 miles north of Welshpool, Powys. [11]

The Walled Garden, Knill, 3 miles from Kington and Presteigne, Powys. [24]

Yew Tree Nursery, Lydart, 2 miles south of Monmouth, Gwent. [25]

◆

Blaengwrfach Isaf, Bancyffordd
MRS GAIL M. FARMER

When we came here fifteen years ago, it was to an almost traditional Welsh longhouse with concrete terrace and land which fell away steeply to a wooded gully and stream. Then there was no vestige of a garden to be seen and we had no grand plan at the beginning, but the garden as it is today has slowly evolved over the years away from the house and has now become an intensively planted acre, the cottage and terrace clothed in old-fashioned roses, jasmine, honeysuckle and *Clematis*.

I have discovered that it is possible in a very small area to fit in many aspects of gardening: scree, water, formal, woodland and rampant.

Directions to Gardens

Blaengwrfach Isaf, Bancyffordd, 2 miles west of Llandysul. [1]

Bodynfoel Hall, Llanfechain, 10 miles north of Welshpool, Powys. [2]

Botany Garden, Penglais Road, Aberystwyth, Dyfed. [3]

Cae Hywel, Llansantffraid-ym-Mechain, 10 miles north of Welshpool, Powys. [2]

The Chain Garden, Chapel Road, 1 mile north of Abergavenny, Gwent. [4]

The Clock House, Cathedral Close, Llandaff, 2 miles northwest of Cardiff, Glamorgan. [5]

Clytha Park, midway between Abergavenny and Raglan, Gwent. [6]

Coedarhydyglyn, 5 miles west of Cardiff, Glamorgan. [7]

The Dingle, 3 miles north of Welshpool, Powys. [8]

Ewenny Priory, Ewenny, 2 miles south of Bridgend, Glamorgan. [9]

Garreg Farm, Glandyfi, 5 miles west of Machynlleth, Dyfed. [10]

Glebe House, Guilsfield, 3 miles north of Welshpool, Powys. [11]

The Graig, Pen-y-Clawdd, southwest of Monmouth, Gwent. [12]

The Hall, Angle, 9 miles west of Pembroke, Dyfed. [13]

The Hill Cottage, Bausley, Crew Green, 8 miles northeast of Welshpool, Powys. [14]

Llanfair Court, 5 miles southeast of Abergavenny, Gwent. [15]

Llyysdinam, Newbridge-on-Wye, southwest of Llandrindod Wells, Powys. [16]

Lower House Farm, Nantyderry, 7 miles southeast of Abergavenny, Gwent. [15]

Maenllwyd Isaf, Abermule, 5 miles northeast of Newtown and 10 miles south of Welshpool, Powys. [17]

7 New Street, Talybont, 6 miles north of Aberystwyth, Dyfed. [18]

Penrallt Ffynnon, Cwm-cou, 3 miles northwest of Newcastle Emlyn, Dyfed. [19]

Powis Castle Gardens, Welshpool, Powys. [20]

Blaengwrfach Isaf in July. A colourful corner with the late double-flowered cranesbill *Geranium pratense* **'Plenum Violaceum', tobacco plants and violas.**

A great love of scented plants and an interest in natural history has led to many old types of flowers being planted, favourites being roses and *Dianthus*. Growing plants rich in nectar gives an extra dimension to a garden with many bees and butterflies encouraged to visit and feed.

The garden is so closely planted that with our very high rainfall, growth is often rampant. We sometimes wonder if we might lose visitors amidst it all in high summer, and special places have to be found for our tiny treasures which would soon disappear out in the open. The answer to this we found was to make our own troughs.

Bodynfoel Hall, Llanfechain

MAJ. AND MRS BONNOR-MAURICE

The original garden was laid out between 1835 and 1840, when the house was built, and in the early part of this century the new garden was added. From 1920 to 1970 the house was let to a succession of families, and when the owners returned in 1970 only the lawn in front of the house was not a jungle. The work of reclamation has proceeded slowly and most of the original garden is now under control.

A small pool has been created, and work is now aimed at linking this to the main garden, with the objective of all-the-year-round colour. The garden is basically informal and is geared to the encouragement of birds, butterflies, and above all tranquillity.

Botany Garden, Aberystwyth

UNIVERSITY COLLEGE OF WALES

This medium-sized garden houses botanical collections of herbaceous plants, shrubs and trees; there is also a general greenhouse collection, including such exotics as pink bananas and insectivorous plants. A large pool has just been constructed in the temperate house; this contains fish and aquatic plants including some young Amazon waterlilies.

Cae Hywel, Llansantffraid-ym-Mechain

MISS JUDITH M. JONES

My garden is on a slope, and has areas of different levels joined by steps and winding paths. The most outstanding feature is the rock garden, steep and south-facing, which is a blaze of colour from early spring through most of the summer, and another interesting feature is the herb garden where I have learned to control the ever-spreading mints by having them in island-beds and mowing around them.

The Chain Garden, Abergavenny

MR AND MRS C.F.R. PRICE

The Chain Garden is a two-acre garden situated on a hill on the outskirts of Abergavenny. Originally laid out by the Baker-Gabb family, and enclosed by stone walls, the garden slopes to the west down to the Cibi stream which flows through the garden from the Sugar Loaf mountain.

Mature trees and shrubs include a very old medlar and mulberry, an evergreen oak, three large deciduous oaks and several yews, many rhododendrons and two old camellias. There are also two hornbeams, an old paeony, and a *Choisya*. We have added a great variety of shrubs, some that are unusual and others slightly tender. These include *Stuartia*, *Halesia*, *Hoheria*, *Parrotia* and many others. *Carpenteria californica* does especially well, and we have taken several cuttings of this shrub, and *Magnolia sinensis*, about ten years old, has now started to flower. Maples, azaleas and heathers also do very well in this garden.

In the spring there are many daffodils, bluebells, crocuses and erythroniums, as well as a special favourite – the indigenous white wood anemone – followed by primulas, *Meconopsis* and spring and autumn *Cyclamen*. There are two rock gardens; a large one which has many varieties of gentians, and a small one which is particularly attractive in the spring. Many ferns grow naturally in the garden and the royal fern, *Osmunda regalis*, has also been established.

More recently several *Clematis* have been added together with wisterias. The conservatory was built two years ago and we are now able to grow a variety of tender plants.

The kitchen garden is more or less unchanged since 1900 and many fruit trees are grown on the walls, including 'Morello' cherries, apricots, peaches, and fine dessert grapes. There is a greenhouse which houses a dessert grape and is also used for propagating and growing bedding plants.

Grassy paths and lawns have linked together the many different aspects of this garden to make it one of interest at all seasons.

The Clock House, Llandaff

PROF. AND MRS BRYAN HIBBARD

The garden is adjacent to Llandaff Cathedral and seems to have absorbed the atmosphere of serenity and timelessness. It is surrounded by high walls, some of which date from mediaeval times.

The irregular form of the garden offers many delightful corners and unexpected vistas. The main lawn is separated from the house by a small patio which, apart from roses, *Artemisia* and pinks, contains mainly early-flowering bulbs and winter and spring shrubs such as the lovely *Daphne × neapolitana*. The lawn leads to a small lily-pond enclosed by old-fashioned roses,

maples, irises and hostas. A nearby grass walk is bordered by lavender and 'Iceberg' roses and leads to a superb mature *Ginkgo*. Under this *Ginkgo* is a well-placed seat which provides a vantage point for the imposing views of the ruined mediaeval bishop's castle on the hillside beyond the garden.

From the lawn, another grass path passes under an arch covered by *Rosa* 'Complicata' into a series of enclosures bordered by yew hedges. The first of these small gardens is a mass of colour in summer with old roses, *Clematis* and delphiniums. Boldly outstanding in these borders are imposing groups of *Inula grandiflora* and *Acanthus spinosus*. On the high stone walls adjacent to this area are several large old-fashioned roses including 'Mme Isaac Pereire', 'Mme Alfred Carrière' and 'Lady Waterlow', all intermingled with *Clematis*. Next to the house is a formal 'ladies garden' with clipped box hedges and a small fountain pool. It is surrounded by hydrangeas, viburnums and a lovely *Ceanothus* 'Trewithen Blue'. On the house wall there are a huge *Rosa* 'Veilchenblau' and a fine *R. banksiae* 'Lutea' and a prolific fan-trained 'Peregrine' peach. Beyond this there is an informal wooded area containing lilacs, azaleas and a lovely *Acer palmatum*. In spring this area is filled with snowdrops, daffodils and fritillaries.

Clytha Park, Nr Abergavenny

R. HANBURY-TENISON, ESQ.

The large garden at Clytha Park has existed in almost its present form for a hundred and sixty years, although the curved kitchen garden wall, the arch on to the main road, and possibly one or two of the trees, are fifty years older than that. Inevitably in recent times, gravel paths have been grassed over and planting out has been more or less eliminated, but visitors can still walk round the 'lake' (formed by damming the stream in around 1820) and enjoy the sudden changes of view so beloved of garden designers in the early nineteenth century. Two of the finest trees are the cedar of Lebanon in front of the house, and the large, somewhat stag-headed, tulip tree overlooking the water garden. Visitors in May are rewarded by a carpet of wild daffodils that cover the slope on one side of the house, but the garden is best in June when rhododendrons and irises add colour to every corner.

As with many eighteenth-century houses, the main part of the garden is enclosed by a hedge and wall some hundred yards behind the house. Until the First World War the park deer were thus able to graze up to the windows.

Coedarhydyglyn, Nr Cardiff

SIR CENNYDD AND LADY TRAHERNE

Coedarhydyglyn has been described in the

past as a large 'palace' in miniature. The parkland and woods were laid out in the second decade of the last century and the building of the house was completed in 1821. The original woods were underplanted with laurel, yews, privet and hawthorns, the two latter types considered as flowering shrubs. The main trees were beech, oak, ash and a number of Lawson's cypresses. During the next fifty years new specimens were planted – monkey puzzles, *Cryptomeria japonica* and *C.j.* 'Elegans', and a large *Sequoia sempervirens*. As *Rhododendron* species became available and popular they were planted in the woodlands, and include a large ancient specimen of *Rhododendron arboreum*, the first rhododendron to be introduced from the Himalayas.

At the beginning of this century a fine Japanese garden was made on the sides of a small stream. Many interesting maples, flowering cherries, bamboos and magnolias were planted and many of these still remain. During the First World War no new activities took place but in 1938 there were many additions to the Japanese garden from the Dyffryn Gardens. Then in 1944 replanting started in the wood where softwoods had been cut for war use. About five acres were planted with over one hundred and ten different species and they are arranged by continent – Asia, Americas, Europe and Australasia. The collection is continually being added to and now after forty years is a very attractive sight. Also in the past forty years many new rhododendrons have been planted in the woods together with a cypress garden including some good specimens of Lawson's cypresses. The house is situated on the side of a glyn with a good view to the north, and land rising to the east and south. There is a small rose garden and pergola near the house and a modern shrub border on the north side. Strong shoes are essential if one wishes to enjoy the grounds and woods.

◆

The Dingle, Welshpool
MR AND MRS D.R. JOSEPH

Right from the start we decided to have generous planting of evergreens for winter, and other bright foliage shrubs for summer, as a background to bulbs, azaleas, roses and herbaceous flowers.

Because of this, it seemed simpler to work to a theme. So, we have lime-green leaves with red and white flowers; silver-foliaged shrubs with blue and yellow; copper and grey-blue with apricot, and white with all shades and textures of green. At present we are experimenting with *Berberis temolaica*, Koster's blue spruce and *Cupressus arizonica* as a foil for acid-yellow day lilies, *Kniphofia* 'Little Maid', *Helichrysum* 'Sulphur Light' and other cream or greenish-yellow flowers.

The garden slopes steeply to the south, down to a half-acre pool with a 'Japanese' bridge. This gives us an opportunity to use reflectors. All year the tapestry colours of the bank are enhanced by its double in the water.

But the pool really comes into its own in winter when, clear of weeds, it reflects all the bright barks round its edge. *Cornus alba* 'Sibirica' looks very splendid flanked by the white plumes of pampas grass. *Cornus stolonifera* 'Flaviramea' and *Cornus* 'Kesselringi' contrast with each other, while the warm tones of *Salix alba* 'Chermesina' echoes the orange twigs and catkins of *Alnus incana* 'Aurea'. Even on the dreariest days of winter, there is something to cheer us.

◆

Ewenny Priory, Nr Bridgend
R.C.Q. PICTON TURBERVILL, ESQ.

The garden has seen many ups and downs since the priory was reconstructed early in the nineteenth century, from a messy grass cover to high Victoriana to present-day form. In all, it covers six acres; however, it cannot be divorced from the twelfth-century remains which consist of a portcullis, South Tower Gate, Columbarium, thirteenth-century tower and a large unspoilt Norman cruciform church, the whole mainly connected by a curtain wall. As is to be expected, there are many mature trees, amongst them lime, beech, yew, pine, horse chestnut, walnut, weeping ash, wellingtonia, Canadian maple, white poplars and *Ginkgo*.

Facing south, in places exposed to east and west, the purpose of this alkaline garden is by degrees to melt into the country and vice versa. To achieve this is not easy as the shape is long and comparatively narrow. The wings on the east and west are partly woodland with primulas, bulbs and shrubs, with small flowing ponds on the east, and on the west a small lake with lilies, white poplars and bog plants.

The south side is close mown grass, bulbs planted annually, daffodils and tulips, followed by annuals, usually the scented tobacco. Mown grass extends to a stream with willows and bog life. Beyond this is a forty-acre field mown around the circumference with a long grass drive to a nineteenth-century copy of an eleventh-century gate house. This garden is at its best in spring and mid-to-late summer; in spring with bulbs and shrubs, cherries, *Amelanchier*, *Viburnum*, *Osmanthus*, *Magnolia*, *Enkianthus*, *Choisya*, *Sambucus*, *Zanthoxylum* and many others; in summer, with fully blown roses (climbing and tea), perennials, lilies, scented annuals and peacocks strutting whilst their tails last, a place of peace and interest.

◆

Garreg Farm, Glandyfi
LT. COL. AND MRS P.A. LATHAM

Our aim in this garden is to provide colour for as long a time as possible. The courtyard walls are clothed with *Pyracantha*, *Cotoneaster*, variegated ivies, *Jasminum nudiflorum* and lots of *Parthenocissus tricuspidata*. *Clematis montana rubens* and *Wisteria* cover one corner and honeysuckle and climbing roses peek over the lower walls from the main garden. Troughs

and raised beds start the year with bulbs, pansies, and wallflowers, to be followed by fuchsias, petunias and pink geraniums, which also feature in window-boxes and huge hanging baskets made from the rims of old bicycle wheels and wire. Doronicums and blue *Pulmonaria* start the colour in the herbaceous border, which later becomes a riot of cottage-garden flowers. Hybrid tea roses are underplanted with *Iberis* and *Aubrieta* which are cut back after flowering to form a green carpet for the rest of the year. Rhododendrons and daffodils provide spring colour in the greener areas of the garden, but summer-flowering shrubs do not like the cold inhospitable grey stony clay. Formerly ailing shrubs and plants have found a home in a small 'do-or-die' corner of salt-marsh near the tidal stream, whose banks have daffodils in spring and, later, yellow flags and other *Iris* among the wild sedges and grasses.

◆

Glebe House, Guilsfield
MRS JENKINS AND MRS HABBERLEY

Glebe House was the domestic half of the old Guilsfield Vicarage, whose mellow brickwork forms a background to many varieties of *Clematis*, some climbing among roses or fruit trees. A flagged, small courtyard, cool in summer, has heathers, alpine strawberries, and rampant hardy *Cyclamen*. The kitchen garden supplies fresh vegetables, while half a dozen 'Müller-Thurgau' vines against a fence show promise. Several old varieties of apple are to be trained into arches; a fruit cage contains raspberries and gooseberries, red and white currants. In a small greenhouse are grown tomatoes and a 'Black Hamburg' grape.

The central lawned area, shaded by a horse chestnut, contains a raised alpine bed, an outdoor grape and mixed borders. Behind the house an orchard of old fruit trees is carpeted with snowdrops and daffodils in the spring and is dominated by a large wellingtonia. A small goldfish pool and bog garden bordered by a mixed *Chaenomeles* hedge finishes off the garden.

◆

The Graig, Pen-y-Clawdd
MRS RAINFORTH

The Graig was originally two very small cottages facing east, with small square front gardens divided by a stone path. This layout was kept to preserve the cottage garden feeling. The centre of one front garden is now a rose bed, while the other has heathers and conifers, and both are edged by stone paths leaving borders for herbaceous plants. The centre path is at a lower level with stone walls giving good conditions for rock plants.

The house is on a hill and in 1960, when a south wing was added, the old orchard became a lawn sloping gently to the ha-ha, giving a wonderful unrestricted view of the valley and the Welsh hills beyond. Where the ground falls away more steeply there are tall old-fashioned shrub roses; seen thus from above one can appreciate the blooms more fully.

Beyond the front gardens was a large hollow, used for rubbish before council collections started. Gradually cleaned, this proved to be a natural bog and is now planted with moisture-loving plants. On the far side is a tall *Salix matsudana* 'Tortuosa' grown from a slip in 1965. The vegetables are divided from the gravel drive by a heather hedge thirty yards long, one part *Erica* 'Arthur Johnson' which flowers from January to Easter, the other *Erica* 'Silberschmelze', white, which usually starts flowering by Christmas. On the other side of the drive are hundreds of *Crocus* species and snowdrops with winter-flowering shrubs, primroses and violets. This concentrates all the winter and early spring flowers between the front gate and the house, where they are constantly seen, and not, like Wordsworth's violet, 'half hidden from the eye'.

The Dingle, Welshpool, in May. Contrasting and complementary foliage, evergreens and coloured twigs provide interest both in winter and summer (see previous page).

The Hall, Angle
MAJ. J.N.S. ALLEN-MIREHOUSE

Angle is situated in the extreme south-west of Pembrokeshire and therefore we have a Gulf Stream garden, although this feature is slightly mitigated by some lack of shelter, particularly from the north and east. Nevertheless, as well as the usual palms we have an outdoor mimosa and our unheated conservatory contains an outstanding *Bougainvillea* and *Plumbago*, *Datura suaveolens*, *Aeonium* and *Nerium oleander*.

The entire garden, which is on the edge of the Haven estuary, has a very slight slope to the north and consists of three virtually separate gardens, the east, the west and a walled garden. This latter is our best protection against the ravages of wind, small children, rabbits and peacocks which take their toll of any new and tender plant. The east garden is quite separate from the west and contains two banks of trees grandly known as 'The Shrubbery'. There are stands of bamboo, *Rhododendron* and *Hydrangea* and a fine bank of camellias about eighty years old. Edging the front lawn are copper beeches and horse-chestnuts, a Judas tree and double-flowered cherries, with a magnificent stand of hydrangeas at their best in August.

The west garden is much newer, having been a field as recently as 1950, and it is here that we are building up a shelter belt of mixed hardwoods and planting shrub roses, hebes, brooms and *Pieris*. The walled garden has three greenhouses in various stages of disrepair, full of clivias, crinums, geraniums, houseplants, carnations, billbergias, vegetables and melons. The garden is used in the best Scottish and Irish traditions, not merely as a kitchen garden but also as an enclosure in which to grow flowers and meander. So we have a totally unfashionable but very colourful and useful mixture of fruit, vegetables and stands of flowers to cut for the house – *Agapanthus*, paeonies, delphiniums, alstroemerias, dahlias, roses, gladioli, tulips and chrysanthemums, all watched over by a venerable *Ginkgo* tree. By growing stocks and sweet peas in the greenhouse we can have cut flowers for the house for ten months of the year.

To summarize, not a plantsman's or specialist's garden, but a spectacular setting on the water's edge and the mild climate compensates for this.

The Hill Cottage, Bausley
MR AND MRS A.T. BAREHAM

Spring and early summer, when most of the alpines are in bloom, are the best times to visit this garden. The garden, which covers just under one acre, has been developed since 1972 from rough hill pasture on an exposed location, and it features island beds and borders, a peat bed and a bog garden formed around a natural spring. All these contain a wide variety of shrubs, conifers and perennial plants. There is also a rockery, rock walls, sink gardens and a sunny bank where alpines are grown.

Those wary of planting conifers in their garden because of their possible rate of growth may find reassurance that many desirable dwarf forms exist after seeing them here.

Llanfair Court, Nr Abergavenny
SIR WILLIAM AND LADY CRAWSHAY

In order to complement the house, we have tried to show examples, on a small scale, of various features carried out in the execution of historical garden plans.

Facing the sixteenth-century side there is a walled courtyard with climbing shrubs such as *Clematis* and roses underplanted with beds of annuals. A door leads through to an eighteenth-century front with lawns divided from fields by a ha-ha; off these is a small rock garden, and a formal water garden with pools, cascades and fountains.

Continuing on, we come to a traditional herbaceous border and a rose garden, half formal and half mixed with hellebores, irises, bulbs, perennials and small flowering shrubs. Clipped yew and *Thuja* hedges separate the gardens and examples of contemporary and classical sculpture are sited between specimen flowering trees and shrubs.

Llysdinam, Newbridge-on-Wye
LADY DELIA VENABLES-LLEWELLYN AND LLYSDINAM CHARITABLE TRUST

Late May and early June, when the old-established azaleas are in flower, is probably the best time to visit this garden, but there is plenty to see at other seasons, from sheets of daffodils in spring to autumn colour and always the superb view across the valley of the upper Wye.

Looking from the house a long sweep of lawn, dominated by a fine Turkey oak, has a partly raised border backed by a yew hedge on one side. The raised part of the border has polyanthus and small bulbs in spring, followed by irises, paeonies and cottage pinks with variegated-leaved geraniums and dahlias for late summer. At the end of the lawn is a small shrub garden and beyond it a fine stand of very old Ghent azaleas backed by woodland.

A lower path leads past a border of flame-coloured *mollis* and other azaleas interplanted with *Hemerocallis*, *Aconitum vulparia*, *Antholyza*, *Kirengeshoma* and *Clematis viticella* 'Alba' for later colour. Below this border a small pond is surrounded by moisture-loving plants including large clumps of *Osmunda*, *Peltiphyllum* and *Lysichitum*. A bridge over the pond leads to what was once a large rock garden and which is now planted with small shrubs and ground-cover plants for easier maintenance. Returning across the main lawn a gate in the yew hedge leads into the kitchen

Lower House Farm, Nantyderry, in July. A gay border of annuals with pink and white *Lavatera trimestris*, cornflowers, *Salvia sclarea* and orange marigolds.

garden with its double herbaceous borders leading to the greenhouses.

Lower House Farm, Nantyderry
MR AND MRS GLYNNE CLAY

This medium-sized garden has been designed to be of interest from early spring to late autumn. We are lucky to have a mildly acid, free-draining soil and a good supply of farmyard manure, but we do suffer damage from wind and late frosts.

A wide range of colourful and unusual plants are grown in mixed beds, and priority is given to those with a long season of interest. Foliage is particularly valued, and many golden, purple and variegated leaves are to be found. Late-rooted cuttings of tender perennials such as *Osteospermum*, *Gazania*, and *Verbena* are overwintered under frost-free conditions and planted out in May.

The yellow trumpets of *Narcissus* 'February Gold' usher in the daffodil season and drifts of later varieties carry it on; 'Binkie' is particularly admired in the drive. A shallow ditch meanders gently through the garden and its margins provide a home for moisture-loving subjects. Here you will find many old favourites such as *Hosta*, *Astilbe*, *Ligularia*, and *Iris sibirica* as well as the more unusual *Gillenia*, *Tricyrtis* and *Roscoea*.

A paved garden created only two years ago already looks mature and the crevices between the York stones are rapidly filling up. Nature has helped with many self-sown seedlings, some quite unexpected!

A short walk, past *Sorbus* and *Betula* species planted for autumn colour, brings one to a small wooded island surrounded by a stream. Here are mossy paths and a collection of ferns; in spring it is carpeted with wood

anemones, bluebells and wood sorrel that all just arrived once the brambles had been removed.

In order to keep the garden interesting we try to make something new every year and do not hesitate to move around the existing plants and features.

Maenllwyd Isaf, Abermule
MRS DENISE HATCHARD

The house is a typical black and white yeoman's farmhouse of about 1580, rundown and pathetic (and not even electricity!) when I bought it in a mad moment thirty years ago. Its assets were a bowling green and a bricked drive, in the eye of the sun, a tall hill to the north and between house and hill a steep little valley and rushing river.

The house and farm buildings are now kempt, much of the work done myself, learning as I went and sacking myself when necessary. The pigsties have been turned into a little orangery with classical leanings.

Of the seventeen acres, about three have been gardened and include a wood and a wild garden. There is now no bowling green but lawns, island beds, trees and shrubs with interesting leaves and conifers for winter interest. There are different vistas from the house windows and a tendency always for the garden to expand, change and be crammed full.

A small, tallish, tufa bed was made this spring and is well-established and nice to lean on. The goldfish pool has to be netted against herons and kingfishers and its spoil made the base of the rockery and an area of scree.

The wood, now thinned (it was impossible to get through it) has encouraged the return of windflowers, bluebells and many ferns.

Hostas and rhododendrons–overflows from the garden–are being planted there. It is lovely to look down on to pale *Rhododendron* flowers surrounded by glaucous hostas in the steep part of the wood and below that the river.

Peat blocks are edging a new peat bed and it is hoped that erythroniums, roscoeas and other delights will enjoy this. A new primula bed at the back of the house shows great promise with morning and evening sun only. It had been the ash tip for generations.

---

7 New Street, Talybont
MISS M.J. HENRY

This garden at the rear of a stone terraced house measures five by twenty-five yards. I have re-made it myself in recent years to give surprise and variety by as many different means as possible. Meandering paths and small flights of steps lead from one aspect and level to another. Little 'rooms' offer sitting places in sun and shade, where plants crowd together to give the effect of a long-established garden. Influences from cottage and Japanese gardens show in the use of pottery and natural objects as ornaments. Home-made troughs display alpines and dwarf conifers. A special feature is the collection of pots and portable troughs containing small trees and brilliant flowers to cheer dull corners. Tall conifers contrast with rock-plants scrambling over low walls and terraced beds. The hard-wearing and easily maintained paths are laid with sea-washed bricks and pebbles from the beach. A handsome plant at all times is the *Hamamelis mollis* trained as an espalier and now extending over many feet. A number of other shrubs have been given restrictive training to make the most of space, and a miniature greenhouse completes this retreat in a busy village.

Penrallt Ffynnon, Cwm-Cou
MR R.D. LORD

This garden of nearly five acres lies on the steep western side of a small valley running north from the Teifi valley. On a naturally windy steep site the wind can be only partially kept out, but neither can the very good views, and in most of the garden one is agreeably conscious of the country outside.

Before the garden was started in 1971 there were two old-style meadows whose wild flowers re-assert themselves at all times among the plantings and whenever mowing is neglected. Garden-making has consisted of digging, planting and mowing the original grass. The result is a number of large beds and borders separated by grass paths and large grass areas. Informal hedges give shelter and form, the most notable being one of *Camellia* × *williamsii* cultivars, which flower well in March and April. Three lines of Japanese cherries also help in this respect; especially pleasing is one of 'Tai Haku'.

Rhoose Farm House, Barry, in July. The rounded hummocks of *Santolina chamaecyparissus* echo the curves of the sculpture.

There are many rhododendrons here, several valued not for flower but for foliage; *R. bureavii* and *lepidostylum* are best, but there are others. Nor should I forget the autumn colours of a patch of the old yellow azalea, *R. luteum*. A great effect, quite different from that of any other tall tree, is made by eight species of *Eucalyptus*.

A list of uncommon genera (*Aronia, Halesia, Meliosma, Trochodendron, Clethra, Stuartia,* and *Colletia*) invites the charge of 'label gardening', but there are also common plants in abundance. For example, many roses (but no modern bedding types), paeonies and day lilies, as well as bulbs, where pride of place goes to over two hundred kinds of *Narcissus* in grass or borders. Unfortunately, crocuses (and *Tulipa tarda*!) though often tried, seem strictly for the mice.

Powis Castle Gardens, Nr Welshpool
THE NATIONAL TRUST

These wonderful gardens with hanging terraces were laid out in 1720, in the Italian style, by an unknown Englishman. Owing to their south-east-facing aspect and well-drained limey soil, they harbour a collection of rare and rather tender plants, including huge shrubs of *Artemisia* 'Powis Castle', which looks well against the red limestone walls.

The kitchen garden is laid out with formal gardens, and surrounded with dwarf apple and pear trees in many ancient varieties.

There is an extensive wild garden on acid soil, with huge oaks, and many exotic trees and rhododendrons.

Rhoose Farm House, Nr Barry
PROF. A.L. COCHRANE

The garden has been developed from a field on one side of an old farmhouse and the farmyard on the other. The soil is alkaline and heavy. On one wall at the front of the house is a fine *Rosa banksiae* and on a raised wall is a collection of alpines in seventeenth-century pig troughs. At the side of the house is a free-flowering *Sophora tetraptera* and a young *Fremontodendron californicum*.

From the pig troughs a lawn leads to Hepworth's 'Meridian' backed by flowering cherries. The lawn is flanked on the right by rose beds at the side of the vegetable garden, which leads to old-fashioned roses. To the right is a shrub avenue, containing shrubs from New Zealand and Australia such as *Phormium tenax, Olearia macrodonta* and *Corokia cotoneaster*.

Continuing past the old-fashioned roses one comes to a secluded area with a large *Magnolia delavayi*, roses and trees in grass. Steps lead to the swimming pool, with stone walls on two sides, sheltering climbers such as *Actinidia chinensis*, shrubs and many paeonies.

Along the top of the garden are sculptures by Hepworth and Nicholas; a lily pool is backed by a striking *Clematis*. A *Cistus* avenue now returns to the front, completing the encirclement of the vegetable garden, part of which is now devoted to collecting varieties of the genus *Phormium*. On the other side of the house are the seventeenth-century arches of Nicholas' gallery, and the scree garden which contains many conifers, *Helichrysum*, bulbs, ground-cover such as *Zauschneria* and cotoneasters which have been trained to criss-cross the area. On one side is a willow-surrounded pool containing a copy of a seventeenth-century Welsh fountain, while on the other is a copy of a tenth-century Welsh cross.

◆

Saundersfoot Bay Leisure Park
IAN SHUTTLEWORTH, ESQ.

This is a garden built in and around a modern caravan park and its success can be measured by the fact that the gardens are now more dominant than the caravans. The garden slopes gently to the east with magnificent views of the Bristol Channel, and great care has been taken to ensure that the gardens blend into the surrounding woodland and pasture land. Because of our location we enjoy a mean temperature a few degrees higher than many parts of Great Britain (this is the early potato county) and advantage has been taken of this, in order to cultivate shrubs and plants not usually seen elsewhere. The grass everywhere is lush and like a lawn, making a perfect background to the many shrubs and flower borders.

Planning the gardens, bearing in mind the need for summer displays, has meant limiting the selection of plants to those that flower from March to early October. Much use is made of hydrangeas – including *H. quercifolia*, *H. serrata* and lace caps – hebes in variety, escallonias, hardy and semi-hardy fuchsias, geraniums, mallows and *Osteospermum*. The season begins with drifts of our native *Narcissus pseudonarcissus* subsp. *obvallaris*, the Tenby daffodil, in March. Amongst the recently planted specimen trees are *Catalpa bignonioides* and its striking golden-leaved variant, *Betula pendula*, *Betula pendula* 'Purpurea' and *B. papyrifera*, *Cordyline australis*, *Liriodendron tulipifera* 'Aureomarginatum' and *Eucryphia* 'Nymansay'. A new feature in 1984 was the planting of a long bed of shrub roses, using selected climbing roses as ground-cover, and in 1985 work was concentrated on a large rock garden and water feature which complements a stream-side border of azaleas and rhododendrons, primulas, astilbes and *Alchemilla mollis*.

◆

Slebech Hall, Nr Haverford West
THE LADY JEAN PHILLIPS

The outstanding feature of this garden is its position on the tidal river Cleddau and the picturesque ruins of the Knights Hospitallers church of St John of Jerusalem which comprise part of the garden.

The orchard and kitchen garden are protected from the north-east by an old wall and the orchard is terraced; above this is a border with many different plants and shrubs including

Carpenteria californica and the golden-leaved *Philadelphus*.

During June the roses are a feature and in early July *Rosa filipes* 'Kiftsgate' is in full flower, cascading spectacularly through the west window of the ruined church. In early May the cherry avenue to the church is worth seeing. In the churchyard there are azaleas and camellias as the soil is acid; the problem – being near the sea – is the westerly wind, but if the site is carefully chosen, quite tender things such as *Hebe hulkeana* can be grown.

◆

Trawscoed Hall, Welshpool
MR AND MRS J.G.K. WILLIAMS

The house was built in about 1560 by Sir Roland Heywood when he acquired vast tracts of land formerly belonging to Strata Marcella. He was Lord Mayor of London and owner of two manors in Kent, and two in Shropshire. The garden slopes towards the south and flows into deciduous primaeval woodland with particularly outstanding oaks.

The soil has a pH of 7, and leafmould is the only fertilizer used. In 1960 the shrubs started to suffer severely from honey fungus, and many of the existing shrubs have been planted since that time. The most spectacular plant is the *Wisteria* covering the house.

In spring drifts of naturalized daffodils are followed by rhododendrons and a succession of flowering plants throughout the summer until the autumn colours take over.

◆

The Walled Garden, Knill
MRS S. VOELKER

The small Norman church of Knill, and the Walled Garden, lie in a valley scooped out by a glacier which also shaped the surrounding tree-clad hills. On the south side the garden is bordered by the sparkling Hindlewell Brook.

The house is encircled by the garden, and its windows look over a spacious lawn sloping down to the stream, on the banks of which grow the huge-leaved *Gunnera*, willows, clumps of *Iris kaempferi* and *Iris sibirica*, ferns, primulas and hostas.

High mellow brick walls abut the house at either end and curve gently round to join the brook, thus enclosing the lawn – and protecting the fruit trees, old roses, wisterias, *Clematis*, a lily-pond with goldfish and, in the spring, a beautiful white paeony and gentians.

To the north of the house are mixed borders against stone walls, full of delphiniums, bearded irises, poppies, geraniums and other summer-flowering perennials.

On the west edge lies a damp area, planted with shrubs and bog-loving plants, happy in

an alkaline soil, provided they receive plenty of leafmould and compost. The area of the property is about three acres and the temptation has been to extend the garden, to create just one more patch, so that outside the walls *Cyclamen* cluster thickly under chestnut trees and a more intimate garden with a stone bench now borders the stream as it runs alongside the drive; on the opposite side (known as the dingle) is a small area of trees underplanted with bluebells, daffodils and lilies-of-the-valley.

It has been of absorbing interest making this garden, which was completely derelict when we arrived twenty years ago – but its real attraction lies in the ever-changing beauty of its setting.

◆

Yew Tree Nursery, Lydart
MR AND MRS JOHN HARPER

The garden, developed since 1955 near the top of a six-hundred-foot escarpment of sand and puddingstone, has marvellous views westwards over the Welsh mountains. The yew tree itself is very old and reduced to a leafy sphere which, with a cap of snow, resembles a traditional Christmas pudding.

The acid soil, together with wooded protection from gales and biting easterlies, is ideal for rhododendrons and a wide collection of unusual trees and shrubs. Thus we are able to grow such half-hardies as *Leycesteria crocothyrsos*, *Clerodendrum bungei* and *Abutilon* varieties. These, with herbaceous plants and alpines in streamside beds, walls and troughs, have become the stock plants for a small nursery to satisfy numerous requests for plants.

A hilly garden of this size presents problems that we must surmount before our vigour diminishes with advancing years. Compost heaps are sited above the areas destined for their products as it is so much easier to carry loose herbage uphill and wheel dense good stuff down. Thick moss on slippery grass slopes is not discouraged for the sure foothold it provides.

From the depths of winter with witch hazels and *Helleborus corsicus* in bloom, there is a constant succession of flower and foliage until the waning days of autumn produce brilliant colours in maples and mountain ashes. Other surprises can be arranged: *Xanthorrhiza simplicissima* with its purple-green leaves has striking yellow underground stems – a few of which can be left exposed as if by accident; grow *Mahonia japonica* in a poor soil and some forms produce contrasting red leaves that last through winter; and *Fascicularia pitcairniifolia* – why not grow it on its side in a specially built nook near the top of a stone wall to show off its brilliant blue inflorescence at the red base to the shuttle-cock of leaves?

WARWICKSHIRE AND WEST MIDLANDS

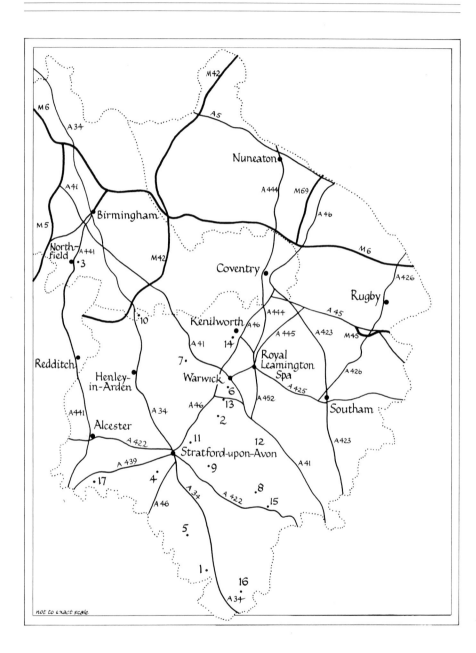

not to exact scale

Directions to Gardens

Barton House, Barton-on-the-Heath, 3 miles east of Moreton-in-Marsh. [1]

Cedar House, Wasperton, 4 miles south of Warwick. [2]

The Davids, Hole Lane, Northfield, Birmingham. [3]

Elm Close, Binton Road, Welford-on-Avon, 5 miles southwest of Stratford-upon-Avon. [4]

Foxcote, 4½ miles west of Shipston-on-Stour. [5]

17 Gerrard Street, Warwick. [6]

Hickecroft, Mill Lane, Rowington, 6 miles northwest of Warwick. [7]

Ilmington Gardens, 8 miles south of Stratford-upon-Avon, 4 miles northwest of Shipston-on-Stour. [5]
> **Crab Mill; Foxcote Hill; Foxcote Hill Cottage; Frog Orchard; Grey Cottage; Loreto; Pear Tree Cottage; Rose Cottage.**

Ilmington Manor, Ilmington (for directions see above). [5]

Ivy Lodge, Radway, 7 miles northwest of Banbury, Oxon. [8]

Loxley Hall, 4 miles southeast of Stratford-upon-Avon. [9]

Packwood House, 1½ miles east of Hockley Heath, 11 miles southeast of Birmingham. [10]

Parham Lodge, Alveston, 2 miles northeast of Stratford-upon-Avon. [11]

Pittern Hill Farm, Kineton, 12 miles southeast of Warwick. [12]

Puddocks, Frog Lane, Ilmington (for directions see Ilmington Gardens). [5]

Sherbourne Park, 3 miles south of Warwick, ½ mile north of Barford. [13]

The Spring, Upper Spring Lane, Kenilworth. [14]

Upton House Gardens, 2 miles south of Edgehill, 7 miles northwest of Banbury, Oxon. [15]

Whichford and Ascott Gardens, 6 miles southeast of Shipston-on-Stour. [16]
> **The Old Rectory; Brook Hollow; Whichford House; Rightons Cottage; The Gateway; Stone Walls.**

Woodpeckers, Marlcliff, near Bidford-on-Avon. [17]

◆

Barton House, Barton-on-the-Heath
DR I.A. BEWLEY CATHIE

Fortunately, and unusually for the Cotswolds, Barton House is sited on top of a hill mainly of clay with a high water table. Rhododendrons are the special feature of the five-acre garden whose only level site is a crown bowling green. The size means that it cannot all be kept immaculate, and successive areas among the shrubberies are devoted either to special plants or to a particular colour.

After drifts of daffodils there are some species rhododendrons, mainly in May (sadly the large-leaved varieties do not survive well), followed by masses of brilliantly-coloured hybrids from then until July. Azaleas follow these, and there are also many fine trees. The

Ilmington Manor, Warwickshire, in May (for description of this garden see page 207). In this view yellow lily-flowered tulips and forget-me-nots are balanced by bluebells and buttercups in the grass.

Scots pines at the gates date from 1945, and visitors like the *Tropaeolum speciosum* which relieves the dullness of the yew and box background.

Cedar House, Wasperton
MR AND MRS D.L. BURBIDGE

This well-matured garden of about three acres faces south, the main lawn dominated by two three-hundred-year-old cedars of Lebanon. The soil is light, sandy and neutral, and offers such a tremendous variety of plants and shrubs that there is always something pretty to pick for the house from January to December. The house was once the Rectory for the little church standing beside it. There are a wealth of places to sit, rest and enjoy, especially a little terrace garden, enclosed by climbing roses, *Hibiscus*, honeysuckle and crinums, looking over a lawn to old-fashioned shrub roses, a wonderfully coloured maple, *Acer negundo* 'Variegatum', cotoneasters, and many others.

Search carefully and you will find a secret garden to sit and admire the rhododendrons, weeping cherry, primroses and forget-me-nots in the spring. Walk through daffodils carpeting the little arboretum of silver birch,

Deciduous azaleas, bluebells, and the leaves of *Helleborus foetidus* at Sherbourne Park in May (for description see page 208).

Japanese maple, medlar, *Acer griseum*, and blue spruce, and on to the woodland we are in the process of replanting. Sit by the fish pond and look across to the *Cotinus coggygria* with the pink poppy 'Mrs Perry' growing through it. Can you spot the hidden entrance to the church? Visit the swimming pool area and see the climbers thriving against the south-facing wall, a riot of colour in summer, helped along by *Clematis montana* and *C. montana* 'Rubens' in the spring.

The Davids, Northfield
MRS J. CADBURY

The Davids is something of an oasis within five miles of the centre of Birmingham. With its fields, trees and shrubs it is a haven for birds and inhabited by three or four foxes. Surrounded by shrubs and flowering trees of all kinds, rhododendrons and azaleas and every shade of green, the house and garden are shielded from the busy surrounding roads.

The sloping ground lends itself to a series of vistas; the terrace leads to the rose beds and herbaceous borders which flank a lawn with a yew hedge, leading on through a gap to an avenue of birch trees.

Up the hill slopes a large lawn leading up to more trees and a collection of ancient cannons and guns, some of which came from the Tower of London having been captured in battle in different parts of the world. Nearby is a natural swimming pool with daffodils, primroses and bluebells on the banks but too cold for those used to heated pools. In spring daffodils and crocuses flourish as harbingers of the colours to come in July.

◆

Elm Close, Welford-on-Avon

MR AND MRS E.W. DYER

Welford-on-Avon is a beautiful village with an attractive church, a maypole, many picturesque beamed and thatched cottages, riverside walks (there is a small weir), and excellent refreshment facilities available from the local inns.

Elm Close has a garden of two-thirds of an acre which five years ago was almost totally devoted to lawn, with just a few shrubs and trees and a dozen lonely daffodils.

Within the garden now the visitor will find a rock garden, a scree, island beds, pergolas with climbing plants, pools, formal borders, sinks and troughs with alpines, numerous dwarf conifers, many varieties of *Clematis*, thousands of small bulbs, a selection of maples and other foliage plants.

The aim has been to provide colour also in winter, both with flowering shrubs and plants, and by the inclusion of a variety of conifers in different shades and textures. From the snowdrops, aconites and hellebores of earliest spring, to the winter-flowering *Iris unguicularis*, *Hamamelis mollis* and *Viburnum* × *bodnantense* there is something in bloom in the garden all the year round.

◆

Foxcote, Nr Shipston-on-Stour

MR AND THE HON. MRS HOLMAN

We came to live here twenty-five years ago when I was totally ignorant about gardens and gardening, and it was only when my children grew up that I suddenly awakened to the fact that here was enormous scope and a great new interest in my life. As we are surrounded by wonderful and well-known gardens, all I had to do was look, listen and learn. We were lucky to find here a formal structure of mature yew and beech hedges, and although I am still no horticulturist, I have now filled the borders with shrubs, roses, irises, lavender and selected annuals, grown at home from seed, all thrown in rather higgledy-piggledy but making wonderful colour for many months. The walled kitchen garden, however, is very orderly and productive with a large range of vegetables, herbs and fruit and some fine old fig trees. All this is thanks to Mr Peachey who starts work with first light and goes on till dusk. He is also a forester and an extra hand on the farm, whistles while he works and is ably assisted by his wife.

We have recently rebuilt the fifteenth-century monastery fish ponds at the bottom of the garden, and now stocked with trout they give an added interest and make a fine setting for the classical early Georgian house.

◆

17 Gerrard Street, Warwick

MISS P.M. AND MR T.K. MEREDITH

This is a small walled town garden of a sixth of an acre, which we bought in 1975, but serious gardening did not start until 1978. There had been a garden here for many decades (the 1855 map of Warwick shows an entirely different layout), at one time in good order, but the previous owner had been defeated by the years so that golden rod and seedling Michaelmas daisies were the main feature.

The removal of four dead apple trees and the making of new steps and flagged paths were satisfactorily accomplished to a very simple design.

The garden now presents a splendid jumble of assorted plants, almost certainly horrifying to the professional garden designer but reasonably satisfying to the owners, who are also well aware of some of its weaknesses. Much remains to be sorted out and improved but all the year round there is something of interest to be seen.

We are strong on *Clematis* with over twenty at present, including *C. rehderiana*, *connata* and *grata*, the last two grown from Kashmir seed. Hellebores, euphorbias, *Geranium* species in variety, *Meconopsis* and lilies are all featured and many other plants reflecting our current, but constantly changing, tastes.

Abutilon vitifolium gives a real show over several weeks as does *Indigofera gerardiana*, planted against a wall and growing to ten feet in a good year. The dark velvety red *Clematis* 'Niobe' links it with the rose 'Grüss an Teplitz'. 'Madame Isaac Pereire' is one of our better roses and in the spring 'Madame Grégoire Staechelin' gives freely of her charms on an east wall.

◆

Hickecroft, Rowington

MR AND MRS J.M. PITTS

The two-acre garden has been designed and created since 1980 around the nucleus of an older garden, surrounding a rambling red-brick house dating back to 1547. The site slopes gently to the west with pleasing views over countryside. One of the main aims of the design has been to create a more sheltered and varied environment to show off a collection of plants consisting primarily of shrubs and herbaceous perennials. Sadly there are few existing mature trees, but now many interesting and less usual trees are becoming established.

Near the house is a small formal lawn surrounded by simple yew and box topiary and borders, some of which are bedded annually. This year's combination of *Helichrysum* 'Microphyllum' and *Verbena* 'Silver Anne'

was most successful. Below this top lawn is a long gravel walk and narrow beds planted with alpines and herbaceous plants bordering what was originally a tennis lawn. From here the eye is drawn to the new yew walk, terminating in a young *Fagus sylvatica* 'Pendula'. To the right of the walk are mixed borders and beds of hybrid musk and bourbon roses, grouped round broad grass paths and a small lawn leading to a formal lily-pond, with plans for a garden pavilion and herb garden beyond. One grouping of note here, particularly at the time of opening, is *Astrantia major involucrata* running through a vigorous seedling of *Artemisia absinthium*, backed by *Pyrus salicifolia* 'Pendula' and *Salix purpurea* 'Gracilis'.

To the left of the yew walk is an area of mown paths through rough grass, devoted to trees and shrubs for autumn colour with spring bulbs. As with any young garden it is forever changing and expanding. Implementing these improvements is made simpler and more effective because they follow the principles of a master plan conceived in the garden's infancy, which is now at the exciting stage where it is beginning to mature.

◆

Ilmington Gardens

Crab Mill (PROF. D. C. HODGKIN)
Foxcote Hill (MR AND MRS M. DINGLEY)
Foxcote Hill Cottage (MISS A. TERRY)
Frog Orchard (MRS C. NAISH)
Grey Cottage (THE MISSES PARKER)
Loreto (MRS E. BLADON)
Pear Tree Cottage (DR AND MRS A. HOBSON)
Rose Cottage (MISS M. JAMES)

On a summer Sunday afternoon every year, eight or so gardens in Ilmington are open to the public for The National Gardens Scheme. These gardens are well contrasted. There are the large Manor gardens (described on page 207) and others of varying sizes and types, the smallest illustrating very ingenious use of deeply sloping ground being terraced and planted with many interesting plants and a variety of vegetables and fruit.

There is another small garden mostly paved, with pockets of unusual and most attractive small plants grouped with great artistry – the whole being bounded by Cotswold stone walls, a perfect background for flowers.

A long, beautifully maintained garden shows immaculately tended lawns, bordered by colourful beds of annuals and perennials and backed by an old orchard of graceful old fruit trees.

A small garden of the true cottage type has flowers, fruit and vegetables all jostling happily together by old fruit trees and some ancient 'out-houses'. Beehives are in a corner of another garden and the pathway to them is past beds abounding in colour, showing to advantage the charm of annuals, perennials and roses planted together – four gardens, all with the village stream flowing through, show great contrasts of planting its banks – astilbes, candelabra primulas, *Iris kaempferi* in one, ferns, shrubs and trees in others.

Views of the rolling Cotswold country are seen as one strolls through these gardens and throughout the afternoon Ilmington's own team of traditional Morris Men dance at each garden and outside the Village Hall.

Ilmington Manor

DENNIS L. FLOWER, ESQ.

This garden was created in 1919 from a rough orchard on a gentle slope by building walls and terracing of Cotswold stone, and growing yew hedges and borders all embellished by topiary and garden ornaments. The principal charm of the garden is the way the eye is drawn from two main vistas, to other parts which reveal smaller self-contained gardens each distinct in character, and all linked by wide lawns which are planted with specimen and fruit trees and a host of daffodils and crocuses. Starting down the drive, the paved pond garden appears with its central goldfish and lily pool, ornamented by carved stone. The surrounding beds partially enclosed by a trellis are planted with scented and aromatic plants and climbers. Next, passing through the forecourt, one may walk up the Pillar Border, named after the stone pillars with urns which flank its entrance and filled with a mixture of shrubs and herbaceous plants in colour groups.

Returning to the forecourt, the visitor should walk up steps into the formal rose garden with its stone summer-house. From here one looks along the main vista which ends in a fine stone seat marking the end of the long double border planted with old and modern shrub roses and softened by herbaceous flowers. Returning to the rose garden and turning left, one finds the Dutch Garden, a square enclosed by yew hedges, a secret and peaceful place planted as informally as a cottage garden. Continuing round one sees another border, the Garden House, trough garden, *Iris* and foliage beds, and then returns to the forecourt past the rock garden, a much loved and cherished feature. A regular visitor will notice that a number of interesting new plants are added each year.

(This garden is open in conjunction with others in Ilmington – see p. 206.)

Ivy Lodge, Radway

MRS M.A. WILLIS

This garden lies along the lower slopes of a steep, wooded ridge which faces north and two factors were pre-eminent in its planning and planting. First, since it covered almost five acres, it had to be labour-saving, and second, since the woods above it dominated the view, it had to seem to be almost a part of them, so foliage was as important as flowers. The trees and shrubs were planted to achieve

A view across the lake at Sherbourne Park in May with the temple and Sir Gilbert Scott's church spire (for description see page 208).

colour contrasts of gold, grey and red using, among others, *Berberis thunbergii atropurpurea*, *Fothergilla monticola*, *Amelanchier*, golden *Philadelphus* and golden elder, weeping pear and *Sorbus* 'Mitchellii'.

The garden is all grass underfoot with wide paths cut very short. There is an old orchard with bulbs thickly planted beneath the fruit trees. There is a pond bordered by water plants and full of waterlilies, and there is a series of big irregularly shaped beds which divide up the view.

From February to May there is a long succession of bulbs and blossom and by June the shrub roses are in flower together with clumps of tall blue campanulas, while drifts of many-coloured cranesbills give ground cover.

Loxley Hall, Nr Stratford-upon-Avon

COL. A. GREGORY-HOOD

Loxley is a garden designed as a series of domestic spaces or rooms, except for the lawns in front of the house which lead directly into the country. Each room has its own character and personality, its own colours and time of flowering.

A very unusual feature is the display of contemporary sculpture from the Juda Rowan Gallery in London. The layout of the garden suits admirably the placing of sculpture in the various rooms which are carefully sited to add a focus, or extra dimension, to the natural environment. Perhaps the most exciting moments in the garden are the daffodil lane in early spring, the *Laburnum* and *Iris* garden in late May, the herbaceous border in the wild rose garden in June, the shrub garden in the autumn and the sculpture at any time.

In addition, Loxley Church, which leads directly into the garden, is well worth a visit.

It is one of the oldest churches in the country, being founded in A.D. 761, and has a genuine Saxon wall complete with leper's squint (now filled in) which can be seen in the sanctuary. In early spring the snowdrops, primroses and anemones transform the churchyard into a carpet of flowers.

Packwood House, Nr Hockley Heath

THE NATIONAL TRUST

Probably the most famous feature of the gardens at Packwood are the famous old clipped yews, but there are also herbaceous plants and shrubs and roses trained on walls.

Parham Lodge, Alveston

MR AND MRS K.C. EDWARDS

We have made this garden since 1977, and have aimed for ease of maintenance with a variety of colour and texture and with foliage and flowers for flower arranging. It is a plantsman's garden with attention paid also to the needs of wildlife.

At the front is a small old woodland of lime, a large cedar, hornbeam, holly and a huge copper beech, with a woodland walk carpeted with ivies and violets. An old cedar throws delightful shadows on the croquet lawn and the paved barbecue area, and can be viewed from the summer house. The paved areas are decorated with hanging baskets, pots of fuchsias and planted sinks. Hostas in large pots give colour and movement and keep free from slugs – tucked into the greenhouse in winter, they provide early spring foliage. Behind the house is a large pond bounded by heathers and rockeries. *Pyrus salicifolia* 'Pendula' underplanted with 'Carlton' daffodils reflect into the pool, with *Salix sachalinensis* 'Sekka' adding form and colour as do the many fish. Island beds form places for the eye to rest; here grey and red foliage contrast and *Cupressus* in variety add texture. Honesty growing under *Betula pendula* is a picture in winter and spring. Bulbs are everywhere and flower throughout the year making a riot of colour or tranquil setting according to season. The long herbaceous bed comes into its own in high summer and the *Buddleja* corner is a delight. In the orchard the grass grows long and paeonies flower in drifts after the daffodils have faded.

Frost comes early and as late as June, so delicate plants are tucked in near the house, ready to cover with leaves or netting when temperatures get really low.

(Several other gardens in Alveston usually open jointly with this one.)

Pittern Hill Farm, Kineton
DR AND MRS M. MACGREGOR

This garden was devised in the 1930s around an eighteenth-century stone farmhouse with contemporary out-buildings. It lies on a southern hillside facing across the valley to Edgehill five miles away, and the garden merges into fields on all sides. The use of the natural contours and stone boundary walls provides diversity of shape and levels in a working garden of about one and a half acres, with orchards and vegetables as well as flowers. The soil is basically a heavy clay and roses grow well. Perhaps the most interesting features are the many mixed rose borders into which bedding plants and perennials are incorporated with pleasing effect.

Puddocks, Ilmington
MISS H.E. SYME

This is a cottage garden, perhaps at its best in spring when primroses pop up everywhere, even in the paths. The village stream runs through the garden and daffodils of many varieties grow on the banks, and the flower beds are a succession of colour – from snowdrops, scillas, *Chionodoxa* and *Anemone blanda* to bluebells. A golden privet hedge cut in an Adam swag helps to shield the fruit cage and small vegetable garden. At the foot of this hedge is a planting of collar or split corona daffodils, so useful in flower arranging.

As the season progresses the pink and silver bed comes into its own, with many pinks and border carnations, grey foliage plants and pink lavender bushes. This bed is backed by a low wall and steps up to the paved garden, where small plants grow in pockets of gravel, and various thymes spread a deliciously scented carpet, beloved by bees. *Crepis incana* generously seeds itself among the sisyrinchiums and rock roses. Dwarf irises cluster among beds of mixed perennials and large bearded irises grow in front of a *Lonicera* hedge – the most striking of these is the pure

white *Iris* 'Cliffs of Dover'. The soil is alkaline so *Clematis* enjoy growing here and *C. tangutica* spreads its seedlings everywhere. Many varieties of *Phlox* and perennial penstemons give colour in summer and *Rosa filipes* 'Kiftsgate' cascades from an old pear tree under which are various viburnums giving a succession of delicious perfumes early in the year. A hedge of lavender 'Munstead' greets one at the lane and a large pampas grass lends height near the drive. (This garden is open in conjunction with others in Ilmington – see page 206.)

Sherbourne Park, Nr Warwick
THE HON. MRS SMITH-RYLAND

I like a garden to be full of surprises, with little gardens incorporated into the whole. Over the last twenty-five years we have created a formal framework, comprising a series of avenues and vistas interspersed with hedges, ornamental walls and gateways, which lead you to a series of smaller gardens.

The Dutch garden, edged with box, is planted in silver and blue with standard honeysuckles. The roses in the middle beds are underplanted with blue violas, violets and primroses which give added colour in the spring. The yew-enclosed white garden leads on to the lake with a temple as a focal point amid a planting of unusual trees, the whole dominated by Sir Gilbert Scott's church spire. The view from the house leads between the croquet lawn borders to the ha-ha, where a lime avenue goes down across the River Avon. There is a cross-avenue of *Sorbus* on the bottom lawn which gives little vistas in four directions. I like to have continual interest in all areas, although the goldfish pond is orientated to spring and the swimming pool, where a *Salvia patens*, *Solanum jasminoides* 'Album' and a *Campsis radicans* give an added bonus, to summer. The mixed borders are planted in two or three colour combinations; by an August pruning a good second flowering in the autumn gives colour and interest all the year round.

The Spring, Kenilworth
MISS H. MARTIN

The garden here is set within a sunken fence, which separates it from surrounding fields and mixed woodland. Interesting features include a fine collection of azaleas, herbaceous and mixed borders, a large formal rose garden, and connecting lawns. The Victorian walled garden is a particularly fine example, and still retains its original use as a fruit and vegetable garden.

Upton House Gardens, Edgehill
THE RT HON. VISCOUNT BEARSTEAD; THE NATIONAL TRUST

Upton is situated on sandstone at an altitude

of seven hundred feet, and has a number of terraces and a rock garden which take advantage of these two natural features. The garden here is on the grand scale, with lawns, lakes and an impressive flight of stone steps, but there are also many interesting plants, particularly perennials and, around the lake, bog plants.

Whichford and Ascott Gardens

These adjoining villages are situated in an attractive valley in Warwickshire, at the northern point of the Cotswolds. Nearly all the houses are of local stone; with many springs in the hills, water in some form adds to the variety of the gardens.

The Old Rectory, Whichford (MR AND MRS R.M. SPITZLEY) Some years ago, the garden was made in a field, with a stream running through it. Three ponds were cleared out, with a waterfall at the foot of a sloping lawn which blends well with the landscape. In contrast, on the other side of the house is a formal paved garden with roses in a retaining wall.

Brook Hollow, Whichford (MR AND MRS J.A. ROUND) The house and garden were completely derelict when the present owners started it and they have some interesting historical photographs. It is a terraced garden, south-facing, with a stream at its foot, crossed by a bridge. There are specimen trees and shrubs, with over forty varieties of conifers, and roses and *Clematis* growing through trees and as ground cover.

Whichford House (MRS OAKES) The present owners took on a large garden with full-time gardener, and have simplified it well, which has, if anything, increased its charm. Pleached trees at the entrance give a formal look. A terrace, with roses to the rear, overlooks a spacious lawn and there is a walk with *rugosa* roses alongside the old churchyard. It is difficult to realize that, except for the mowing, Mrs Oakes does the garden herself at weekends.

Rightons Cottage, Ascott (COL. AND MRS C.R. BOURNE) This is a small garden, planted to merge into the rural background, and provides a variety of aspects. A heather bed, a shady border, shrub and ground cover roses, contrasting evergreen shrubs, and a secluded patio with small fish pond and views over rolling farmland, are its main features, all created for tranquil retirement.

The Gateway, Ascott (MRS M.W. THORNE) This is a spring garden with two magnificent trees of *Prunus conradinae*, a stream with primulas and *Lysichitum americanum* and a paved area near the house with a fish pond and an attractive lawn enclosed with fine box hedges.

Stone Walls, Ascott (MRS SCOTT-COCKBURN) A small garden surrounded by walls, and a cobbled area, has provided a

This view of the herbaceous border at Woodpeckers in May is dominated by a large clump of *Euphorbia griffithii* 'Fireglow'; in the background are *Rheum palmatum atropurpureum*, a silver *Salix lanata* and *Acer pseudoplatanus* 'Brilliantissimum'.

home for many alpines and rock plants. There are *Cistus* everywhere and several *Clematis*, notably 'Edith', growing flat among junipers.

Woodpeckers, Marlcliff
DR AND MRS J. COX

Woodpeckers was so named because the old plum and apple orchard upon which we built our house in 1965 was much frequented by greater spotted and green woodpeckers. Unfortunately our horticultural activities have made their appearance rare, but we have tried to retain the atmosphere of a country orchard. We have two and a half acres of roughly level ground two hundred yards from the River Avon, subject to occasional flooding and late spring frosts. The soil has a pH of 7, and is heavy but fertile. The outlook is over water-meadow and rising pasture. As far as possible we have no formal boundaries so the garden is part of the landscape. The informal design has evolved with our enthusiasms. It is never finished – we are always incorporating new ideas.

There is always something to see; in winter, trees with interesting bark, winter-flowering heathers, snowdrops, aconites and early crocuses; in spring, snake's head fritillaries and daffodils in the meadow garden, alpines grown in scree and stone troughs (twenty at the last count); a pond and bog garden – a nice place to sit in June; a white and apricot garden – very cool in hot July. We have many old roses, and *Clematis* and rambler roses climb into the old apple trees. A michaelmas daisy border, hardy chrysanthemums, colchicums, *Cyclamen* and crocuses brighten autumn days.

Slightly tender subjects are grown in a twenty-foot circular unheated greenhouse. *Abutilon megapotamicum*, *A. × milleri*, *Clematis australis*, *C. fosteri* and *Myrtus* thrive here. *Clematis florida* 'Sieboldii' is spectacular in June, flowering six weeks before a specimen outside. We love having visitors to share gardening experiences with, and welcome them by appointment at any time of year.

WILTSHIRE

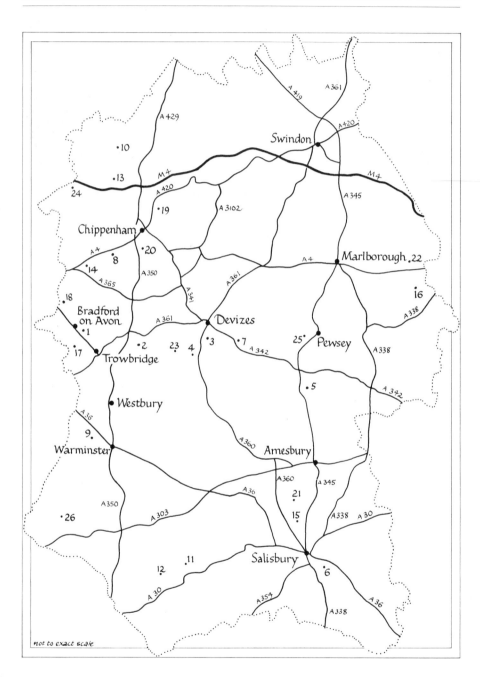

not to exact scale

Directions to Gardens

Belcombe Court, Bradford-on-Avon. [1]

Blagden House, Keevil, 4 miles east of Trowbridge. [2]

Broadleas, south of Devizes. [3]

Cheverell Mill, Little Cheverell, 5 miles south of Devizes. [4]

Chisenbury Priory, 6 miles southwest of Pewsey. [5]

Clarendon Park, 3 miles south of Salisbury. [6]

Conock Manor, 5 miles southeast of Devizes. [7]

Corsham Court, 4 miles west of Chippenham. [8]

Corsley Mill, Corsley, between Warminster, Westbury and Frome. [9]

Easton Grey House, 3½ miles west of Malmesbury. [10]

Fitz House, Teffont Magna, 10 miles west of Salisbury. [11]

Fonthill House, 3 miles north of Tisbury. [12]

Foscote Stables, Grittleton, 5 miles northwest of Chippenham. [13]

Hazelbury Manor, near Box, 5 miles southwest of Chippenham. [14]

Heale Gardens, Middle Woodford, 4 miles north of Salisbury. [15]

Hillbarn House, Great Bedwyn, southwest of Hungerford. [16]

Hillier's Cottage, Little Cheverell, 5 miles south of Devizes. [4]

Iford Manor, 2½ miles southwest of Bradford-on-Avon. [17]

Inwoods, Farleigh Wick, 3 miles northwest of Bradford-on-Avon. [18]

Kellaways, 3 miles north of Chippenham. [19]

Lackham College of Agriculture, Lacock, 4 miles south of Chippenham. [20]

Lake House, Lake, 7 miles north of Salisbury. [21]

Littlecote House, 3 miles west of Hungerford. [22]

Monastery Garden, Edington, 4 miles east of Westbury. [23]

The Old Vicarage, Edington, 4 miles east of Westbury. [23]

Pound Hill House, West Kington, 8 miles northwest of Chippenham, exit 18 on M4. [24]

Sharcott Manor, 1 mile southwest of Pewsey. [25]

The Stable House, Keevil, 4 miles east of Trowbridge. [2]

Stourhead Garden, Stourton, 3 miles northwest of Mere. [26]

Stourton House, Stourton, 2 miles northwest of Mere. [26]

Wedhampton Manor, 5 miles southeast of Devizes. [7]

Belcombe Court, Bradford-on-Avon
MRS A.J. WOODRUFF

The garden of Belcombe Court is at the end of a winding valley near Bath on the River Avon. It is still worthy of the consecration it appeared to have in pagan times when the ancient Britons dedicated it to their god Belenus.

In the garden there is an octastyle pavilion, a model of the temple in Delphos provided by a stonemason in 1735. However, the proportions did not please John Wood as he writes in his descriptions of Bath (1765). The temple stands by a pond shaped as a half moon; this pond ends in a stone grotto floored with ammonites and other fossils. The stones are said to be taken from an ancient stone circle which stood in the fields above. Here one rests on seats in the cool, contemplating the garden and watching the graceful carp glide through the water-lilies, while the ceiling of the grotto dances with light reflected by the water. It is one of the delights of a Georgian garden that one always looks onwards and upwards. Above the grotto is a chamber with stone seats which I call the banqueting hall. It is rather like a double-decker sight-seeing bus open to the sky. Here one can sit elevated above the garden peering through giant stones as if one had climbed the highest peak in Switzerland, watching unseen the life in the garden – pillars, statues, all glisten in the sunlight. Cascades of roses tumble from the flower beds intermingling with the border flowers, all tended with such care but so very close to nature in their plenty.

The park stretches beyond the ha-ha, and beyond stand the woods, into which one is enticed by more arches and follies to discover the source of Belcombe Brook.

In the garden there is an octagonal house open to the sky rather like a bandstand but contemporary with the rest of the garden.

On either side of the path as you walk to the octagonal house flower beds are planted with *Nepeta* underplanted with *Achillea* and giant double poppies, giving a haze of colour. This tended garden is only a backdrop to nature stretching beyond.

Blagden House, Keevil
MAJ. AND MRS ANTHONY CARR

This is a summer garden, and roses and *Clematis* love our heavy soil. It is essentially an old-fashioned garden, as we are lucky to have weathered red-brick walls and a two-hundred-and-fifty-year-old yew hedge. These walls and hedge dictate the shape of our planting, with a rose garden by the house, a fountain in the middle, and on one side an old stable block of red brick with *Clematis* and climbing roses on it. One feels compelled to see the other side of the hedge, so we have planted two long herbaceous borders, with lower yew hedges to back them. These lead up to a young cherry avenue with a pergola at the top, covered in roses, *Clematis* and honeysuckle. There one can sit and look back at the borders, and the pretty roofs of the house and stable block beyond the hedge.

The rest of the garden is now a productive kitchen garden with many greenhouses. In the spring we have hundreds of naturalized bulbs in the orchard and in a small nut grove leading to the church beyond. It is a pretty, tranquil garden in a lovely setting.

A mass of shrub roses at Cheverell Mill in early July. The pale pink 'Fritz Nobis' and 'Buff Beauty' cover the end of an old barn.

Broadleas, Nr Devizes
LADY ANNE COWDRAY

At Broadleas, situated on upper greensand, we are fortunate in being able to grow all types of plants, and full use has been made of this advantage. In the 'dell', which is the site of an old water course, can be found a large number of magnolias, maples, camellias, rhododendrons and other rare, unusual and beautiful trees and shrubs, under a canopy of oak and beech. In spring both sides of the 'dell' are covered with daffodils and other spring flowers, and there is always something here to discover in the way of bulbs, trilliums, *Sanguinaria, Meconopsis* and small plants, continuing right through to a glorious autumn display. Having a path along the top of the 'dell' is another bonus, as a lot of the taller trees can be viewed to advantage from above.

Near the house there is the rose garden, with hedges of shrub roses, the grey border and the perennial 'secret garden', full of a wide variety of plants. Broadleas is now the holder of the National Collection of deciduous *Euonymus*, and the species already collected are now being planted in the woodland walk, an extension to the garden that has been gradually opened up during the last two or three years.

Cheverell Mill, Little Cheverell
BRIG. AND MRS ROBERT FLOOD

Cheverell Mill is mentioned in the Domesday Book, and its history can also be traced through the criminal records of various millers. The mill was rebuilt in 1840, when an iron overshot wheel, with seven spokes, replaced the original wooden wheel, but part of the mill cottage is sixteenth-century.

When we bought the mill in 1972, the mill pond was silted up and the water had been diverted to the original stream line with a drop of nine feet in the level. The surrounding area had become a wilderness and, apart from some old willows and apple trees, the only appeal to a gardener was a mass of naturalized snowdrops along the stream line and the unusual lie of the land.

Our first major task was to dig the mill pond down twenty-one feet to the level of our new drawing-room french windows and to make a courtyard using the millstones, old window mullions and other large stones which we found in the collapsed mill pond walls. We resisted the temptation to make herbaceous borders and concentrated on climbing roses, *Wisteria*, shrubs and shrub roses on the walls of the house and the mill pond.

The stream has given us great pleasure and has made a natural home for primulas, *Iris, Mimula* and other water-loving plants, and also for groups of old-fashioned roses set back on the banks and in the lawns.

With the loss of the elms in the county, we have planted a number of new trees including a London plane which loves having its feet in water. Four years ago we built a conservatory which is the home of a large *Plumbago* and other tender plants and also provides lovely shelter on sunny days when the wind is cold.

Chisenbury Priory, Nr Pewsey
MR AND MRS ALISTAIR ROBB

Chisenbury Priory lies in a fold of the Downs on Salisbury Plain, sheltered by mature trees. As you drive down the avenue of sycamores, looking to your right you see the vineyard recently planted on a southern slope, which we believe is the site of the original priory vineyard. The drive opens out on to two

Conock Manor in June. A view of the copper-domed cupola of the stable block from the Gothick thatched dairy.

either side of which we are starting to plant trees and shrubs.

The walled garden with its sweeping lawns retains some of its original Tudor formality; the walls are again covered with roses and *Clematis*, and through this garden runs the leat, flanked by shrub roses such as 'Nevada' and 'Complicata' and damp-loving plants – ligularias, astilbes, hostas and willow gentians. Here also are old apple trees into which climb the 'Rambling Rector' and many others.

Clarendon Park, Nr Salisbury
MR AND MRS A. W. M. CHRISTIE-MILLER

This is a wild garden, laid out in the 1920s by the present owner's grandparents and covering an area of about twelve acres. A very interesting collection of trees and shrubs is set in a beautiful woodland situation amidst magnificent mature oak and beech. The acid soil supports a wide variety of azaleas and rhododendrons together with magnolias and camellias. Of particular interest are fine specimens of *Eucryphia* 'Nymansay', *Magnolia acuminata*, *Cercidiphyllum japonicum* and *Davidia involucrata*. Primulas abound in the woodland walks and valleys and the gardens are at their best in late May and early June.

Conock Manor, Devizes
MR AND MRS BONAR SYKES

'A Georgian house of great charm', according to the architectural historian, Nikolaus Pevsner. An early Gothic revival stable block, with a copper-domed cupola and a Gothick thatched dairy and *cottages ornés* provide the setting. Around the house, lawns with specimen trees and ha-has frame views of Salisbury Plain to the south and the Marlborough downs to the north. The soil is greensand, slightly alkaline, with rainfall of about thirty-two inches. A long brick wall shelters a mixed shrub border between house and stables, planted with roses, 'Roseraie de l'Haÿ', *Rosa multibracteata* and others, underplanted with *Dianthus deltoides*; *Rosa* × *cantabrigiensis*, underplanted with *Limnanthes douglasii* and blue and white *Linum perenne*; each of the four sections has groups of Oregon irises, various alliums and groups of annuals.

Beyond the stables, brick walls, beech and yew hedges provide the framework for the kitchen garden and shrub walk. The latter, planted in about 1930, has been described as 'an ingenious formal arrangement of beech hedges and clipped box . . . an intriguing variety of spaces, alternately broad and narrow, and given continuity and perspective by pairs of box balls'. Plants here include ornamental *Malus*, many paeonies, *Cornus nuttallii*, *C. kousa*, *C. florida*, *Callicarpa bodinieri* var. *giraldii* with *Tricyrtis formosana*, blue and white *Meconopsis betonicifolia*, with groundcover of *Geranium endressii*, *G. clarkei* 'Kashmir

forecourts in front of the main house. The priory is said to date from the eleventh century and now shows its beautiful early eighteenth-century façade of warm red brick with stone mullions. The main courtyard is flanked by magnificent flint and chalk walls coped with tiles; along these walls are two herbaceous borders.

Inside the west gate lies one of our favourite corners with shrubs and climbers tumbling over themselves, showing good colour

throughout the summer. This show starts in spring with *Akebia*, followed by old-fashioned roses, honeysuckle, *Cytisus battandieri*, many *Clematis* and perennial peas, ending with the sweet-smelling *Clerodendrum trichotomum*.

Following on down the red-brick path, you come to the terrace garden, facing south-west. In this intimate corner we are trying to introduce more unusual plants. From this garden you look down to the lily-pond on

White', *Pulmonaria*, *Alchemilla alpina*, and *Viola cornuta*.

The gardens on either side of the stables are linked by a short avenue of pleached limes. Nearby are small paddocks planted with *Magnolia*, *Sorbus*, *Prunus*, *Acer*, *Malus* and *Crataegus*. Narrow borders contain *Geranium*, *Cistus* and *Dianthus* with cordon apples screening the kitchen garden. The surrounding parkland and shelter belts were planted mainly with beech in about 1820, and extensive planting has taken place since 1970. Severe losses were suffered in the drought of 1976, and further planting has been necessary. A woodland walk surrounds the park.

◆

Corsham Court, Nr Chippenham
THE LORD METHUEN

Ethelred, the Saxon king of Wessex, was the first recorded owner of the 'Manor of Cosseham'. From that period the Manor, finally to become known as Corsham Court, had various owners, royal and otherwise and, in 1745, it passed into the ownership of the Methuen family. Subsequent alterations to the house and grounds by Capability Brown, Nash and Bellamy, have produced notable architectural styles.

The gardens contain magnificent views to the north, south and particularly east. Here the lake, originally created by Brown in 1763 on the north side of the house and altered by Repton to its present location in 1796, provides a tranquil aspect. Brown's ha-ha is still in evidence around the northern perimeter of the gardens.

The secluded gardens and lawns contain many beautiful specimen trees including the great oriental plane, *Platanus orientalis*, measuring some two hundred and forty yards round the perimeter of the canopy. A walled area of herbaceous borders, with many newly planted shrubs and plants, rose gardens and lawns surround the lily-pool. Adjacent stand the stone Bath House and Bradford Porch, both of historical interest.

Some of the many fine trees to be seen here include *Nyssa sylvatica*, *Juglans nigra* (the black walnut) and *Paulownia*.

◆

Corsley Mill, Corsley
MR AND MRS CHARLES QUEST-RITSON

We opened our garden for the NGS when it was less than two years old. Visitors would see it when all mud and weeds, and return when the garden was established. And so it was. Most of our visitors were enthusiastic and offered advice; we have learnt much from them. You cannot go wrong with four acres of greensand round a Queen Anne house. We sprayed it all with Round Up, harrowed it and sallied forth with miles of lawyer's red tape to mark out the beds and borders. These were treated with Simazine to prevent weed germination, while the grass was allowed to grow where we intended lawns and paths. It worked.

We like: strong design, long vistas, right angles, rich planting, clever contrasts, visiting gardens, Hidcote, Sissinghurst, Russell Page, NCCPG, dendrologists (most), alpines (in the Alps). We planted: a wood of *Sorbus* and birch; a wheel of colour; a conventional rose garden; a bog garden; an avenue of golden elders (vulgar, yes, but effective); a hot garden; a winter garden; a glade of spindles, and lots more.

We have four hundred different old roses, mostly on their own roots. Cuttings come easily from hardwood taken in autumn, and floribundas are just as easy as gallicas. They usually grow very much better than grafted plants. We have the National Collection of European primulas and find that old primrose varieties grow best in the shade of the rankest weeds; a tip for lazy gardeners. But we are generalists rather than specialists, and will try to grow anything rare or curious, anything from seed or collected on our travels. All is of interest; everything has something to contribute.

◆

Easton Grey House, Nr Malmesbury
MRS PETER SAUNDERS

There has been a house on the site of Easton Grey since the Domesday Book. We bought the present Georgian house, with its wrought-iron staircase and unique views over Easton Grey village and its ancient bridge over the infant Avon, about twenty years ago. It had been rented in the 1920s by the then Prince of Wales as a hunting box. I like to think we only made tactful changes to the garden, which we thought beautiful as it was:

a walled enclosure of about two acres, which we divided into four quarters – one for a tennis court, one for a swimming pool and poolhouse, one for a rose garden and one for greenhouses and a kitchen garden. Quite a large part of the park was taken in and planted with brimming beds of labour-saving shrubs and flowering trees. About ten years ago, Peter Coats advised on further embellishments – notably the twin terrace borders, planted in his special style for year-long effect, with coloured-leaved plants such as silver *Senecio* 'Sunshine', red *Berberis*, blue *Ruta graveolens* and golden *Euonymus*. He reorganized the central path borders in the walled garden rather in the same way, colourful and weed-suppressing, and added a summer house modelled on the 'greene seats' at Rousham, and a circular tree-seat in the Gothic taste. I am American and wanted a typically English garden, which so many Americans aim at, at home, and do not quite achieve. I'm not an expert gardener, but one thing I have learned is to listen attentively to my betters!

◆

Fitz House, Teffont Magna
MAJ. AND MRS MORDAUNT-HARE

Fitz House garden of four acres surrounds a beautiful group of stone buildings; sixteenth- and seventeenth-century mullion-windowed farmhouse, a fourteenth-century thatched tithe barn and a seventeenth-century cottage by a trout stream in one of Wiltshire's most lovely villages. The original garden was laid out in the 1920s in the seventeenth-century style and is still being extended by the present owners. Lying in a valley on a south-east-facing hillside, the garden is partly terraced and includes rooms within yew, beech and

The extensive collection of old roses, some of which are seen here with the silver-leaved *Elaeagnus commutata*, provide a setting for the Queen Anne house at Corsley Mill.

box hedges. Higher up the hillside rolling lawns among the remaining ancient orchard apple trees form a setting for the larger shrubs and climbing roses. A tulip tree and a *Fraxinus ornus* are of interest – beyond them the trees and cow-grazed fields form a truly rural backdrop.

We have been influenced by Vita Sackville-West at Sissinghurst in the late 1940s, by Christopher Lloyd, by the books of Graham Stuart Thomas and by much garden visiting. In our planting we have made wide use of all kinds of roses, *Clematis*, aromatic and silver-leaved plants, mixed with herbaceous perennials. So far as possible, we believe that, for example, shrub roses should not be planted at the back of borders but given individual positions where their arching beauty and scent can best be appreciated. We also believe that one must be ruthless in moving or cutting out plants that have been wrongly sited, even to the extent of moving them in full flower! Given a good rootball and loving after-care this is perfectly possible. In our view it is a mistake to over-regiment plants and a certain amount of self-expression must be allowed! In spring, bulbs and flowering trees and shrubs are a cheerful welcome for our visitors and in the autumn their leaves and berries give them a red and golden farewell.

Fonthill House, Nr Tisbury
THE LORD MARGADALE

The gardens at Fonthill House face south and have complete protection from the north wind. Built on a ridge of high ground at the east end of Fonthill Park, the house and gardens enjoy magnificent views south towards Cranborne Chase, Wyn Green and the Dorset border, and west, over the lake adjacent to the sites of earlier mansions, towards Fonthill Abbey woods in which are situated the ruins of Beckford's stupendous Gothic construction.

The gardens divide into two sections with a woodland garden on the side of the ridge behind and to the north of the house, and more formal lawns and beds to the south of the house. The woodland garden, largely developed in the 1930s, is planted under a thin canopy of old oaks and several magnificent beeches. There is a wide selection of cherries, crab apples, maples, rhododendrons and azaleas which are a particular feature, amidst a carpet of daffodils and bluebells. Later there is a fine array of autumn colouring.

The formal gardens include a variety of roses, mostly old-fashioned, but with some of the more attractive modern types, together with herbaceous plants and many small shrubs. These gardens are also blessed with walls providing extra shelter and a framework for a multitude of climbing and wall shrubs. The soil at Fonthill is mostly greensand but with some clay enriched with centuries of leaf-mould. Thus, most shrubs and plants prosper, and as the gardens are high on a

hillside there is no frost pocket and spring frost damage is very limited.

Fonthill House is approached by the public road from Fonthill Bishop to Fonthill Gifford, originally a private drive, which passes through Fonthill Arch, reputedly designed by Inigo Jones, and the private road which passes over the lake is lined with daffodils and azaleas for much of its mile length to the house.

Foscote Stables, Grittleton
MR AND MRS BERESFORD WORSWICK

Foscote Stables garden was started twelve years ago, before the stables were converted into a house, on a sloping three-acre site of mostly alkaline soil, but with a small area of neutral soil ideal for azaleas. On what was open field, there are now lovely Cotswold walls built by a wonderful stonemason. Trees and shrubs of all kinds, usual and unusual, were planted with an emphasis on scent – the very fragrant *Elaeagnus* and balsam poplar and of course *Philadelphus* and honeysuckles in variety.

The garden falls naturally into divisions. The lower lawn is square with richly planted borders each side with delphiniums, *Phlox, Hemerocallis* and the beautiful *Paeonia mlokosewitschii*, backed by walls on which roses and *Clematis* grow. From here wide steps lead to the upper lawn, which is circular and planted round with more paeonies and roses, including 'Ispahan', specimen trees underplanted with bulbs for the spring, with catmint and carpeting plants to follow on.

A yew arch, not yet fully grown, leads to a larger lawn for croquet. On one side are pleached limes, and on the other a bog garden for moisture-loving plants, where there is also *Cornus kousa*, quite beautiful in June. A screen of trees and shrubs conceals a fox-proof enclosure for ornamental ducks with one large and two smaller ponds where wild trees and plants grow vigorously.

From here at the top of the garden, you can return to the house down a grass walk between high beech hedges and borders filled with old shrub roses and through a gate into a little walled garden with a standard *Wisteria* as its star attraction. Throughout the seasons pots and troughs are used to add interest and colour. These are filled with tulips, pansies, lilies, petunias and *Agapanthus* and an occasional tender shrub.

Hazelbury Manor
MR AND MRS I.D. POLLARD

When we arrived at Hazelbury Manor in 1972 we were dismayed by the state of the gardens and set out not only to restore what once had been but also to enhance the gardens further.

We inherited a mediaeval archery walk complete with the original teller's seat and a croquet lawn, but most interesting of all is the

yew topiary around a sunken garden. Following through the theme, a yew chess set has been created to one side of the lawn, from which you can pass into a variety of individual planting areas or 'rooms' enclosed by yew hedging. Here you discover an orchard crammed full in spring with thirty or so varieties of daffodils, there a formal Elizabethan rose garden, its fifteen beds in traditional patterns, and so on to a foliage garden with its leafy plants chosen for shape, colour and texture.

The sunken garden, complete with fountain, is edged with borders which range in colour through white, yellow, red and orange on one side and through pink and lilac to blue and purple on the other.

While some areas have been painstakingly thought out, others happened almost by accident. A huge mound of soil – debris from clearing away part of the drive – was transformed, in an inspired moment, into a beautiful rockery containing a waterfall and ponds.

The most important aspect of the garden is its very human scale, a place where one can feel at home. Intimacy is created by the garden 'rooms' in various sizes; then suddenly, as you turn a corner, long vistas through the garden and beyond greet the eye and delight the senses.

Heale House and Garden
MAJ. DAVID AND LADY ANNE RASCH

Heale garden – although based on a much more formal concept created at the beginning of this century by the present owner's great uncle, the Hon. Louis Greville, with help from Harold Peto – maintains the shape and layout of the original intention. The garden provides interest almost throughout the year, helped by the basic 'bones' of that original design. The earlier herbaceous planting has given way to shrubs and ground-covering plants creating the feeling of a large-scale cottage garden.

In spring the water garden surrounding the Japanese tea house (imported at the end of the last century) is at its best. Intersected by streams from the nearby River Avon, the spring bulbs are succeeded by *Lysichitum, Primula, Rodgersia* and giant *Gunnera* growing under *Magnolia, Acer palmatum, Liquidambar* and an enormous *Cercidiphyllum*. Many of the shrubs supporting rambling roses provide interest throughout most of the summer until the autumn colours take over.

In summer the many roses, both old and new varieties, grow in an orderly confusion with paeonies, delphiniums and other plants and shrubs, their flowers and foliage providing a gentle colour scheme to enhance the beautiful seventeenth-century manor house.

The walled garden is crossed with tunnels of espalier-trained apples (a fine sight in May), vines, *Clematis, Laburnum* and roses, and these provide a foil to the vegetables. Surrounding beds are planted with the more tender and scented shrubs.

In all, eight acres of garden provide a varied selection of plants and shrubs; many of the less common ones are for sale in the small nursery.

◆

Hillbarn House, Great Bedwyn
MR AND MRS A.J. BUCHANAN

This is really a series of small gardens within a garden, in a two-acre area right in the middle of the village. Visitors always remark on their surprise as they step through the small door off the village High Street to discover such an unexpected garden.

Some of the more unusual features are a hornbeam tunnel with windows, a summer-house in clipped hornbeam, a hornbeam hedge on stilts, pleached limes, clipped topiary box, a chessboard herb garden decorated with standard species roses, a paeony garden, a rose garden of pegged hybrid musk roses, hornbeam trees growing in boxes, quince arches and a nut arch, all trained by the talented young gardener John Last.

The garden has been formed over the last twenty-five years by three separate owners, and is probably at its best when the old-fashioned roses are flowering in June. Some of the more interesting borders were planned by Lanning Roper using chalk-loving plants, with muted flowering colours, and interesting leaf colours and shapes.

◆

Hillier's Cottage, Little Cheverell
MRS M.L. WORT

When I bought this cottage in 1964 the local Council told me it had outlived its useful life and was only fit to be pulled down. The garden had been a complete wilderness for many years.

It is an interesting small garden with a stream running through it. I grow many varieties of *Hosta*, *Iris sibirica*, *Astilbe*, *Primula japonica*, *P. florindae* and 'Garryarde Guinevere' along the banks. A lawn runs down from the cottage to the stream and I have a mixed shrub and herbaceous border down the side of the garden. This is beautiful throughout the year. *Sorbus hupehensis* 'Rosea', *Sorbus* 'Joseph Rock' and a 'Victoria' plum tree provide shade on the lawn. The front garden is on the other side of the lane from the cottage, rising steeply on two terraces with an old thirteen-foot brick wall keeping it in place. This front garden faces south, the soil is greensand and requires endless compost, peat etc; but is ideal for growing pinks, campanulas, dwarf irises and helianthemums which hang over the wall. In spring many groups of daffodils and tulips give early colour.

As I have no help, I have planted beautiful shrubs and shrub roses on these terraces which more or less look after themselves: *Anemone blanda* and *Scilla* grow in profusion beneath the shrubs and many hellebores and bergenias help to suppress the weeds.

A wonderful specimen of *Cornus alternifolia* 'Argentea', planted close to *Clerodendrum trichotomum* with its turquoise berries and pink bracts in October, gives much pleasure to passers-by. My three bee-hives live in safety on the top terrace.

◆

Iford Manor Gardens, Nr Bradford-on-Avon
MR AND MRS J.J.W. HIGNETT

In the eighteenth century, Iford was renowned for its woodland walks and classical views. Traces of these remain above Harold Peto's Edwardian garden in the Italian style which overlooks the steep valley of the River Frome with its ancient bridge. The classical façade of the house conceals its Tudor origins. The garden is terraced and has many architectural features, in accordance with Peto's ideas. There are pools, statues, a colonnaded terrace, a Japanese garden and a cloister.

The structural quality of the garden is enhanced by plantings of box, cypress, *Phillyrea* and yew. Martagon lilies are naturalized in the rough grass and up into the beechwoods, and there are other plants of horticultural and historical interest.

◆

Inwoods, Farleigh Wick
MR AND MRS D.S. WHITEHEAD

This garden was laid out in 1927 by Captain H. Whitehead. The main features are the herbaceous border, the collection of flowering shrubs, and the wild garden. The garden backs on to a wood, with a notable collection of wild flowers in the spring. In this mildly alkaline soil rhododendrons will not grow in the open, but they flourish when planted in the wild garden under oak trees.

◆

Kellaways, Nr Chippenham
MRS D. HOSKINS

This is an informal garden extending to approximately two acres, and has been designed and planted since 1949 by the present owner, around the late seventeenth-century Cotswold stone house. Situated on the famous Kellaways limestone, the garden enjoys exceptionally good drainage.

The garden comprises a walled garden with exceptional herbaceous borders, a large collection of old roses, and some rare plants. There are a great many species of paeonies, and the collection of *Clematis* is of particular interest. The rock garden is always colourful, but the miniature *Cyclamen* make it particularly so after Christmas. There are many interesting trees, and the shrubbery has much varied foliage, a special feature being a well-established *Aralia elata* 'Aureovariegata'.

Lackham College of Agriculture, Lacock, Nr Chippenham
WILTSHIRE COUNTY COUNCIL:
PRINCIPAL: PETER W. MORRIS, ESQ.

Lackham is situated in a great crook of the river Avon which forms a part of the boundary of this ancient estate whose history stretches back to Aelfstan of Boscombe – before the Norman Conquest. The present Lackham House is Georgian with an attractive Italian garden terrace to the south and a carved stone balustrade over which roses, including 'Albertine', make a special July feature. There are lawns, borders, great trees and there is space; the river walks include one really ancient garden feature with the few relics of a hornbeam walk which probably stretched for maybe a mile or so, and there is also a lime walk, heavy with scent and the sound of bees in early July. Part of the joy of visiting Lackham is the view from a high point on the one-mile front drive which overlooks the verdant college farms and onwards towards the Plain of Lacock to the south and the more wooded Bowden Hill to the east. The walled garden is a splendid haven for the traditional gardener with very special beds of vegetables, herbs, herbaceous plants, fruits and also glasshouses featuring their own special collections of tender shrubs as well as orchids, hoyas and columneas. Most of the plants are labelled, and there is usually expert advice available since this is the Wiltshire County Council's centre for agricultural and horticultural education.

◆

Lake House Garden, Nr Salisbury
CAPT. O.N. BAILEY, RN

The modern garden at Lake, about seven acres in all, was developed from 1922 onwards and in the last few years has been further adapted, to cope with the problems of upkeep, without changing the basic design. With the Avon running along the fringe of the garden it was natural that the river became an important feature in this design. A sidestream runs through the garden and forms a charming water garden with connecting streams, ornamental trees and bridges, the whole area covered in drifts of daffodils and in the shady parts anemones and woodland lilies.

Nearby, the old rose garden, surrounded by clipped yew hedges and flint walls, has been replanted in the last few years, the hybrid tea roses being replaced by old and modern shrub roses. 'Constance Spry' and 'Moonlight' live happily on the chalk with 'Blanc Double de Coubert' and 'Fantin-Latour' and only need a modest feed and a gentle shaping each year.

Like many Wiltshire gardens, walls and yew hedges form very important features between one area and another as well as providing valuable shelter against the north and east winds. Near the house itself is a group of shrub borders and a lawn, known as the 'bowling green'; the yews surrounding

Campanula poscharskyana cascades down a flight of steps at Fitz House (for description see page 213). In the background the rose 'Rambling Rector' is climbing into a tree, and the greyish leaves of *Vitis vinifera* 'Tomentosa' are beginning to cover the arch.

this are reputed to be at least two hundred years old. Here, and under the house, much new planting has taken place to provide a balance of colour all the year round with a minimum of labour. Euphorbias in the shady areas mix with *Erica carnea*, potentillas, *Cytisus* and *Hemerocallis* to the fore, while *Philadelphus coronarius*, viburnums, shrub roses and *Clematis* help to form a background of organized chaos.

The main sweep of the lawn extends south-eastwards to a pleached lime alley which borders the croquet lawn. To the right is the drive and a sweep of mature trees, while to the left a magnificent arched yew hedge some twenty-five feet high leads into the tall wattle wall of the original vegetable garden (later a small rose garden and now a swimming pool area), and then to the curved outer wall of the vegetable garden. Outside the pool wall are more old-fashioned shrub roses and in the narrow border following the line of the curved wall a new planting scheme has been carried out to mix decorative shrubs with sturdy perennials. Here clumps of del-phiniums are supported by variegated *Weigela*, paeonies by sedums and white *Phlox* by a wide variety of hostas. Along the wall itself, climbing roses like 'Pink Perpetue', 'Handel'

Lime green *Alchemilla mollis* and blue *Campanula* around a thatched dovecote at Fitz House in July.

and 'Aloha' mingle with *Clematis* species and hybrids and a fine specimen of *Garrya elliptica*.

Many fuchsias and geraniums are grown in the greenhouses and a feature of the garden in high summer is the quantity of urns filled to overflowing with standard and ornamental fuchsias and variegated and ivy-leaf geraniums. They demonstrate vividly how such a display can add vital touches of colour to the garden all summer as well as giving a special ounce of elegance.

Littlecote House, Nr Hungerford
PETER DE SAVARY, ESQ.

The grounds of the lovely seventeenth-century Littlecote Manor, situated in beautiful countryside on the Wiltshire–Berkshire border, have something for both the keen gardener and the historian. The herbaceous border with its canal-type trout stream, running along the north boundary of the gardens, is of special interest during July and August. The gardens are surrounded by ancient walls and well-trimmed yew hedges. The parkland at the front of the house with its wooded area is especially attractive in spring, with its naturalized daffodils clothing the south slopes of the park.

In the front garden is a fine Tudor bank with a single bowling green at the top – this is a unique feature of Littlecote, as there are few to be found in any other part of the country. On the lawn at the bottom of the bank is a *Catalpa bignonioides*, and on the walls of the house are perhaps two of the oldest plants in the garden – two fine *Magnolia grandiflora* with their large white flowers in late summer. On the lawns at the rear of the house is a fine specimen of *Davidia involucrata* with its delicate paper-handkerchief flowers, seen at their best in late May.

The gardens were neglected during the war, and are at present undergoing a large amount of restoration, with the terraces and paths being replaced around the lawns, new borders, new rose gardens and many other features of interest. The theme for the gardens is the seventeenth century, and the planting of shrubs and roses has been chosen to represent many of the plants found around the grounds in the Cromwellian period. The house was a garrison for Colonel Popham and his soldiers, whose armour and buff coats now hang on the walls of the house, making what is the largest and most complete collection of Cromwellian armour and musketry in England today.

Monastery Garden, Edington
THE HON. MRS DOUGLAS VIVIAN

Monastery Garden is entirely surrounded by high stone walls built from the ruins of the fourteenth-century Bonshommes Monastery. Little else remains except, of course, the large and beautiful Priory Church overlooking the

Dodecatheon meadia at The Old Vicarage, Edington, in June. This damp-loving plant is a member of the *Primula* family, the American counterpart of the European *Cyclamen*.

garden and the ruin of what some say is the monks' well-house, now covered in *Clematis*.

The lower part of the five-and-a-half-acre garden is an old and roughly kept orchard, containing apples, pears, plums and ancient quince trees with gnarled and twisted trunks. The upper half is less wild, though with few formal beds. Successive generations added trees and there are now many well-established birches, beeches, firs and a magnificent tulip tree.

During the past ten years I have taken care to retain the informal character of the garden adding many trees and quantities of spring bulbs, as well as shrub roses. Springs fed from Salisbury Plain above enabled me to create a small pond, now surrounded by irises, ornamental reeds, *Cornus*, primulas and *Mimulus*. Perhaps I have been responsible for one addition that is less informal than the rest of the garden – that is, a small rose and herb garden alongside part of the walls that are said to have formed one side of the monks' cloisters.

The Old Vicarage, Edington
JOHN D'ARCY, ESQ.

The Old Vicarage garden at Edington lies on the steep, northern escarpment of Salisbury Plain, and, although surrounded by chalk downland above and stony clay below, the soil is acid greensand and easy to work. The lawns and terrace formed part of a long-established vicarage garden, but the planting areas have been greatly extended and will be framed in time by beech, yew and holly

hedges to give protection from the frequent winds coming from many sides.

Few parts of the garden remain in the sun all day and a number of mature yew, ash and hazel trees shade terraces and borders where lilies, *Cyclamen*, hydrangeas and daphnes flourish. *Daphne* × *houtteana*, a seldom-seen cross between *D. mezereum* and *D. laureola*, has purple leaves and lilac-purple blooms along the bare stems in March and April; it is perfectly hardy, tolerates shade and looks well with Welsh poppies self-sown around. *Daphne glomerata* collected from the Caucasus has been slow to establish but is now happy growing under an azalea, as it was found on the Georgian Military Highway at 6,000 feet. *Echium rubrum*, a Soviet red version of our Viper's Bugloss from Armenian forest meadows, provides a useful new addition to the herbaceous border.

A collection of *Oenothera* species and named hybrids has been started here under NCCPG's scheme; it is a confusing family, with many differently named species that appear identical, some not garden-worthy. Generally yellow, some have pink or white flowers over a long season.

In the spring irises and tulips collected in the wild in the Caucasus, Russian Central Asia and Iran flower well in bulb frames, where all summer water can be excluded.

Pound Hill House, West Kington
MR AND MRS PHILIP STOCKITT

The garden is set around a fifteenth-century house in Cotswold stone and is divided into six separate areas. Surrounding the house there is a flagged terrace in which grow a wide

Primula 'Kinlough Beauty' at Stourton House in April (see page 218). This striking plant is a hybrid of *Primula juliae*, a dwarf purple primrose from the Caucasus.

range of alpine and climbing plants. Beyond the terrace there is a rectangular grass courtyard, around which are beds edged with dwarf box and backed by stone walls, well-covered with climbers. In the borders are clipped yews, silver, white and pink plants and quarter-standard 'Ballerina' roses; one side of the courtyard is another paved area, containing dwarf shrubs and alpines.

Beyond the courtyard there is a sweep of grass leading up to the wild garden, and there is a small water garden with primulas, irises, lilies and other moisture-loving plants. A group of *Betula papyrifera* is underplanted with miniature bulbs, including *Fritillaria*. To the west of the house is an orchard and, running through this, a pergola covered with roses, *Wisteria* and honeysuckle, which leads into a small rose garden planted with old-fashioned roses, lilies, lavender, *Phlox* and silver plants. Another courtyard surrounded by raised beds gives a wonderful opportunity to show some of the five hundred different alpines which grow in the adjacent nursery.

Sharcott Manor, Pewsey
CAPT. AND MRS DAVID ARMYTAGE

Within lovely old walls and yew hedges, we have redesigned and planted this garden since 1977. On fertile greensand and with water, the scope is endless. In the New Year snowdrops and *Crocus* species abound. *Hamamelis mollis* 'Pallida' is a magnificent sight above a carpet of snow against a clear blue sky, and frost permitting, the camellias will soon be flowering.

From March to May mown rides through rough grass lead us past thousands of named daffodils, planted in bold drifts near a small lake. By the stream a huge clump of *Gunnera manicata* frames a pretty brick bridge. Throughout the summer, shrubs, roses, and perennials flower in perfect harmony. *Rosa* 'Bobbie James' cascades from an old yew, and over the summerhouse tumbles 'New Dawn', with *Stachys* 'Silver Carpet' at its feet, and *Clematis* 'Hagley Hybrid' scrambling over it and up the rose.

It is not only flowers that bring beauty to the garden, but the many variegated plants and contrasting leaf colours that give pleasure for months on end. As autumn approaches the arboretum of young trees take on their varying shades. *Malus tschonoskii* stands in all its glory at the end of a long vista. Soon winter will be here.

The Stable House, Keevil
MRS E.C. CRAWFORD

My garden, which was started on the site of an old kitchen garden in 1964, is a monument to my fickle tastes, total inability to estimate the ultimate spread or height of any shrub planted, and the carelessness with which the birds, my cat and I distribute weed seeds.

It is small, about a third of an acre, bounded by an old and beautiful brick wall on three sides, and dominated by a superb copper-beech in one corner. The only other large trees are a *Robinia*, and a silver birch planted twenty-odd years ago which has attained a magnificent height and girth. In winter the ground below it is carpeted with *Cyclamen*, snowdrops and aconites and *Crocus* species set off by the red stems of various *Cornus*. In spring we have blossom: *Forsythia*, *Prunus* 'Cistena', *Amelanchier*, and my favourite, the snowy little pompoms of *Prunus glandulosa* 'Albiplena'. *Primula denticulata* are massed in a half-shady border, and the little 'Garryarde Guinevere' edges the paths, while daffodils are everywhere, causing havoc later with their foliage.

The real peak of the year is mid-June, when the shrub roses are in full swing: from moderns like 'Fritz Nobis' and 'Constance Spry' to the glorious scented oldies – 'Fantin-Latour', 'Celestial', 'Maiden's Blush', the delectable 'Mme Hardy' and more, with irises, paeonies, delphiniums and hardy geraniums for company.

From then onwards I try to keep up a succession of colour in the borders; in late summer there are seven or eight different *Clematis* making huge curtains of purple, red and blue. We sign off with a display of berries from a six-foot hedge of *Pyracantha* surrounding the vegetable plot, and autumn colour from the *Amelanchier* and various *Berberis*.

Stourhead, Stourton
THE NATIONAL TRUST

One of the earliest and greatest landscape gardens in the world, created by the banker Henry Hoare in the 1740s on his return from the Grand Tour. Inspired by the paintings of Claude and Poussin he strove to create a 'romantic' landscape, and over the last two centuries rare trees, rhododendrons and azaleas have been added to the original scheme.

Stourton House, Stourton
ANTHONY AND ELIZABETH BULLIVANT

This is a four-acre, plant-lovers' garden. It lies, hidden, just before the car park of Stourhead's famous landscape garden. Not many people realize that this second garden, so close to its world-famous neighbour, exists at all, let alone being so big, so varied, colourful and complementary to it, through being a plantsman's garden. The grass paths lead through many varied vistas of charming shrubs, lovely trees and many unusual plants. It is a garden that combines formality and informality. It is full of surprises and ideas to stimulate creative thoughts for one's own garden. It is worth a special journey to see the very unusual daffodils and the wealth of herbaceous plants.

The garden is well-known for its production of Stourton Dried Flowers; these dried herbaceous flowers retain their original colouring for years. Many people enjoy seeing how much in the garden is used for drying, and discovering how it is done. The garden specializes in hydrangeas, and well over twenty varieties are usually for sale, as well as being represented by good specimens in the garden.

Wedhampton Manor, Nr Devizes
MRS E.L. HARRIS

Wedhampton Manor is a fine Queen Anne house, placed on a glorious site with magnificent views from the garden, south to Salisbury Plain, north to Chenhill Downs. Homeliness is the key to the design of the gardens and colour throughout the year is provided by bulbs, herbaceous borders and many annuals. There are various trees, including a fine hundred-year-old cut-leaved lime.

Index

Numbers in bold indicate illustrations